Dr. Guttma

PREGNANCY, BIRTH
& FAMILY PLANNING

Dr. Guttmacher's

PREGNANCY, BIRTH & FAMILY PLANNING

Completely Updated and Revised by

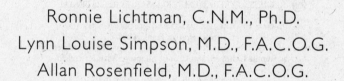

Ronnie Lichtman, C.N.M., Ph.D.
Lynn Louise Simpson, M.D., F.A.C.O.G.
Allan Rosenfield, M.D., F.A.C.O.G.

New American Library

New American Library
Published by New American Library, a division of
Penguin Putnam Inc., 375 Hudson Street,
New York, New York 10014, U.S.A.
Penguin Books Ltd, 80 Strand,
London WC2R 0RL, England
Penguin Books Australia Ltd, 250 Camberwell Road,
Camberwell, Victoria 3124, Australia
Penguin Books Canada Ltd, 10 Alcorn Avenue,
Toronto, Ontario, Canada M4V 3B2
Penguin Books (N.Z.) Ltd, Cnr Rosedale and Airborne Roads,
Albany, Auckland 1310, New Zealand

Penguin Books Ltd, Registered Offices:
Harmondsworth, Middlesex, England

This edition first published by New American Library, a division of Penguin Putnam Inc.

First Printing (Second Revised Edition), April 2003
10 9 8 7 6 5 4 3 2

Illustrations new to this revised edition by Laura Hartman Maestro
Charts by Mark Stein

 REGISTERED TRADEMARK—MARCA REGISTRADA

LIBRARY OF CONGRESS CATALOGING-IN-PUBLICATION DATA:
Guttmacher, Alan Frank, 1898–
Dr. Guttmacher's pregnancy, birth & family planning—Completely updated and revised
/ by Ronnie Lichtman, Lynn Louise Simpson, Allan Rosenfield.
p.   cm.
Includes bibliographical references and index.
ISBN: 0-451-19889-1 (alk. paper)
1. Pregnancy. 2. Childbirth. 3. Birth control. I. Title: Doctor Guttmacher's pregnancy,
birth, and family planning. II. title: Pregnancy, birth, and family planning. III. Lichtman,
Ronnie. IV. Simpson, Lynn Louise. V. Rosenfield, Allan. VI. Title.
RG525 .G82 2003   2002031527
618.2'4—dc21

Set in Adobe Garamond, Gill Sans
Designed by Ginger Legato

Printed in the United States of America

Irwin H. Kaiser, M.D., who was closely associated with Dr. Alan F. Guttmacher during Dr. Guttmacher's lifetime, prepared the first revision of the work in 1986 at the request of Dr. Guttmacher's widow, Lenore Guttmacher, and prepared subsequent revisions in 1996. Dr. Kaiser's 1986 revision contained an acknowledgment by Lenore Guttmacher which included the statement ". . . to me, Irwin Kaiser represents the best of his specialty—Obstetrics—as did his mentor, Alan Guttmacher."

ACKNOWLEDGMENTS

Any project of this magnitude is always a collective effort. We have many people to thank. As a group, we thank Sally Guttmacher and Ann Loeb, the daughters of Alan Guttmacher, who trusted us to update their father's classic book. We thank Hugh Rawson, Alan Guttmacher's editor at Penguin Press, for his enthusiastic support, helpful suggestions, and patience. We wish him the best in his new endeavors. We thank Marie Timell, who took over the editing job with energy and excitement, and Claire Zion, the editor who carried the manuscript to fruition with great care and concern. Marjory Garrison was also very helpful in pulling everything together. We were fortunate to have a line editor, Jill Parsons, whose expertise, to our amazement, encompassed not only grammar, but pregnancy. We thank the late Dr. Irwin Kaiser, who was responsible for the previous update and generously allowed us to take over.

Maria Tancona-Kupfer, C.N.M., M.S., assisted with research. Anne Showers performed many tasks for us. Gillian Williams and Burkina Morgan helped put together the final manuscript. Amalia "Mali" Kelly, M.D., read the section on infertility with extreme care. Her suggestions were invaluable. Jacques Moritz, M.D., a great supporter of natural birth and midwifery, volunteered to read the proofs and we thank him. We especially thank Elin Waring, Ph.D., Tom Abernathy, and Linnea and Bobby Abernathy, whose support and encouragement went way beyond the ordinary or expected. They gave time, caring, and expertise. This project might not have been finished without their help.

Finally, we thank our many family members and friends, whose love has been sustaining.

Of course, we take full responsibility for any and all omissions or errors.

CONTENTS

⸺∞⸺

Chapter 3 · Are You Pregnant?   32
EARLY PREGNANCY SYMPTOMS
> Presumptive Signs. Probable Signs. Positive, or
> Definite, Signs

Chapter 4 · Duration of Pregnancy   50
CALCULATING DELIVERY DATES
> A Word on Terminology. Calculating the Delivery
> Date from a Known Day of Insemination. Calculating
> the Delivery Date from Ultrasound. Calculating the
> Delivery Date from Uterine Size. Calculating
> the Delivery Date from the First Fetal Movements.
> What Are the Chances of Delivering on Time?
> Prolonged Pregnancy. Legal Problems Associated with
> Duration of Pregnancy. Laboratory Tests for Paternity

Chapter 5 · The Fetus   59
A REASSURING WORD
THE FERTILIZED CELL
SUMMARY OF DEVELOPMENT FOR EACH PERIOD OF PREGNANCY
LIFE IN THE UTERUS
> The Amniotic Fluid. The Umbilical Cord. The
> Placenta and Its Function in Fetal Nutrition. The
> Bloodstreams of Mother and Fetus Are Separate. Blood
> Cells Can Cross the Placenta. Heat Exchange.
> Hormone Production by the Placenta. Most Drugs
> Cross the Placenta to the Baby. Beneficial Effects of
> Drugs on the Fetus
OVERVIEW OF TERATOGENESIS
> Overview of the Time Frame in Pregnancy for
> Teratogenic Effects. Specific Drugs Possibly Harmful to
> the Fetus. Historical Examples of Teratogenic Drugs.
> Drugs with the Potential for Abuse. Therapeutic
> Drugs: Prescription and Over-the-Counter
METABOLIC DISEASES WITH FETAL EFFECTS
INFECTIOUS DISEASES WITH FETAL EFFECTS
> Sexually Transmitted Infections. Other Infections with
> Fetal Effects

PREFACE

The Meaning of Pregnancy

We have written this book in the spirit of Dr. Alan Guttmacher. We have respected his belief in a woman's right to information about her body. We have attempted to present this information as he would have—thoughtfully and thoroughly. Our commitment, like his, is to give each woman the ability to make intelligent decisions about her care, to enter into a partnership with her physician or midwife.

To provide a comprehensive picture of pregnancy and its care today, we have necessarily spent many pages describing pregnancy problems and medical interventions. We have discussed pregnancy in women who have illnesses. We have identified complications of pregnancy. We have covered ultrasound and amniocentesis, in vitro fertilization and fetal surgery. We have enumerated genetic disorders and toxic exposures. We have reviewed forceps deliveries, vacuum extraction, and cesarean birth.

In the midst of all this information we hope the most important message has not been lost. Pregnancy is not a medical event. Being pregnant is not like having a broken leg or gallstones. It is not an instance of the body breaking down or malfunctioning. It is quite the opposite. Pregnancy is the body doing one of the things it is biologically competent to do.

Pregnancy is a profound personal experience. It is a family and a social event. It is a life transition.

For every human being who has ever inhabited this earth, a woman has been pregnant. Most of these pregnancies, throughout history, have proceeded without incident. In quite an amazing way, babies are created and grow inside their mothers and are born. Most are born healthy.

The essence of pregnancy is the new life it creates. This life enters

xxvii

into your own to change much of what you have ever known—forever.

Your physician or midwife is first and foremost an observer. A guardian of nature's ways. Someone whose job usually involves doing very little. Watching, waiting, keeping track. An invited guest into the most deeply meaningful moments, perhaps, of your life.

Technology works wonders when it is needed and can have harmful consequences if it is used inappropriately. Our lengthy discussions of technology are offered to provide you with options and choices, to make sure that nothing is done *to* you, but rather everything is done *for* you and *with* you. With your full consent and understanding of risks and benefits.

Few interventions are totally risk free. Sometimes, the risk is justified, clearly and simply. Other times, the choice is among shades of gray. We want you to understand and evaluate the choices and make them knowledgeably.

We wish all our readers wanted, healthy pregnancies, pregnancies in which the major events are the baby's first movements, the sound of its heartbeat, the pleasure of gaining weight, the anticipation of birth. We wish our readers who develop pregnancy-related problems the satisfaction of being full participants in decision making and of seeing every problem resolved. We wish those few women whose outcomes are less than optimum support from their loved ones and the ability to seek professional help as necessary.

We wish our readers a sense of trust in their own bodies and the common sense to do what is best for their baby-to-be.

We are fortunate to live in an era in which most of the few complications that do arise during pregnancy have solutions. We are fortunate to be living in an era in which women and their families have a voice in their own care, in how they want their labor to be conducted, in how and where they want to deliver their babies. We are fortunate in the knowledge that human beings have acquired. We would like to see this knowledge utilized in ways that never dehumanize or diminish any person. We hope this book helps each reader to maintain her humanity throughout pregnancy, labor, and birth, and in planning her family.

INTRODUCTION

⁓⊱⊰⁓

Childbearing and parenthood are two of life's greatest endeavors. They forge human bonds that cannot be broken, bonds we have to our own bodies, to our co-parent, to our children. Our feelings for our own mothers and fathers change once we join the community of parents. We develop strong and lasting friendships with the parents of our children's friends. Current affairs affect us in a more immediate way. We may, for a time at least, become somewhat oblivious of the outside world, but, in fact, we care more deeply about its events as we now have an intimate and permanent commitment to another generation.

That men have become more involved in pregnancy, birth, and parenting is not only a help to women, but a gift they have given themselves. Human interactions become more meaningful as you provide not only love, but care and comfort. Men are finding new dimensions to themselves as they participate intimately in all aspects of baby care.

Reproductive freedom provided by safe, effective, and affordable birth control with emergency contraception and safe, legal abortion as backups has made parenthood voluntary. For the first time in human history, recent generations have had the ability to bear only wanted children. Although this goal has not been achieved entirely, it is worthy and possible.

Generally improved health, accessible care, and advances in medical knowledge and techniques have made childbearing safe, and women themselves have made it dignified and family centered. Together with responsive physicians and midwives, they have assured that birth options are available. Women today can choose to have their babies in a traditional hospital setting, an in-hospital birthing room, an out-of-hospital birthing center, or at home. With careful selection of an appropriate environment, most births are normal and happy. Even hospitals that serve poor women and families increasingly offer women a consistent physician or midwife for their prenatal care and provide childbirth education and pleasant atmospheres for birth.

This is a wonderful time to be pregnant. Contrast this with pregnancy and birth in 1937, when the first edition of this book was published.

Imagine you are pregnant in 1937. If you live in an urban area and are poor, you might go to a clinic and have your baby in a hospital where a revolving array of medical students, interns, and residents will take care of you. If you live in an urban area and are middle class or wealthy, you will see a private doctor who will deliver your baby, but your hospital birth experience may not be substantially different from the poor woman's experience. Your family will drop you off at the hospital and you will be attended by a nursing staff you have never met. The father of your baby and other family members will wait anxiously in a room down the hall. After the baby is born, you will be separated from it. You will stay in the hospital for at least a week, confined to bed. You will only see your baby at assigned times.

If you are poor and live in a rural area, you might have your baby at home with a midwife. The midwife will probably have lots of experience but little formal education. If all goes well, as it almost always does, you will be fine. Your loved ones will be nearby, perhaps even assisting with the birth.

In any of these situations, if you have a problem, you or your baby might become seriously ill. Either of you might even die.

At that time in history, women's rights were not considered as a component of childbirth. In a tribute to Alan Guttmacher, written in 1974 and published in the journal of the Alan Guttmacher Institute, Frederick S. Jaffe, the Institute's first president, stated:

In the early 1930s, long before it became fashionable, he [Alan Guttmacher] decided that women had the right to a straightforward account of what they could anticipate in pregnancy, that the useful knowledge hoarded by organized medicine had to be demystified and made more generally available. He began to write a series of books, revised periodically . . . which were read and reread by . . . young women who wanted to manage pregnancy, delivery and aftercare successfully. In 1961, he broke ground by authoring the first paperback on birth control . . . Today he might be described as a premature "consumer advocate," a pioneer in "informed consent," and an early voice in support of women's rights to know about and control their bodies. But when Alan Guttmacher began his educational program for American women, he received few plaudits from his colleagues, some of whom viewed writing for the laity as professionally disreputable.*

Alan Guttmacher wrote:

No woman is completely free unless she is wholly capable of controlling her fertility; and . . . no baby receives its full birthright unless it is born gleefully wanted by its parents.*

In 1937, a book with information for women was revolutionary. Now, many such books are available. In 1937, it would have been most unusual for a physician and midwife to collaborate on such a book. Today, collaborative practice among various kinds of health care providers is increasingly the norm.

This book would have been a different work if we hadn't had the privilege to rewrite a classic. It would have been different if any of us had written it individually. That physicians and a midwife were able to work together and all feel comfortable with the information presented is a metaphor for the future of health care delivery in this country. Collaborative practice undoubtedly provides consumers of health care the most options, the best of various possible worlds. It is to the goal of health-fulfilling and personally satisfying choices in all of reproductive life that together we dedicate this edition of *Pregnancy, Birth and Family Planning.*

*From *Family Planning Perspectives* 6, no. 1 (1974):1–2.

CHAPTER ONE

‒‒‒∞‒‒‒

You Were a Long Shot

When babies grow up to be winners of marathons or authors of great books or presidents, they are considered to have done so in part as a result of chance. Yet in none of these happenings does chance play so large a part as in the miracle of birth. The selection of parents is most fortuitous; if your father and mother had not been who they were, you would not be you. Then, too, at the moment of conception any one of four hundred million male cells—spermatozoa—had an equal chance of becoming your particular biological father; only one did. And no two of these four hundred million spermatozoa were exactly alike. Each had a slightly different chromosomal makeup. The chromosomes containing helixes of *deoxyribonucleic acid*—DNA—are those constituents of the body cells that carry the blueprint of the offspring. When the two sets of blueprints—one from the father and one from the mother—are followed, a unique product results. In your case, by one chance in four hundred million, that unique product was you.

REPRODUCTION

The complex, seemingly magical process of fashioning a baby is by now quite well understood. And this process is a far cry from the primordial beginnings of life on this planet. The earliest life was probably a single-celled organism that reproduced by division into two similar organisms. And when those two organisms had grown to adult size, each of them divided into two. There were no special sex cells and no separate sexes.

Some simple animals such as amoebas and paramecia still adhere to this primitive reproduction pattern.

The process of the union of the sex cells, as it occurs in humans and other mammals, did not just happen; it evolved through many steps, some of which we can trace. More primitive forms of life such as simple marine animals like the starfish have a very wasteful form of sexual reproduction. There are two sexes, but the sperm and eggs are discharged haphazardly without any physical awareness or even proximity between the two parents. A more advanced stage in the evolution of the union of the sex cells is illustrated by fish. There is a strong physical awareness between male and female during mating, but absence of physical contact. The male swims above the female and as she discharges her eggs he discharges his sperm. In the frog, which has a still more advanced pattern of mating behavior, there is not only sex awareness, but actual physical contact. The male clasps the back of the female with a specialized clasp organ and as she discharges her eggs, he discharges his sperm upon them. All varieties of external insemination, however, are relatively wasteful and inefficient.

Internal insemination, as practiced by humans, by the other mammals, and by many submammalian forms, is far more efficient. In this pattern of reproduction, a special organ of the male—the penis—is inserted into a special organ of the female—the vagina. In addition to depositing the semen well on the way to the precise area where it is to function, this method of introducing the male ejaculatory organ deep within the body of the female protects the spermatozoa by releasing them in a highly favorable environment. Such conditions as temperature and moisture within the cervical canal, the uterus, and the fallopian tubes of the female reproductive tract are optimal for the conservation of sperm.

The Biological Advantage of Two Sexes

If a single parent cell simply divides into two new cells, and they split into two and all the new individuals also reproduce by division, each of the progeny in this species is an exact or almost exact duplicate of the original parent. If some adverse environmental influence such as drought or extreme cold comes along and the organism is especially susceptible to it, the whole species will be wiped out.

However, if elements from two separate parent cells fuse and this new combination of genetic materials then divides, the progeny is never an exact duplicate of either parent, but has some characteristics of both. When this progeny mates with a similar organism from a set of different parents, still greater variation results. These variations enhance survival and development of a species.

LIBIDO

The ageless, unhurried process of evolution has granted animals immense protection by making vital functions pleasurable. It is pleasant to eat, drink, void, defecate, sleep—and impregnate or be impregnated. This pleasure in sex is termed *libido*. Libido is created by body chemicals known as sex hormones. Reproduction and sexual pleasure are so closely intertwined that the sex cells that unite to form the embryo and the sex hormones that create the appetite for mating in each of the sexual partners are produced in one and the same organ—the ovary of the female and the testis of the male.

Mating among mammals may be restricted to a single annual season, as in deer, bears, and seals; or it may take place in isolated recurrent estrus periods (mating periods), as in cats, dogs, and the domesticated rodent. Still a third type of sexual rhythm is demonstrated by the primates—humans, apes, and monkeys: a willingness to mate at all times without restriction of season or estrus period, though, to be sure, with fluctuations of desire, particularly on the part of the female.

The Nature of Sexuality

Dr. William H. Masters and Ms. Virginia E. Johnson, in their excellent studies of human sexual behavior, underscored the fact that sexual difficulties among human beings are rarely caused by physical disease, but are ordinarily psychological in origin. That is why it is so important that adolescents be introduced to the miracle of sexual reproduction in a sensitive, intelligent fashion. The Masters-Johnson study proves that it is dangerous to create an aura of sin, dirt, and taboo around human sexual activity. Sexuality should be viewed as a beautiful gift which, when used intelligently with freedom, joy, and consideration, greatly enriches all facets of life.

THE SEX CELLS

Eggs

The eggs (*ova*) of all the higher mammals are similar in both size and appearance: round with a clear, thin, shell-like capsule as rigid as stiff jelly. The capsule encloses liquid in which hundreds of fat droplets, proteins, and other materials (including the nucleus) are suspended. The egg, the largest cell of the whole body, is approximately 1/200 of an inch in diameter—about one-fourth the size of the period punctuating the end of this sentence. The eggs of mice, rabbits, gorillas, dogs, pigs, whales, and humans are all about the same size.

Spermatozoa

The spermatozoa of different species can show greater differences in form than the eggs. The human spermatozoon consists of an oval head 1/6000 of an inch in diameter, mostly occupied by the nucleus. With the aid of the additional magnification provided by the electron microscope, it has become evident that the head is covered by a saclike structure. This structure is called the *acrosome* and provides an outer membrane, the acrosomal membrane. The acrosome is attached by a short neck to a cylindrical middle piece that terminates in a thin tail about ten times as long as the head. The tail, which consists of several hairlike fibers resembling a horse's tail, is capable of rapid side-to-side lashing movements. These movements propel the spermatozoon.

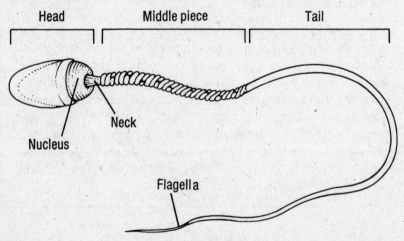

A human spermatozoon enlarged 5,000 times.

A spermatozoon can swim an inch in 4 to 16 minutes, depending on whether it is traversing watery uterine or tubal fluid, or relatively thicker cervical mucus. Easily blocked by the slightest obstruction because of its small size, its path is seldom a straight line, and it frequently takes more than the minimum time to progress an inch.

When ejaculated, spermatozoa are suspended in *seminal plasma*, a thick mucoid fluid produced by the male during sexual orgasm. Semen, which arises from the prostate, the seminal vesicles, and the other accessory reproductive glands, is a homogenous fluid immediately upon ejaculation. Within a few minutes it sets to a gel called *coagulum*. After about 15 to 20 minutes, this gel is fully redissolved into a viscous fluid. In some cases this transformation is not complete; then the semen is very viscous and may have tapiocalike lumps.

> The amount of semen ejaculated depends in part upon the interval between successive ejaculations. In humans the normal quantity varies from one-half to one-and-one-half teaspoons. By comparison, in the stallion, the quantity is ordinarily two ounces—ten to twenty times as much as in the human.
>
> The average human ejaculate contains almost half a billion spermatozoa, a seemingly extravagant number, since only one spermatozoon fertilizes the egg.

A fresh drop of semen seen under a microscope suggests the rush of traffic in a crowded city street. Myriad spermatozoa dash here and there, now steering straight ahead, now halted by a speck of dust, now free again to scurry out of the microscopic field.

FERTILIZATION

The essential step in the initiation of a new life is *fertilization*, the penetration of the ovum by a spermatozoon and the fusion of a portion of the two cells into a new single cell. From this united parent cell originate all the billions of cells that form a new being.

Nucleus

The part of each cell that fuses is called the *nucleus*. On a properly prepared microscopic slide it is the part of the cell that stains dark with aniline dyes. The nucleus is not a solid mass of tissue, as it may appear under low magnification, but is made up of a network of little rods called *chromosomes*.

Chromosomes

There is a specific number of chromosomes characteristic for each species, and every cell in the body of each animal belonging to that particular family contains this number of chromosomes. The famous fruit fly, which has contributed so selflessly to our knowledge of genetics, possesses only four pairs of chromosomes. In humans there are forty-six single chromosomes, but each has a counterpart; thus there are twenty-three different pairs. Before fertilization is accomplished, the chromosome number of each *human parent cell*—sperm and ovum—has been halved from forty-six to twenty-three, one member of each of the twenty-three pairs remaining in the fully mature sex cell. Thus when the two mature human sex cells fuse, each brings twenty-three chromosomes to the process of fertilization, and their union restores the human species' number of forty-six chromosomes. Research has shown that these minute rods are the all-powerful agents in the transmission of hereditary characteristics. To them, each of us owes not only our sex, but our body build, coloring, and, in large measure, our mentality, emotional makeup, and longevity.

Genes

Chromosomes, in turn, are made up of chains of smaller genetic units called *genes*. The total number of genes in our twenty-three chromosomes is estimated at between fifty thousand and one hundred thousand. Since the individual genes are the ultimate determinants of genetic inheritance, the almost infinite variety of combinations explains why all humans differ so markedly, unless they are identical, one-egg twins. One-egg twins have exactly the same chromosomal-gene makeup, since the egg divides after fertilization and from each half an independent embryo develops. Thus a pair of one-egg twin children contain exactly the same chromosomes and genes. For more about twins, see Chapter 23.

~~~

CHAPTER TWO

Becoming Pregnant

The biology of pregnancy as detailed in Chapter 1 certainly seems straightforward: egg and sperm meet, cellular material fuses, genetic composition is determined, and billions of cells grow and divide to create a new member of your family.

Yet the joining of egg and sperm is the result of many fascinating events in your—and your partner's—body. To begin the process of conception, the sperm and the egg each need to be produced. Next, they must find each other. Then, they have to make intimate contact. Finally, the fertilized egg must make its way to the uterus and create a bed for itself in the rich and nourishing uterine lining, which must have been made ready for its arrival.

The Three Stages of Pregnancy

Fertilization is a two-part process that begins when the spermatozoon or sperm cell enters the ovum or egg cell; it is completed when the nuclei of the male and female cells (called *pronuclei*) unite.
Conception is the onset of pregnancy marked by implantation of the fertilized ovum. These two processes lead to pregnancy.
Pregnancy is the condition of having a developing embryo or fetus in the body after successful conception.

To understand the process of pregnancy, it is first helpful to understand the basics of male and female anatomy.

FEMALE ANATOMY AND PHYSIOLOGY

The Structure and Function of Female Sex Organs

The reproductive organs of the female—the vagina, ovaries, fallopian tubes, and uterus—serve six purposes:

- They provide a receptacle for the male semen.
- They produce the ovum (egg cell).
- They serve as a meeting place for sperm and egg.
- They furnish a safe and secure site for the fertilized ovum to develop into a fetus.
- They manufacture chemicals, most notably estrogen and progesterone, essential for carrying out the female's role in reproduction.
- They offer a source of sexual pleasure and satisfaction.

The Vagina

The *vagina* is the body cavity adapted to the reception of the semen. In actuality, the vagina is a *potential* cavity. Unless opened by the penis or by passage of an infant during birth, the front and rear walls are virtually next to each other. In the woman who has not had sexual intercourse with vaginal entry, the entrance to the vagina is generally closed in part by the *hymen*, a skinlike membrane that stretches across the vaginal entrance and contains one or more small openings. Normally the membrane is pierced at the initial sexual intercourse. However, the hymen is a highly variable structure, absent at birth in some female newborns and complete without any opening in others. It can be destroyed through activities other than intercourse, such as bicycle riding. The condition of the hymen cannot be considered as evidence of virginity or not.

The entrance to the vagina is guarded on either side by both a small and a large fold of skin, called the *labia*, or lips of the vagina. Since the inner pair is relatively small and the outer pair large, they are termed *labia minora* and *majora*. At the upper end of the vagina, just above the urethra from which the urine exits, is the *clitoris*. When unerected, it is usually about a half-inch in length, and when erected, almost twice as long. In its unerected state, a hood of skin covers the clitoris. The sole function of the clitoris is to react to sexual stimulation, enhancing the female's pleasure and response.

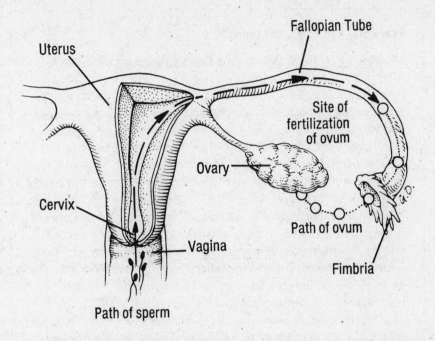

Fallopian Tube

Uterus

Site of
fertilization
of ovum

Ovary

Cervix

Path of ovum

Vagina

Fimbria

Path of sperm

The female internal reproductive organs. A window cut into the wall of the
uterus shows the path taken by sperm through the uterus enroute to the site of
fertilization. The drawing also shows the path of the ovum from the ovary to
where it meets the sperm in the tube.

The Ovaries

The two ovaries, the size and shape of almonds, lie in the lower part of
the abdominal cavity and produce the ova or egg cells. Normally one
ovum matures each month. This process begins just before or soon after
the first menses (*menarche*) and continues until the last (*menopause*), except during the nine months of pregnancy and a period of time thereafter.
Usually only one of the ovaries matures an egg during each monthly cycle
with no discernible plan. Sometimes they alternate; at other times the
same ovary produces the ovum several months in succession. If one ovary
is surgically removed, the remaining one takes over the complete job of
egg production, maturing an ovum each month, usually with no reduction in fertility.

Fraternal and Identical Twins

In perhaps 5 to 10 percent of cycles, two eggs are ovulated, one from each ovary or both from the same one. If both eggs are fertilized and then implant and develop, which occurs in less than 1 percent of cycles, two-egg, or nonidentical or *fraternal* twins result. Since two eggs and two sperms are involved, the twins are no more genetically alike than single-born siblings. One could say that fraternal twinning is not true twinning, since "twin" comes from the Old English "getwin," dividing into two. Fraternal twins are more common among certain populations (seen as frequently as 1 in 25 births in certain groups in Nigeria and as infrequently as 1 in 150 births among Japanese women). In the United States, twin births occur naturally in about 1 in every 73 births among African Americans and 1 in every 93 among Caucasian women. Twins also reflect a family tendency on the mother's side; a female relative of a woman who has fraternal twins has an increased chance of having fraternal twins herself.

True, or *identical*, twinning is an even rarer event, accounting for only about 30 percent of twins. Identical twins are born approximately once in 250 to 300 pregnancies. There appear to be no geographic, racial, or hereditary factors in the occurrence of identical twins. It appears to be an accidental event. Identical twins develop when a single ovum, fertilized by a single sperm, divides into two. The genetic material contained in each twin is thus exactly the same—hence the term identical twins. This division can occur anytime between two days and two weeks after fertilization. If the division occurs later in this time frame, it is likely to be incomplete and cause the twins to be conjoined. (A complete discussion of multiple pregnancy is provided in Chapter 23.)

The ovary, like the male testicle, is an endocrine gland. It manufactures the two female hormones, estrogen and progesterone, in quantities that depend upon the phase of the monthly cycle. It also manufactures androgens, such as testosterone, although in much smaller quantities than are manufactured in the male. Most of these are changed to estrogens. The ovary produces another reproductive hormone, *folliculostatin,* also called inhibin. Inhibin suppresses or inhibits FSH, or follicle-stimulating hormone, produced by the pituitary gland. This is further described on pages 13 to 18.

The Fallopian Tubes

The two *fallopian tubes*, or oviducts, one on either side of the uterus, lead from the abdominal cavity near each ovary to the interior of the uterus. They are each approximately five inches long. They form the pathway for the upward swim of the spermatozoa and the downward journey of the ovum. The *tubal canal*, or channel, is constantly moist with secreted fluid, the amount of which increases significantly at the time of ovulation. The fallopian tube itself resembles a cornucopia. The wide bowl-like ovarian end is fringed with many fingerlike *fimbria* (see the drawing on page 9). During most of the monthly cycle, the fimbria are flaccid and inert. Just preceding ovulation, they become erect and constantly lick the surface of the adjacent ovary like hungry tongues seeking to sweep the surface of the freshly ruptured follicle and lick the egg into the open end of the tube. If by mischance the tiny egg is spilled into the abdominal cavity near the vicinity of the tube, the tube acts like a siphon and attempts to suck the spilled egg into it.

Ectopic Pregnancy

Fertilized ova are able to implant elsewhere in the reproductive tract. These are *ectopic* (Greek: *ektopos* = out of place) pregnancies. They almost all miscarry early but may cause severe internal bleeding. Rarely, an ectopic pregnancy may carry to the age of viability or even to term. This occurs in the extremely rare event that the fertilized ovum implanted in the abdominal cavity—called an *abdominal pregnancy*. The most common site of an ectopic pregnancy is the fallopian tube—called tubal pregnancy.

Ectopic pregnancy occurs in approximately 1 percent of all pregnancies. Among these, more than 95 percent are tubal. Women with ectopic pregnancies often discover they are pregnant and shortly thereafter start to bleed. Others may have what appears to be a late period but is actually bleeding from an ectopic pregnancy. Indeed, in any sexually active woman of reproductive age, ectopic pregnancy should be considered when there is abnormal vaginal bleeding. Severe pain usually accompanies the bleeding and shoulder pain may develop if bleeding is heavy. If you experience any of these symptoms, immediately call your physician or midwife, or go to the emergency room. Diagnosis of ectopic pregnancy is made by examination, laboratory test for pregnancy, and ultrasound. Usual treatment is surgical removal of the pregnancy, and often the tube.

Recently, some types of ectopic pregnancies have been treated without surgery. These cases have been diagnosed early and have not resulted in serious bleeding. A more detailed discussion of ectopic pregnancy appears in Chapter 12.

The Uterus

Finally, there is the pear-sized, pear-shaped two-to-three-ounce muscular uterus, enclosing a slitlike, highly distensible cavity. The lining of the cavity is called the *endometrium*. It is here that the fertilized ovum embeds or implants and the fetus develops. The uterus consists of two parts: the *corpus*, or body, and the cervix. The corpus is the upper section. The top part of the corpus is called the fundus. The fallopian tubes attach to each side of the fundus, allowing the fertilized egg to enter the uterus. The *cervix*—the neck or mouth of the uterus—has a tiny opening, called the *os*. Before a woman has ever given birth, the os looks like a tiny dimple in the middle of the cervix. During birth, the os opens to allow passage of the baby. After a woman has given birth, the os will look more like a slit than a dimple.

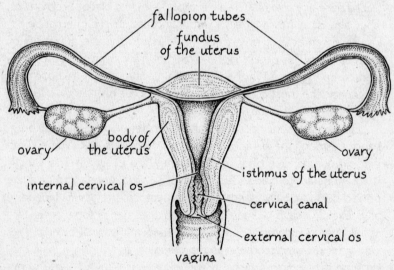

Uterus, cervix, vagina.

During pregnancy the uterus will grow in weight from less than a quarter of a pound to almost three pounds. Its volume will increase from virtually nothing to about five quarts.

THE THREE FEMALE CYCLES

The *cyclic menstrual period* is the most obvious manifestation of the reproductive cycle in women. In fact, the female reproductive cycle consists of three interrelated cycles, working in exquisite concert with each other to create the conditions necessary for fertilization and implantation. We will call these the hormonal cycle, the uterine or endometrial cycle, and the ovarian cycle. The *hormonal cycle* is the secretion, in precise order and with perfect timing, of the chemical messengers or hormones necessary to control the entire female reproductive process. The *uterine* or *endometrial cycle* is the preparation each month of the endometrium, the lining of the uterus (Greek: *endo* = inside; *metra* = uterus) for possible implantation of a fertilized egg. Without a fertilized egg, the endometrium is shed, to build up again in the next cycle. The *ovarian cycle* refers to the monthly development and expulsion of the egg cell from the ovary to the fallopian tube, where it meets the sperm, or, without a fertilization encounter, disintegrates.

The Hormonal Cycle

Hormones are chemical messengers produced by *endocrine* glands (Greek: *endo* = internal; *crine* = secretion). Chemically, they are either steroids (related to lipids or fats) or proteins. These messengers circulate within the body and have specific influences on particular organs, called *target organs*. These organs include the brain and hypothalamus, where mood and emotions are controlled. Thus, reproductive hormones may have an influence on the emotions.

Female Reproductive Hormones

> *Hypothalamic Hormones*
> Gonadotropin Releasing Hormone (GnRH)
>
> *Pituitary Hormones*
> Follicle-stimulating Hormone (FSH)
> Luteinizing Hormone (LH)
> Prolactin
>
> *Ovarian Hormones*
> Estrogen

> Progesterone
> Androgens
> Folliculostatin (Inhibin)

Hormones are manufactured in several locations in the body. The hormones of female reproduction are made in the hypothalamus, the anterior pituitary gland, and the ovary.

The *hypothalamus*, situated at the base of the brain, makes Gonadotropin Releasing Hormone (GnRH), which is transported to the pituitary gland. This hormone stimulates the pituitary to cyclically release several hormones, called *gonadotropins* (Greek: *gonad* = sex organ and *tropin* = acting upon), which then act on the ovary.

The *pituitary* is about the size of a seedless grape and is located in a socket in the skull and attached to the base of the brain by a short stalk. The pituitary secretes three gonadotropins:

• **Follicle-stimulating hormone (FSH)** causes the ripening of the part of the ovary containing the egg—called a *follicle*. FSH also stimulates the secretion of estrogen.
• **Luteinizing hormone (LH)** causes the ripe follicle to rupture, releasing the egg to be caught up by the fallopian tube. This is called *ovulation*. LH then stimulates the ovary to convert the empty follicle into the hormone-secreting structure known as the *corpus luteum* (Latin: *corpus* = body, *luteum* = yellow). It is so named because of its yellowish appearance. The corpus luteum secretes somewhat more estrogen and much progesterone.
• **Prolactin** may have an effect on maturation of the follicle and may also help maintain the corpus luteum. In pregnancy, it stimulates and maintains lactation and breast development. In the nonpregnant woman, it reduces the response of the pituitary to GnRH and of the ovary to FSH and LH. An excess of prolactin can be involved in some instances of infertility (see Chapter 13).

The *ovaries* produce estrogen and progesterone which bring about secondary sexual development and the possibility of reproduction. Throughout the potentially reproductive years, estrogen and progesterone influence changes in the endometrium—the lining of the uterus. Progesterone also plays an important role in the initial maintenance of pregnancy. The ovarian hormones influence the secretion of the pituitary hormones through feedback mechanisms. This means that low or high levels of hormone secreted by one organ influence whether another organ will secrete or not secrete its hormone at a given time.

The Feedback Mechanism and Ovulation

Low levels of estrogen in the early part of your menstrual cycle stimulate the manufacture of the gonadotropins, FSH and LH.

Higher levels of estrogen, in the midportion of the cycle, suppress FSH. FSH stimulates the secretion of inhibin (folliculostatin), and in turn, inhibin suppresses the secretion of FSH.

After ovulation, high levels of progesterone inhibit the secretion of both gonadotropins from the pituitary by inhibiting GnRH secretion in the hypothalamus. If gonadotropins remained high, the ovarian follicles would be subjected to constant stimulation—meaning that ovulation could occur at any time. Instead, the exquisite timing of the feedback mechanisms provides for ovulation only once each cycle.

The graph below shows the differing reproductive hormone levels at each stage of the menstrual cycle.

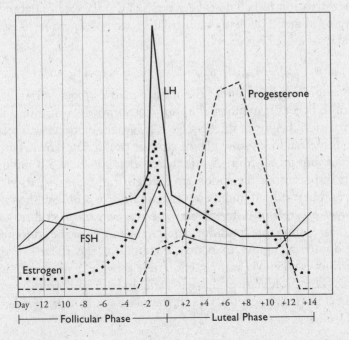

The Uterine or Endometrial Cycle

The cycle of the uterine lining consists of three distinct phases:

- Menstrual
- Proliferative
- Secretory

Each phase is controlled by the hormones discussed in the previous section.

The Menstrual Phase

Because we count the beginning of the reproductive cycle from the first day of menstruation, this phase begins the endometrial cycle. *Menstruation* is the shedding of the lining of the uterus that had been built up during the previous two phases. As the ovarian corpus luteum slows and stops functioning, secretion of estrogen and progesterone decreases. In response to the dropping levels of these hormones, the blood vessels of the endometrium go into spasm, there is oxygen loss to the tissue (*necrosis*), and the lining sloughs off. Menstrual flow consists of blood, mucus, and cells from the lining of the uterus. No other organ in the body sheds and regenerates cyclically for years as does the uterus.

Menstruation usually lasts between 3 and 6 days, although it can be shorter or longer. Following menstruation, the *proliferative* phase of the endometrial cycle begins.

The Proliferative Phase

During this phase, under the influence of estrogen secreted by the ovarian follicle as it matures, the endometrium, which is thin following menstruation, begins to thicken. Cells lengthen, blood vessels reform in the endometrial lining, and glands grow or proliferate. The height of the endometrium grows from .5 millimeter to as much as 5.0 millimeters. This is important as the endometrial height can be measured via sonogram; and beyond 5.0 millimeters may indicate a problem known as *endometrial hyperplasia* (Greek: *yper* = above; *plassein* = to form). If not treated, over time this condition can lead to cancer of the endometrium. An endometrial biopsy in which a sample of the tissues of the endometrium is taken via a tiny suction tube provides a more definitive diagnosis. The proliferative phase is variable in length from woman to woman and from cycle to cycle in the same woman. It may last from 7 to 21 days.

The Secretory Phase

Once ovulation has occurred, progesterone becomes the dominant ovarian hormone as it is the main hormone secreted by the newly created *corpus luteum*—formed from the follicle through which the egg just ruptured. Under the influence of progesterone, the endometrium enters its secretory phase. This phase is consistently 12 to 16 days long. During this phase, the endometrium continues to thicken, blood vessels grow and open, and glands grow and secrete a fluid rich in *glycogen* (sugar). As many as fifteen thousand endometrial glands open onto the endometrial surface during the secretory phase of the cycle. The lining of the endometrium becomes more dense, but growth in height is inhibited.

The Ovarian Cycle and Ovulation

The Follicular Stage

During a girl's fetal life, the ovaries contain hundreds of thousands of eggs, which are scattered around in the connective tissue of the ovary. Most of these eggs disappear prior to birth. As she grows older some of them are surrounded by specialized cells that eventually form a capsule called the *follicle*, much like the shell of a hen's egg. As sexual maturity approaches, the pituitary gland, under the stimulation of GnRH from the hypothalamic part of the brain, begins to secrete follicle-stimulating hormone, FSH.

Under the influence of FSH, some of the follicles now develop a fluid, and those that are near the ovarian surface may bulge through the surface. These are called *graafian follicles*. In an entirely random manner, one or, at most, a few grow far larger than the rest. This growth begins during menstruation, and is called the *follicular* phase of the ovarian cycle. Follicles that do not grow simply shrivel and disappear. The follicular stage of the ovarian cycle, which takes place simultaneously with the menstrual and proliferative phases of the endometrial cycle, is variable in length.

Ovulation

When a certain level of growth is reached, the graafian follicle falls under the influence of another hormone from the pituitary gland—*luteinizing hormone* or LH. At midcycle there is a surge of LH, which follows the peak of estrogen secretion by about 24 hours—see the graph on page 15. LH stimulates further development of the follicle until, within 12 to 36 hours of the LH surge, it bursts through the surface of the ovary and pops the egg with its surrounding mantle of follicle cells into the waiting folds of the fallopian tubes. This is called *ovulation*. From the estrogen peak to actual ovulation is considered the *ovulatory phase* of the ovarian cycle.

Ovulation and Becoming Pregnant

Data gathered on ovulation shows that it most often occurs between 8 and 19 days after the onset of menses, the exact day being influenced by the length of the individual menstrual interval. Whether you have a short menstrual interval (for example, 25 days from the first day of bleeding to the next first day of bleeding) or longer intervals (31 to 35 days), you will ovulate about 12 to 14 days before the onset of your next menstrual period.

When an egg is fertilized, however, there is no next menstrual period, ovulation occurring about 14 days before the woman would have menstruated had she not become pregnant.

Since most women menstruate approximately every 28 days, if one counts the first menstrual day as day one, the usual time of ovulation is day 13 or day 14, which explains the fact that pregnancy is most likely to occur in midcycle, midway between menstrual periods. In very rare instances, however, pregnancy may result from intercourse at virtually any time during the menstrual month—which implies that ovulation in exceptional cycles occurs at exceptional times. There is evidence that female orgasm infrequently may trigger an aberrant ovulation in some women. All experienced clinicians can cite examples of women becoming pregnant at odd periods in the cycle. Anecdotal reports of pregnancies being established during menses and very early and very late in the nonbleeding part of the cycle abound. In truth, such pregnancies are quite rare.

The two times in the month when pregnancy is least likely to occur, the relatively "safe periods" for sexual relations without causing conception, are the first week of the cycle including the menses, and the last week, that is, the week prior to menstruation.

In humans, ovulation is totally independent of sexual intercourse, occurring with equal frequency in the sexually developed virginal woman and the sexually active woman. If fertilization does not occur—obviously its occurrence is relatively infrequent—the tiny unfertilized egg quickly dies and fragments into many pieces, which white blood cells then eat up.

The Luteal Phase

Following ovulation, the follicle walls fall inward and, under the influence of LH, the follicle changes into the corpus luteum. The corpus luteum secretes some estrogen, but more progesterone. This phase of the ovarian cycle is termed the *luteal phase*. The luteal or progesterone-dominant phase of the ovarian cycle corresponds in its timing to the secretory phase of the endometrial cycle. It is relatively constant in length, varying from 12 to 16 days in all women.

When a woman becomes pregnant, the corpus luteum will remain viable for several months, secreting progesterone necessary to maintain the pregnancy. The corpus luteum is maintained by *human chorionic gonadotropin* (hCG). (In medical literature, a lower case "h" is often used to distinguish naturally occurring human hormones from synthetic ones.) Human chorionic gonadotropin is a hormone secreted first by the fertilized egg, starting about 6 days after fertilization, and later by the placenta. The chorion is the layer of the embryo from which the placenta and the outer of the two fetal membranes develop.

When a woman does not become pregnant—which is true for most of her cycles—the corpus luteum will regress, progesterone levels will then drop, and the menstrual flow will begin.

The elegant interplay and miraculous coordination of multiple mechanisms to make reproduction work successfully is a source of ceaseless amazement. Many more eggs are fertilized than babies born. Fertilization, implantation, and early development of the ovum are each so complex that something frequently goes wrong and further growth ceases. If this occurs within the first 10 to 12 days, the menstrual period is not even late. If development of the ovum is arrested, say, around the fifteenth day, the menses are delayed a week or so but no recognizable tissue is passed. However, if pregnancy progresses several weeks before it comes to a halt, a discernible miscarriage occurs. Some experts believe that at least 40 to 50 percent of fertilized eggs never end up as a baby.

MALE ANATOMY AND PHYSIOLOGY

Structure and Function of the Testes

Throughout a man's reproductive life, which sometimes continues after the age of eighty or ninety, *spermatozoa* or sperm cells are constantly being formed by the two testicles (or *testes*) suspended in the *scrotum*, a thin-walled sac of skin. In adult males, the testicles are the size and shape of plums. The scrotum is a highly specialized structure that, because of its external location and its large area of skin surface, constantly maintains the testicles at around 92.6° Fahrenheit, a temperature about six degrees Fahrenheit lower than the interior of the body. The sperm-making cells of the testicle are extremely sensitive to heat and, within 24 hours after being exposed to a temperature as high as that of the body's interior, stop producing spermatozoa.

In warm weather the scrotum is large and flaccid, exposing a large skin area for heat loss through evaporation, while in cold temperature the scrotum is small and contracted to conserve heat. In short, the scrotal pouch is a highly effective air conditioner.

In a boy's early fetal life the testicles are situated high up within the abdomen, and they gradually migrate downward, reaching the scrotum about 8 weeks before birth. Many premature male babies and occasionally boys delivered at full term are born with *undescended testicles*; in most the condition corrects itself within the first few months or years of life. Undescended testicles after the first few years of life generally require a surgical procedure to guide the testicle or testicles into the scrotum and to be sewn in place. The operation is usually successful in preserving potential fertility. The ideal time to perform such an operation is before age 5 or 6. Otherwise, by adolescence, the sperm-producing tissue of the testicle is already so irreparably damaged by chronic exposure to the relatively high intra-abdominal temperature that reposition has uncertain value.

Sperm Production

Spermatogenesis, the creation of sperm cells, is a continuous process beginning in early adolescence and usually not ceasing until death. Each testicle contains hundreds of thousands of little round chambers, lined with cells called *spermatogonia,* from which *spermatids,* the forerunners of spermatozoa, are derived. When the formation of a spermatozoon has been completed, it is delivered into a collection duct that interconnects with larger ducts, through which it finally passes into the *epididymis,* a long, narrow, much-coiled tube lying above each testicle. The canal of the epididymis is continuous with the canal of the *vas deferens*, a tube that runs from the upper scrotum to the abdominal cavity behind the bladder. Here it joins the seminal vesicle duct that empties into the *urethra* of the penis, from which the sperm cells are ejaculated. Millions of sperm cells enter the *vas* daily to be stored there until ejaculation.

At *orgasm*, the muscle cells in the wall of the seminal vesicle go through a series of contractions, expelling its fluid swarming with spermatozoa into the urethra. Other glands, most notably the prostate, also contract during ejaculation, expelling their fluids as well. All these secretions form the *semen*. Because of their tiny size, the hundreds of millions of sperm cells make up a negligible amount of the semen. Therefore, male *sterilization*, tying and severing each *vas* near the testicle to obstruct the upward journey of the sperm cells from the testicle, does not noticeably diminish the volume of ejaculated semen. The seminal vesicles, prostate, and other glands still discharge their fluids during orgasm, precisely as they did before the operation. The volume and quality of the semen is the same whether ejaculated during intercourse or masturbation.

Hormone Production

The second type of testicular cell, the *interstitial* or *Leydig* cell, produces *testosterone*, which is absorbed directly into the bloodstream from the testicle. Carried in the blood, it affects such masculine characteristics as body form, libido, sexual potency, voice register, and body and facial hair. Leydig cells are not sensitive to heat and, unlike spermatogonia, continue to function normally in an intra-abdominal testicle. Therefore, males with undescended testicles are wholly masculine except for the absence of spermatozoa in ejaculated semen. In the *castrated* or *eunuchoid* male, however, the removal of the testicles causes profound modification of masculine characteristics because of the lack of testosterone in the bloodstream.

Structure and Function of the Penis

The *penis* has a conical end, the *glans*, which in the uncircumcised male is partially protected by a thin elastic, retractile skin cover, the foreskin. The *urethra*, the tube from which the urine ordinarily flows and from which semen is ejaculated during orgasm, runs through the center of the shaft of the penis and terminates in a small oval opening at the tip of the glans (the urethral meatus).

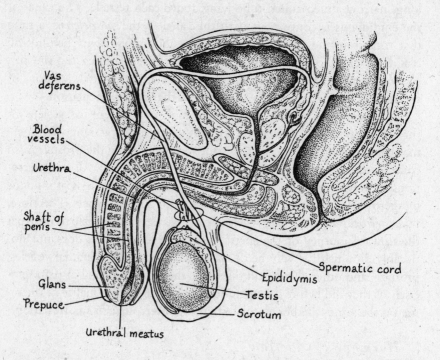

Vas deferens

Blood vessels

Urethra

Shaft of penis

Glans

Prepuce

Urethral meatus

Spermatic cord

Epididymis

Testis

Scrotum

Male Genitals

Erection is accomplished by the rapid and greatly increased flow of blood into the special spongy tissue that forms the penis, and by the temporary imprisonment within it of this increased blood under pressure—which comes about through the closure of exit valves in the veins that return the blood from the penis back into general circulation.

Orgasm consists of a series of muscular contractions involving the whole male tract, which drives out the semen in spurts, after which the valves of the veins open, releasing the imprisoned blood and allowing the penis to soften.

During the process of erection, a temporary valvelike structure forms at the junction of the bladder with the urethra, which prevents urine from being discharged with the semen during ejaculation.

The Male Reproductive Process

The hormones controlling the male reproductive processes are secreted by the hypothalamus, the anterior pituitary, and the testes.

Male Reproductive Hormones
   Hypothalamic Hormones
   Gonadotropin Releasing Hormone (GnRH)

   Pituitary Hormones
   Follicle-stimulating Hormone (FSH)
   Luteinizing Hormone (LH)

   Testicular Hormones
   Androgens
      Testosterone

Control of the reproductive process in men begins, as it does in women, in the hypothalamus. GnRH is produced in both men and women. Similarly, GnRH, in turn, causes production and secretion of LH and FSH by the anterior pituitary gland in men, just as it does in women.

In men, LH and FSH cause sperm production in the testes. This takes place in the *seminiferous tubules*. There are approximately 250 wedge-shaped *lobules* in each testis. Each lobule contains up to three seminiferous tubules.

LH and FSH also stimulate the production and secretion of *androgens* or male hormones, including testosterone. The production of testosterone begins early in the embryo, causing development of the internal and external male reproductive organs. Later in puberty, it causes male secondary sexual characteristics, and also is responsible for further development of male reproductive organs, as well as sexual drive.

THE PROCESS OF FERTILIZATION

The Journey of Spermatozoa Through the Male Ducts

From each testicle the spermatozoa slowly pass upward through the epididymis. The trip through the ducts requires 2 to 4 weeks, the spermatozoa maturing as the journey progresses.

Sperm Motility and Fertility

If the male does not ejaculate for some time, the spermatozoa that complete the journey from the testes are stored in the ducts and epididymis and may suffer effects of aging. The first ejaculation after a long interval, therefore, may produce cells of impaired motility. For this reason, physicians and midwives recommend frequent intercourse— optimally, every 24 hours during the days immediately preceding ovulation—for most couples desirous of pregnancy who are having difficulty in conceiving.

Spermatozoa do not make their own way up the male ducts, since they are motionless at this stage, but are propelled upward by imperceptible contractions of the muscular tissue forming the walls of the epididymis and vas. It is only after the mass of sperm cells is diluted during orgasm by fluid from the prostate and other male glands that they are thrown into vigorous movement. Spermatozoa remain actively motile for as long as 72 hours in the upper reaches of the female reproductive tract.

The Journey of the Egg Down the Tube

After ovulation, the egg, having passed from an ovary into the fallopian tube, travels down the five-inch tube. The muscular walls of the tube encircle a canal that is wide at the ovarian end and narrow at the uterine end. The diameter of the tube at the uterine end is as small as a single broomstraw. Although it would make sense that an egg released from the left ovary would be picked up by the left tube, women who have had one tube and the opposite ovary removed have been known to achieve pregnancy, attesting to the remarkable action of the tubes.

The mechanism that propels the egg downward through the tube toward the uterus seems to be a combination of fluid currents and rhythmic muscular contractions. Many of the cells lining each fallopian tube are *ciliated*: they possess hairlike projections from the surface that beat vigorously. Under the microscope, they look like a field of wheat being blown by the wind. The beating of the cilia causes a fluid current that mostly flows down the tube from the ovarian end toward the uterine end. When the ovum is ovulated from a ripe ovarian follicle, it is surrounded by a thick, loosely adherent covering of some three thousand small cells, the *cumulus cells* that envelop the egg completely during its residence in the follicle. Some of the cells are brushed loose by the egg's contact with the sides of the tube, especially with the ciliated cells of the tubal wall.

The Upward Journey of the Spermatozoa

The midportion of the fallopian tube is the rendezvous point for egg and sperm. Explanations of how spermatozoa ascend from the vagina into the uterus, and from the uterus to the meeting place in the tube, have shifted as knowledge of the subject has increased and clarified. A hundred years ago a spermatozoon was believed to be endowed with instinctive, bloodhound-like qualities which directed it along the proper path to insure fertilization. Today it is known that the fate of the several hundred million spermatozoa depends in part on the phase of the recipient's menstrual cycle.

During the 3 or 4 days before ovulation and the day of ovulation itself, the canal of the *cervix*, the opening into the uterus from the vagina, is filled with a profuse, transparent, watery, stretchy mucus through which the sperm cells swim with ease. The mucus at this time can be stretched between the fingers for several inches, like the white of an egg or a strand of wool as it is stretched out on the spinning wheel. This characteristic is called *spinnbarkeit*. The appearance of this profuse mucus explains why some women notice a colorless vaginal discharge each month for 3 to 5 days in midcycle.

Some women occasionally spot or even bleed lightly for up to 48 hours in midmonth, at the time of ovulation. Many experience pain in occasional cycles for 4 or 5 hours on one side or the other of the lower abdomen, depending on whether the egg that particular month was ovulated from the left or right ovary. This is called *mittelschmerz* (German: *mittel* = mid; *schmerz* = pain). At times of the month other than these several days in midcycle, the cervical canal contains a scant, sticky, opaque mucus, onto which sperm are entrapped, quite like flies on flypaper.

During intercourse, the spermatozoa are catapulted into the upper vagina, near the cervix. The sperm cells swim haphazardly in all directions, some into the upper recesses of the vagina, some toward the outside, others away from the middle of the vagina far to one side or the other. Most spermatozoa never reach the protective confines of the cervical canal, but remain in the vagina, exposed to the acidic environment of vaginal secretions. Sperm cells are sensitive to an acid medium, and those remaining in the vagina become motionless and dead within a few hours. A relative few, by sheer spatial accident, immediately gain the

sanctuary of the alkaline cervical mucus. This was demonstrated by studies in the 1970s in which cooperating couples notified research physicians as soon as male orgasm had been accomplished. The physicians
then took samples of mucus from high up in the cervical canal. Much to
the surprise of the scientific community, the cervical mucus was already
swarming with sperm cells. Some sperm reach the site of fertilization in
the fallopian tube within 5 minutes of ejaculation; the majority, within
4 to 6 hours.

Some of the sperm swim straight up the one-inch canal with almost
purposeful success, while others bog down on the way, getting hope-
lessly stranded in tissue bays and coves. A small proportion of the total
number ejaculated eventually reach the cavity of the uterus and begin
their upward two-inch excursion through its length. This progress is
aided by muscular contractions of the uterus. The undaunted sperm reach
the openings of the two fallopian tubes—one on each side of the uterus.
From there, they continue their upward journey into one of the tubes.

If the egg has reached the midportion of a tube, a spermatozoon
swimming up the opposite tube has no chance of meeting it. Only a few
thousand of the four hundred million cells ejaculated ever reach the
trysting site, the midsegment of the fallopian tube containing the egg,
two or three inches above where the uterus meets the tube. Only a few
hundred sperm ever come near the egg cell.

The one sperm that achieves its destiny has won against gigantic
odds, several hundred million to one. The baby it engenders has a far
greater mathematical chance of becoming president than the sperm had
of fathering a baby. No one knows just what selective forces are responsible for the victory. Perhaps the winner had the strongest constitution;
perhaps it was the swiftest swimmer of all the contestants entered in the
race. Perhaps it was merely the luckiest in finding a fluid current leading
straight to the ovum.

The method by which the tiny sperm cells locate the egg is not
clearly understood. Because of the few spermatozoa, just several thousand, in the relatively long tube at the time of fertilization, many investigators feel some process other than random encounter is involved.
One suggested explanation is that the egg exerts a *chemical trapping effect*, increasing sperm concentration by making them swim more rapidly
when they are headed toward it and less rapidly when going away from
it. When sperm-egg collision occurs, the sperm immediately becomes
bound to the egg's surface.

If ovulation occurred within several minutes to 24 hours before the
sperm's journey ends, the ovum will be in the tube, awaiting fertiliza-

tion. If ovulation took place more than 24 hours before the sperm's arrival, the egg cell will have begun to deteriorate and fragment by the time the spermatozoon reaches it. If ovulation has not yet occurred, but takes place within 2 or 3 days after intercourse, living spermatozoa will be cruising at the tubal site waiting for the egg.

We have followed the sperm and egg to their meeting place, and we can now observe what happens when they meet—that is, the actual process of *fertilization*.

Capacitation

Before fertilization can be accomplished, the sperm must undergo the process of *capacitation*—the process by which sperm become transformed and thus able to enter the egg cell. Freshly ejaculated spermatozoa are incapable of causing fertilization. Capacitation is accomplished by exposure of the sperm to secretions of the uterus, the fallopian tube, or the ovary's graafian follicle. Capacitation requires as little as 2 hours in the hamster and as long as 11 hours in the rabbit. It requires about 7 hours in the human being.

Use of an electron microscope, which permits magnification from ten thousand to more than one hundred thousand times, has shown that each sperm head is surrounded by two membranes, a *plasma membrane* closely applied to it and a loose, veil-like outer membrane, called the *acrosomal membrane*. As far as can be observed, a capacitated sperm appears the same as a sperm before capacitation. However, several hours' exposure to fluids of the female reproductive tract enables it to undergo the acrosomal reaction, which ruptures the outer membrane surrounding the sperm head and releases enzymes beneath the membrane. These enzymes dissolve cumulus cells, cutting a path through the *corona radiata*—the halo surrounding the egg's surface. Next, the enzymes must carve out a pathway through the *zona pellucida*—the egg's covering.

The egg capsule, the zona pellucida, is relatively firm and rigid: its thickness is approximately one-tenth the diameter of the egg. Precisely how a spermatozoon gets through the capsule is not completely known. One effect of capacitation is to increase the speed of the sperm. This may be important in allowing it to move through the zona. Once a sperm passes through the zona pellucida, the zona undergoes a reaction called the *zona reaction*. This makes it impervious to other sperm.

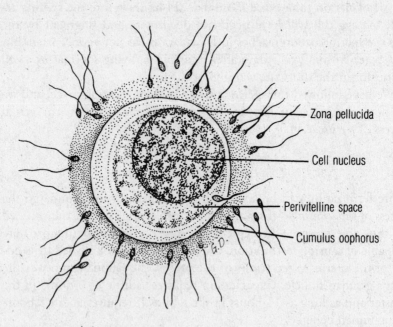

- Zona pellucida
- Cell nucleus
- Perivitelline space
- Cumulus oophorus

A human ovum at the moment a sperm has penetrated the zona pellucida. The egg is about ³⁄₁₀₀₀th of an inch in diameter, one hundred times the size of the head of a spermatozoon.

Only a single sperm—one that has undergone the acrosomal reaction—makes its way through the *perivitelline membrane*, just beneath the zona pellucida, to pair the twenty-three chromosomes of its nucleus with the twenty-three chromosomes of the nucleus of the egg.

Fusion of the Two Nuclei

Once the sperm has entered the cytoplasm of the ovum, its head enlarges to form what is called a *pronucleus*—the nucleus of the mature sperm cell. The ovum also completes its final maturation after entry of the sperm, also forming a pronucleus. Both the male and female pronuclei enlarge and migrate toward the center of the cell. The membranes of each pronucleus disintegrate, and the two nuclei fuse into one nucleus. When this has been accomplished, fertilization is completed. The fertilized ovum now has forty-six chromosomes—twenty-three from the father and twenty-three from the mother. It has become a *zygote* (Greek: "yoked together").

Cleavage—or rapid cell division—ensues within 30 hours of fertilization. The fertilized ovum divides into two cells; the two cells divide into four, the four into eight, and so on, creating—after an average of 266 days from the moment of fertilization or 280 days from the beginning of the last menstrual period—a fully developed baby, weighing from 5½ to over 10 pounds.

The Enigma of When the Fetus First Becomes a Living Being

Legalizing elective abortion has had the consequence of reviving discussions on when life begins. In many cultures and in a number of religions, life is not considered to begin until either the mother becomes aware of independent fetal movement or at some other time when ensoulment is assumed to have taken place. Others who have thought about this consider that human life begins with the union of the sperm and egg and the reestablishment of the normal number of chromosomes and therefore the potential of a unique human being. For still others this is not the beginning of life, since a free-floating structure such as a fertilized egg must accomplish implantation in the wall of the mother's uterus before developing the true potential of independent existence. Another large group of people believes that life commences only at the point when the fetus is able to maintain an independent existence. At present, with the best available perinatal care, this is around the twenty-fourth week of pregnancy. About 50 percent of fetuses of this developmental age today survive to adulthood. Many other people believe that the fetus achieves life only when it is actually born and has left its mother's body.

Our own conviction is that the only scientific resolution to all this is that life is a continuum; that the sperm and the unfertilized egg are living structures like any cells, and that, although their union creates a potentially unique individual, it does not create life. Unfortunately, we doubt that the social and political issues that are related to this discussion will be resolved on a scientific basis.

THE EARLY HOURS OF THE FERTILIZED EGG

In the mouse the two-cell egg appears 24 hours after fertilization, and the four-cell stage after 38 to 50 hours. In the human a two-cell stage has been observed within 30 hours after fertilization and sixty-four-cell development in 72 hours. By the fifth day the human embryo is made up of about five hundred cells, the cells having doubled their number about every 12 hours since the time of fertilization.

In all mammals, the developing egg in its earliest phase, while still a traveler down the fallopian tube, is a solid mass of cells, aptly termed a *morula* (Latin: *morum* = mulberry, which it resembles). It is still round and has increased little if at all in diameter, its contents merely having divided into smaller units.

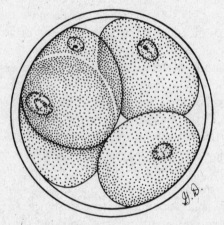

A four-cell human embryo, ready for transfer to the uterus in the course of in vitro fertilization.

The egg passes from the tube into the uterus on day 4 or 5, when it is no longer a solid mass of cells, the cells having arranged themselves about the outer surface of the sphere, the center now occupied by fluid. It is termed a *blastocyst* (Greek: sprouting bladder). By the fifth day the multicellular conceptus begins to increase in size. It floats about the slit-like uterine cavity for about 3 more days and then adheres to its inner cell lining, which has been prepared by the special hormone progesterone, fed by the ovary into the bloodstream from which it reaches the uterus. Progesterone has made the lining succulent and full with a network of new and enlarged blood channels coursing through it. The developing egg, possessing an enzyme that digests away the surface cells to which it has adhered, then sinks down into the rich depths of the uterine lining. The process is something like hoeing the firm, dry earth above to plant corn in the soft, moist, nourishing earth beneath. Implantation occurs around the eighth day. By the twelfth day the human egg is already firmly implanted, but the damaged, superficial uterine lining cells through which it passed have only partially healed to roof over the tissue nest in which the egg now rests. About 6 out of 10 pregnancies implant on the *posterior*, or rear, wall of the uterine cavity, and 4 in 10 on the anterior, or front, wall. Either site is normal.

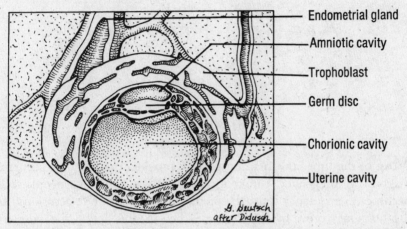

Endometrial gland

Amniotic cavity

Trophoblast

Germ disc

Chorionic cavity

Uterine cavity

G. Deutsch
after Didusch

A cross section of a 12-day-old human embryo and the site in the uterine lining in which it has implanted. The tubular structures are maternal blood vessels, two of which have opened into that portion of the embryo destined to become the placenta, inside which the fluid-containing membranes are taking shape. In the very midst of all this is the germ disc, the part of the embryo which will become the fetus. The actual measurement of the structures shown in this illustration is about 1/64 of an inch across.

When studied under a microscope, the 12-day egg already shows a specialized accumulation of cells which later will form the embryo. The remaining cells become the placenta and membranes. At about the time of implantation, the fertilized egg secretes the pregnancy hormone hCG. This keeps the corpus luteum from regressing. The progesterone secreted by the corpus luteum is necessary for the maintenance of pregnancy. Again, this reminds us of the wondrous interactive rhythms that are required to create new life.

The process of becoming pregnant is now completed, yet the mother-to-be has not even had time to miss her first menstrual period, and will not experience other symptoms suggestive of pregnancy for several days.

CHAPTER THREE

_____

Are You Pregnant?

Most of the time, a woman or her care provider can make an accurate diagnosis of pregnancy. Unlike many conditions for which people seek health care, pregnancy is usually prediagnosed. Yet on rare occasions, its diagnosis may prove more puzzling. When there is doubt, the woman's _symptoms_—certain bodily changes assessed by a physician or midwife—and specific laboratory tests provide the information to make a definitive diagnosis.

EARLY PREGNANCY SYMPTOMS

There are three broad categories of signs of pregnancy:

- **Presumptive signs** are those changes that the woman herself experiences, such as a missed period. It could be argued that some of these signs, like feeling the first movements of the fetus, are definitive signs, but because they are being reported by the pregnant woman as feelings she is having rather than being confirmed by medical/scientific evidence, doctors do not consider them definite indicators of pregnancy.
- **Probable signs** include changes in the mother's body that can be documented on physical examination, such as growth of the uterus.
- **Definitive signs** are changes that are directly due to the presence of a fetus, such as a fetal heart rate and ultrasound demonstration of a pregnancy.

Presumptive Signs

Absence of Menses

A missed menstrual period (*amenorrhea*) is usually the earliest evidence of pregnancy. A missed period in a woman between ages 15 and 45 with previously regular cycles suggests pregnancy as the most likely possibility. It is not a definitive sign, however, since there are many other causes for a delayed or even a skipped period.

Periods may be quite irregular toward the beginning and the end of the menstrual years, confusing the issue of whether or not a woman is pregnant. Recent childbirth, especially when a woman is nursing, may eliminate menses temporarily or lengthen the interval between periods. Illnesses, including untreated diabetes, thyroid gland disturbances, substance abuse, and high fever from infection may create menstrual irregularities. Severe malnutrition may lead to an absence of menstruation. Amenorrhea may occur in women who have lost weight rapidly on a very strict diet.

Ballet dancers and athletes, particularly those who train intensely for long-distance running, often stop menstruating. Psychological stress may also be responsible for the temporary disappearance of menses. Among the stresses might be adjustment to living in a new country or a change of occupation. Emotional upsets such as the death of a loved one can precipitate amenorrhea. Missed periods are not uncommon among young women who leave home for college.

False Pregnancy

A common cause of amenorrhea is the sudden fear that an unwanted pregnancy has occurred, and, at the other end of the spectrum, the conviction by a woman, perhaps with a history of infertility, that she has achieved pregnancy. This is called *pseudocyesis*, or false pregnancy. This condition can mimic pregnancy sufficiently to mislead not only family but physicians and midwives. The woman with a false pregnancy may present any and all the symptoms of a true pregnancy. She may feel nauseated; her breasts may be tender; she may gain weight and even think she feels the baby move. A *pregnancy test*, which detects the presence in urine or blood of human chorionic gonadotropin (hCG), the hormone produced by the placenta, may even be positive due to certain rare tumors. The diagnosis of false pregnancy depends on physical and pelvic examination and repeated negative hCG tests and sonographic examinations.

Pseudocyesis can be the result of, or lead to, serious psychological problems. Psychiatric consultation often is needed, particularly at the time the diagnosis is made.

To confuse the issue further, you may be pregnant and still appear to menstruate during the early months. On close observation, such menstrual periods are different. Ordinarily they are shorter and scantier. A woman may menstruate 3 days instead of 5 at the normal time her period is due. A month later she menstruates half a day, the following month for an hour, and then her periods cease entirely for the remainder of pregnancy. Women may develop menstrual-like cramps at the time of the first missed period without any bleeding. They fully expect to menstruate each hour, but do not. The discomfort lasts for up to 3 or 4 days, then stops.

Breast Changes

Many women experience breast changes premenstrually. These changes include fullness and tenderness. These symptoms subside rapidly just before or with the onset of menstruation. When pregnancy occurs, the feelings of fullness and tenderness continue instead of disappearing, and become even more marked. In the very first weeks after conception, you may feel a tingling in your breasts, and they may become extra tender, with hypersensitive nipples. If you haven't realized that your period is late, you may dismiss these feelings as premenstrual symptoms, but the tenderness usually is more intense than it is premenstrually. In fact, you may feel breast tenderness even before a missed period. In a second or later pregnancy, you will often recognize this intense sensitivity as an early sign of pregnancy.

Breast sensations in pregnancy usually are of short duration; the breasts remain large, but the feelings of tenseness and tenderness gradually disappear by the end of the third or fourth month of pregnancy. In preparation for lactation the mammary glands continue to increase in size during the remainder of pregnancy, the enlargement due in part to growth of the milk-secreting glandular tissue and in part to a greatly enriched blood supply. The latter is often manifested in the second half of pregnancy by the appearance of a delicate tracery of blue veins beneath the skin on the chest, especially noticeable in women with very fair skin.

The nipple and the colored circle of skin surrounding it—the *areola*—enlarge and their pigmentation darkens. Arranged in a circular fashion around the periphery of the areola, near the skin edge, are a number of small, roundish elevations, or *oil glands*—in the inimitable words of William Fetherstone H. Montgomery, who first described them, "a constellation of miniature nipples scattered over a milky way." These glands, called Montgomery's glands or tubercles, become more prominent in pregnancy. In some women breast enlargement is accompanied by the formation of stretch marks in the skin, or *striae*. Since they appear more extensively over the abdomen, they will be discussed later in this chapter under "Abdominal Changes."

Nipple Secretion

After the first few months a sticky, yellowish, watery fluid—*colostrum*—may be expressed from the nipple by gently squeezing the breast. This finding is not absolute evidence of pregnancy, however. Women who have borne and nursed children may retain colostrum in the breasts for years. In the later months of pregnancy drops of colostrum may flow from the nipples spontaneously. As term is approached, the colostrum takes on an opaque, whitish appearance, more resembling milk.

Nausea and Vomiting

With today's early pregnancy testing, most women already know they are pregnant by the time they feel nauseated or vomit. However, nausea and vomiting in pregnancy are so common that they are considered reliable presumptive signs. These symptoms most frequently occur from 5 to 12 weeks after the last menstrual period, although you may feel nausea as early as 2 to 3 weeks after your last period. For some women this is the first clue that they are pregnant.

Nausea occurs in 50 to almost 90 percent of pregnant women and is often, though not always, accompanied by vomiting. In popular speech these symptoms have been cheerfully termed *morning sickness*, since the most usual time to experience nausea or to vomit is when you first awaken. Unfortunately, this term is not accurate since the symptoms can occur at any time of day.

Certain foods and odors, even familiar ones, can cause nausea and vomiting. Some pregnant women have difficulty cooking specific foods. Some women have the fortunate problem of becoming nauseated by the smell of smoke and so stop smoking early in pregnancy.

A variety of reasons for nausea and vomiting have been proposed, but no one really knows why they occur. In the past, they were said to be *psychosomatic*, indicating perhaps ambivalence toward, or even aversion to, pregnancy, intercourse, or the baby's father. In some studies, a *placebo* (or pretend pill) alleviated symptoms, which could be construed as supporting a psychological cause for their occurrence. Other studies, however, found women *without* nausea and vomiting to be more prone to psychological difficulties during pregnancy and after birth. Another possible reason for nausea and vomiting is *hormonal changes*, a theory supported by the fact that women on birth control pills, which contain the hormones of pregnancy (estrogen and progesterone), also frequently experience these symptoms.

The woman who vomits during the early months of pregnancy may notice that what she vomits is flecked or streaked with blood. This generally is not a cause for concern, as repeated vomiting may rupture a tiny blood vessel in the throat or esophagus. Such a small vessel clots quickly and heals spontaneously. You should notify your physician or midwife if you notice more than a minute amount of blood in the vomit or if it occurs more than once.

Many instances are recorded of particularly suggestible husbands who vomit with their pregnant wives; there are even cases in which the husband vomited though his wife did not.

In general, nausea and vomiting subside by 10 to 12 weeks of pregnancy, but may persist. If severe or prolonged, the vomiting may be a pregnancy complication called *hyperemesis gravidarum*, discussed in Chapter 12.

Remedies for nausea and vomiting are discussed in Chapter 11.

Ptyalism, or excessive salivation—up to three or four quarts a day—sometimes occurs with pregnancy. This symptom is likely to appear 2 or 3 weeks after the first missed period, persist throughout pregnancy, and disappear promptly after delivery. It is a most disturbing symptom. See Chapter 11 for some suggested remedies.

Changes in Appetite

Newly pregnant women may notice a temporary decrease in appetite, and ordinary amounts of food may lead to fullness and bloatedness. Women often naturally find themselves ignoring scheduled mealtimes and instead eat frequent small meals—an excellent way to eat during pregnancy. It's not harmful to the fetus to reduce your food intake in the first trimester, although you should take multivitamins that contain folic acid. If you experience nausea, however, try to avoid going for long periods of time without food. If your stomach is empty, you are more likely to become nauseated—and even to vomit—when you do eat. Of course, eating frequently to avoid nausea may mean that you may gain more than the few pounds usually gained in the first few months of pregnancy. Chapter 10 details healthful eating during pregnancy.

Some pregnant women develop a craving for one particular food almost to the exclusion of anything else. Earlier obstetrical texts gave more space and emphasis to what they termed *pica*, or cravings for unusual foods or nonfood substances, than newer texts. But the condition remains a relatively common one. Unquestionably diets are more diversified and better balanced today, and the opportunity to obtain milk, fruits, and vegetables at all seasons of the year is greater. Nonetheless, some women still describe such cravings during pregnancy.

Geophagia and Amylophagia

One remarkable present-day form of pica consists of eating dirt or clay (*geophagia*) or related thick materials like moistened laundry starch (*amylophagia*). The taste for these specific substances may be at least in part related to dietary shortages, especially a deficiency of iron and trace elements, although whether this is the cause of pica remains unclear. Certainly, pica can result in nutritional deficiencies and women with pica are generally quite anemic. Another explanation is that pica relieves nausea and vomiting. Women have also reported that eating these substances relieves hunger pains.

Geophagia and amylophagia are most frequently observed among African-American women from rural areas, although they may occur among women of all races and from all geographic areas. They are associated with a family history of pica and with pica occurring in childhood—in other words, pica may have a social component. Past generations of women may have believed that these substances helped with delivery, and passed on these beliefs. Overcoming nutritional deficiencies with good eating habits, prenatal vitamins, and iron supplementation may correct pica, but will not automatically do so as the practice usually is an ingrained habit. Pregnant women are often motivated, however, to stop or reduce habits that are not healthful. Pica is one such habit.

Fatigue and Sleepiness

In many women one of the early symptoms of pregnancy is an un-usual degree of sleepiness. The reason for this is unknown. The fatigue generally disappears after the end of the first 3 months, or trimester, of pregnancy, usually to recur near term.

Frequent Urination

Sometimes frequency of urination begins as early as the first day of a missed period. This is caused by pressure on the urinary bladder from the growing uterus. Urinary frequency disappears about the twelfth week, as the uterus grows out of the pelvis, relieving the bladder pressure. It often recurs a few weeks before delivery, when the baby's head drops into the pelvis, again creating bladder pressure.

Abdominal Changes

As pregnancy progresses, a woman is likely to become conscious of the gradual filling of her lower abdomen. At first she might notice that she is "losing" her waistline. Next, when her bladder is full, she may be able to feel a small, soft mass, just above the pubic bone (the bone felt behind the pubic hair). The bladder is simply pushing the pregnant uterus up to where it can be felt through the relaxed abdominal wall. The uterus gradually grows upward during the pregnancy, by 12 weeks reach-ing to where it can be felt above the pubic bone without a full bladder. It grows to the level of the navel or umbilicus at about 20 weeks.

Most pregnant women begin to "show" at some time between 14 and 20 weeks, although this varies greatly from woman to woman. Some women look obviously pregnant at week 14 while wearing ordinary street clothes, and others wear tight blue jeans through the sixth month and barely look pregnant at all to the casual observer.

As the size of the uterus increases, *stretch marks* or striae may appear. This common term is something of a misnomer. The marks are only partly due to the mechanical stress of the growing uterus on the skin and connective tissue of the abdominal wall. They also result from the hormonal influences of pregnancy, and in fact appear in areas where there is no actual physical stretching. Above the navel they tend to look something like the upper half of a circle; around the navel they form a circular pattern, and in the lower abdomen they characteristically form lines slanting downward and inward. The marks are very slightly de-pressed below the level of the normal skin, making the skin look frayed.

Stretch marks may appear no matter how little weight a woman gains. Some women may have an inherited tendency toward developing them. They tend to increase as the pregnancy progresses, and have a red or brownish color from the growth of tiny blood vessels. (Their color may depend on skin tone.) After delivery they gradually fade as the blood vessels become less prominent. They become shiny and pearl white, and narrower than they were during pregnancy, but they do not entirely vanish.

In some women, the navel begins to protrude during the latter months of pregnancy. Although completely normal, this may be embarrassing to some women in certain clothing. Covering the navel with a Band-Aid is usually comfortable and will prevent it from being seen as a protrusion beneath almost all clothing.

The end of the sternum or breastbone, called the *xiphoid*, is attached by a hinged joint. Under ordinary circumstances, this bone cannot be felt, but in late pregnancy it may loosen up and rotate outward so that a bump can be felt in the V-shaped space between the lower margin of the ribs. This is quite normal.

The long muscles of the abdominal wall—the *rectus abdominis*—which run from the rib cage down to the pubic bone are stretched by the growing uterus. As a result, in the later part of pregnancy, they separate in the midline of the abdomen. When the abdomen is filled with the pregnant uterus, this is not particularly noticeable, but as soon as the baby is delivered, separation of the rectus muscles—the *diastasis recti*—may be quite obvious. Sometimes you can see or feel a vertical indentation in the middle of the abdomen, usually starting at or below the navel and going to the breastbone (*sternum*). If you can't see this clearly, you can lie down and contract your abdominal muscles by lifting your chin. This will exaggerate the diastasis and you can more easily see or feel it. You can reduce the degree of separation with exercises for the stomach muscles (for example, bent-leg sit-ups) but the muscles may never completely close. This usually is not a problem, but if the diastasis remains large, in subsequent pregnancies there may be less support for the growing uterus and sometimes extra discomfort as pregnancy progresses.

Quickening

Somewhere between 16 and 22 weeks, the mother is first able to feel the movements of the fetus. Fetal movements are felt more readily when the placenta is attached to the rear wall of the uterus. A woman having her first baby will probably notice the movements about 2 weeks farther along than she will in later pregnancies, when she may recognize them as early as the sixteenth week. Tell your midwife or physician when you first definitely feel the fetus move because this can help to time the pregnancy.

The subjective sensation of these first movements has been likened poetically to the faint flutter of a caged bird's wing and, more prosaically, to the bursting of a bubble of thick syrup.

At the onset the movement is so gentle, particularly since the baby is floating in an amount of water greater than its size, that the woman may not be certain what she has felt. Only after these light taps against her uterine wall have been repeated several times can she be certain that this is fetal movement. Of course, later in pregnancy, the movements of the arms and legs, the stretching of the trunk, and the movement of the baby's head become very much more powerful, to the point where anyone is able to feel them by placing a hand on the mother's abdominal wall. Often, fetal movements can be seen beneath the skin. Sometimes the movements are so active that women become convinced that they are carrying twins or triplets.

Once women perceive fetal movements they come to expect to feel them every day, but at the beginning, several days may pass when they are not felt at all. In later pregnancy, certainly by week 24, fetal movements are felt daily. Fetuses in general tend to be more active late in the day, after supper and stretching into bedtime, to the point where they may sometimes make it difficult for the woman to fall asleep.

Ultrasound examinations have confirmed that at quiet times the fetus is in fact asleep. In general, fetal cycles of sleeping and awakening tend to run on about a 90-minute schedule. In the third trimester, starting about week 26 of pregnancy, if a fetus goes more than 24 hours without activity, call your care provider immediately, since lack of movement may be a warning signal of fetal distress. A marked decrease in the number of fetal movements is also a reason to notify your physician or midwife.

Probable Signs

Pregnancy Tests

Today, pregnancy can be determined by both blood and urine testing—early and with great accuracy. However, since pregnancy tests are not quite 100 percent accurate, a positive result (one indicating a pregnancy) is considered as only a probable sign of pregnancy, not a definitive one.

Pregnancy tests are based on the presence of human chorionic gonadotropin (*hCG*). This hormone, made by the blastocyst as early as the fourth day of its existence, and later by the developing placenta, is sent into the mother's bloodstream and excreted in her urine. It can thus be detected in either blood or urine. Today's methods can detect hCG in minute amounts.

The most commonly used pregnancy tests today for both in-office and at-home pregnancy testing actually test for an antibody that is specific to a particular part of hCG, called the *beta subunit*. These tests are approximately 99 percent accurate and can detect pregnancy as early as the first day of the missed menstrual period. The test directions must be followed very carefully and if a test is negative, it should be repeated in a week if menses hasn't yet occurred.

A physical examination of a pregnant woman reveals that virtually every organ and tissue of the body is affected to some degree by the physiologic changes of pregnancy. These changes result, directly or indirectly, from the action of the chemicals produced by the *placenta*—the afterbirth. (Placenta is from the Latin, meaning "flat cake.") The placenta's primary function is to deliver oxygen and food essentials from the mother's bloodstream to the baby and to excrete the baby's waste products, but it is also an amazingly efficient chemical factory.

Since the most striking pregnancy changes occur in the reproductive organs, an examination of these organs will be used to confirm pregnancy.

Special Circumstances and hCG Titers

There are several circumstances in which a *quantitative hCG test*, which shows the actual amount of hCG in the blood, is useful. The amount of hCG detected is called a titer. In *ectopic pregnancy*—an abnormal condition in which implantation occurs outside the uterus— the normal rise in hCG titer is not observed; low values are seen instead. This usually corroborates the mother's impression that she may be pregnant but that it doesn't feel right. With a positive pregnancy test in the woman at risk for ectopic pregnancy (such as somebody who has had a previous ectopic pregnancy or somebody who has had a serious pelvic infection), the physician or midwife must find out where the pregnancy is located. As was mentioned earlier, ultrasonography can identify very early pregnancies. The combination of an hCG titer and ultrasound has greatly accelerated our detection of ectopic pregnancies.

The hCG hormone is also formed in the presence of a few rare tumors of the ovary, and its values in blood can be useful in following the treatment of women with these problems. Human chorionic

gonadotropin is also positive in the presence of tumors of the placenta such as *hydatidiform mole* (Greek: *ydatis* = drop of water;
Latin: *forma* = form). If the uterus is abnormally large and there are
other signs of hydatidiform mole (see Chapter 12), a quantitive
hCG and sonogram are warranted.

Examination of the Breasts

Your physician or midwife will ask if your breasts are fuller and/or
more sensitive. He or she will inspect them to see if the nipple and the
areola appear darkened. Since the breasts do change in pregnancy, early
signs of breast cancer may be inadvertently disregarded. It is important
on this first examination, therefore, to palpate carefully for lumps and
other abnormalities.

Flat or Inverted Nipples

Some women have flat nipples and may wonder if they will be able
to nurse their baby. If you are concerned, ask your midwife or physician to check to see if the nipples become erect or everted when
squeezed. If they do, then nursing will not be a problem. Even if the
nipple is inverted, and does not become everted, you can be reassured that most times, by the time the pregnancy is over, the nipples
will be erectable. Even if your nipples remain flat or inverted, the
baby can usually pull them out by sucking. Some people recommend using *breast shields*, also called breast shells or breast cups, to
help evert flat nipples. These are plastic dome-shaped cups placed
inside your bra. They can be worn in the third trimester of pregnancy
and during the first few weeks of breast-feeding. There is no research
available to demonstrate whether or not they are effective. Discuss
with your physician or midwife whether he/she thinks the shells will
help you. You also can check with a lactation consultant. They are not
to be worn when you are lying down. You will probably need a
larger-sized bra to accommodate the shells comfortably. Most times,
the baby does just fine at bringing the nipple out.

You may notice, particularly in later pregnancies, a leakage of colostrum from the nipple. The examiner can confirm this by gently palpat-

ing the glands around the nipple. Women who have previously nursed, particularly if they have done so recently, may have small amounts of milk in the breasts even in the absence of pregnancy.

Abdominal Examination

An abdominal examination begins with palpation of the upper abdomen. The liver and spleen are found under the ribs on the right and left sides respectively. When you take a deep breath and your diaphragm drops, the liver may be pushed down to the examiner's hand, but the spleen cannot be felt unless it is enlarged. The lowermost part of a normal kidney can be felt occasionally deep in the abdomen of a slender woman during a deep breath. The other organs, such as the stomach and the small and large intestine, cannot be felt unless they contain masses. In the second half of pregnancy, the uterus can be felt above the navel and obscures palpation of these other organs.

The examiner next checks for ruptures (*hernias*) at the navel and in the groin. If you have had a previous pregnancy, the muscles of your abdominal wall may still be separated and this should be called to your attention so you can do exercises to strengthen them.

The lower abdomen is examined next. From week 13 onward, it contains the rising uterus. The uterus at first is a small, vaguely definable midline swelling, globular and somewhat soft. It can usually be distinguished from masses such as uterine fibroids and ovarian cysts, both of which feel quite different to the experienced examiner's hand.

At about the twentieth week the uterus has risen to the level of the umbilicus. One month later it may become possible to feel the fetus within the uterus, as though feeling a doll through several thicknesses of blanket. The larger the doll the easier it is to be certain of its outline; the thinner the blanket the more clear the identification of the doll's various parts. The first portion of the fetus that can be felt with any certainty is the head. By week 28 it may be possible to make out the arms and legs and to locate the buttocks, which feel softer and less roundly shaped than the head. Past week 32 an examiner can outline the fetus with considerable certainty in slender women and even more easily in women having later pregnancies, since their uterine muscles, and often abdominal muscles, are more relaxed than they were the first time around.

The Pelvic Examination

This is the examination of the external and internal genitalia. You should empty your bladder before it is carried out, as a full bladder can be mistaken for a pregnant uterus. A full bladder will also make the examination more uncomfortable and confuse the accurate measurement of the uterus.

You will be asked to lie on your back, with your buttocks on the edge of the examining table, your heels in footrests, and your knees relaxed and wide apart. Many women feel very exposed and vulnerable in this position and have trouble relaxing. Most women are more comfortable with their head and back propped up. In this upright position, you can be actively involved in the examination. With the help of a small hand-held mirror you can observe everything the physician or midwife is doing. You hold the mirror with one hand against your inner thigh, angled toward your vagina and a bit off to the side so as not to get in the way of the light that the examiner uses. A magnifying mirror might make it easier to see. You will be able to see the urethra, the anus, and the opening of the vagina as well as the vaginal walls and cervix after the speculum is placed (see page 45). You may be able to see the bluish tone to the cervix that is associated with pregnancy. To allow for better visualization, and also because drapes tend to be a barrier preventing eye contact between patient and examiner, some providers prefer to use minimal or no drapes during a pelvic examination.

If you like the idea of this style of pelvic examination, and those providing your care do not customarily employ it, there is no reason you cannot request it. You can consider taking your own mirror with you to the examination and ask that the head of the examining table be raised. Ask the physician or midwife to show you what he or she is observing and palpating.

The principal changes in the vagina during pregnancy are threefold:

1. **Increased blood supply.** Pelvic circulatory changes appear early in pregnancy, usually before the second missed period. These changes cause the tissues around the entrance of the vagina and within it to take on a purplish, dusky color instead of the nonpregnant pink. The color change is called *Chadwick's sign.* The color deepens as pregnancy advances, and is likely to be more striking in those who have already borne children.

2. **Softening of the tissues.** As pregnancy advances, the vagina becomes increasingly elastic and distensible because of the softening of the tissues that form its walls.

3. **Extra secretions.** The increase in vaginal secretions that usually occurs with pregnancy is largely due to an increase in activity of the mucus-secreting glands of the cervix.

A pelvic examination begins with inspection—looking at the tissues for their normalcy. The entire vaginal area is inspected, including the vulva, the vaginal lips, the clitoral area, the area between the vaginal entrance and the anus (the *perineum*), and the anal area. The examiner uses one hand to separate the labia to observe the urethral opening and to see if there are unusual secretions from the glands (*Skene's glands*) surrounding the urethra. The examiner will palpate or gently squeeze the lower part of both sides of the vagina to see if there is any tenderness or swelling in the area of the Bartholin's glands. You may be asked to cough or bear down to check whether you have a weakness in either the upper (anterior) or lower (posterior) vaginal wall. Some examiners may then insert two fingers slightly into the vaginal opening and ask you to squeeze your vaginal muscles around their fingers. This tests the strength of your vaginal muscles, important for pushing in labor and for preventing problems later in life such as loss of urine with coughing or laughing and prolapse of the uterus, a condition in which the uterus descends into the vagina. If these muscles are weak, your care provider will suggest Kegel exercises to improve muscle tone (see Chapter 9).

Following observation of the external genitalia, the examiner inspects the inner vagina and cervix. This is done by opening the vaginal walls with an instrument called a *speculum*. The examiner may press against the vaginal walls to help insert the speculum, which hopefully is warmed and slightly lubricated with warm water. The speculum may be made of sterilized steel or disposable plastic. The plastic speculum may feel warmer, but often makes a clicking sound when removed which might be somewhat startling.

Once the cervix is visualized, the examiner can take material for a Pap smear. Using either a small cotton-tipped applicator (similar to a Q-tip with a longer handle) or a small plastic brush, the examiner will gather cells from the opening of the cervix. These are rotated in the cervical opening or *os* (Latin: *os* = mouth). A small wooden spatula, looking like a narrow tongue blade, is often used to gather cells from the outside of the cervix. Newer brushes take cells from both the inner and outer cervix simultaneously, so the spatula may not be needed. These cells are placed on a slide or in a small jar to be sent to a laboratory for analysis. You may have some slight spotting right after this examination, especially if the brush is used. This is perfectly normal and should not be a cause for concern, unless the bleeding continues or is very heavy.

Cervical sampling usually is painless, although some women report sensitivity when the applicator touches the cervix. The whole thing takes less than a minute. After the Pap smear, cultures are taken for *sexually transmitted diseases*—gonorrhea and chlamydia. The technique is similar: an applicator is inserted gently into the cervix, rotated, removed, and placed into a special solution to be sent to the laboratory. This takes about another 30 seconds.

In the laboratory the Pap smear specimen is studied under the microscope by a *cytologist* (Greek: *kytos* = cell). The cytologist can detect cancerous cells, precancerous cells, and cells that may not be pre-cancerous but are unusual. The specimen can also show some types of infections. The laboratory's report may not be ready until several days or even a few weeks after the smear is obtained.

After the Pap smear and cultures are taken, the speculum is removed and the bimanual examination is performed. Two fingers are inserted into the vagina to feel the internal organs and the other hand placed on the abdomen just above the pubic bone. The cervix can be felt as a slightly firm structure protruding into the upper vagina and attached to the uterus, which is more or less enlarged and softened depending on the duration of the pregnancy. The examining fingers feel the uterus, getting an idea of its size, shape, and consistency. The tissues to either side of the uterus are palpated to identify the ovaries, if possible, and any abnormal structures, such as ovarian cysts or fibroids that are coming off the side of the uterus.

One very important part of the pelvic assessment in pregnancy, especially if the first visit is in the first trimester (3 months), is to compare size of the uterus to the expected size based on the woman's last menstrual period. In very early pregnancy, the body of the uterus remains firm while the midportion between the body and the cervix softens. This is called *Hegar's sign* and is suggestive of pregnancy. Still later on, the body of the uterus softens and becomes increasingly spherical and, in the presence of a single fetus, enlarges in an entirely predictable manner. By the eighth week of pregnancy the bulk of the uterus is approximately doubled and by the twelfth week it is tripled.

If the uterus is smaller than expected, the pregnancy may be growing abnormally or the dates may be off. An unexpectedly large uterus may indicate fibroids or a multiple pregnancy, or just that the dates are off in the opposite direction. In either of these cases, correct diagnosis is established by watchful waiting or by sonography, depending on when in the pregnancy the examination is done and how many weeks off the exam is from projected dates. A discrepancy of 2 weeks between the expected date by last menstrual period and the size of the uterus is perfectly within the realm of normal.

At the time of the first pregnancy pelvic examination, the examiner often makes an estimation of the adequacy of the bones of the pelvis for the passage of a normal-sized infant. Nowadays contraction of the bony pelvis sufficient to obstruct birth is an exceedingly rare event, unless the fetus is extraordinarily large. Congenital abnormalities of the pelvis are rare, and the marked deformities due to rickets and malnutrition seen four or five generations ago rarely exist today. Many practitioners, however, like to know whether the pelvis is on the smaller or larger side of normal. They can also assess its specific shape.

Pelvic Shape and Predictions for Labor

There are four pelvic types:

- **gynecoid,** or normal female, which is round inside;
- **android,** or normal male, which is a narrow oval and may indicate that there will be a problem;
- **anthropoid,** elongated from front to back but generally normal; and
- **platypelloid,** elongated from side to side but also generally adequate in size.

While any of these pelvic shapes, except android, is a variation of normal for women, your specific pelvic shape may influence the position of the baby during labor and help explain a labor that is proceeding slowly, but normally. For example, a woman with an anthropoid pelvis (seen more commonly among African and African-American women) may be more likely to have a fetus who faces forward, causing the back of his or her head to press on the mother's back. This can result in so-called back labor and possibly a longer time for dilation (or opening of the cervix) to occur.

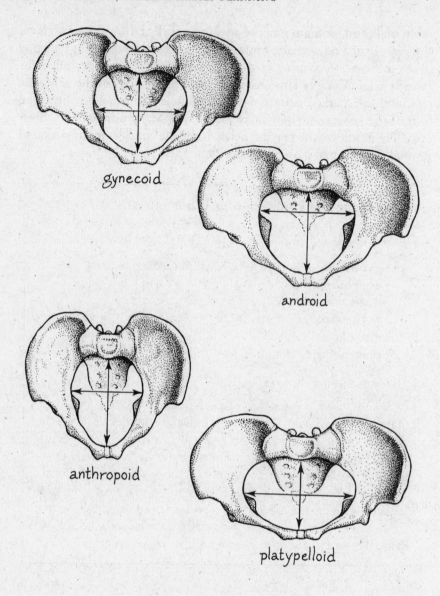

gynecoid

android

anthropoid

platypelloid

Positive, or Definite, Signs

The changes in the vagina, cervix, and uterus found on pelvic examination are considered only probable evidence of pregnancy, since other conditions also can cause the same changes. The earliest conclusive proof of pregnancy is the demonstration by sonography of a live embryo. It can ordinarily be visualized at the seventh week of pregnancy, surrounded by the gestational sac and the uterus.

By the ninth or tenth week of pregnancy the fetal heart can be heard with an ultrasound detector. Sound waves encounter tissues and bounce back in an echo phenomenon, and moving tissues will change the pitch of the sound. This is known as the *Doppler effect*. Ultrasound waves at two million cycles per second—the frequency that is used—cannot be heard by the unaided human ear, but changes in the pitch of their echoes from a moving object can be converted electronically and made audible. This means the beating heart of the fetus can be "heard."

If you are heavy, or the fetus is in a particular position, it may be difficult to pick up the heart tones at this early stage of pregnancy. Generally, if your uterus is growing normally and you have not experienced any problems such as cramping or bleeding, this is no cause for concern. Some physicians and midwives do not even attempt to locate the fetal heart tones this early in pregnancy, waiting instead until around 16 weeks to hear with a Doppler or even until 20 weeks to hear with a special stethoscope called a *fetoscope*. The heartbeat can be heard with an ordinary stethoscope or specially designed fetoscope at about 20 weeks, although again, if the uterus is growing normally and the woman is heavyset or the fetus is lying in certain positions, there is no cause for concern if this is not possible for 2 or more weeks beyond the twentieth week of pregnancy.

Fetal Movement

At about 20 weeks of pregnancy, the movement of the fetus can be felt, not only by the mother, but by an outside observer using a hand on the mother's abdomen. The mother's perception of movement is called *quickening* and is considered a presumptive sign of pregnancy. By the time an outside observer can feel fetal movement it can be considered a definite sign.

Fetal Ultrasound

Today, ultrasound performed through the vagina (transvaginal ultrasound) can detect a *gestational sac*—the earliest positive evidence of pregnancy—in the uterus at about 10 days after implantation. This is just about the time of the first missed menstrual period. Using ultrasound performed with the instrument placed on the abdomen, a pregnancy may be confirmed by 4 to 5 weeks after your last menstrual period—about 2 to 3 weeks after fertilization. These are definitive signs of pregnancy.

CHAPTER FOUR

—∞∞∞—

Duration of Pregnancy

CALCULATING DELIVERY DATES

Just about all pregnant women want to know when their baby is due to be born. Once given a "due date," this often seems to get writ in stone. The reality is that this date is only an estimate. It should be considered as the midpoint of a month-long possibility of due dates.

Physicians and midwives can be very impressive in figuring out due dates. If you tell one of us that the first day of your last mentrual period (LMP) was March 18, for example, we can tell you, almost instantly, "Your baby is most likely to be born on Christmas Day." In fact, we have several methods we use to determine the due date and once you know them, you, too, can figure out your own or someone else's expected date of childbirth.

Calculating Your Due Date

For consistency among women we consider the number of weeks of pregnancy as the weeks that have elapsed since the first day of the last normal menstrual period. Since most months are longer than 4 weeks, the estimations by weeks and months do not correspond in a simple way. The most common length of pregnancy is 280 days after the start of the last period. This is 40 weeks, or 9 months and 1 week. Counting from the day of fertilization, the duration of pregnancy averages 266 days, or 38 weeks, or 1 week less than 9 months.

Naegele's Rule: Add 7 days to the first day of the last normal menstrual period and count back 3 months. Using March 18 as an

---

example: 18 + 7 = 25, then count back—February, January, December. Your expected due date is December 25. This formula is actually a shortcut for counting 280 days from any fixed date.

Wheel Calculators: Some practitioners use pregnancy "wheels" to figure out the expected date of delivery. These are pocket-sized, low-tech devices that are designed to calculate when a baby is due, also based on the first day of a woman's last menstrual period. The wheels can also pinpoint exactly how many weeks pregnant a woman is at any given date. Wheels are slightly more accurate than Naegele's rule because they take into account the varying number of days in each month. These wheels also track *fetal development* (usually length and weight) for each week of pregnancy. You can ask your doctor or midwife to give you one if you want to keep track.

We must stress, however, that the 280 days is the *average* length of pregnancy. A vast number of pregnancies end before day 280, a vast number after it, and relatively few on the exact day. At best the calculated or expected date of birth is an approximate date. The pregnant couple as well as relatives and other interested persons ought to remember this. It is all too common for panic to become general when "D" day arrives, then passes, and yet there is no sign of labor. Telephones soon begin ringing, and on each occasion the expectant mother is greeted by a well-meaning friend or relative with the query, "Hasn't the baby come yet?" For many women, the days past the due date are the most trying of the entire pregnancy. If you and your loved ones could heed this warning these days might not be quite so difficult.

A Word on Terminology

Medical textbooks call the due date the *Expected Date of Confinement*, and it is usually abbreviated EDC. This terminology stems from the era when newly delivered mothers were kept in the hospital for days, even a week, after birth, and were truly confined. Today's new mothers are up and about shortly after birth, and may deliver at home or in a birth center from which they go home after as few as 6 hours. Even women delivering in hospitals leave after 1 or 2 days. Women who have had cesarean births return home after 3 to 5 days. So, the term confinement no longer applies. Many of today's practitioners call the EDC the *Expected Date of Childbirth*, or have rewritten the acronym as EDD—*Expected Date of Delivery*, or *Expected Due Date*.

Pregnancy weeks, or *gestational age*, always refer to completed weeks of gestation. So you are considered 4 weeks pregnant until you have finished your fifth week.

Calculating the Delivery Date from a Known Day of Insemination

By calculating the expected date of childbirth from 425 cases in which a purported single sexual act led to a pregnancy, an old study found that the average woman delivered 269.9 days after intercourse. However, there was wide variation, from 231 to 329 days.

A second study, involving fifteen cases of artificial insemination, yielded an average duration of pregnancy of 272 days from the day of the insemination, with a span of 261 to 288 days. Obviously, calculating the anticipated delivery date from data on sexual intercourse and presumed fertilization has little or no advantage over the more standard technique of utilizing the first day of the last menstruation.

Calculating the Delivery Date from Ultrasound

For women who are sure of the start of their LMPs and whose periods are fairly regular, ultrasound adds little to the estimation of the age of the fetus (*gestational age*) or the expected date of delivery. There are, however, instances in which an ultrasound is useful in determining the age of the fetus and predicting a delivery date:

- When a woman doesn't know the date of her last menstrual period
- When her last menstrual period was the bleeding that occurred when she completed her last pack of birth control pills
- When the size of her uterus doesn't match the size expected for her last menstrual period
- When a woman is late in registering for prenatal care
- When a woman has very irregular periods

When an ultrasound is used to calculate the delivery date, it does so by determining the number of weeks of gestation of the fetus at the time of the test. With current technology an ultrasound that is done through the vagina, using a narrow instrument called a *transducer*, can identify a gestational sac at approximately 3 to 4 weeks of gestation. The size of the sac can be used as a good estimate of the age of what is then the embryo. The embryo itself can be identified at approximately 6 weeks gestation through transvaginal sonography and at 7 weeks by placing the transducer on the abdomen.

Starting at about 7 weeks, an ultrasonographer can measure the crown-rump length (or the *sitting height*) of the embryo or *fetus* (after the eighth week, the embryo becomes a fetus). This measurement is considered highly accurate in judging gestational age as there is little variability in development at this time. The error is plus or minus 3 or 4 days (meaning the actual age can be 3 or 4 days older or younger than reported).

From age 10 to 26 weeks, the crown-rump length (CRL) can also be used as a determinant of fetal age, but becomes less accurate. Starting at about 12 weeks, the *biparietal diameter* (BPD) of the fetal head provides a more accurate assessment of fetal age. The biparietal diameter is the widest part of the fetal head—the *parietal bones* are the large bones on the left and right sides of the skull. After 26 weeks, the length of the *femur* or thigh bone is generally used to assess gestational age. Often, a variety of measurements are taken to be certain that the baby is growing symmetrically. Many ultrasonographers estimate gestational age by averaging a number of these measurements.

From 12 to about 18 weeks, the error of ultrasound is just over a week on either side—the fetus's real age could be one week earlier or one week later than reported by ultrasound. From about 18 weeks to about 24 weeks, the error is closer to 2 weeks on either side of the date given—similar to the error of using LMP or fundal height measurements to estimate gestational age. From about 24 to 30 weeks of pregnancy, errors in measurement using the BPD can be more than 2 weeks (plus or minus) while measurement using femur length varies by just about 2 weeks. From 30 weeks to 36 weeks, the error using femur length approaches 2½ weeks (plus or minus) and after 36 weeks, the error is more than 3 weeks. This increase in error is due to increased variation in individual fetuses as they get closer to full term.

In summary, the most accurate time to use ultrasound to determine gestational age and delivery date is either between 7 and 10 weeks of pregnancy or 12 and 18 weeks. After 36 weeks, this measurement has little value. Chapters 8 and 17 provide more information on ultrasonography and its other uses in pregnancy.

Calculating the Delivery Date from Uterine Size

The uterine size can be assessed accurately—with an error of about 2 weeks on either side—by an experienced examiner before 36 weeks of pregnancy. In the first 12 weeks of gestation (counting as always from the first day of the LMP), the uterus can only be felt through a pelvic examination. Before 6 weeks gestation, it is not enlarged. At 6 weeks, it is perhaps a bit enlarged, or what the examiner might call "upper limit normal" size. At this time, the softening of the lower segment may be felt.

Many practitioners compare the size of the uterus in early pregnancy to the size of fruits—knowing, of course, that fruits vary greatly and that uterine size may vary as well. The uterine size for a woman having a second or third (or more) baby may be larger than that of the woman having a first baby. Keeping in mind that these are estimates at best, a uterus at about 6 weeks from LMP is about the size of a lemon. At about 8 weeks past the LMP, the uterus is less oval in shape, becomes more round and assumes the approximate size of an orange. At 10 weeks past the LMP, the uterus is grapefruit-sized and at 12 weeks is about the size of an average cantaloupe.

After 12 weeks, the uterus can be felt through the abdominal wall, just above the *pubic symphysis* (the bone felt behind the pubic hair). At 16 weeks, the uterus is usually midway between the pubic bone and the mother's navel or umbilicus. At 18 weeks it is about a *fingerbreadth* (the width of a finger) below the umbilicus. It reaches the umbilicus at 20 weeks. After 20 weeks, examiners usually measure the uterus in centimeters, often using a tape measure. (There are 2.2 centimeters in one inch.) Conveniently, between 20 and 36 weeks, the measurement in centimeters from the pubic bone to the top of the uterus (the *fundus*) equals the number of weeks gestation—give or take 2 centimeters. At 36 weeks, the uterus reaches the *xiphoid*—the bottom of the sternum. After 36 weeks, the uterus may actually move down in the abdomen and measure fewer centimeters as the baby's head moves down.

From 36 weeks to the end of pregnancy, uterine size is not considered an accurate measure of gestational age. In any case, with ultrasound available, practitioners rarely rely on uterine measurements alone when determining gestational age.

Calculating the Delivery Date from the First Fetal Movements

Another method of computing the due date is to count 18 or 20 weeks from the time you first feel fetal movements or *quickening*. This method is even less exact than the calculations from LMP, uterine size, or the date of fertilization because of a variety of factors that may influence your perception of fetal movement, including your weight or whether this is a first pregnancy. The date of quickening, however, can be added to other data and used to help support or dispute the calculated due date.

What Are the Chances of Delivering on Time?

After considering all available modern scientific data, we come to the conclusion that the generalization first made decades ago about the duration of pregnancy is relatively correct. If the date is calculated from the onset of last menses, almost 50 percent will deliver within the week before or after day 280, and 75 percent within 2 weeks of it. In a study of over 17,000 pregnancies carried beyond week 27, 54 percent delivered before 280 days, 4 percent on day 280, and 42 percent later. Forty-six percent had their babies either the week before or the week after the calculated date, and 74 percent within a 2-week period before or after the anticipated day of birth.

Another reliable study found that 40 percent of women go into labor within a 10-day period—5 days before and 5 days after the calculated date—and nearly two-thirds within plus or minus 10 days of the expected time.

Factors Affecting the Delivery Date

Several factors may influence when within the 280-day average you may deliver:

• **Menstrual cycle:** If you have a consistent, regular menstrual cycle, you are more likely to have a baby on day 280 than the woman who menstruates irregularly. A short menstrual interval, such as 25 days, counting from the first day of bleeding in one cycle to the first day of bleeding in the next, is frequently associated with delivery a few days early. A lengthy menstrual interval often corresponds to a delivery later than the calculated due date. If your periods are not 28 days apart, calculate your estimated due date by increasing or decreasing one day for each day your cycle exceeds or falls short of 28 days.

• **Boy vs. girl:** In a study of almost 15,000 first births of a single infant in Aberdeen, Scotland, 24 percent of women with a male infant delivered during the thirty-ninth week and 28 percent in the fortieth week (total 52 percent). Twenty-three percent of mothers in a first labor who gave birth to daughters bore them during week 39 and 30 percent in week 40 (total 53 percent). This slight difference in delivery dates between boys and girls is not statistically significant.

• **Birth weight:** A study of over 20,000 pregnancies at the University of Chicago showed that women giving birth to babies weighing over ten pounds averaged 288 days to delivery instead of 280 days.

• **Multiple births:** The average woman who carries twins delivers them about 4 weeks early—on day 252 instead of day 280. Triplet and quadruplet pregnancies are usually briefer than this, triplets commonly arriving about 7 weeks early and quadruplets up to 12 weeks before term. In 1997, the McCaughey septuplets were born in Iowa at 31 weeks and the Thompson sextuplets were born in Washington, D.C., at 29 weeks and 6 days.

• **Other factors:** Neither maternal age, race, size, nor the previous number of children seems to influence the length of pregnancy.

Prolonged Pregnancy

A small percentage of pregnancies will continue beyond 42 weeks (294 days after the last menstrual period). There have been cases in which pregnancy extended to 336 and 337 days, and one in which the duration was 343 days (49 weeks). Estimates vary that from 2 percent to more than 10 percent of all pregnancies will not have delivered by 42 weeks gestation. This statistic reflects some errors in dating pregnancies rather than pregnancies that actually exceed 42 weeks. For example, if a woman doesn't exactly remember her last menstrual period, or when the timing between a woman's periods is longer than 28 days, and this isn't accounted for when initially deciding the due date, her calculated delivery date may be off by several weeks. To prevent a miscalculation of pregnancy dates, all women should:

1. Keep track of the first day of every menstrual period so you always know your last one should you become pregnant.
2. Have a preconception care visit several months before planning a pregnancy (see Chapter 6).
3. Seek early prenatal care as soon as you believe you are pregnant.

The Effect of Prolonged Pregnancy on the Fetus

When a pregnancy is genuinely prolonged beyond 42 weeks, there is a chance that the welfare of the fetus may be jeopardized. Prolonged pregnancy may result in a condition known as *placental deficiency* or *uteroplacental insufficiency*—in which the placenta ceases to function well enough to supply the fetus with needed oxygen. Many such fetuses tolerate the stress of labor poorly. They often have diminished amniotic fluid, decreasing the cushion they need to withstand contractions. They are prone to pass meconium (the thick green material that fills the fetal large intestine) into the amniotic fluid, making a dense mixture. They tend to gasp in response to the stress of uterine contractions and thus to breathe in the meconium. Meconium is very irritating to the lung tissue and breathing it in can result in respiratory difficulty after birth.

Some babies born after 42 weeks gestation develop "postmaturity syndrome." These babies lose some of the fat under their skin so they appear thin. Their fingernails are characteristically long. They often lose the protective creamy coating on the skin called *vernix caseosa*, as well as the fine hair covering the newborn's body, called *lanugo*. This makes their skin dry, peeling, and unusually wrinkled. They are born with an especially alert look.

When pregnancy is prolonged, with the possibility of postmaturity, a number of tests are utilized to check the baby's well-being. These tests are fully described in Chapter 17. When midwives or family physicians have been the primary providers for the pregnancy, an obstetrician should be consulted after 42 weeks. If there is any question about whether the baby is in danger, labor usually will be induced. Induced labor is discussed in Chapter 22.

Cesarean delivery is not a treatment for a postdates pregnancy unless fetal assessment has given evidence of serious fetal distress, indicating that induction will be dangerous to the fetus, or when a planned induction does not succeed.

Legal Problems Associated with Duration of Pregnancy

In the past, before testing for paternity was possible, knowing the duration of pregnancy had an important legal aspect beyond its medical implications. It was used to resolve matters such as inheritance and child support. The laws and the court decisions on these issues have never been consistent over time or region. Some countries, for example, recognize a married couple as the legal parents for any baby born after the marriage of the couple. Elsewhere the child is considered the "legitimate" offspring of a married couple only if the baby is born 8 months or more after the date of the marriage. Babies born as long as 355 days after the supposed fertile contact have been declared the legal offspring of a married mother and father. And in one celebrated case, according to testimony, the date of the last coitus between the couple preceded birth by 360 days. This particular decision was overthrown, on appeal by the husband, as being biologically unreasonable.

Of course, while the courts may make rulings regarding "legitimacy," many people are questioning the entire concept. Illegitimacy is a stigma that should no longer be attached to any human being. As single women or homosexual couples or lesbian couples, for instance, opt to have babies through artificial insemination, with surrogate mothers, or through intercourse with a willing male who is not their husband, the issue of legitimacy becomes almost moot. Social mores often change more rapidly than legal precedents, and changing family types is truly a modern-day—and in many cases highly acceptable—phenomenon.

Laboratory Tests for Paternity

Obviously, the duration of pregnancy doesn't give sufficient evidence regarding paternity. When a dispute arises regarding who the baby's father is, genetic testing on blood or tissue may be used. A minute amount of the infant's blood, obtainable from a heel or finger stick, is sufficient for today's highly sophisticated and specialized tests.

A child's blood and tissue types are inherited following strict rules of genetics. A child's genetic makeup comes, in part, from *each* parent. If the child has a type, whether red cell or tissue, not present in a presumed parent, that person is biologically excluded. A high likelihood of parenthood can be demonstrated by the matching of many types; however, it takes only *one* mismatch to exclude parenthood.

Until the very recent past, it was possible by blood or tissue typing to prove only that the presumed father (or mother) *could not be* the actual biologic parent. With currently available testing, a parent can now be excluded with greater than 99 percent accuracy. However, in the past decade, the science of genetics has advanced to the extent that the likelihood of a shared type of DNA "fingerprint," or DNA sequence, is so small that demonstrating such a shared DNA fingerprint virtually proves parenthood. Using this particular DNA testing, paternity can be proven with greater than 99.9 percent accuracy.

CHAPTER FIVE

∞∞∞

The Fetus

A REASSURING WORD

Much of this chapter is devoted to problems encountered by the fetus from drugs, the environment, and various types of infections, and a pregnant woman could be justifiably quite nervous after reading it. We want to emphasize that we include this information so that all pregnancies may be as safe as possible, all newborns as healthy as possible, and that all expectant parents have as much information as possible. We do not want to imply that there is a large chance of any fetus encountering difficulty. The vast majority of pregnant women are healthy and the vast majority of fetuses grow without problems.

THE FERTILIZED CELL

At the moment of fertilization, the precursor of the child is of microscopic size, two cells so very tiny they are invisible to the naked eye, a mass so light that its weight cannot be expressed in even thousandths of an ounce. Within nine months this minute dot of tissue develops into a twenty-inch, seven-and-a-half-pound crying infant.

The initial 10 days in the life of your future baby are described in detail in Chapter 2. As reported there:

• The ovum implants itself into the substance of the uterus, excavating the home that it will occupy for more than 8 months by digesting its way into the interior lining of the uterus.

• In the process it taps very, very small maternal blood vessels and soon finds itself surrounded by a veritable lake of its mother's blood, into which it dips vigorous, hungry cells.
• These cells, called *villi*, grow like streamers from the surface of what is called the *blastocyst* at this stage of development. The villi absorb minerals, vitamins, carbohydrates, proteins, and fats essential to growth.
• With nourishment, the fertilized ovum increases rapidly in size.
• A specialized mass of cells soon appears; this mass is called the *inner cell mass* or *embryonic area*, and it is from these cells that the embryo itself develops.

SUMMARY OF DEVELOPMENT FOR EACH PERIOD OF PREGNANCY

Physicians and midwives calculate the weeks or months of pregnancy by counting from the first day of the last menstrual period. As fertilization generally takes place midcycle, or about the fourteenth day after a period begins, the actual age of the embryo or fetus is 2 weeks behind the calculated duration of pregnancy. To prevent confusion, we shall discuss embryonic and fetal development in terms of duration of pregnancy, not in actual fetal age. This is called *gestational age*.

End of the Second Week of Calculated Pregnancy
Fertilization occurs. The fertilized ovum is now called a *zygote*. By the third day following fertilization, the cells of the zygote have divided and formed daughter cells. This process is called *cleavage*. The zygote is now called a *morula* and is a round, solid, mulberrylike mass of cells.

End of the Third Week: First Week After Fertilization
The morula travels down the fallopian tube; on the seventeenth day it enters the uterus. The morula then transforms into a *blastocyst*, an outside layer of hundreds of cells with fluid in the center, like a tiny rubber ball filled with liquid. The blastocyst is about $\frac{1}{100}$ of an inch in diameter and floats in the uterus for about a week.

Beginning of the Fourth Week
Implantation of the blastocyst into the uterine wall begins about 7 days after fertilization. Implantation can take up to a week. The blastocyst is still barely visible to the naked eye. After implantation, it be-

gins to grow rapidly, doubling its size every 24 hours. Cells forming the embryonic area (from which the embryo will grow) appear on the inner wall of the blastocyst (the inner cell mass). The placenta begins to form on the part of the outer wall of the blastocyst deepest within the maternal tissues—the *trophoblast* (Greek: *trophe* = nutrition).

Beginning of the Fifth Week
This is when the pregnant woman might expect a period—but it doesn't come. The part of the blastocyst that burrows into the uterus also produces a hormone—human chorionic gonadotropin (hCG)—that passes into the maternal blood and is secreted by her urine. Enough hCG is now present in the mother's system that a pregnancy test of blood or urine will be positive. Sometimes, a woman will have bleeding around this time from the site of implantation. The bleeding is usually lighter than a normal period, but will often make her think she is not pregnant.

The growing being is now called an *embryo*. The sac containing the embryo is ⅖ of an inch in diameter, and already contains some fluid in addition to three layers of cells, called *germ layers*: the ectoderm, mesoderm, and endoderm. These cells give rise to all the tissues and organs of the embryo. Rapid embryonic development occurs at this time. The primitive streak that will become the spine is laid down.

End of the Fifth Week
The backbone is forming and five to eight vertebrae are present. The foundation for the child's brain, spinal cord, and entire nervous system are established. When this first appears, at about 18 days of fetal life, it is called the *neural plate*. By this time, the neural plate has converted into a neural tube. Shortly afterward, the ends of the tube close. Congenital anomalies of the brain or spinal cord in which the tube doesn't close or closes incompletely are called *neural tube defects*, and can occur as early as this stage of pregnancy—when a woman still may not even realize she is pregnant.

The cardiovascular system is now developing. Blood vessels begin to form and blood cells are made. The heart, shaped like a tube, begins to beat on about the thirty-fifth day following the last menstrual period.

Rudiments of the eyes develop 20 days after fertilization. The embryo is under one-quarter inch long.

The Sixth Week
The sixth week is one of rapid growth. All major structures develop during the sixth to tenth weeks of gestation.

By the end of the sixth gestational week, the entire backbone is laid down and the spinal canal closed over. The brain is increasing conspicuously. The beginnings of arms and legs can be seen; these are called upper and lower *limb buds*. The embryo now has a visible tail. Depressions form beneath the skin where the eyes and ears are to appear. The length is now one-quarter inch or slightly larger. Germ cells, to become either ovaries or testes, have appeared.

The Seventh Week

The chest and abdomen are now formed. The head is growing rapidly compared to other body structures. The eyes are clearly perceptible through closed lids. The face is flattening, with shell-like external ears. The mouth opens. Lung buds appear. The tail has almost disappeared. The body may begin to move slightly. The great bulge of brain predicts that this creature is destined to feel, think, and strive beyond the capacity of all other animals on earth. The embryo is now approximately ½ to ⅝ of an inch and weighs ¹⁄₁₀₀ of an ounce.

The Eighth Week

The face and features are forming. The jaws are now well formed, and the teeth and facial muscles are beginning. Rudiments of fingers and then toes become evident; these are called *digital rays*. Cartilage and bone may be seen in the forming skeleton. The 8-week embryo is about ¾ of an inch long. Its weight is ³⁄₁₀₀ of an ounce (one gram)—less than an aspirin tablet.

The Ninth Week

The baby's face is now completely formed. Arms, legs, hands, and feet are partially formed. The eyelids are beginning. Stubby toes and fingers can be seen. From this time on, the embryo looks very much like a miniature infant. It is almost one inch in length and weighs about one-tenth of an ounce (3 grams).

The Tenth Week

This marks the end of the embryonic period and the beginning of the fetal period. The eyes, which were at the side of the head, are moving to the front. The face is quite human. The heart is forming four chambers. The external genitalia have begun to differentiate into male and female. In the male, the scrotum is appearing. The palate to form the roof of the mouth is closing. Major blood vessels are assuming final form and the muscle wall of the intestinal tract is forming. The fetal heart rate is 120 to 160 beats per minute.

The fetus at this age resembles a teensy top-heavy doll, approximately one inch in height with its head making up almost half its size. The 10-week-old fetus has gracefully formed arms and legs, slitlike closed eyes, small ear lobes, and a protuberant abdomen.

The End of the First Trimester (About 13½ Weeks)

Arms, legs, hands, feet, fingers, and toes are fully formed. Nails appear. The ears are completely formed. The external genital organs begin to show clear gender differences. Now when the brain signals, muscles respond and the fetus kicks, even curling its toes. Arms bend at the wrists and elbows, and fingers close to form tiny fists. With eyes tightly shut, the face squints, purses its lips, and opens its mouth.

The fetus may swallow amniotic fluid, excreting it back into the fluid as urine. Reflex movements from the spinal cord are made. The brain is not yet organized sufficiently to control them. The fetal length is about three inches, its weight one ounce (thirty grams).

About 18 Weeks

The casual observer could distinguish gender in fetuses miscarried or aborted at this phase of development. Fine, downlike hair, called *lanugo*, covers the body. The fetal skin, less transparent than previously, is covered with a cheesy material called *vernix caseosa* which protects it from the harshness of the amniotic fluid. Eyebrows and eyelashes appear. The fetus is now about eight-and-a-half inches long and weighs about six ounces (180 grams).

22½ Weeks

Hair appears on the head and fat is deposited under the skin, although the fetus is still very lean. By this time, the mother is feeling fetal movements and the heart can be heard with a special stethoscope called a *fetoscope*. If born, the fetus may live a few minutes. The fetal length is now about twelve inches and the weight about one pound (452 grams).

24–26 Weeks

By 24 weeks, a lipid (or fatty) substance called *surfactant* is produced in the lungs. Surfactant allows the lungs to expand once the baby is born—its absence or presence is one of the main determinants of whether a baby born prematurely will survive. By 26 weeks, the lungs usually are sufficiently developed for the baby born at this gestational age to have a reasonable chance of survival, if given appropriate intensive care. The fetus's eyes start to reopen at 26 weeks, the toenails are visible, and the amount of body fat increases.

At about 24 to 26 weeks, the fetus is about fourteen inches long and weighs about two pounds (960 grams).

The Eighth Month (32–35 Weeks)

In the male fetus, the testicles begin to descend into the scrotum. A child born alive during this month has an excellent chance of survival. The age-old superstition that a baby born in the seventh month will do better than one born in the eighth is entirely untrue. Each day nearer term makes the child's chances for survival that much better. The average 8-month-old fetus is about sixteen inches long and weighs about four pounds, eleven ounces (2,100 grams).

The Ninth Month (36–40 Weeks)

A full-term baby is any baby born after the thirty-seventh week of gestation. The baby's skin is smooth and still covered by cheeselike material. A bit of downlike hair remains over the shoulders and arms. The chest is prominent and the breasts protrude a bit in both girl and boy babies. The head hair is about one inch long. Nails have grown beyond the ends of the fingers and toes. The eyes usually are a slate color; their final color is not predictable. The weight of term babies varies; the average is about seven and a half pounds (3,400 grams). Babies who weigh less than five and a half pounds (2,500 grams) at term usually are considered *low birth weight*.

At birth the various body systems of the newborn human are developed sufficiently to carry on the necessary activities for survival outside of the uterus, provided the baby is protected and nourished. But a newborn is far from being an independent individual. The complicated muscular coordination necessary for sitting must wait six months and for walking a year or more. This is in bold contrast to lower animals. A newly hatched chick trots off almost at once in search of food. The newborn wildebeest on the plains of Africa is delivered during herd migrations and five minutes after birth must trudge after its mother if it is to survive. Human parents have the privilege and duty to watch the final stages of development of their young in the nursery.

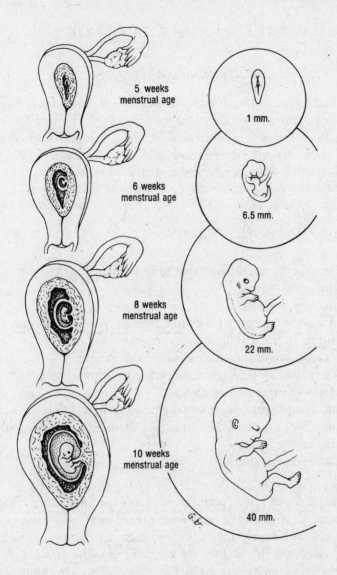

The fetus early in its development and its size relative to the uterus. Only one tube and one ovary are shown.

A. 5 weeks after the start of the last normal period—21 days after fertilization: $^{78}/_{1,000}$ of an inch long.

B. 6 weeks after last menses—4 weeks ovulation age; ¼ of an inch long.

C. 8 weeks after last menses; ¾ of an inch.

D. 10 weeks after last menses. The fetus is almost fully formed; about 1 inch long.

LIFE IN THE UTERUS

The Amniotic Fluid

The colorless *amniotic fluid* that surrounds the fetus is mostly water. As pregnancy advances, the fluid contains skin cells shed by the fetus, fetal hair, specks of *vernix* (the oily, cheeselike material that covers much of the fetal skin), various minerals and sugar in weak solution, and products of fetal urine, such as uric acid and creatinine.

The Useful Fluid
Amniotic fluid serves many purposes:

• It prevents the membranes that form the fetal sac from growing into the fetus.
• It stops the walls of the uterus from cramping the fetus and allows for unhampered and symmetrical movement and growth, thus aiding in the development of muscles and bones.
• It is particularly necessary for lung development.
• It is a marvelous insulator against cold and heat, protecting the fetus from changes in temperature.
• Its antibacterial activity protects against fetal infection.
• It can give us valuable information about the well-being and maturity of the fetus.
• It is an excellent shock absorber.

It is easy to appreciate a pregnant woman's special concern if she falls precipitously, is struck hard on the abdomen, or is badly shaken in an accident. Of course pregnancy does not lessen her chance for injury, but the fetus usually is shielded by the cushioning amniotic fluid. A blow on the mother's abdomen often merely jolts the fetus, who floats away. A puncture wound, however, may cause bleeding from the placenta, which is dangerous to both mother and fetus. Rarely, an accident may initiate premature labor, usually by an associated rupture of the membranes. Accidents occurring during pregnancy never cause birthmarks. Malformations only occur when an object such as a bullet or knife penetrates the abdomen and uterus.

The Dynamic Fluid

Amniotic fluid is by no means stagnant; about 95 percent of it is replenished every day. It is constantly reabsorbed into the mother's blood system and replaced. This happens in a variety of ways:

• Some fluid is exchanged through the fetal membranes and some through the wall of the uterus.
• Fluid is exchanged through the fetal skin.
• Fluid is secreted by the fetal lungs.

During the second half of pregnancy, most amniotic fluid is lost because the fetus swallows it. Most of it is returned through fetal urination. In the last two-thirds of pregnancy, the fetus swallows about one pint a day, and urinates a similar quantity. (Usually, the fetus does not have bowel movements before birth.)

At the twelfth week of pregnancy the volume of amniotic fluid in the uterus measures about two ounces, in midpregnancy somewhat less than a pint. The fluid reaches a maximum volume of about a quart at 36 to 38 weeks gestation. At term (the end of 9 months) there is a little less than a quart.

In rare circumstances, the uterus may swell with up to eight gallons of amniotic fluid. When the amount of fluid exceeds two quarts, the abnormal condition is called *hydramnios* or *polyhydramnios* (Greek: *Hudra* = water serpent; *poly* (*polus*) = much, many). This condition can occur, for example, when the fetus is unable to swallow. Women with diabetes are also prone to polyhydramnios (see Chapter 12).

In other circumstances, the volume of the fluid can be greatly reduced. This condition is called *oligohydramnios* (Greek: *oligos* = few, little). Oligohydramnios occurs when the fetus cannot urinate. As a result of losing its cushioning fluid, the fetus may be less able to withstand the pressure caused by labor contractions. Polyhydramnios and oligohydramnios are discussed further in Chapter 12.

The Umbilical Cord

The umbilical cord begins its formation by the twenty-sixth day of embryonic life. It forms from a structure called the connecting stalk that appears around day 14 of life. The connecting stalk goes from the embryo to the cells that eventually become the placenta.

The umbilical cord is a moist, dull white, semitransparent, jellylike rope that runs from the navel, or *umbilicus*, of the fetus to the inner or fetal surface of the placenta. The cord is the lifeline of the fetus, a vital cable connecting the developing being to the nourishing placenta. Fetal blood, which is low in oxygen and high in waste products, travels

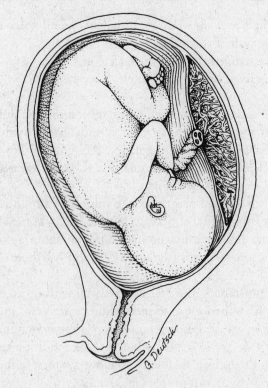

A fetus at about 28 weeks menstrual age. The placenta and umbilical cord have assumed their final shape.

through two umbilical arteries to the placenta. There, the blood is purified and takes up oxygen and nutrients from the mother's blood. The cleansed, well-oxygenated, richly nourishing placental blood returns to the fetus through a single umbilical vein.

The diameter of the cord is about three-quarters of an inch. It averages twenty-two inches in length at term, although cords from a half-inch to fifty inches have been reported. Some cords are straight, others twisted, and some, in rare instances, become knotted by fetal gymnastics. A "false knot" in the cord occurs when a part of the blood vessel within it is folded on itself. This causes a nodulation on the surface of the cord that is not dangerous to the fetus. A "true knot" is a rare occurrence. If tight, it can restrict blood flow to the fetus, which is a danger-ous condition. In most cases of true knots, however, the jelly inside the cord, called *Wharton's jelly*, cushions and protects the umbilical vessels.

The Placenta and Its Function in Fetal Nutrition

The placenta is a temporary, though complex, organ through which the fetus absorbs food and eliminates waste products. The blood of the mother and the blood of the fetus come in close proximity in the sub-stance of the placenta, and materials pass over from one blood system to the other. If, for example, the mother's blood contains more sugar than that of the fetus, the excess passes over into the fetal blood until relative equality is reached. In this way sugar that the mother eats is fed to her baby. In the other direction, the excess carbon dioxide of the fetal blood goes over to the mother's blood and is exhaled by her lungs. The mother, in essence, breathes for her child. The mother likewise absorbs other fetal waste products and eliminates them through her kidneys. The deli-cate interchange between mother and fetus is illustrated by the observa-tion that cigarette smoking by the mother temporarily increases the fetus's heart rate.

Not all vitamins, minerals, and hormones are in exact equality in the maternal and fetal circulations. For example, the amount of vitamin C in the fetal blood is several times that in the maternal blood. Calcium to build fetal bones passes from the mother to the fetus at twenty times the rate it passes back from the fetus to the mother.

The fetus's growth is governed largely by the development and func-tioning of the placenta. In some abnormal situations the placenta per-forms poorly, causing a problem termed *uteroplacental insufficiency*, which may adversely affect the growth and well being of the fetus. A condition called *intrauterine growth retardation* or *intrauterine growth restriction* (IUGR) may occur. In this condition, fetal growth in the uterus is slowed. This can occur throughout pregnancy or late in pregnancy. When it occurs throughout pregnancy, IUGR usually results in a small baby whose body is proportional. This may be called *symmetrical IUGR*. When it occurs late in pregnancy only, the growth restriction "spares" the fetal head. The head at birth is proportionally larger than the body. This may be called *asymmetrical IUGR*.

The Bloodstreams of Mother and Fetus Are Separate

The bloodstreams of the mother and fetus are ordinarily quite separate. The exchange of materials from the blood is carried on through a multi-celled membrane, or partition. Some of the smaller molecules pass intact back and forth through the separating membrane. The larger ones, including fats and proteins such as antibodies, are broken down on one side of the barrier and pass through to be reformed on the other side. This all sounds quite remarkable, and it is. To feed a rapidly growing organism, to keep it supplied with oxygen, and to excrete its waste products are huge complex tasks. The placenta, a relatively small organ, weighing one-fifth to one-sixth as much as the fetus, accomplishes these vital tasks with unmatched efficiency.

Blood Cells Can Cross the Placenta

Until the end of the eighteenth century, scientists believed that the blood cells of the mother intermingled freely with those of her fetus. At that time an English obstetrician performed an experiment by injecting a dye into the blood vessels of a woman who had died while pregnant. The dye did not appear in the blood vessels of her fetus. This was thought to prove the independent integrity of the two vascular systems, and the scientific world believed that mother and fetus never interchanged blood.

In the 1940s, when the fetal disease *erythroblastosis* was first described, some doubt was thrown on this concept. Erythroblastosis occurs when an immune response is produced in the mother to some factor present in the fetal red-blood cells—a factor the mother lacks. For the immune response—or *sensitization*—to occur, fetal red blood cells must pass into the maternal circulation.

We now know that fetal blood may pass into the mother's system when the placenta separates from the uterine wall after the birth of the baby. In the separation process the placenta can tear, even in a tiny place, allowing fetal blood to leak into the uterine cavity. The uterine contractions, so necessary to halt bleeding from the placental site, help squeeze some of the fetal blood into the mother's circulation.

Erythroblastosis

Leaks of fetal blood into the mother also can occur during pregnancy through minute breaks in the placenta. If the fetus has Rh-positive red blood cells inherited from its father, and its mother is Rh-negative, the transfer of even a few fetal cells can result in sensitization of the mother to Rh (a blood factor she lacks and is therefore perceived by her body as foreign to its system). This causes her to produce antibodies, which in essence fight off the foreign Rh factor. The maternal antibodies can then leak back across the placenta and damage the fetus's Rh-positive cells, causing erythroblastosis. *Erythroblastosis* is severe anemia. Once the mother's body begins to manufacture antibodies, the process is lifelong; these antibodies are ready to attack any Rh-positive red cells encountered in this and future pregnancies.

Your blood will be tested to determine whether you are Rh-positive or Rh-negative either at your first prenatal visit (see Chapter 7) or your prepregnancy visit if you have one (see Chapter 6). To prevent sensitization, an injection of *human anti-Rh gamma globulin* (a blood protein), called RhoGAM, is given to all Rh-negative mothers at about the twenty-eighth week of pregnancy, whenever an amniocentesis is done, or at the time of an abortion or miscarriage. The only exceptions are when the father is known to be Rh-negative or the woman has already been sensitized in a previous pregnancy. When the father is Rh-negative, the baby also will be Rh-negative, so the mother's body will not need to make antibodies against the foreign Rh factor. When a woman has already been sensitized, her body is already involved in the lifetime task of manufacturing antibodies, and injecting antibodies will have no benefit. When the Rh antibody is acquired externally through injection, the body processes that would otherwise manufacture it are halted. The injected antibodies are short-lived, so the red blood cells of the fetus of this pregnancy and the fetuses of future pregnancies are not harmed by the mother's antibodies, although the injection must be repeated in the postpartum period and in all future pregnancies, unless there is a different father, known to be Rh-negative.

Heat Exchange

The placenta, with rapid flow of blood on both sides of its separating membrane, acts as a medium of heat exchange. Normally, the fetal temperature is almost a degree Fahrenheit (or about half a degree centigrade) above the maternal. When the maternal temperature goes up, the temperature of the fetus rises too, because it has no way to lose the extra heat except through the placenta. Since the amniotic fluid provides insulation, the fetus's temperature will rise somewhat later than the mother's.

This efficient transfer of heat means, unfortunately, that when the pregnant woman's core body temperature is elevated, the fetus can be harmed. A maternal fever of 102° Fahrenheit (38.9° Celsius) or greater for more than 24 hours in the first trimester may be related to the development of neural tube defects in the fetus (see page 61). Prolonged use of a hot tub or sauna, especially in the first trimester, may have similar effects, although research has not demonstrated this conclusively. Hot tubs are more likely to pose a threat because saunas permit heat loss through evaporation of perspiration.

Hormone Production by the Placenta

As mentioned earlier, the placenta produces a variety of hormones. These include human chorionic gonadotropin (hCG), human placental lactogen (hPL), and the female sex hormones, estrogen and progesterone. HCG is the hormone whose presence is detected in pregnancy tests to determine whether a woman is indeed pregnant. In early pregnancy, it maintains the progesterone-producing part of the ovary—the corpus luteum.

After about 6 weeks of pregnancy, the placenta starts to produce female sex hormones. Progesterone, acting as the brake on uterine activity to prevent the uterus from expelling the fetus before it is mature, increases slowly throughout pregnancy. Estrogen is produced by the placenta in large quantities—at the end of pregnancy the daily amount is one thousand times the amount produced by the ovary at ovulation. As pregnancy progresses, the estrogen is manufactured from substances made by both mother and fetus. This is one of many ways that the two work as a synchronous unit. Because these hormones are necessary to maintain the pregnacy, their production is not influenced by the gender of the fetus.

Most Drugs Cross the Placenta to the Baby

Virtually all drugs taken by the mother cross the placenta to the fetus. The obvious danger is that a particular drug, even if it is beneficial to the mother, may damage the fetus. Recreational drugs or substances taken by the mother for nonmedical reasons may also be harmful to the fetus. Drugs or other substances that cause embryonic and fetal abnormalities are known as *teratogens*. Other ways of saying this are that these drugs or substances are *teratogenic* or capable of *teratogenesis* (Greek: *teras* = monster; Latin: *genesis* = birth). The risk of teratogenesis is greatest in the first trimester when the major organ systems are taking shape.

Beneficial Effects of Drugs on the Fetus

The transfer of drugs, however, can also be put to beneficial use to provide treatment to a fetus prior to birth. Treatment of maternal syphilis with antibiotics that cross the placenta is an example of drug therapy that benefits both mother and baby. The fetus is usually infected when the mother has active syphilis and is usually cured when the mother is cured, if appropriate treatment is received before the last third of pregnancy. (Of course, treatment should be given at any time in pregnancy that syphilis is diagnosed; if given late, however, the baby may still be born with the disease.)

Probably the first therapeutic intervention given to the mother solely to treat the fetus was oxygen. Given to the mother, its purpose was to improve the fetal oxygen supply when slowing of the fetal heart indicated fetal distress in labor. This therapy is still in widespread use.

Abnormalities of fetal heart rate that result from improper electrical regulation of the heartbeat and not from infection or labor stress can be treated by giving cardiac drugs to the mother, though her heart beats normally.

Giving corticosteroids to the mother when a delivery prior to 34 weeks of pregnancy is anticipated may reduce the difficulty that the premature baby has in breathing. In late pregnancy, the fetus forms these steroid hormones from its own adrenal glands, but premature babies may not have had enough time in utero to produce them. When given to the mother, steroids may speed maturation of the fetal lungs, which is crucial for survival of the premature infant.

OVERVIEW OF TERATOGENESIS

Throughout most of human history, people believed that congenital anomalies were due to witchcraft or experiences of the pregnant woman impressing themselves upon the fetus. Early twentieth-century scientific thinking held that congenital anomalies were always genetic, despite the recognition a century or more earlier in Britain of the effect of alcohol on infants born to drinking mothers. Scientists and clinicians envisioned the placenta as a perfect barrier—protecting the fetus entirely from the environment.

Today, approximately 45–50 percent of congenital anomalies are believed to be due to a variety of inherited or chromosomal factors. Environmental substances, including drugs, are thought to account for approximately 7–10 percent of congenital anomalies, with drugs considered responsible for 2–3 percent of these. Current knowledge cannot explain the remaining 40–50 percent of birth defects.

Guidelines for the use of medications in pregnancy to reduce the possibility of teratogenic effects

- If you need medications for chronic or other conditions, do not stop or change these medications without consulting your physician or nurse practitioner. The effects of illness can be more devastating to you, your pregnancy, or your baby than the medication.
- If you are on long-term medication you should let your physician or nurse practitioner know before you start trying to become pregnant. Medications can have the most devastating effects on the embryo before you even know you are pregnant, so don't wait until your periods stop or you have a positive pregnancy test. Discuss the safety of your medication with your physician, midwife, or nurse practitioner before you stop using birth control.
- Effective drugs that have been used for some time and are generally considered safe are preferable to newer medications whose effects in pregnancy are less known.
- When necessary, medications should be changed to those that are known to have less risk in pregnancy *before* you stop using birth control. You should continue to use birth control until the

effectiveness of the alternative medication can be determined and additional adjustments made and evaluated as necessary.

- If you become pregnant unexpectedly while taking any medication, you should consult with your physician, nurse practitioner, or midwife as soon as possible to determine the possibility of teratogenesis. Do not, however, stop the medication if it is necessary for your health. In the first 2 weeks of pregnancy—the 2 weeks before your first missed period—drugs and other substances are not teratogenic. They either have no adverse effects or cause a miscarriage—often before you even realize you are pregnant.

- Before you take any drug in pregnancy, remind the prescriber that you are pregnant and ask whether the drug is known to be reasonably benign or, if not, is so essential in treatment that some risk must be incurred.

Because teratogenic effects are often specific to the species, animal studies do not always provide definitive evidence regarding human teratogenesis. For obvious ethical reasons, scientists cannot conduct experimental studies in which a drug is given to some pregnant women and not to others to assess its effect on the newborn. Most information about the safety of drugs or other substances in pregnancy is based on reports of women exposed accidentally or because they simply needed a particular medication—regardless of possible adverse effects. The babies of women exposed or medicated can be compared to babies of women not exposed or medicated—the control group. These studies do not allow for as valid or reliable conclusions as experimental studies do.

Based on this sometimes imperfect knowledge, the Food and Drug Administration has developed the following classifications of drugs in pregnancy:

- **Category A:** Controlled studies in women fail to demonstrate a risk to the fetus; the possibility of fetal harm is remote.

- **Category B:** Animal studies do not indicate a risk to the fetus and there are no controlled studies in humans, *or*
Animal studies show adverse effects but controlled studies in humans have not shown a risk to the fetus.

• **Category C:** Animal studies have shown the drug to cause adverse effects but there are no controlled studies in humans, *or* No studies are available in animals or humans.

• **Category D:** Definitive evidence of risk to the human fetus exists, but the benefit in certain situations (e.g., life threatening situations in which safer drugs are unavailable or ineffective) may justify the use of the drug in those situations.

• **Category X:** Studies in animals or humans have demonstrated fetal abnormalities or there is evidence of fetal risk based on human experience or both, and the risk clearly outweighs the possible benefits.

Approximately one-third to two-thirds of all pregnant women take at least one medication during pregnancy. Some of these are taken throughout the pregnancy, others taken briefly to treat a particular condition that arises during pregnancy.

No drug can be considered *completely* safe in pregnancy. Yet, many diseases are worse for both mother and baby than are the drugs used to treat them.

Overview of the Time Frame in Pregnancy for Teratogenic Effects

Teratogens have their greatest effect when fetal organs are forming. This is called the *critical period* and varies for different organ systems. Teratogens will not cause deformities before the stage of organ formation—from fertilization to implantation, or the first 2 weeks following fertilization—the 2 weeks before you miss your period. During this time, they may, however, cause the pregnancy to miscarry. This may happen around the time of your expected period; your period may seem normal or may be somewhat heavy.

The critical period for brain development is from 5 to 18 weeks gestational age (or 3 to 16 weeks fetal age). Major anomalies, including neural tube defects, develop during the fifth and sixth weeks of gestation; this crucial stage starts about a week after the first missed menses, so you can see why a woman may not yet realize that she is pregnant. Since the brain grows rapidly throughout pregnancy, however, medications and other substances such as alcohol can produce mental retardation at any time during fetal development. This is true even during the first 2 years of life. The critical period for the skeleton and teeth also extends into childhood, so environmental substances may continue to affect the bones and teeth after birth.

The following are critical periods for major organs (using gestational age—weeks from the last menstrual period):

ORGAN	CRITICAL PERIOD FOR MAJOR ANOMALIES (weeks from last period)	CRITICAL PERIOD FOR LESS MAJOR ANOMALIES AND DISTURBANCES OF FUNCTION
Brain and Central Nervous System	5 to 18 weeks	throughout the rest of pregnancy (and beyond)
Heart	5 to 8 weeks	9 to 10 weeks
Upper Limbs	4 to 7 weeks	8 to 10 weeks
Lower Limbs	just over 5 weeks to just over 7 weeks	just over 7 weeks to 10 weeks
Eyes	just over 5 weeks to just under 10 weeks	throughout the rest of pregnancy
Ears	just beyond 6 weeks to about 11½ weeks	until about 18 weeks
Teeth	just under 9 weeks to 10 weeks	throughout the rest of pregnancy (and beyond)
Palate (roof of the mouth)	just under 9 weeks to just over 11 weeks	just over 11 weeks to just over 12 weeks
External Genitalia	approximately 9½ to almost 11 weeks	throughout the rest of pregnancy

Specific Drugs Possibly Harmful to the Fetus

The following sections discuss a variety of prescribed and over-the-counter drugs. The discussion, although lengthy, is far from complete. A summary of selected substances with harmful effects on the fetus or pregnancy is provided in the table on pages 98 to 105. Where it is known, the pregnancy category of the drug is given. Illegal drugs such as heroin are not categorized.

If you are prescribed a drug that is not listed, do not assume that it is safe in pregnancy. Conversely, if you need a medication that appears on the table, do not stop it without consulting your physician. Your own health is vital for the health of your baby.

If you currently use any of these medications, discuss possible alternatives with your physician or nurse practitioner *before* you become pregnant or as soon as you know you are pregnant if the pregnancy was not planned. If you have been exposed to possible teratogens in the early pregnancy months, your physician or midwife may refer you to a genetics counselor with whom you can discuss the specific risks of the exposure to your developing child.

Historical Examples of Teratogenic Drugs

If anyone ever doubted that drugs taken by the mother, with minimal maternal effects, could be disastrous for the fetus, the frightening experiences with thalidomide and DES (diethylstilbestrol) dispelled this.

Thalidomide was introduced in Europe in the 1960s as a mild sedative to encourage sleep. Unfortunately, pregnant women often have difficulty sleeping and many of them took the drug. Within a year the disaster became obvious. Large numbers of malformed babies were born. They had one form or another of what is technically referred to as *phocomelia* (Greek: *phokos* = seal; *melus* = limb). The children lacked long bones in their arms and legs and had flippers for hands and feet.

The unfortunate experience with DES came to light in the early 1970s. This synthetic estrogen was given to women who had a multitude of problems with their pregnancies. Motivated by the mistaken expectation that it would improve the outcome of pregnancy, doctors prescribed DES for pregnant women who had diabetes and bleeding. It was given early in pregnancy to women who had previous miscarriages or unexplained second-trimester pregnancy losses. Four to six million pregnant women were treated with varying amounts of DES for varying durations of their pregnancies during a period of over twenty years, from the late 1940s into the early 1970s.

Articles doubting the benefit of DES appeared in medical journals as early as 1953. Yet, the adverse effects of DES on the daughters of women who took the drug during pregnancy did not make themselves known until the daughters were well into adolescence, explaining the 20-year delay in identifying the problems DES produced. Researchers took even longer to verify the less noticeable changes in the sons, a small percentage of whom have some anatomic abnormalities.

The first DES warning was the appearance in Boston of an unusual kind of cancer of the vagina among young women. This unusual cancer had been seen before in older women, but the occurrence over a short time in a substantial number of adolescents pointed to an environmental cause. Investigators rapidly made the connection with DES given to the mothers.

The epidemic of cancer among DES daughters appears to be over, although whether there will be additional carcinogenic effects as this group of women ages remains unknown. In addition to various non-malignant changes in the anatomy of the vagina, cervix, and uterus, a number of DES daughters have had difficulty becoming pregnant or maintaining their pregnancies. They have more frequent miscarriages, ectopic pregnancies, and premature labors.

If you were born before 1972 and think you may be a DES daughter, ask your mother whether she took any drugs during her pregnancy. Since memory is inexact and since DES-type drugs were marketed under numerous trade names, also ask your physician or midwife to examine you specifically to look for the typical anatomic changes produced by DES.

Drugs with the Potential for Abuse

Opiates
Opiate drugs—derived from the opium poppy or made synthetically in the laboratory to mimic the natural substances—include both legal and illegal substances.

Legal opiates are used for pain relief. Historically, they were one of the first medicines ever used. Because they induce feelings of euphoria and tranquility, these drugs have a high potential for abuse. They also cause physical dependence, meaning that withdrawal of the drug causes unpleasant symptoms—the opposite of those desired by the person using the drug. These drugs have the potential for harming the fetus and can cause unpleasant and dangerous withdrawal symptoms in the newborn.

Legal opiates include morphine, codeine, methadone, meperidine (Demerol), fentanyl, oxycodone (Percodan), hydromorphone (Dilaudid), pentazocine (Talwin), nalbuphine (Nubain), and butorphanol (Stadol). Some of these are given in controlled doses for pain relief in labor. Given only during labor, these drugs will not cause fetal addiction. It is too late at this point for them to cause adverse effects on fetal growth or development. However, if the medication is given too close to the time of birth, the newborn may have difficulty breathing or be sleepy at birth and for some time afterward. More detailed discussion of pain relief in labor is in Chapter 20. Although they can be prescribed legally, they can be a source of drug abuse, similar to the illegal opiates, like heroin. Because these drugs do not cause congenital malformations, they are not technically teratogens.

In addition to enduring withdrawal, babies born to opiate users may suffer from low birth weight, small head size, and prematurity. They have an increased risk of sudden infant death syndrome (SIDS). Mothers who use these drugs frequently have poor nutrition, with vitamin deficiencies and anemia. They risk medical complications, including hepatitis and human immunodeficiency virus (HIV), from the use of dirty needles. Hypertension (high blood pressure) can be a side effect. Users of opiates have an increased likelihood of miscarriage, infection, and toxemia (see Chapters 12 and 14).

Illegal or so-called street drugs may be mixed with impurities and pollutants, which can have additional ill effects on both mother and fetus—compounded by the fact that the substances are not known, obscuring diagnosis and complicating treatment. If a pregnant woman stops using these drugs abruptly, her fetus may die from the effects of sudden drug withdrawal. For these reasons, methadone, a legal opiate, is recommended as a heroin-substitute during pregnancy. This allows the mother to be maintained at a prescribed dose of a drug without impurities.

Women maintained on methadone during pregnancy are better nourished, have better participation in prenatal care, and show fewer obstetrical complications than those who take heroin on the street. Although methadone withdrawal for the infant can be more severe than heroin withdrawal, this treatment is still recommended in pregnancy for its advantages to mother and fetus.

Because the infants born to opiate users may suffer from acute drug withdrawal after birth, the pediatrician must be aware of the mother's problem. The withdrawal symptoms of an addicted newborn may appear as early as eighteen hours or as late as one week after birth. The child becomes irritable and overactive, may have tremors, and tends to cry with a high-pitched tone. In severe cases convulsions occur. When the pediatrician knows that an infant was exposed to addictive drugs in utero, appropriate drug treatment can be prescribed to allow the baby to withdraw gradually.

In many communities babies born to substance abusing mothers are subject to protection by the courts and can be taken away from their mothers. Many mothers know this and conceal their addiction. However, if you are a substance abuser, the best way to prevent the state from placing your child in foster care is to be in a drug treatment program. If you have been a user of illicit drugs, the benefit to you and your fetus is great if you inform your physician or midwife and allow them to refer you to social services and a treatment program.

Some states require drug testing of the urine of all newborns, so, ultimately, drug use is difficult to conceal. While the ethics of this practice, without requiring informed consent of the parents, are questionable, where it is a law, the test will be done.

If you use other drugs, such as alcohol or cocaine, in addition to opiates, then you must be in treatment for each of these substances. You should be in contact with a social worker throughout your pregnancy, hospitalization for birth, and afterwards.

A final problem among babies of women who use drugs by injection is that infection with HIV can be passed through contaminated needles. When the mother is infected, the virus can cross the placenta and be passed to the fetus. Treatment of the infected mother with antiviral medications during pregnancy and labor and of the newborn after birth substantially reduces the possibility of the newborn's acquiring the infection. The long-term effects of antiviral treatment are unknown, but the immediate benefit is so apparent in reducing the possibility of newborn infection, that the Centers for Disease Control and Prevention and HIV specialists strongly advise its use in pregnant HIV-infected women and in their newborns. Preconception or prenatal testing for HIV is advised for all women who have not been previously diagnosed.

Stimulants

Stimulant drugs include today's most commonly used and abused substances—nicotine, caffeine, amphetamine, and cocaine. Amphetamines include "speed" and newer drugs like MDMA ("ecstasy"). Stimulants work on the central nervous system, causing symptoms that people find pleasurable.

CAFFEINE   Caffeine is the most popular drug in the United States. It is found in coffee and tea, cola, chocolate, and cocoa. It is also a component of a number of medications, available both over-the-counter and by prescription. The undesirable effects of caffeine, including irritability, sleeplessness, nervousness, and anxiety, may be worsened in pregnancy as the drug stays in the body longer in a pregnant person than in a non-pregnant person. (We say its "half-life" is increased—this refers to how long it takes for half the drug to be eliminated from the body.)

Caffeine is considered addictive at high doses. People who drink more than six cups of regular coffee a day (600 mg) may have withdrawal symptoms if they stop. Symptoms might include headache, irritability, and lethargy.

Extremely high doses of caffeine have been found to be teratogenic in mice. This finding led the Food and Drug Administration in 1980 to caution women to reduce their caffeine intake during pregnancy. Since that time, studies have not found the same effects in humans as in the mice, but little is known about very heavy coffee consumption during pregnancy. Some studies have shown slightly lower birth weight among babies of heavy coffee drinkers, but many women who drink a lot of coffee also smoke, and we know for sure that smoking reduces birth weight.

Although some researchers have looked at the relationship of caffeine intake to miscarriage (spontaneous abortion), findings are not consistent or conclusive. Heavy intake of caffeine may be associated, however, with a delay in becoming pregnant.

In general, the prudent approach is to limit caffeine during the pregnancy planning stage and during pregnancy. Drink no more than two cups of percolated coffee per day. This is especially important if you have other risks for a low birth weight baby. (Risks include a previous premature or low birth weight baby, smoking, or having diabetes or high blood pressure.)

Tea has about two-fifths the amount of caffeine as coffee and cola beverages have about one-fifth. You can make your coffee or tea weaker and add increasing amounts of milk, so you are eventually drinking milk with coffee rather than coffee with milk. Mild herbal teas can be substituted, such as peppermint or lemon tea. (Check with your physician or midwife to ascertain that a specific herbal tea isn't dangerous in pregnancy.) Decaffeinated beverages can be substituted as well, but we are uncertain if other substances contained in these drinks may affect birth weight or affect the baby in other ways. Water and unsweetened juice are nature's best drinks.

NICOTINE   Numerous studies have shown that babies born to heavy smokers weigh less at birth than the babies of nonsmokers. The lesser weight does not seem to prejudice the baby's chances for survival, unless it is also born prematurely. However, the babies of heavy smokers also may have a tendency to be born earlier. The size of the deficit in birth weight is in proportion to the number of cigarettes smoked daily. The most apparent effects are seen in babies of women who smoke fifteen or more cigarettes a day (three-quarters of a pack). The fetus also may be affected by passive smoking, so even if you are a nonsmoker, you should avoid cigarette smoke while pregnant.

Heavy smokers may be more prone to miscarriage and ectopic pregnancy; some researchers have found increased rates among smokers of placental problems including *abruptio* (separation of the placenta) and *previa* (the placenta covering the cervix). Some of these may occur even among women who smoke only prior to pregnancy. Smoking is not known to cause congenital malformations, although a few recent studies have suggested that defects of the heart, limbs, and urinary system may be increased among children of smokers. One study found these slightly increased rates of defects when either the mother or father smoked.

The infants of women who smoke have higher rates of SIDS and apnea (intermittent episodes of no breathing). This may be as much from the effects of passive smoking on the newborn after birth as from in utero exposure. Smoking may decrease milk supply, and smoking during lactation is best avoided.

Nicotine is known to constrict blood vessels, resulting in decreased blood flow to the uterus. Cigarette smoke contains thousands of different chemicals, including carbon monoxide gas, cyanide, and sulfides. Since we do not know the extent to which other cigarette components contribute to the harm done by smoking, experimenting with cigarette brands credited with low tar and low nicotine content is unlikely to be helpful. Carbon monoxide, for example, binds to the hemoglobin in the blood, interfering with the hemoglobin's ability to carry oxygen, reducing the amount of oxygen available for vital body functions and for the baby.

Since 1984, all cigarette packs have carried the warning, "Smoking by pregnant women may result in fetal injury, premature birth, and low birth weight." Still, up to one-fourth of all pregnant women smoke. Giving up smoking takes conviction and the motivation to go through the discomfort of abandoning a true physical dependence.

Nicotine chewing gum and the nicotine patch, while useful in smoking cessation, currently are not advised in pregnancy. If you smoke, we recommend the following:

- Try to stop smoking before becoming pregnant. If you need help, you can use nicotine gum or the patch at this time, weaning yourself from it before you start trying to become pregnant.
- If you are pregnant and still smoke, we strongly advise stopping during pregnancy. If you haven't been able to stop to protect your own health, then consider the health of your newborn for extra motivation. Since passive smoking is also dangerous, your partner and other family members should join you in stopping smoking. At the very least, people should not smoke around you.
- If necessary, ask your physician or midwife for a referral to programs such as those offered by the American Lung Association.

- If you cannot stop smoking completely, cut down. While not as good as stopping, reducing the number of cigarettes smoked is a step in the right direction and can benefit your baby.
- Try not to resume smoking after the baby is born, but if you do, do not smoke around the baby. Do not allow others to smoke around the baby. Especially do not smoke while nursing or feeding the baby.

COCAINE   Cocaine is a major source of drug abuse. Cocaine can be inhaled, swallowed, or injected into a vein or under the skin. Injection into a vein carries a high risk of overdose. Freebase, or crack cocaine, a form of the drug that is smoked, is particularly powerful.

Cocaine has potent effects on the heart and blood vessels and can lead to high blood pressure, heart attack, stroke, and even death. Pregnant women who use cocaine may be poorly nourished and are at increased risk of infections, including HIV. Cocaine use may be associated with miscarriage and placenta abruptio (see Chapters 12 and 14). Cocaine users have an increase in premature babies and stillbirths. Labor and delivery may be what is called "precipitous"—quick and powerful.

Babies born to women who use cocaine may show low birth weight, small head size, brain hemorrhage (bleeding) or blood clots, and short sleep cycles. A few reports have appeared of congenital malformations of the brain, heart, abdomen, urinary tract, and limbs related to cocaine use. The numbers of babies reported with such problems, however, are small.

Symptoms of cocaine withdrawal in babies include irritability, feeding difficulties, seizures, and breathing problems. Withdrawal is generally milder than withdrawal from opiates. Whether there are other long-term effects on infants and children exposed to cocaine in utero is currently unknown.

AMPHETAMINES   Amphetamines are contained in diet pills and some recreational drugs. Their effects are similar to those of cocaine.

If you use any type of stimulant drug, let your physician or midwife know. Programs are available to help you stop the drug use. You need assistance and support—your physician or midwife can make sure you receive it.

Hallucinogens

Nature is full of hallucinogens that have been used throughout human history in all parts of the world. These drugs cause changes in mood and perception. They include natural substances such as mescaline and psilocybin (PCP) and laboratory-made substances, including lysergic acid diethylamide (LSD). Marijuana (cannabis) is sometimes labeled a hallucinogen. Scopolamine, which was given to women in labor until about the mid-twentieth century to cause them to forget the experience, has hallucinogenic effects. Besides memory loss, it causes bizarre delusions, disorientation, and difficulty thinking—hardly effects most women would choose for their birth experience.

There are no documented adverse effects on pregnancy or the fetus from these drugs, other than the effects of overdosage on the mother. Overdosage with PCP can be fatal. Marijuana may increase the adverse effects of alcohol use. There also may be some reduced fertility among men who smoke marijuana daily. In the absence of firm evidence, the wise thing to do is to abstain from these drugs when you are trying to become pregnant, in pregnancy, and during nursing.

Alcohol (Ethanol)

Women who abuse alcohol may give birth to babies with *fetal alcohol syndrome* (FAS). This syndrome involves deficient growth before and after birth, mental retardation, behavioral disturbances, and an unusual facial appearance. Typically, the baby's eye openings are small, the eyelids droop, the skin is webbed between the eyes and the base of the nose, the nose is short and upturned with a sunken bridge, and the groove between the nose and upper lip is flat or not present. The baby's jaw is small and its ears are low-set and may be poorly formed. Congenital defects of the heart and brain are common. The baby may have a heart murmur or more serious heart defects. Its brain may be small and it may suffer from learning disabilities such as a short attention span and hyperactivity. Specific impairments differ among babies and children with FAS. Some babies with FAS suffer from mental retardation, although usually not severe retardation. FAS occurs in 30 to 40 percent of newborns born to women who have eight or more drinks per day, or at least four ounces of absolute alcohol daily.

Lesser effects, called *fetal alcohol effects* (FAE), occur when a pregnant woman drinks less than three or four ounces of absolute alcohol daily. This could be as few as two drinks a day or several drinks a week. Even one episode of intense drinking during pregnancy—called "binge" drinking—can cause FAE. No absolute safe level of alcohol can be determined, so abstinence is the best policy. The alcohol content of wine or liquor burns out in cooking, so you can indulge in coq au vin and other foods prepared with alcohol. Babies with FAE usually do not show the obvious facial abnormalities shown by babies with FAS. For this reason, the condition is less easy to diagnose early. These children, however, may have serious impairments such as learning disabilities.

The message is clear: if you have problems with drinking, let your physician or midwife know and seek treatment. Get help before you get pregnant, or early in your pregnancy. Your child's future may depend on your getting help.

Therapeutic Drugs: Prescription and Over-the-Counter

The following notes may be of some value if you have doubts about a drug you have been advised to take. The drugs are listed in alphabetical order by type. Any physician or other health care provider who prescribes a drug for you can check with your obstetrician or midwife, or you can check yourself to get another opinion regarding the drug's use in pregnancy. If there is disagreement, ask the prescribing health care provider to discuss the treatment with your obstetrician or midwife. Health care providers are very comfortable discussing such matters with each other. In this discussion, we speak of a drug as "contraindicated." This means that the drug should not be used in a given specific situation—in this case, pregnancy.

Mild Analgesics (Pain Relievers): Aspirin and Acetaminophen

A 1987 study of 1,000 women found that almost half used either aspirin or acetaminophen (Tylenol) during pregnancy. Technically, these drugs do not fall into the same category. Aspirin is a nonsteroidal anti-inflammatory drug (NSAID, page 92) and acetaminophen is not an anti-inflammatory. It is used for relief from pain and fever. These drugs are considered together because they are taken so commonly, often interchangeably, for mild pain.

In usual doses, acetaminophen is not dangerous to the fetus, but it can cause liver problems and even fetal death in maternal overdoses. High doses of aspirin have been reported to be associated with cardiovascular defects in fetuses whose mothers had used it in pregnancy, especially in the first trimester. For mild pain or fever in pregnancy, acetaminophen in low doses is a wiser choice than aspirin. Take only the number of pills advised on the bottle or package label and do not take the pills more frequently than the instructions prescribe (depending on the dose, generally take one or two tablets, every 4 to 6 hours). Chapter 11 outlines measures other than medications that may help relieve pregnancy discomforts, including headache.

Antiacne Drugs

Isoretinoin (Accutane), used for severe cystic acne, is teratogenic. It can cause shortening of the limbs of the fetus and is contraindicated in pregnancy. Many Accutane users are young women; they must use effective birth control while on this medication (see Chapter 27). A similar preparation is available for topical (skin) usage. Based on the currently available evidence, topical tretinoin (Retin-A or Renova) does not appear to be teratogenic, but should still be avoided in pregnancy just to be cautious. A woman who conceived while using the topical medication should not be unduly concerned, however.

Anticoagulants (Blood Thinners)

Anticoagulants are sometimes called *blood thinners*. There are several available anticoagulants, used in a small number of persons with artificial heart valves and in some that have had repeated episodes of excessive blood clotting—thrombophlebitis. One of the common anticoagulants, warfarin (Coumadin), causes an abnormal appearance of the baby's face if given in early pregnancy. This is similar to the facial changes produced by alcohol (see page 85). In extreme cases, it may cause fatal hemorrhage in the fetus or newborn. There are other anticoagulants, such as heparin, which can be used with less risk in pregnancy.

Anticonvulsants

Anticonvulsants, such as Dilantin (phenytoin), and barbiturates (phenobarbital, for example) are used to control epilepsy and other seizure disorders. A number of abnormalities have been associated with these drugs, but some of the problems may be related to the disorder for which the drug is prescribed rather than the drug itself.

If at all possible, anticonvulsant doses should be reduced in pregnancy. Some anticonvulsants are more potentially damaging to the fetus than others. Whenever possible these medications should be changed before pregnancy begins. Valproic acid (Depakene, Depakote) can cause failure of the neural tube to close when given in very early pregnancy. Trimethadione (Tridione), also used for epilepsy, is a known teratogen and must be avoided.

Women taking antiseizure medications should never try to adjust dosages or switch medications without the supervision of their physician, as seizures are dangerous for the fetus and the pregnant woman. The neurologist or physician who manages your seizure disorder should work in collaboration with the physician caring for your pregnancy.

Anti-Infective Agents

Drugs given for infection can be classified according to the type of infection against which they are effective—infections caused by bacteria, fungi, viruses, and parasites. This section discusses possibly teratogenic agents in each of these categories. Alternative medications are available to replace ones that cause fetal problems.

ANTIBIOTICS   Antibiotics are used for infections caused by bacteria. There are many classes of antibiotics, with new ones frequently being developed. Many can be used with a high degree of safety in pregnancy; others are contraindicated. For each contraindicated antibiotic, a substitute is usually as effective or reasonably close in effectiveness.

Streptomycin and gentamicin are the most familiar of a group of antibiotics called *aminoglycosides*. Aminoglycosides can produce deafness by damaging the acoustic nerve. Since these drugs can cross the placenta, the fetus can be affected. The drug must be taken for a long time to cause nerve deafness in mother or baby. This is sufficiently well known, so that it is very unlikely that a pregnant woman would be treated with these drugs long enough to produce injury.

Tetracyclines cross the placenta and are deposited in the fetus at the growing ends of bone and in the enamel of teeth. This may interfere with growth of the long bones of the arms and legs. Tetracycline in tooth enamel causes a yellow to brown discoloration in the baby teeth. Despite the odd appearance there is no other damage and these will fall out. The permanent teeth are normal, unless the drug is used for long-term therapy during childhood. Doxycycline and minocycline are also tetracyclines.

Sulfur drugs are a class of antibiotics often used to treat common infections such as urinary tract infections. These drugs are contraindicated in the last trimester of pregnancy as their use may cause the baby to develop *hyperbilirubinemia*—a condition in which too much bilirubin in the blood causes jaundice or yellowing of the skin. Bilirubin is a normal by-product of red blood cell destruction, which is a normal daily occurrence in all humans. Bilirubin is usually bound to other substances in the blood. When bound, it cannot cause damage. It eventually is cleared by the liver. In babies, the immature liver has trouble clearing this chemical. Sulfur drugs bind to the same sites as the bilirubin. Unable to find binding sites, which are used up by the sulfur drugs, unbound bilirubin builds up in the blood and causes the jaundice. This is a particular problem in preterm babies, whose livers are especially immature.

Bactrim and Septra are trade names for another antibiotic used to treat urinary tract infections. This medication is made of a sulfur drug (sulfamethoxazole) and another drug called trimethoprin. Trimethoprin is a *folic acid antagonist*. This means it kills bacteria by working against the bacteria's folic acid. Because folic acid is so important to human development, some experts do not advise using this combination antibiotic in pregnancy. When studied, however, infants exposed to this drug in early pregnancy have not shown increased numbers of congenital problems. Nevertheless, in general, combination drugs are best avoided in pregnancy if other medications can be used instead.

Another antibiotic commonly used to treat urinary tract infections is *nitrofurantoin* (Macrodantin or Macrobid). This drug is not known to cause congenital anomalies but in pregnant women with a rare condition called glucose-6-phosphate dehydrogenase deficiency (G6PD deficiency), it could cause anemia. This deficiency is very rare, however, and most times this drug does not cause problems when used in pregnancy.

The *fluoroquinolones* are a recently developed class of antibiotics. They include ciprofloxacin (Cipro) and norfloxacin. In immature dogs, they are associated with irreversible arthritis; therefore, their use in pregnancy is not advised.

Several very powerful antibiotics are not recommended in pregnancy. Vancomycin (Vancocin) is used for infection of the heart in people allergic to penicillin and in certain types of colitis. Like the aminoglycosides, it can be toxic to the ears. It also can cause kidney damage. Although there are no studies available, the possibility that these effects may be seen in the embryo or fetus makes this drug inadvisable in pregnancy. Chloramphenicol (chloromycetin) is a very potent antibiotic recommended only for serious infection when other drugs are ineffective or cannot be used. It causes abnormalities of the blood. In infants it causes potentially fatal vascular problems known as the *gray syndrome*. One case of the gray syndrome has been reported in a newborn after the drug was given to its mother in labor. This drug should not be used in pregnancy.

The antibiotics with the longest history of use in pregnancy are the *penicillins* and *cephalosporins*. These are not considered to have risks to the fetus and can be used in pregnant women who are not allergic to them. Common examples of these antibiotics are listed in the box below.

Fifteen percent of people allergic to penicillins are also allergic to cephalosporins. A category of antibiotic called the *macrolides* can be used in allergic individuals. These include erythromycins and zithromycin (Zithromax). Zithromax is an inexpensive medication that can be used in some cases in a single dose (such as for treatment of genital chlamydial infections). Macrolides also can be used in pregnancy for infections that otherwise would be treated with a tetracycline.

Penicillins	Cephalosporins	
Benzathine penicillin (Bicillin)	Cefaclor (Ceclor)	Cefpodoxime
Penicillin V potassium	Cefixime (Suprax)	(Vantin)
(Pen-Vee K)	Cefoperazone (Cefobid)	Ceftazidime (Fortaz)
Procaine penicillin (V-cillin K)	Cefuroxime (Claforan)	Ceftizoxime
Ampicillin (Omnipen)	Cefoxitin (Mefoxin)	(Cefizox)
Amoxicillin (Amoxil)	Cefotaxime	Ceftriaxone
Carbenicillin (Geocillin)	(Ceftin; Zinacef)	(Rocephin)
	Older ("first generation") cephalosporins still in use:	
	Cefadroxil (Duricef)	Cephalexin (Keflex)

ANTIFUNGAL AGENTS   Some infections caused by a fungus, such as vaginal yeast infections, are somewhat common in pregnancy. Most antifungal agents are not known to be teratogenic, although griseofulvin (Fulvicin, Grifulvin, Grisactin, Gris-PEG), given orally for the treatment of ringworm or yeast infections of the skin, nails, and scalp, has been associated with congenital anomalies. It is contraindicated in pregnancy. Vaginal yeast preparations are not considered teratogenic. Fluconazole (Diflucan) is an oral antifungal used to treat vaginal yeast with a single dose, but it is classified as a Category C drug (see page 76) and not recommended in pregnancy.

ANTIVIRAL AGENTS   Antiviral medications are relative newcomers to the fight against viral infections. They are used to treat HIV, herpes simplex virus, and varicella (chicken pox). Zidovudine (AZT) is given widely to pregnant HIV-positive women to prevent transmission of the virus to the newborn. Although long-term studies are not available, animal studies do not show teratogenesis, and to date the benefits of treatment are considered to far outweigh any potential risk to the fetus. Less information is available about the newer drug treatments for HIV.

Acyclovir (Zovirax) and ganciclovir are used to treat herpes and varicella. No pattern of anomalies can be traced to these drugs, although their use in pregnancy has not been widespread. In any individual case, the benefits must be weighed against potential risks.

Ribavirin is used as an inhalant to treat viral respiratory infections in infants and young children. Women working in intensive care nurseries may be exposed to it. Although human studies are not available, animal studies have shown this drug to cause *hydrocephalus* (water on the brain) and limb defects. It is contraindicated in pregnancy.

ANTIPARASITIC AGENTS   Infections by parasites are very common. They include head and pubic lice, scabies, and vaginal trichomoniasis. Metronidazole (Flagyl) is used to treat trichomoniasis. In animal studies, it is carcinogenic. It also causes mutations in certain bacteria. For many years, it was contraindicated in pregnancy, especially during the first trimester. In a study published in 1987 of more than 1,000 infants born to women who used metronidazole during the early weeks of pregnancy, no increased number of congenital defects was seen. Some physicians and midwives still avoid the drug in the first trimester, although it is often used later in pregnancy.

Lindane is a prescription-strength medication used to treat lice and scabies. In adults, systemic absorption of this medication can be toxic to the central nervous system. For this reason, it is not recommended in pregnancy. Pyrethrins and piperonal butoxide can be used for lice; these are available over-the-counter as shampoos or lotions in products such as A-200 and RID. Shampoos are preferred in pregnancy as they always wash off completely. Permethrin cream or sulfur in petrolatum are used to treat scabies in pregnant women.

Head lice may be a particular problem for women who have a child in day care or school. Nontoxic home remedies can be tried before the chemical agents are used. Rubbing petroleum jelly into the scalp and hair, then covering it overnight with a plastic shower cap may suffocate the lice.

Anti-inflammatory Agents

Steroids are anti-inflammatory drugs that are derived from the hormones of the adrenal gland. When used briefly while a woman is in premature labor to accelerate the development of the fetal lungs (see Chapter 15), steroids show no adverse effects. When mothers are on steroids for long periods of time to treat maternal diseases such as lupus and arthritis, the development of the fetal adrenals may be delayed. This is considered a rare complication, however. Women with asthma, for example, may need to use steroid inhalants and in severe cases may need oral steroids. For these women, the benefits of breathing outweigh the small risk of the medication, especially after the first trimester of pregnancy. (If asthma is to worsen in pregnancy, it usually happens in the last trimester.) If you use these medications regularly in pregnancy, notify your pediatrician, who can check the baby and make certain that there have been no adverse effects.

In recent years, the nonsteroidal anti-inflammatory drugs (NSAIDs) have become popular. Like aspirin, NSAIDs such as ibuprofen and naproxen are readily available over-the-counter. Some NSAID trade names are Advil and Aleve. NSAIDs are also available in prescription strength in medications such as Naprosyn or Anaprox. Of course, their common use for menstrual cramps is not an issue in pregnancy, but women also use them for headache and arthritis pain or after minor injuries such as sprains. Although these drugs are considered Category B (see page 75) in pregnancy, they should be used cautiously in the late third trimester as they might have adverse effects on the fetal cardiovascular system. As with acetaminophen, do not take these medications in a higher dose or more frequently than instructed.

If you rely on these drugs for functioning, as women with arthritis may, your physician or midwife will likely recommend careful monitoring of the fetus during the second half of pregnancy with ultrasound and fetal echocardiography (ultrasound of the fetal heart). Your dose should be kept as low as possible, especially during the last few weeks of pregnancy.

Antithyroid Agents

Antithyroid drugs can cross the placenta and suppress the development of the fetal thyroid. As with so many diseases, treatment of thyroid problems is necessary for a successful pregnancy. However, radioactive iodine, which is used in the treatment of thyroid abnormalities in adults, readily crosses the placenta and is accumulated by the thyroid gland of the fetus. Since it is radioactive it will affect the growth of that gland and the fetus may be born with an underactive thyroid gland. Radioactive iodine should not be administered to a pregnant woman.

Cancer Chemotherapeutic Agents

Some anticancer drugs cross the placenta and severely affect the fetus. A number of these are listed in the table on page 98. If you need treatment for cancer in pregnancy, you should carefully discuss the safety of any proposed drug and its alternatives with your *oncologist* (cancer physician) and obstetrician.

Recently, thalidomide has reemerged as a treatment for a type of cancer known as multiple myeloma. Because of the devastating experience with use of this drug during pregnancy, any woman taking thalidomide during her childbearing years must be warned not to become pregnant. Any sexually active woman using this drug must use a highly effective contraceptive method (see Chapter 27).

Cardiac Drugs

Although the drugs used for heart problems cross the placenta, most have not shown harmful effects when they are used at ordinary dosage levels. Cardiac drugs include those that regulate heart rhythm, lower blood pressure, or cause blood vessels to relax (vasodilators).

Digitialis (Digoxin, Lanoxin, Digitek) has been used for many years to regulate the heartbeat and is beneficial rather than harmful. The regulation of heart rhythm is vital in women with some types of heart disease. Although digitalis crosses the placenta, it is not known to cause adverse effects on the fetus. Propanolol (Inderal) is another commonly prescribed drug for cardiovascular disease. Although Inderal is used in pregnancy when necessary, intrauterine growth restriction (slowed fetal growth) has been reported in newborns whose mother received the drug. If given in labor, Inderal can cause a slowed heartbeat, lowered blood sugar levels, or difficulty breathing in the newborn. When the benefits of Inderal use are considered to override these risks, the baby should be monitored closely at birth. Among the drugs used to treat high blood pressure (*hypertension*), those falling into the category of angiotensin-converting enzyme inhibitors (*ACE inhibitors*) should be avoided in pregnancy as they can cause kidney abnormalities in the fetus. Captopril and Enalapril are examples of ACE inhibitors. Many alternative antihypertensive agents are available.

Diuretics

Diuretics or "water pills" used to be prescribed extensively in pregnancy for swollen ankles and for the prevention and treatment of toxemia (see Chapter 12). In excessive doses they can lower the maternal blood volume enough to interfere with blood flow through the placenta. Therefore, diuretics should not be used except for specific medical indications in pregnancy. An example of this is *pulmonary edema* (water in the lungs) due to heart failure, an event fortunately quite rare. Diuretics should not be given for swelling of feet and ankles or for the treatment of toxemia.

Hormones

The adverse effects of the estrogen DES have already been mentioned (see page 78). Some of the synthetic progestins (related to the natural hormone progesterone) can cause abnormalities of the external genitalia of female fetuses if given in pregnancy. Although surgically correctable, these are certainly undesirable effects. Fortunately, these hormones are rarely administered.

We used to believe that use of *oral contraceptives* (birth control pills) in the first three months of pregnancy was responsible for fetal abnormalities, but research has not supported this. If a woman gets pregnant while using "the pill," she should stop using it, but not worry about its effect on the fetus.

An antiestrogen hormone, danazol (Danocrine) has been observed on rare occasions to have a virilizing (or masculinizing) effect on female fetuses when given inadvertently in early pregnancy. These effects include an enlarged clitoris and partial closure of the vaginal lips, which can be corrected, if necessary, with surgery after birth. Prior to pregnancy, when it may be used for endometriosis, this drug does not have any such effect. (*Endometriosis* is a condition in which the endometrial tissue—tissue from the lining of the uterus—is found in patches elsewhere in the body such as the ovaries or the fallopian tubes; it causes pain before and during menstruation.) Pregnancy itself is often a cure for endometriosis and the symptoms do not occur during pregnancy.

Premature Labor Drugs

The class of drugs technically known as beta-adrenergic receptor agonists or beta-mimetics are used to stop premature labor. Beta-adrenergic receptors are cells present in muscle and other tissues. In the uterine muscle, stimulation of these cells slows or stops contractions. Several drugs in this class have been tried in the effort to prevent premature birth. Examples are ritodrine (Yutopar) and terbutaline (Brethine). They share in common the effects of increasing the fetal heart rate and inducing abnormalities of fetal heart rhythm while being administered. Otherwise they appear to have no long-term adverse effects on the fetus. They ordinarily are given intravenously to hospitalized mothers and must be given with great care since they also have profound maternal side effects. These include an increased heartbeat, decreased blood pressure, chest pain or feeling of tightness, and swelling in the lungs as well as changes in some body chemicals. Women on these drugs may have vomiting, headaches, fever, and hallucinations.

Psychotrophic Drugs

A variety of drugs that act on the central nervous system are used to maintain mental health. Antipsychotics, antidepressants, sedatives-hypnotics, and barbiturates are all psychotropic drugs. Bear in mind that your mental health is important to your fetus; when these drugs are necessary for your well-being, they must be continued in pregnancy.

ANTIPSYCHOTICS   A variety of drugs are used to treat serious mental illness such as schizophrenia. Commonly known as antipsychotics, or major tranquilizers, these include chlorpromazine (Thorazine), haloperidol (Haldol), thioridazine (Melaril), and trifluoperazine (Stelazine). The safety of these drugs in pregnancy is undetermined, although animal studies have suggested the possibility of teratogenesis with Thorazine and Haldol. If you take any of these medications, your psychiatrist should work with the provider who is caring for you during pregnancy.

ANTIDEPRESSANTS   Tricyclic antidepressants (e.g., amitriptyline or Elavil, desipramine, doxepin, imipramine or Tofranil, nortriptyline) are used to treat depression and sometimes to prevent migraine headaches or to treat involuntary loss of urine (incontinence). Imipramine, amtriptyline, and nortriptyline might be associated with congenital anomalies although studies are not conclusive. Clomipramine, desipramine, and imipramine pose a risk of newborn withdrawal. If you rely on any of these medications, their benefit must be weighed against their potential for harm. This is a topic to discuss with your therapist and obstetrician. Remember, always, your well-being is essential to your fetus.

Because of their current popularity, perhaps most important in the discussion of psychotrophics are the selective serotonin reuptake inhibitors (SSRIs). These include Prozac, Paxil, and Zoloft (chemical names: fluoxetine, paruxetine, and sertraline). These have become the drugs of choice for depression because of their selective activity on serotonin, a chemical involved in the transmission of central nervous system signals. Interference with this transmission is considered a causative factor in depression. By being so selective in their action, these drugs have fewer undesirable side effects.

Because these medications have become so widely prescribed in the past few years and because depression, one of the main reasons for their use, is so often seen in women, questions naturally arise regarding the safety of these drugs in pregnancy. Prozac also is used in the treatment of the eating disorder bulimia, another condition seen most commonly in women. (Other uses of the SSRIs are the treatment of obsessive-compulsive disorder and anxiety or panic attacks.)

Animal studies have not shown teratogenesis with SSRIs although the manufacturers of these drugs report an increase in stillbirths or death among newborn animals whose mothers took the medications at the end of pregnancy and during lactation. As human studies are not available, these drugs are classified as Category C (see page 76).

Paxil has been reported to possibly interfere with the making of sperm (spermatogenesis), so if a woman has difficulty conceiving with a man who takes this drug, he should consider consulting with his provider to discontinue or change medication, if possible.

Lithium, a drug used to treat manic-depression, also called bipolar disorder, may be teratogenic. Its use is not advised in pregnancy. Again, however, the benefits must be measured against the possible risk—always in consultation with your psychiatrist and obstetrician or midwife.

SEDATIVES-HYPNOTICS, BARBITUATES, MINOR TRANQUILIZERS
A number of drugs are used for their calming effect, to decrease anxiety, and to encourage sleep. They are among the most widely prescribed drugs in the world. Well-known drugs like diazepam (Valium), chlordiaze-poxide (Librium or Limbitrol), ativan, phenobarbital, and secobarbital (Seconal) belong in this category. These drugs can cause tolerance—the dose must be increased over time to cause the desired effect. They also cause physical dependence—abruptly stopping the drug causes with-drawal or unpleasant symptoms. The possible adverse effects of these drugs on the fetus include facial anomalies with first trimester use and newborn dependence with chronic use.

Vaccines

In principle, the use of live virus vaccines is inadvisable in pregnancy, because they can cross the placenta and infect the fetus. The measles, mumps, German measles or rubella (MMR), and yellow fever vaccines are derived from live viruses. In actual practice they are rarely danger-ous. Special registries have followed hundreds of babies born to women who have been vaccinated against rubella during pregnancy with no evi-dence of any fetal effect.

Rubella vaccine is routinely given just after delivery to women who are not immune to rubella. It does not affect nursing newborns.

The killed bacterial vaccines, such as those against cholera, typhoid, and whooping cough, can be used if necessary, but since they tend to cause fever are probably best avoided. The toxoids, such as diphtheria and tetanus, are safe. Rabies vaccine, a killed virus, is probably not un-safe, but is only given when exposure is known or suspected.

The flu vaccine can be given in pregnancy as the viruses contained in it are inactivated (killed). Because pregnant women are more likely to develop complications from the flu than nonpregnant women, the Cen-ters for Disease Control and Prevention (CDC) recommend that women who will be beyond the first three months of pregnancy during the flu season should get a flu shot. The best time to get a flu shot is from Oc-tober through November. Flu activity in the United States generally peaks between late December and early March. The CDC further recommends that pregnant women who have medical problems that increase their risk for complications from the flu should get a flu shot before the flu season, no matter their stage of pregnancy. Discuss your risk with your doctor or midwife. You should not have a flu shot if you have ever had a severe allergic reaction to eggs or to a previous flu shot or you have a history of *Guillain-Barré Syndrome* (GBS). GBS is a disease in which the body damages its own nerve cells (outside of the brain and spinal cord). It causes muscle weakness and sometimes paralysis. GBS can last for weeks to months and 5 to 6 percent of the people who develop the disease die. Most people eventually recover completely or nearly completely, but some people have permanent nerve damage. In 1976, vaccination with the swine flu vaccine was associated with getting GBS. Since then, several studies have been done to evaluate if other flu vaccines were associated with GBS. Only one of the studies showed an association. That study suggested that one out of one million vaccinated people may be at risk of GBS associated with the vaccine.

Vitamins

The amounts of vitamins in the usual prenatal pills are safe but—for many pregnant women—unnecessary, with the exception of folic acid. Folic acid is a B vitamin that, in very early pregnancy, helps in the prevention of neural tube defects. All women trying to become pregnant should take 0.4 mg of folic acid daily. In fact, any woman of childbearing age should take this supplement since its benefit is in the time period before you usually know you are pregnant. Women who have had a baby with a neural tube defect, or had an abortion because such a defect was discovered during prenatal tests, should take 4.0 mg of folic acid daily for three months before getting pregnant and throughout the first trimester. Tablets containing 1 mg can be obtained via prescription. If you have multivitamins that contain 0.4 mg, do not take extra tablets to reach the 4.0 mg dose as this may increase the doses of vitamins A and D to harmful levels.

Note: Although you can buy unlimited quantities of vitamins over-the-counter, do not fall into the trap of thinking that if some is good, ten times as much is better. The Food and Drug Administration has warned that excessive intake of vitamins can be harmful. Vitamin A is teratogenic at doses higher than 10,000 international units (IU) a day. Pregnant women must not take multivitamins containing more than 10,000 IUs of vitamin A. Very high doses of vitamins D and C also may be harmful to the fetus.

Chapter 10 discusses maternal nutritional needs in depth and includes a section on vitamin supplementation.

Other Medications

Pregnant women commonly take a variety of other medications. They take medications for nausea and vomiting, heartburn, hemorrhoids, itching skin, and the ordinary discomforts of life—colds, coughs, and allergies. These symptoms and treatments are discussed in Chapter 11. Additional information on medications is found in Chapter 12.

DRUGS WITH POSSIBLE TERATOGENIC OR OTHER ADVERSE EFFECTS ON THE FETUS*			
DRUG (General Name, Trade Name, Category)	**TYPE OF DRUG OR USUAL USE**	**POSSIBLE FETAL/ NEWBORN EFFECTS**	**TIME IN PREGNANCY OF MOST POTENTIAL DANGER**
ACE Inhibitors (e.g., Captopril, Enalapril) Category C: First trimester Category D: Second and third trimesters	Antihypertensive, to treat high blood pressure	Severe kidney damage	Second and third trimesters
Aminopterin	Anticancer (antifolic acid)	Multiple anomalies, especially of the skeletal and central nervous systems, can cause intrauterine death in the embryo	First trimester
Aminoglycoside antibiotics (e.g., streptomycin, gentamicin) Category D	Antibiotic, to fight infection	Damage to the auditory nerve (causing hearing problems)	Anytime in pregnancy
*Androgens (e.g., testosterone) Category X	Male hormones	Masculinization of female fetus	Second and third trimesters
Antilipemic agents (cholesterol-	Antilipemic, used to lower	With Lipitor, for example, report of	First trimester, but not to be taken at

*A star next to the drug's name means it is Category X in pregnancy—contraindicated.

DRUG (General Name, Trade Name, Category)	TYPE OF DRUG OR USUAL USE	POSSIBLE FETAL/ NEWBORN EFFECTS	TIME IN PREGNANCY OF MOST POTENTIAL DANGER
lowering drugs) The "Statins": atorvastatin (Lipitor), cerivastatin (Baycol), fluvastatin (Lescol), lovastatin (Mevacor), pravastatin (Pravachol), simvastatin (Zocor) All category X Other cholesterol-lowering drugs: Clofibrate (Atromid-S) Category C but contraindicated Colestipol (Colestid) Not categorized but interferes with absorption of fat-soluble vitamins Fenofibrate (Tricor), gemfibrozil (Lopid), niaspan (Niacin) Category C Colesevelam (WelChol) Category B	cholesterol levels	bone deformity, tracheoesophageal fistula (opening between the eating and breathing tubes), and anal atresia (failure of development of the anus). Studies in rats show delayed development	all during pregnancy
Barbiturates (e.g., phenobarbital) Category D	Used to control seizures, for sedation, sleep, muscle relaxation	Newborn withdrawal with chronic use. Evidence for congenital malformations.	Withdrawal: use throughout third trimester. Possible malformations: First trimester use.
Bisulfan and 6-mercaptopurine	Anticancer agents	In alternating courses, have caused multiple severe anomalies; either used alone	Throughout pregnancy, if used in alternating courses

DRUG (General Name, Trade Name, Category)	TYPE OF DRUG OR USUAL USE	POSSIBLE FETAL/ NEWBORN EFFECTS	TIME IN PREGNANCY OF MOST POTENTIAL DANGER
		does not appear to cause major anomalies	
Chlorambucil Category D	Chemotherapy in selected cases of leukemia or lymphoma	Malformations of the genitals and urinary organs	Anytime in pregnancy
Chloramphenicol (Chloromycetin) Category C	Potent antibiotic, used only when other antibiotics are ineffective.	Possible increased risk of "gray baby syndrome" (a vascular disease); known to increase this syndrome if given to the newborn—effect on fetus if given to mother is unknown	Third trimester
Chlorpropamide (Diabinese) Category C	For noninsulin dependent diabetes	Decreased sugar levels (hypoglycemia) in newborn	Third trimester
Clomipramine Category C	Treatment of obsessive-compulsive disorder (OCD)	Newborn withdrawal symptoms	Third trimester
Cocaine Topical solution: Category C Street cocaine— not categorized	No therapeutic use except for topical (local) anesthesia	Increased risk of miscarriage, placental problems, prematurity	Anytime in pregnancy
Cortisone	Steroid hormone, anti-inflammatory, used in many diseases	Increased risk of cleft palate; slight chance of low birth weight or underactive adrenal gland in newborn	Cleft palate: First trimester. Low birth weight or underactive adrenal gland: Throughout pregnancy. Use with caution; weigh risks against benefits

DRUG (General Name, Trade Name, Category)	TYPE OF DRUG OR USUAL USE	POSSIBLE FETAL/ NEWBORN EFFECTS	TIME IN PREGNANCY OF MOST POTENTIAL DANGER
Cyclophosphamide (Cytoxan) Category D	Chemotherapy for certain cancers; may be used in treatment of systemic lupus erythematosus (SLE)	Various congenital abnormalities including malformations of the digits (fingers and toes)	First trimester
Cytarabine Category D	Anticancer agent	Various congenital malformations, including limb defects and ear deformities	First and second trimesters
*Danazol (Danocrine) Category X	Antiestrogen, used for endometriosis	Masculinization of female fetuses, genital abnormalities	First trimester
*Diethylstilbestrol (DES) Category X	Female hormone	Vaginal, cervical, and uterine anomalies; infertility	Anytime in pregnancy
Disulfiram (Antabuse)	Used to assist in discontinuing alcohol use	Malformations of the lower extremities and others	Anytime in pregnancy; use only when benefits outweigh risks
Ethanol (alcohol)	No therapeutic use— "recreational" drug	Fetal alcohol syndrome	Anytime in pregnancy, chronic use or even one binge use; avoid in pregnancy
*Etretinate (Tegison) Category X	Severe psoriasis	High risk of major congenital malformations, including open neural tube defects, facial abnormalities, limb deformities	Anytime in pregnancy

DRUG (General Name, Trade Name, Category)	TYPE OF DRUG OR USUAL USE	POSSIBLE FETAL/ NEWBORN EFFECTS	TIME IN PREGNANCY OF MOST POTENTIAL DANGER
Fluoroquinolones (e.g., ciprofloxacin or Cipro and norfloxacin) Category C	New class of antibiotics	Irreversible arthritis seen in immature dogs; animal studies show no adverse effects in pregnancy, but no studies on pregnant humans are available	As effects are as yet unknown, not advised anytime in pregnancy
Griseofulvin (Fulvicin, Grifulvin, Grisactin, Gris-PEG)	Antifungal agent; used for ringworm infections of the skin, hair, and nails	Conjoined twins	First trimester; contraindicated in pregnancy or in women contemplating pregnancy
Heroin	No therapeutic use— "recreational" drug only	Newborn withdrawal	Anytime; avoid in pregnancy; substitute methadone for chronic users
Hydroflu- methiazide (Diucardin) Category C	Diuretic— "water pill"	Some evidence of increased risk of malformations	First trimester
Iodide or *radioiodine radioiodine: Category X	Potassium iodide is used in cough mixtures, may be used as part of asthma therapy. Radioiodine is used to treat thyroid hyper- activity. Povidone- iodine is used in vaginal douches and is absorbed into the bloodstream.	Congenital goiter (thyroid enlargement), hypothyroid (underactive thyroid)	Anytime in pregnancy
*Isotretinoin (Accutane) Category X	Severe acne	Very high risk of congenital anomalies	Anytime in pregnancy

DRUG (General Name, Trade Name, Category)	TYPE OF DRUG OR USUAL USE	POSSIBLE FETAL/ NEWBORN EFFECTS	TIME IN PREGNANCY OF MOST POTENTIAL DANGER
Lithium Category D	Manic-depression (bipolar disorder)	Cardiovascular defects	First trimester
Methadone	Heroin addiction	Newborn withdrawal	Anytime in pregnancy; use only when benefits outweigh risks (i.e., for treatment of heroin addiction)
*Methotrexate Category X	Anticancer chemotherapy, used in other conditions including rheumatoid arthritis and psoriasis	Many congenital anomalies	First trimester
Methylthiouracil	Thyroid disorders	Hypothyroid (underactive thyroid)	Anytime in pregnancy
Minor tranquilizers (Diazepam— Valium; chlordiazepoxide— Librium or Limbitrol; meprobamate— Miltown) Diazepam: Category D	Antianxiety; muscle relaxant	Anomalies of the head and face; newborn dependence with chronic use	Malformations: First trimester. Newborn dependence: throughout pregnancy. Avoid in first trimester.
Penicillamine	Removal of excess copper in persons with Wilson's disease—in which there is an abnormality in metabolism of copper; also used for rheumatoid arthritis	Skeletal defects, cleft palate, however discontinuation may be deleterious to mother with Wilson's disease.	First trimester. Use only when risks clearly outweigh benefits. Should not be used in pregnant women for conditions other than Wilson's disease.

DRUG (General Name, Trade Name, Category)	TYPE OF DRUG OR USUAL USE	POSSIBLE FETAL/ NEWBORN EFFECTS	TIME IN PREGNANCY OF MOST POTENTIAL DANGER
Phenytoin (Dilantin) Category D	Antiseizure	Cleft lip and palate and other possible anomalies: "fetal phenytoin syndrome"	Anytime in pregnancy. Use when benefit outweighs risk. Abnormalities may be related to disease rather than the drug.
Progestins	Synthetic form of progesterone—a female hormone	Effects on genitals; cardiovascular problems	Anytime in pregnancy
*Ribavirin (Virazole) Category X	Antiviral agent, used for severe respiratory tract infections	Testicular lesions in rodents; various teratogenic effects in all animal species in which tested	
Sulfur Drugs (e.g., sulfa-methoxazole, contained in Septra and Bactrim) Category C	Anti-infection, often used for urinary tract infections	May cause newborn jaundice	Third trimester
Tamoxifen Category D	Anti-estrogen effects; used in treatment of endometrial cancer and prevention of breast cancer	Increased risk of miscarriage or fetal damage	Anytime in pregnancy
Tetracycline	Antibiotic	Discoloration and defects of teeth and altered bone growth	Anytime in pregnancy. Use only when benefits outweigh risks—can substitute safer antibiotics.

DRUG (General Name, Trade Name, Category)	TYPE OF DRUG OR USUAL USE	POSSIBLE FETAL/ NEWBORN EFFECTS	TIME IN PREGNANCY OF MOST POTENTIAL DANGER
*Thalidomide Category X	Previously used for sleep; recently shown to be an effective treatment for multiple myeloma, a type of cancer	Shortened or absent long bones of limbs	First trimester
Tricyclic antidepressants (e.g., amitriptyline or Elavil, desipramine, doxepin, imipramine, nortriptyline) Category D	Antidepressants; sometimes used to prevent migraine headaches or to treat involuntary loss of urine (incontinence)	Possible congenital anomalies with imipramine, amtriptyline, nortriptyline. Possible newborn withdrawal with clomipramine, desipramine, and imipramine	Possible anomalies with first trimester use. Newborn withdrawal with third trimester use. Use only when benefits outweigh risks.
Trimethadione (Tridione) Category D	Antiseizure	Many anomalies	Anytime in pregnancy
Vaccines, live virus (e.g., MMR— measles, mumps, rubella [German measles], oral polio) Category C	Prevention against viral infection	Risk of fetal infection	Anytime in pregnancy
Valproic acid (Depakene, Depakote) Category D	Antiseizure	Congenital anomalies, especially spina bifida	Anytime in pregnancy
*Warfarin (Coumadin) Category X	Anticoagulant (blood thinner)	Facial anomalies; central nervous system abnormalities; growth retardation; risk of newborn bleeding	Facial and other anomalies: first trimester. Risk of bleeding: third trimester.

METABOLIC DISEASES
WITH FETAL EFFECTS

Metabolic diseases are those in which there is a defect in the chemical processes essential to life. One example is diabetes mellitus (sugar diabetes). In diabetes, glucose is not used efficiently as a source of energy for the body and accumulates in the blood. Women with diabetes may become pregnant or a woman may develop *gestational diabetes*—a type of diabetes specific to pregnancy. Pre-existing diabetes (sometimes called pregestational diabetes) may have different effects on the fetus and newborn than does gestational diabetes, which is generally milder.

Gestational diabetes can result in extra fetal growth so that the newborn will be large, while pre-existing diabetes can result in either increased growth or, if serious enough, reduced growth. Women with a family history of diabetes or other reasons why they may be prone to this disease should be tested for diabetes in pregnancy. Reasons include having had a very large baby, having had a previous unexplained stillbirth, having had gestational diabetes in a previous pregnancy, and obesity. Many physicians and midwives routinely test all pregnant women for diabetes with a blood sugar test. This is usually administered between 24 and 28 weeks of pregnancy, but may be given earlier and repeated if negative, for women who may be prone to the disease. Women who enter pregnancy with pregestational diabetes should be followed closely by an expert in high-risk pregnancy or in the specialty of maternal-fetal medicine, also called perinatology. Diabetes as a complication of pregnancy is discussed in greater detail in Chapter 12.

Another metabolic disease is *phenylketonuria* (PKU). This metabolic defect results in an accumulation of phenylalanine, one of the amino acids or building blocks of body proteins. This accumulation damages the central nervous system and causes mental retardation if untreated. Dietary restriction of phenylalanine limits the damage when initiated within the first 3 weeks of life. Because newborn screening has been mandated for many years, there are now adults with PKU who are healthy but have an increased phenylalanine blood level. If a woman with this metabolic defect does not follow dietary restrictions during pregnancy, especially in the earliest weeks, her fetus is at risk of nervous system injury. Although most women with PKU are aware of their diagnosis, PKU blood levels should be measured in any woman who has given birth to two or more infants with *microcephaly*—an abnormally small head—for whom the cause is unknown.

INFECTIOUS DISEASES
WITH FETAL EFFECTS

Infectious organisms can pass through the placenta. Minor infections usually pose no risk to the fetus, but a few diseases do. Some diseases that are mild or go almost unnoticed in the mother can have serious consequences for the developing fetus.

Sexually Transmitted Infections

Sexually transmitted infections (STIs) including human immunodeficiency virus (HIV) and syphilis can be passed to the fetus through the placenta. Treatment of both these diseases is recommended during pregnancy if the mother is infected. Syphilis is routinely tested for during prenatal care. Some states require specialized counseling and testing for HIV as well, although women have the right to refuse. Since there is now effective treatment available to protect the baby from HIV, we strongly recommend being tested before pregnancy or early in its course. This treatment is given to the mother during pregnancy and labor and to the newborn.

Herpes simplex virus is another sexually transmitted infection that causes only sporadic, localized problems in adults with intact immune systems, but can cause serious, even fatal, systemic illness in newborns who've acquired it from their mothers. Babies born with herpes simplex may show microcephaly, abnormalities of the eyes, and mental retardation.

Herpes virus is rarely transmitted through the placenta. Most often, babies acquire the virus at birth, from a herpes blister present in the birth canal as they pass through.

Women who have recurrent herpes usually pass their antibodies against the virus to the baby along with the virus, so their babies are protected. A woman who acquires herpes during pregnancy for the first time is more likely to transmit it to her newborn.

Gonorrhea and chlamydia trachomatis are not teratogens as they do not cause congenital anomalies. If the mother's cervical canal is infected with these organisms during the birth process, however, they can cause serious eye problems in the newborn. All babies are required by law to have preventive treatment of their eyes shortly after birth. This is discussed further in Chapter 19.

Other Infections with Fetal Effects

GERMAN MEASLES OR RUBELLA   German measles (sometimes called 3-day measles) is an example of an infection that may cause only a mild fever and slight rash in the mother but can result in serious congenital anomalies in a fetus exposed to it during organ development. When the mother has rubella during the first trimester, there is a very high likelihood that her fetus will be infected and show symptoms of congenital rubella syndrome. This syndrome affects development of the heart, eyes, ears, and brain. During the second trimester, there is a minimal chance that rubella will cause congenital anomalies, but hearing loss or mental retardation may still occur. Fetal anomalies are rare when the mother is infected after the fifth month of gestation (20 weeks). Some infants who are affected only mildly may not show symptoms until months or even years after birth—with heart problems or deafness showing up later in life.

CYTOMEGALOVIRUS (CMV)   CMV causes minimal or no problems in adults, but can have serious consequences when acquired during fetal development. In very early pregnancy, the infection is thought to be so devastating to the embryo that a miscarriage usually occurs. When the infection is acquired later, it can cause a variety of problems including decreased fetal growth, brain damage, blindness, deafness, cerebral palsy, and an enlarged liver and spleen.

CHICKEN POX, OR VARICELLA   Chicken pox may cause fetal anomalies in the first few months of pregnancy. About 20 percent of exposed fetuses develop anomalies. These might affect the eyes, skin, brain, limbs, urinary tract, and genitals. In the second half of pregnancy, this virus does not have teratogenic effects. If a mother passes the chicken pox virus to her fetus shortly before birth, however, or during the birth process, the newborn can develop a serious form of the disease.

HUMAN PAROVIRUS B19   Human parovirus was identified in 1975. It causes a disease called erythema infectiosum (EI), more commonly known as Fifth disease. Up to 20 percent of people infected with B19 are asymptomatic. Most others have a mild illness with a facial rash looking like a "slapped cheek," and a lacy rash on the trunk, arms, and legs. Sunlight, changes in temperature, and emotional stress may cause the rash to recur over several weeks. Often, mild symptoms occur 1 to 4 days before the rash appears. In adults, joint pain, weakness, or inflammation may be the only symptoms of EI. When a woman is infected between weeks 10 and 20 of pregnancy, there is a small possibility (probably less than 10 percent) of fetal death. Although some animal paroviruses are teratogens, the evidence regarding whether there is an increased rate of congenital anomalies in infants born to women who had this infection in pregnancy is conflicting.

LYME DISEASE   Lyme disease is a bacterial infection passed by tick bites. Rarely, it can be passed to the fetus and even cause stillbirth. Lyme disease is most prevalent in the Northeast, from Massachusetts to Maryland, the North Central states, especially Wisconsin and Minnesota, and the West Coast, particularly northern California. Symptoms include a rash with a clear center like a bull's-eye, fever, fatigue, headache, muscle and joint pain (even occurring years later), and swollen lymph nodes.

HEPATITIS B   Hepatitis B is not a teratogen as it does not cause congenital abnormalities but a baby born to an infected mother may be infected during birth. These babies may develop lifelong hepatitis infections with resulting liver damage later in life. Many physicians and midwives routinely test all women for this infection (see Chapter 7). See Chapter 16 for more information about hepatitis B and its prevention in newborns.

GROUP B STREPTOCOCCUS   This organism may be present in the birth canal of a mother who has no illness. It is not teratogenic but is a leading cause of serious infection in newborns. The Centers for Disease Control and Prevention, in conjunction with the American College of Obstetricians and Gynecologists and the American Academy of Pediatrics, have developed guidelines for prevention of group B streptococcal disease in newborns. These are outlined in Chapter 15.

TOXOPLASMOSIS   This disease, acquired from cat feces or raw or very rare meat, may go wholly undiagnosed in the mother. In the fetus, it damages the brain and the eyes. Early in pregnancy, toxoplasmosis may even cause fetal death.

More information on these and other infectious diseases is found in Chapter 16.

Infectious Disease Guidelines

1. Have a preconception visit before you start trying to become pregnant so your risks for various diseases can be assessed, screening and diagnosis carried out, and treatment initiated whenever possible before you are pregnant. See Chapter 6 for information on preconception care.
2. Have a blood test to see if you are immune to rubella, varicella, and toxoplasmosis before pregnancy or very early on. If you are not immune, follow these guidelines strictly:
   Before you are pregnant, be vaccinated against rubella

and wait 28 days to get pregnant or have the vaccine in the postpartum period—before your next pregnancy. You can breast-feed if you are vaccinated right after birth.

3. Be tested for syphilis and, if indicated, Lyme disease, before pregnancy or as soon as possible in pregnancy. Get treatment if necessary as soon as a diagnosis is made.

4. **Hepatitis B**
   - If you live in a household with someone who has hepatitis B, work in a job that exposes you to blood, share needles for injecting drugs, or have sex with an infected person, be tested for hepatitis B before or during pregnancy. If you have recently immigrated from a country where this disease is very common, such as some Asian countries, also consider having the test for hepatitis B.

     If you are not immune to hepatitis B, consider being vaccinated before you get pregnant. The vaccinations are given in a series of three injections, so several months will pass before you can try to get pregnant once you start the series.

5. **Toxoplasmosis**
   Before you plan to conceive:
   - Have a blood test to see if you are immune to toxoplasmosis. If you are not, or don't know whether you are immune, follow these guidelines.
   - Avoid changing the cat litter during pregnancy or use gloves if you must do so. Wash your hands thoroughly with warm soap and water after handling the cat litter. The biggest danger of toxoplasmosis is from the excrement of kittens. Since it takes at least 2 days for toxoplasmosis in cat feces to become infectious at room temperature, changing the litter every day is a good protective measure.
   - Do not allow your cat to go outdoors where its chance of acquiring toxoplasmosis is increased. Do not feed raw meat to your cat. Feed it dry or canned cat food.
   - Do not take a stray cat or kitten into your home if you are pregnant. Avoid contact with any cat that might have been fed raw meat or might have been an outdoor cat.

6. **Safe Food Handling**
   - Avoid eating raw or rare meat in pregnancy. Cook eggs well and do not drink unpasteurized milk and milk products.

- Cook meat thoroughly—until it is no longer pink in the center or until the juices run clear. Do not taste meat before it is completely cooked.
- Wash hands thoroughly with hot soap and water after handling raw meat and before eating.
- Avoid touching your eyes and lips while preparing uncooked meat.
- Wash cutting boards, the sink, utensils, and counters well after meat has been on them. Use hot soapy water.
- Wash fruits and vegetables well before eating them.
- Clean your refrigerator regularly.
- Use a refrigerator thermometer to make sure that the refrigerator always stays at 40° F or below.
- Wear gloves for garden work and wash your hands well with soap and water after touching soil or sand.

7. **Foods to Avoid**
- Do not eat hot dogs, luncheon meats, or deli meats unless they are reheated until steaming hot.
- Do not eat soft cheeses such as feta, Brie, Camembert, blue-veined cheeses, and Mexican-style cheeses such as *queso blanco fresco*. Hard cheeses, semisoft cheeses such as mozzarella, pasteurized processed cheese slices and spreads, cream cheese, and cottage cheese can be safely consumed.
- Do not eat refrigerated pâté or meat spreads. Canned or shelf-stable pâté and meat spreads can be eaten.
- Do not eat refrigerated smoked seafood unless it is an ingredient in a cooked dish such as a casserole. Examples of refrigerated smoked seafood include salmon, trout, whitefish, cod, tuna, and mackerel which are most often labeled as "nova-style," "lox," "kippered," "smoked," or "jerky." This fish is found in the refrigerated section or sold at deli counters of grocery stores and delicatessens.
- Do not drink raw (unpasteurized) milk or eat foods that contain unpasteurized milk.
- Use all perishable items that are precooked or ready-to-eat as soon as possible.

8. **Highly Infectious Diseases**
- Stay away from anyone who has a fever or rash or known German measles, chicken pox, or Fifth disease.

• If you are exposed to chicken pox, call your physician or midwife so you can be tested for immunity, and if not immune, receive an injection of antibodies within 96 hours after the exposure.

9. **Lyme Disease**

• In wooded areas or areas with tall grass, wear long sleeves, shirts tucked into pants, and long pants tucked into socks. Wear light-colored clothing to help you see ticks. Walk in the center of trails and avoid overhanging grass and bush. Keep the grass short in your own area, especially in the eastern U.S., where most transmission of Lyme disease occurs near the home. Remove plants that attract deer (they carry ticks) and put up barriers to keep deer away from your home.

• If you have been bitten by a tick or develop a rash with a clear center, like a bull's-eye, inform your physician or midwife, as Lyme disease is treatable with antibiotics.

10. **HIV**

• Have an HIV test before pregnancy, or early in the course of pregnancy. Ask your partner to be tested as well, as it takes up to 6 months for you to show a positive result if you were recently infected.

• If you are HIV positive, consider treatment during pregnancy and labor and treatment for the newborn. Discuss this fully and carefully with your provider.

• Practice safer sex. This means using a condom even during pregnancy unless you are certain that you and your partner are disease free, are both monogamous, and don't use intravenous drugs.

• Do not breast-feed if you are HIV-positive.

ENVIRONMENTAL AND OCCUPATIONAL HAZARDS

Modern life, with its constant exposure to automobile exhaust, noise, smoke, and food additives, can make any pregnant woman nervous about fetal defects. Fortunately, there is no evidence that fetal abnormalities today are any more common than they were a hundred years ago, and newborn survival has vastly improved.

Environmental Exposures

Several environmental exposures are of concern, however. Mercury, PCBs, and lead are particularly dangerous to the developing fetus. Other chemicals may also pose dangers for the embryo or fetus. Arsenic, formaldehyde, benzene, and ethylene oxide may cause miscarriage. Learn to read labels and avoid products such as hair dyes, relaxers, or permanents that contain any of these substances. When using household cleaners, make sure the area is well ventilated and don't use aerosol sprays. Plain white vinegar, lemon juice, club soda, and borax work well for many household cleaning needs.

Insecticides and pesticides should be avoided as much as possible. If you need to paint home furniture or walls—as many expectant parents do when preparing for the baby—use latex-based paints rather than oil-based paints. Avoid using paint removers or solvents. Open the windows. Best of all—have someone else exterminate, paint, or refinish furniture for you, and leave the house until the work is finished.

Mercury

Mercury is a chemical that exists in many forms. One form has gotten into our air as a result of industrial waste, largely from coal-burning power plants, incinerators, and mines. The mercury in the air rains down into waterways, where bacteria in the water convert it to methylmercury. Methylmercury accumulates in the fatty tissues of fish and in animals that eat the fish. The consumption of fish is the major source of mercury in the body.

The effects of low levels of methylmercury are unclear, but in the 1960s and 1970s, thousands of people were seriously harmed in Japan and Iraq after eating food that contained heavy concentrations of methylmercury. Many died or suffered brain damage. The fetus is most vulnerable to mercury's toxicity.

Fortunately, the most commonly eaten fish in this country have relatively low levels of mercury. The Food and Drug Administration (FDA) considers 1 part per million or less to be a safe level in seafood. Tuna, shrimp, pollock, salmon, cod, clams, flounder, crab, and scallops all contain less than this level of mercury. The larger, longer-lived fish that feed on other fish accumulate the highest levels of methylmercury and should be avoided in pregnancy, whenever you might become pregnant (if you are trying to become pregnant or not using effective contraception), or when you are nursing. These fish include shark, swordfish, king mackerel, and tilefish. However, fish is a source of low-fat, high-quality protein and can be a part of a pregnant woman's diet if a variety of fish are chosen and limited to an average of 12 ounces per week. As a usual serving is three to six ounces, you can choose fish two to four times a week, unless you eat smaller portions. If you eat more fish than this in a given week, don't panic. You can cut down the following week.

You can check with your state or local health department to find out if fish caught in freshwater lakes or streams in your area are safe to eat. You can also contact the United States Food and Drug Administration. Contact information is provided in the Appendix.

Polychlorinated Biphenyls

PCBs are also found in freshwater fish from contaminated waters. These chemicals can cause intrauterine growth retardation and skin discoloration. In Japan and Taiwan, PCBs have been found in contaminated cooking oil.

Lead

Another environmental teratogen, lead can cause miscarriages, fetal anomalies, intrauterine growth retardation, and other defects. Lead is found in old paint, soil, dust, and water. Certain occupations and hobbies such as pottery or stained-glass making may result in lead exposure. The pregnant woman might be exposed from a family member who inadvertently brings home lead dust on skin and clothes. The box on page 114 lists various ways that women can be exposed to lead. The box on page 115 lists various ways to reduce lead exposure. If you believe you might be exposed to lead at the workplace or if you live in an old building with peeling paint, you should consider a blood test for lead before getting pregnant. The FDA has approved several drugs that bind to, or *chelate*, lead molecules so the body can remove them in urine and stool. Calcium disodium versenate (edetate calcium disodium or EDTA) requires injections or intravenous infusion in the hospital. It may be used with another injected medication, BAL (dimercaprol). A third medication, Chemet (succimer), is given to children orally.

Possible Sources of Lead Exposure

Paint: Since 1977, the Consumer Product Safety Commission has limited the lead in most paints. Paint for bridges and marine uses may contain more than the recommended level. In the U.S., 74 percent of privately owned housing units built before 1980 contain lead-based paint.

Auto emissions: Lead is no longer in gasoline, but lead from dust in automobile emissions has been deposited in soil. Soil near roads and freeways may be lead contaminated. This is hazardous for children who play near these roads.

Drinking water: Water can be contaminated from lead-soldered pipes. The U.S. Environmental Protection Agency has a toll-free Safe Drinking Water hotline at 1-800-426-4791. You can receive information on how to have your water tested and what to do if it has unsafe levels of lead.

Food: Food may be contaminated from lead-soldered cans. Few lead-soldered cans have been produced in the U.S. since 1980, but imported food may be packed in these cans. Imported glazed ceramic pottery contains lead.

Folk remedies: Folk remedies that may contain lead include greta and azarcon, alarcon, alkohl, bali goli, coral, ghasard, liga, pay-loo-ah, rueda.

Occupations: Occupations with the possibility of lead exposure include plumbers, pipe fitters, lead miners, auto repairers, glass manufacturers, shipbuilders, printers, plastic manufacturers, lead smelters and refiners, police officers, steel welders or cutters, construction workers, rubber product manufacturers, gas station attendants, battery manufacturers, bridge reconstruction workers, firing range instructors.

Hobbies and other activities: Activities that might involve lead exposure include glazed pottery making, target shooting at firing ranges, lead soldering (e.g., electronics), painting, preparing lead shot or fishing sinkers, stained-glass making, car or boat repair, home remodeling.

Cosmetics: Surma or kohl used around the eyes for medicinal or decorative purposes may contain lead.

Nutritional supplements: Calcium supplements derived from animal bone sources (dolomite) may contain lead.

Household items: Old painted toys and antique furniture, including cribs, may contain lead, as do miniblinds made outside the United States before July 1996.

Moonshine whiskey

Gasoline "huffing"

Source: Centers for Disease Control and Prevention, *Case Studies in Environmental Medicine: Lead Toxicity,* 9/1/92; and American Academy of Pediatrics, *Lead Poisoning: Prevention and Screening: Guidelines for Parents,* 1998.

Ways to Reduce Lead Exposure at Home

Clean and cover any chalking, flaking, or chipping paint. You can apply a new coat of paint or use duct tape or contact paper. Be especially careful of windows and window sills as opening and closing windows send leaded dust into the air. Contact your local department of health about lead hazard abatement if you live in an old dwelling, especially if the paint is chipped or peeling. Wells are another potential source of lead.

If your house was built before 1960 and has hard-surface floors, wet mop them at least once a week with a high-phosphate solution (5 to 8 percent phosphate—check the label or buy trisodium phosphate in a hardware store).

If your home was built before 1960 or is near a major highway, plant grass or other ground cover. Plant bushes around the outside of the house so that the exterior paint is not accessible.

Avoid eating paint or dirt (see Chapter 10 on "pica"); do not put your hands in your mouth if you have paint or dirt on them. Wash children's hands and faces before they eat; wash toys and pacifiers frequently.

Store food in glass, stainless steel, or plastic containers, rather than ceramic or lead cans. Never store food in open cans, especially if they are imported.

Do not use ceramic pottery for food if it was inadequately fired or is meant for decorative use only. Imported glazed ceramics may contain lead and should not be used for food storage. If you make pottery, use lead-free glazes.

Do not use leaded crystal for food storage over long periods of time. Do not use leaded crystal to hold baby formula or juices. Do not use lead-soldered tea pots.

Do not use lead solders to repair food containers or to make or repair cooking utensils.

If the lead content of your water exceeds the drinking water standard (see box above), use only fully flushed water from the cold-water tap for drinking, cooking, and infant formula. This means running the water every morning for 2 minutes before using it.

Do not burn lead-painted wood in home stoves or fireplaces. This generates lead fumes and lead-contaminated ashes that contaminate backyard soil.

If you have a home garden and are concerned about the

amount of lead in the soil used for the food you grow, contact your state department of agriculture about testing the food.

If you or anyone in your household works in an occupation listed in the box above, make sure your skin and clothes are free from dust before going home. Wash your hands and face and change clothing if possible before leaving work.

As lead is absorbed most efficiently from an empty stomach, eat regularly and make sure your children eat regularly.

Make sure your diet and your children's diet contain plenty of iron and calcium, which help protect against lead absorption. (See Chapter 10 for good food sources of these minerals.)

Source: Centers for Disease Control and Prevention, *Case Studies in Environmental Medicine: Lead Toxicity*, 9/1/92; and American Academy of Pediatrics, *Lead Poisoning: Prevention and Screening: Guidelines for Parents*, 1998.

Workplace Exposures

Dangerous chemicals may be used in the aerospace industry, the printing industry, the semiconductor industry, and the production of microchips. The fetus may be damaged by exposure to *organic solvents*—a group of liquids of low-molecular weight that can dissolve other organic substances. Examples of these are aliphatic, aromatic, and halogenated hydrocarbons; aliphatic alcohols; glycols; and glycol ethers. Gasoline, for example, is a mixture of various hydrocarbons. Vapors from gasoline, lighter fluid, spot removers, aerosol sprays, and paints can be dangerous to the fetus. Exposure can cause malformations and miscarriage. In industries such as dry cleaning and any that involve regular work with paint removers, paint thinners, floor and tile cleaners, glue, and laboratory reagents, you have a high risk of exposure to dangerous levels. Adequate ventilation and protective equipment are important, especially in the first trimester.

Women who think they may be exposed at work to possibly toxic chemicals should check with their employers. The U.S. Occupational Safety and Health Administration (OSHA) is a resource employers and employees can use to find out about potential hazards at their worksite. Many states have OSHA offices. Your local department of health may be able to refer you to the appropriate agency. The OSHA website provides information about OSHA-approved state plans or regional and area OSHA offices for residents of states without state offices. Contact information is provided in the Appendix.

X Rays

We are all exposed today to a variety of types of radiation—from X rays, microwaves, ultrasound, diathermy (therapeutic use of heat energy), and radio waves. Except for radiation from X rays, these are all low-energy wavelengths and considered to have few biological effects. X rays, however, are high-energy rays, with the potential for potent biological effects. X rays are a form of ionizing radiation.

Ionizing radiation in very high doses can be harmful to the fetus. This was tragically demonstrated after the bombings of Hiroshima and Nagasaki during World War II. Babies who had been exposed to radiation between 10 and 27 weeks gestation had severe mental retardation. Those exposed between 10 and 18 weeks were harmed at lower radiation dosages than those exposed after 18 weeks. Other evidence of x-ray damage to fetuses has come from studies of babies born to women treated with high-dose radiation for certain cancers and other conditions during pregnancy. These babies showed an increased incidence of mental retardation and other anomalies.

The x-ray dosages (measured in "rads") used today for most diagnostic studies are considered safe for the developing fetus, especially when the body part being x-rayed is far from the uterus (such as the chest or teeth or ankle). A total pregnancy dose of five hundred millirads or less is considered to be safe for the fetus. (A millirad is a thousandth of a rad.) A common chest X ray, for example, results in a dose to the fetus of about 1 millirad.

X rays are not transported around the body in the bloodstream, so their effects are limited to the areas where they actually hit, although there can be some "scatter" effect. Use of an abdominal shield is wise. X rays should be done before the tenth week of pregnancy or after the twenty-seventh week, whenever possible. Multiple x-ray examinations should be avoided during weeks 10 to 27 of pregnancy, especially between 10 and 18 weeks. The screening machines for carry-on baggage at airports are well shielded and do not constitute a risk to pregnancy.

X rays of body parts near the uterus may pose some risk and should be avoided if possible during pregnancy. If you need special x-ray studies, such as a barium enema or angiogram, the benefit to you versus the risk to your fetus must be carefully discussed with your physician. Such x-ray exposure to the fetus can be as high as 2 rads which is four times the recommended amount for the entire pregnancy. If necessary, a medical physicist can be consulted regarding dosage and ways to minimize it.

Treatment doses of radiation, such as those used for certain cancers, should be avoided in pregnancy if at all possible. When these are deemed necessary for your health, the benefits and risks must be discussed fully with your physician.

Until the latter part of the twentieth century, X rays were used frequently to measure the pelvis when labor was prolonged or the baby was in the breech presentation. This exposure was found to be associated with an increase in childhood leukemia. Today, x-ray measurement of the pelvis is rarely used and sonography has almost entirely replaced the use of X rays to visualize babies in the breech presentation.

Computed Tomography (C-T Scans)

Sometimes a woman needs a C-T scan when she is pregnant. In a C-T scan, multiple thin x-ray beams are passed through a body part from different directions. The images are interpreted by computer. As with X rays, the amount of fetal exposure depends on how close the part being scanned is to the uterus. When a C-T scan is called for, discuss the potential benefits against the possible risks with your physician or team of health care providers.

Obstetrical uses of C-T scans are being developed. C-T scans are used before intrauterine fetal surgery to clarify abnormalities noted on sonogram. In some major medical centers today, C-T scans are used for viewing babies in the breech presentation and for measurement of the pelvic bones in labor on the rare occasion that such measurement is considered necessary (see Chapters 21 and 22). Before it is utilized for this purpose, however, the radiation dosage must be known to be lower than the dosage from X rays.

Ultrasound

Ultrasound is the use of very high frequency sound waves to create images. The frequencies used are higher than the frequency of audible sound. The principle behind sonography or ultrasound imaging of the body is that these high frequency sound beams are reflected to different degrees depending on whether they hit soft tissue, bone, air, or fluid. Most of the sound beam is scattered as it passes through the body, but some is reflected directly back and picked up by an instrument called a transducer. These echoes also can be translated electronically into images and displayed on monitor screens, or photographed or taped, usually in one or two dimensions, although three-dimensional sonography is now in the experimental stage.

Sonography is in daily use in obstetrics today. Currently the technique most utilized is called real-time ultrasound, which allows a continuous picture of the moving fetus to be shown on a monitor screen. Ultrasound is used for imaging of fetal parts and to pick up and amplify the fetal heart. The small handheld device used to locate fetal heartbeat, the Doptone, operates on the principles of ultrasound. Its use gives parents audible reassurance that their baby is alive. It can be adapted to a larger apparatus with several microphones and used in late pregnancy to make a continuous record of the fetal heart rate. The rate is printed on a moving strip of paper as part of the evaluation of fetal well-being late in pregnancy and in labor. Both of these Doppler devices take advantage of the fact that sound waves change in frequency when they echo from a moving target. The change in the echoes from a beating heart is converted electronically to an audible and recordable heartbeat.

How Safe Is Ultrasound?

At present there is no clear scientific evidence that ultrasound is in any way damaging to either fetuses or adults when used for diagnosis as described above. Theoretically, and in some laboratory studies, ultrasound can cause tissue damage. This can happen in either of two ways—through heat created by the technique or through a phenomenon known as *cavitation*. Cavitation occurs when there is a bubbling in the cells. Most experts believe that the intensity of ultrasound used for fetal diagnosis is much too low for either of these effects to occur, although higher intensities and longer exposure times have shown problems in laboratory animals. One study reported in 1993 showed somewhat lower birth weights among babies born after frequent, repeated ultrasound examinations. Although ultrasound has been in use for more than two decades, and some studies have followed children past infancy, long-term risk cannot be entirely ruled out.

Following an intense study of this subject, the National Institutes of Health wisely took the position in 1984 that it was not possible to say that ultrasonography was completely safe. Accordingly, the National Institutes of Health and the American College of Obstetricians and Gynecologists recommend ultrasound only for selected purposes. Whether every pregnant woman should have at least one routine ultrasound during pregnancy is a source of considerable controversy. This is discussed further in Chapter 8. In its 1984 statement, the National Institutes of Health presented the medically necessary indications for sonography— and there are many! These are found in Chapter 8.

Magnetic Resonance Imaging (MRI)

Magnetic resonance imaging (MRI) is a body imaging technique that utilizes a large magnet and radio waves. A magnetic field is created which causes the nuclei of hydrogen atoms to leave their normal position. (The human body, consisting of mostly water and fat, is about 63 percent hydrogen atoms.) When the nuclei go back into their usual position, they send out radio signals that can be analyzed by a computer and converted into an image of the body part being examined.

Several studies have looked at the effects on the fetus from MRI. No adverse effects have been noted to date. However, the National Radiological Protection Board advises against using MRI in the first trimester of pregnancy. MRI currently does not provide better images of the fetus than ultrasound so there is no reason to use it to obtain information about fetal anatomy or growth. Sometimes a chemical is used with MRI to increase the contrast in various body parts. Among the chemicals used, the gadolinium-based magnetic resonance contrast agents may be harmful to the developing fetus and should be avoided in pregnancy.

Low-Frequency Electromagnetic Fields

Recently concerns have been raised about exposure to low-frequency electromagnetic fields in the environment. Electric blankets and electrically heated water beds are common examples of devices that create these fields. Video display terminals also produce low-frequency electromagnetic fields. Most current evidence does not show a risk of developmental defects or other pregnancy problems such as miscarriage, prematurity, or low birth weight from such exposure. Some experts believe, however, that studies to date are not strong enough to conclude that exposure to low-frequency electromagnetic fields is completely safe. For sure, no major problems have emerged as use of electric and electronic devices has become widespread. As with any possible exposure in pregnancy, a prudent approach is warranted. Electric blankets and water beds heated by electricity are perhaps best avoided in pregnancy. Sit far from the television and keep electronic machines turned off if you are not using them. In general, however, do not worry about this exposure, which is difficult if not impossible to avoid in today's world.

Other Concerns

Microwaves are not a form of ionizing radiation. Although extensive exposure to microwaves can cause problems such as cataract development, the microwaves from the ovens used in cooking are not known to cause any fetal problems. They all have a shield that prevents the waves from escaping. However, the most prudent approach is not to stand in front of the microwave oven while you are using it.

An additional source of fetal damage comes from extreme heat. Although the likelihood of damage is small, avoid hot tubs, saunas, steam rooms, and tanning salons. Keep the temperature in your regular bath under 100° F.

The automobile is a hazard, but driving while pregnant poses no additional danger as long as you wear a seat belt. The lap belt should be below the pregnant uterus. The shoulder harness should be adjusted to rest between your breasts and off to the side of the pregnant uterus. If late in pregnancy you find driving awkward or you don't feel comfortable under a steering wheel, turn the driving over to someone else if possible.

BIRTH WEIGHT

Why is birth weight important? Other than its being of cultural interest in our society, appearing on birth announcements and always one of the first questions asked of new parents, it can influence the health of the newborn.

Average Birth Weight

The average newborn in the United States who is born at term weighs between 3,000 and 3,600 grams or approximately 6 pounds, 10 ounces and 8 pounds. Birth weight is influenced by many things, including race, economic status, size of mother and father, and sex of the baby. Boys are about 100 grams, or 3 ounces, heavier than girls, on average.

Low Birth Weight

A low birth weight is generally considered to be less than 5 pounds 8 ounces or 2,500 grams, although this standard of birth weight may not apply to all people. Some people are genetically smaller than others and will have perfectly normal and healthy babies who weigh less than this standard.

True low birth weight increases the risk for stillbirth or newborn death. Babies whose growth was interfered with during pregnancy are said to have had intrauterine growth retardation or restriction (IUGR) or to be "small for gestational age." These babies often have difficulty maintaining their body temperature after birth and their blood sugar levels often will be low. They may require intensive neonatal care. Of course, as with any other risk, low birth weight does not predict with certainty that a baby will have problems. Many do quite well, especially those born at or near term.

Factors Affecting Birth Weight

Many things affect the baby's size at birth. Some do not imply a problem and smaller weights are not always indicative of growth retardation. Girls, for example, ordinarily weigh a few ounces less than boys. A woman's first child usually weighs less than her subsequent babies. Mothers who themselves were large newborns tend to have large babies. The size of the baby's father also plays a role in its birth weight.

Heredity

Heredity plays a large role in fetal size. Ordinarily, parents descended from a lineage of big people breed infants of large size, and those with small parents and grandparents produce babies of less than average birth weight. The size of members of the paternal line is at least as important as of those of the maternal line.

Gestational Age

Of course, birth weight depends a lot on gestational age at birth—how many weeks pregnant the mother is when the baby is born. A baby who weighs four pounds because she or he was born prematurely at 32 weeks is at an appropriate weight for its gestational age. However, this baby will still have a more difficult time than a baby who weighs four pounds at term. A baby who is born at 32 weeks and weighs two pounds is small for that gestational age as well as premature. This baby will have the most problems.

Maternal Weight and Weight Gain

Nutrition is important. How much the mother weighed when she began pregnancy and how much weight she gained during pregnancy can influence birth weight. The exact relationship of maternal weight gain to infant weight is not entirely clear or simple. Among malnourished women, low weight can lead to poor fetal growth and low birth weight. This is more common in developing nations than in industrialized countries, but certain populations in industrialized countries are at risk for poor weight gain and poor infant growth. These include young adolescents and women with eating disorders (anorexia and bulimia). Excess maternal weight gain may be a risk for the baby becoming an extra-large baby, which can result in problems such as difficult birth. Maternal obesity and excess weight gain may also result in maternal complications. More discussion of recommended weight gain is in Chapter 10.

Race

Birth weight also varies according to race. African-American infants tend to be smaller than white infants of the same gestational age. Experts therefore advise that African-American women should have weight gains in pregnancy reflecting the upper limit of the recommended range of weight gain (twenty-five to thirty-five pounds). Asian women have smaller babies than white women, but this may simply reflect smaller size among Asian people.

Mother's Age

Although research shows conflicting results, young adolescent women also tend to deliver smaller babies and should gain toward the higher end of the recommended spectrum. These and other nutritional recommendations are discussed in more detail in Chapter 10.

Environmental Influences

Substance use—including cigarettes, alcohol, and drugs—can affect infant size. In terms of numbers alone, smoking is one of the most important influences on birth weight in this country, where most women of childbearing age are well nourished and in good health.

Maternal Illness

Chronic maternal illnesses may affect birth weight, in general producing babies smaller than expected. Diseases that affect the circulatory system, including high blood pressure, or diseases causing chronic kidney damage adversely affect the growth of the fetus.

Large Size

The only condition commonly associated with babies of excessive size is diabetes, although the relationship is complex. The babies of women with gestational diabetes tend to grow large. Women with long-standing diabetes may have kidney damage, however, and have a small baby rather than a large one. As medical science has learned in recent years about the importance of controlling maternal blood sugar levels through diet and the use of insulin, the problem of excessively large babies has declined, since the extra growth of the baby in many instances is a response to abnormal elevations of the mother's blood sugar.

Less than one-tenth of 1 percent of babies born weigh more than eleven pounds. The birth of a sixteen-pound baby made the news in the United States in 1979. In 1879, a twenty-four-pound baby was born.

We are interested in excessive birth weight because very large babies may have some trouble being born. Large infants often have broad shoulders so that even after the head has been born, there may still be serious difficulty with the birth.

Large Babies and Cesarean Delivery

Although some experts have suggested that babies whose weights are estimated at over 9½ or 10 pounds be delivered by cesarean, this is *not* accepted practice. First, neither physical examination nor ultrasound provides a completely accurate estimate of weight. Second, most large babies are born vaginally without problems. Size is not the sole determinant of whether the baby has enough room to fit through the mother's pelvic bones. Indeed, some smaller babies have shoulders that have difficulty fitting through some maternal pelvic structures. The shape and size of the bones, the position of the fetus in the uterus, and the strength of the contractions play a role. The mother's position for birth may slightly change the shape of her pelvis to create more or less room.

One hospital with a large obstetrics service reported that more than 99 percent of infants weighing between 9½ and 10 pounds delivered vaginally without problems and over 96 percent of fetuses weighing more than 10 pounds delivered safely through the vagina.

THE SEX OF THE FETUS

Whether the baby will be a boy or girl is decided at the critical moment of fertilization. Merely looking at the fertilized egg, however, would give us no clue about the baby's sex. The sex organs are identical in boys and girls until about the ninth week of pregnancy. The external genitalia do not begin to have male or female characteristics until the tenth week of pregnancy.

Determining Sex at Conception

The mother's egg does not appear to be involved in determining the sex of her offspring. The father ejaculates two types of sperm cells in apparently equal numbers. The two types differ from each other by a mere chromosome, yet this small variation makes a major difference to the sex of the individual.

Normally every person receives twenty-three chromosomes from each parent, so that most individuals have a total of forty-six chromosomes. Of the twenty-three chromosomes in all sperm cells, twenty-two appear the same. Called *autosomes*, these affect the inheritance of all bodily structures and functions except sex and some characteristics associated with sex. The twenty-third chromosome, the sex chromosome, differs markedly in the two kinds of sperm cells. In half, the sex chromosome is relatively large and is a replica of the sex chromosome of the egg. It is called the *X chromosome*, because when it was first identified scientists did not know its significance. In the other half of the sperm cells, the sex chromosome is much smaller and very different in appearance; it is called the *Y chromosome*. When an ovum is fertilized by an X-bearing sperm cell, the fetus is 46XX or female; when it is fertilized by a Y-bearing sperm cell, the fetus is 46XY or male.

Is Sex Affected by Heredity?

There is a popular fallacy that the tendency to produce a preponderance of males runs in some families and an equally strong tendency toward the creation of girls runs in other families. This concept has been investigated repeatedly by geneticists and statisticians, leaving no doubt that the production of a child of one sex or the other is not affected by heredity; the sex of an infant is purely a matter of chance. Your chances for having a girl in the next pregnancy are precisely the same whether you have already had six sons in six pregnancies, or six daughters, or any combination of the two.

Sex Ratio

Sex ratio, by definition, is the number of males to every hundred females. There are several kinds of sex ratio:

- Primary: the number of male embryos conceived per hundred female embryos;
- Secondary: the ratio of males to females at birth; and
- Tertiary: the number of living males at any time during the postnatal period per hundred females.

Since X-bearing and Y-bearing spermatozoa are produced in approximately equal numbers, in theory the primary sex ratio should be one-to-one. In reality, we do not know this ratio. It could be surmised from the sex of miscarried fetuses, but gender usually cannot be ascertained by appearance in such early pregnancies.

The secondary sex ratio is uniformly between 105 and 106 males to 100 females in almost all populations that have been studied. We know that the death rate among male newborns is somewhat higher than the death rate among females, so that the tertiary sex ratio more closely approaches one-to-one. Among stillborn infants, the ratio of males to females is 150 to 100.

How Can Fetal Sex Be Diagnosed?

Today's expectant parents can find out the sex of their child well before it is born. There are two basic ways of determining fetal sex. One is by analyzing genetic sex, based on the information encoded in the sex chromosomes. The present techniques for doing this in the first and second trimesters, chorionic villus sampling and amniocentesis, each incur a risk of miscarriage. In families where there is an inherited disease such as hemophilia that appears only in males, determination of fetal sex might be important.

The rate of correct diagnosis of genetic sex by study of the chromosomes is close to 100 percent. The diagnosis of anatomic sex on the basis of genetic sex cannot be 100 percent, however, since there are rare instances in which the anatomic and genetic sex are not identical. When such a difference exists, anatomic sex generally determines the gender of the individual.

Sonography—using ultrasound to look at the appearance of internal and external genitalia—eliminates the early pregnancy risk of spontaneous abortion or miscarriage that occurs with chorionic villus sampling or amniocentesis. However, if a decision on abortion for sex-linked genetic disorders is at stake, an error rate of approximately 10 percent seriously limits its usefulness.

Although prospective parents may be tempted to have an ultrasound merely to satisfy their curiosity about the sex of their baby, this practice is discouraged as ultrasound, like most medical interventions, cannot be determined to be completely safe. Its use requires a benefit beyond mere curiosity. The American Institute of Ultrasound in Medicine stated in May 1999, "The use of either two-dimensional (2D) or three-dimensional (3D) ultrasound to only view the fetus, obtain a picture of the fetus or determine the fetal gender without a medical indication is inappropriate and contrary to responsible medical practice."

Fetal sex also can be ascertained in the second trimester by fetoscopy, described in Chapter 8. The risks of fetal injury with this technique are considerable and failure to see the genitalia frequent. Again, the method is not used purely to determine sex.

Can We Control the Sex?

Chance controls the sex of the fetus, and by definition we cannot affect chance. But there are now methods to separate X and Y sperm from each other *in vitro*—in the test tube. Specialized laboratory techniques select sperm based on differences between the X and Y sperm in speed, swimming ability, and microscopic appearance. The proportion of X to Y sperm is thus altered in a sperm sample, then used for artificial insemination. The likelihood that the resulting newborn will be the desired sex is increased, although guarantees of a particular sex cannot be made.

Some parents try a less high-tech way to choose their infant's sex. A study conducted in the 1970s of more than 3,500 births found that more boys were born when sexual intercourse took place at least two days after ovulation than when it occurred closer to ovulation. Of course, timing ovulation in this way offers no assurances and exposes the parents to disappointment if the less-desired sex is conceived.

Chorionic villus sampling has become a reliable method for the identification of the sex of an embryo in the first trimester. Combined with the availability of safe abortion, it is possible to continue to carry only a baby of the desired sex. The same degree of safety of abortion for the mother is not present later in pregnancy, when determination of fetal sex is made by amniocentesis or sonography.

Should We Control the Sex?

Of course, aside from the matter of feasibility, selecting sperm or choosing abortion based on the sex of the fetus poses a host of ethical questions. Besides the personal and family meaning of rejecting a child of a particular sex, what if these methods led to an altered sex ratio among certain populations? What would be the long-term evolutionary effects of such a change?

Feminists and others have even questioned the ethics of simply knowing the sex of the baby before birth. There certainly are advantages in being able to narrow the choices in baby names and to choose a gender-based layette if so inclined. On a much more meaningful level, expectant parents may feel better able to bond with a baby they can visualize as either a boy or girl. Yet, there may be less obvious drawbacks to knowing the baby's sex in advance of birth. Might there be conscious or unconscious behaviors by the mother or father that would differ depending on whether the unborn child was known to be a boy or girl, such as tone of voice or amount of stroking of the uterus, that could subtly affect development and gender roles later in life? As there is no way to answer this question even regarding behaviors directed toward a newborn girl or boy, we merely raise it for readers to consider.

We have rarely seen a new mother or father express disappointment about the infant's sex at the moment of birth. And when that disappointment is expressed, it is fleeting. The reality of the new life and the tangible presence of the squirming, crying infant, who may even look like one or both of the parents, supersede any and all disappointment in its gender. Yet, expectant parents may be disappointed when they discover infant gender during pregnancy—and spend time grieving the loss of the child of the desired sex.

And, of course, there is always that rare, but possible, error in diagnosis.

THE FETAL POSITION IN THE UTERUS

Early texts in obstetrics taught that the fetus might assume any position in the uterus, the number of positions limited solely by an author's imagination. Accurate observations gradually eliminated the more fanciful.

The positions which the child assumes in utero may be divided into two general classes: *longitudinal* and *transverse*. In the longitudinal, the spinal column of the child is parallel to the spinal column of the mother; in the transverse it is at right angles to the mother's, forming a cross with it. We call these positions the *lie of the fetus*.

More than 99 percent of fetuses are in the longitudinal lie. The transverse lie is rare, occurring in less than 0.5 percent of pregnancies.

Occasionally a baby lies diagonally to the mother's back. This is called an *oblique* lie and always changes to either a transverse or longitudinal lie before labor or shortly after it begins.

The classifications of fetal lie may be subdivided into more exact groups called *presentations*, a term referring to the part of the fetus which is in position to be born first. At term, 96 percent of fetuses lie longitudinally and present by the head (*cephalic presentation*); 3.5 percent present by the buttocks (*breech presentation*). When the child lies transversely, the shoulder always presents.

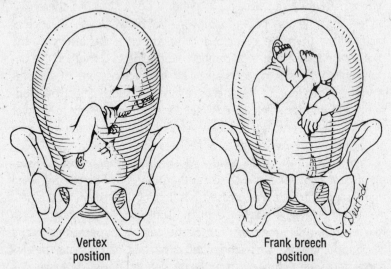

Vertex position   **Frank breech position**

On the left, a fetus near term, lying with its spinal column parallel to its mother's, head down, in the mother's pelvis. On the right, also lying parallel, the fetus has its buttocks down into the pelvis—a frank breech presentation. The legs of the fetus are extended.

In a cephalic presentation, the back is convex or curved inward, the thighs flexed over the abdomen, the legs bent at the knee joints, and the feet crossed. The arms are either crossed over the chest or straight and parallel to the sides. This is the typical fetal position. The umbilical cord nestles looped in the abdominal space between the arms and legs.

Cephalic Presentations

When the head presents, it ordinarily flexes before or during labor, so that the infant's chin rests on its breastbone. When this occurs, the crown of the head first enters the mother's pelvis and is the part of the fetus first visible as the birth takes place. This is the most common variety of cephalic presentation, seen in almost 99 percent of the babies in which the head presents. This presenting part is the *vertex*—the top of the skull.

Babies born with the vertex as the presenting part frequently have a temporary swelling over the area that the hair whorl will later occupy; the swelling is caused by pressure, since this area is the lead point in the birth process. These babies' heads are often cone-shaped as the bones overlap each other to allow the head to fit through the pelvis. This is quite normal and the head will assume its round shape within a few days.

Occasionally, instead of being flexed, the head of the fetus is extended or thrust backwards during labor, and the infant delivers with the face presenting. When the face presents, the features may appear as swollen as those of a beaten prizefighter, but within 48 hours the contusions and swellings disappear. If the head is only partially extended, said to be *deflexed* or in the military position, the baby's brow is the lead point. As a baby in this position won't fit through the mother's pelvis, most of these heads eventually flex or extend during labor. If this doesn't occur, a cesarean birth is necessary.

Breech Presentations

A breech presentation and even a transverse lie are relatively common during the early months of pregnancy, when the fetus has lots of room to move around. Babies have been observed to turn 180 degrees from breech to head down right up to the onset of labor. Approximately 3 to 4 percent of all babies present as breeches. Breech presentation is more common in premature labors than at term. There are three types of breech presentation: frank, footling, and full.

Frank Breech

The most common breech presentation is one in which the baby's legs are flexed up over the abdomen, with the knees straight so that the toes touch the shoulders and the two buttocks present over the pelvis. If not for the very loose joints of the fetus, this position would be almost unattainable and, to say the least, uncomfortable. After delivery it is not uncommon for the baby who delivered as a frank breech to keep its legs flexed at the hip and straight at the knee for several hours. Since the buttocks and genital area are the lead points in the birth of a frank breech, they are often swollen and discolored at delivery. This clears up rapidly without permanent damage.

Footling, or Incomplete, Breech

One or both legs are held straight downward, as in the standing position, and act as the lead point in labor and delivery. One foot or both feet present first, and, on occasion, if the water has broken, may wiggle out through the cervix, either during labor or before it starts. Sometimes, one or both of the baby's legs are straight down at the thigh, but flexed at the knees, which are then the presenting part. This variation is sometimes called a *kneeling breech*.

Full, or Complete, Breech

The fetus sits cross-legged in the mother's pelvis, like a tailor on his sewing bench. In this type of breech presentation, which is the least common type of breech, the feet and buttocks present together.

Transverse Presentations

In 1 of every 400 to 500 pregnancies, the fetus lies transversely at the start of labor, with its head to one side of the uterus and its buttocks to the other side. A shoulder or hand may enter the pelvis or the baby may be lying back down and the only part that can be reached through the mother's vagina is the baby's back. Vaginal birth under these circumstances is impossible.

Presentation of Twins

When there are twins, there are a variety of possible presentations, as both twins may or may not present in the same way. Most commonly, both children present by the head. In another common variation, one fetus presents by the head and the other by the breech. Both may present by the breech or one may present transversely, with the other presenting by the head or the breech. Both twins in the transverse lie is seen least frequently.

How the Fetal Position Is Diagnosed

The position of the fetus is usually diagnosed by feeling or palpating the mother's abdomen. From about the twenty-eighth week or so, the physician or midwife can usually identify the fetal head, at the top or bottom of the mother's uterus. The fetus's back and extremities can sometimes be felt this early, sometimes a few weeks later. Lie and presentation can be confirmed by ultrasound where there is doubt. Once the cervix dilates (opens), the fetal position can be determined by a vaginal exam in which the examiner can actually feel the presenting part.

Changing the Fetal Position: External Version

The position of the fetus ordinarily is not fixed until at least 34 or 35 weeks of pregnancy, although the fetus has been seen to change position as late as just before labor. There has been a recent revival of interest in an old hands-on technique to turn babies from *breech* or in transverse lies to *cephalic* presentations. The fetus is moved to a head-down presentation externally, through the mother's abdominal wall. If this is done early enough in pregnancy it's rather easy and probably also unnecessary, since the great majority of babies who present by the breech prior to the thirty-fourth week convert spontaneously to head-down presentations anyway. Today, external cephalic version is usually done at about 37 weeks gestation or later. It can even be done in very early labor if the membranes have not yet ruptured.

Before this technique, called *version*, is attempted, a sonogram must be performed to demonstrate that there is a single fetus, that the placenta is not obstructing the cervix (*placenta previa*), that there are no fetal anomalies, and that the umbilical cord is not around the baby's neck. The fetal heart rate must be monitored before, during, and after version. Up to 40 percent of fetuses may have some decelerations due to external version, but these are usually not dangerous. Often, medications are given to relax the uterus, especially if labor has begun. One of the medications that might be used is terbutaline sulfate, given in a *subcutaneous* injection (under the skin). Terbutaline sulfate causes muscle relaxation and may also be used to stop premature labor. The version might cause discomfort to the woman and will be stopped if this becomes excessive. With a transverse lie, if external version is not successful, a cesarean must be done to deliver the fetus.

Women can perform specific exercises in late pregnancy if they know their baby is in the breech presentation. In these exercises, the pregnant woman makes use of gravity to turn the fetus. She lies with her hips higher than her uterus and remains in that position for about ten minutes several times a day. A good way to do this is to lie on your back on a bed that is next to a wall. Put a pillow under your hips. Lift your legs straight up and rest them on the wall.

Women have also reported that putting a radio or tape or CD player with music familiar to the baby near the pubic bone causes the baby to bring its head down. While we don't know whether breech exercises or playing music is more effective than just waiting to see if the baby turns on its own, which most do, these self-help measures are certainly not harmful.

ACTIVITY OF THE FETUS IN THE UTERUS

While we obviously lack subjective descriptions of intrauterine life, ultrasound has revealed many secrets of the life of the fetus. We know that the fetal kidneys function in utero and that the fetus urinates into the amniotic fluid. The fetus also swallows amniotic fluid, although whether or not to quench its thirst will likely never be known. The intestines are also active, and a thick, viscid, tarlike substance called meconium is found in the lower bowel. Usually, meconium is not excreted until after delivery, although it may be squeezed out of the bowel of a baby in breech presentation, or when the baby has been stressed during labor and delivery.

The fetal movements felt by mother, father, physician, and midwife are usually the thrusting and bending of arms and legs. The motion of the legs is more extensive than that of the arms, so if movements appear most active in the upper abdomen, the head is most likely down.

Dr. Johann Friedrich Ahlfeld, a German scientist, was the first to claim that the fetus sucks its fingers in utero. He reported the case of a child born with a swollen thumb; immediately after birth it put the swollen finger into its mouth and sucked. Now that we have been able to watch babies with sonography, such activity has been recorded on movie film and videotape.

The fetus also hiccups somewhat frequently. Mothers can feel or see these movements through the abdomen. They are short, quick, regular jerks of the child's shoulders and trunk, fifteen to twenty a minute. They resemble ordinary hiccups except for the absence of the stridor, the harsh noise. An attack of intrauterine hiccups usually lasts about 15 minutes and may recur several times before birth.

In the very strictest sense the fetus does not breathe in utero simply because there is no air inside the uterus. Exchange of gases between the mother and the baby and therefore between the baby and the outside environment is carried on by the placenta and the maternal circulation. However, steady chest movements of the infant clearly play a role in the development of the lungs. Respiratory movements of the fetal thorax were first observed over 100 years ago by noting a rhythmic rising and falling of the abdominal wall of the mother near the navel.

The Fetal Heart

Contractions of the fetal heart muscle begin about 35 days following the last menstrual period. The motion of the tiny heart can be demonstrated by sonography when the embryo is only a few weeks old. As early as the ninth week of pregnancy, counting from the first day of the last period, the fetal heart can be detected with an ultrasound device (commonly called a *Doptone*) in the lowermost portion of the mother's abdomen. Detection of fetal heartbeat as early as nine weeks depends on the mother being slender and the uterus in a forward position, so that the distance from the fetus's heart to the microphone is minimal. Inability to pick up the fetal heart by Doptone is not really meaningful this early. Typically the Doptone will detect most fetal heartbeats by 12 weeks. The fetal heart can be heard with a stethoscope at about the twentieth week of pregnancy.

It is our preference to use the fetoscope to listen to the fetal heart, and use the Doptone only very briefly for the mother or other family members to hear the heartbeat more easily than they can hear it with the fetoscope. During prenatal examinations with the mother on her back, a jellylike contact material is placed on the handheld device and the unit is pressed gently against the mother's abdominal wall. The fetal heart has a double beat like the tick of a watch and it has a soft nonmetallic pitch. The fetal heart rate normally is between 120 and 160 beats per minute throughout pregnancy.

A common misconception is that a pregnant woman can feel the baby's heart pulsate as she lies on her back. Actually she may be sensing any of several other phenomena:

• Pulsations of her own aorta, the large main artery in the trunk, as the pregnant uterus rests upon it. This rate, being synchronous with the mother's heartbeat, is easily recognizable as her pulse.
• Substantial fetal hiccups, which, except for their slower rate, could be mistaken for a heartbeat.
• Baby's breathing movements in the uterus. Slender women occasionally are able to see, though not to feel, these movements. They may see the skin around their belly button moving up and down rhythmically about fifty times a minute. Again, this rate is substantially slower than the fetal heart rate.

Late in pregnancy our ability to record the fetal heart by ultrasound becomes a means of testing the baby's state of health. When the baby is in good health in the last few months of pregnancy, the heart rate fluctuates, depending on whether he or she is asleep or active. If the uterine blood flow and the placental circulation have begun to fail, these fluctuations no longer occur. This is called *loss of variability*. Such a loss also may be a response to sedative drugs taken by the mother or to anesthetic agents used for pain relief in labor.

A severely stressed baby will respond to the stress by slowing down its heartbeat from time to time. This is usually in response to the decrease in maternal blood flow in the placenta, resulting from uterine contractions that occur in pregnancy and labor. The slowed heartbeat is referred to as a *deceleration*. It may simply be from pressure on the baby's head from the contraction, but could have a more ominous significance. Use of the fetal heart rate to test the baby's well-being during pregnancy and in labor is covered more fully in Chapters 17 and 20.

Fetal Heart Rate Does Not Indicate Sex

The superstition still exists that the sex of the fetus can be determined by counting the fetal heart rate. This is simply not so. We now can identify fetal sex by chorionic villus sampling in the first trimester of pregnancy, by amniocentesis in the second trimester, and by sonography after 20 weeks, all with considerable accuracy. But fetal heart rate counting will not tell the sex any more precisely than tossing a coin. Fifty percent of the time the guess will be correct.

Disorders of Heart Rate and Rhythm

Even in the absence of distress, abnormalities of the fetal heart rate and rhythm can occur. A rate as high as 220 beats per minute may be picked up on a routine prenatal visit by Doptone, although it has not produced symptoms in the mother. A rate this fast cannot be counted by listening with a stethoscope, although the listener can certainly perceive that the heart is beating faster than the normal range. This increased heart rate, called *tachycardia* (Greek: *takhus* = swift; *kardia* = heart), is due to an overreactive electrical system in the heart. Since the fetus can suffer heart failure if it persists for several days, tachycardia must be treated by cardiac drugs given to the mother, unless the fetus can be easily and safely delivered.

A very slow heart rate, down to fifty beats per minute, is the result of incomplete conduction of electrical signals and may reflect anatomic defects in the fetal heart. Other defects in conduction may cause the fetal heart to be markedly irregular.

In each of these cases, *echocardiography*—a special form of sonography—should be used to study the muscle and valves of the fetal heart to establish an exact diagnosis to form the basis for proper treatment.

Fetal Sensibility and Learning

In recent years we have accumulated an astonishing variety of evidence of fetal sensibility and learning in the uterus. These phenomena are apparently limited to late pregnancy. The fetus has brisk responses to light. If a sonography unit is focused on the fetus's face and a bright light flashed at the baby through the mother's abdominal wall and uterus, the baby can be seen to blink.

That babies are able to hear in utero has been known for several decades. At term, their heartbeats accelerate in response to the sound of an ordinary tuning fork. In a fascinating study reported in 1984, psychologists at the University of North Carolina discovered that a newborn sucked on a pacifier in one way when it heard its own mother's voice and in a different pattern when it heard a strange voice. It didn't seem to matter whether the babies were breast-fed or bottle-fed, or how young the babies were. The researchers found, however, that the babies had to be at least a few weeks old before they had a clear preference for their fathers' voices.

The researchers wondered whether the babies did any of this learning in the uterus, since they manifested the preference at such an early age. They played for the newborns tape recordings of a maternal heart-beat and a male voice and were able to demonstrate that the babies sucked considerably more often upon hearing the heartbeat than the male voice. They then carried the test an ingenious step further. A group of women in the last seven weeks of pregnancy read Dr. Seuss's children's book *The Cat in the Hat* aloud in a voice directed at their pregnant abdomens twice a day every day. By the time the babies were born each had heard the story for about five hours. After birth the babies were tested with a tape recording of their mothers' reading *The Cat in the Hat* or another children's book by Dr. Seuss, also a poem but with a very different meter. The babies showed a clear preference for *The Cat in the Hat*. This is scientific evidence of what we have believed for many years about prenatal impression. Obviously, the extent to which prenatal impression occurs is an area open to further research.

CHAPTER SIX

—∞∞∞—

Care Before Pregnancy

THE BENEFITS OF PLANNING

Not all pregnancies can be planned. Both human and technological errors occur with all methods of family planning. Planning, however, has definite benefits; healthy pregnancies are most likely to occur in healthy women. Effective methods of contraception should be used until you know you want to get pregnant. These are discussed in detail in Chapter 27. Once you make the decision that you are ready for children, or more children, the best advice is to continue using birth control until you have had a prepregnancy health care visit.

Although many forward-thinking doctors and midwives have informally provided preconception care to women for decades, the concept that this is a distinct type of care visit has only recently gained wide acceptance. In 1989, an Expert Panel on the Content of Prenatal Care, convened by the Public Health Service of the United States Department of Health and Human Services, advocated that pregnancy care begin in the preconception period.

If you are planning to become pregnant within a year, or are actively trying to get pregnant, and have not discussed your plans with your gynecologist, midwife, or nurse practitioner, you should call for an appointment. Screening tests that can pick up potential problems for a pregnancy were probably not conducted at your routine annual gynecologic visit, nor were you likely to have been given information regarding self-help measures and practices to aid in preventing birth defects and other problems that can occur in pregnancy. These measures can be most important even before you know you are pregnant.

A few birth control methods, such as Norplant or the IUD, require a health care visit for removal. This would be a good time to have preconception care. If you use Depo-Provera, you can combine a preconception visit with your last shot.

THE PRECONCEPTION VISIT

The preconception visit gives you and your practitioner the opportunity to review specific risks that might complicate your pregnancy, to screen for and treat undetected conditions that could affect your pregnancy adversely, and to discuss pregnancy-specific health promotion activities. These include nutrition and nutritional supplementation, smoking cessation, and avoidance of toxic substances such as alcohol, drugs, and even some over-the-counter medications.

Assessment of pregnancy risk and health screening are carried out through a complete health history, a physical examination that includes a pelvic exam, and certain laboratory tests. The history will cover medical, menstrual, obstetric, and gynecologic issues. Any previous pregnancies will be discussed in detail, especially if you had problems. You will be asked questions about your psychological well-being. An assessment will be made of your environment to see whether you are exposed to workplace hazards or other toxic substances. Your ethnic and racial background will be noted to determine risk for certain diseases. A nutritional assessment should be made. You will be queried about smoking, drinking, drug use, and eating disorders.

You will be asked questions about your sexual health, including any history of sexual abuse and your risk of acquiring sexually transmitted diseases. Your physician or midwife should also ask about any experience you have had with domestic violence. These questions are not prying or frivolous; they help your care provider identify your needs for specific types of health care and, if necessary, make appropriate referrals.

The health of your partner will be included in the history taking. In addition, your family history will be reviewed, focusing on conditions that have a genetic component, including fraternal (nonidentical) twins or other multiple pregnancies.

The physical examination will be head-to-toe. Your physician or midwife will look specifically for signs of anemia and thyroid disorders, high blood pressure, varicose veins, poor nutritional status, including under- or overweight, and any pelvic pathology, such as fibroids.

Laboratory tests will be done for anemia, sexually transmitted diseases, cervical cancer, and German measles (rubella). You may be tested for chicken pox (varicella) if you can't remember having the disease, and tuberculosis if you live in an area where it is common. Long thought to be a health problem largely of the past, tuberculosis has been making a resurgence in many U.S. communities. It is seen especially in crowded inner-city neighborhoods, among people infected with HIV, and in immigrants from Africa, Asia, or Latin America. Health care workers who serve people at risk should also be tested.

Your sugar may be checked if you are at risk for diabetes or show diabetic symptoms. This can be done through a urine or blood check. You may be more prone to develop diabetes during pregnancy (gestational diabetes) if someone in your family has the disease, if you are overweight, if you had gestational diabetes during a previous pregnancy, or if you have had many pregnancies. Common symptoms are increased thirst, hunger, and urinating.

Some women are at risk for *hepatitis B*, a serious viral infection of the liver that can be passed to the fetus during pregnancy. The federal government's Centers for Disease Control and Prevention recommend that all pregnant women be screened for this infection. Depending on your ethnic and racial background, you may be tested for sickle-cell anemia or to see whether you carry the gene for sickle-cell or Tay-Sachs disease. *Tay-Sachs* disease is a rare but fatal illness seen most commonly among persons of Ashkenazi Jewish descent (from Eastern or Central Europe). You may be tested for one of the genes that carries cystic fibrosis. If you carry a gene for one of these diseases, your partner also can be tested. If he tests positive, you can meet with a genetics counselor to discuss the possible risk to your baby.

If you have a cat or eat rare or raw meat, you can be tested for toxoplasmosis, although this is not commonly done. This disease, which is passed to you through cat feces or undercooked meat, rarely causes symptoms in adults but can be harmful to the fetus if the mother becomes infected during pregnancy. You should be offered in-depth counseling and possible testing for HIV. These various tests appear as a table in Chapter 7, on pages 168 to 173.

PRECONCEPTION PREVENTIVE MEASURES AND TREATMENTS

Such extensive testing in the preconception period makes it possible to treat conditions that might adversely affect pregnancy. Anemia can be corrected, usually through nutrition and iron supplements. High blood pressure, diabetes, or other conditions also can be treated, allowing you to start your pregnancy with reduced risk.

Research has shown preconception care to be especially beneficial to women with certain diseases. For example, if you have diabetes, tight control of blood sugar during *and before* pregnancy can help improve the chances of having a healthy baby. For women with *phenylketonuria* (PKU—an uncommon condition in which the body cannot digest this particular protein), specific dietary measures beginning before pregnancy can help prevent fetal anomalies such as small head size and heart defects that can occur with this disorder.

If your tuberculosis skin test is positive, you can have a preconception chest X ray to diagnose whether you have active disease. If you need tuberculosis medication—possible even if you are not actually ill—it is far preferable to take this before you are pregnant.

If you are not immune to German measles, you can be given the option of vaccination and postponement of pregnancy for a short time so that you need not worry about exposure during pregnancy. A 28-day waiting period is usually recommended, although there have been no documented defects from rubella in babies born to women vaccinated within three months before or after conception. Now that an approved vaccine exists for chicken pox, you might consider being vaccinated before you start trying to get pregnant if you have never had the disease and the blood test shows that you are susceptible.

If the test for hepatitis B shows that you are not immune to this virus, you might want to have this vaccination also. The hepatitis vaccine has three doses and the third is usually given six months after the first, so pregnancy should be postponed for at least six months. If you do get pregnant accidentally during these six months, however, the vaccine is not considered to pose risks to the fetus as it contains only noninfectious viral particles. The vaccine is recommended for people in certain groups whose likelihood of exposure is considered high. You are in one of these groups if you are a health care or public safety worker; if you live with someone who has hepatitis or carries the virus (also detectable by this blood test); if you have sex with someone who has hepatitis or is a carrier; or if you are from an area where this disease is very common or endemic. People from such areas include Alaskan Natives, Pacific Islanders, and many refugees or immigrants. Since hepatitis B is a sexually transmitted disease, you may be at increased risk if you have more than one sexual partner.

The test for hepatitis B might show that you are infected, which is possible even without symptoms. You then should postpone pregnancy as this infection can be passed to the fetus. Once your blood test shows that the infection has passed, you can safely become pregnant. However, some people who have had hepatitis become carriers and can pass the disease to others, including their own fetus. If your blood test shows that you are a carrier, the baby's pediatrician will need to know so that the baby can be treated shortly after birth.

If the test for toxoplasmosis shows that you have never had this disease and not built up immunity to it, you should avoid cat feces and raw or rare meat. Somebody else can change the cat litter or you can wear rubber gloves. You also should wear gloves if you garden in a yard visited by neighborhood cats. Wash your hands thoroughly after you prepare raw meat for cooking.

When you have a preconception visit, your first prenatal visit, discussed in detail in the next chapter, will be shorter and less involved. Most of what needs to be done will already have been accomplished!

SELF-HELP MEASURES AND PREVENTIVE CARE

There are many things women can do for themselves before becoming pregnant and during pregnancy to increase their own health and the health of their babies. There are even measures to help you become pregnant.

Optimizing Your Chances for Becoming Pregnant

Once a couple makes the commitment to start, expand, or complete a family, it often becomes crucial to them to accomplish this goal as soon as possible. In their fervor to achieve pregnancy, many couples diminish their chances by having sex too often. Daily sex may lower sperm counts, reducing the chance of one reaching the egg. The best advice for getting pregnant is to continue your normal sexual activity, without contraception, of course, and see if you get pregnant within a few months.

If this doesn't happen, you can optimize your chances by having sexual intercourse every other day (or night), starting about a week after your menstrual period begins. If you know when you ovulate (see Chapters 2 and 13), recent studies suggest that daily intercourse in the few days preceding ovulation may give you a greater chance for getting pregnant than sex every other day. Your partner should not wear pants or underwear that is too tight, and avoid excess alcohol and marijuana. These substances can adversely affect the number or quality of sperm. Some evidence shows that cigarette smoking also may affect sperm quality.

A variety of easy-to-use home kits that demonstrate the fertile time in a woman's cycle through urine testing are now available. They are expensive, however, and for most couples, unnecessary. You may want to try one for a cycle or a few cycles if several months of "leaving it to nature" prove unsuccessful. More information on problems with fertility is provided in Chapter 13.

If you are under 35 years old and have regular menstrual cycles, you should wait for at least a year after first planning a pregnancy before you become worried about not becoming pregnant, unless you know that you or your partner has a particular problem. If you are 35 or over, you might consider seeking the advice of a fertility specialist after six months of consciously trying to become pregnant.

If you have not been keeping a record of your menstrual periods, this is a good time to start. Physicians and midwives use the first day of your last menstrual period to determine how pregnant you are. The more exact you are about this date, the easier it is to date your pregnancy. Your menstrual pattern, especially your cycle length, may also influence when you will have your baby. Cycle length is the number of days from the first day of one period to the first day of the next. Although the date your baby is due can never be determined exactly, women who usually have *short cycles*—less than 28 days apart—may have their babies a bit before their due date. Women who usually have *long cycles*—more than 28 days apart—may have their babies a bit after their due date. Menstrual record keeping is a good health practice not only when you are planning a pregnancy, but for your entire life.

Birth Control and Planning

If you use a *barrier method* of contraception, including the diaphragm, the male or female condom, the cervical cap, or contraceptive creams, foams, or film, you can safely become pregnant anytime you stop using it. This is true for an IUD as well.

If you take oral contraceptives ("the pill"), many physicians and midwives recommend that you have one regular menstrual period before trying to become pregnant. Although the hormones in the pills do not accumulate in your body and there is no danger in becoming pregnant as soon as you stop taking the pills, dating your pregnancy is harder if you haven't had at least one period. You or your partner can use a barrier method until you have a period and then start trying. Plan, then, to stop the pill at least a month before you wish to become pregnant.

If you use Depo-Provera ("the shot"), it may take a while for the hormone to clear your system. There is no danger in getting pregnant right away, but only about half of women who stop using Depo-Provera become pregnant within 10 months of the last injection. Be patient. About 93 percent of women using Depo-Provera become pregnant within 18 months after the last injection. This doesn't mean the shot causes infertility—the percentage is no lower than the percentage of the general population who try to get pregnant and succeed within this time period. The rate of pregnancy at 18 months after the last shot is the same as the pregnancy rate following use of all reversible methods of birth control, but women should expect a longer delay in getting pregnant after discontinuing Depo-Provera than after discontinuing other methods.

Couples who rely on natural family planning methods have an advantage in becoming pregnant. These methods, discussed in Chapter 27, can also help you achieve pregnancy. You can continue using them, not to see when you are infertile, but to see when you're most fertile.

Avoiding Exposures

From the time you stop using contraception, you should be cautious around potentially toxic substances. These include radiation, smoking, alcohol, and drugs—not only illegal ones, but also some over-the-counter and prescription medications. This might be the time to enroll in Nicotine Anonymous or join Alcoholics Anonymous; the health of your future baby is certainly a powerful motivation to stop harmful habits. The American Cancer Society, the American Lung Association, or the local March of Dimes can refer you to a local program to help you stop smoking. More information on *teratogenesis* (the effects of such exposures on the fetus) is provided in Chapter 5, pages 73 to 122.

If you regularly use medicines—whether prescription or over-the-counter—discuss with your physician or midwife whether or not you should continue, discontinue, or change them. Do not make these decisions on your own. Most often, if you need medication, it is better for your developing baby that you receive treatment than suffer the consequences of not being treated. This is true even if the medication carries some risks to the fetus. For some illnesses, such as epilepsy, certain drugs are preferable to take in pregnancy. You may need some time to adjust to new medications and dosage schedules, so if you are on continuous treatment for any condition, you and your regular physician can use the prepregnancy months to find the medication regimen that is best for you and your developing baby. Meanwhile, you can use birth control.

If you think you may be exposed to chemicals or other toxic substances at your workplace, you can ask for a copy of the Material Safety Data Sheet (MSDS) that your employer is required to keep on file. While this sheet will be unlikely to identify which workplace materials are reproductive or developmental hazards, you can bring it to your physician or midwife for review. Although you or your care provider may not be familiar with everything listed, a number of resources can provide up-to-date information. These include the local March of Dimes, REPROTOX, an on-line database, and The Reproductive Toxicology Center's Clinical Inquiry Program (2440 M Street, NW, Suite 217, Washington, DC 20037-1404, 202-293-5137). Your state may also have a hotline to call regarding reproductive hazards. Your physician or midwife should know how to contact this resource, if available.

If you live or work in an old building with peeling paint, or use imported lead-glazed pottery for food storage or serving, you may be exposed to lead. Exposure can occur among workers in the following industries: mining, welding, smelting, printing, painting, shipping, and automobile manufacturing. Working with storage batteries also poses a possible risk. Elevated blood levels of lead—above 10 micrograms per dL—may be harmful to the developing fetus. If you are concerned about such exposure, your practitioner can order a blood lead test before you become pregnant. The National Lead Information Center at 1-800-LEADFYI can provide useful information about lead removal.

It is wise to see your dentist before you start trying to have a baby. If you need X rays or treatments requiring medications, these can be accomplished before there is any possibility of fetal effects, however miniscule they may be. If you are already trying to get pregnant, and there is any possibility that you might be, you must inform the dentist or any other care provider of this. If you aren't using birth control, then schedule your dental checkup when you have your period, so you can be reasonably certain that you are not yet pregnant. If you need X rays, insist on an abdominal shield. If your dentist recommends medication or surgical treatment, consider using birth control again until the treatment is completed, just to be extra safe.

If you are near or over 40, discuss having a mammogram with your physician or midwife. As mammography is not recommended during pregnancy and mammograms may be difficult to read in breast-feeding women, it could be several years before your next opportunity. Be sure you are not yet pregnant when you have this X ray.

Nutrition

Women who are either overweight or underweight should use this planning time to try to achieve a healthful weight. Women who are underweight at the start of pregnancy tend to have smaller babies, even if they gain as much weight during pregnancy as somebody who starts her pregnancy at a normal weight for height. Optimal weight should be achieved through a well-balanced diet. This is discussed in more detail in Chapter 10. A recommended eating plan is also found in Chapter 10. If you have an eating disorder, such as anorexia, bulimia, or pica (eating nonfood substances), this is the time to seek help from therapists and care providers skilled in these areas and to consider joining a support group.

Little is known about whether the father's nutrition can affect the developing fetus. It is known, however, that four nutrients are essential in making sperm: vitamins A and E, linoleic acid (a type of fatty acid), and zinc. In general, a well-balanced diet will supply these nutrients.

Folic Acid

Recent research has shown that *folic acid*—a type of B vitamin—is important in the prevention of several types of birth defects called *neural tube defects*. The neural tube forms the brain and spinal cord. Neural tube defects, such as spina bifida, occur during the early weeks of fetal development if the tube doesn't close completely. These conditions may be so slight as to be unnoticed or they may cause physical and mental disability along a continuum from mild to severe.

To exert its preventive effect, folic acid must be taken before conception and in the earliest weeks of a pregnancy. For this reason, women planning a pregnancy should take folic acid supplements as soon as they stop using birth control. In fact, the Centers for Disease Control and Prevention (CDC) recommend that all women of childbearing age have 0.4 mg of folic acid every day.

National survey results estimate that most American women eat foods containing about 0.2 mg of folic acid daily. The additional recommended 0.2 mg can be achieved through diet. Foods high in folic acid include:

- leafy green vegetables
- liver
- yeast
- other green vegetables
- legumes
- nuts
- whole grains
- fortified foods, such as cereals anad breads

At least one serving of these foods a day in the preconception period and during pregnancy is recommended.

Several factors may interfere with folic acid intake:

- Much of the vitamin's activity can be lost in storage and cooking.
- The hormones in oral contraceptives may interfere with absorption and metabolism of folic acid, so women who have been on oral contraceptives over long periods may have slight folic acid deficiencies.
- Excessive alcohol intake can also lead to a folic acid deficiency.

If you are uncertain whether your diet gives you an adequate amount of folic acid you should take an over-the-counter supplement of 0.4 mg (400 micrograms) of folic acid or a multivitamin tablet containing the same amount of folic acid. Read the label. Today, just about any vitamin that calls itself a prenatal supplement has 0.4 mg of folic acid.

For women who have already had a baby with a neural tube defect, the CDC recommends taking 4 mg (4000 micrograms) of folic acid per day from 4 weeks before conception through the first 3 months of pregnancy. If there is a chance that you may have a vitamin B12 deficiency (*pernicious anemia*), discuss having a B12 blood level drawn before you start taking such a high dose of folic acid. A vitamin B12 deficiency sometimes occurs in strict vegetarians or vegans or after prolonged antibiotic therapy. The folic acid can mask the diagnosis of this condition, which can cause you to have neurologic damage unless treated. A 4 mg dosage of folic acid is available only by prescription. Do not take extra multivitamins to get more folic acid as there is a possibility that vitamins A and D can be harmful to the developing fetus if taken in too high doses.

A Final Word

Remember, becoming pregnant should be pleasurable! With a little advance planning, it also can be a time for you and your partner to optimize your health and health care. A simple preconception visit, combined with good nutrition, vitamin supplementation, and common-sense avoidance of exposures will provide an excellent start to a healthful pregnancy.

———— ∞∞∞ ————

CHAPTER SEVEN

Care During Pregnancy

Care for pregnant women has changed greatly over the past half-century. Birth used to be thought of as a medical event associated with illness. Prenatal care was seen as a technical task. Its goal was simple: to conduct pregnancy so that it ended up with a healthy mother and a perfect infant. The concept that the process of having a baby could and should be a full, happy, family-centered experience, free of fear and anxiety, was virtually nonexistent. Paternalistic attitudes were common; doctors saw pregnancy and labor as their concern, not the woman's or her family's. The concept of giving women emotional support or confidence through childbirth education was foreign. Physicians and hospitals rarely believed that a woman could make decisions about her pregnancy, labor, or birth.

The publication of the first edition of this book in 1937 gave recognition to a woman's right to information about her body, her pregnancy, and her birth. In the same decade, an English physician, Grantly Dick-Read, fostered the idea of childbirth without fear. Yet formal childbirth education was not introduced in the United States until the 1950s. The psychoprophylactic or Lamaze method of childbirth was brought to France from Russia by Dr. Ferdinand Lamaze in 1951, and to the U.S. several years later by Marjorie Karmel, a woman who had experienced the method in Paris. Later, the Bradley—or husband-coached—method of childbirth was introduced and still later, the cooperative method of childbirth developed. These methods, in addition to offering nonmedicated ways to cope with labor pain, sought to demystify the process of reproduction by explaining the facts of conception, pregnancy, labor, and infant care.

The concepts of gentle birth, advocated by Dr. Frederick Leboyer in 1975, and of mother-infant bonding, researched and popularized by Drs. Marshall Klaus and John Kennel in the 1970s and 1980s, increased our awareness of the needs of the newborn in the birthing process. The birthing center and home birth movements have changed the atmosphere surrounding birth so that it has become a profound personal experience associated with individual development, growth in interpersonal relationships, and enhanced self-esteem for women. This increased consciousness has affected not only out-of-hospital birthing, but in-hospital childbirth as well. The increasing use of midwives, with their strong commitment to family-centered care, has also contributed to the movement to involve women in their own pregnancies and childbirth experiences.

The women's rights movement has influenced the conduct of prenatal care and birthing so that women now routinely determine how they want their pregnancies and births carried out. Fathers or other support persons are involved without question in the process. Siblings may be included, to the extent their parents choose, and classes are available especially for them. You should be completely at ease raising any concern with your physician or midwife; in fact, a major criterion for choosing any provider is the comfort you feel broaching and discussing intimate subjects with her or him.

PRENATAL CARE: AN OVERVIEW

The first clinic in the United States to give periodic care to pregnant women who were not ill, had no noticeable symptoms of problems, and were not in labor was established in Boston in 1909. Its main concern was the early detection of toxemia of pregnancy (high blood pressure with liver and kidney complications) among women who appeared healthy. These women received regular blood pressure checks, weighing, and tests of urine for protein. Because of early detection, toxemia today is not the threat to maternal life that it once was, except in countries where regular prenatal care is not available.

The goals of prenatal care today, while still focused on concluding pregnancy with a healthy mother and baby, have expanded impressively. In 1989, the Expert Panel on the Content of Prenatal Care of the Public Health Service of the U.S. Department of Health and Human Services proposed the following objectives for prenatal care:

For the pregnant woman:
- to increase her well-being before, during, and after pregnancy and to improve her self-image and self-care
- to reduce maternal death and disease, fetal loss, and unnecessary medical interference in pregnancy
- to promote the development of parenting skills

For the fetus and the infant:
- to increase well-being
- to reduce prematurity, poor fetal growth, birth defects, and failure to thrive
- to reduce neurologic, developmental, and other illnesses
- to reduce child abuse and neglect, injuries, preventable acute and chronic illness, and the need for extended hospitalization after birth

For the family:
- to promote family development and positive parent-infant interaction
- to reduce the number of unintended pregnancies
- to identify for treatment behavioral disorders leading to child neglect and family violence

---

Recommended Reading

A good first step in promoting a healthy and satisfying pregnancy is to become as educated as possible. Many books for pregnant women are available besides this one. Some are general information books, similar to this; others cover such specific topics as pregnancy and parenting for the working woman, nutrition and special diets for pregnancy, herbs to use in pregnancy, exercises to prepare for and recover from delivery, and care of the newborn. Many books are devoted entirely to breast-feeding. Some volumes focus on the emotional or spiritual aspects of pregnancy, others on lovemaking during pregnancy. You can find books that describe each of the several approaches to psychological and physical support for the woman in labor. There are books about home birth and books that help you decide how you would like your birth carried out. There are books on midwifery. Books for pregnant women with diabetes and for women who have had cesarean births are available. There are books to help women cope with pregnancy loss. Books have been written for expectant fathers and for children expecting a sibling. A recently published book provides a guide to pregnancy expressly for African-American women. If you are a reader, you will not be at a loss for material. For our specific suggestions, see the Appendix.

Besides books, there are several other excellent resources. These include the American College of Obstetricians and Gynecologists, the American College of Nurse-Midwives, the Midwives Alliance of North America, the March of Dimes, La Leche League, the International Childbirth Education Association, and the American Society for Psychoprophylaxis in Obstetrics. Addresses and phone numbers of these and other helpful organizations are provided in the Appendix. Some of these organizations have web pages, and we have also listed these and other Internet resources.

Your public library most likely has a special section of books and videos on pregnancy, breast-feeding, and baby care. Your neighborhood video store may be a resource for tapes on childbirth and pregnancy exercise. Childbirth education groups in your community also may be able to supply you with audio and videotapes.

HOW TO CHOOSE YOUR SUPPORT SYSTEM

Your Physician or Midwife

The majority of the births in the United States today are managed by specialists in obstetrics. The American Academy of Family Physicians reports that about 20 percent of births are attended by family physicians. Midwives currently attend about 9 percent of the vaginal births in this country, approximately 7 percent of all births. Many physicians and midwives offer one visit, either before pregnancy or during its early weeks, just to talk. There often is no fee for this visit. Sometimes it is conducted as a group orientation or a telephone conversation. Take advantage of such offers to "shop around" if you are undecided about a provider during the pregnancy planning stages or at the beginning of the pregnancy.

Obstetricians

There are about thirty-nine thousand members of the American College of Obstetricians and Gynecologists (ACOG). Obstetricians have graduated from medical school and then completed four or more years of residency in obstetrics and gynecology. At the conclusion of this training program they are authorized to take a more-than-three-hour written examination on the factual basis of the practice of this specialty. Those who pass the examination may represent themselves as Board-eligible. This means they have met the qualifications set by the American Board of Obstetrics and Gynecology (ABOG).

The American Board of Obstetrics and Gynecology is one of more than twenty member-Boards of the American Board of Medical Specialties. It was established in 1927, making obstetrics the third oldest medical specialty in the United States. The Board is sponsored by the American College of Obstetricians and Gynecologists, the Association of Professors of Gynecology and Obstetrics, the American Gynecological and Obstetrical Society, and the American Medical Association.

After two or more years of practice as Board-eligible physicians, the candidates submit to the ABOG a list of all the women they have cared for and all procedures they have performed during the last full year of practice for review by the Board. If this review indicates that the quality and quantity of practice are sufficient to meet the standards of the Board, the individuals are invited for a three-hour oral examination. This is intended to scrutinize the level of their knowledge and the style of their practice. If all this is completed successfully, the individuals are authorized to identify themselves as Fellows of the American Board of Obstetrics and Gynecology. Most Fellows are required to be recertified by examination at regular intervals so that the Board can be certain that they have kept themselves up-to-date with the changing standards of practice.

Some obstetricians and gynecologists become subspecialists. ABOG currently certifies physicians in four subspecialties: gynecologic oncology (care of women with reproductive-related cancers); maternal and fetal medicine (care of women and fetuses with obstetrical problems or risks); reproductive endocrinology and infertility (care of women with problems related to the chemical or hormonal component of reproduction, with a particular emphasis on infertility); and female pelvic medicine and reconstructive surgery (care of problems of the urinary tract and disorders resulting from loss of muscle support of organs in the pelvis). Physicians who become subspecialists have completed an advanced educational program in one of these areas. If you have a serious medical or obstetrical problem complicating your pregnancy, you may choose to have a subspecialist in maternal and fetal medicine care for you, or your regular obstetrician may consult with a maternal and fetal medicine subspecialist. Sometimes these subspecialists are called *perinatologists*.

You can find out whether the physician that you intend to go to is Board-eligible or a Fellow (or Diplomate) by consulting the local medical society, the local medical library, or the office of the administrator of the hospital where your physician practices. The contact information for the national offices of both ABOG and ACOG is listed in the Appendix to this book. The doctor's office can also give you information about his or her qualifications. The directories listing those physicians who are Board-certified also list their age, where they went to medical school, and where they took their training. You can always reinforce the available information by consulting people in your own community whose opinion you value, including physicians in other fields. Incidentally, you should be warned that the Yellow Pages of the telephone directory is not a solid reference for doctors' qualifications.

Family Practitioners

Family practice is the medical specialty that provides care to all members of a family. Family physicians have not spent nearly as much time on their education in obstetrics, although they have done work in the field in the course of their training. The American Academy of Family Physicians, known until October, 1971, as the American Academy of General Practice, has more than eighty-five thousand members. Since 1969, examinations have been conducted in this specialty to certify and recertify practitioners. The Academy also requires continuing education of all its members. Its contact information is listed in the Appendix.

Approximately 25 percent of family practitioners provide maternity care. Most hospitals that are accredited by the Joint Committee on the Accreditation of Hospitals authorize such practitioners to take care of normal pregnant women and their births. Most often, the hospitals specify that major problems and operative obstetrics be referred to physicians with obstetrical qualifications. Approximately two thousand family practitioners, however, are credentialed to perform cesarean births in hospitals in the U.S. today. Such credentialing is determined on an individual basis. Some family practice residency programs include preparation in cesarean section. Most family physicians take an advanced training program or fellowship to learn this skill. Once again, local sources of information can be used to indicate a particular doctor's experience and credentials.

Why would somebody choose a general or family practitioner to attend a birth? There are a number of reasons. Perhaps the physician has been your family's doctor for a number of years—taking care of you and other family members. This is a distinct advantage; the physician with whom you already have an ongoing and trusting relationship can provide your maternity care and then care for the newborn. He or she can follow your children throughout their lives. Because, like midwives (see below), they often don't care for women with serious complications, and generally need to call in an obstetrician for a complication or for a forceps or cesarean birth, family physicians generally are less likely to utilize technological interventions, which may carry the risk of causing one problem while correcting another. Finally, in some communities, the only obstetrical provider is the general or family practitioner. This may be especially true in rural areas.

Midwives

Midwifery is a growing profession in the United States. It has evolved over time and continues to evolve as a variety of educational pathways have developed in recent years for professional midwives. Of course, the roots of the profession can be traced back through human history. Midwifery can make a claim as the oldest profession—or perhaps the second oldest, following motherhood. Indeed, the term obstetrics is derived from the Latin *obstetrix*, which means midwife. Early midwives were not necessarily educated in the art or science of maternity care; they were community women who were called upon to help other women in childbirth. Oftentimes, such women passed on their acquired knowledge to younger women—perhaps a daughter, niece, or granddaughter.

The history of midwifery in the United States is a rich subject, revealing much about social trends in the nation and its health care. It is well described in *Midwifery and Childbirth in America*, an extensive work by Judith Pence Rooks listed in the Appendix, and recommended to anyone who wishes further information on midwifery.

A History of Midwifery in the United States

Of course, midwives existed in America among Native American populations before the colonists arrived. Midwives also came to the United States as colonists and as enslaved Africans. Later immigrant groups included midwives. Training varied depending on where the midwives were from, but formal midwifery training was not available in the early days of this country. Although a few schools of midwifery opened in the nineteenth century, most were short-lived. By the early part of the twentieth century, they had all closed. Many midwives were illiterate; many believed that since childbirth was normal, there was no need for formal education. Most preferred to let nature take its course and did not want to learn interventions.

A variety of factors led to the decline in midwifery in the United States. As medicine became a profession in the eighteenth and nineteenth centuries, its schools were largely open only to men, mostly from the upper classes. Although early physicians disdained childbirth as a area for their practice, in the mid-eighteenth century a doctor in Philadelphia began to attend the births of upper-class women. This physician, Dr. William Shippen, established a maternity hospital for poor women and offered training to both men and women, but eventually restricted his students to males.

By the late nineteenth century, there was a physician-led movement in the United States to eliminate midwifery. A number of social changes occurring in the United States at the turn of the century influenced the further decline of midwifery. In summary, these social changes included:

• A rapid increase in the number of hospitals and improvements in transportation increasing access to hospital birth.
• The introduction of "twilight sleep" for childbirth—a combination of a pain killer and an amnesiac which made women forget the pain of labor and birth. Seen as a great advance and accepted by upper-class women, this motivated increasing numbers of women to use physicians for childbirth and to have their babies in the hospital.
• The increasing power of physicians through professional organizations while midwives, mostly poor and often poorly educated, remained unorganized.

Although today statistics on indicators of health such as infant and maternal mortality are readily available, this was not so in the past. The collection of data on health only began in the first few decades of the twentieth century. These initial data documented the poor health care received by American women and children. While conditions such as maternal mortality actually increased with the move of childbirth to the hospital due to *postpartum infection* ("childbed fever") spread by personnel who hadn't yet discovered hand washing, midwives became the scapegoat for these poor statistics.

One good consequence of this poor publicity for midwives was the development of formal schools of midwifery in a number of U.S. cities. The first such school opened at Bellevue Hospital in New York City in 1911 and remained open until 1935. By 1929, twenty-nine states provided some form of education to midwives. Indeed, in 1923, a White House Conference on Child Health stated that untrained midwives had records almost as good as physicians and that trained midwives surpassed the record of physicians in normal deliveries. Despite this good record, the percentage of births attended by midwives declined so that by 1935, midwives attended only 12.5 percent of all births in the United States. Most of these were in the rural South.

It was not until the 1920s and 1930s that the idea of educating nurses to be midwives began to take hold in the United States. A nurse, Mary Breckinridge, was almost single-handedly responsible for this. A well-educated woman from a prominent Southern family, she was widowed at age 25. She remarried, but following divorce and the loss of both her children, she made a commitment to devote her life to improving conditions for children. She completed a midwifery course in England and returned with two British nurse-midwives to start a midwifery service in rural eastern Kentucky. This was the beginning of the Frontier Nursing Service (FNS), the first nurse-midwifery service in the United States. The early nurse-midwives in this service traveled to births on horseback, delivered most babies at home, and, keeping superb records, demonstrated huge decreases in stillbirths, neonatal mortality, and maternal mortality.

FNS maintained its midwifery service by sending American public health nurses to England to become midwives. In 1931, a New York organization, the Maternity Center Association, established the first school of nurse-midwifery in the United States, the Lobenstine Midwifery School. It was affiliated with the Lobenstine Clinic, the second nurse-midwifery service in the U.S. From 1932 to 1958, midwives of the Lobenstine Clinic provided care to poor women in New York City, performing mostly home births, with a maternal mortality rate lower than the national average. It was not until the 1950s that major medical centers—first in New York City at Sloan Hospital of the Columbia-Presbyterian Medical Center and later at Johns Hopkins in Maryland—hired nurse-midwives.

Today, nurse-midwives practice in many major medical centers, in smaller community hospitals, in hospital-based birthing centers, in freestanding birthing centers, and in home birth practices. Midwives may be hired by a hospital to staff its clinic and attend the births of the women who use the clinic. There are municipal hospitals, such as North

Central Bronx Hospital in the Bronx, New York, where midwives pro-. vide the bulk of care to all pregnant women and attend most of the births. Midwives may be in independent private practice with privileges at private hospitals. They may work as partners or as employees of physicians. Nurse-midwives today provide full-scope health care to women so that women need not leave midwifery care once their maternity needs have ended—or before they have begun.

Although in the early part of the twentieth century, the introduction of nurse-midwifery was seen as a progressive step, today many women question the need to be educated first as a nurse in order to be a midwife. In many European countries, midwives are not necessarily educated first as nurses. In the United States today, midwives may be nurses or not, depending on their prior education and the state in which they practice.

Every state recognizes and accepts the national certification examination administered by the American College of Nurse-Midwives' Certification Council (ACC). Graduates of schools accredited by the American College of Nurse-Midwives (ACNM) are eligible to sit for this examination. ACNM is recognized as an accrediting body by the U.S. Department of Education. Most graduates of ACNM-accredited educational programs are nurses first. On successful completion of this examination, these nurse-midwives use the title C.N.M.—*Certified Nurse-Midwife*. Currently, one ACNM-accredited program educates women who are not nurses to be midwives and additional such programs are in development. These midwives carry the credential C.M.—*Certified Midwife*. To use these initials, they must have passed the same national examination as the nurse-midwives.

Another type of midwife licensed in a number of states is the C.P.M.—*Certified Professional Midwife*. These midwives have also passed a certifying examination developed by the North American Registry of Midwives (NARM), which was started by the Midwives Alliance of North America (MANA). MANA is an organization of both nurse-midwives and midwives but is more oriented towards the concerns of the latter—direct-entry midwives. Some NARM-certified midwives have attended excellent schools of midwifery, such as the Seattle School of Midwifery, and others have been educated through apprenticeships. These schools can be accredited by the Midwifery Education and Accreditation Council (MEAC), which, at this writing, is applying for recognition from the Department of Education as an accrediting body. Apprentice-trained midwives, or midwives with many years of experience but without formal education, may become eligible to sit for the

NARM certification examination after approval of an extensive portfolio documenting their qualifications.

You must check with an individual state's Department of Health or Department of Education for its acceptance or nonacceptance of NARM certification. One difference between NARM certification and ACC certification is that ACC certification mandates knowledge of gynecologic and other women's health care issues while NARM certification makes such knowledge optional. Another difference is that NARM certification includes a skills test while the ACC accepts validation of skills provided by the educational program.

Some states require C.M.s and C.N.M.s to meet standards for continuing education. Midwives certified by ACC since 1996 must meet recertification requirements at established intervals. Both ACNM and MANA expect their members to continuously update their education.

There is yet another group of midwives—*Licensed Midwives* or L.M.s. These midwives are recognized only in selected states. Standards for licensure vary greatly from state to state. If you are considering using an L.M. you should carefully research their credentials, including what kind of education she or he has had and what the state requirements for licensure are.

There are also people calling themselves midwives who are neither certified by examination nor licensed by state law or regulation. In some states such persons are practicing illegally; in other states, these practitioners are not breaking any law. Controversy exists regarding the appropriate term for such practitioners. Some people call them traditional midwives or independent midwives or *traditional birth attendants* (TBAs—as they are called in many other countries). Although many such midwives provide excellent care, there is no standardization of their education or guarantees of safety to the public such as there are for certified and licensed midwives. Anyone choosing to use a traditional midwife must be fully confident of her or his qualifications, but aware that this midwife's competency is not assured through the passing of a state or national examination or graduation from an accredited educational program. Another difference is that C.M.s and C.N.M.s must work within the health care system, with formal affiliations with physicians and hospitals. Traditional midwives are not regulated and therefore their affiliations, if they have them, are informal.

The American College of Nurse-Midwives and the Midwives Alliance of North America are listed in the Appendix at the back of this book. You can get information about certification of a particular midwife from these groups as well as from the individual state Department of Education or Professional Licensure.

Why would somebody choose a midwife over an obstetrician or family physician for maternity care? The word *midwife* means "with woman" (Middle English: *mid* = with; *wif* = wife or woman—explaining why men can be called midwives). The midwife believes in being with a woman throughout most of labor and birth and the postpartum period.

Some midwives advise women who wish a type of birth experience different from what they provide to seek services elsewhere; others respect the woman's wishes even when they differ from their own philosophy. Sometimes, this will depend on where the midwife attends births; the midwife in a hospital setting has more flexibility in terms of getting assistance from other personnel such as a nurse-anesthetist or anesthesiologist in providing epidural anesthesia, for example, while the midwife attending births at home may believe that most, or even all, pain medications are too dangerous to use at home.

The midwifery model of care actively promotes childbirth as a natural experience, a part of one's life cycle, a developmental task, as opposed to an illness or a medical event. In keeping with this philosophy, most midwives consider themselves the guardians of normal. They tend to let nature work in her best way, saving interventions for those situations where they are absolutely necessary. Of course, in order to protect the normal, midwives screen scrupulously for complications. They want to find them before they cause major problems.

When a complication or potential complication is found, the midwife may continue to care for the pregnant woman, providing ever-watchful surveillance to make sure that the problem does not worsen or lead to an adverse maternal or fetal outcome. In many instances, the midwife will consult with a physician—usually the obstetrician or family practitioner with whom she practices, but possibly a specialist in internal medicine, endocrinology, or other area of medicine. Sometimes, a midwife will have to refer you for part or all of your care to a physician. Whether or not the midwife will continue to be involved in your care, and the extent of her involvement, depends on the severity of your potential or actual problem as well as the practice agreements the midwife has with her collaborating physician.

A further tenet of midwifery philosophy is the active participation of the woman and the people she chooses to include in her pregnancy and birth. While midwives vary in the practices they are willing to implement, such as the use of medication and epidural anesthesia, most, if not all, believe that women should have as much education as possible to make informed choices at all times.

Licensed midwives always work in collaboration with obstetricians. Most often, you will have the opportunity to meet the obstetrician or obstetrical group with whom the midwife works. Then, if you develop a problem and need to have your care transferred to the obstetrician, this will be a comfortable transition. Occasionally, you will not have this opportunity when you are working with a midwife, and the transition may be stressful. Many problems, however, are amenable to collaborative care, where the midwife continues to care for the pregnancy and attend the birth while the physician manages the problem. Sometimes the woman needs the full care of a physician, as when there is severe fetal distress or other serious complication or when a cesarean becomes necessary. Many times, the midwife will continue to be involved, providing supportive care and even remaining with you during the cesarean and providing postpartum care. Some midwives receive training to assist in the cesarean. At other times, the midwife may not have hospital privileges or be otherwise unable to participate in your care when certain problems develop.

Collaborative Practices—A Team Approach

Health care practices today are increasingly following the team model. An obstetrician will often work, for example, with a midwife, a physician assistant, and a nurse practitioner. A physician assistant (PA) is specially trained to provide some components of medical care and work directly under the supervision of a physician. A *nurse practitioner* (NP), also called an advanced practice nurse, provides primary health care. In a maternity care service, the NP might be an *adult nurse practitioner* (ANP), a *woman's health nurse practitioner* (WHNP), an *obstetrical and gynecological nurse practitioner* (Ob/Gyn NP), or a *family nurse practitioner* (FNP). PAs and NPs generally provide in-office care, but usually do not attend births.

In group practices such as these, you may or may not have a choice of provider. Sometimes prenatal care is rotated among the many different types of practitioners and either a physician or midwife will attend your birth, depending on who is on-call when you go into labor. In other such practices you can choose your birth attendant; the midwives and physicians see separate groups of women. This is based on your preference, your health, and whether your pregnancy is complicated by problems. Of course, in any of these cases, an obstetrician is always available for emergency care should the need arise.

Many women feel that collaborative practices offer the best of all possible worlds. In many of these practices, other health care personnel also are available to provide components of care. These may include, for example, a nutritionist, a childbirth educator, a massage therapist.

Be Comfortable with Those Who Give You Care

Most important in choosing a physician, midwife, or group practice for your maternity care is that you be comfortable with the thought of working with this person or group. You must have confidence in the individual or individuals, and this in itself is a good reason for looking into their qualifications and attitudes before making a commitment to them. If, for example, you have strong feelings that you wish to breast-feed, it is not good for you to get your care from someone who is cool to the idea.

The same goes for the conduct of labor. If you have attitudes about or experience with fetal monitoring, you should find out whether it is the practice where you intend to deliver to require it or to individualize its use. If you have had a previous birth by cesarean and wish a vaginal birth, you should find out the attitudes toward such care on the part of those you choose to assist you in labor. What do you want your main source of pain relief to be? If you want to use relaxation, breathing, support, massage, and other nonpharmacologic remedies as much as possible, make sure your physician or midwife is comfortable with these options and won't pressure you into medications or epidural anesthesia. If you want an episiotomy only on indication and not routinely, make sure that your obstetrician or midwife doesn't believe in routine episiotomy. If you want rooming-in with your baby 24 hours a day, but the hospital where your physician or midwife delivers does not provide for that, you might think about switching providers. If you want an intravenous (IV) feeding tube only if you are dehydrated or need it for labor augmentation or medication, but the hospital at which your physician or midwife attends births insists on routine IVs, then you might want to find a provider at another facility, or consider a birthing center—or compromise and have an IV.

The fact that you have gone to a provider or facility does not mean that you are contracted to stay with it, if it turns out in the course of prenatal care that you are not at ease. If necessary, discuss this candidly with the people who have been providing your care so some resolution of the problem can be worked out amicably. Most of us who provide maternity care consider prenatal care as a commitment to follow through. We are often aware of the women who are uncomfortable in our care and are quite accepting when such women transfer themselves elsewhere. Of course, care will not be refused when you don't exactly see eye-to-eye with your practitioners. Try to continue to raise your concerns and come to compromise solutions if you have no choice, as when you live in a small town and there are no alternative providers.

If you have trouble raising your concerns, something is amiss. You should never feel silly asking any question; you should not feel rushed; you should never feel that your concerns are made to seem trivial. It's an old cliché, but the only silly question is the one you didn't ask!

If you discover at the end of pregnancy that you are unhappy with what your practitioner is offering for labor and birth, you can certainly switch providers even at that late date, although some practitioners and birthing centers will not accept a woman late in pregnancy.

Doulas

A *doula* (Greek: *doula* = woman's servant) is an old concept and a new profession. A doula is somebody who provides support to the laboring woman and/or the new mother. Labor doulas are sometimes called labor coaches or *monitrices* (a word coined by Dr. Lamaze). They are often on-call, like obstetricians, midwives, and other birth attendants, and will be with you for labor and birth. The advantage of a doula is that she (generally she) is especially trained or experienced in attending births and can provide excellent psychological and physical support. She can be great at massage, assisting with breathing techniques, helping with relaxation. She can often act as an advocate for you, intervening when hospital policies and your wishes seem incompatible.

The disadvantage of a doula, for some women, is that she is another professional. She is not a loved one and can interfere with the bonding that can occur during childbirth between a woman and somebody she loves. In well-staffed hospitals, nurses can provide the type of care that doulas provide. As midwifery, by definition, means "with woman," many midwives provide the same type of support that doulas provide, as well as managing the labor and birth.

In some cultures men are prohibited from being present during childbirth, or are not allowed to touch the woman in labor. In such cultures, a female doula may provide invaluable support. Some partners travel or may be otherwise unavailable for birth and again, in this situation, a doula may be a big help. Well-conducted, controlled studies in a variety of countries and settings consistently have shown that a trained support person in childbirth has definite benefits in labor, including reduced use of pain medication, lowered incidence of vacuum or forceps delivery, and fewer cases of a 5-minute Apgar score below 7 (see Chapter 21).

Support has been shown to shorten labor. Many doulas also provide care for the mother at her home after the birth. Unlike a baby nurse, doulas focus on the physical and emotional needs of the mother. Some doulas provide only postpartum care.

Some hospitals offer doula services or a doula can be located through several doula organizations, listed in the Appendix of this book.

Your Family and Friends

Thanks to the prepared childbirth movement, it has become almost customary for laboring women to have a loved one with them. Almost all institutions providing maternity care now accept the fact that most women will be accompanied by somebody during labor and for delivery.

Many women choose to have the baby's father with them—whether or not he is their husband—or the baby's second mother; others choose to have their sisters, mother or mother-in-law, or a friend. Some women or couples wish to have their older children present at birth. Other women choose to have more than one support person.

Who and how many people are admitted to a labor room may vary, however, from institution to institution. If you want your mother, your best friend, your sister, and your partner, you must make sure that there is no policy prohibiting more than one person from attending your birth. It is way too late to make your birth plans and then discover as you enter the labor room of a hospital that you cannot bring the people you had chosen to be with you.

In some institutions, more than one person can be with you, but not at the same time. In others, several people may be in the labor room, but not present for the birth. If you wish to have a child with you, make certain that the hospital policy will allow for that. If so, it should also allow for an extra support person, who is there to care for the child. In general, birthing centers have been designed for women to choose their own style of birth, including who and how many support persons to have. In your own home, of course, the decision is entirely your own.

PRENATAL VISITS

Ideally, prenatal care should begin prior to conception, as outlined in the previous chapter. We realize, however, that not all pregnancies are planned, not all providers educate women about the importance of a prepregnancy visit, and readers of books like this are usually already pregnant. The fact is, most pregnant women today have their first pre-natal visit during the early weeks of their pregnancy.

The Initial Visit

As soon as you think or know you are pregnant (see Chapter 3), you should contact a specific pregnancy care provider—see the preceding pages. The initial pregnancy visit should occur sometime in the first 12 weeks—or first trimester—of pregnancy. Optimally, it should take place when you are about 6 to 8 weeks pregnant. If you haven't had a precon-ception visit, the first pregnancy visit will be lengthy, and include all the components of the prepregnancy visits described in Chapter 6. If you had a preconception visit, the first pregnancy visit will be fairly short; it will involve updating your health history, reviewing the laboratory tests already completed, perhaps repeating a few of these, and redoing parts of the physical examination. It will include an abdominal exam and a pelvic assessment, depending on how pregnant you are.

The update of your health history will cover any early pregnancy danger signs that you may have had, such as bleeding and cramping, as well as normal but troublesome symptoms, such as nausea, vomiting, and headache. Your physician or midwife will ask if you have had any X rays since becoming pregnant, if you have been sick or exposed to any diseases, and if you are taking any medications.

The abdominal and pelvic examinations are to measure your uterus and compare its size to the size expected for how pregnant you are, based on your last menstrual period. If you are less than 12 weeks preg-nant, your uterus is still too small to be felt in the abdomen, so it can only be measured by feeling it through the vagina. A nurse, midwife, or doctor will check your weight and blood pressure, as they will on all pre-natal visits. Your urine also will be checked.

Some practitioners routinely perform *clinical pelvimetry* on a first pre-natal care visit. This means they feel, with their fingers, the size and shape of the pelvic cavity by palpating, through the vagina, the circle of bones that create the pelvis. This makes the vaginal examination slightly longer and a bit more uncomfortable. It alerts the practitioner to any structural abnormalities and gives a rough estimate of the likelihood that a normal-sized baby will fit through. Many practitioners, however, have given up this practice in prenatal care, believing that the pelvic bones loosen and expand in labor and that the strength and frequency of contractions as well as the position of the baby are more important indicators of whether the baby will pass through the pelvic cavity. Pelvic abnormalities were more common in the days—long gone in this country—when women suffered in childhood from rickets, a vitamin D deficiency. Yet many physicians and midwives still feel that knowing that a woman has an adequate pelvic size can be reassuring if labor proceeds slowly, and simply do not wish to lose this old-fashioned skill. A history of a fractured pelvis or structural abnormality is certainly a reason for your physician or midwife to perform clinical pelvimetry. Otherwise, this assessment is optional.

Whether or not you have had a preconception visit, one of the goals of the first pregnancy visit is to determine your due date—once known as the expected date of confinement and now called the *expected date of childbirth* (EDC) or *expected date of delivery* (EDD) (see Chapter 4). At the end of your first prenatal visit, you will usually know how pregnant you are and approximately when you can expect to deliver. Remember, of course, that this date is only an estimate. It is really the midpoint of a 4-week period. The baby can be born any time two weeks before or two weeks after this date.

Of course, the first prenatal visit is a time for you to ask all the many questions that have come to mind since you discovered that you are pregnant. These may include questions about prenatal care, fetal growth and development, exercise, sex, work, childbirth education, discomforts you might be experiencing or expect to experience, medications, infant feeding, maternity clothing—just about anything. Many of these should have been answered in advance if you had a preconception visit.

Other family members, including your husband or partner, your children, and your parents, may have questions. They can ask these if they come with you to the visit or you can ask for them if they are unable to attend or if you prefer coming by yourself or with only one family member.

Whether or not you ask questions, your physician or midwife may raise certain issues with you. These include physiologic and emotional changes of pregnancy, nutrition, vitamin and iron supplementation, the important option of in-depth HIV counseling and testing, safer sex, avoidance of toxic substances and drugs, giving up smoking and drinking, activity and exercise, and early pregnancy danger signs.

Routine Testing in Prenatal Care

The following table of laboratory tests utilized routinely in pregnancy, or within a year prior to pregnancy, was adapted from the recommendations of the Expert Panel on the Content of Prenatal Care. Some tests are advised for all women, others only for women at risk for particular problems. Most of these are performed to look for conditions that share a number of characteristics: these conditions are found somewhat commonly in young women yet most often have no obvious symptoms and they may affect pregnancy, the developing fetus, or the newborn. Chapters 12 and 16 provide greater details about some of the conditions that can be uncovered with these tests. Some physicians or midwives may choose to alter the specific tests used or the timing of such tests. Some women may need additional tests; these are discussed in Chapters 8 and 17.

You may notice that ultrasound, which has become widely used in pregnancy care, does not appear in the table of routine tests. Although generally considered a safe procedure whose benefits usually outweigh any possible adverse effects, its safety cannot be totally assured. For this reason, neither the National Institutes of Health nor the American College of Obstetricians and Gynecologists recommends routine ultrasound in pregnancy. Its use is reserved for selected reasons, of which there are many. These are discussed in Chapters 8 and 17.

ROUTINE TESTS IN PRENATAL CARE
Blood Tests

Test	What It Tests For	Timing in Pregnancy	Normal Values*	Follow-up When Values Suggest a Problem
Blood type and Rh factor	Possibility for incompatibility between mother's and baby's blood	Preconception or first visit	Any result normal, but if mother is Rh negative, possibility for incompatibility exists	Test for antibodies in blood; test baby's father's blood; if baby's father has Rh positive blood, or is unavailable for testing, repeat antibody testing later in pregnancy; treat with RhoGAM at 26–28 weeks and

*Where numeric, the interpretation of normal values may vary among laboratories and practitioners.

Test	What It Tests For	Timing in Pregnancy	Normal Values*	Follow-up When Values Suggest a Problem
				postpartum (see Chapter 8)
Chlamydial culture or screening test	Chlamydia infection (the most common sexually transmitted disease)	Preconception and/or first prenatal visit; may be repeated at 36 weeks	Negative	Treat with antibiotic; test and treat partner; retest for cure
Cystic fibrosis	Carrier for cystic fibrosis; most common among Caucasians	Preconception or first prenatal visit	Negative	Test partner; genetic counseling
Diabetes screen (1-hour Glucose Challenge Test—GCT)	Possible diabetes	26–28 weeks of pregnancy; earlier in women at risk for diabetes	Usually <135 or <140	Retest with 3-hour Glucose Tolerance Test (GTT) for definite diagnosis
Gonococcal culture or screening test	Gonorrhea infection	Preconception and/or first prenatal visit; may be repeated at 36 weeks	Negative	Treat with antibiotic; test and treat partner; retest for cure
Hemoglobin electro-phoresis	Sickle-cell anemia or trait (carrier state)	Preconception or first visit for women at risk (women from Africa, the Mediterranean, or Asia, or of such backgrounds)	Hemoglobin AA (normal adult hemoglobin)	Test partner; if partner has disease or is carrier, genetic counseling to discuss risk of infant's having disease; prenatal diagnosis of fetus available
Hemoglobin or Hematocrit	Low levels of this oxygen-carrying	Preconception and/or first visit; repeated	Hemoglobin ≥12 Hematocrit	Treat with diet and iron; retest after

Test	What It Tests For	Timing in Pregnancy	Normal Values*	Follow-up When Values Suggest a Problem
	chemical in the blood, or anemia. Often due to low iron, the major constituent of this chemical	in third trimester	≥36	treatment; if values remain very low, have additional laboratory testing for specific cause
Hepatitis B	Hepatitis B infection or immunity	Preconception or first visit	Negative antigen; may show positive antibody, indicating previous infection and possible immunity. If antigen is present, you may have the disease or be a carrier of the disease	If infectious, retest later in pregnancy; supportive care; treat baby
HIV testing after in-depth counseling	Presence of antibodies to virus causing AIDS	Preconception or first visit; may be offered again at 36 weeks. Many states have regulations regarding HIV testing, which have been under recent revision because of changing knowledge regarding prevention of transmission to the baby. Testing of the	Negative	See provider with experience caring for pregnant women with HIV; have counseling regarding treatment options to reduce possibility of transmission to fetus

Test	What It Tests For	Timing in Pregnancy	Normal Values*	Follow-up When Values Suggest a Problem
		mother can be refused, but testing of the newborn may be mandatory		
Maternal serum alpha-fetoprotein (AFP)	Possibility of some types of genetic defects (open neural tube defects— see Chapter 8)	14–18 weeks of pregnancy	Levels appropriate for timing in pregnancy	Sonogram to check dating of pregnancy; repeat test; if level remains abnormal, genetic counseling and amnio-centesis (see Chapter 8)
Pap smear	Cervical cancer or precancerous conditions, other cervical and/or vaginal problems such as infections	Preconception or first prenatal visit	Negative (Class I)	Repeat Pap smear after 3 months, further testing, or treatment, depending on findings
Random blood glucose	Possible diabetes	First prenatal visits for women at risk for diabetes	Usually <120	Retest with more specific blood test for diabetes
Rubella titer	German measles; shows susceptibility, immunity, or possible infection	Preconception or first visit; if susceptible, may need repeat test if exposure or symptoms occur	Negative test or low titer indicates susceptibility; high titer indicates possible infection; moderate titer, immunity	If susceptibility discovered pre-conceptionally, consider vaccination and avoid pregnancy for 28 days; if pregnant, avoid exposure and have vaccine after pregnancy. If possible in-

Test	What It Tests For	Timing in Pregnancy	Normal Values*	Follow-up When Values Suggest a Problem
				fection, retest to confirm; if pregnant and infected, seek genetic counseling to discuss risks to fetus
Serologic testing for syphilis (RPR or VDRL)	Syphilis	Preconception and/or first visit; may be repeated in third trimester in women at risk for sexually transmitted diseases	Negative results	Treat with penicillin or other antibiotic, unless previously treated, then retest for reinfection; test and treat partner; retest for cure
Serologic testing for toxoplasmosis	Toxoplasmosis infection for immunity	Preconception or first visit	Negative or low levels indicate susceptibility; moderate levels show infection with immunity; high levels may indicate current infection	Retest may be necessary to ascertain infection; if mother infected, treat with antibiotic to prevent fetal transmission; if susceptible, avoid cat feces, rare or raw meat
Tay-Sachs	Carrier of Tay-Sachs disease	Preconception or first visit in persons of Ashkenazi Jewish background	Negative carrier	Test partner; genetic counseling if both parents are carriers; prenatal diagnosis of fetus available

Test	What It Tests For	Timing in Pregnancy	Normal Values*	Follow-up When Values Suggest a Problem
Tuberculosis skin test (Tine or PPD)	Exposure to tuberculosis or possible past or present infection	Preconception or first prenatal visit or following known exposure	Negative (no or minimal redness or swelling at site)	Chest X ray after 20 weeks of pregnancy; possible treatment
Urine culture and/or urinalysis	Urinary tract infection	First prenatal visit; may be repeated if symptoms occur later in pregnancy or if at risk	Negative (no bacterial growth) on culture; no white blood cells or chemical called nitrite on urinalysis	Treat with antibiotic; self-help preventive and curative measures; retest for cure
Urine dipstick	Protein and sugar in urine, which may indicate kidney problems, preeclampsia (see Chapter 12), or possible diabetes	Preconception visits and first visit; repeated at all subsequent visits, although value as a routine test has been questioned	Negative	May necessitate further testing

Subsequent Prenatal Visits

At all prenatal visits, your physician or midwife will review how you are feeling and whether you have experienced any danger signs (see Chapters 12 and 14). A nurse or your doctor or midwife will weigh you and take your blood pressure. Blood pressure measurements are especially important in the second half of pregnancy (after week 20). The growth of your uterus will be assessed abdominally; most physicians or midwives measure the height of the *fundus* (the top of the uterus) at each visit. They may measure with their fingers, using fingerbreadths above or below certain body landmarks, such as your navel, to ascertain whether or not your uterus is growing appropriately. They may measure with a tape measure in centimeters; there are 2.2 centimeters in 1 inch. From 20 weeks of pregnancy, when the fundus just about reaches the navel, to 36 weeks, the uterine measurement should approximately equal your weeks of pregnancy, plus or minus two centimeters. So, if you are 28 weeks pregnant, your uterus should measure 28 centimeters, or between 26 and 30 centimeters.

At about 20 weeks of pregnancy, the fetal heart can be heard with a special stethoscope called a *fetoscope* and will be listened to at each visit. If the tubing on the fetoscope is long enough, you might be able to hear your baby's heartbeat, especially as the baby grows larger. Your partner can listen also; so can your other children or anybody who accompanies you to a prenatal visit. Many practitioners today use a Doptone or Doppler to hear the fetal heart; this instrument uses *ultrasound* (or sound waves) to amplify the fetal heart tones so that you can hear them loudly and earlier in pregnancy. The intensity of ultrasound used with this type of Doppler is so far below the level considered dangerous in humans, and the duration of exposure at each visit so short, experts have not questioned the safety of this application of ultrasound. The fetal heart can be heard quite early with a Doppler—sometimes at 10 weeks of pregnancy or even before. The value of this remains uncertain as not hearing it doesn't mean there is a problem; it may just make you and your provider nervous.

Leopold's Maneuvers

Starting at about 26 weeks of pregnancy, your physician or midwife will perform hand maneuvers on your abdomen known as *Leopold's maneuvers*—to feel the baby's position inside the uterus. These maneuvers help the practitioner determine the *lie*—whether the baby is in an up-down position (longitudinal lie) or lying sideways (transverse lie). They help assess the baby's *presentation*—which part, usually the head or buttocks, is nearest the pelvis. They tell the *position*—on which side the baby's back and legs are. They tell something about *descent*—whether the baby has entered the mother's pelvic cavity or not. With these maneuvers, the practitioner can help you and your partner feel the baby's various parts.

Vaginal examinations generally aren't necessary during the normal course of pregnancy, except to take a specimen for screening or when infection is suspected, or if you show signs of premature or preterm labor. Although some women like to know whether their cervix is thinning out (*effacing*) or opening (*dilating*) as their due date approaches, this doesn't provide much useful information. The state of the cervix in late pregnancy is not a reliable predictor of either the onset of labor or its duration, but if pregnancy has exceeded the due date by at least 1 or 2 weeks, a cervical check may help decide the advisability of induction (see Chapter 22).

Several additional activities are important in prenatal care. Time should always be made available for you and your partner to ask questions. No topic should be considered silly or taboo. Danger signs appropriate to the timing of pregnancy should be reviewed at each visit. Plans for infant feeding and the conduct of labor should be discussed by the third trimester (approximately 24–26 weeks). Information should be provided to you about the signs of labor, including preterm labor; what to do when labor begins; and choices available for pain relief in labor, with discussion of their advantages and disadvantages. Information about childbirth education classes should be given fairly early in pregnancy. While most classes begin at the eighth month or thirty-second week, some types of childbirth education start earlier in pregnancy and these options should be made available (see the following section).

The Timing of Prenatal Visits—Recommendations of the Expert Panel on the Content of Prenatal Care

For many years, practitioners have scheduled prenatal visits on a monthly basis until about 7½ or 8 months (30 or 32 weeks), followed by visits at 2- or 3-week intervals until the last month (36 weeks), when they become weekly. Some practitioners vary this schedule by seeing women every 3 weeks between 6 and 7½ months, which adds one additional visit (i.e., visits at 24, 27, 30, and then 32 weeks, instead of 24, 28, and 32 weeks). Women following one of these schedules have between 12 and 15 prenatal visits. The Expert Panel on the Content of Prenatal Care questioned the value of such frequent care and recommended fewer visits for women with healthy pregnancies. For women having their first baby—*nulliparas*—the following schedule was suggested:

Preconception visit: in the year preceding pregnancy
First visit: 6–8 weeks
Second visit: within 4 weeks of first visit
Third visit: 14–16 weeks
Fourth visit: 24–28 weeks

Fifth visit:	32 weeks
Childbirth education classes:	weekly from 32 to 38 weeks
Sixth visit:	36 weeks
Seventh visit:	38 weeks
Eighth visit:	40 weeks
Ninth visit:	41 weeks

For *multiparous* women—women who have already had a baby—the recommendations allowed the second visit to be a telephone contact.

In our experience, few if any providers have actually adopted this pregnancy visit schedule. We provide it here to demonstrate that the timing of visits in pregnancy can be flexible. We must emphasize that a reduced number of visits in pregnancy is safe only when certain conditions are met:

1. The pregnancy must be normal and free from risk; otherwise, visits must be more frequent. They must become more frequent if the pregnancy changes from normal to abnormal. Risks include, for example, preexisting diseases, such as high blood pressure, diabetes, sickle-cell anemia, blood clotting disorders, and severe asthma; pregnancy-induced diseases such as gestational diabetes or pregnancy-induced hypertension (*preeclampsia*); a previous poor pregnancy outcome, such as a premature or low birth weight baby; a poorly growing fetus; problems with the placenta; or the development of signs of preterm labor.

2. Extensive health education must be provided at each visit, focusing especially on danger signs to report before the next visit.

3. Childbirth education classes must be offered—either a series of five or six classes or two refresher classes for women who attended a series in a previous pregnancy. If a woman does not choose to attend classes, then more frequent prenatal visits should be considered.

4. Support services such as smoking cessation programs and psychological counseling must be available as integral parts of prenatal care whenever needed.

PREPARED CHILDBIRTH

Childbirth has often been called a life crisis. Crisis in this sense of the word is not negative, but means a time of great change and upheaval. It is a time for growth and restructuring of many relationships. It is a time to assume a new role and new responsibilities. Childbirth also is a time of discomfort and a time of hard work. For a great deal of human history, however, childbirth was a family or social event. Women delivered at home and loved ones were nearby, if not actually present at the birth. It wasn't the mystery it became when laboring women began to be escorted to the hospital, left there, and brought home with a new baby a week or more later.

The childbirth education movement began in the 1930s in Europe, Asia, and Africa and has had a variety of thrusts to it. A now-famous story was told by the English obstetrician Grantly Dick-Read, who worked in South Africa and England. He asked a woman whose birth he attended if it hurt. "No," she responded. "Was it supposed to?" This inspired Dr. Dick-Read's thinking that a good deal of pain in childbirth is based on fear. He developed the concept of the fear-tension-pain syndrome and published a book called *Childbirth Without Fear*. At that time, heavy doses of analgesia and anesthesia were commonly used in English hospitals. Dr. Dick-Read advocated providing information to women on the physiology of labor and what to expect at birth. He encouraged exercises and breathing techniques for relaxation.

Dick-Read's book did not appear in the United States until the 1940s. Its publication led to a movement for natural childbirth and the establishment of classes for pregnant women. Later, childbirth educators in the United States added their own approaches and developed new methods of prepared childbirth.

In the early 1950s, a French obstetrician, Dr. Ferdinand Lamaze, visited Russia with a colleague to learn how the concept of conditioned reflexes was used to help women tolerate labor. This was based on the work of the Russian physiologist Ivan Pavlov and his famous salivating dogs. Dr. Lamaze taught Pavlov's concepts in childbirth preparation classes. He focused on a series of deliberate breathing techniques, practiced until they became conditioned responses to contractions. These were meant to distract women from the pain of labor. The babies' fathers participated in these classes and worked with their wives in exercising, relaxing, and breathing. Known as the Lamaze method, this is probably the most widely used technique for preparation for childbirth in the Western world today—although with great modifications since its introduction.

The Lamaze method was brought to the United States not by a professional, but by a mother—Marjorie Karmel—who had delivered one baby in France with Dr. Lamaze and another using his techniques. Karmel's *Thank You, Dr. Lamaze* was published in the U.S. in 1959 and led to the development of ASPO, the American Society for Psychoprophylaxis in Childbirth. Psychoprophylaxis refers to the use of psychological methods (*psycho*) to prevent *prophylaxis* (pain) in childbirth.

Most Lamaze teachers today have modified the rigid breathing techniques developed by Dr. Lamaze and concentrate on more natural forms of breathing. In the early days of Lamaze classes, some women complained about feeling like "failures" if they didn't breathe "properly" or if they required medication. Today, childbirth teachers often focus more on self-determination, on women having the knowledge to choose the way they want their childbirth to be conducted (to the extent possible given the many natural variations in labor and delivery). They provide women with a variety of tools to use for pain relief, such as relaxation, psychological support, breathing, the application of heat and cold, massage, position changes including walking, and, if necessary, various types of pain medication. Many childbirth educators teach more eclectic methods, borrowing from the Lamaze or Psychoprophylactic method and utilizing other techniques such as imagery and a relaxation program called *progressive relaxation*, not specific to childbearing. Some instructors use principles of hypnotherapy, massage, or acupressure.

Several other concepts have been introduced in childbirth preparation so that today it is much more than simply a way of dealing with pain. Robert Bradley, an American obstetrician, emphasized the role of the husband, developing "husband-coached childbirth," or the Bradley Method. Other childbirth educators stress the emotional or spiritual aspects of birth.

In the 1970s and 1980s, the emphasis of childbirth education broadened to include the immediate needs of the newborn. Another French obstetrician, Frederick Leboyer, helped focus attention on the entry of the baby into the world. He encouraged reducing the stimuli that could affect the baby by turning down the lights, speaking quietly in the delivery room, and stressing gentleness in the management of the delivery. Dr. Leboyer recommended that the newborn be placed in a tub of warm water, which has the unhappy effect of separating the baby from the mother. While Leboyer may not have been entirely sensitive to the needs of the birthing mother, his concept of gentle birth has increased our awareness of the emotional needs of the newborn. More recently, yet another French obstetrician, Michel Odent, advocated for waterbirth, allowing the mother to gently birth her newborn directly into a pool of water. (This is a controversial topic which should be discussed with your provider.) The earlier work of the U.S. pediatricians Marshall Klaus and John Kennel on maternal-infant bonding also led to change in the ways births have been conducted in the past several decades. They too are proponents of compassionate care of the newborn from the moment of birth, and for immediate support of the mother-infant relationship.

Today, generally accepted principles of childbirth education or preparation include:

- That women know what is happening during the processes of pregnancy, labor, birth, and the postpartum period
- That women have choices in the way they want their births conducted
- That women are active participants in all aspects of birth (an early book on childbirth education written by an American obstetrician, Irwin Chabon, was called, appropriately, *Awake and Aware*)
- That women have loved ones with them in childbirth, and that these loved ones also can participate in the birth process (the number of participants may be limited, however, by the logistics or policies of the birth setting)
- That the maternal-newborn relationship be fostered by the birth and the immediate period afterward

Formal Childbirth Education

Today, childbirth classes are conducted under a number of auspices: hospitals, the American Red Cross, childbirth education groups, midwifery groups, doctors' offices, community centers, college- and university-sponsored graduate education, churches, and visiting nurses services. A number of organizations train and certify childbirth educators, including ASPO, the International Childbirth Education Association (ICEA), and the American Academy of Husband-Coached Childbirth. National organizations such as these have set up specific outlines for classes and for training courses for childbirth educators. Many labor and delivery nurses and midwives also teach childbirth education classes without additional certification. Often, your midwife or physician will recommend a particular childbirth course or instructor.

Remember that hospital classes will largely tell you about the specific policies of the hospital. Privately taught classes may provide you with more options, but not all of these may be possible if you are delivering at a hospital with set policies. You may want to talk with several childbirth educators before registering for classes to learn about their education, philosophy, and approach. You can check with the childbirth organizations listed in the Appendix to this book to learn whether a teacher has met any of their standards.

Classes in preparation for childbirth are generally started somewhere about the twenty-eighth week, although some educators offer early pregnancy classes. Early classes may focus on topics such as nutrition in pregnancy and common discomforts of pregnancy—things you have already experienced by the twenty-eighth week. Some teachers offer a brief series, or a single class, as a "refresher" for women and partners who took their classes for a previous birth. Special preparation classes are available for women planning to birth at home. You may wish to set up a schedule for your own needs with your childbirth educator.

There are also classes devoted to the care of the newborn. Indeed, hospitals often offer such teaching sessions to new mothers following delivery. These include the obvious features, such as diapering, feeding, and bathing a newborn baby; the basic pattern of newborn urination and bowel movements; and the advantages and disadvantages of breast- and bottle-feeding. It may seem strange to the experienced, but women who are mothers for the first time sometimes are quite unsure of how to respond to a crying baby. They may be hesitant to follow their instincts, although these usually direct them toward bonding with the baby.

Exercise is another subject that may be stressed in classes in preparation for childbirth, not necessarily as part of a "method" but under the general heading of physical fitness. Little research has been done on exercise in pregnancy and exercise standards have not been developed for pregnant women. In general, if a woman is accustomed to strenuous exercise it will harm neither her nor her baby if she continues the activities during her pregnancy. If complications should develop, your physician or midwife may modify or restrict your exercise program. If you are used to being sedentary, begin exercise slowly in pregnancy and increase gradually. Chapter 9 discusses exercise in pregnancy more specifically.

Unsolicited Advice

A pregnant woman is a ready target for a wide range of well-meant but unasked-for instruction. Even in today's very medically oriented society, superstitions about pregnancy abound. Few pregnant women have escaped the warnings of well-wishers who caution them against going swimming, reaching up to high shelves, wearing high heels, indulging in intercourse, eating certain foods, and so on. The list is apparently endless. Many claim to be able to predict the sex of the fetus by gazing into the eyes of the mother-to-be or by looking at the shape of the bulge, or through a variety of other mysterious ways. Pregnancy is a very public state and even strangers do not hesitate to communicate their prediction to the mother. Of course they are correct about 50 percent of the time.

The best way to handle advice that you readily recognize as pure superstition is to listen to it politely and then follow the dictates of your own common sense. Remember that there is no truth to the old tale that *port wine stains* or *strawberry marks*, which are actually diffuse collections of blood vessels within the skin, are produced by experiences of the mother during pregnancy. But it has been scientifically proven that the baby does experience events in the world outside the uterus and after birth can remember sights and especially sounds experienced in the late months before birth. A baby may be born knowing the rhythm of his or her mother's voice through hearing it repeatedly while in utero. Sensitive fetuses can even learn a melody this way. Evidence exists that the higher centers of the fetal brain are working in the last trimester, or last three months, of pregnancy. There is no evidence, however, that visual, auditory, or other sensory stimuli received by the mother during pregnancy can cause any physical changes in the fetus.

Women also love to tell pregnant women their own birth stories. Unfortunately, too many women whose births are normal feel that their stories are too boring to tell or that once the baby came, nobody was interested in their experience anymore. This means that often we don't hear birth stories until we are pregnant and that most birth stories we do hear are the ones in which something went terribly wrong. A pregnant woman today could easily get the feeling that birth is a very scary and dangerous event, when in fact most births are totally normal. Ask women who do not volunteer their birth stories to tell them to you. Most often they will be reassuring and medically uneventful, but there will be something to learn in them. Do not try to plan your birth, however, on anyone else's. Each birth is different—even for the same woman.

THE ENVIRONMENT FOR LABOR

Along with changes in health care and in education has come a change in concepts of what labor facilities should look like. In the 1940s a labor room in a major hospital might have been a rather large room done in gray ceramic tile. A low bedspring, coming to about eighteen inches off the floor, without either headboard or footboard nor in any way adjustable, covered by a thin mattress, might have stood in the middle of the floor. The only other furniture in the room might have been a bedside table. The windows were likely to be barred by heavy wire mesh, and the room looked for all the world like the isolation room in a psychiatric hospital.

In the half-century since, we have changed to labor beds with ample springs and innerspring mattresses, sometimes with bolsters and other appurtenances of bedroom luxury. Floors may be carpeted and comfortable overstuffed furniture are often provided for both the woman in labor and her support team. The electronic gear that we have come to employ so extensively can be stored inconspicuously and everything done to attempt to simulate a comforting home environment. Music is occasionally piped into the room, lighting is indirect and soft, curtains are hung in the windows, and it is taken for granted that a maximum of privacy will be assured.

Not every hospital is able to provide environments as pleasant as this, but more and more the effort is being made in modern obstetrical facilities to make the surroundings homelike and comfortable.

Perhaps an even more far-reaching change is the option of choosing a birthing center to have a baby, or to birth at home. In the middle of this century, home birth was considered something to do only if you were very poor and couldn't afford the hospital. The hospital was the place for educated, middle- and upper-class women. More recently, however, as women have been seeking more control in the conduct of their births, women in these socioeconomic categories have opted to deliver in out-of-hospital settings. Several large studies published in major medical journals have shown that with careful selection of women for these births and with the births attended by educated providers, birthing center and home birth can be as safe as hospital birth for mother and baby. Readily accessible medical consultation and a back-up hospital are essential. Currently, the overwhelming majority of babies in the U.S. are delivered in hospitals.

Women and their partners should think about what it is they want for their birth. They should read as much as possible—see the reading list in the Appendix. They should talk to friends and family members who have had babies about the quality of their experience. They should discuss with their physician or midwife his or her views on the use of routine fetal monitoring or other technologies. Later chapters of this book will help in making these decisions. Before pregnancy, women should talk to current gynecologic care providers to see if they attend births. If so, find out where your physician or midwife delivers and something about his or her approach to pregnancy care and birth.

Your Place for Birth

There are four types of birth places from which to choose. The overwhelming majority of women in the United States today give birth in hospitals. Three other choices include in-hospital birthing centers, freestanding birthing centers, and one's own home. Where you choose to birth will depend on a number of factors.

The most important considerations in deciding where to birth are your own health and your own preferences, as well as those of your partner or support persons. If you are completely healthy, you can choose any place and your birth will be safe, assuming it is attended by a qualified midwife or physician, as discussed in the previous section. However, you need to be comfortable. If you are fearful of being at home, then you shouldn't be there. If you are fearful of the interventions that are sometimes unavoidable in hospitals, like speeding labor if it does not adhere to a certain time frame, then perhaps that is not the best place for you. If you want nonintervention if at all possible, but do not want the responsibility of preparing the environment for birth, then perhaps a birthing center is where you should have your baby.

Each individual will assess the advantages and disadvantages of various birthing options differently. For example, having lots of personnel available at a hospital may be an advantage to one woman and her partner and a disadvantage to another woman who wants a quiet, private birthing experience. The accompanying table provides generally accepted pros and cons of each birth setting, but remember that your own interpretations may differ. Remember, also, that anybody can have a baby in a hospital but only healthy women with uncomplicated pregnancies can deliver in an out-of-hospital setting. Women and families should not merely consider the number of advantages and disadvantages at each site, but what each of these advantages and disadvantages means to them—how important each is. Worrying about a transfer may be enough to negate all other advantages of an out-of-hospital site.

ADVANTAGES AND DISADVANTAGES OF BIRTH SETTINGS

HOSPITAL

Advantages	Disadvantages
1. Has a variety of health care professionals available should you or your baby need immediate attention beyond that provided by your obstetrician or midwife.	1. Personnel may enter and leave your room without asking; you may sacrifice privacy and may find the interruptions disruptive.
2. In addition to your own support person you will have an obstetrical nurse to care for you during labor.	2. You may hear noise from other rooms and other laboring women.
3. Has available a variety of pharmacologic and nonpharmacologic measures for pain relief such as narcotics and epidurals.	3. The hospital may have policies that its staff, including your physician and midwife, are compelled to follow. These may or may not be consistent with your wishes for the conduct of your own birth (see pages 189–192 for some of these).
4. Has facilities available should you need emergency care, such as a blood bank for transfusion and operating room for a cesarean birth.	4. There may be pressure to use interventions, such as epidural anesthesia, as it is the hospital's usual way of managing labor.
5. May be equipped to care for newborns with special needs such as low birth weight or very low birth weight, or babies with serious birth defects. If it is a community hospital without this ability, it will have a transport system available.	5. The availability of technology, making its use more widespread, can create a "slippery slope" of intervention—one intervention leading to another.
6. Most obstetricians, family practitioners, and nurse-midwives attend births in hospital, giving you a wider choice of providers when you choose this birthing option.	6. You may have restrictions both on whom you have with you for labor and on how many support people may be present.
7. You may have in-hospital classes on newborn and maternal care during your postpartum stay.	7. The baby may be taken to a newborn nursery for a short time or may be kept in a nursery and only brought to you at regular intervals.
8. You may have a newborn nursery available for the baby should you wish some rest time.	8. The type of care you receive may be dependent on how busy the service is at the particular time when you are in labor. Staffing, for example, may be patterned after an "average" day but you may have your baby on a busy day.
9. A breast-feeding specialist or lactation consultant may be on staff to assist you.	9. A lack of privacy may interfere with the initiation of breast-feeding and some nurses may feed formula in a bottle even if you wish to breast-feed.
10. There may be restrictive visiting policies, such as limitations on siblings; the newborn may have to be moved to the nursery when visitors come.	

IN-HOSPITAL BIRTHING CENTER

Advantages	Disadvantages
1. Has a variety of health care professionals available should you or your baby need immediate attention beyond that provided by your obstetrician or midwife. 2. In addition to your own support person you will have an obstetrical nurse to care for you during labor. 3. Most obstetricians, family practitioners, and nurse-midwives attend births in the hospital, giving you a wider choice of providers when you choose this birthing option. 4. You may have in-hospital classes on newborn and maternal care during your postpartum stay. 5. A breast-feeding specialist or lactation consultant may be on staff to assist you. 6. You are close to the hospital; you may be a floor away or even just down the hall, yet the environment is more home-like, less technology is utilized, and fewer interventions are routine. 7. Although you are in the hospital, you will have more control over the conduct of your birth, such as being able to walk in labor and to birth in a variety of positions. 8. You may be able to eat and drink in labor. 9. You can usually have whomever you want with you at birth and as many support people as possible. 10. If you need/desire pain medication or labor augmentation, your physical transfer is easier; you need not change buildings. 11. If you need emergency care, for yourself or your newborn, it is as readily available as it is for women delivering in a more traditional	1. There still may be a number of personnel in and out of your room. 2. If the personnel are not really committed to nonintervention, they may still use technology and other invasive procedures routinely or liberally; a pretty room or suite of rooms does not a philosophy make. 3. The availability of a bed in the birthing center may not be guaranteed; you may have to use the regular hospital with all its routines and policies if the birthing center is "filled" when you arrive in labor. 4. You may still need to be transferred to a postpartum unit after birth and subjected to the same postpartum policies (e.g., those regarding the newborn and maternal-newborn separation; breast-feeding support or nonsupport, etc.) as the women delivering in the attached hospital. 5. The type of care you receive may be dependent on how busy the service is at the particular time when you are in labor. Staffing, for example, may be patterned after an "average" day but you may have your baby on a busy day.

hospital setting. If your newborn has a problem, you will already have been admitted to the same institution as the baby. 12. If you need to be transferred to the regular obstetrical unit, you may be cared for by the same doctor or midwife and perhaps the same nurses. 13. Many in-hospital birthing centers are beautifully designed and equipped with amenities such as Jacuzzis and double beds.	

FREESTANDING BIRTHING CENTER

Advantages	Disadvantages
1. There are fewer routines to follow; care is more individualized; you have more say in how you want your labor and birth conducted. 2. You can usually have whomever you want with you at birth and as many support people as possible. 3. You can usually choose your position for labor, including walking as much as you want. 4. You will most likely be able to drink and eat in labor; an intravenous is not started routinely. 5. You are not separated from your baby at all. 6. There is a formal transfer arrangement made with a nearby hospital so that in the case of an emergency, you have a system of care already set up. 7. There are few personnel working in a birthing center so you will have more privacy for your labor and birth. 8. Most birthing centers have a limited number of births per month and are staffed for one-on-one, one-on-two, or at most one-on-three care so your care is less de-	1. You will need to transfer to a hospital should a complication arise before, during, or after your birth. Rarely, a transfer may have to occur rapidly. 2. If your birth attendant, or those on staff at the birthing center, does not have hospital privileges, your entire care will then be transferred to the hospital if you are no longer deemed eligible for birthing center care. 3. There may be a group approach at the birthing center and you may not know who will be your birth attendant; it may be one of many midwives or physicians on staff—generally midwives, in most free-standing birthing centers. 4. There are restrictions on the type of pain medication available; if you need or desire something that is not offered at the birthing center, such as epidural anesthesia, you will need to be transferred. 5. If your labor does not progress according to set standards, you will need to be transferred to a hospital. 6. If your newborn has a problem

pendent on how busy the center is when you arrive in labor. 9. Many birthing centers have outdoor areas and, in good weather, you can spend some of your labor outside. 10. Many birthing centers are beautifully designed and equipped with amenities such as Jacuzzis and double beds.	and needs to be transferred to the hospital, you may not be admitted as well.

YOUR HOME

Advantages	Disadvantages
1. Your own home offers you the most flexibility—and responsibility—in terms of ways of conducting labor: whom you want with you and how long your labor can progress before you need to be transferred (as long as there are no maternal or fetal problems). 2. You have the most privacy in your own home. 3. You need not move yourself and your belongings in the midst of labor (or within a few hours or days after birth to return home). 4. Your newborn is never separated from you and you can establish immediately your own sleeping arrangements and patterns of nursing and family living. 5. Your other children can be at the birth and still be in the protected atmosphere of their own home; they can play in their own rooms while you are in labor or wander in and out of the labor area. If they need to go to sleep, they can be awakened to see their new sister or brother. 6. You can have music or rituals of your choosing and alter the environment in any way you choose. 7. If you and/or your practitioner are	1. You will need to transfer to a hospital should a complication arise before, during, or after your birth. Rarely, a transfer may have to occur rapidly. Transfer may pose more difficulties from home if a system has not been established. 2. If your birth attendant does not have hospital privileges, your entire care will then be transferred to the hospital if you are no longer deemed eligible for a home birth. 3. There are restrictions on the type of pain medication available; if you need or desire something that is not offered at home, such as epidural anesthesia, you will need to be transferred. 4. If your newborn has a problem and needs to be transferred to the hospital, you may not be admitted as well. 5. You need to assume a large share of the responsibility for the birth, from preparing the bed linens to cleaning up afterwards. 6. You need to have a plan for transfer to a hospital should you need to transfer. This must be worked out and tested out in advance of labor. 7. You may have difficulty finding a qualified practitioner to attend your birth at home.

familiar with herbal or homeo-pathic remedies, you will be able to use these at home. 8. You may find yourself part of a supportive community of home-birth parents and families. 9. Women and families often feel that home birthing provides the most emotionally and spiritually satisfying place for birth.	8. Unexpected complications may be more difficult to manage at home than in the hospital. 9. You will need a caregiver to super-vise other children during labor and birth. 10. You may have to defend your deci-sion to your community—your friends and family. You will find that the majority of obstetricians with whom you may consult are strongly opposed to home birth because of concerns about complications.

Naturally, if you have any medical complications at the start of pregnancy, or develop a pregnancy complication at any time during prenatal care or labor, or even following the birth, you will need to be in a hospital. This may require a transfer from the birthing center or home. If you are uncomfortable with the idea of transferring, possibly during the throes of labor, then you should choose a hospital from the outset. If you are willing to take the risk of having to transfer, but would prefer to be out-of-hospital if at all possible, then you can choose an out-of-hospital site. The willingness to be transferred to a hospital should the need arise is absolutely essential for anyone choosing to have a baby outside of a hospital.

Of course, another criterion for where you birth is where your physician or midwife will attend. Some practitioners only attend births in a hospital, or only attend birthing center deliveries. Others have exclusively home birth practices. Some women and their partners will first choose the place of birth and then find a practitioner who will attend their birth at their chosen location. Some women, however, have already established a close relationship with a provider and will choose to have that provider attend their birth regardless of the location.

In general, our philosophy is that the attitude and practices of the physician or midwife are more important than the place of birth. You can choose an in-hospital birthing center, for example, because it has carpeted rooms with patterned wallpaper and dainty sheets, and an old-fashioned wooden cradle for the baby, but hidden behind the wall is every piece of technological equipment that will fit. If your physician or midwife believes rigidly in the use of that technology, you can be sure it will come out from behind those closed doors, regardless of whether it is really needed, and regardless of your wishes. So, be certain you and your provider agree philosophically.

The appearance of the birthing environment is not necessarily indicative of the birth experience you will have. One of us used to work in a large inner-city hospital. The rooms were small and had minimal adornments but most births were in the labor rooms and technology was used only as necessary—even with a population considered high-risk by socioeconomic need. If the personnel attending a birth truly believe that pregnancy is a normal, nonmedical event, then even in the most hospital-looking environments, birth can be kept natural with minimal interventions. Conversely, unless the personnel are committed to a philosophy of nonintervention, the most homelike room will not make for a natural birth.

In addition to learning about the philosophy of your physician or midwife, you need to discover something about the policies of the institution. You can ask your physician or midwife about the policies at the institution or institutions with which he or she is affiliated: sometimes you have a choice of birth place even with the same practitioner. Or you can go on a tour of the facility. Many childbirth education classes, especially if given at a hospital, will take you on a tour. This, however, is usually late in pregnancy. Call the facility and see if tours are available outside of the childbirth class or call the instructor and see if you can attend the tour early in your pregnancy. If you have limited choices, you can sometimes have a birth experience more to your liking by staying home as long as possible, assuming, again, that everything remains normal. (When to go to the hospital, of course, is something to discuss in advance with your physician or midwife.)

Both in-hospital and free-standing birthing centers are eligible to apply for accreditation by the National Association of Childbearing Centers. We recommend choosing centers that are so accredited. Freestanding birthing centers are more likely to follow safe guidelines if accredited and in-hospital birthing centers are more likely to be more family-centered if accredited.

Birthing Choices

Here are some questions to think about with your partner and to ask your physician or midwife. They relate to a variety of decisions about birth. Generally, when a woman and her partner have no preference, the physician or midwife will do what she or he is accustomed to doing. Therefore, it is good to know what the usual practices of your provider are and what restrictions are put upon her or him by the institution where your birth will be. If you don't know what your own preference would be in answer to any of the following questions, continue reading this book. See the book list in the Appendix. Talk to other mothers and fathers. Look at videos; watch television. Search the internet. And think. Think about what feels best for you. Nobody can really tell you that except yourself.

The prenatal care:
• How many members are there in the practice? What are their specialties?
• Will you have a primary provider, or will you see all members of the group during your pregnancy? Will this provider be of your own choosing and can you choose between a physician and midwife?

The labor:
• Will your primary provider be your birth attendant or will you be cared for in labor by whomever in your group practice is on-call that day?
• Can you choose between a physician and midwife to attend your birth?
• Will your physician or midwife meet you in the admitting area of the hospital or birthing center or will you be examined initially by a resident who will then contact your provider?
• Will you have a routine pubic shave (not shown to be effective in reducing infection rates)?
• Will you have a routine enema (not shown to be effective in stimulating or shortening labor and may have side effects)?
• Will you be allowed to walk around in labor (shown to help reduce the length of labor)?
• Who and how many people will be able to accompany you in labor?
• Will children (if you wish) be able to be present in labor?
• What is the provider's rate of epidural anesthesia? The institution's? What other pain relief measures does the provider generally utilize or recommend? If you have an epidural, will it be a low-dose, "walking" epidural?
• Can you bring your own pillows, clothes, food?
• Will you be able to eat/drink in labor? (See Chapters 18 and 19 for more discussion of this.)
• Will you routinely have intravenous (IV) tube feedings?

• Will you have routine continuous electronic fetal monitoring, intermittent electronic fetal monitoring, or intermittent monitoring of the fetal heart tones by fetoscope? Will the type of monitoring be determined by your risk status? (See Chapter 20 for a complete discussion of the pros and cons of each of these types of monitoring.)

• What is the limit to how long each stage of labor will be able to go on, as long as progress is being made?

• What is the limit to how long you will be able to push as long as progress is being made?

• Will you be able to push in a variety of positions, such as knee-chest, side-lying, squatting, on the toilet?

The birth:

• Will you be able to birth in the same room as your labor?

• Will you be able to birth in a variety of positions, including squatting or side-lying, as you prefer at the time?

• Who and how many people will be able to be with you at the birth?

• Will children (if you wish) be able to be present for the birth?

• Will your partner or other support person be able to cut the umbilical cord? Will he or she be able to put hands on the baby at the delivery?

• Is there a policy regarding audio or video taping of labor and/or birth should you want this option?

• What is the physician's or midwife's rate of episiotomy (should be very low as routine episiotomies have not been shown to be beneficial)?

• What is the provider's rate of cesarean birth? (This may be difficult to evaluate as it will depend on the type of practice the provider has; for example, if the provider is known as a "high-risk" physician, or is certified in the subspecialty of maternal and fetal medicine, other physicians may send women with serious problems to this physician, increasing her or his cesarean birth rate. In any case, it should be as low as possible. The Healthy People 2000 goals of the U.S. Public Health Department advised a cesarean birth rate of 15 percent by the year 2000. While this takes into consideration not only what is desirable, but what is possible, it can be used as a reasonable cut-off for a cesarean birth rate, even by a specialist in problem pregnancies.)

• Will your partner/support person(s) be able to accompany you if you have a forceps, vacuum, or cesarean birth?

• Will you be able to have epidural anesthesia for a cesarean birth, except in the situation of severe fetal distress requiring the fastest type of anesthesia available (most likely general anesthesia)?

The period after birth (postpartum):

• Will you be able to hold the baby immediately? Will the physician or midwife put the baby on your abdomen as soon as s/he is born?

• Will you be able to nurse immediately after birth?

• Will you ever need to be separated from the baby—i.e., will you have 24-hour rooming-in starting immediately?

• Will the baby's physical examination be at your bedside or, if not, can you go to the newborn nursery for the examination?

• How many hours/days will you and the baby need to stay in the hospital/birthing center?

• Will you be able to stay in the hospital if the baby needs to remain there longer than you do?

• What kind of emergency care is available should the baby need special care? Is this care on-site or via transfer? If transfer, what is the transfer system?

• Will the nurses give the baby formula if you do not have 24-hour rooming-in or will they wake you up to nurse?

• Does the hospital have a breast-feeding specialist or lactation consultant on staff?

• What, if any, type of classes for newborn and mother care are available postpartum?

• What are visiting policies postpartum—for your partner, other family members, friends, other children? Does having visitors mean the baby will have to go to the nursery?

• If your baby needs special care, is kangaroo care available (see Chapter 25)? What are visiting policies for the mother/father/others in the special care nursery (often called the NICU—Neonatal Intensive Care Unit)? Can the parents participate in the newborn's care in this nursery?

FINANCING YOUR MATERNITY CARE

Health care financing has been undergoing rapid change in the past decade. For this reason, it is impossible to write with any certainty what services will be covered by insurance companies and to what extent. Coverage changes at a phenomenal rate and varies by state, by plan, and even within plans, depending on the employer. We can only provide some general guidelines regarding the questions to ask and the pitfalls to watch out for.

With the increasing reliance on what is called *managed care*—or should be called managed payment—families need to be very careful in choosing health care plans, where they have a choice, to make sure that what they want for birth will be covered. Some states, for example, mandate that health insurance cover midwifery care for pregnancy, birth, and the postpartum period. In states that do not mandate this, women must check to make certain their policy covers the services of midwives, should they want this option. In more than fifteen states, there are laws prohibiting the denial of access to any licensed provider, with two provisos: their education and scope of practice includes services covered by the plan and they are willing to meet the plan's conditions.

If appropriate, you should check to determine whether birth at a birthing center will be covered (it usually is since these births are less expensive, relying on fewer technological interventions and with shorter stays). A home birth is less likely to be covered; again, if this is the option you want, you must check in advance with your insurance company.

We discussed previously that you might have a preference for a particular physician or midwife or place for birth. Remember, some plans only provide coverage if you use a provider within the plan's network. If you can only use in-network providers, get the list of your plan's obstetricians, midwives, or family practitioners who provide maternity services and see what information you can find out about them, including where they attend births. You might want to make an appointment to have a gynecological visit with a potential obstetrical provider or group and find out something about the philosophy of the provider or members of the group. You might want to ask women (or men who've participated in a birth) whose opinions you value and whose philosophy is similar to yours.

If your health plan allows you to use out-of-network physicians or midwives, but pays only a percentage of their fees, then find out what these fees are. Determine whether or not you can afford the percentage of the fees for which you will be responsible—often 20 percent, up to a maximum out-of-pocket expense, beyond which you will be reimbursed for the whole fee, if the insurance company determines that it is reasonable and customary. If the insurance company deems the fee beyond its usual and customary reimbursable fee, which varies by state, city, or even county, then you will be responsible for any amount above the usual and customary. The provider's office can provide you with its standard maternity service fee. Maternity services are generally covered in a package—one fee for the entire prenatal care, the birth, and the 6-week postpartum visit. You can call your insurance company to see if your provider's fee is usual and customary. You may need to send in a form. Remember, of course, that tests such as ultrasound, blood work, and amniocentesis, for example (see Chapters 8 and 17), will have additional fees. The services of additional team members, such as genetic counselors, radiologists, anesthetists or anesthesiologists, will be billed separately. It is up to the insurance company to set each usual and customary fee and decide how much it will pay.

Another concern is whether you need to pay any of the provider's fee up-front. Insurance companies will often pay for only the prenatal care at the start of the pregnancy, not paying for the birth until it has occurred. In-network providers cannot bill you for anything except your standard co-pay, but those out-of-network may ask you to pay before your insurance company is willing to reimburse. Generally, hospital fees are billed directly to the insurance company as are fees for services rendered at the hospital, such as anesthesia.

With the change in laws to assure that "pre-existing conditions" are covered, it is not as imperative as it was previously to get the coverage you want before you are pregnant. However, in many places of employment you can only change plans at certain times of the year. If you marry, or have a baby, you can update your plan to reflect this changed status—a baby need not wait until the usual change of plan time to be put on your insurance. But in ordinary circumstances, where there is no major life change, you must change during the weeks set aside for this. In smaller places of employment, you may not have a choice. In this case, you may choose to have your partner's plan cover you. Again, these are things that should be investigated as soon as you are thinking about a pregnancy. Even before it seems like a reality, check the maternity coverage of your plan so you are not taken by surprise in the event of an unplanned pregnancy, or even a planned one.

PREGNANCY DISABILITY

The federal Pregnancy Disability Act of 1978 prohibited discrimination against pregnant workers. Under this act, employers must treat pregnancy in the same way they treat any other medical condition, although specific benefits are not guaranteed. If an employer does not offer disability for other medical conditions, they may not offer it for pregnancy. Where disability is a benefit, 6 weeks are generally allowed for an uncomplicated labor, delivery, and postpartum period. Information about more specific state laws can be obtained from the regional office of the Department of Labor. You can also contact this office if you believe your employer is not complying with the law.

CHAPTER EIGHT

Early Fetal Testing

Our ability to learn about the fetus was revolutionized in the second half of the twentieth century. At the middle of the century, we were just able to see the fetal skeleton by X ray at about the fourteenth week of pregnancy (although not a common practice) and hear the fetal heart with a stethoscope at 20 weeks. Physicians were just learning to make in utero estimates of the severity of fetal Rh disease (*erythroblastosis*). Today, far less mystery surrounds fetal life. We can visualize the fetus and scrutinize it for anatomical and functional disorders. We can carry out a variety of blood tests that may indicate possible fetal problems. We can obtain samples of the early placental structures, amniotic fluid, fetal cells, and fetal skin to make precise diagnoses. We can do in utero surgery, and treat a variety of medical problems of the fetus.

THE IMPORTANCE OF FETAL ASSESSMENT

By the 1970s, the concept that the fetus could be assessed before birth had become somewhat commonplace. Today, fetal assessment allows for life-saving treatment in the womb for some abnormalities, or for preparation for treatment immediately after birth. Fetal assessment and diagnosis give parents the option of an abortion for a fetus who would die shortly after birth or require endless medical care and whose quality of life would be severely diminished. Conversely, the availability of fetal testing has made safe childbirth possible for individuals and couples who might otherwise choose not to risk childbearing, such as those who are known to carry genes for certain illnesses. Utilizing fetal assessment is one of many ways that parents today can control their lives.

In this chapter, we repeatedly use the words "defect," "disorder," "anomaly," and "abnormality." We realize that for babies born with problems, and for parents and families of these children, these words may be offensive. We use them for want of other language and to express that the conditions discussed here adversely affect quality of life, for most people, in ways ranging from minor to severe. In no way is this discussion meant to minimize the lives of individuals born with congenital problems.

There are many reasons a fetus might have a disease or defect. Birth defects may be caused by infections the mother contracts during pregnancy or other diseases she may have, such as diabetes mellitus. Other defects are the consequence of exposures, including alcohol, medication, recreational drugs, radiation, and environmental toxins. These teratogenic effects are discussed in depth in Chapter 5. Still other birth anomalies result from abnormalities in chromosomes or particular genes. Some anomalies are *multifactorial*—they cannot be traced to a single cause but are the result of a variety of factors working together—a genetic predisposition, for example, combined with an environmental exposure. The origin of many defects, unfortunately, remains unknown.

There are a variety of ways the fetus can be examined in pregnancy. Some are noninvasive, or relatively so, and considered safe; others are invasive and carry risks to the pregnancy or the fetus. Noninvasive techniques include ultrasound, testing of the mother's blood, and sometimes testing of the father's blood. Invasive techniques include chorionic villus sampling (CVS), amniocentesis, cordocentesis or percutaneous umbilical blood sampling (PUBS), and fetoscopy or direct viewing of the fetus through a scope. The newest technique—very much in experimental stages—is *embryoscopy*, direct viewing of the embryo before 11 weeks of pregnancy.

Prenatal genetic testing, and pre-conceptional testing of parents to determine whether they carry the genes for certain diseases, is becoming more commonplace. Over time, the likelihood is that more diseases will be tested for early in pregnancy, or even before pregnancy.

Of course, despite the availability of these technological and scientific methods of fetal assessment and the continuing refinement and expansion of their ability to detect fetal conditions, no test or series of tests can guarantee the health of any fetus. Approximately 1 to 2 percent of babies are born with a congenital problem; about 1 percent of these are serious. Some of these babies are born to women who did not have a reason to have fetal assessment; other are babies whose conditions defy diagnosis in the womb.

THE SCIENCE OF GENETICS

To understand how each fetal assessment technique described in this chapter determines fetal well-being or its lack requires some understanding of the science of genetics or heredity. This science is the basis for many recent medical advances and will continue to be central to medical progress in the foreseeable future. Of course, a complete discussion of genetics requires at least its own book, so what follows is merely a glimpse.

Chromosomal Abnormalities

Chromosomes carry genetic material or *genes*. The normal number of chromosomes in human beings is forty-six, made up of twenty-three pairs. Twenty-two pairs, the *autosomes*, carry the genes that encode the information necessary to develop a person from a single-celled *ovum* (egg). The autosomes are numbered in order of size, the largest labeled number 1 and the smallest, number 22. The additional pair of chromosomes is the pair of sex chromosomes. This pair determines the individual's genetic sex. Each sex chromosome is designated X or Y. A female has two X chromosomes and is designated XX. A male has an X and a Y chromosome and is designated XY. The sex chromosomes also contain genes, but most traits are carried on the autosomes.

The chromosomes consist of short arms and long arms, with relatively inactive material at the point where the arms cross each other, the *centromere*. The short arms, designated as *p*, and the long arms, designated as *q*, are always on the same side of the centromere—the short arms are uppermost.

Every cell in the human body undergoes division into "daughter" cells at some time in its life—*mitosis*. During mitosis, the chromosomes divide into two equal sets of twenty-three pairs. This process gives rise to two new cells with genetic makeup identical to that of the parent cell. In the formation of reproductive cells, however, the process of division produces a sperm or egg cell equipped with only one of each pair of chromosomes. This process is called *meiosis*. Because of meiosis, egg and sperm merge in fertilization to form a potential human being consisting of twenty-three chromosomes from one parent and twenty-three from the other.

During the ordinary working life of a cell, when it is not in the process of division, the material of the chromosomes is not visible even under the microscope. At the time of cell division the chromosomes become thicker and more easily take up a chemical stain for visualization. At this time the chromosomes can be analyzed. A complete picture of the chromosomes is taken and they are mapped in order. This is called a *karyotype*.

Defects in Chromosome Number

Chromosomal defects may be the result of either abnormal chromosome number or structure. Abnormal chromosome number, called *aneuploidy*, can result from a missing chromosome or one or more extra chromosomes. Extra chromosomes may occur in either the autosomes or sex chromosomes. A fetus cannot survive the loss of an autosome—each autosome carries too much genetic material. A fetus can form and develop, however, lacking one sex chromosome, but only if it has an X but no Y chromosome. Not even an embryo will form if there is a Y but no X.

Embryos with one X, designated as 45X (previously denoted as 45XO), have a high rate of miscarriage in the first trimester and of fetal death in the second. Some do develop to full term, however. Their condition is called *Turner syndrome*. They ordinarily look like females but have rudimentary sex organs. They are commonly short in stature. There is an increase in heart and kidney problems among individuals with Turner syndrome. Deficiencies in sexual development can be corrected with hormone therapy, but 45X individuals cannot reproduce.

Occasionally when sperm or ova form during cell division they acquire excess numbers of chromosomes, either autosomes or the sex chromosomes. *Trisomy* is the addition of an extra autosome for a total of forty-seven chromosomes. Trisomy occurs because of *nondisjunction*—when the chromosomes fail to separate (disjoin) or to separate completely—during the formation of a sperm or ovum. Rarely, this can happen during early cell division of the fertilized egg, explaining why it is possible for only one of a pair of identical twins to have a trisomy.

There are also individuals with extra sex chromosomes, as many as two or three extras, for a total of forty-eight or forty-nine chromosomes. Individuals with forty-seven chromosomes who are 47XXY are said to have *Klinefelter syndrome*. They tend to be tall, gangly males with small genitalia and even smaller testes who cannot produce sperm. The individuals who are 47XXX are externally normal females with normal fertility; a small proportion of these suffer from a mild degree of mental retardation. The even rarer individuals with forty-eight and forty-nine chromosomes all manifest minor degrees of mental retardation and are infertile. They may be externally male or female.

Trisomy of the larger chromosomes ordinarily results in a fertilized ovum that cannot survive embryonic life. The pregnancy miscarries. When trisomy of the chromosomes having very short arms occurs, a live birth is possible, although these fetuses and infants tend to be smaller than usual. The most common trisomy involves chromosome number twenty-one and is responsible for *Down syndrome*.

An abnormal chromosome number may occur simply by accident, as an inherited characteristic, as a consequence of advanced maternal age, and rarely as a consequence of advanced paternal age. Most forms of nondisjunction become more frequent as the mother's age increases. The accompanying table will give you some idea of the likelihood of having a baby with Trisomy 21, a baby with any one of the three trisomies compatible with life, and a baby with any chromosomal abnormality at given maternal ages. Although older mothers are more likely than younger ones to conceive an infant with a trisomy, the actual number of such babies is greater in women under 30 today. This is because there are so many more babies born to women under 30 and because mothers over 35 are offered routine testing for the condition and, on its discovery, often choose not to carry the fetus to term.

The figures in the table are lower than the number of trisomies found by first trimester chorionic villus sampling because some of the affected fetuses do not survive to be born alive. Trisomies 13 and 18 are compatible with live birth, but the children have serious problems and do not survive early childhood.

APPROXIMATE INCIDENCE OF TRISOMY			
Mother's Age	Down Syndrome (Trisomy 21)	Trisomies (Trisomy 13, 18, and 21)*	All Chromosomal Abnormalities
20–24	1 in 1,490		1 in 500
25–29	1 in 1,120		1 in 450
30	1 in 950		1 in 420
31	1 in 900		1 in 385
33	1 in 620		1 in 285
35	1 in 250	1 in 200	1 in 134

36	1 in 200	1 in 160	1 in 109
37	1 in 150	1 in 126	1 in 89
38	1 in 120	1 in 98	1 in 71
39	1 in 100	1 in 76	1 in 58
40	1 in 75	1 in 59	1 in 46
41	1 in 60	1 in 45	1 in 37
42	1 in 45	1 in 34	1 in 29
43	1 in 35	1 in 26	1 in 23
44	1 in 30	1 in 19	1 in 18
45	1 in 20	1 in 15	1 in 15
47	1 in 18		1 in 13
48	1 in 14		1 in 10
49	1 in 11		1 in 8

* NOTES:
a. Various sources give slightly different estimates of the risk of having these chromosomal abnormalities. These figures are not exact and have been rounded off.
b. The figures up to age 35 are estimates of these abnormalities at birth. The numbers from age 35 on are the estimates at a 16-week amniocentesis.
c. A large international study found the following rates of sex chromosome abnormalities: Klinefelter syndrome (XXY) 1 in 600; XYY 1 in 900; Turner syndrome (45X) 1 in 2000; XXX 1 in 1000.

The likelihood of Down syndrome reaches approximately 1 in 100 at about age 39 and the likelihood of all trisomies reach 1 in 100 slightly earlier than this. Women with Down syndrome, since they have an extra chromosome 21, can be expected to have many more children with the chromosome abnormality than will women without it, and indeed that is the case.

Defects in Chromosome Structure

Chromosomes can be changed in a number of ways. A part of one chromosome can switch over with a part of another chromosome. This is called a *translocation*. There can be an *inversion*, where there is a break in two places on a single chromosome with a resulting rearrangement of the genetic material. There can be a *deletion*, loss of a segment of a chromosome, or a *duplication*, an extra segment within a chromosome. The ends of the chromosomes can come together to form a ring, which usually involves a deletion.

Changes in chromosomes may or may not cause problems. For example, a translocation may be *balanced*, when there is no loss or gain of genetic material. In this case, the person with the translocation will be unaffected by it. If an amniocentesis shows a child with a balanced translocation, the blood of the parents will be drawn for a karyotype. If either parent shows the same balanced translocation, the child can be assumed to be similarly unaffected by the chromosomal change.

In the formation of the sex cells, however, the translocation will not always remain balanced in the daughter cells. Genetic material can be lost. This is called an *unbalanced translocation*. A child of a parent with a balanced translocation can then be born with a chromosomal abnormality that can cause difficulties. Sometimes, the unbalanced translocation may be incompatible with life, causing a miscarriage. Recurrent miscarriage is a cause to perform chromosomal analysis of the parents.

One form of translocation is called a *Robertsonian translocation* and involves chromosomes 14 and 21. In cell division, this may result in a trisomy of chromosome 21, causing Down syndrome. Approximately 5 percent of the incidence of Down syndrome is caused by a Robertsonian translocation. The risk of conceiving a child with Down syndrome if either parent has a Robertsonian translocation is about 33 percent, but many of these will spontaneously miscarry. Such a parent has a 33 percent chance of having a child without the translocation, and a 33 percent chance of having a child with a balanced translocation—in short, a 66 percent chance of a pregnancy occurring without a problem caused by this chromosomal change.

Among the other structural changes in chromosomes, inversions usually cause no problems. Persons who carry inversions have normal offspring or, if abnormal, the changes are incompatible with life and result in miscarriage. Deletions usually result in problems while duplications are highly variable in their effects.

Amniocentesis, the withdrawal of amniotic fluid from the uterine cavity, or *CVS*, the sampling of early placental structures, are the tests currently used to verify the presence or absence of trisomy and other chromosomal abnormalities in the fetus. After growing the cells in culture, which allows them to be harvested in the dividing state, the investigator takes a photograph through a microscope of a dividing cell. The individual chromosomes are identified and arranged in order. In skilled hands this forms a reliable chromosomal map or *karyotype*. A firm diagnosis of a chromosomal abnormality can be made.

Defects of Genes

Genes are combinations of *amino acids* (protein parts), arranged in sequences as part of a large molecule, *deoxyribonucleic acid* (DNA), located on the chromosome. Each gene occupies a specific position on a specific chromosome. There are between fifty thousand and one hundred thousand genes in every human cell. "Gene mapping" was a major scientific endeavor of the late twentieth century and several thousand genes have been located on particular chromosomes. Scientists project that most, if not all, genes will be located by the year 2003. The gene map is called the *human genome*.

Chromosomes are visible under the microscope, but the DNA molecule is too small to be seen this way and therefore cannot be mapped in the same way that chromosomes are. Researchers have developed biochemical techniques for identifying specific genes and, even more significantly, determining their absence. They can also identify abnormal biochemical products of abnormal genes. As an example, the biochemist can demonstrate the absence of the enzyme, hexosaminidase A (hex A). Its lack causes *Tay-Sachs disease*, a fatal metabolic disorder seen most frequently in Jewish people from Central and Eastern Europe (Ashkenazi Jews).

Autosomal Gene Defects

When a disease is carried on a specific gene, its inheritance can follow a number of identified patterns including *autosomal dominant* and *autosomal recessive*. Sometimes this is referred to as *Mendelian genetic inheritance*, after Abbe Mendel, whose experiments with peas led to the discovery of these genetic patterns.

Not all genetic traits, however, are so simply derived as to conform to such rules. We know, for example, that eye color shows a complex pattern of inheritance involving several genes. Neural tube defects are another example of apparent deviation from a Mendelian pattern. This may be because several genes, possibly on more than one chromosome, are involved in producing the defect.

AUTOSOMAL DOMINANT INHERITANCE   Autosomal dominant diseases are carried in genes on one of the twenty-two autosomes. The disease occurs even though the matching autosome from the other parent is perfectly normal. The severity of the disease cannot be predicted, but that it will appear is certain.

Huntington's disease (also called *Huntington's chorea*), a severe neurological disorder, follows this pattern. Since a parent with one gene for the disease passes either that gene or the normal gene, his or her children each have a 50 percent chance of receiving the gene for the disease. Regardless of whether they receive a gene for the disease from their other parent or not, they will have the disease, as it is a dominant trait.

Huntington's disease does not make itself known until about age 40, by which time the carrier of the gene may have already had a family. Recently tests have been developed that can detect the gene in people before they develop the disease itself. As this disease cannot be identified currently in the fetus, people with the gene can choose not to have children, to seek donor sperm or ova, or to chance the 50 percent possibility that any offspring will not have the disease.

AUTOSOMAL RECESSIVE INHERITANCE   Autosomal recessive diseases become manifest only when both chromosomes of a pair carry the gene for the defect. This is called the *homozygous state* (Greek: *homeo* = likeness, resemblance; *zyotos* = yoked). In the *heterozygous state* (Greek: *eteros* = other), when one chromosome of the pair lacks the gene, the individual appears normal, although sensitive tests may disclose a relative deficiency in, for example, an enzyme produced by the gene. The heterozygous state makes the person a carrier of the gene for the disease.

A carrier can pass the gene to his or her offspring. With autosomal dominant diseases, carriers are also afflicted. With autosomal recessive diseases, carriers are healthy. In autosomal recessive inheritance, should the offspring of a carrier be conceived with a partner who has the disease (is homozygous for it), then the offspring will be either diseased (a 50 percent chance), or will be a carrier (an equal chance). In the case of two carriers, each offspring has a 50 percent chance of being a carrier, a 25 percent chance of having two normal genes, and a 25 percent chance of having the disease. Offspring conceived by a carrier and a person who does not have a gene for the disease will never have the disease but will have a 50 percent chance of being a carrier. Prenatal diagnosis is not needed when there is no chance that the offspring will have the disease.

The boxes on pages 205 to 207 show how one particular autosomal recessive disease—sickle-cell anemia—is inherited. Like all autosomal recessive diseases, sickle-cell anemia occurs only when someone has two genes for sickle—or abnormally shaped—hemoglobin, called hemoglobin S. That person's genotype for hemoglobin is SS. A person with two normal genes for hemoglobin (called hemoglobin A) is disease free and cannot transmit it. That person's genotype for hemoglobin is AA. A person with one gene for the disease and one normal gene—AS—is a carrier. Depending on the hemoglobin gene carried by this person's partner, the resulting offspring may have only normal hemoglobin genes, may be carriers for sickle-cell anemia, or may have the disease.

In the diagrams shown, the outer boxes reflect each of the two genes for hemoglobin in each parent and the inner boxes reflect the possible genetic makeup of their children. The boxes show various possible combinations of parents. Boxes A, B, and C represent parents with the matching genotypes: both parents AA (nondisease, noncarrier state); both parents SS (disease state); and both parents SA (carrier state). Boxes D, E, and F show combinations of parents: AA mating with SS; AA mating with AS; and SS mating with AS.

When one or both parents are heterozygous, then the child's condition will depend on which gene the child gets from each parent. This is a random event—it is not planned. Box C, for example, shows how, by chance, when two carriers mate, each of their offspring has a 25 percent chance of being unaffected by the disease (AA), a 25 percent chance of having the disease (SS), and a 50 percent chance of being a carrier (AS), just like the parents.

When both parents are carriers (box C) or when one parent is a carrier and the other has the disease (box F), fetal testing should be done.

INHERITANCE OF SICKLE-CELL ANEMIA—AN AUTOSOMAL RECESSIVE TRAIT		
A. Neither parent is diseased or a carrier (AA)		
	PARENT 1 ↓	
PARENT 2 ↓	A ↓	A ↓
A →	AA (disease-free state)	AA (disease-free state)
A →	AA (disease-free state)	AA (disease-free state)

No genetic tests of fetus required; all children disease free. If mother shows AA hemoglobin, no need to test father.

B. Both parents have disease (SS)

	PARENT 1	
	↓	
PARENT 2 ↓	S ↓	S ↓
S →	SS (disease state)	SS (disease state)
S →	SS (disease state)	SS (disease state)

No genetic testing of fetus required; all offspring will have disease. If mother tests SS, father should be tested, as genetic testing is available if he is AS (see box F).

C. Both parents are carriers (AS)

	PARENT 1	
	↓	
PARENT 2 ↓	A ↓	S ↓
A →	AA (disease-free state)	AS (carrier state)
S →	AS (carrier state)	SS (disease state)

Genetic testing of fetus available. If mother shows AS hemoglobin, father should be tested. If he is AA (see box E), offspring will have no chance of having disease.

D. One parent is disease-free (AA), other parent has disease (SS)

	PARENT 1	
	↓	
PARENT 2 ↓	A ↓	A ↓
S →	AS (carrier state)	AS (carrier state)
S →	AS (carrier state)	AS (carrier state)

No need for fetal testing; all offspring will be carriers. If mother is AA, no need to test father.

E. One parent is disease-free (AA), other parent is carrier (AS)

PARENT 2	PARENT 1	
	A ↓	A ↓
A →	AA (disease-free state)	AA (disease-free state)
S →	AS (carrier state)	AS (carrier state)

No need for fetal testing; all offspring will be carriers or disease-free. If mother is AA, no need to test father.

F. One parent has disease (SS), other parent is carrier (AS)

PARENT 2	PARENT 1	
	S ↓	S ↓
A →	AS (carrier state)	AS (carrier state)
S →	SS (disease state)	SS (disease state)

Fetal testing available. When mother is SS, father should be tested, as no genetic testing is required if he is also SS or AA.

The blood test called a *hemoglobin electrophoresis* detects which hemoglobin a person carries. This test is recommended for all persons at risk for this disease. Risk groups include people from Africa or the Mediterranean or with ancestors from these parts of the world. If the mother is known to have the disease (which should be manifest by the child-bearing years), or found to be a carrier, the father should be tested. If he is known to have the disease, or found to be a carrier as well, then the parents should seek genetic counseling to understand the risk that each of their children has for having the disease. If the risk is 100 percent (the mating of two people each with the disease), then this couple can choose not to have children, seek donor sperm or donor ova, or accept that they will have a child with the disease. If the risk is 25 or 50 percent (see boxes C and F), then the couple may consider fetal testing, which can be accomplished via biochemical testing after CVS or amniocentesis or via the removal of blood from the umbilical cord, as discussed later.

Mediterranean people are also at risk for *thalessemia*, sometimes called Mediterranean anemia. This disease has many forms. The form thalessemia major may cause severe anemia. Females with thalessemia major often do not ovulate, so we rarely see a diseased mother reproducing (as is shown in boxes B, D, and F in the diagram for sickle-cell anemia). However, two people with the carrier state may mate. Hemoglobin electrophoresis can show the carrier state for thalessemia major. Fetal testing can then be utilized to diagnose a fetus with the disease.

Tay-Sachs disease is another disease inherited as an autosomal recessive trait. People who have two genes for the disease die within the first few years of life. Inheritance shown in boxes B, D, and F, where one or both parents have the disease, is impossible for people with Tay-Sachs disease. Heterozygous parents may reproduce. They lack the gene on one chromosome and are normal in all respects except for a slight deficiency of hexosaminidase A (hex A). The deficiency, which does not affect their health, can be found by laboratory testing of blood, thus identifying the carrier state. As with sickle-cell anemia, if both parents (or prospective parents) are carriers, their children have a 25 percent chance of being disease-free, a 50 percent chance of being a carrier like the parents, and a 25 percent chance of having the disease.

Tay-Sachs disease is most common among Jewish people from Europe (Ashkenazi Jews), so when two people who share this background are planning a pregnancy, preconceptional testing is advised. If the woman is already pregnant, the father should be tested, as a test in pregnancy is difficult to interpret. If the father is not a carrier, then the baby cannot have the disease, regardless of the mother's genes for the disease. If both parents are carriers, the diagnosis in the fetus (who has a 25 percent chance of having the disease) can be determined by amniocentesis and CVS. Some French-Canadian people from the East St. Lawrence River Valley of Quebec are also at increased risk for Tay-Sachs disease, as are members of the Cajun population in Louisiana. These groups, like the Ashkenazi Jews, have a risk that is one hundred times the risk of other ethnic groups. Depending upon how it is done, the blood test for Tay-Sachs disease will detect 95 to 98 percent of carriers.

Ashkenazi Jewish people are also at increased risk for *cystic fibrosis* (CF) and *Canavan disease*. Cystic fibrosis is a disease of the lungs and digestive system. Some treatments exist for CF, and have extended the lives of affected individuals to an average of 30 years. Still, many people with cystic fibrosis die in their twenties. Canavan disease is a neurological problem resulting from an enzyme deficiency. Sufferers get progressively worse and usually die during adolescence.

Of these two diseases, cystic fibrosis is the more common. How often it occurs varies with ethnicity. The more common the disease is in a particular ethnic group determines how likely the screening test will be able to detect it. The table below shows the incidence of CF, the frequency of carriers in a particular population, and the ability of the screening test to detect the gene for the disease, as reported by the March of Dimes. The screening test does not pick up all carriers because there are many different gene changes that are associated with CF and the test cannot screen changes for them all.

Ethnic Population	Disease Incidence	Numbers of Carriers in the Population	Detection Rate of Screening Test
Northern European	1 in 2,500	1 in 25 to 1 in 29	85 to 90 percent
Southern European	1 in 2,500	1 in 25 to 1 in 29	70 percent
Ashkenazi Jewish	1 in 2,800	1 in 26 to 1 in 29	97 percent
Hispanic	1 in 8,100	1 in 46	57 percent
African-American	1 in 14,500	1 in 60 to 1 in 65	72 percent
Asian	1 in 32,000	1 in 90	30 percent
Other Populations	Variable	Variable	Approx. 70 percent

In October, 2001, the American College of Obstetricians and Gynecologists (ACOG) and the American College of Medical Genetics (ACMG) issued new guidelines for screening for cystic fibrosis. These guidelines made a distinction between "offering" the screening test and "making it available." *Offering* screening means providing the information before the care provider sees the patient and following this up with a discussion at the prenatal visit. Making screening *available* means providing information but not following up with a discussion at the care visit. The guidelines advise offering the test to individuals with a family history of CF, partners of affected people, and, because the highest risk is among Caucasians, to Caucasians seeking prenatal care or planning a pregnancy. The test should be made available to other populations. Of course, there is a case to be made that the test should be offered to all groups, providing discussion of the disease in a person's ethnic group and the value of the test in that group. That way, each person can make an informed decision.

Ideally, both partners are screened before conceiving. Ideally, insurance covers testing for both partners. In reality, most women who are screened are already pregnant, and the partner's insurance will not cover the test.

The guidelines for CF screening reflect the advances in identifying genes that have come from the Human Genome Project. It is quite likely that CF screening will provide a model for future genetic screening that will encompass a wider range of genetic problems.

Sex Chromosome Gene Defects

Defects on the sex chromosomes, with a few exceptions, are recessive and carried on the X chromosome—hence, the terminology *X-linked trait*. These defects rarely are seen (expressed) in the female body. She would have to receive two X chromosomes for the disease to express itself. This occurs only in the extremely rare instance that the mother is a carrier and the father has the disease. If the embryo is a male, defects in genes located on the X chromosome can express themselves, since there is no equivalent gene on the Y chromosome to be dominant. Each son of a carrier has a 50 percent chance of having the disease.

X-linked defects include *hemophilia* and most of the *muscular dystrophies*. The mother of an affected son is necessarily a heterozygous carrier. Her daughters may also be carriers if they receive her X chromosome with the defect. A number of X-linked diseases result in death in early childhood, so the fathers never have the chance to pass on their X gene for the disease. Some do not result in early death, particularly with newer treatments. This is true for hemophilia so, rarely, women are affected.

Sisters of brothers with X-linked diseases should consider being tested before pregnancy to see if they are carriers. If so, they can consider prenatal testing for their fetus.

When parents are apprehensive that their child may have a sex-linked disease, the sex of the embryo often can be identified by CVS as soon as the cells are collected. If it is female, the parents can be reassured that it will not have the problem. If the embryo is a male, it is still possible that it may not be afflicted, and the mother can await the culture of the cells from CVS or later from amniocentesis before deciding whether to continue to carry the pregnancy. She can, of course, choose to defer sex determination until she can have an amniocentesis, for its advantage of having a lower rate of fetal loss.

Genetic Testing

Not all defects have been traced to specific genes; thus biochemical testing will not necessarily bring to light all disorders that run in families. However, the list of inherited abnormalities that can be detected occupies entire pages in books on the subject. When a disease is known to run in a family, a *genetic counselor* can help parents determine whether it is detectable by prenatal testing, whether or not to have a test, and which test to choose. Genetic counselors are individuals with special training and expertise in birth defects, genetic disease, and mental retardation.

No discussion of genetic testing can be complete without some mention of the personal and social issues it raises. On a personal level, there is often extreme anxiety surrounding the testing procedures. Once a blood or other sample is obtained, women and families become quite anxious about the results. Should testing show a parent to be a carrier, or reveal a fetus with a disease or defect, parents may react not merely with sorrow, but with guilt. Genetic counseling, and possibly psychological or crisis-intervention counseling, may be appropriate at times. Prospective parents should be reassured, of course, that most often fetal assessment reveals a fetus without problems.

The father of the baby or other support person should be welcomed to be present during any of the procedures described in this chapter.

On a social level, questions related to privacy have emerged. How are persons with chromosomal or genetic abnormalities, for example, protected when employers ask for health examinations as part of a routine hiring procedure? The discussion of these issues is beyond the scope of this book, but they are raised for readers to consider.

FETAL ASSESSMENT: NONINVASIVE TECHNIQUES

Ultrasound

The high quality of the images produced by ultrasound today has made possible the correct prenatal identification of a wide range of defects. Ultrasound allows us to look at the fetus in the womb, to see structural abnormalities including defects of the skeletal system, the urinary tract, the gastrointestinal (digestive) system, and the heart. Some aspects of function also can be assessed, as ultrasound shows fetal movement. Ultrasound has made it easier and safer to place a needle or catheter (tube) into the chorionic villi, amniotic sac, or body cavity of the fetus.

Ultrasound uses high-frequency sound waves, higher than the waves that can be heard by humans. When these waves are transmitted through body tissues with a large water content, an echo is sent back and an image is created. Because the fetus floats in fluid, ultrasound produces images clear enough to show anatomic details.

Today's ultrasound technique is called *real-time imaging*. This picture, in shadowy tones of gray and black, shows the fetus in motion, allowing, for example, for the beating heart to be recognized. Fetal echocardiography is a sonogram focused on the heart. It might be performed in instances where there is a family history of congenital heart disease; in maternal disease including diabetes, lupus erythematosus, or phenylketonuria; or maternal drug exposure or alcoholism. It might also be performed when there is *polyhydramnios* (extra fluid), when the fetal heart sounds irregular, when other fetal abnormalities have been identified by chromosome analysis or sonogram, and when there is intrauterine growth retardation or restriction. Fetal echocardiography is not performed before the second trimester.

When there is a high suspicion of a fetal problem, a comprehensive ultrasound may be performed in the second trimester. This is often referred to as a *Level II ultrasound*. Very high quality equipment and skill are needed and a Level II ultrasound is best performed or interpreted by an expert in maternal-fetal medicine or a *perinatologist* (see Chapter 7).

Advances in ultrasonic technique continue to be made, increasing its usefulness. Vaginal ultrasound has made it easier to view the fetus at very early gestational ages. The addition of color, available in some major medical centers, can enhance the detail of some sonograms. Techniques allowing more realistic three-dimensional visualization of the fetus are among the newest innovations and may add even greater accuracy to obstetrical ultrasound in the future. Color Doppler techniques, which permit visualization of the motion of blood through vessels, are sometimes used in large medical centers in late pregnancy when there is a question of intrauterine growth retardation or restriction (see Chapter 17). Doppler techniques are still new and require a very skilled ultrasonographer to be useful. Even with skill, opinions differ as to the value of Doppler studies in contributing to determining the well-being of the fetus or newborn.

Should Ultrasound Be Routine?

Whether or not every pregnant woman should have at least one ultrasound screening for fetal anomalies is a question engendering considerable debate. A number of studies have evaluated the extent to which ultrasound can reliably detect fetal abnormalities and whether such detection improves the outcome of pregnancy. Conflicting results have been obtained. Two large studies are often cited, one supporting the argument that every pregnant woman should have a routine ultrasound and the other supporting the argument that ultrasound should be reserved for instances of specific need.

While most researchers believe ultrasound to be safe, the National Institutes of Health (NIH) and the American Institute for the Use of Ultrasound in Medicine (AIUM) advise prudent use of the technique, meaning that it should be used only when there is an identifiable reason for its use—some kind of a problem or known risk factor. These groups note that, with current knowledge, future adverse effects of ultrasound exposure cannot be ruled out entirely.

The major study supporting routine use of ultrasound was carried out in several countries in Europe. Called the *Eurofetus Project*, its findings were reported in 1997. In this study, which involved sixty European hospitals, ultrasound detected approximately 56 percent of fetal anomalies, including 73 percent of major abnormalities. Eighteen percent of sonograms, however, reported abnormalities where there were none. In half of these instances, a second sonogram proved more accurate, showing the fetus to be without the anomaly. Based on these results, most women in Britain, Germany, and France have routine sonograms and average more than one per pregnancy.

Results from a United States study, supported by the National Institutes of Health, differed from the Eurofetus Project. *RADIUS* (Routine Antenatal Diagnostic Imaging with Ultrasound Study) reported in 1993 that in low-risk pregnancies, ultrasound screening detected less than 17 percent of major fetal anomalies when performed before 24 weeks of gestation and just under 35 percent of defects when performed later in pregnancy. RADIUS did show that multiple gestations were picked up more frequently with a routine ultrasound, but overall, the pregnancy outcome in this study was not different for the group of women who received a routine ultrasound and the group who received an ultrasound only when the care provider felt there was a specific need to perform one.

One possible difference in the research conducted in Europe and the United States was the expertise of the person performing the ultrasound. In the Eurofetus study, ultrasounds were more likely to be performed by specialists in the technique. In fact, some ultrasound experts report higher rates of detection of anomalies than were found in either study.

Detection rates alone, however, do not answer the question of whether or not finding an anomaly helps the baby do better after birth. What detection does do, if performed early enough, is allow the mother to have an abortion so babies with serious anomalies will not be born. Studies that have shown an improvement in outcome based on routine sonogram have all attributed this improvement to abortion of fetuses with major anomalies.

When the parents choose not to have an abortion, detection may help them better prepare for the birth of a baby with a problem. It may also allow for delivery in a major medical center with a team of pediatric experts available at the moment of birth. Again, the extent to which this helps improve outcome is unclear at this point.

The recommendations of the National Institutes of Health for obstetric ultrasound appear in the box on pages 216 to 218. The NIH recommends twenty-eight specific uses of ultrasound in maternity care. Some of these are performed as part of treatment for infertility, before the woman is actually pregnant, or in later pregnancy. These topics are covered in detail in Chapters 13 and 17.

In general, the most common uses of ultrasound for early fetal assessment are confirmation of early pregnancy when there is a doubt, especially if there is a history of ectopic pregnancy (a pregnancy outside the womb) or bleeding that might suggest ectopic pregnancy or miscarriage (see Chapters 12 and 14). A gestational sac can be seen as early as 4½ weeks gestation. If the fetus is not in the uterus and a pregnancy test is positive, the ultrasound can search for the fetus outside the uterus. The earlier an ectopic pregnancy is found, the less chance of its causing a serious problem for the pregnant woman.

Fetal heart motion can be demonstrated by 7 weeks. This is a reassuring finding when there is vaginal bleeding, suggesting a possible miscarriage. Ultrasound is also used to assess gestational age if the woman does not know the first day of her last menstrual period, if her periods are irregular, or if she became pregnant while taking oral contraceptives or shortly after discontinuing them—before she reestablished regular periods. Ultrasound can determine a due date and sometimes spare a woman the need for a "post-dates" workup (see Chapter 17). It can be used to assess fetal growth where there is doubt, as in the case of the uterus measuring smaller or larger than would be expected by the date of the last period.

In early pregnancy, the gestational age of the fetus usually is determined by a measurement called the *crown-rump length* (CRL), the length from the top of the fetal head to the bottom of its buttocks. This is made between 7 and 13 weeks gestation and is considered accurate to within 3 to 5 days. Prior to this—before the fetus itself can be visualized—a sonogram can estimate gestational age by measuring the sac in which the fetus grows. The measurement used is called the *mean sac diameter* (MSD) and is obtained by measuring the sac's three largest perpendicular dimensions and averaging them.

In the second trimester, after 13 weeks, gestational age is assessed by measuring the *biparietal diameter* (BPD). The BPD is the widest diameter of the fetal head, measured from one side to another just above the ears. Early in the second trimester, BPD measurement is considered accurate to about 1 week more or less than the actual gestational age. Later in the trimester, from about 17 to 26 weeks, the accuracy is about 10 days more or less. In the third trimester, as there is more variation in head size among babies, the estimate of gestational age becomes less accurate. After 29 weeks, the accuracy is reduced to plus or minus 3 weeks or more. The femur length (the length of the thigh bone, the longest bone in the body) may be used in later pregnancy for gestational age assessment. Often, measurements of BPD, femur length, and abdominal circumference are made and gestational age is decided by averaging the three together. This is discussed further in Chapter 17.

Early ultrasound also may be performed when the examiner hears two or more heartbeats or when the uterus measures larger than would be expected by the date of the last period. The sonogram is very accurate in showing the number of fetuses in the uterus. Ultrasound can also demonstrate increased or decreased amniotic fluid (*polyhydramnios* or *oligohydramnios*). Since there is an increase in fetal anomalies in these conditions, the ultrasound also will scrutinize the fetus for abnormalities. Sometimes, when the uterus is enlarged in early pregnancy, it is due to a rare condition known as *hydatidiform mole*, in which a tumor develops in the uterus (Greek: *hydatid* = watery vesicle; Latin: *mola* = millstone). This is discussed in Chapter 12. When hydatidiform mole is present, the sonogram displays a mass of small round images without an embryonic sac. On extremely rare occasions, a fetus can be seen with a molar pregnancy, but it cannot grow to term. Early ultrasound can also find *fibroid tumors* of the uterus, benign growths that cause an enlarged uterine size, but do not affect the baby.

The placenta is quite accurately identified by sonogram. Sonogram is utilized whenever invasive testing is done to show the fetal and placental positions.

Among those who recommend routine ultrasound screening for all pregnancies, there is disagreement on the number of scans a woman should receive, and exactly when they should be performed. Many experts recommend one routine screen at 18 to 20 weeks to look for malformations, multiple pregnancy (twins, triplets, or more), and the placenta. This is still early enough for the woman to choose an abortion should major malformations be shown conclusively or to have further testing should the sonogram be suggestive of a genetic abnormality.

Some sonogram proponents also recommend a routine screen at about 6 to 8 weeks to confirm the pregnancy, and get an early, accurate assessment of fetal gestational age. Finally, a scan may be recommended at about 34 weeks to assess fetal growth. The National Institutes of Health do not support a routine third-trimester ultrasound examination and acknowledge that there exists conflicting data regarding the value of an earlier screen.

National Institutes of Health (NIH) Recommended Indications for Ultrasound Screening in Pregnancy

- **Estimation of gestational age** when there are uncertain dates or verification of dates for women who will have elective repeat cesarean delivery, induction of labor, or other elective termination of pregnancy. This is recommended to avoid premature interventions.
- **Evaluation of fetal growth.** Indications for this include a reason for uteroplacental insufficiency (a poorly functioning placenta) such as severe preeclampsia (see Chapter 12), chronic hypertension, chronic kidney disease, severe diabetes mellitus, or other medical complications of pregnancy where fetal malnutrition, i.e., intrauterine growth retardation or macrosomia (unusually large fetus), is suspected.
- **Vaginal bleeding of unknown cause in pregnancy.**
- **Determination of fetal presentation,** when it cannot be accurately assessed in labor or late pregnancy.
- **Suspected multiple gestation** based on hearing more than one fetal heartbeat or fundal height (uterine height) larger than expected for dates, or use of fertility drugs.
- **Adjunct to amniocentesis.** This avoids endangering the placenta and the fetus and increases the chances of obtaining fluid.
- **Significant uterine size/clinical dates discrepancy.** This is when the uterus measures smaller or larger than is expected for the gestational age based on last menstrual period. This oc-

curs, for example, when there is polyhydramnios or oligohydramnios, in multiple gestation, or intrauterine growth retardation, with certain anomalies, or inconclusive dates.

• **Pelvic mass detected on pelvic examination.**

• **Suspected hydatidiform mole.** This pregnancy complication (see Chapter 12) is suspected when there is high blood pressure, protein in the urine, and/or ovarian cysts felt on pelvic examination, or a failure to detect fetal heart tones with a Doppler ultrasound device after 12 weeks.

• **Adjunct to cervical cerclage placement.** This is a *suture* (stitch) put in the cervix for women who have cervical incompetence (see Chapter 12)

• **Suspected ectopic pregnancy.** Sonogram is utilized to screen for an ectopic pregnancy when pregnancy occurs after repair of a fallopian tube or when a woman has had a prior ectopic pregnancy.

• **Adjunct to special procedures,** such as fetoscopy, intrauterine transfusion, shunt placement, in vitro fertilization (see Chapter 13), or CVS.

• **Suspected fetal death.**

• **Suspected uterine abnormality.** These include fibroids or defects in the uterine structure—such as a double uterus.

• **Intrauterine contraceptive device (IUD) localization.**

• **Ovarian follicle development surveillance.** This is used in certain treatments for infertility.

• **Biophysical evaluation for fetal well-being** after 28 weeks of gestation (see Chapter 17). This assesses amniotic fluid, fetal muscle tone, fetal movement, fetal breathing, and heart rate patterns.

• **Observation of intrapartum events,** including external version (see Chapter 5).

• **Suspected polyhydramnios or oligohydramnios.**

• **Suspected abruption placentae** (see Chapter 12).

• **Adjunct to external version from breech to vertex presentation** (see Chapter 5).

• **Estimation of fetal weight and/or presentation in premature rupture of membranes and/or premature labor.** This helps guide decisions on timing and method of delivery.

• **Abnormal serum alpha-fetoprotein (AFP) value** for clinical gestational age when drawn. Sonogram will confirm gestational age, which may point to an error in the determination of normalcy of the AFP value and may also show several conditions that may cause elevated AFP values, such as twins or *anencephaly* (absence of brain tissue, a form of neural tube defect).

• **Follow-up observation of identified fetal anomaly.** This may show change or lack of change in an abnormal condition.

• **Follow-up evaluation of placenta location for identified placenta previa** (see Chapter 12).

• **History of previous congenital anomaly.** This may show a recurrence or reassure parents that there is no recurrence.

• **Serial evaluation of fetal growth in multiple gestation.** Ultrasound permits recognition of discordant growth of the fetuses, guiding patient management and timing of delivery.

• **Evaluation of fetal condition in women who register late for prenatal care.** Accurate knowledge of gestational age assists in pregnancy management decisions for this group.

How Ultrasound Is Performed

An ultrasound is generally a painless procedure, although a full or nearly full bladder usually is required to help transmit the sound waves and this may be quite uncomfortable. An ultrasound performed through the vagina does not require a full bladder.

For an *abdominal ultrasound,* you will be instructed to drink about a quart of water an hour before the exam. You will be lying down for the ultrasound. For a *vaginal,* or *transvaginal, ultrasound* your legs may be in stirrups as they are for a vaginal examination. You need not undress for the abdominal ultrasound as only your abdomen needs to be exposed. For a transvaginal ultrasound, of course, you will be asked to undress from the waist down.

In an abdominal ultrasound, a gel is applied to your skin to help transmit the sound waves. The examiner, who may be a physician, an ultrasound technician, or another specially trained care provider will move a handheld device called a *transducer* (or probe) slowly over your abdomen until the fetus is visualized. The transducer, about the size of an average bar of soap, sends out the sound waves and receives the echoes returning from them. The motion of the tranducer over the abdomen is gentle and does not hurt. Sometimes you will be asked to urinate a little if the examiner finds the bladder to be too full. Although this can be challenging, most women are able to accomplish it! The entire procedure usually takes anywhere from 15 minutes to half an hour.

In a transvaginal ultrasound (sometimes called an *endovaginal sonogram*), a small probe is placed into a protective latex covering (perhaps a glove or a condom will be used) and gently placed into the vagina. The diameter of the probe is small, about the size of a medium to large tampon. Many women find the vaginal ultrasound less uncomfortable because there is no bladder pressure. Often, both an abdominal and a transvaginal sonogram are performed to get the best possible visualization.

As the sound waves are transmitted through the transducer, an image is produced on a monitor or screen. The image is two-dimensional in shades of gray. The examiner can show you the parts of the fetus as the exam is done.

Maternal Blood Testing: AFP or Triple Screen

Another screening procedure requires only a small sample of the pregnant woman's blood, hence its consideration as a noninvasive technique. Blood sampling of the mother allows the measurement of certain chemicals that have passed from the fetus to the amniotic fluid and through the placenta into the mother's circulation. A screening test does not provide a definite diagnosis; it indicates an increased possibility that a condition is present. Maternal blood testing can screen for open neural tube developmental defects (see Chapter 5) and genetic disorders including Down syndrome or other trisomies. Abnormal values of these chemicals suggest that parents consider further testing for proof of a fetal defect.

Alpha-fetoprotein (AFP) is a protein found in all fetuses. When a fetus has unusual openings in the skin, such as characterize the open neural tube defects (NTDs) like *spina bifida*, the level of this protein in the amniotic fluid and in the mother's blood is unusually high. In these defects, which form early in gestation (see Chapter 5) and result from a failure of the structures that become the brain and spinal cord to close properly, nervous system tissue is on the outside of the body. NTDs cause a variety of problems, from mild to severe.

Maternal blood is tested between 15 and 20 weeks of pregnancy. The test is sometimes abbreviated as MSAFP, standing for *maternal serum alpha-fetoprotein*. The protein actually is measured in the serum or liquid portion of the mother's blood, separated in the laboratory from the solid substances in the blood, such as red and white blood cells.

There is no absolute amount of AFP in maternal blood that positively identifies NTD. The amount is reported as MoM—*multiples of the mean* for the gestational age. This represents how far from the mean or average the measured value of AFP falls. The analysis takes into consideration other factors that influence AFP, including mother's weight, race, and whether she has diabetes mellitus or is carrying more than one fetus (if known). The cutoff score that indicates risk is set to miss as few actual NTDs as possible, but the majority of fetuses whose mothers show an elevated value do not have the defect.

MSAFP will be accurate in showing a neural tube defect in 80 to 85 percent of fetuses who actually have the defect, but as many as 90 percent of fetuses whose AFP screening test shows an elevation will turn out to be normal. This is called a *false positive* result.

An elevated AFP is reason for sonographic study of the fetus's central nervous system to look for a neural tube defect or other abnormality associated with an increased maternal AFP level. As AFP normally increases each week between 15 and 20 weeks of pregnancy, an elevated AFP could be due to an error in dating the pregnancy, so that the gestational age is actually greater than that calculated by last menstrual period. This can be determined by a sonogram and the AFP value reinterpreted according to the revision in the gestational age. Multiple pregnancies can also cause an increase in the mother's AFP levels. Sonography is very accurate in confirming multiple gestation. Other fetal defects associated with elevated AFP and are demonstrable on sonogram include fetal death and defects in the formation of the fetal abdominal wall and umbilical cord. *Anencephaly*, a neural tube defect in which the skull is absent, can be diagnosed definitely by sonogram, but other NTDs can be missed.

At the other end of the spectrum, an unusually low concentration of AFP in maternal serum may be associated with a trisomy. This must be corroborated by amniocentesis, although sometimes a well-performed comprehensive sonogram can find anomalies that are strongly indicative of Down syndrome. The accuracy of such sonograms depends in large part on the experience of the person performing the test. Even a slight change in the placement of the transducer or probe may cause an error in findings. A *karyotype*, or mapping of the chromosome pairs, is the only way to make a definitive diagnosis of Down syndrome.

Low AFP levels may also signify a molar pregnancy (see page 315), confirmable by ultrasound, or an overestimate of gestational age. If the gestational age is shown on sonogram to be less than calculated by last menstrual period, the AFP can be reassessed in the laboratory and may prove to be normal, rather than low.

Recently, two other assessments have been added to the maternal blood screen. These are *beta hCG* and *unconjugated estriol*. Beta hCG is a specific part of the pregnancy hormone, human chorionic gonadotropin, and estriol is one of the estrogens that normally increase in pregnancy. When all three are used, this is called the *triple screen*. These values may be high or low in some of the conditions already discussed and may help make the test more precise. For example, in a neural tube defect, while the MSAFP is unusually high, the unconjugated estriol may be normal or low and the beta hCG normal. In a fetal death, the MSAFP is high while both other values will be low. In a multiple pregnancy, all three *markers*, as they are called, will be high. The table below shows the three values in various fetal problems.

INTERPRETATION OF THE TRIPLE SCREEN			
	Alpha-fetoprotein	Beta hCG	Unconjugated Estriol
Neural tube defect	High	Normal	Low or Normal
Trisomy 21 (Down syndrome)	Low	High	Low
Trisomy 18	Low	Low	Low
Fetal death	High	Low	Low
Hydatidiform mole	Low	High	Low
Multiple pregnancy	High	High	High or Normal
Gestational age actually less than estimated (error in gestational age assessment)	Low	High	Low

Abnormal results of either MSAFP alone or of the triple screen still only provide a suggestion of a disorder. Any abnormal result requires confirmation.

Because maternal blood screening is noninvasive, some experts have suggested that the triple screen be used instead of amniocentesis in women over the age of 35 to check for chromosomal anomalies. Amniocentesis would be reserved for women whose blood screening showed the possibility of abnormality. Unfortunately, while this would pick up most of these anomalies, it would miss 10 to 15 percent of babies with Down syndrome and up to 40 percent of other anomalies. Amniocentesis picks up very close to 100 percent of these.

Some experts urge that MSAFP or the triple screen be routinely utilized for the early detection of fetal central nervous system abnormalities in all pregnancies. In Scotland and Ireland, countries with very high rates of neural tube defects (and also in Appalachia in the United States, an enclave of descendants of Scotch and Irish immigrants), there is little question that this screening is justified, but there is no agreement as to whether it should be applied to all women. The usual rate of occurrence of NTDs is approximately 1 in 1,000 pregnancies in the United States.

Women who have previously had infants with neural tube defects have only a slightly increased likelihood of having another such fetus. They are nevertheless usually screened for alphafetoprotein. At the least, all pregnant women should be informed of the availability of the test. The Centers for Disease Control and Prevention recommend screening when it is performed with counseling and the availability of follow-up testing. When MSAFP or the triple screen is offered routinely to all pregnant women, the disadvantages of its high false positive rate are an increase in invasive tests, anxiety in pregnant women and their partners, increased expense of maternity care, and a small number of complications due to the amniocenteses performed.

Research is currently under way to assess markers that would identify increased risk for Down syndrome in the first trimester of pregnancy. Some of these might even be measurable in the mother's urine. This would not eliminate the need for second-trimester screening for neural tube defects, however.

FETAL ASSESSMENT: INVASIVE TECHNIQUES

Invasive techniques for fetal assessment are reserved for pregnancies in which there is a reason to suspect an abnormality. This is because any "invasion" of the uterine cavity carries a risk to the pregnancy or the fetus.

Invasive techniques allow direct analysis of fetal cells. These may come from the chorionic villi, the amniotic fluid, or a specimen of fetal blood or even skin. These techniques can detect *all* chromosomal abnormalities but only selected genetic defects or diseases. In general, the genetic conditions looked for are those for which there is a high level of suspicion in a particular fetus.

Invasive techniques, including amniocentesis, may be appropriate in the following situations:

• **Women 35 years of age and older.** This designation as high risk for a fetal defect is somewhat arbitrary, but 35 is the age at which the risk to the pregnancy of amniocentesis is approximately equal to the risk of having a baby with a *trisomy*, the most common of the chromosomal abnormalities. Both risks are about 1 in 200 at this maternal age. Some experts recommend testing when the father is 44 years or older, although a link between father's age and Down syndrome has not been shown routinely.

• **Parents who have had a child with Down syndrome** or another chromosomal abnormality.

• **Parents who are known carriers** of a chromosome rearrangement, such as a translocation.

• **Parents who have a family history** of a genetic condition for which testing is available. A few of the more common ones are shown in the box below, although there are over 60 metabolic diseases that invasive testing is able to detect.

• **Exposure to a teratogen,** like certain medications, early in pregnancy that might increase the risk of an open neural tube defect, such as spina bifida. (See Chapter 5 for discussion of such exposures.)

• **An elevated MSAFP or triple screen result** indicating an increased risk for a neural tube defect or other condition, including a trisomy. As the mother's blood levels are measured at or after week 15 of pregnancy, an amniocentesis, not CVS, is the appropriate follow-up test.

• **Parents who are first cousins** (called consanguinity).

• **History of unexplained stillbirths** or multiple miscarriages.

SAMPLE CONDITIONS THAT CAN BE DIAGNOSED THROUGH FETAL ASSESSMENT			
Ultrasound	CVS	Amniocentesis	Fetal Blood Sample (PUBS)
• Congenital heart disease (echocardiogram) • Neural tube defect (sometimes) • Cleft lip and/or palate • Skeletal disorders • Disorders of	• Chromosomal abnormalities • Cystic fibrosis • Hemophilia • Duchenne muscular dystrophy • Becker muscular dystrophy • Sickle-cell anemia	• Chromosomal abnormalities • Neural tube defects • Hemophilia • Duchenne muscular dystrophy • Becker muscular dystrophy • Sickle-cell	• Hemophilia • Sickle-cell anemia • Toxoplasmosis • Cytomegalovirus • Syphilis • Fetal abnormalities diagnosed by ultrasound

the urinary tract or gastrointestinal (digestive) system • Exposure to teratogens: alcohol, radiation, chemicals, toxoplasmosis, rubella, cytomegalovirus, syphilis • Maternal insulin-dependent diabetes • Multiple pregnancy • Fetal loss	• Tay-Sachs disease • Fetal abnormalities diagnosed by ultrasound	anemia • High level of MSAFP • Fetal abnormalities diagnosed by ultrasound	

Chorionic Villus Sampling (CVS)

At the tenth week of pregnancy the embryo is developing inside the sac of membranes, which also contains the amniotic fluid. The sac is formed by two membranes. The *amnion* or inner membrane is closer to the fetus and the *chorion* or outer membrane is closer to the uterine wall. By this time, the chorion has formed a very large number of *villi*, the beginnings of the placenta. Some villi reach out into the lining of the uterus (the *endometrium*) at the point where the placenta will soon be located. Others lie loosely free in the endometrial cavity. Once the placenta is fully formed, the villi will shrink and disappear, but at 10 weeks they are growing rapidly. Since the placental and fetal tissues have the same origin, samples of villi can be used to determine fetal genetic disorders.

Under ultrasonic guidance, a CVS can be done either *transabdominally*—through the abdomen—or *transcervically*—through the vagina and cervix. The transcervical route is more commonly used, although which route is chosen may depend on the location of the villi, or the preference of the physician performing the test.

In the transcervical route, a narrow plastic tube or catheter is directed through the vagina to the cervix and through the cervix to the chorionic villi. In the transabdominal route, a needle is introduced through the abdominal wall. With either procedure, a small amount of villus material—about the size of a pea—is suctioned into the catheter.

CVS is performed between 10 and 12 weeks of pregnancy. Since the villi are dividing rapidly, some cells may show distinct chromosomes even before they are grown in culture. When this is possible, an immediate diagnosis of an abnormality of chromosome number is feasible and fetal sex can be determined. Generally, however, the cells are put into a culture medium and grown. This allows for chromosome mapping or karyotyping to be readily accomplished as described on page 227. Results take approximately 10 days to 2 weeks. Fetal sex and fetal trisomies can be identified by CVS. Cultured villi also can be studied for chemical evidence of other genetic disorders.

Parents must decide before they have this test, sonogram, or amniocentesis whether they want to know the sex of the baby. Of course, in a sex-linked disorder like hemophilia, or if there is an abnormality of the sex chromosomes, this is important information. In other circumstances, it is a personal choice. If you decide you do *not* want this information, you must let your physician or midwife know in advance and inform the person performing the test. You can change your mind at any time during the pregnancy from not knowing to knowing; once the test has been performed, the information is available.

There is little risk to the mother from CVS. Most women feel some pressure or cramping during CVS, but it is usually slight. When the procedure is performed through the abdomen, local anesthesia may be injected at the site where the needle is introduced. A full bladder enables a better ultrasound view of the pregnancy. This may cause some discomfort. A small amount of bleeding may be noted for a few days following the procedure. Most women rest immediately following CVS, but resume normal activities shortly afterwards. The incidence of intrauterine infection is greater than that experienced with amniocentesis, but these infections occur in less than 1 percent of the women having the procedure. They usually respond promptly to antibiotic therapy.

Estimation of risk of fetal loss after CVS varies, but is usually reported as approximately one-half to 1 percent. As with many medical procedures, this will depend on the experience of the person performing the test. The risk is higher than the risk following amniocentesis, and for this reason more women who desire genetic testing choose amniocentesis.

Following CVS, you must call your physician or midwife if you have any vaginal leakage of fluid, fever, severe cramps, or bleeding.

Some studies have suggested an increased risk of deformity of the fetal extremities following CVS. This may be due to a disruption of the blood supply to the fetal arms or legs. Although studies show conflicting results, the overall risk appears to be slightly increased over the usual expected rates; with CVS the risk of a limb deformity is no more than 1 in 3,000 to 1 in 1,000 procedures. The higher rates occur when the procedure is performed before 9 weeks gestation. For this reason, procedures today are not performed before the tenth gestational week—counting, as usual, from a woman's last menstrual period.

CVS is considered quite accurate. About 98 percent of the time, adequate tissue is obtained. Sometimes, however, the results are inconclusive and an amniocentesis is necessary for clarification.

Amniocentesis is needed when the villus sample shows a chromosomal pattern called *mosaicism*. In mosaicism some cells show chromosomal abnormalities, while others do not. Mosaicism may not be present in the fetus, although it is seen in the placental tissue. Only an amniocentesis can determine whether the pattern is fetal. Also, CVS does not detect neural tube defects. Since only tissue, and not fluid, is collected, alphafetoprotein cannot be measured by this procedure. Women who have a CVS are still advised, therefore, to have maternal serum AFP testing at 15 to 18 weeks of pregnancy. If this value is elevated, the woman will need a sonographic evaluation and possibly amniocentesis. If the main reason to have fetal assessment is because of an increased risk of a neural tube defect, an amniocentesis is the more appropriate test. Approximately 3 percent of women who have CVS also have an amniocentesis for various reasons.

The main advantage of CVS is that it can establish the diagnosis early enough so that abortion can be carried out late in the first trimester or early in the second trimester of pregnancy, which is safer for the mother than a later abortion.

Amniocentesis

In an amniocentesis (Greek: *amnion* = little lamb; *kentesis* = puncture), the *amniotic sac*—commonly called the bag of waters—is punctured to collect amniotic fluid and cells shed into it by the fetus. Amniocentesis for fetal diagnosis can be performed between 14 and 17 weeks of pregnancy. Recently, some physicians experimented with performing amniocentesis earlier, but a study of more than 4,000 women in Canada, reported in 1998, showed that amniocentesis at 11 or 12 weeks was associated with a rate of fetal loss higher than both later amniocentesis and CVS. In addition, the babies born to women after early amniocentesis showed an increase of clubfoot.

Amniocentesis (*amnio*) is always accompanied by sonography to localize the fetus and the placenta and to find a pool of amniotic fluid. The pregnant woman lies on her back, her abdomen is cleansed with a sterile solution, and a small needle is inserted through her skin and muscles into the fluid. Some physicians inject a small amount of local anesthetic under the skin. A tiny needle is used for this and it feels like a pinprick. Other physicians feel that this is not necessary and that it limits their ability to change the area of injection if the fetus moves just before they are about to insert the amniocentesis needle. For this and other procedures, you may want to discuss in advance whether or not you have a preference for local anesthesia, or whether it is the physician's practice to inject it or not, so you are prepared.

The needle used for the amniocentesis is about the same diameter as a needle used to draw blood from an arm vein, but is longer, since it must go through the mother's skin and abdominal and uterine muscles to reach the fluid. For most women, the procedure causes minimal pain. The needle's entry is felt as a slight pinprick sensation, but there may be pressure as the needle moves into the uterus. The uterus lies against the mother's abdominal wall, so there is no risk of injuring other abdominal organs.

Once a suitable fluid sample is obtained, usually about 30 cc or 2 tablespoons, the needle is withdrawn and a small bandage is placed over the puncture site. Withdrawing the fluid takes less than a minute.

Shortly after the test is completed, most women can get up and go about their business. There may be soreness at the site of the needle stick for a day or two. Generally, women are advised not to lift anything heavy for 2 days. After an amniocentesis, you must call your physician or midwife if you have any vaginal leakage of fluid, fever, severe cramps, or bleeding. Slight cramping might occur for the first day and is normal. A small amount of fluid leakage from the vagina is often normal as well, but you still should report it so it can be evaluated and followed if necessary.

Once the amniocentesis is completed, the fluid is placed into sterile tubes and sent to a laboratory. There, it is placed onto a culture medium that allows the cells to grow. Cell growth takes about 1 to 2 weeks. The cells are then "harvested" and treated with chemicals. These chemicals stop the process of cell division at the stage when the chromosomes can be seen most clearly and cause the chromosomes to swell and spread apart. The cells are stained and viewed under a high-power microscope. The chromosomes are photographed and mapped for analysis. The analysis determines whether there are errors in the numbers of chromosomes (*aneuploidy*), such as extra chromosomes or missing chromosomes, and whether there are errors in the structure of chromosomes, such as missing pieces of chromosomes or mixing up of chromosomes (*translocations*).

The amniotic fluid is assessed for evidence of markers of disease, such as elevated alpha-fetoprotein, as described in the section on screening of maternal blood. Direct analysis of alpha-fetoprotein in amniotic fluid is considered to be 99 percent accurate in diagnosing neural tube or other defects. Fresh amniotic fluid and the liquid culture medium also can be examined for the presence of enzymes and other biochemicals whose presence indicates various genetic disorders such as Tay-Sachs disease, cystic fibrosis, combined immune deficiency, sickle-cell anemia, and thalessemia major, as well as other less common diseases.

Amniocentesis has been employed for fetal treatments to administer medication to the fetus. It is a part of the process of in utero fetal blood transfusion.

Amniocentesis is also used in late pregnancy to assess the amount of a *lipid* (fatty) chemical which gives an estimate of fetal lung maturity. This is one of the possible tests performed when there is a question as to whether a baby who is not growing properly would thrive better if left to develop to maturity inside the mother or if delivered and cared for in a neonatal intensive care unit. This is discussed further in Chapter 17.

A recently developed technique called FISH (*fluorescent in-situ hybridization*) may speed diagnosis in some cases. This technique requires knowing the DNA sequence where a specific gene is located so that a probe for that gene can be applied to allow visualization of the part of the chromosome of interest. It can also be used to demonstrate abnormal chromosome numbers. FISH has two advantages over currently used procedures: it is accurate when there are only a few cells obtained and it does not require capturing the cells at the time of division. Because of the first advantage, FISH might be used eventually on the fetal cells that find their way into the maternal blood, in the future perhaps decreasing the need for some amniocenteses. Because of the second advantage, results from CVS and amniocentesis could be obtained without the delay of growing the cells over time.

Cordocentesis or
Percutaneous Umbilical Blood Sampling (PUBS)

With the continuing improvement in sonographic images, a method of inserting a long needle into the umbilical vein as early as week 17 of pregnancy has been developed. In percutaneous (Latin: *per* = through;

cutis = skin) umbilical blood sampling, or PUBS, a small volume of fetal blood is withdrawn, approximately 1 to 4 milliliters, or less than one-eighth of an ounce. This sample can be analyzed directly, without the need to grow cells in culture. This simplifies and speeds the diagnosis of some fetal abnormalities. The risk of PUBS or *cordocentesis*, also called funipuncture (Latin: *funis* = cord), is estimated at about 1 to 3 percent, less than that of fetoscopy (see next section) but greater than amniocentesis. This technique is performed under the strictest sterile technique. Before the needle is inserted, the pregnant woman's abdomen is cleansed with a sterile solution. As with amniocentesis, a local anesthetic may be injected into the site where the needle will be inserted.

PUBS is always performed under ultrasonic guidance to localize the umbilical cord. Because there is some bleeding from the cord following the procedure, the ultrasound is continued after the needle is withdrawn to make sure the bleeding stops rapidly—which it usually does. The fetal heart is also monitored during and immediately following the procedure.

PUBS is performed only at specialized centers and is reserved for specialized circumstances. These might include:

- **A woman seeking fetal diagnosis** because of a high likelihood of a chromosomal or genetic abnormality, but requiring a very rapid assessment because her pregnancy is close to the legal limit for an abortion
- **The need to diagnose certain blood disorders** including sickle-cell anemia and hemophilia
- **The need to diagnose certain metabolic disorders or fetal infection** with organisms known to be teratogenic, including toxoplasmosis, rubella, cytomegalovirus, varicella (chicken pox), or parovirus B19 (Fifth disease), discussed in Chapters 5 and 16
- **Evaluation of Rh disease** in the fetus as well as in utero treatment of Rh disease by blood transfusion
- **The need to treat the fetus** directly with drugs, for example, in fetal heart disease
- **In later pregnancy** (see Chapter 17)**, to assess the fetal condition** when there is intrauterine growth retardation or restriction
- **In later pregnancy, to perform a rapid karyotype** when there is fetal distress and a sonographically demonstrated major abnormality; a karyotype may show the abnormality to be fatal and thus the mother is spared a cesarean delivery for a newborn that would not survive

Some obstetric experts believe that as physicians become more proficient in performing this technique, thus reducing its potential risks, PUBS will become more widely utilized.

Fetoscopy/Embryoscopy

A viewing instrument called a *fetoscope*, tiny enough to pass through a needle, can be introduced into the amniotic cavity, making it possible to view the fetus directly. The method of inserting the fetoscopy needle is the same as for amniocentesis, done under strict sterile precautions, though for this purpose the needle is wider.

Unfortunately, the fetal view is not always clear, since the amniotic fluid may be cloudy, due in part to the fetal cells floating in it. The field of vision is also limited, so that only very small parts of the fetus can be viewed at any one moment. Defects can be found of tiny parts such as fingers and toes. By maneuvering the fetoscope around, the physician can see fetal blood vessels, especially on the surface of the placenta. With specially developed miniature instruments, the physician can obtain samples of fetal blood and bits of fetal skin, which can then be used for studies of cells and biochemicals.

Recently, *embryoscopy*—a technique for viewing the embryo—has been developed. This allows for visualization of the embryo as early as 9 or 10 weeks of pregnancy. Like amniocentesis and fetoscopy, embryoscopy is performed through the mother's abdomen. It is an experimental technique, made possible by fiber-optic technology. The instruments used are tiny. The risk of pregnancy loss is estimated at approximately 12 percent—more than 1 in 10. This technique is reserved for fetuses in families known to have recurrent severe genetic diseases whose manifestations can be recognized exclusively by visual examination. Until its risk can be lowered, it will not become widely utilized.

Risks of Invasive Procedures

Despite careful attention to sterile technique, infection can occur with any procedure that disturbs the integrity of the uterine environment. Infections usually respond to antibiotics. The hole made in the membranes may be delayed in healing, or may not heal at all. In either case, the amniotic fluid will drain through the membranes, into the uterine cavity, and out through the cervix. The fetus may die or be born prematurely with incompletely developed lungs. The puncture itself may damage fetal blood vessels; such an accident can cause fetal death due to hemorrhage.

Most experts report the fetal loss rate from amniocentesis at about .25 to .50 percent (1 in 400 to 1 in 200 procedures). The loss rate from CVS is about double this, and from fetoscopy it is probably 10 times this. Fetoscopy has a risk of miscarriage in the realm of 5 percent. Embryoscopy is associated with a fetal loss rate more than double that of fetoscopy. Fetoscopy and embryoscopy are currently limited to the very few hereditary diseases that cannot be diagnosed in any other way, or for fetal treatments (see below). Fetal treatments are reserved largely for those situations where the alternative—no treatment—is fatal.

During any invasive procedure, the maternal and fetal blood may mix. All Rh negative women, unless known to be pregnant by an Rh negative man, must receive an injection of RhoGAM to prevent Rh sensitization after any invasive procedure (see Chapter 5).

Follow-Up of Genetic Defects

As invasive procedures carry risks, some experts believe they are unjustified in the situation where a woman knows she will carry the pregnancy regardless of the outcome of the test. Some women and their families, however, feel that they can be better prepared to cope with a baby with a health problem if they can anticipate it. In some cases, still relatively rare, diagnosis can allow for fetal treatment. Whether to carry a pregnancy or consent to fetal treatment is a personal and family decision, although, of course, the medical implications of the discovered defect and the safety of proposed treatment will play an important role in the decision making. Prior to any invasive procedure, the mother should be informed of the likelihood of having the condition for which the procedure is being performed and of the risks to her and to her fetus, including the possibility of errors in diagnosis. The decision whether to have an abortion is entirely the woman's.

Selective abortion, where one fetus in a multiple pregnancy has a defect, is possible, as is selective abortion—sometimes called *selective reduction* or *selective birth*—when large numbers of embryos develop after infertility treatment (see Chapters 13 and 23). This is technically a difficult procedure, though high success rates have been reported.

Obviously, if chromosomal or genetic defects occur in your family or if you are over the age of 35, you should get as much information about your individual situation as possible. Ask your physician or midwife for information and request a referral to a genetics counselor early in pregnancy. Genetic counseling is available at major medical centers in the United States. If you live in a small town or rural area and are not near such a center, which is usually a large hospital associated with a medical school, you are well advised to make a trip to such a center for at least one visit if you fall into a category as described above, or if your physician or midwife recommends such a visit. A genetic counselor also can be located through the National Society of Genetic Counselors (see Appendix).

The role of the genetic counselor and the obstetrical care provider is to explain the genetic, pediatric, developmental, and social implications of the particular genetic problem involved. A genetic counselor will be able to teach parents, or prospective parents, about the genetic aspects of the particular problems with which they are most concerned, as well as the influences of environment and other relevant factors on genetic inheritance. For example, although a plant may have a gene for tallness, which is dominant over its gene for shortness, it may end up short because it is growing in a shallow pan or is not exposed to sufficient sunlight.

Your partner should attend the counseling session so you can make an informed decision together. For some mothers or couples, there is no alternative to abortion if the presence of a defect is verified, regardless of whether or not the extent of disability can be determined prenatally. Other families may want to consider the extent of the potential burden. They may consider what familial supports they have, what community services are available, how their particular life situation might influence the difficulties involved in raising a child with serious disabilities. Many mothers wish to share their problem with a spouse, a counselor, a parent, or a friend, to help them choose a comfortable course of action.

In most cases, genetic counseling will be reassuring about the outcome of the pregnancy, but if that is not possible, it will point the woman and her partner in the direction of competent diagnosis and care, as well as possible alternatives, such as use of donor sperm or ova.

TREATMENT OF THE FETUS IN UTERO

In utero blood transfusion to the anemic fetus was the first treatment ever given directly to the unborn child. This was introduced more than 40 years ago by Sir Albert W. Liley when he gave the blood through a needle placed into the fetus's peritoneal cavity, the potential space that contains the abdominal organs such as the stomach, liver, intestines, and spleen. He did this as early as week 28 of pregnancy. It was, of course, first necessary to develop methods of in utero diagnosis of the severity of fetal anemia. Fetal transfusion continues to be used today, with good success rates. If the anemia will be fatal in utero before the fetus is mature enough to survive birth and subsequent transfusion, then in utero transfusion can be performed.

In Utero Surgery

Highly accurate diagnosis of fetal diseases as well as accurate placement of devices necessary to treat them have been made possible by improved ultrasound techniques. As a result, in utero surgical therapy has been expanding steadily in the last several decades. The drainage of excessive fluid accumulations in the urinary tract and the nervous system were the earliest procedures performed.

In the urinary tract, *obstruction* can occur where the bladder connects with the *urethra*, the short tube through which the baby urinates. Obstruction can also occur where the *renal pelvis*, the small reservoir for urine in the kidney, connects with the *ureter*, the tube that carries urine down to the bladder. If such obstructions are present, the urine that continues to form blows up the drainage system to astounding size. This, in turn, damages the kidney. Treatment of urinary tract obstructions has been accomplished by placing fine catheters into the stretched organs and allowing the fluid to drain into the fetus's peritoneal cavity or the amniotic sac. This treatment has been highly successful and Dr. Frank Manning, who performed the first such surgery in 1980, recently reported an 80 percent survival rate following surgery, compared to a 2 percent survival with this condition before the availability of surgery.

The same treatment principle has been applied when there is obstruction of the flow of cerebrospinal fluid, the fluid that functions as a shock-absorbing cushion within the brain and spinal cord. Obstruction to the flow of this fluid results in *hydrocephalus*, a swelling of the brain with fluid (Greek: *hydro* = water; *cephalos* = head). This procedure has been shown to improve survival rates of babies with hydrocephalus from one-third of affected infants to two-thirds, but among babies who survive, 60 percent have serious problems including seizures, mental retardation, and blindness. In 1988, physicians stopped performing this fetal surgery because of this high rate of complications.

When first introduced, fetal surgery was reserved for fetuses with conditions that would almost certainly be fatal. Today, physicians are performing surgeries with the goal of reducing the disability caused by certain conditions. In some specialized centers, physicians have closed open neural tube defects in utero, rather than waiting until birth, because of the irritating effect of amniotic fluid on the exposed nervous system tissue.

Because of the risks associated with fetal surgery, ethical questions arise anytime the surgery is performed to improve function, rather than to save the life of the fetus. Families who choose these surgeries must receive complete information regarding potential risks and benefits and make their choices without any coercion.

An example of fetal surgery performed through a fetoscopy was the transplantation, through injection, of bone marrow from a father to the fetus. This male fetus had a severe, usually fatal X-linked condition called *combined immune deficiency*. The bone marrow was obtained under general anesthesia, posing a slight risk to the father.

Fetal surgery has been used successfully in a condition known as *twin-to-twin transfusion syndrome* (TTS). TTS occurs in a particular type of twinning in which the twins share the *chorion*, the outer of the two membranes forming the bag of waters (see Chapter 23). Sometimes, these type of twins share some part of the placental circulation, with one baby getting too much blood and the other too little. Untreated, both twins usually die. Several intrauterine treatments are available, including *serial amniocentesis*, a withdrawal of fluid from the twin who has an excess. A more recent procedure involves laser interruption of the blood vessels that the twins share. This is done in only a few centers around the world. A small incision is made in the mother's abdomen and the instruments are inserted through this incision. The mother is put to sleep with general anesthesia for the procedure. In another type of procedure, where one twin is severely affected with a certainty of dying, the umbilical cord to that fetus may be tied off. This has a high success rate of saving the less severely affected fetus, who would otherwise die or have brain damage as a result of the death of the sicker twin.

Some of the more complex intrauterine surgical procedures, such as repair of neural tube defects, are called *open uterine surgeries*. The mother receives general anesthesia and a larger surgical incision is made in her abdomen and uterus to reach the fetus. This carries not just a risk to the fetus, but a small risk to the mother. Some conditions for which open uterine surgeries have been successfully reported include open neural tube defects, certain fetal tumors, and congenital diaphragmatic hernias. A diaphragmatic hernia causes major anomalies and is fatal, as may be some tumors.

These advances in technology, as spectacular as they seem, actually benefit a small proportion of pregnancies and contribute little to fetal and newborn survival statistics—statistics often used to judge a country's overall health.

In Utero Treatment of Genetic Defects

Sophisticated biochemical techniques have allowed scientists to introduce genes into living beings—first into animals and now into humans. The gene is attached to a virus known not to cause disease in the species. Because viruses live inside cells, when injected, the virus is able to insert the gene into selected cells such as bone marrow cells.

Such "gene therapy" is very much in experimental stages. It has been used on a very small number of people with *hemophilia*, an X-linked recessive clotting disorder. Once gene therapy becomes more widespread, there is no reason to think that it could not be done with fetuses, and for a number of conditions.

Of course, genetic therapy raises enormous ethical questions, a discussion beyond the scope of this book. International conferences have been convened to discuss the ethics of genetic therapy. Most experts currently agree that the use of genes should be restricted to treatment of conditions that are life threatening or require difficult long-term treatments. Gene *manipulation*, gene *enhancement*, and genetic *engineering* are terms used to refer to making changes in genes for the purpose of altering characteristics that do not cause disease, but may be considered undesirable in some situations. At the present time, this is considered unethical by most scientists, ethicists, government agencies, and others interested in such questions. These ethical issues must continue to be pursued with as much vigor as the research is carried out.

CHAPTER NINE

━◦◦◦━

The Pregnant Months

There are great differences of informed opinion about the conduct of normal pregnancy. Further, each woman's pregnancy is individual. Our comments here are not intended to displace or alter those of your own physician or midwife. We believe that the foundation of a healthy pregnancy is prenatal care, beginning early in pregnancy—ideally *before* pregnancy—and continuing throughout.

Until the middle of the twentieth century pregnancy was a risky condition for women in the U.S. In 1930, the maternal mortality in the United States was 670. This means that for every 100,000 babies born alive, 670 women died during pregnancy, delivery, or the first 6 weeks following delivery. Since 1930, pregnancy has become 80 times as safe for women in this country. From 1982 to 1996, the maternal mortality rate was fairly steady at 7.5 per 100,000 births or approximately 1 in 13,000 births. (As the number of births in 1997 was 3,880,884, there were approximately 291 deaths among pregnant women that year.) The United States government has set a goal that, in this new millennium, deaths among pregnant women be reduced to just over 3 deaths in every 100,000 live births, or 1 maternal death in about every 33,000 live births.

Risk Factors in Childbirth

The risk of childbirth is not uniform among women. Worldwide, maternal mortality remains a major individual and public health concern. In the United States there is a dramatic difference in ma-

---

ternal mortality for white women and African-American women. From 1992 to 1996, the maternal mortality of U.S. white women was 5.0 per 100,000 live births, and for African-American women it was 20.3. This shocking four-fold difference in mortality rate derives from social and economic factors such as a lack of accessible or quality prenatal care, lifelong inadequate nutrition dating back to the mother's own prenatal experience during her mother's pregnancy, living conditions associated with poverty, and overall poor health and poor health education among African-American women. Reducing this disparity is another health goal for the twenty-first century.

The chief causes of maternal death are:

- Pregnancy-induced high blood pressure
- Hemorrhage
- Blood clots (*emboli*)
- Ectopic pregnancy
- Infection

The last has diminished greatly since the near disappearance of illegal abortion, which was a principal cause of death through infection. Most of these causes of death are preventable or treatable.

As pregnancy in the United States no longer poses a major risk to life, women's concerns are how to achieve optimal health and comfort during pregnancy and how to best contribute to the well-being of the child they are carrying.

SUBJECTS YOU MAY BE WONDERING ABOUT

Exercise

Before offering advice about exercise during pregnancy, we stress that you should consult with your physician or midwife before continuing or beginning an exercise program during your pregnancy.

Scientific evidence about exercise in pregnancy has been gathered only recently. In the past, obstetrical care providers relied on a combination of common sense and myth to give advice about exercise. Older textbooks often urged moderation in physical activities during pregnancy. They frequently advised fresh air and told women that they could continue "housework." At the same time, if a woman had a previous pregnancy loss or symptoms of a threatened miscarriage, she often was told to go to bed. Then, of course, if she actually suffered a miscarriage, she would search her life for the cause and with no difficulty discover it either in some minor accident or the simple exertions of her everyday existence. With advances in knowledge about the real causes of miscarriage, our attitude toward exercise during pregnancy has changed. We realize that the majority of miscarriages are deliberate—even blessed—acts on the part of nature to avoid the further development of an abnormality of the ovum, sperm, the embryo, or the fetus.

Exercise in pregnancy has many of the same benefits it has at any time: it boosts physical and mental health. In 1996, the National Institutes of Health reported that 30 minutes a day of moderately strenuous exercise such as walking, cycling, or gardening on most or all days is beneficial, even if the exercise is in short bouts of only 10 minutes each.

Exercise also may ease some of the common discomforts of pregnancy such as backache, fatigue, constipation, and varicose veins. Regular exercise may help promote sleep, which is often a problem in pregnancy.

Recent studies have shown both moderate and vigorous exercise to be without adverse effects on the fetus in low-risk pregnancies. Babies born to women who exercise in pregnancy and babies born to women who do not exercise show no important differences in birth weight. One recent study comparing 34 babies of women who exercised to 31 babies of women who did not exercise found that at 5 days after birth, babies of the exercising mothers were more alert and less fussy.

Studies also have shown that exercise does not trigger premature labor, but no evidence at this time supports claims that exercise helps speed the process of labor or birth.

Guidelines for Exercising in Pregnancy

• Mild to moderate exercise can be continued throughout pregnancy, if the pregnancy is and remains low-risk. Regular exercise, at least three times a week, is better than sporadic exercise.

• Exercise should be avoided in the presence of the following pregnancy complications (see Chapters 12, 14, 15, and 23):

Preterm labor or a history of preterm labor
Vaginal bleeding

Cervical incompetence
Ruptured membranes (broken bag of waters)
Fetus who is not growing properly on ultrasound examination
Pregnancy-induced high blood pressure
Twins or other multiple pregnancy

• Pregnant women with the following medical conditions should consult with their physician before beginning an exercise program:

High blood pressure
Diabetes
Heart disease
Thyroid disease

• After the first trimester, pregnant women should avoid exercising flat on their backs as this causes pressure on the *vena cava*, the main vein carrying blood to the heart. This can slow the heart, cause dizziness, and even reduce the blood flow to the uterus.
• Do not exercise to exhaustion; instead, stop when you become fatigued.
• Avoid exercise that might interfere with balance, cause injury to the abdomen, or has a high risk of falling.
• Unsafe exercises in pregnancy include water skiing, surfing, horseback riding, diving, and snowmobiling. Downhill skiing may be difficult, especially in the third trimester, due to the risk of falls as balance changes. Women who are skiers should stick to easy slopes. Cross-country skiing is safer. A stationary bicycle is safer as pregnancy progresses, even for experienced cyclists.
• Make sure you continue to gain an adequate amount of weight. Exercise should not be used in pregnancy to lose weight or to limit pregnancy weight gain. Guidelines for weight gain in pregnancy are discussed in Chapter 10.
• Avoid overheating, especially early in pregnancy:

Drink plenty of fluids.
Wear clothes that breathe, such as loose pants and T-shirts rather than leotards and tights.
Dress in layers.
Avoid exercise on hot, humid days.
Avoid immersing yourself in a hot tub or sauna; the body heat it creates may be associated with birth defects.

• Stop exercising immediately if you have:

Shortness of breath
Dizziness or faintness
Weakness
Headache
Nausea
Chest pain or tightness
Uterine contractions or cramps
Back or pelvic pain
Vaginal bleeding or leakage of fluid
Rapid heart beat at rest

Although exercise can be continued throughout pregnancy, exercises that don't involve weight bearing are easier to maintain at a consistent level of intensity. These include stationary cycling, swimming, and water aerobics. Most pregnant women who do aerobics or jog find that they need to reduce the exercise intensity as pregnancy progresses. Your own body is your best guide. You may wish to replace jogging with brisk walking. Singles tennis, squash, or racquetball may become too strenuous. It also may be too dangerous because of the possibility of falling due to the many sudden starts and stops in these activities, not to mention the risk of getting hit with the fast-moving ball. Late in pregnancy, you may decide to play doubles instead of singles.

The American College of Sports Medicine recommends drinking two glasses (sixteen ounces) of water or a sports drink 2 hours before exercising and five to twelve ounces every 15 to 20 minutes during exercise. Other good exercise tips include always starting with a warm-up and ending with a cool-down. A warm-up consists of light aerobic activity such as stationary cycling or walking, possibly followed by stretching, before you begin more vigorous activities. A cool-down should include walking in place and stretching. Wear good, well-fitting athletic shoes. As your feet may swell, you may need to buy a larger-sized pair for pregnancy.

Women often ask if there is a minimum amount of exercise required in a normal pregnancy. The answer is that it depends on you. It is an entirely individual decision related to what you are accustomed to and comfortable with. Exercise is always beneficial to general health, and it is no different in pregnancy.

Women who did not exercise before pregnancy can begin a slow and gradual exercise program during pregnancy. Brisk walking is a good beginning exercise. Swimming is also good because it uses both arm and leg muscles and the water supports the body. Late in pregnancy, however, diving is dangerous.

During exercise, position changes, especially from sitting or lying to upright, should be accomplished slowly to prevent dizziness. If possible, when getting up from lying, turn to your side and push off with your arms. This spares the lower back muscles.

Yoga is frequently recommended in pregnancy. It can help with pregnancy discomforts and contribute to a general sense of well-being and calm. Standing in any one position for a long time, as some yoga postures require, can lead to dizziness in pregnancy, so be careful.

There has been a proliferation of books and videotapes recommending particular exercises for childbirth and for recovery from the delivery. A number of these are listed in the Appendix.

Sexual intercourse, a special kind of exercise, is also not harmful to mother or baby. Nor is there any evidence that orgasm has anything other than transitory effects on uterine contractions and fetal heart rate. However, an increase in uterine activity may be undesirable in women who have a risk of premature delivery.

Kegel exercises may help maintain the tone of the pelvic floor muscles in pregnancy. This exercise strengthens the muscles that circle the vagina, anus, and clitoris, and consists of tightening and releasing these muscles. The pelvic floor muscles are sometimes hard to find; they are the muscles you use when you are holding in urine when you can't get to a toilet. Your sexual partner will be able to tell you whether you are using the correct muscles as he can feel them tighten around his penis or fingers. You can ask your midwife or physician to show you the exercise during a pelvic examination and get feedback on whether you are using the right muscles or not.

Once you can identify the correct muscles, pelvic floor exercises can be done anytime during the day. You can work on holding the muscles in the tightened state for increasingly more seconds, and on increasing the number of repetitions done at any one time.

This is also a good exercise for postpartum comfort and healing (see Chapter 25).

Employment

You need not change or stop your ordinary work just because you are pregnant. Today, the majority of pregnant women work. Indeed, federal legislation prohibits employers from excluding women from job categories because they are or might become pregnant.

There are a few possible dangers in the workplace. One is toxic chemicals, discussed in Chapter 5. Several studies have shown that standing in the same position for hours at a time, unusually heavy workloads, and long working hours may be associated with a slightly increased risk of preterm delivery or reduced birth weight. Of these, the most consistent research finding seems to be about standing for long hours.

We recommend frequent rest periods and position changes on any job. If you have a job requiring prolonged standing, make sure you take breaks every few hours. A midmorning and midafternoon break, in addition to a lunch hour, should be enough in a regular 8-hour day. During breaks, sit or lie down, preferably on your left side, which allows the most blood flow to the uterus. While on the job, try to walk around a bit in the area where you are standing. Change positions whenever possible. If possible, put one leg up on a stool for at least part of the day. Do some arm stretches and shoulder lifts and circles. If you sit all day, stand up at least every few hours and stroll. If you can, put your legs up on a chair or stool while sitting.

We have each provided care to many women who have worked right up to the time of delivery. They may be more tired than their nonpregnant colleagues, but for the most part, in most jobs, working was not harmful to them or their babies.

Travel

There are only two arguments against travel in pregnancy:

1. Miscarriage or labor can happen at any hour on any day. If the pregnant woman happens to be traveling at the time of such an occurrence, or is residing in a community other than her own, it can be inconvenient and frightening. One way to lessen the difficulty is to obtain the name of an obstetric facility in the area you plan to visit. Put the information in your wallet and expect not to need it—almost certainly you will not. Usually the second trimester is a time of few untoward happenings, so if you can schedule your trips, travel between 13 and 26 weeks of pregnancy.
2. Traveling can be fatiguing and uncomfortable, especially in late pregnancy. You undoubtedly will be uncomfortable sitting in a cramped position for several hours. Put your legs up

if possible. If traveling by car, stop every 2 to 3 hours, get out of the car, urinate, and walk about for a few minutes. In a train or airplane, stand up at least every few hours, go to the bathroom, and walk around the aisles.

There is no evidence that traveling by any means of locomotion brings on labor, miscarriage, or any complication of pregnancy. Naturally, if a thousand women who are 8 to 12 weeks pregnant travel, a certain small percentage will miscarry, or if a thousand are 34 to 35 weeks pregnant, a small proportion will go into premature labor. However, the same thing is almost certain to happen to the same women if they stay home in bed. Studies of the pregnant wives of armed-services personnel in World War II showed no significant difference in the incidence of spontaneous abortion, premature labor, or any other obstetric complication between two groups of women—those who traveled about with their husbands and those who remained at one post.

Travel in the third trimester (the last 13 weeks) of pregnancy is inadvisable for a woman with a history of premature labor, the diagnosis of multiple pregnancy, or other pregnancy complications. During her last month, the woman should stay within easy reach of a hospital.

Decisions as to mode of travel during pregnancy should be governed mainly by common-sense considerations. For example, if you are prone to motion sickness, the train is probably best. Long distances are usually accomplished with least fatigue and discomfort by air. Since commercial airplane cabins are always pressurized, there are no grounds for worrying that air travel during the first 3 months might cause a fetal abnormality due to decreased oxygen at this formative period. The equipment used by security personnel at airports to screen passengers and baggage poses no danger to mother or fetus.

Check with the airline when you make reservations about whether they have any policies regarding pregnancy and flying. The airline may require special medical forms to be completed or may curtail flying after a certain number of weeks gestation. You can request an aisle seat in the bulkhead for extra room, or a seat over the wing for the smoothest ride. Make sure you drink a lot of fluids during a plane trip as the low humidity in the cabin can be dehydrating. In addition to walking frequently, you can flex and extend your ankles when the SEAT BELT sign is on. Fasten the seat belt in the pelvic area, beneath the uterus.

The Centers for Disease Control and Prevention (CDC) has published guidelines for international travel. The following conditions make a destination hazardous:

- High altitudes
- Areas with ongoing outbreaks of life-threatening food or insect-borne infections
- Areas with *Plasmodium falciparum* malaria that is resistant to chloroquine
- Areas where live-virus vaccines are required and recommended

The CDC has also developed a checklist for pregnant international travelers. Included in this list are:

- Making sure that health insurance can be used abroad
- Determining who will provide prenatal care, if it will be needed on the trip
- Checking the medical facilities at your destination. If you travel in the third trimester, available facilities should be able to treat complications of pregnancy, including toxemia, and perform cesarean deliveries.
- Checking beforehand whether blood is screened for HIV and hepatitis B
- Checking the destination for the availability of safe food and drinks, including bottled water and pasteurized milk

The CDC also has guidelines for vaccines—which ones are safe and which are not during pregnancy. Before you travel to an international destination, you must check to see what vaccinations are required or recommended. You or your care provider can then check with the CDC regarding the advisability of these vaccines during pregnancy. You can find this information at the CDC website, listed in the Appendix. Click on Traveler's Health, then Special Needs Travelers.

Automobile Travel

It is perfectly fine for a pregnant woman to drive a car herself, and you may continue to do so as long as you can sit comfortably behind the wheel. The previous edition of this book suggested that during the last trimester it would be inadvisable to drive alone at night, or on little-frequented roads, because of the potential problems that might arise from a flat tire or other automotive emergencies. Today, with the wide availability of cell phones and easily reached 24-hour emergency road services, this advice seems outdated. Also, today almost all cars are equipped with power steering, making obsolete the concern that urban parking might be overly exhausting during a pregnancy's final months.

Safe Use of a Seat Belt

Seat belts protect both mother and fetus. The main reason for death of a fetus in an automobile accident is death of the mother. Pregnant women should always wear three-point restraints. The lap belt goes under the abdomen and across the upper thighs. The shoulder belt goes between the breasts. Both belts should be as snug as comfortably possible.

Sleep

In early pregnancy, the average woman requires an unusually large amount of sleep; this need disappears between 12 and 16 weeks. The last months may be marked again by increased fatigue and sleeplessness.

Sleeplessness in late pregnancy usually is due to difficulty in finding a comfortable position or due to activity of the fetus. The fetus often chooses nighttime to cut capers. As there is no way to diminish fetal movements, the remedy is anything that will make you relax and sleep despite them.

A warm bath followed by a cup of warm milk is often helpful, with soft music in the background. The old home remedy, using warm milk as a sleep aid, is actually rather scientific. Milk contains *tryptophan*, a natural sleep inducer, and warming it helps release this amino acid. A back rub can be very relaxing and help with sleep.

Pregnant women may wonder whether it is harmful to sleep on the back or stomach. No possible harm can result from any position, since the fetus is so well protected that pressure on the pregnant woman's body does not affect it. If you lie on your back, prop your upper body up with pillows to avoid too much pressure on the *vena cava*, the large vein carrying blood to the heart, which could interfere with blood supply to the placenta and thus the fetus.

A side-lying position with lots of pillows to support as many joints as possible is often the most comfortable. A pillow can go under the head and neck, behind the back, under the uterus, and between the two knees or under the upper leg, which can be bent and crossed over the lower leg. If the upper elbow is crossed over the abdomen, it also can be supported with a pillow.

The amount of sleep you get should be governed by habit and desire; the safest rule is to sleep enough to awake well rested. So much of good care in pregnancy is determined by your own body's messages and your lifetime of common sense. If convenient, naps during the day can be quite refreshing.

Care of Your Breasts

The breasts require no special care during pregnancy. There is no benefit in massaging them with or without ointments or attempting to initiate lactation by manipulating the nipple and the *areola* (the darkened area around the nipple).

Whether to wear a bra during pregnancy is a matter of personal comfort. The breasts do become heavier and comfort may be enhanced by wearing a bar with cups large enough to hold all the breast tissue, especially the breast tissue that extends out to the armpit. The shoulder straps should be wide enough not to cut into the shoulder.

Many women buy nursing bras in late pregnancy, rather than purchasing a regular larger-sized bra. Nursing bras have flaps that open downward, to facilitate the infant's access to the nipples. The breasts usually increase in size in early pregnancy and then after birth, so if you purchase a nursing bra, buy it a cup size larger than you need in late pregnancy.

Manipulating your nipples or breasts as a preparation for breast-feeding is not only unnecessary, but can stimulate uterine contractions. Signals go via the nervous system to the hypothalamus, which reacts by causing release of the hormone oxytocin from the pituitary. The oxytocin in turn causes the uterus to contract. This response is best avoided by women who have a history of previous premature labors or even premature contractions, women who have had any treatment for the *incompetent cervical syndrome* (see Chapter 14), and women who have had threatened premature labor in the present pregnancy.

Even educated, motivated women may be anxious about their ability to breast-feed, often based on the size of their breasts. The success of breast-feeding is not related to the size of a woman's breasts. Larger breasts are larger mostly because of fatty tissue, not functional breast tissue.

Your nipples do not need to be toughened during pregnancy to prevent the development of cracks or soreness while nursing. Scrubbing them with a nail brush or wash cloth, as used to be advised, or applying alcohol just creates the conditions it is meant to prevent. Chapter 26 on breast-feeding discusses ways of preventing nipple soreness or cracking during nursing.

Most nipples project normally and babies have no trouble grasping them. Some nipples appear flat, but will project easily once the baby sucks. To test this, pinch the areola, the pigmented circular area around the nipple, between your fingers and see what happens. If the nipple projects, you definitely will have no problem. If the nipple appears to remain flat or even turns inward, you may have what are called *inverted nipples*. Your physician or midwife may have checked this on your initial prenatal or preconception visit and already discussed the potential problem with you. Most of the time, the condition corrects itself during pregnancy, and by 9 months, the nipple can be erected. Even if not, the baby's sucking usually will cause the nipple to evert.

There is much disagreement among breast-feeding experts about how to treat inverted nipples, if at all. Plastic dome-shaped breast shells (also called *breast shields* or *breast cups*) are specially designed to pull out the nipple, although there is no clear evidence that these are effective. They can be worn during the third trimester of pregnancy and the early weeks of breast-feeding. They are worn between feedings; they are not the same as *nipple shields*, worn during feedings—which are definitely not recommended.

Some women find breast shells uncomfortable, although wearing a larger bra or attaching a bra extender to the bra hooks can help make them more comfortable. They should not be worn for sleeping as lying on them causes undue pressure. In the last few weeks of pregnancy, they are worn for gradually increasing time periods during the day, starting with half an hour. During the early weeks of nursing, they can be worn for half an hour before feeding. Breast shells are available from La Leche League (see Appendix).

Whether or not to use breast shells is a topic to discuss with your midwife or physician or with a *lactation consultant*. Lactation consultants may work in the hospital or birth center or in a private practice, often coming to your home. Any of these professionals can assess your individual situation and help you find a solution if inverted nipples persist as a problem toward the end of your pregnancy or early in the postpartum weeks.

During the last 6 weeks of pregnancy and while nursing, wash the breasts only with plain water. Soap is drying to skin and its use may increase the chances of cracking. Normal pregnancy secretions, called *colostrum*, help prepare the breasts for sucking and need not be washed off.

It is not unusual for one breast to be larger than the other during pregnancy. This difference in size may become accentuated as pregnancy progresses. Some asymmetry between anatomic structures on opposite sides of the body is common and normal. It is almost always present, just not always apparent.

Your Abdomen

Throughout the ages, women have used various remedies to prevent loss of abdominal muscle tone or to restore tone after delivery. The preventives have been most elaborate and consisted of two types: the wearing of an abdominal support and the anointment of the abdomen with some greasy medicament. In earlier times, supports were of two varieties: either a specially treated animal skin, or a broad linen swatch "made fir the purpose to support her Belly." The rubbing ointments were legion, and many authors had several of their own special concoctions; the very number leads one to suspect their efficacy.

Some women, especially women who have had many children or who are carrying a very large fetus or more than one fetus, lose muscle tone during pregnancy, causing the uterus to fall forward. This is uncomfortable and may cause backache and interfere with balance even more than the usual changes of pregnancy do. Some women with this problem like to wear a *maternity girdle*. A girdle will not work to maintain or restore abdominal muscle tone; it is worn purely for comfort.

Even women who have good muscle tone during pregnancy may find that their navel or umbilicus protrudes in late pregnancy. This should not be a cause for concern. If it bothers you esthetically, placing a Band-Aid over the navel will keep it from showing through your clothing. The navel will return to normal in the postpartum period.

Rubbing the abdomen with various oils or creams does not help with either muscle tone or the *striae*—stretch marks—of pregnancy. However, if you enjoy doing it, it is not harmful, provided you use a nonmedicated substance such as cocoa butter or plain olive oil.

Even if the abdominal wall bulges and sags immediately after delivery, it will spontaneously regain much of the tone it previously possessed within the first 10 postpartum weeks. Abdominal exercises are certainly helpful. Again, a girdle will do nothing to restore tone and may make you less likely to exercise. It certainly is neither necessary nor recommended in the postpartum period. Striae eventually will fade. The *linea negra* or dark line that appears in the middle of the abdomen also fades in the postpartum period.

Bathing

Raising the core body temperature in pregnancy has been associated with a risk of birth defects. Hot tubs and saunas can cause the core body temperature to rise and should be avoided in pregnancy. Showers are certainly safe throughout pregnancy. The temperature in tub baths should be less than 100° F. If the water is warm and comfortable, then it should be the appropriate temperature and safe. Late in pregnancy, as your sense of balance changes, you have to be careful getting in and out of the tub, and sometimes may need some assistance.

No Douching

No special hygiene of the genitals is recommended during pregnancy. They should be cleansed with soap and water as usual. You may notice increased vaginal secretions during pregnancy. This is called *leukorrhea* (Greek: *leukos* = white; *roia* = flow). Leukorrhea is normal as long as there is no associated odor, itching, burning, pain, or other discomfort.

Vaginal douching is unnecessary during pregnancy or at any other time. Women have been taught to think of their genitalia as dirty and requiring frequent cleaning. The vagina maintains its own cleanliness quite efficiently. Vaginal infection is not due to poor hygiene, and if the vagina does become infected, it requires specific treatment. Douching is unquestionably hazardous for a pregnant woman who has vaginal bleeding or whose membranes have ruptured. A bulb syringe douche should *never* be utilized in pregnancy as it can send air into the amniotic fluid space, causing a serious problem. If you do douche (which we really do not recommend), you must not hold the bag more than two feet above the level of your hips nor put the nozzle more than three inches into the vagina.

Deodorant douches and deodorant sprays are unnecessary. A surprising number of women are allergic to some of the chemicals in these preparations and can do themselves harm, however minor, by using a product that has no health benefits.

Clothing

We have already considered the issue of bras. Clothing in general should be loose and comfortable and, if possible, hang from the shoulders to prevent constriction of the waist. Tight circular garters should not be worn; they act as tourniquets and increase the likelihood of varicose veins, which are common in pregnancy because of the normally increased pressure in the veins of the pelvis and legs. Pantyhose can be worn instead. Loose, low socks are preferable to tighter knee socks.

Shoes with broad toes and low, flat, rubber heels are usually more comfortable as pregnancy progresses. The extra weight that the woman carries in front tends to disturb the sense of balance, and low heels help to prevent tripping and falling forward. If balance remains undisturbed and shoes with heels are comfortable, they can be worn.

Teeth and Dental Care

"For each child a tooth," was a common saying about pregnancy in past years. The damage to women's teeth with each repeated pregnancy was almost certainly a consequence of nutritional inadequacy and a lack of dental care. Modern dental care and diet has largely eliminated dental problems during pregnancy.

Use pregnancy, or pregnancy planning, as an occasion for securing good dental care. It is preferable to go to the dentist before you become pregnant, although regular cleanings can be carried out in pregnancy. Tooth enamel is laid down long before pregnancy, and is not a part of the mobile body store of calcium, so the calcium content of your diet is not directly important to the integrity of your teeth.

Some women's gums have a tendency to bleed when the teeth are brushed. If you have increased discomfort when brushing or flossing, or if your gums hurt, you should see your dentist, who will instruct you in a special program of oral hygiene. Drink a lot of water throughout the day, especially if you have vomiting that causes stomach contents to come into your mouth. A little lemon squeezed into the water might help if you have a bad taste in your mouth.

Remember, of course, to tell your dentist that you are pregnant, or that you are trying to become pregnant. Dental x-ray machines, combined with the extremely fast films that are used for dental X rays, expose teeth to very small radiation doses. The radiation dose to the baby, or your reproductive organs a foot or more away, is probably not even measurable. Nevertheless, your dentist will want to place a lead apron over your abdomen to be on the safe side.

Local anesthesia like Novocaine can be used for dental procedures if necessary. Sometimes epinephrine is added to the local anesthesia; this causes the blood vessels to constrict and should not be used in pregnancy. General anesthesia is best avoided in pregnancy. Nitrous oxide (*laughing gas*) should not be used either.

Sexuality

Sexual desire, or *libido*, varies greatly from one woman to another in pregnancy, and even in any one woman at different times during pregnancy. Nausea, for instance, may not make for sexual desire.

Women who previously regarded intercourse only as a way of becoming pregnant and not as a source of love or gratification may have a drop in their sexual drive. In other pregnant women, sex interest and response are increased. This may be true for women for whom contraception was seen as a bother. Occasionally, a pregnant woman develops an aversion to intercourse, perhaps because of some unexpressed fear that sexual activity might adversely affect the fetus, or perhaps because of feelings about her changed body, especially in this thinness-oriented society. These reactions are by no means fixed and may be present at one stage of pregnancy and disappear in another.

The pregnant woman's partner also may experience changes in libido. He or she may be unusually excited by his or her partner's changing body, or find that it is less appealing sexually. Partners may also have a fear of hurting the growing fetus. These issues should be discussed as openly as possible. If either of you has a problem that seems to be interfering in any way with your relationship, your provider may be able to offer some good advice, help with your communication if you are both present, or work with you if you are having trouble communicating your feelings to your partner. A referral to a marriage counselor, psychologist, psychiatric social worker, or psychiatrist may be helpful in some instances. Usually, however, these feelings pass, and, with good communication, cause no major problems.

In the absence of vaginal bleeding, ruptured membranes, or a history of repeated miscarriage or premature labor in this or prior pregnancies, sexual intercourse is safe at any stage of pregnancy. Bleeding following intercourse calls for examination. Unless some abnormality exists, abstinence during pregnancy is entirely a matter of choice by the partners.

In general, orgasm during pregnancy has no adverse effects on either the mother or the fetus, although orgasm does induce uterine contractions. These contractions may be hazardous in women who have a history of incompetent cervix or of premature labors or premature contractions (*threatened labor*). Discuss this with your physician or midwife, who will advise you on whether you should refrain from orgasm in the middle or later weeks of pregnancy, before your baby reaches a safe size to be born.

There is no reason to believe that masturbation or *fellatio* (female to male oral sex) is dangerous in pregnancy. *Cunnilingus* (male to female oral sex) is dangerous if it is associated with blowing air into the vagina but otherwise there is no known danger.

The positions of the couple during intercourse may have to be modified on simple physical grounds as pregnancy progresses. It's fine to experiment with a variety of positions. A woman is often more comfortable when she is on top, lying on her side, or on her hands and knees. The vagina is ordinarily quite well lubricated during pregnancy. If you have discomfort on penile entry, discuss this with your physician or midwife. When intercourse is uncomfortable, as it may be, for example, if you have varicose veins of the pelvic area, or when your physician or midwife advises against intercourse, you and your partner can explore alternative ways of mutual pleasuring, such as kissing, caressing, and touching.

In today's age of HIV/AIDS and *sexually transmitted infections* (STIs), of course, the issue of intercourse or oral sex during pregnancy may pose additional problems for some women. You should use a condom if:

- your partner is infected with AIDS or an STI (although abstinence is preferable in these situations)
- you think your partner may be infected
- your partner is at risk for acquiring a sexually transmitted infection (has other sexual partners or uses intravenous drugs)

You can contract an STI, including HIV, during pregnancy, and these can be harmful to the fetus or infect the baby during the birth process (see Chapters 5 and 16).

Drugs

The best general rule is not to medicate yourself during pregnancy. This is especially important in the first trimester of pregnancy. A few drugs, however, such as aspirin and ibuprofen, are more dangerous in the third trimester and should be avoided during the last three months of pregnancy. A few common over-the-counter preparations are probably safe:

- Mild analgesics, such as acetaminophen (Tylenol), although aspirin is best avoided
- Drugs for indigestion and heartburn
- Preparations for constipation
- An over-the-counter antihistamine like Benadryl (diphenhydramine) is preferable to a sleeping pill for insomnia

The use of aspirin and acetaminophen (Tylenol) is discussed in Chapter 5 and other medications in Chapter 11.

Emotional Changes of Pregnancy

Pregnancy is a time of great change and adjustment for most women. It is a time of role change, relationship change, family change. For each woman, each pregnancy is unique. Each one is a new transition, with its own set of concerns and expectations.

Each trimester has its expected feelings, although no woman follows any set emotional plan during a pregnancy. The first trimester is often marked by ambivalence about the pregnancy. A woman may feel regretful that she has become pregnant, depressed, or fearful. Remember, these are normal feelings, experienced by many women. They should not be cause for guilt or shame. Fatigue or physical discomfort, common in the first trimester, may make adjustment even more difficult. Women who have experienced previous miscarriages may spend all or part of the first trimester worrying.

Body image is a frequent issue for pregnant women. Although women usually don't gain more than a few pounds in the first trimester, they will not yet be "showing" and may be concerned about how these extra few pounds make them look. In the early second trimester, this feeling may be exacerbated as the weight gain increases but the pregnancy itself still is not apparent. Perhaps the parents-to-be have decided not to announce the pregnancy if they are going to have fetal assessment tests performed.

When *antepartal fetal testing* is advised, the woman and her partner may go through periods of extreme anxiety, especially as they await the results of tests. Again, this is normal. If any tests show a fetal problem, a woman may feel intensely guilty, despite reassurance that the problem is in no way her fault.

Many women report the second trimester as the easiest time in pregnancy, physically and emotionally. Results of any fetal testing become available and are usually reassuring. The physical discomforts of the first trimester are relieved and the fatigue and awkwardness of the last weeks of pregnancy haven't yet set in.

Quickening usually occurs in the mid to late second trimester, between 16 and 20 weeks of pregnancy. This is when the woman first feels the baby moving. It occurs later in a first pregnancy. Some women undergoing fetal assessment tests report quickening shortly after they receive the results of these tests, as if they fear acknowledging the fetus until they know it is safe to do so. Once quickening occurs, the pregnancy often takes on a new meaning and the woman may begin to see herself as a mother, especially in a first pregnancy. This often leads a woman to become rather introspective. Childbirth classes, although they often do not begin until the third trimester, are a good place to find support.

The third trimester has been described as a time of anxious waiting. Most women begin to make plans for the new baby. Toward the very end of pregnancy, a phenomenon called *nesting* often occurs—a woman becomes incredibly busy preparing the baby's room or even cleaning the whole house. The largeness of the pregnant body at the end of the last trimester may make a woman feel awkward and clumsy. This, too, is a normal and common feeling.

Throughout pregnancy, women report a great variety of pregnant dreams. One of our pregnant patients continually delivered bunny rabbits in her dreams. Dreams often reveal worries that the baby will not be normal. Fear of labor and birth may also be expressed in dreams. Discuss your dreams with your partner, your friends, your midwife or physician. This will help alleviate the fears.

A common late pregnancy feeling is grief or depression as a woman realizes that soon she will no longer be pregnant. Of course, for some women, the end of pregnancy is greeted with welcome relief. Nonetheless, the idea that the baby will soon have its own existence, outside of the womb, may trigger feelings of loss.

The important point to remember about the emotional ups and downs and changes of pregnancy—and there are usually many—is that they are normal, experienced by most pregnant women, and do not signal anything about your worth as a woman, your readiness to be a mother, or your ability to be a sexual and life partner.

Partners also experience a variety of emotional changes in pregnancy. A phenomenon called *couvade* (French: *couvade* = to brood upon) is often seen. This is when the pregnant woman's partner experiences some of the same changes she is undergoing, such as weight gain or nausea and vomiting.

Stress in Pregnancy

For many years, researchers have investigated the relationship of stress to the outcome of pregnancy. One of the problems with this research is the difficulty in defining stress. Most people today live stressful lives. Stress can be encountered in everyday hassles like public transportation or traffic, long lines, or bills to pay. Stress can be chronic, as in a situation of domestic violence. Stress can be acute, as in divorce or the death of a loved one. Stress can also lead to behaviors that can be harmful such as smoking and drinking.

Studies looking at the effects of such stress on pregnancy have shown inconsistent results, but in general, if stress does have an effect on such pregnancy outcomes as prematurity and low birth weight, it is extremely minimal. You can be reassured that your fetus will not be harmed if you are unusually stressed during pregnancy. The human reproductive process appears to be remarkably resilient in its ability to withstand the vagaries of the human emotional experience.

~∞~

CHAPTER TEN

Nutrition During Pregnancy

We don't know all the ways a fetus may be affected by what its mother eats. We do know, from studies of babies born during famine in World War II, that adequate nutrition, or at least an adequate number of daily calories, is important for the fetus to grow to an optimal size. In early pregnancy, severe nutritional deficiencies may have an adverse effect on development and even survival of the embryo. In late pregnancy, severe deficiencies may inhibit fetal growth. The fetus is somewhat protected, however, against less severe nutritional inadequacies in the mother's diet, so that infants whose prenatal nutrition has been suboptimal grow and develop without apparent detriment.

In the United States today, most pregnant women eat well enough so that most babies are not harmed by the eating habits of their mothers. Nor is the mother robbed of most nutrients. She does not suffer tooth or bone loss or most other deficiencies. Whether there are subtle effects of minor nutritional deficits on the developing fetus or on the pregnancy is not known.

Still, eating well is one way to provide the best environment for your developing child.

When we think of optimal nutrition in pregnancy, several questions come to mind:

1. How much weight should a pregnant woman gain? How much should she gain in each week of pregnancy?
2. What foods are most healthful to eat in pregnancy and how much of these should a pregnant woman eat?

3. Should a pregnant woman take nutritional supplements and,
    if so, what supplements should she take? At what doses?

Additional questions relate to the special needs of certain groups of
women: adolescent women, underweight and overweight women, women
at risk for low birth weight babies, and women on restricted diets, by
need or choice, including women with eating disorders.

This chapter will address these questions.

WEIGHT GAIN IN PREGNANCY

In the course of pregnancy you will build another human being—on
some occasions even more than one. To equip your body to do that, to
nurture and deliver the baby, and to feed it for months afterwards, your
body needs to add new tissue. The first new additions are the tissues of
the baby itself, the umbilical cord, the placenta, and the amniotic fluid.
Second is the growth of the maternal organs directly involved in pregnancy: the uterus, the breasts, and the solid and fluid parts of the circulating blood. Next is the increased fluid that accumulates within body
tissues. Finally, the addition of fat is a small part of the process.

Distribution of Pregnancy Weight Gain	
Baby	7–8.5 lbs.
Placenta	2–2.5 lbs.
Amniotic fluid	2 lbs.
Growth of the breasts	1–3 lbs.
Growth of the uterus	2–3 lbs.
Increase in tissue fluid	3–5 lbs.
Increase in maternal blood	4–5 lbs.
Increase in maternal "stores" (mostly fat)	4–6 lbs.
TOTAL	25–35 lbs.

Over the years, recommendations about weight gain in pregnancy
have followed a sweeping pendulum. Before 1970, women were limited
to gaining twenty pounds, or at most twenty-five pounds. Stepping on
the scale at prenatal visits was dreaded by many women whose natural appetite led to higher weight gains. Low weight gain was believed to
reduce the problems associated with the birth of large babies and help

prevent toxemia of pregnancy. *Toxemia,* discussed in Chapter 12, is a pregnancy illness marked by rapid weight gain and swelling, along with high blood pressure and protein in the urine. We now know that the increased weight gain is the consequence of toxemia, not its cause.

In the 1970s, research began to show that restricted, rather than excess, weight gain could lead to problems for the developing fetus. Low weight gain was found to be associated with lowered birth weight in newborns, a cause of newborn illness and death. Starting in the 1970s, women were told to gain approximately twenty-four pounds, with a range of twenty to twenty-five pounds. The pattern of weight gain also received attention at that time. Less than two pounds per month was considered inadequate and more than six pounds per month, excessive. These limitations were still difficult for many pregnant women.

A new approach to pregnancy weight gain was advocated in 1990, following the publication of an extensive report by the Institute of Medicine of the National Academy of Sciences. To determine optimal weight gain, this group studied a large number of births. They assessed the range of weight gain associated with what they defined as a *favorable pregnancy outcome*—birth between 39 to 41 weeks gestational age and birth weight of 6.6 to 8.8 pounds.

In this new approach, widely accepted today, recommended weight gain varies according to whether the woman is normal weight, underweight, overweight, or obese. These categories are based on a calculation of a woman's prepregnant weight for height. This calculation is also called the BMI or *body mass index.* Once a woman's BMI is calculated, it is compared to a cutoff score and the woman is assigned into one of the four weight categories. Within each weight group, the recommendations span a range of ten to fifteen pounds. With these guidelines, pregnant women should no longer go hungry or feel guilty for gaining weight.

The BMI is calculated by dividing weight (in kilograms) by height (in centimeters) squared. Your physician or midwife should have a table of BMIs so your BMI can be determined easily at your first pregnancy visit or preconceptional visit. Underweight women are those whose weight for height is <90 percent of the normal weight; overweight is 120 to 135 percent of the normal; obese is >135 percent of the normal weight. The adult female cutoff weights for the four categories are shown in the table.

WEIGHT CATEGORIES FOR HEIGHT IN WOMEN			
Height	Underweight	Overweight	Obese
4'10"	≤95 lbs.	≥128 lbs.	≥141 lbs.
4'11"	≤97 lbs.	≥130 lbs.	≥145 lbs.
5'0"	≤98 lbs.	≥136 lbs.	≥152 lbs.
5'1"	≤106 lbs.	≥141 lbs.	≥156 lbs.
5'2"	≤108 lbs.	≥145 lbs.	≥161 lbs.
5'3"	≤110 lbs.	≥147 lbs.	≥165 lbs.
5'4"	≤112 lbs.	≥152 lbs.	≥169 lbs.
5'5"	≤118 lbs.	≥157 lbs.	≥176 lbs.
5'6"	≤121 lbs.	≥163 lbs.	≥180 lbs.
5'7"	≤125 lbs.	≥167 lbs.	≥185 lbs.
5'8"	≤129 lbs.	≥173 lbs.	≥191 lbs.
5'9"	≤134 lbs.	≥178 lbs.	≥198 lbs.
5'10"	≤136 lbs.	≥183 lbs.	≥205 lbs.
5'11"	≤139 lbs.	≥187 lbs.	≥209 lbs.
6'0"	≤144 lbs.	≥195 lbs.	≥215 lbs.

Note: These weights were adapted from a table presenting the data in kilograms for weight and centimeters for height. The weights are not exact.

Range of Recommended Weight Gain in Pregnancy
by Weight Classification
Underweight   28–40 lbs.
Normal weight   25–35 lbs.
Overweight   18–30 lbs.
Obese   15–30 lbs.

These weight gains are meant to create the most likely environment for the best possible outcome for the infant. As African-American infants weigh less at any given gestational age, the Institute of Medicine recommends that the weight gain for African-American women be at the upper end of the range. This is also true for infants of very young women, those who have been menstruating for less than 2 years at the time of their pregnancy. Very short women (<5'2") should keep their weight gain to the lower end of the normal range; even a few pounds less is considered acceptable for short women. While the minimum weight gain for obese women is fifteen pounds, obese women may gain less than fifteen pounds without adverse effects on the newborn. Women should never lose weight during pregnancy, regardless of their prepregnant weight. The recommended total weight gain for women carrying twins is thirty-five to forty-five pounds.

For women whose weight falls within the normal range, the recommended pattern of gain is one pound per week during the second and third trimesters. Most women gain only a few pounds (two to five pounds) during the first trimester. Women who suffer from nausea and vomiting may gain even less during the first trimester without untoward effects on the pregnancy or fetus. In the second and third trimesters underweight women should try to gain slightly more than a pound per week and overweight women should gain about two-thirds of a pound per week. Of course, no one weekly reading is able to indicate poor or excessive weight gain. Some women show slightly more erratic patterns but over time gain appropriately.

A FOOD PLAN FOR PREGNANCY

Weight gain, of course, is only one component of good nutrition in pregnancy. What you eat is important too.

To gain the recommended amount of weight in pregnancy usually requires eating two hundred to three hundred extra calories a day in the second and third trimesters. According to the National Research Council, the average woman requires twenty-two hundred calories a day. This means that the average pregnant woman needs twenty-five hundred calories daily. This will vary, of course, according to your height and activity. The taller you are and the more active you are, the more calories you will need. For example, a nonpregnant woman who is 5'2" tall (with 2" heels), has a small frame, and is sedentary may only require about sixteen hundred calories a day, while an active, large-framed woman who is 5'6" tall may require as many as twenty-five hundred calories daily.

The common phrase "eating for two" is rather misleading. Adding three hundred calories to your diet does not mean adding a lot of extra food. The following list offers four ways to add approximately three hundred calories to your diet:

- 3½ to 4 glasses of skim milk (eight-ounce glasses)
- 2½ to 3 glasses of skim milk and 1 medium apple
- 2 glasses of skim milk and 3 ounces of chicken (approximately 1 breast)
- 2 glasses of skim milk, 1 apple, and 1 egg

In addition to extra calories, pregnant women should eat extra protein and increase their intake of certain vitamins and minerals. Protein is especially important to promote the growth of tissue in the body and support the increased volume of circulating blood. Some researchers have suggested that protein deficiency is responsible for the development of *preeclampsia* or toxemia of pregnancy (see Chapter 12), but these claims have not been supported. Protein supplementation in the form of protein drinks or protein powders are not recommended, except perhaps among women who are severely protein deficient, as occurs in conditions of famine or near starvation.

About 10 to 15 grams of extra protein a day are needed in pregnancy, for a total of 60 grams of protein. Three ounces of most meat, fish, or poultry (three ounces is about an average serving) supply about 20 grams of protein. Two cups of milk provide 16 grams of protein. If you drink four cups of milk a day (eight ounces each), and eat two average servings of meat or fish or legumes (three to four ounces at each serving or, say, a chicken breast or a cup and a half of beans with rice), you will have sufficient protein.

The pregnant woman needs at least 1,200 milligrams of calcium a day. Calcium is needed for formation and growth of the bones and teeth. Calcium is needed most in the third trimester. A quart—or four eight-ounce glasses—of milk provides the daily required amount of calcium. One and a half ounces of hard cheese, 1½ cups of soft cheese, or 1 cup of plain yogurt is equal to about an eight-ounce glass of milk in calcium content.

Lactose Intolerance

Many adults lack the digestive enzyme (*lactase*) that converts *lactose*—the sugar in cow's milk—to simpler sugars, which are easier to digest. This condition is called *lactose intolerance*. When people with lactose intolerance drink milk, they get stomach upsets and diarrhea. Frequently, people with a lactose deficiency can tolerate dairy products such as yogurt, cottage cheese, and aged hard cheeses. They can get sufficient calcium from these milk substitutes.

Several products are available to help lactose intolerant people digest milk. Lactaid is a company that produces milk pretreated with the lactase enzyme. The company also markets enzyme capsules that can be swallowed or chewed before drinking milk and enzyme drops to be added to milk. Other choices for lactose intolerant women include taking calcium supplements (see page 274) or drinking calcium-fortified soy milk or calcium-fortified orange juice.

Legumes, nuts, dried fruit, and some green vegetables have calcium. Among the green vegetables, the calcium in spinach, chard, and beet greens is not available to the body because these vegetables also contain oxalic acid, which binds the calcium.

Most people prefer to think in terms of food groups rather than grams of nutrients. Following the daily plan shown in the table below will ensure that you have adequate calories, protein, calcium, and other vitamins and minerals.

EATING PLAN FOR PREGNANCY			
Food Group	Recommended Daily Intake: # of Servings	Serving Size Example	Comments
Milk, cheese	4 servings milk or milk products	8 ounce glass milk 1½ ounce hard cheese 1½ cups soft cheese 1 cup plain yogurt	Skim milk or fat free products recommended.
Eggs, meat, poultry, fish, legumes (beans), nuts, seeds	4 servings	1 egg or 3–4 ounces of meat, poultry, fish 1½ cups of legumes	Low fat choices recommended, e.g., white meat poultry. 1–2 eggs per day can be eaten in pregnancy. Liver 1–2 times per week in second and third trimesters for iron. Limit shark and swordfish to no more than 1 serving per month (see Chapter 5). Avoid freshwater fish from contaminated waters.
Grains, breads, cereals	4 or more servings	1 slice (approximately 1 ounce) bread	Choose whole grains (cereals, for example, must say

Food Group	Recommended Daily Intake: # of Servings	Serving Size Example	Comments
		¾–1 cup cereal ½ cup noodles or rice	"whole wheat"; "bran"). Choose dark breads, brown rice.
Green and yellow vegetables	1–2 servings	1 cup cooked vegetables 1 carrot 1 ear corn	Choose fresh or frozen vegetables, avoid canned. Do not overcook.
Citrus fruits and other vitamin-C rich fruits and vegetables (e.g., tomatoes)	2 servings	1 medium orange ½ grapefruit 1 medium tomato	
Potatoes and other vegetables and fruit	1 or more servings	1 small potato 1 cup vegetables	Wash well with brush. Eat skins if possible for increased nutrients and fiber.
Fats—margarine, butter, oils	1–2 servings	1 tablespoon	
Iodized salt	Use to taste		Do not avoid salt in pregnancy (as recommended in past years).
Sweets—candy, cake, cookies, pastry, soft drinks	Sparingly		Do not substitute for healthful foods.

If you have questions about the adequacy of your diet, write down everything you eat over a one-to-three-day period, and the amount in each serving, and then compare your list with general recommendations such as those above, or the much more detailed recommendations in books specifically on nutrition in pregnancy.

Here is an example of how one pregnant woman filled out a chart to help her see how well she was eating.

24-HOUR FOOD DIARY		
Meal	Food Eaten	Food Group/ Number of Servings
Breakfast	I bowl bran cereal ½ cup milk I cup orange juice I cup coffee with ¼ cup milk	Milk—¾ Breads/cereals—I Citrus fruit—I
Snack(s)	I apple	Fruit—I
Lunch	I sandwich—2 slices whole wheat bread with I small can tuna fish in water mayonnaise (small amount) celery and onion I glass milk I orange	Milk—I Fish—I Breads—2 Vegetable—I Citrus fruit—I Fat—I
Snack(s)	2 pieces whole wheat bread with 2 slices cheddar cheese I glass milk	Milk—I Cheese—I + Breads—2
Dinner	I turkey burger (broiled) I burger roll broccoli mashed potatoes salad with dressing (lettuce, tomatoes, cucumber, green peppers) I glass milk I cookie	Milk—I Meat—I Breads—2 Vitamin C vegetable (tomato)—I Green vegetable—2 Potato—I Sweets—I
Snack(s)	I (8-ounce) glass milk I chicken leg and thigh (baked)	Milk—I Meat—I
Total Number of Servings per Food Group		Milk—5+, okay Meat/fish/poultry/eggs/ nuts—3, okay but could be I more serving Breads/cereals/grains—6, okay, perhaps high Citrus (vitamin C) fruit or vegetable—3, okay Green or yellow vegetable—2, okay

Meal	Food Eaten	Food Group/ Number of Servings
		Potato or other fruit or vegetable—2, okay Fats—2 or possible 2+, okay, perhaps high Sweets—1

This one-day food diary reflects good eating. This woman drank only one cup of coffee, with milk. She had few sweets, which supply empty calories and sometimes lots of fat. She lacked one serving of meat, but with the extra serving of milk, she has had far more than 60 grams of protein. She could have added one egg to her breakfast for protein and iron. Her diet was a bit heavy in the breads/cereals/grains family, but most were whole grains. It might be heavy on fats, depending on what type and how much salad dressing was used, and how the mashed potatoes were cooked. The food diary could have indicated how the food was prepared and whether butter or fats were used in cooking. The type of milk used was not specified. Skim (nonfat) or 1 percent milk is preferable to whole milk or 2 percent milk.

If this daily food pattern is representative of this woman's regular eating, she is doing well, although depending on her height, activity level, and prepregnant weight, she might gain a bit too much. Based on her weight at her prenatal visits, she might want to adjust her intake from the breads/cereals/grains group and the fat group, and make sure that her milk is skim or low fat. If she is very tall or very active, however, she might not gain enough on this diet and might have to add to the breads/cereals/grains group, preferably with whole grains.

When you write your food diary, choose days that represent your usual eating habits. Don't chart a day you go to your friend's wedding, for instance, or have twenty people at your house for dinner. Add up and then analyze your food group intake. Use your weight gain and food diary to make adjustments as necessary.

Your physician or midwife can help you assess your eating patterns. Some prenatal practices or clinics routinely refer all pregnant women for at least one visit with a dietitian or nutritionist who can be of even greater assistance.

Meals Versus Grazing

Pregnant women often find large meals difficult to eat, especially in later pregnancy when the abdominal organs are somewhat scrunched by the large uterus. In early pregnancy, nausea and vomiting may be exacerbated by going long periods without food and then eating a large meal. Many pregnant women find it more comfortable to "graze." *Grazing* means eating lightly throughout the day. This is perfectly fine, as long as a balanced diet is maintained and sufficient caloric intake is achieved, especially in the second and third trimesters.

A Word About Culture

Food is entwined with our cultural and personal identities. As eating is one of our earliest experiences, food reminds us of our childhood and bespeaks maternal love. Immigrants often cite familiar foods as one of the things they most miss in a new country. In fact, groceries selling ethnic food products usually spring up in immigrant communities.

The suggestions in this chapter are not meant to alter the eating habits of any cultural group. Almost always, healthful choices can be made using familiar types of food.

A Note on Salt

One of the symptoms associated with toxemia or preeclampsia of pregnancy is retained fluid. Because salt (*sodium*) holds water in the body, the belief used to be that pregnant women should limit or even avoid salt to prevent toxemia. Many women who do not have toxemia also have an increase in fluid retention in pregnancy with swelling, or *edema*, of the legs and ankles. In actuality, the clearance of salt by the kidneys is increased substantially in pregnancy and pregnant women naturally lose more sodium than nonpregnant women. Some edema is quite normal and restricting salt will not eliminate it. Pregnant women should not restrict salt. Babies born to women who restrict salt may have low blood sodium at birth, a condition called *hyponatremia*.

Using salt to taste provides an adequate and not excessive intake of this mineral. Choose iodized salt, as the fetus needs the iodine to develop. Iodine excess is nearly impossible to achieve in any normal diet.

FOOD PROGRAMS

The federal government has two food programs to help pregnant women in need. The Special Supplemental Food Program for Women, Infants, and Children (WIC) provides vouchers for specific foods for women in economically needy communities who are at nutritional risk. Factors for nutritional risk include:

- Anemia
- Underweight or overweight
- Multiple pregnancy
- Substance abuse
- Closely spaced pregnancies (less than 2 years apart)
- Adolescence
- Poor fetal growth
- Poor pregnancy weight gain
- Prior premature or low birth weight baby
- Diabetes
- Other conditions determined by the physician or midwife

The WIC program also provides nutritional counseling.

The Supplemental Commodities Distribution Program distributes surplus foods such as meat, poultry, fruits, vegetables, eggs, beans, peas, dairy products, and grains to women with low incomes.

If you think you qualify for these programs, request a referral from your physician or midwife.

VEGETARIAN DIETS

There are several types of vegetarian diets. A *lacto-ova* vegetarian consumes milk, milk products, and eggs. *Vegans* do not eat any animal products, including dairy and eggs. They rely on legumes (beans), nuts, seeds, grains, and vegetables for protein.

Protein is composed of amino acids. A *complete protein* is one that provides the body with all the essential amino acids—those we need to get from food sources. Meat, fish, eggs, poultry, and dairy provide complete proteins. Vegetable and grain sources of protein can provide adequate nutrition, but many nutritionists recommend specific combinations of them to be sure that you get all the essential amino acids.

Legumes—mainly dried beans, peas, and lentils—are deficient in trypto-phan and methionine. The nuts and seeds such as sunflower seeds, peanuts, and sesame seeds lack lysine and isoleucine.

Complete proteins can be ensured through the following combinations:

Rice and legumes
Corn and legumes
Wheat and legumes
Wheat and peanuts and milk
Wheat and sesame and soybeans
Rice and brewer's yeast
Beans and corn
Soybeans and rice and wheat
Soybeans and peanuts and sesame
Soybeans and peanuts and wheat and rice
Peanuts and sesame and soybeans
Sesame and beans
Sesame and soybeans and wheat
Sesame seeds or Brazil nuts or mushrooms and: green beans, lima beans, brussels sprouts, cauliflower, or broccoli
Greens and millet or rice

The additional protein requirement of pregnancy can be satisfied with the following food choices in a vegan diet, while increasing the caloric intake by 300 calories:

2 cups soy milk (plain)
9 ounces tofu
3 ounces tempeh
1 cup cooked beans

Since vegans do not eat dairy, they need to get calcium from other sources. These might include calcium-fortified soy milk or orange juice with calcium. Greens, such as broccoli and kale, have calcium, but it is hard to get enough from these sources. Tofu can be made with calcium sulfate or carbonate. Blackstrap molasses, tahini, and figs all have calcium. Depending on the amount of dietary calcium, a supplement may be advised. The recommended dosage is 1,200 mg (in divided doses of 300 or 600 each) and 10 micrograms (400 IUs—*International Units*) of vitamin D daily.

Because vitamin B_{12} is found only in animal sources of foods, a 4 microgram supplement of vitamin B_{12} is advised for people on vegan diets. If soy milk is used, the need for supplementation depends on whether or not the milk is fortified with these nutrients. Other sources of vitamin B_{12} are fortified cereals and yeast powder. Red Star Vegetarian Support Formula has been tested for active B_{12}. One teaspoon of yeast powder should provide the day's requirement of this vitamin for women on a vegan diet.

Some pregnant women are accustomed to following special weight loss diets such as high protein, low carbohydrate diets. Others follow restrictive diets such as the macrobiotic diet. These are too limited for pregnancy and should be modified to include foods from all the groups listed in the table on pages 262–263.

FOOD PREPARATION: PROCESSING, ADDITIVES, COOKING

Processing

In general, fresh foods are preferable to processed foods. Many vitamins are destroyed in some of the processes used to package foods. Canned foods are high in sodium. While sodium restriction is not advised in pregnancy, the amount in canned foods is too high for anyone's health.

As pregnant women today work outside the home and lead busy lives, we know that many rely at least occasionally on packaged or processed food to feed themselves and their families. As a general rule, frozen foods retain the most nutrients and use the fewest chemicals.

Additives

Additives are commonly used today in packaged foods. Some are added to prevent bacteria or fungi from spoiling the food and harming people who eat it. Some preservatives are actually food nutrients and are considered safe. Examples of these are calcium propionate, citric acid, ferrous gluconate (iron), ascorbic acid (vitamin C), and alpha tocopherol (vitamin E). Some preservatives such as BHT (butylated hydroxytoluene) or sodium nitrate may be cancer-causing and are best avoided in pregnancy (or at any time).

Other additives include food dyes and colorings and sweeteners. These are also best avoided or limited. The sweetener cyclamate has been banned in the United States. Saccharin is still used as a sweetener. Saccharin may be associated with bladder cancer, especially when exposure occurs in utero or when the mother is exposed to high doses prior to pregnancy. This sweetener is best avoided, or used sparingly, by pregnant women or women planning a pregnancy.

Aspartame is the most widely used artificial sweetener today. Aspartame increases the circulating levels of phenylalanine in the blood, so concerns have been raised about adverse effects on the fetus. Studies to date have shown that in usual doses, the levels of phenylalanine after aspartame ingestion are not high enough to cause fetal damage. Of course, women with phenylketonuria should avoid this substance. No other birth defects have been associated with aspartame use, but as a general guideline, use of any artificial chemical in pregnancy should be sparing.

Some chemical contaminants in food, such as mercury and lead, are discussed in Chapter 5. Do not eat more than one serving of swordfish or shark per month. Pottery made outside of the United States and crystal may contain lead. Do not use these for food storage. As some pesticides are dangerous, wash all fruits and vegetables vigorously. Use a brush and soap and rinse well. Although expensive, and inaccessible in some communities, organically grown fruits and vegetables are best.

Cooking

A quick note on cooking: heat destroys many vitamins. Boiling vegetables depletes their nutritional value. Steam vegetables whenever possible or eat them raw.

SUPPLEMENTS

Nutritional supplements have become a fixed feature of prenatal care in the United States. In its 1990 report, the Institute of Medicine concluded that, except for iron, all nutritional needs of most pregnant women can be met through diet. Since that report, scientists have discovered the importance of folic acid in preventing neural tube defects and a folic acid supplement is now advised.

Women in nutritional risk groups may benefit from supplementation. These include women with poor diets or women suffering from substance abuse.

Many midwives and physicians routinely recommend a prenatal supplement for all pregnant women. If you either take an over-the-counter prenatal vitamin or are prescribed a prenatal vitamin, read the label before you take any of the individual supplements discussed in the following sections to make sure you don't get too much of a particular supplement. If you are unsure, discuss supplementation with your physician or midwife.

Folic Acid

The discovery of the relationship between deficiencies in folic acid, a B vitamin, and neural tube defects (NTDs) was one of the most important breakthroughs ever in preventive health care. Folic acid is particularly important in the earliest weeks of pregnancy, when the neural tube is developing (see Chapter 5). All women planning pregnancy and, in fact, all women in the childbearing years should take 0.4 mg (4 micrograms) of folic acid daily. Women who have had a child with a neural tube defect should take 4 mg of folic acid, a prescription strength dosage. This supplementation should be begun in the pregnancy planning stages and continued for at least the first 3 months of a pregnancy. Researchers estimate that this supplement can prevent up to 50 percent of NTDs.

Foods rich in folic acid include:

Artichokes
Asparagus
Avocados
Bran and granola cereals
Broccoli
Brussels sprouts
Chili
Fortified cereals and breads
Liver
Okra
Orange juice
Pinto, navy, and other dried beans
Spinach

Overcooking will destroy the heat sensitive folic acid.

Recently, foods such as breads and cereals have been fortified with folic acid, although there was vigorous debate before this occurred. The main argument against fortification was that high folic acid intake may mask a vitamin B12 deficiency. Vitamin B12 deficiency, also called *pernicious anemia*, can cause neurological problems. Pernicious anemia is rare in people under the age of 50, however, so this is not an issue with folic acid supplementation or fortification in the childbearing age group.

Prenatal vitamins usually contain between 0.4 mg and 1 mg of folic acid. If you take a prenatal multivitamin read the label so you do not unnecessarily take an extra folic acid tablet.

Iron

Pregnant women need extra iron to make the hemoglobin in the fetus and in the extra maternal blood required for pregnancy. The Institute of Medicine recommended a daily supplement providing 30 mg of iron. This recommendation was based on the following evidence:

1. Pregnant women who take iron supplements have higher hemoglobin levels.
2. Hemoglobin is necessary for body function.
3. Iron at low doses poses no dangers to the mother or fetus.

Iron is so needed by the baby that it is the only nutrient for which the fetus will act as a parasite, taking what it needs from the mother. Resulting anemia in the mother will cause fatigue and increased susceptibility to other illness. It puts a strain on her heart and puts her in danger should she bleed too much at delivery.

Although it is possible to get sufficient iron for pregnancy through diet, the average woman's diet does not supply adequate iron. Before supplements are taken, however, the hemoglobin level in the mother's blood can be measured and the need for supplementation determined individually. In fact, a hemoglobin test is a routine part of the first prenatal visit or preconception visit. If a woman does not take supplements, the hemoglobin level should be repeated early in the third trimester (about 26 to 28 weeks) to see if her need has changed. If her hemoglobin at either time is low enough to be considered anemic, further testing can be done to determine the precise cause of the anemia. Iron deficiency is only one possible reason for anemia.

Foods high in iron include:

Blackstrap molasses
Dried legumes (beans)
Liver
Oysters
Prunes
Shellfish
Some meats, especially beef and pork

Foods somewhat high in iron include:

Brown or fortified white rice
Eggs
Fish, chicken, lamb
Oatmeal
Shredded wheat
Vegetables: greens, potatoes, broccoli, acorn squash (for greens, the greener the vegetable, the more iron it supplies)
Wheat germ
Whole wheat or fortified white bread

The iron in meat (*heme* iron) is absorbed more readily than the iron in vegetables or grains (*nonheme* iron). A cup of cooked green beans, for example, contains the same amount of iron as a cup of beef stew, but the person eating the beef stew will get more iron. While vegetarian diets can be more than adequate in iron, especially with a high intake of legumes, vegetarians may have to be somewhat more careful about making sure they eat enough iron-rich foods.

The absorption of iron from the diet is enhanced by vitamin C. Take your iron with orange juice, grapefruit juice, or tomato juice.

Certain foods or medications, including antacids and dairy, interfere with iron absorption. Iron should not be taken with milk. This may be somewhat of a challenge to organize as pregnant women drink milk frequently.

The amount of iron contained in vitamin tablets generally is not sufficient to meet the needs of late pregnancy. Women should take separate tablets of iron.

Iron tablets come in several forms—ferrous sulfate, ferrous gluconate, and ferrous fumarate—and under various trade names. The amount of total iron in a supplement is not the amount of elemental iron in the supplement. Elemental iron is the available or absorbable part of the tablet. To allow you to absorb 30 mg of iron, the tablet strength should be 150 mg of ferrous sulfate, 300 mg of ferrous gluconate, or 100 mg of ferrous fumarate. As iron can suppress zinc levels, do not take more than this dosage, unless you are anemic and your physician or midwife advises extra iron.

If you develop digestive distress after taking iron on an empty stomach, you can take it with meals. In this case, drink milk between meals. Some women find liquid iron preparations easier on the stomach.

Excessive iron intake tends to make the stools dry and firm, causing constipation. An occasional woman responds to iron with diarrhea. In either circumstance, you can try changing the type of iron you take from a tablet to liquid or from one of the three available compounds to another (e.g., ferrous fumarate to ferrous sulfate). If this doesn't help, the supplement strength may have to be reduced. You may have to experiment a bit to see which type and how much iron you can take comfortably. If you reduce your supplement, be sure to compensate with an increase of iron-rich foods on a daily basis.

An iron overdose can be dangerous. Keep your iron tablets where small children cannot get them. The second most common form of poisoning seen in pediatric emergency rooms comes from children eating their mothers' iron tablets.

Calcium

Calcium is needed for the development of the baby's bones and teeth. Recent studies point to a likely link between calcium deficiency and the development of *maternal hypertensive disorders* (high blood pressure) in pregnancy. Calcium may also play a role in preterm birth. Neither of these associations has been proven. Calcium supplementation is not a routine requirement. Sufficient calcium can be achieved through diet.

Four eight-ounce glasses of milk a day, or its equivalent in cheese or yogurt, supply enough calcium for the pregnant woman's needs. (Ice cream is high in calcium, but the caloric and fat load is high too!) If you don't drink milk or eat dairy products, you can take a calcium supplement—1,200 mg a day in divided doses.

Calcium citrate is absorbed whether or not you take the supplement with food while *calcium carbonate* needs to be taken with food. The disadvantage of taking a calcium supplement over getting enough calcium from dietary sources is that dairy products also supply a lot of protein, at low cost. If you don't drink milk or eat other dairy, you need 32 grams more protein than the woman who drinks a quart of milk a day. This is the equivalent in protein of 4 eggs, about 4–5 ounces of meat, 1 cup of most nuts, or 1½ cups of legumes. Calcium supplementation might cause constipation in some women. Remedies for constipation are discussed on page 285.

Zinc

Zinc deficiency has been associated with birth defects in animals, and possibly in humans. Zinc deficiency also has been associated with low birth weight. Studies in which pregnant women were provided with zinc supplements have shown inconsistent benefits, however. To date, zinc supplements are not advised. Foods highest in zinc include seafood, meats, eggs, corn, beets, and peas. Foods with moderate zinc content include carrots and whole wheat bread. Zinc-rich foods should be included in the diet of every pregnant woman. Zinc supplementation may be recommended when high doses of iron are prescribed as the extra iron decreases zinc absorption. The recommended amount during pregnancy is 15 mg.

Magnesium

Low magnesium levels have been associated with leg cramps, a common complaint in late pregnancy. For women who have leg cramps, increased magnesium may be helpful. Nuts, soybeans, wheat germ, wheat bran, and green vegetables are good sources of magnesium. You could also try a magnesium supplement of 100–250 mg daily. Be careful with magnesium supplementation if you are anemic as it may reduce the absorption of iron. Research is currently under way to determine whether there is a role of magnesium, or of the balance among magnesium, calcium, and phosphorus, in preeclampsia or preterm labor and whether or not these disorders can be prevented nutritionally.

Vitamin B6 (Pyridoxine)

Supplementation with vitamin B6 is not needed in pregnancy, but may have a role in the relief of nausea and vomiting. Supplements of 25 mg taken every 8 hours were found to benefit women with severe nausea and vomiting in at least one study. They did not help women with milder forms of nausea and vomiting (see Chapter 11).

Possibly Dangerous Supplements

Excessive Vitamin Intake

The recommended dose of 60 mg of vitamin C in pregnancy is much lower than many people take today. Many people commonly take hundreds of milligrams of vitamin C to ward off colds and other infections. Excessive doses of vitamin C in the fetus, however, may lead to symptoms of vitamin C deficiency in the newborn. Eating at least two servings a day of a vitamin C–rich food is sufficient during pregnancy. Megadoses should be avoided.

Vitamin D in large doses also may be harmful to the infant. Doses that have been identified as dangerous, however, are above what anybody gets with just about any amount of sunlight and milk. If a woman does not drink milk, a supplement of 400 IUs of vitamin D a day is safe. This is especially important in winter months or climates where you receive little sunlight. Half this dosage might be taken by women whose intake of fortified milk is low.

Vitamin A has the greatest potential among the vitamins to cause problems in the fetus. Both vitamin A deficiency and vitamin A excess can be dangerous to the fetus. The recommended dose of vitamin A in pregnancy does not differ from the recommendation for nonpregnant women. Most women in the U.S. have adequate stores of vitamin A (fat-soluble vitamins, including A, D, and E, are stored in the body, unlike vitamins B and C, which are water soluble and excreted in the urine).

As vitamin A deficiency is rare in this country, overdose is a greater concern. There are consistent reports of malformation in infants born to women who take more than 25,000 IUs of vitamin A daily. Reports of fetal malformation among women who take more than 10,000 IUs have also appeared. The Teratology Society recommends that women take no more than 8,000 IUs of vitamin A daily during pregnancy and the American College of Obstetricians and Gynecologists recommends limiting intake to 5,000 IUs. If you take a multivitamin or prenatal vitamin, you *must* read the label to see how much vitamin A you are getting. Stop the tablet immediately if the dose is greater than 8,000 IUs. Beta-carotene, the form of vitamin A available from plant sources, is safe.

The anti-acne medication *isotretinoin* (Accutane) is a vitamin A product and is teratogenic in pregnancy. The teratogenesis of drugs is discussed in Chapter 5.

Phosphorus

Phosphorus is widely available in the American diet. Calcium and phosphorus need to be in balance in the blood or muscular irritability, such as leg cramps, may occur. In pregnancy, because of the stress on the body's calcium reserves and the wide availability of phosphorus in processed and snack foods and many soft drinks, this balance may be disturbed. Pregnant women should limit their intake of processed and snack foods and soda in pregnancy, especially if they get leg cramps.

Caffeine

Caffeine is discussed in detail in Chapter 5. In general, the prudent approach is to limit caffeine during the pregnancy planning stage and during pregnancy. Drink no more than two cups of percolated coffee per day. This is especially important if you have risks for a low birth weight baby. (Risks include a previous premature or low birth weight baby, smoking, or having diabetes or high blood pressure.)

Tea has about two-fifths the amount of caffeine as coffee and cola beverages. You can make your coffee or tea weaker and add increasing amounts of milk. Mild herbal teas can be substituted, such as peppermint or lemon tea. (Check with your physician or midwife to ascertain that a specific tea isn't dangerous in pregnancy. Lobelia, sassafras, coltsfoot, comfrey, pennyroyal, ginseng, licorice, hops, sage, golden seal root, and blue and black cohosh are among those that might have adverse side effects in pregnancy.) Decaffeinated beverages can be substituted as well, but we do not know for sure that these don't contain other substances that might adversely affect the baby. Of course, water and unsweetened juice are nature's best drinks. Caffeine is contained in some combination medications that are not recommended in pregnancy—check the labels of any nonprescription medication.

Alcohol

Alcohol is discussed in Chapter 5. At present, we simply do not know what constitutes a safe intake in pregnancy. Abstinence is the best policy, although wine or other alcohol can be used in cooking as its alcohol content burns out.

Raw Meat and Fish

Raw meat can cause *toxoplasmosis*, a mild disease in adults that may have severe consequences on the fetus, discussed in Chapters 5 and 16. Even rare meat should be avoided in pregnancy, unless you have had a blood test that shows you are immune to toxoplasmosis. Wash hands well after preparing meat and clean all surfaces such as counter tops and cutting boards that the meat has touched.

Raw fish or sushi may carry bacteria or parasites. While it is rare for a person to get sick from eating sushi, the safest route is to avoid eating raw fish in pregnancy.

SPECIAL PROBLEMS

Pica

Pica is the name for unusual food cravings (Latin: *pica* = magpie, a bird known for its unusual appetites). The condition is the basis for jokes about the yearning for odd combinations of foods, such as pickles and ice cream. In fact, women with pica often eat substances like clay, dirt, laundry starch, baking powder, baking soda, ashes, or ice.

Nobody quite knows the reason for pica. Some researchers speculate that it is caused by nutritional deficiencies, including iron. Some women say it helps with nausea and vomiting. Other women find it relieves nervous tension. In some cultures, pica is passed on from mother to child, although pica is not limited to any particular geographic areas or cultural groups. What is clear about pica is that it can lead to nutritional deficiencies, especially iron-deficiency anemia.

A few simple suggestions may help you overcome your pica habit. Think of things you might do when you get the urge—go for a walk, go to the movies, call a good friend. You can try chewing sugarless gum. These are techniques people use in conquering any harmful habit.

Pica is a health problem, not a cause for embarrassment. If you have pica, even pica for ice, which may not seem at all unusual, tell your physician or midwife, who can assist in making sure that your nutrition remains adequate.

Eating Disorders

A variety of factors, including society's emphasis on thinness, has resulted in an alarming number of people with the eating disorders anorexia and bulimia. These disorders mostly affect young women in the childbearing years. Anorexia is seen in as many as 1 percent of female high school or college students. Bulimia affects from 3 to 19 percent of young women.

Few young women with anorexia become pregnant because the condition interferes with the menstrual cycle and reproductive ability. Bulimia is usually less severe. If you suffer from either of these eating disorders, you should work with your physician or midwife and a team of specialists, including a psychologist and clinical nutritionist, to ensure that you gain enough weight in pregnancy and that you and your fetus get adequate nutrients. Remember, you should never lose weight in pregnancy. Remaining the same weight is equivalent to losing weight. Pregnancy is a good time to work against these illnesses as the health of your baby is at stake as well as your own.

EATING IN SPECIAL SITUATIONS

Diabetes

Women who enter pregnancy with diabetes or develop gestational diabetes need to follow special food plans. These are based on guidelines provided by the American Diabetic Association (ADA). The number of calories and how they are allotted by food group is determined by a dietitian or specialist in the care of pregnant women with diabetes. The specifics of the plan are worked out according to your weight, level of activity, and weeks of pregnancy. Diabetic diets follow a food group plan so they are not difficult to implement. In general, carbohydrate "loads" or large portions of carbohydrate at one time are to be avoided, as are simple sugars, or sweets.

Once you receive your individualized food plan, you will be taught how to test your blood sugar so adjustments can be made as necessary. Some pregnant women will also need insulin, even if they never took it before. More discussion of diabetes in pregnancy is included in Chapter 12.

Phenylketonuria (PKU)

Phenylketonuria (PKU) is a rather rare disorder of metabolism in which the body cannot utilize the amino acid phenylalanine. In the past, this disease had serious consequences, including interference with brain development. Since 1968, all newborns have been screened for the disease. Those affected are placed on phenylalanine-free diets. Today, women with PKU are healthy and becoming pregnant, but they often have elevated levels of phenylalanine in their blood. These levels are enough to cause serious damage to the fetus, including *microcephaly* (small head), heart problems, and mental retardation.

Any woman who knows she has been diagnosed with phenylketonuria must receive careful assessment and dietary counseling, optimally beginning in the preconception period. She needs referral to a special center as her diet will need to be restricted greatly and she will need nutritional supplementation.

Any woman who bears a child with microcephaly for whom a cause cannot be ascertained should have a test for PKU.

RESOURCES

Many fine books on diet in pregnancy have been published. A few are listed in the Appendix.

CHAPTER ELEVEN

Common Discomforts of Pregnancy

Pregnancy is a healthy state. Yet, pregnant women are more prone to physical discomforts than nonpregnant women. Some of these are caused by pregnancy, others exaggerated by it.

NAUSEA AND VOMITING

One of the most common discomforts in pregnancy is nausea, with or without vomiting. Nausea and vomiting are usually mild and self-limited to 6 or 8 weeks. The symptoms can appear anytime from about 5 to 8 weeks of pregnancy. They usually subside after about 13 to 15 weeks of pregnancy. Nevertheless, they can be quite disconcerting and interfere with usual activities. As many as half of all pregnant women experience nausea and vomiting.

Nobody knows exactly what causes nausea and vomiting in pregnancy. Theories suggest that they are due to increased hormone levels, low blood sugar, slowed digestion, an enlarging uterus, and emotions. On the plus side, a few studies have found that nausea and vomiting are related to a good pregnancy outcome, although this, too, is only a theory.

Because nausea and vomiting in pregnancy often occur in the early hours of the day, the condition has been called *morning sickness*. In fact, nausea and vomiting are by no means limited to the morning. On occasion, the vomiting becomes severe or persists beyond the first trimester. This is called *hyperemesis gravidarum* (Greek: *yper* = above; *emesis* = vomiting; Latin: *gravida* = pregnant). Hyperemesis is discussed as a complication of pregnancy in Chapter 12. For women whose nausea and vomiting are annoying rather than pathologic, a number of home remedies can be effective to varying degrees for varying women.

Nutritional Remedies

A number of nutritional remedies work for some women with nausea and vomiting. These measures are safe and certainly worth a try, especially if you are very bothered by the symptoms.

Pregnant women often vomit when they eat a big meal following several hours of not eating. If this seems to be the pattern for you, avoid large meals and, even more important, don't let your stomach become empty. You can *graze*—eat small amounts throughout the day. Or you can eat regular meals, but snack frequently between meals. Dry carbohydrates sometimes provide relief. Pregnant women often carry a small box of crackers with them and eat a few every 15 minutes or so.

If you really have "morning" sickness, place several dry, crisp crackers in a tin box on your bedside table before going to bed. You can also put a can of ginger ale or a container of juice and a straw with the crackers. Papaya juice has been reported to be especially good for nausea and vomiting. When you wake, eat the crackers and sip the soda or juice, without raising your head from the pillow. Continue lying on your back for 15 to 20 minutes. Get up and eat a regular breakfast.

Some women find eating a hard candy or drinking fruit juice before going to bed at night and before getting up in the morning works better than crackers. Sour-flavored candy such as lemon may relieve nausea better than sweet-flavored candy.

If brushing your teeth in the morning induces or exaggerates your queasiness, postpone that ritual until later in the day when your stomach feels settled; in the interim simply rinse your mouth.

Pregnant women often find that their stomach stays calmer if they avoid eating fats and fried foods. Sometimes smells alone cause queasiness. If this is the case, of course limit foods with strong smells. You may be able to eat them, but not able to cook them. Let someone else do the cooking.

If you do vomit, make sure you have sufficient fluids throughout the day. Over a short period, fluids are more important to health than solids. Very often iced liquids are tolerated best. Many women in early pregnancy find plain water nauseating, but if a little lemon or orange juice is added it becomes drinkable. Almost all women, no matter how nauseated, can tolerate teaspoons of crushed ice flavored by fruit juice, which is a splendid source of fluid. The same may be said for sherbet or ices, which make an excellent midafternoon snack. While not really healthful, ginger ale and nondiet soft drinks are high in carbohydrates and can supply energy for you during the weeks you are bothered by nausea and vomiting. Don't get into the habit of drinking these for the whole pregnancy, of course.

Other Remedies

In a review of scientific studies of various alternative remedies for nausea and vomiting, three remedies were shown to be effective in controlled trials. These are vitamin B6, ginger root, and acupressure.

Vitamin B6 can be taken in a dose of 25 mg three times a day. Higher doses should not be taken, as the cutoff for a safe dose in pregnancy has not been established. Ginger root can be taken in capsules of 250 mg four times a day for severe nausea and vomiting, although its value with less severe symptoms is unknown. Adverse effects on the fetus have not been seen with this dosage of ginger, but have not been evaluated extensively. You can also make ginger tea from 1 teaspoonful of freshly grated ginger. You should not drink more than 4 cups a day of the ginger tea. Ginger will work best if taken at the onset of nausea. Other herbs have been suggested for nausea and vomiting, including red raspberry and wild yam, but have not been tested scientifically.

A number of studies have found that acupressure relieves nausea and vomiting. All studies have used an acupuncture point called the *pericardium 6* (P6) or *Neiguan point*. This is on the *palmar* (inner) surface of the forearm about the width of three fingers above the wrist. Several regimens of acupressure have been studied, with women applying pressure themselves to the Neiguan point four times a day for 10 minutes at a time or wearing wrist bands which apply continuous pressure to this point. The wrist bands can be purchased in many health food or drug stores. They come with clear instructions.

Hypnosis and behavior modification have been suggested as beneficial for nausea and vomiting during pregnancy but have not been studied. *Homeopathic remedies,* which use extremely small doses of natural substances to stimulate the body's ability to heal itself, are also available in many health food stores and pharmacies. Again, these have not been evaluated scientifically to date. A therapy such as behavior modification may appear to be beneficial but actually the symptoms would have abated anyway simply due to the time passed between treatments.

The nausea and vomiting of pregnancy usually do not clear up dramatically. Improvement is gradual, with the appearance of good days that soon gain ascendancy over bad days. The bad days become fewer and fewer and finally disappear.

Pharmacologic Remedies

Until a number of years ago, a drug called Bendectin was available for women with nausea and vomiting. Bendectin contained vitamin B6 and an antispasmodic. This is the only drug approved by the Food and Drug Administration for the treatment of nausea and vomiting in pregnancy. Bendectin was taken off the market in 1983 after several lawsuits claimed that it caused birth defects. The association of this drug and birth defects was never shown in scientific research, but the drug has not returned to the market in the United States. In Canada, a drug containing the same ingredients is available under the name Diclectin. This drug was reviewed in Canada in 1989 by a panel of experts in the fields of teratogenesis, obstetrics, and pediatrics. The panel concluded that this drug is safe in pregnancy and prevents nausea and vomiting from becoming severe. Bendectin, however, is unlikely to reappear in the U.S.

HEARTBURN

Heartburn is a fiery, burning sensation in the chest. The name is a partial misnomer because the condition has nothing to do with the heart but results from a *reflux*, or regurgitation, of acid stomach juices into the lower esophagus. Heartburn may occur in anyone but is more common during pregnancy. This is due to the upward displacement and compression of the stomach by the enlarged uterus and the slowing of the muscular contractions of digestion as a result of the hormone progesterone.

Heartburn is a type of indigestion. It frequently is associated with the burping of small amounts of bitter, sour fluid. The omission from the diet of rich, greasy food, such as mayonnaise, cream, and fried foods, or, in fact, any food that the woman learns by her own experience to associate with heartburn, helps, as do smaller and less hurried meals.

Heavy foods and large meals should especially be avoided before bedtime. Although fatty meals may cause heartburn, some women find relief if they eat a very small amount of fat (like a pat of butter) about a half hour before a meal. Other helpful dietary measures might include:

• Small frequent meals
• Drinking fluids between meals, rather than with meals

- Avoiding very cold foods with meals
- Avoiding spicy foods or other foods that cause heartburn for you
- Drinking skim or cultured milk, eating lowfat ice cream
- Chewing gum after meals

In addition to dietary measures, maintain good posture and avoid lying down after meals. Stretching the arms over the head after eating gives the stomach more room to do its job of digestion. (There is a superstition that lifting the arms above the head can harm the baby—this is not true.) When you go to bed at night, use an extra pillow (or several) to elevate your head.

If specific dietary and other self-help measures don't work, over-the-counter antacids are available. You may obtain relief from heartburn by taking a level teaspoonful of milk of magnesia or a milk of magnesia tablet after each meal and again when heartburn occurs. (Some milk of magnesia is combined with mineral oil—do not use that.) If milk of magnesia causes loose stools, you can substitute other antacids. A few of these are made from aluminum hydroxide and are not recommended for long-term use in pregnancy. These include Amphojel and Rolaids. Tums are made from calcium salts and are okay to use in pregnancy, as long as the dose is kept to less than 20 grams a day (read the label as Tums come in different strengths). Calcium may cause constipation. Other antacids combine magnesium and aluminum hydroxide and so have a lower dose of aluminum than the purely aluminum antacids. These include Gelusel, Riopan, Mylanta, and Maalox. They work well and because of the combination of the two chemicals, they do not cause constipation or diarrhea. They should not be taken more often than recommended in the instructions that come with them.

If heartburn continues over time in pregnancy, milk of magnesia or Tums are probably the best antacids to use long-term, although remedies that don't rely on medications are preferable. We don't recommend these medications in the first trimester. Fortunately, heartburn is more of a problem later in pregnancy.

Antacids are available in tablet or liquid form, some in both. The liquid form may work better and is more palatable if you keep it refrigerated and drink it ice cold.

Make sure you don't take antacids with your iron supplement as the antacid interferes with iron absorption.

If heartburn is severe and persistent, you should consult your physician or midwife. It could indicate a health problem such as gallstones. What might seem to be heartburn could also be the pain that occurs in the upper part of the abdomen with *toxemia of pregnancy* (pregnancy-induced hypertension, discussed in great detail in Chapter 12). If your "heartburn" occurs with headache, any visual disturbances, or unusual swelling of your face, make sure you have it checked as soon as possible.

EXCESSIVE SALIVATION (PTYALISM)

This uncommon complaint, caused by excessive secretion of the salivary glands, is very annoying and difficult to cure. The secretion of saliva virtually floods the mouth and is so profuse that the woman cannot manage to swallow all of it, so she must continually expectorate (spit). Sometimes eating starch leads to ptyalism. If this is the cause, stopping the starch ingestion should stop the ptyalism. More often, there is no apparent cause for this problem.

Ptyalism often is accompanied by a foul taste, which can be relieved somewhat by sucking peppermints or chewing gum. Some women find relief by sucking on a lemon or drinking water with a bit of lemon juice in it. Ptyalism frequently persists throughout pregnancy but tends to diminish in the latter half. It always disappears promptly with delivery.

CONSTIPATION

Some women become constipated only when pregnant, and others prone to constipation find that pregnancy increases the difficulty. The condition results from decreased contractions of the intestinal tract caused by the hormone progesterone and from the displacement of the bowels by the growing uterus. Iron supplements may cause or increase constipation. If this occurs, the type of iron supplement may have to be changed, or the dosage reduced and more food sources of iron included in the diet (see Chapter 10).

The hazards of constipation are greatly exaggerated in the public mind, in part from the emphasis on a daily bowel movement in pharmaceutical advertising in popular media. No harm comes to the person who does not have a daily movement. If constipation causes discomfort, the following measures minimize the problem:

• Get daily exercise.
• Maintain adequate fluid intake (eight to ten glasses of water a day).
• Eat whole grains, such as whole wheat bread and bran cereal.
• Eat fresh fruits and vegetables throughout the day.
• Eat fruit at night before going to bed. Certain fruits are especially beneficial, notably prunes, apples, figs, dates, and raisins. A glass of prune juice at night followed by bran cereal in the morning works wonders.
• Develop the habit of a regular visit to the bathroom at the same time each day. This is the best preventive against constipation. Also, do not ignore the urge to go when you have it; you will lose the urge and over time, this will interfere with your ability to have bowel movements.

If these measures do not relieve the constipation, and it is uncomfortable, you can try a mild laxative. A good choice is one of the natural-fiber laxatives such as psyllium hydrophilic mucilloid, marketed under several trade names including Metamucil. It causes the stools to become soft and bulky so they are passed readily.

Mineral oil is not advised as it interferes with intestinal absorption of nutrients. Milk of magnesia, which is not absorbed from the intestinal tract, may be tried. Dulcolax (bisacodyl) is another safe laxative, and is available as oral pills or as a rectal suppository. Colace (docusate sodium) or Senokot is not a laxative, but a stool softener, and may be used in pregnancy. Rectal suppositories of glycerin can also be tried. In general, dietary measures that maintain the body's natural processes are preferable.

GAS

Distention of the stomach and intestines by gas, resulting in a bloated feeling and the frequent need to pass flatus, is a common complaint during pregnancy. Avoidance of gas-producing foods such as beans, parsnips, corn, onions, cabbage, fried foods, and sweet desserts may help, but this condition does not cause serious problems. If you have constipation, helping regulate the bowels, as discussed above, may alleviate much of the gas. If gas becomes very uncomfortable, lying with your knees pulled toward your chest may relieve the cramping.

HEMORRHOIDS

As pregnancy advances, the veins at the anal opening become enlarged by the relaxing effect of progesterone and the gradually increasing pressure within the venous system of the lower half of the body. Hard bowel movements and straining at stool have a tendency to cause these veins to protrude through the anal opening and to cause local pain, bleeding, and itching.

The best treatment for hemorrhoids is the prevention of constipation through use of the measures listed above. Placing your feet on a small footstool when sitting on the toilet puts your body in a more physiologic position to have a bowel movement, approximating the way the body used to be positioned when people squatted to move their bowels. This helps prevent straining, a major cause of hemorrhoids.

If you have slight rectal bleeding without pain or a bulging lump, apply cold cream or petroleum jelly (Vaseline) to the anus with the finger in the morning, before bed, and after each bowel movement. If this does not stop the rectal bleeding within a few days, or if the bleeding is profuse, notify your physician or midwife.

If there is a tender, swollen mass protruding through the anus, you should attempt to replace it gently into the anus after each bowel movement with a finger well lubricated with petroleum jelly or another lubricant like K-Y jelly. If this is painful or difficult, first sit for several minutes in a tub of comfortably warm water. Once the hemorrhoid is inside the anus, you can tighten the muscles around the anal area to keep the hemorrhoid in place. (This is the "Kegel" exercise described in Chapter 9.)

If you cannot replace the hemorrhoid into the anus, lie on your back with the hips slightly elevated and apply a washcloth or cotton swab that has been soaked in iced water—or iced witch hazel—to the anal region. Keep the washcloth moist and cold. This treatment may shrink the hemorrhoid sufficiently to permit its reposition. If the pain does not subside with this regimen, you can try a commercial product like Preparation H. If this is still ineffective, ask your physician or midwife for a prescription for a medicated suppository such as Anusol.

Occasionally a painful clot occurs in the hemorrhoid. This is called a *thrombosed hemorrhoid*. If you have unusual and unrelenting pain in the rectal area, see your physician or midwife. Rarely, you may need an incision and evacuation of the clot under local anesthesia. Surgery for hemorrhoids is inadvisable either during pregnancy or at delivery, since even the severe ones disappear during the postpartum period—even though they often get worse at first.

VARICOSE VEINS

Varicose veins are common during pregnancy due to a number of normally occurring changes. The hormone progesterone causes relaxation of the walls of the veins and the muscles surrounding them. The pressure of the uterus on the pelvic veins when a woman stands or sits inhibits blood from returning from the lower extremities, especially in the second and third trimesters. If a woman lies flat, pressure is put on the vena cava, also interfering with blood return. Finally, heredity plays a role. A familial tendency toward the occurrence of varicose veins may be inherited from either parent.

Studies have shown varicose veins to be present in 11 to 20 percent of pregnancies. Varicose veins can appear as early as the second month of pregnancy, although they are more common later.

In susceptible women, varicosities may be noted in a first or second pregnancy. In each succeeding pregnancy they tend to reappear earlier and are more severe. Fortunately, the enlarged veins regress between pregnancies. After the first few pregnancies they regress almost completely. They may regress only partially after later pregnancies.

The vessels first involved are most frequently on the inner aspect of the calf, but the process may begin in the space behind the knee or on the thigh, and may involve one leg or both. A less common site is the outer vaginal area.

In the early stages, the veins may appear as a superficial spidery network, but when more advanced they stand out as soft blue cords just beneath the skin. They may be straight, tortuous, or knotted.

Varicose veins may cause either no symptoms or considerable discomfort. Once the veins become large, they may cause a feeling of heaviness and fatigue. A dull ache is not infrequent. True pain only occurs if the veins become inflamed.

A number of comfort measures may help lessen varicosities or relieve the discomfort associated with them. Do not stand if you can sit and, when you sit, sit with your legs elevated so that your heels are above the level of the hips. When sitting, if you can't elevate the legs, the feet and toes should be exercised frequently by flexing and extending them. Don't cross your legs. A rocking chair can be helpful as the muscles in the legs contract a bit as you rock. This helps return the blood from the feet and legs to the heart. Do not sit if you can lie down, and when you lie down, lie with your legs raised on a pillow. Lying on your left side is best for circulation.

Some exercise during the day, including walking, helps with circulation. Standing in place for long periods of time is not good. If you work as a cashier, bank teller, or at another job that requires constant, stationary standing, try to walk in place and exercise your legs by circling your ankles or flexing and extending them one at a time. Rise up on your toes from time to time. Take frequent rest periods and sit or lie down during these breaks.

When you can, lie in bed several times a day with the legs lifted to rest high on a wall. You can do this when you get home from work and repeatedly on days off.

Do not wear constricting clothing. Avoid garters and tight stockings or socks. Maternity-support stockings or panty hose, elastic stockings, or Ace bandages can be used to compress the varices from the time they appear until several days after delivery. They can be worn from the toe to the knee for varicose veins involving the lower leg, although panty hose will avoid constriction at any place on the leg. With enlarged thigh veins, if you use the Ace bandages, a second bandage is wound from the knee upward.

Ideally, the support hose or bandage is put on in the morning *before* arising, with elevated legs. This means bathing or showering the night before. If you put the panty hose, stockings, or bandages on during the day, make sure to first elevate your legs for several minutes and, again, keep the legs in a raised position as you put the hose on.

Elastic stockings are marketed over the counter, in a variety of lengths and sizes. A more effective stocking requires individual measurements and is substantially more expensive. You can get a prescription for these stockings, in which case health insurance may pay for them. The amount of bother and expense you wish to go to obviously will be related to the severity of your symptoms.

Sometimes there are large varicosities on the labia or the vulva. These may give sensations of fullness or heaviness in this area, but again are no threat to health. Kegel or pelvic-floor exercises, described in Chapter 9, may help with circulation in this region. A maternity girdle may relieve pressure on the pelvic area and lessen the varicosities somewhat. Warm baths may be soothing. Lying in bed with the hips elevated on a full pillow or several pillows will help return the blood from the pelvic area to the heart.

A variety of treatments, surgical and nonsurgical, are now available for varicose veins. These are not recommended during pregnancy. The veins almost always recede dramatically after delivery and may need no further care.

NOSEBLEEDS AND
NASAL CONGESTION

Nosebleeds are common during pregnancy, particularly during the winter months; they are usually brief and rarely present a serious problem. The most common cause is a drying and crusting of the membrane lining the nasal cavity, a membrane that in pregnancy has a greatly increased blood supply.

If you have a tendency for nosebleeds, you can lubricate the mucous membranes of the nasal lining with a saltwater solution, available as a liquid or in spray form in most pharmacies. The solution can be dropped or sprayed into each nostril every 2 to 3 hours or as often as feels comfortable. You can use a lubricant like plain petroleum jelly (Vaseline) on the nostrils at night. If your bedroom air is very dry, consider using a humidifier. A pan of water placed on the radiator will add moisture to the air. In summer, air conditioning shouldn't be too high, although the cool air helps with other discomforts. In general, try to avoid straining, while lifting or at bowel movements, and don't blow your nose forcefully. If you sneeze, open your mouth to reduce the force of the sneeze.

When you have a nosebleed, do not extend the head backward. Sit still and pinch the nostrils until the bleeding stops. This may take up to 5 or 7 minutes. If the bleeding continues, gently blow out any clots from each nostril and hold the nostrils for another 5 to 7 minutes. If the bleeding still continues, call your physician or midwife or go to the nearest emergency room.

Frequently, throughout pregnancy, the pregnant woman feels as though her nose is swollen by a perpetual cold that interferes with breathing. This is called *allergic rhinitis* of pregnancy. Nose drops or sprays such as Neosynephrine that cause the vessels to constrict or decongestant tablets like Sudafed produce temporary relief but should be used seldom and sparingly; their excessive use only creates resistance to their effects. Saltwater drops are preferable. Boiling a large pot of water and breathing over the steam may provide some temporary relief. Be careful not to burn yourself, of course! As with almost all the miseries mentioned in this chapter, there is a cheerful addendum: allergic rhinitis clears up with delivery.

HEADACHE

Headaches occur somewhat more commonly in pregnant women than in nonpregnant women. If they result from nasal congestion, follow the relief measures outlined above. If they are from sinusitis, you might need prescription medication. Discuss this with your physician or midwife. An examination by an eye doctor can determine if the headaches are caused by eyestrain.

Headaches can be treated with rest, warm or cold compresses, and massage. If these measures are ineffective, mild analgesia, such as acetaminophen, can be used. Usually headaches will become less severe in the second half of pregnancy. At that time, a severe headache, especially if accompanied by visual disturbances such as flashing lights in front of your eyes or double vision, or unusual hand or facial swelling, may be a sign of *preeclampsia* or pregnancy-induced hypertension (high blood pressure). Call your physician or midwife immediately if you have any of these symptoms.

LEG CRAMPS

Spasms of the calf and foot muscles are a common and painful experience during pregnancy. The problem is likely to begin about midpregnancy, but is usually less frequent in the last month. It comes unannounced; most of the time you will be aroused from sleep to find the calf muscles of one leg knotted into a painful, firm ball. The best treatment is to stretch the muscle. You can stand up, or press your knee down and flex your toes toward your knee. Your partner can help you with this as it may be too painful for you to manage even to flex your foot. Massaging the muscle with a kneading motion may relax it.

The muscle may remain tender for several hours after the cramp. Such a muscle spasm is not damaging, nor does it denote any abnormality of health. As with most discomforts, prevention is the best measure. Sometimes leg cramps are related to an insufficient intake of calcium or an excess of phosphorus in the diet. Phosphorus is in milk and dairy products, but also in soft drinks and many processed and snack foods. If you have plenty of milk and dairy but also have a high intake of soda or processed foods, you may have too much phosphorus. Give up the snacks and soda—not the milk. Some evidence suggests a lack of magnesium in the diet as a cause of leg cramps. You can try a magnesium supplement of 100 to 250 mg daily, although its value has not been studied. A lack of potassium might also cause cramping, but if you eat fruits and vegetables, you most likely get enough potassium. You can try eating a banana or half a banana a day to see if this helps the leg cramps.

SWELLING OF THE ANKLES AND LEGS

About 10 to 20 percent of the normal weight gain during pregnancy results from an increase in the amount of water held by the body's tissues. This excess fluid tends to pool into the lower part of the body, so that the feet and ankles show the most evidence of it. Many pregnant women complain of *edema* or swelling of the ankles, the lower legs, and the feet toward the end of the day. This is aggravated by standing for long periods and is worse in warm weather.

If you have swollen ankles or legs you should elevate your feet whenever possible—prop them on a chair or bench, or stretch yourself out on the sofa or bed. You may need to buy shoes in a larger size in late pregnancy to allow for the swelling of your feet. If the swelling in your feet is accompanied by a tight feeling and burn, you can soak them in cold water and Epsom salts for relief. Ordinarily the swelling subsides during the night, and by morning the normal contours of the ankle are visible once again.

The fingers are the next most common site of pregnancy tissue swelling. Your fingers may feel stiff and your rings uncomfortably tight and difficult to remove. Soaking your hand in cold water and soaping your finger and ring may make it easier to remove jewelry.

One important point when you have swelling—do not limit fluids. Drinking less will actually make the body retain more fluid. If you increase your fluids, you will urinate more often and lose fluid more readily.

Swelling of the face may occur normally to a limited extent, causing features to look relatively thick and soft. A marked accumulation of fluid in the face, causing puffy eyes that are difficult to open, could be a sign of toxemia of pregnancy. It *must* be brought to the attention of the professionals who are helping you in your pregnancy care.

FREQUENCY OF URINATION AND NOCTURIA

Many women experience an increased urge to urinate both at the beginning and the end of pregnancy. The sensation in early pregnancy results from the hormone-induced increase in local blood flow in the pelvis and the initial enlargement of the uterus, causing direct pressure on the urinary bladder. In the second trimester, when the uterus grows larger, it becomes less of a pelvic organ and more of an abdominal organ, relieving much of the pressure on the bladder.

The cause of increased urination toward the end of pregnancy is somewhat different, related to the marked increase in the circulating blood volume that occurs as pregnancy proceeds. Thanks to gravity and the enlarging uterus, fluid accumulates in the legs during the day. When you lie down, with your legs at approximately the same level as your heart, water flows back out of the legs into the general circulation. If you rest on your side, so that the weight of the uterus on the abdominal blood vessels is removed, movement of water out of the lower half of the body is even greater. The kidneys promptly respond by increasing the rate at which they form urine and therefore, some hours after you stretch out, you may find that your bladder fills up rapidly. You may be awakened at night to urinate. This is called *nocturia*.

You may be able to reduce the number of times you have to get up at night by limiting fluid intake in the evening and by lying down while you are still awake in the early evening. Lying down before bedtime helps you eliminate some of the extra water before you are asleep. Don't limit fluids entirely. Make sure your total intake of water for the day is at least eight glasses.

You may also have increased daytime urination in the last weeks of pregnancy, after the baby "drops," or moves downward in the uterus, its head entering the circle of bones formed by the pelvis. This puts renewed pressure on the urinary bladder.

If frequent urination is combined with burning upon urination or a feeling of intense urgency when you have to go, especially if the urgency is coupled with only a small amount of urine actually passed, you may have a *urinary tract infection* (UTI). If you have these symptoms with fever and chills and a low backache toward the side of the back (the flank area), especially if this is limited to one side, you may have a *kidney infection*. If you have these symptoms, call your physician or midwife. Don't wait.

ROUND LIGAMENT PAIN

The round ligaments are two rubber-bandlike structures on either side of the uterus that help support it. These ligaments stretch as the uterus grows and this stretching can cause pain. The pressure of the uterus on the ligaments can also cause pain.

Round ligament pain is felt in the lower abdomen, on one or both sides, and can extend into the groin area. It can occur rather early in pregnancy, when the uterus first begins to grow, and can worsen or occur for the first time late in pregnancy when the uterus is very large. Sometimes the pain is particularly noticeable when you are walking, changing position, such as getting up from a chair, or when you are lying on your side, with the uterus pressing against one of the ligaments. In the side-lying position, the pain is often one sided.

If the pain is persistent and intense, bring it to the attention of your physician or midwife, who can make sure it isn't from a health problem like appendicitis. If lower abdominal pain is suddenly acute and unrelenting, call your physician or midwife immediately—you may be having a medical emergency.

Round ligament pain can be quite uncomfortable. The goal of pain relief measures is to reduce the stretch or reduce the pressure of the uterus on the ligaments.

When you walk or get up from sitting, you can help the round ligaments do their job by cupping the bottom of the uterus with your hands, one on either side of the uterus. A maternity girdle may provide the same type of support, if the pain is persistent and frequent, especially late in pregnancy. If the pain occurs when you are sitting or lying on your back, try flexing your knees onto your abdomen. This may reduce the pull on the ligaments. If the pain occurs on one side, try leaning toward the painful side to reduce the stretch. If it occurs in the side-lying position, put a pillow beneath the uterus, between your knees, or under the upper leg, which is bent over the lower one. These pillows provide extra support and reduce the stretching and pulling on the ligament. Finally, a warm bath or heating pad may feel soothing. Heat should only be used if you are sure the pain is not from appendicitis.

BACKACHE

The hormones of pregnancy cause a loosening of the joints of the pelvis. This is purposeful, as it provides additional space for passage of the newborn. Sometimes, however, this causes discomfort at the *pubic joint*—just behind the pubic hair—and in the lower back. The round ligaments, discussed above, are attached to the *sacrum*—the back of the pelvis. As they are stretched from the growing uterus, there is increased pressure on the sacrum. This pressure, combined with the change in the center of gravity caused by an enlarged and protruding uterus, causes most pregnant women to walk with a waddling gait. As the pregnant woman leans backward to counterbalance the weight of her pregnant uterus up front, an unaccustomed strain is put on muscles. Women who have good muscle tone from exercise are somewhat less likely to experience this discomfort.

Upper backache may occur in pregnancy as well, due to the increase in the size of the breasts. Upper backache sometimes begins earlier in pregnancy than lower backache as the breasts enlarge in the first trimester.

Backache is very common. As with most discomforts, the best treatment is prevention. Using the body correctly will help prevent backache. We call this *good body mechanics*.

The following are guidelines for good body mechanics to prevent backache:

• Always bend from the knees, not the waist.
• Keep your feet spread apart when bending; place one foot slightly in front of the other.
• If you are lifting something heavy (like a toddler), bend your knees, pick up the weight close to your body, look up, and lift by straightening your legs.
• Avoid excessive lifting, bending, and walking. If you must do these activities, take rest periods.
• If you do work requiring standing in one position, even an activity like washing dishes, rest one foot on a low stool to relieve strain on your back.
• Do stretching exercises of the arms. Lift them high above the head. Do not worry about hurting the baby by doing this—that is an old superstition.
• Sleep on a hard mattress. Use pillows for support under all joints.
• When arising from your back, turn to your side, or even to all fours, and push off with your arms.
• Wear supportive low-heeled shoes.
• Wear a well-fitting supportive bra. Choose one with wide straps

and with a cup large enough to encompass your entire breast. This will be larger than the bra you wore before you got pregnant. You may even consider wearing the bra for sleeping. A sports bra may be most comfortable for sleep.

If you have backaches despite the above measures, a warm tub bath or heating pad can provide some relief. Some women prefer an ice pack. A massage can be very relaxing and comforting. There are specialists in maternity massage who often have special equipment and techniques to accommodate your pregnant body. If necessary, a maternity girdle may provide additional relief.

The pelvic rock is a good exercise to stretch the lower back and both prevent and relieve aches. You can do this exercise in several positions, but the easiest is probably on your hands and knees. Alternately flatten and round your back by rhythmically tucking your pelvis in toward your navel, then releasing it. You also can do the pelvic rock lying on your back on a flat surface. With bent knees, press the small of your back into the surface and hold it for several seconds.

Physical therapy might help relieve or diminish persistent backache. You can ask your physician or midwife for a referral to a therapist.

A few pathologic conditions can cause backache. Pain from a herniated disc occurs in pregnant women with about the same frequency as in the nonpregnant. A kidney infection is more common in pregnant women than nonpregnant women and may cause pain in the mid to lower back—usually on one side and more often the right side than the left. If you have chills and fever or pain with urination, then the backache is most likely a symptom of kidney infection and you must call your physician or midwife immediately.

SCIATICA

The sciatic nerve goes from the lower back through the buttocks to the legs. Pressure on this nerve can cause pain, tingling, or numbness in the buttocks, hips, or thighs. If the feeling moves from the buttocks down the leg, it is likely to be from pressure on the sciatic nerve, called *sciatica*. Pressure comes from the enlarging uterus or the position of the baby.

Sciatica is hard to treat, but it is not permanent. It will be relieved after the pregnancy. Warm baths or warm compresses may provide some relief. Pelvic rocking and acetaminophen may be useful. Massage and chiropractic care may be of benefit. A firm cushion support for the lower back can be purchased through a physical therapy office. Ask your physician or midwife for a referral to a physical therapist, massage therapist, and/or chiropractor.

FAINTNESS

A tendency to light-headedness and even fainting may occur at any time during pregnancy. Lying on your back for too long may result in a drop in the return of blood to the heart and therefore a sudden drop in blood pressure. This accounts for brief periods of dizziness when you sit up suddenly from lying flat.

To avoid this feeling, don't lie flat on your back in the second and third trimesters. Always prop your head up with pillows or lie on your side. When getting up from lying or sitting, move slowly; turn to your side and push off with your arms. At any time when you feel faint during pregnancy, either sit down with your head between your knees or stretch out on your left side.

INSOMNIA

Despite the increasing fatigue and the desire for additional rest that most women feel in the last trimester, sleep may be seriously disturbed by the nocturnal athletic pursuits of the fetus, not to mention the difficulty of finding a comfortable position for rest. A bath before bed may provide much needed relaxation. Warm milk often induces sleep. Soothing music and a massage may help. Use of pillows under all the joints provides some comfort. In the heat of the summer, an air-conditioned bedroom is a welcome relief. If the insomnia is severe and causes you concern, discuss it with your physician or midwife.

For some women, insomnia creates major disruptions in life, interfering with the ability to work or carry on usual activities. If this happens to you, and the above remedies do not work, discuss the problem with your physician or midwife. If you are in the second or third trimester, he or she may suggest some medication to help you sleep. Generally, an over-the-counter antihistamine like Benadryl is preferable to a sleeping tablet. Take this about half an hour or an hour before you are ready to go to bed. If you fall asleep easily but wake up after a time and cannot resume sleeping, take the pill just before going to bed.

PAINFUL CONTRACTIONS

The uterus, like all smooth muscle structures, is constantly alternating between a phase of contraction and a phase of relaxation. This is not noticeable to you until the middle of pregnancy, when you may feel a hard lump at the fundus, or top of the uterus. This lump remains for up to 30 seconds and disappears, only to reappear 10 or 15 minutes later. Such contractions ordinarily are not painful. They are called *Braxton-Hicks contractions*, named after the physician who first described them.

In some women—usually in a second or later pregnancy—these contractions may become painful during the late pregnancy months. Such painful contractions, or *false labor pains*, may be difficult to differentiate from true labor. In true labor, the pains gradually get closer together, longer, and harder. True labor pains may be accompanied by a show of blood, whereas false pains are not.

If you have painful contractions before the end of week 37 of pregnancy, it is important to determine whether you are having real labor, as a baby born before 37 weeks gestation is considered premature. Premature labor can sometimes be stopped, but only before the cervix has opened. If these pains are accompanied by an increase in vaginal discharge or by blood or *rupture of membranes*—a gush of fluid or any watery discharge from the vagina—and you are less than 37 weeks pregnant, call your physician or midwife immediately. Whether or not you have these other symptoms, if the pains continue for more than 1 hour and are not relieved by drinking water and resting, if they are closer than 8 minutes apart, if you have four or more pains in 20 minutes or eight or more in 60 minutes, contact your physician or midwife. The only definitive way to know whether these pains are real or false labor is to check the cervix to see if it is opening (dilating). Preterm labor is discussed in great depth in Chapter 15.

If you have some painful contractions and are more than 37 weeks pregnant, we recommend rest, a warm bath, a massage, and taking comfort in the knowledge that these contractions may be helping prepare the cervix for labor.

VAGINAL SECRETIONS (LEUKORRHEA)

A certain amount of pale yellow, thin vaginal secretion is normal during pregnancy, resulting from the increased activity of the glands within the cervix. If the discharge becomes very profuse or thick, develops an odor, or is associated with vaginal itching or burning, consult your doctor or midwife. When these other symptoms accompany the vaginal secretion, you may have a vaginal infection. There are three common types of vaginal infections, any of which could occur in pregnancy: *trichomoniasis* (caused by *Trichomonas*); *monilias* or *candidiasis* (caused by *Monilia* or *Candida*); and *bacterial vaginosis* (BV).

Trichomoniasis is caused by a parasite called a *trichomonad*. Moniliasis or candidiasis is caused by a yeast or fungus. Bacterial vaginosis is caused by an overgrowth of a number of organisms in the vagina. Trichomoniasis is almost always transmitted sexually, although neither candidiasis nor BV is sexually transmitted.

The proper diagnosis can be made readily by a pelvic examination and a look at the secretions under the microscope. Each type of infection produces specific symptoms that can be seen on pelvic examination, but the exact diagnosis is made via microscopic identification of the organism or changes in the vaginal cells associated with the infection.

Vaginal infection should be treated in pregnancy. Trichomoniasis and BV are among the conditions that may cause premature rupture of membranes, possibly leading to premature delivery (see Chapter 15). While candidiasis is not one of the infections implicated in premature rupture of membranes, it can be passed to the baby during birth, causing a thrush infection of the mouth. Each infection has a specific treatment.

The treatment for trichomoniasis is an antibiotic called *metronidazole* (Flagyl, Protostat) in a dose of 2 grams, to be taken by mouth in a single day. Since the couple will pass this infection back and forth between them, the woman's partner should be treated at the same time. If the partners are not treated simultaneously and do not use a condom before both are treated, the infection will probably not clear up.

Of course, having a sexually transmitted infection (STI) during a pregnancy can be an emotional upset for a woman. This is something to discuss with your partner. Discuss it also with your physician or midwife, who can help you deal with the issue and refer you for further counseling should that be necessary. If you have any STI during pregnancy, you should use condoms during intercourse to protect yourself from being infected again with the same infection, or with another STI. These can have adverse effects on the baby (see Chapter 5).

Like most effective drugs, metronidazole can have side effects. It may be associated with abdominal discomfort if you drink alcoholic beverages during or after the treatment. Of course, pregnant women shouldn't drink alcohol at all, but both partners should be aware that there is an additional reason to avoid alcohol during treatment with metronidazole and for 24 hours after treatment has ended. Metronidazole produces mutations in bacteria and tumors in mice if given to the mice over long periods in large doses. We have no evidence of such effects in humans, however, to whom the drug is given in much smaller doses for brief periods. As metronidazole is overwhelmingly the most effective treatment for trichomoniasis, it may be prescribed after the first trimester, once the infection is diagnosed. Additional side effects include a metallic taste in the mouth, nausea, and other symptoms of gastrointestinal distress. Metronidazole may cause an overgrowth of *Candida*, which then requires treatment.

Bacterial vaginosis also is treated with metronidazole—250 mg by mouth three times a day for 7 days. One dose of 2 grams can be used as an alternative treatment as can 300 mg of another antibiotic, clindamycin, orally twice a day for 7 days.

In pregnancy the vagina offers an unusually hospitable environment for yeast overgrowth. Throughout pregnancy the vagina is rich in glycogen, on which *Candida* thrive. If *Candida* is the cause of vaginal discharge, an antifungal agent such as miconazole (Monistat) can be prescribed for vaginal insertion at bedtime for 7 days. These medications are now available over the counter. As any medication should be used in pregnancy only when needed, we strongly recommend an examination to make sure that your vaginal symptoms really are a yeast infection before beginning any treatment.

Yeast infections have a tendency to recur during pregnancy and treatment may have to be repeated on several occasions. When the pregnancy ends, the environment of the vagina changes and the complaint tends to subside.

Before you can get to see your physician or midwife, applying plain yogurt or witch hazel to the labia and lower vagina may give some relief from itching or burning. Soaking in an oatmeal bath (Aveeno) may be soothing.

SHORTNESS OF BREATH

Shortness of breath occurs in pregnancy in part because the diaphragm is raised almost 2 inches as a consequence of the increasing size of the uterus. This is mostly a problem in the third trimester. Earlier in pregnancy, a woman may find herself *hyperventilating*—taking quick and shallow breaths. This helps eliminate carbon dioxide from the fetus—a job the mother must perform in pregnancy.

Because the changes in breathing are related to specific changes of pregnancy, little can be done about them. Just knowing that they are normal should be reassuring. You can concentrate on breathing deeply and slowly. You can give your lungs a bit more room if you maintain good posture—don't slouch! You can stretch your arms over your head from time to time, also giving the lungs extra room. You can do this in any position—standing, sitting, or lying down.

If shortness of breath interferes with sleep, prop up your head and shoulders with several pillows to a semisitting position. If you find that you are markedly short of breath climbing stairs and have to stop several times before getting to the top, or if sleep is difficult no matter how high you are propped up, you should report this promptly to your physician or midwife.

In many women, particularly in those with first pregnancies, shortness of breath may be relieved somewhat a few weeks before labor, when the uterus drops an inch or two as the baby's head descends part way into the opening of the bony pelvis.

SKIN CHANGES

Rashes

Pregnant women are subject to the same kind of annoying skin rashes as anyone else. Heavyset women tend to develop skin rashes beneath the breasts or in the groin. This is particularly common in warm humid weather, and is caused by the irritating effect of perspiration against rubbing skin surfaces. The best treatment for this is cleansing and keeping the skin dry by dusting it with plain cornstarch.

In the last few decades, a new condition has been described, called PUPPP. These initials stand for *Pruritic Urticarial Papules and Plaques of Pregnancy*. Pruritic means itchy. Urticaria are hives. Papules are raised areas of the skin, but without exudate or pus.

PUPPP occurs predominantly among women having their first child. Small red elevated patches appear and tend to run together to form larger itching areas. Surprisingly, although women have difficulty refraining from scratching, loss of the top layers of the skin is unusual. The plaques ordinarily begin on the skin of the abdomen and about half the time are limited to the area right around the navel. They also may be distributed over the buttocks, hips, thighs, and upper inner arms. The face is usually spared.

There are no known maternal or fetal complications from PUPPP. It tends not to recur in later pregnancies or when nonpregnant women take oral contraceptives (which sometimes cause side effects similar to some of the discomforts of pregnancy). PUPPP responds to the external use of corticoid ointments, the anti-inflammatory drugs that are related to the hormones of the adrenal cortex. With severe symptoms the oral administration of corticoids has been tried, with relief in a limited number of women.

There are other diffuse rashes that occur in pregnancy, but they are in no way different from those occurring in nonpregnant women.

Increased Pigmentation

About half of all pregnant women develop "stretch marks" in the skin of the abdomen or the breasts or thighs. These appear as pinkish to reddish, slightly indented lines. They will fade in the postpartum period into shiny silver or white lines. They are technically called *striae gravidarum* (Latin: *stria* = channel or groove; *gravida* = pregnant).

Striae are caused, at least in part, by stimulation of the pigment-producing cells (*melanocytes*) in pregnancy, possibly as a result of the increased amount of estrogen and progesterone in the body. The increased activity of the melanocytes also causes a number of other changes:

- Darkening of the nipple and areola (the circular part surrounding the nipple)
- The *linea negra*, a dark thin line that goes from the navel to the pubic hair in the center of the abdomen
- *Chloasma* or mask of pregnancy

Chloasma (Greek: *chloazein* = to be green) is a darkened, usually brownish, pigmentation that appears on the face, mostly over the nose and cheeks, forehead, and possibly the neck. As chloasma is most likely to occur with sun exposure, wearing sun screen or a wide-brimmed hat is recommended in the second half of pregnancy, when these changes in pigmentation become noticeable. Some women who develop chloasma in pregnancy also develop it if they take oral contraceptives. These changes usually disappear or at least fade after pregnancy. They are not at all dangerous or suggestive of illness.

Palmar erythema is another skin change that occurs in the second half of pregnancy. It is a redness of the palms of the hands. If palmar erythema occurs in the first trimester of pregnancy, it might indicate *hepatitis* (an inflammation of the liver), but later in pregnancy it is a normal, benign change causing no pain or discomfort.

Some women develop noticeable vascular patterns on the face, neck, chest, or arms. These are small reddish-purplish areas looking somewhat like a spiderweb, hence the name *vascular spiders* or *spider angiomas*. These changes do not persist after the pregnancy is over.

CARPAL TUNNEL SYNDROME

Carpal tunnel syndrome is a compression of a nerve called the *median nerve*, which passes through a tunnel-like area at the base of the palm as it travels from the forearm to the hand and fingers. The area through which this nerve passes is called the *carpal tunnel*. Compression is common in pregnancy due to the fluid retention in the tissues.

When the median nerve is pinched or compressed, a woman may have tingling or numbing in the hand and fingers or shooting pains in the wrist or forearm. These sometimes travel to the shoulder, neck, chest, or even the foot. She may have difficulty clenching her fist or grasping small objects. Unfortunately, these symptoms may flare up at night and she may be awakened with numbness or pain in one or both hands.

Most of the time carpal tunnel syndrome resolves itself after delivery. If it is severe, even disabling, your physician or midwife can refer you to an orthopedist who can fit you with a splint to be worn at night. A physical therapist can show you helpful exercises. As some experts believe that a vitamin B6 deficiency is related to carpal tunnel syndrome, supplements of this vitamin—in doses not to exceed 75 mg a day—might be helpful.

WHAT TO DO IN THE CASE
OF A FALL OR ACCIDENT

If you fall or have an accident during pregnancy, first discover whether you have injured yourself. Determining this does not differ from doing so when you are not pregnant. Do you hurt? Are you bleeding from any wounds? Are your movements restricted?

Next, turn your attention to the pregnancy. If there is no vaginal bleeding or leakage of fluid and the fetus continues to move, pregnancy was likely unaffected. If you are too early in pregnancy to have felt fetal movements, the only criteria regarding the status of the pregnancy will be vaginal bleeding and abdominal cramping. The fetus is so protected by the cushioning amniotic fluid surrounding it and the veritable shock absorbers built into the uterus that only rarely does even the most direct blow disturb either the infant or the fortress in which it is ensconced.

If you have any concerns, however, after an injury, don't hesitate to call your physician or midwife, even if just for reassurance, or go to the nearest emergency room. If you have a serious injury, of course, call 911.

CHAPTER TWELVE

⎯⎯ ⊶⊷⊶ ⎯⎯

Occasional Complications
of Pregnancy

Complications specific to pregnancy are uncommon, and your chance of developing any one is slim. When complications do occur today, they can almost always be resolved safely. Most important is to know the danger signals so if you do develop a problem you can get prompt attention.

ECTOPIC PREGNANCY
(PREGNANCY OUTSIDE THE UTERUS)

An *ectopic pregnancy* is a pregnancy outside the uterus (Greek: *ek* = out; *topos* = place). Most ectopic pregnancies occur in the fallopian tubes and are called tubal pregnancies. Ectopic pregnancies also can occur in the cervix, the ovary, and the *peritoneal cavity*—the area of the body containing the abdominal organs.

In recent decades, ectopic pregnancy has become more common throughout the United States. This is due, at least in part, to an increase in sexually transmitted infections (STI). STIs can lead to infection in the tubes, called *salpingitis* or *pelvic inflammatory disease* (PID). One study of more than 700 women who had PID showed a 6 percent rate of ectopic pregnancy among those who were able to conceive. This compares to an overall rate of ectopic pregnancy of less than half of 1 percent.

Although uncommon among all pregnancies, ectopic pregnancy accounts for 9 percent of deaths among pregnant women. Of every 2,000 women who have an ectopic pregnancy, approximately 1 will die. The death rate among African-American women is disproportionately greater than among Caucasian women, possibly due to a lack of early care.

These rates, however, are far lower than they were in 1970. New diagnostic techniques permit very early detection of ectopic pregnancies, with increased survival for women and increased possibility of future successful pregnancies.

Besides a history of PID, other risks for ectopic pregnancy include:

- Previous ectopic pregnancy.
- Previous surgery on the tubes. This includes a previous sterilization procedure. A recent study found that among every 1,000 surgical sterilizations, 7 resulted in an ectopic pregnancy at some time within 10 years after the procedure. This was most common among women sterilized before the age of 30. Sterilization reversal also may result in ectopic pregnancy.
- Infertility treatments, including ovulation induction, stimulation of the ovaries, and in vitro fertilization (see Chapter 13).
- Previous pelvic surgery—such as appendectomy or ovarian surgery—that causes scar tissue or adhesions among various organs, putting undue pressure on the fallopian tubes.
- A pelvic mass like a fibroid or ovarian cyst that presses on the tubes.
- Douching. Studies have shown a relationship between the length of time of douching and ectopic pregancy. A recent study among African-American women found that women who douched once a month for more than 5 years had 4 times the risk of ectopic pregnancy as women who never douched, while women who douched for 10 years had 6 times the risk.
- *Endometriosis* (a condition in which the tissue that normally lines the uterus grows outside the uterus).
- Smoking.

If a pregnancy occurs accidentally when a woman is using an intrauterine device (IUD) or the "mini-pill" for contraception, it is more likely to be ectopic than a pregnancy occurring in somebody not using these contraceptives. The *mini-pill*, described in Chapter 27, is an oral contraceptive that contains only one hormone: progesterone. This is also true after the use of emergency contraception, or the *"morning-after" pill*. If the morning-after pill fails to prevent a pregnancy, then that pregnancy has a greater chance of being ectopic than the average pregnancy.

How does ectopic pregnancy come about? The sperm meets the egg in the fallopian tube as it normally does. Formation of an embryo proceeds to the point where it is a tiny hollow ball of cells. This growth takes place, as usual, in the fallopian tube. The interior of the tube is a complex labyrinth with many folds in its lining. It is not surprising that an occasional embryo loses its way, becomes stuck in the maze, and makes efforts to implant there. With a previous tubal infection, the tissues along the folds of the lining of the tube may be scarred and adherent to each other. This creates pockets in which the embryo can be trapped. Patches of *tubal endometriosis*, or uterine tissue, provide an attractive area for implantation during the normal passage of the embryo.

Whatever the reason, the embryo tries to implant in this unsuitable location. It immediately begins to form hCG (see Chapters 2 and 3), which gets into the mother's circulation and signals to the ovary that a pregnancy is under way. The estrogen and progesterone of pregnancy together cause an increase in the local blood supply. As the beginning parts of the placenta burrow into the tubal wall, they seek and invade these blood vessels, causing local hemorrhage. The placenta itself frequently is damaged and dislodged.

Neither the lining of the tube nor its muscular wall is adapted for maintaining a pregnancy. The blood supply is inadequate and the wall too thin. As a consequence, an occasional tubal pregnancy will burst through the wall of the tube and implant itself secondarily on a surface elsewhere within the peritoneal cavity. These surfaces are equally ill suited for maintenance of a pregnancy.

As ectopic pregnancies are not supplied with nutrients, there is a very high incidence of embryonic damage and consequent death of the embryo. There is reason to believe that some ectopic pregnancies actually cure themselves following early embryonic death. Only the rarest of the rare ectopic pregnancy continues to the point at which the fetus might survive.

Symptoms of Ectopic Pregnancy

Ectopic pregnancy may not be apparent in its early stages. A woman may experience irregular bleeding rather than the complete cessation of menses seen with a normal pregnancy. Some ectopic pregnancies are uncovered at the time of elective early abortion when the material removed from the uterus fails to contain embryonic tissue.

As the ectopic pregnancy grows and pushes against the tube or bleeds into its walls, the pregnant woman may have lower abdominal discomfort, along with the usual vague sensations of early pregnancy. These include breast tenderness and possibly nausea if the pregnancy continues long enough for nausea to develop. Episodes of internal bleeding from the tube may cause severe cramping pain. If any substantial amount of blood gets into the peritoneal cavity, the woman may notice urgency to urinate or defecate due to irritation of the bladder and the rectum by the blood on their walls. This much bleeding ordinarily is associated with dizziness and fainting, symptoms that are frequently seen in advanced ectopic pregnancies, along with severe lower abdominal pain. Often the pain is only on the side of the ectopic pregnancy, but it may be on both sides. A woman may feel bloated and her abdomen may feel hard. She may have a sense that her heart is racing.

Ectopic pregnancy can cause shoulder pain if it has ruptured out of the tube with extensive bleeding. The blood in the peritoneal cavity irritates the diaphragm, whose nerves are felt in the shoulder. If ruptured ectopic pregnancy is not treated and hemorrhage occurs, the woman can go into shock.

Diagnosis of Ectopic Pregnancy

The diagnosis of ectopic pregnancy has improved immensely in the past few decades due to the combination of the blood test for hCG and early pelvic sonography. When caring for women with risk factors for ectopic pregnancy, the physician or midwife should maintain what is called a "high level of suspicion." Anytime a sexually active woman presents with a missed period followed by unusual bleeding, a pregnancy test is necessary. Anytime a sexually active woman experiences a missed or delayed period, or even an uncharacteristically light period, followed by unusual pelvic or abdominal pain, a pregnancy test should be performed. The sooner an ectopic pregnancy is discovered, the better the chances of recovery. The early nonsurgical diagnosis of ectopic pregnancy, coupled with improved treatment options, constitute a major advance in obstetrics.

A positive pregnancy test in the presence of any unusual pain or bleeding warrants a pelvic examination and a transvaginal sonogram. When symptoms suggest an ectopic pregnancy, but a urine pregnancy test is negative, a blood test for hCG should be performed. As the level of hCG in ectopic pregnancy ordinarily is lower than usual, even very accurate urine tests may not be able to detect the hCG. The blood test picks up lower levels of hCG than the urine test can identify.

On pelvic examination, a mass may be felt in the area of the fallopian tube, making the diagnosis of ectopic pregnancy very likely with a positive pregnancy test. There may be pain in the tubal area, or pain when the cervix is moved—called *cervical motion tenderness*. However, due to the influence of the pregnancy hormones, the uterus may be softened and enlarged, as in an intrauterine pregnancy, and the mass in the tube too small to feel. A normal pelvic examination thus does not eliminate the possibility of an ectopic pregnancy.

As noted in Chapter 8, the early embryo can be seen with transvaginal ultrasound by 5½ to 6 weeks of pregnancy (1½ to 2 weeks after a missed period). If an embryo is found outside the uterus at the same time that the uterus is seen to be empty, the diagnosis of ectopic pregnancy is made. If nothing suggests pregnancy in the uterus, but pregnancy is not detected elsewhere, ectopic pregnancy is possible, but the ultrasound cannot be considered definitive. Often a sonogram can show blood in the pelvis, a highly suggestive finding.

Newer ultrasound techniques available in major medical centers have been utilized in the early diagnosis of ectopic pregnancies. These include *pulsed Doppler flow ultrasonography*, which shows patterns of blood flow. Patterns consistent with placental blood flow can be demonstrated outside of the uterus even when a fetal sac cannot be seen. This technique requires very expensive equipment and highly skilled practitioners.

On a very rare occasion a pregnancy exists in the uterus along with an ectopic pregnancy. These unusual pregnancies are called *heterotopic pregnancies*. They are reported to occur in anywhere from 1 in 4,000 to 1 in 20,000 pregnancies. Heterotopic pregnancies may be missed if the sonographer does not look beyond the intrauterine pregnancy.

Because ectopic implantation occurs in tissues unsuited for a pregnancy, the level of hCG in the mother's blood does not rise at the rate anticipated with an intrauterine pregnancy. If there is doubt about whether a pregnancy is ectopic or not, the concentration of hCG in the blood can be measured every 48 hours. This is called *quantitative serial hCG measurement*. The value should increase by at least 66 percent in these 48 hours or double in 72 hours. If it does not, then the suspicion of ectopic pregnancy rises, regardless of the sonographic findings. Low hCG values or values that do not rise at the expected rate may indicate a threatened or inevitable miscarriage rather than an ectopic pregnancy. These are discussed in Chapter 14.

A number of other tests may be performed to help make a diagnosis or determine appropriate treatment. Blood tests include measurements of hemoglobin and hematocrit. With significant blood loss these values can be reduced. Some physicians measure the level of progesterone in the blood. Low values are associated with a *problem pregnancy*—one that will result in a miscarriage or may be ectopic. Physicians do not agree on the usefulness of measuring progesterone. The white blood cell count may or may not be increased in an ectopic pregnancy and may be included in an overall workup.

When there is bleeding into the peritoneal cavity from rupture of an ectopic pregnancy, suggested by symptoms of severe pain and vaginal bleeding, blood in the peritoneal cavity can be demonstrated by a procedure known as *culdocentesis*. The part of the vagina behind the cervix is directly in front of a pouch of the peritoneal cavity, which comes down behind the uterus. This is known as the *cul-de-sac*, or pouch, *of Douglas*. Using a needle similar to the one used to draw blood from the arm, an attempt is made to draw fluid from the cul-de-sac. If the withdrawn fluid contains blood that does not clot, this means there has been hemorrhage in the peritoneal space. Combined with other compatible findings, this confirms the ectopic pregnancy.

With accurate sonography and measurements of hCG, culdocentesis is used less than it used to be. In fact, the goal today is to find an ectopic pregnancy before it ruptures—eliminating the need for this procedure.

On occasion a physician may perform *curettage*—a scraping of the uterine cavity. This is done to differentiate between an incomplete abortion or miscarriage and an ectopic pregnancy. If the scraping reveals tissue of embryonic, fetal, or placental origin, then it is not an ectopic pregnancy. This might be particularly helpful if the symptoms are present earlier than a sonogram is able to show a gestational sac. This will not be done if there is any possibility of a viable intrauterine pregnancy that the woman wants to keep.

The most accurate diagnosis of ectopic pregnancy comes from actually viewing the pelvic organs. This is usually accomplished via *laparoscopy*. Some people call laparoscopy the "belly button operation." In this technique a very small telescope-like instrument is placed through a tiny incision just below the navel. A laparoscopy can also be used to remove the ectopic pregnancy. Laparoscopy requires general anesthesia to ensure that the woman is relaxed sufficiently.

In the presence of heavy bleeding or previous infection with adhesions, even laparoscopy may not allow an accurate diagnosis. In these cases, *laparotomy*—an operation with a larger incision into the abdominal cavity—is needed. Usually, the incision can be made just above the pubic hair line. A laparotomy is necessary if the woman comes for care in the midst of a massive hemorrhage, possibly in shock. This then is a life-saving operation.

Treatment of Ectopic Pregnancy

The mainstay of treatment for ectopic pregnancy has been surgery. Today, some ectopic pregnancies can be treated with medications that cause the embryo to stop growing and reabsorb into the maternal tissues. Ectopic pregnancies sometimes cure themselves, when the embryo becomes reabsorbed without medication. On occasion an ectopic pregnancy can be watched for a short period of time to see if it can resolve. This is called *expectant management*, and requires careful monitoring.

The following discussion of treatment for ectopic pregnancy assumes the pregnancy is in the fallopian tube, as this is most common, accounting for about 95 percent of all ectopic pregnancies. When the pregnancy is located in another organ, the treatment will vary somewhat.

The choice of treatment for an ectopic pregnancy will depend on how early in the pregnancy the ectopic is found and how large it is. It will depend on where in the tube the pregnancy is found—whether it is in the part that attaches near the uterus or the part distant from the uterus, near the open end of the tube. Treatment will depend on whether or not the ectopic pregnancy has ruptured out of the tube. It will depend on the extent of bleeding the woman has experienced and whether she is in shock. It will depend on the experience and preference of the physician providing the care. Treatment may depend somewhat on whether the woman desires future fertility, although preservation of her life must be the main consideration.

Surgical treatments for ectopic pregnancy may be performed via a laparoscopy or laparotomy. Oxygen, intravenous fluids, and possibly blood transfusion may be components of needed care.

Salpingectomy and *salpingostomy* are the surgical procedures used to actually remove the ectopic pregnancy. Salpingectomy means removal of the fallopian tube. Salpingostomy (or salpingotomy) means making an incision in the tube through which the pregnancy is removed. Part of the tube may be removed, with repair accomplished at a later date, after healing has taken place. Salpingostomy is called "conservative" treatment as it saves the tube.

The method of surgical removal depends on the extent of damage to the tube. It also may depend on whether the opposite tube appears normal or diseased and whether the woman wishes to have future pregnancies. A procedure in which the pregnancy was "milked" out of the tube used to be performed if the pregnancy had not ruptured, but recent findings indicate that this procedure results in a very high rate of repeat ectopic pregnancy.

If the other tube appears diseased, then surgery that spares the tube containing the ectopic will increase the likelihood that the woman will be able to get pregnant again and carry the pregnancy. After such conservative surgery, however, there is also a higher risk of a repeat ectopic pregnancy. If the other tube appears normal, then future fertility is likely to be the same whether a salpingectomy or salpingostomy is performed.

Since 1985, medications have provided an alternative to surgery for treatment of ectopic pregnancy. Several medications have been used, most frequently *methotrexate*—an anticancer drug. Methotrexate works by inhibiting growth of the embryonic cells, in much the same way as it stops growth of cancer cells.

Methotrexate can be used only when the ectopic pregnancy has not ruptured and when the diagnosis was made without surgery. The woman must not show any noticeable signs of blood loss. Her blood values, such as hematocrit and hemoglobin, must be normal and stable. The mass in the tube cannot be larger than three to four centimeters (less than two inches). The woman must be able and willing to return for follow-up care. She must not have medical reasons that make methotrexate dangerous or contraindicated. Such contraindications include breast-feeding; diseases of the blood, liver, kidney, lung, or immune system; alcoholism; peptic ulcer disease; or a known allergy to methotrexate.

Methotrexate is given as an injection either into the muscle or into the veins. It also can be placed via injection through the vagina directly into the fallopian tube. Women who receive methotrexate must contact their physicians immediately if they show signs of rupture: vaginal bleeding, abdominal or shoulder pain, weakness, dizziness, rapid heart beat, or faintness. Alcohol must be avoided during methotrexate treatment and folic acid cannot be taken as a supplement or in multivitamins, as it decreases the body's response to the methotrexate. Sexual intercourse should be avoided until there are no detectable levels of hCG in the blood.

Follow-up After Treatment

A small percentage of women have a persistent ectopic pregnancy after tube-sparing treatment. The blood is tested for hCG levels at frequent intervals following surgical or medical treatment. If the levels do not drop appropriately, additional methotrexate or surgery will be needed.

Following salpingostomy, tubal healing takes at least 3 months. A woman who has had this procedure should not get pregnant during that time. With any of the treatments used, sonogram and quantitative levels of hCG should be performed early in the next pregnancy to make sure it is not ectopic.

Rh-negative women should have an injection of RhoGAM after an ectopic pregnancy, unless they are already sensitized or certain that the father of the baby is also Rh-negative.

Future Fertility After an Ectopic Pregnancy

About 60 to 80 percent of women treated for ectopic pregnancy are able to get pregnant again. The risk of infertility is greater in women who have damage in the tube that did not contain the ectopic pregnancy. Among the pregnancies that occur after an ectopic pregnancy, approximately 15 percent are again ectopic. When a woman has had two or more ectopic pregnancies her chances of ever having a term pregnancy are less than 50 percent no matter what efforts have been made to save her tubes.

With a high index of suspicion and early diagnosis, the risks to the woman, should a repetition of ectopic pregnancy occur, are not very great. The decision whether to try for another pregnancy after an ectopic has to be personal. Some women choose *in vitro fertilization* (IVF) after an ectopic pregnancy, especially after repeated ectopic pregnancies. When there is destruction of both tubes, for whatever reason, women can also turn to IVF. IVF is described in Chapter 13.

An ectopic pregnancy can be a traumatic experience. The personal implications may be lost in the medical efforts to save the woman's life, especially if the diagnosis is made in the condition of severe hemorrhage and shock. Grieving is normal. The parents grieve the loss of a potential child, just as parents grieve after any miscarriage. There may be additional grief over the possibility of reduced fertility and the risk of another ectopic pregnancy.

Discuss your feelings with your partner, your family, your friends. Discuss them with your physician or midwife. Many hospitals have bereavement teams who will work with you, giving you the opportunity to express yourself. Support groups of other women or families who have had similar losses may be therapeutic. If necessary, you can get a referral for in-depth individual or couple counseling. Do not allow yourself to become depressed without seeking help. Grief and sorrow are normal reactions following this loss, but knowing how normal these feelings are should not deter you from seeking help.

314 PREGNANCY, BIRTH & FAMILY PLANNING

HYPEREMESIS GRAVIDARUM

Unlike the nausea and vomiting of the first trimester of pregnancy which is seen in up to half of all pregnant women, *hyperemesis gravidarum* is a rare complication in which the nausea and vomiting are severe and continue past the first trimester. Hyperemesis gravidarum can lead to weight loss, dehydration, and imbalances in the body's necessary chemicals—called an *electrolyte imbalance*. It can lead to serious changes in the *pH of the blood*—how acid or alkaline it is. These effects can be life threatening if not treated. Hyperemesis gravidarum can cause changes in liver function and result in jaundice (yellowing of the skin).

Hyperemesis gravidarum is treatable. All its associated problems can be corrected. However, the condition can be serious enough to warrant hospitalization and special intravenous feeding, although sometimes it can be managed with intravenous fluid replacement without hospitalization.

The cause of hyperemesis gravidarum is not known. For many years, it was believed to be due to ambivalence about the pregnancy, but that belief has been discarded. There is some evidence that hormone levels are unusually high in hyperemesis but the reason for nausea and vomiting with high hormone levels is not clear. Because sometimes a woman's vomiting subsides when she is in the hospital only to recur when she is discharged, there is speculation that social problems at home play a role in causing hyperemesis gravidarum. Again, this is not proven. However, social services and psychological counseling can be beneficial if you have hyperemesis.

Hyperemesis gravidarum can subside and recur throughout pregnancy, requiring repeated hospitalizations. The physician should look for other pathologic causes of the vomiting such as gastroenteritis, hepatitis, ulcer, or disorders of the gall bladder, kidney, or pancreas. For some women, the condition returns in subsequent pregnancies. At the least, it makes pregnancy less than an enjoyable experience.

If you have severe nausea and vomiting for a short period of time, try to sip fluids throughout the day. If at any time in pregnancy you are unable to hold down any food for 24 hours, you must contact your physician or midwife. The treatment may be as simple as getting some fluids via an intravenous line in the care provider's office or as extensive as prolonged hospitalization. Treatment depends on the extent of symptoms and the results of urine and blood tests to determine your electrolyte balance.

HYDATIDIFORM MOLE

Hydatidiform mole is also called *molar pregnancy*. This is a rare complication, occuring in approximately 1 in 1,000 pregnancies in the United States and Europe. It is more frequent in parts of Asia. In this condition, the chorionic villi of pregnancy are converted into a mass of grapelike cysts. (Greek: *ydatis* = a drop of water; Latin: *forma* = form.) In a complete mole, there is no embryonic or fetal tissue. In a partial mole, there will be fetal tissue. On an extremely rare occasion, a twin pregnancy may result in one viable fetus and one mole. Such pregnancies have gone to term with the birth of a normal baby, but this is extraordinarily rare.

Hydatidiform mole is most frequent in women at either end of the childbearing years—young adolescents and women over the age of 45. There is a ten times higher chance of having a molar pregnancy if you get pregnant at age 45 than there is if you get pregnant at a younger age. Molar pregnancies have been seen in women at the age of 50, whereas a normal pregnancy at that age is practically unknown, except with assisted reproductive technologies (see Chapter 13). Molar pregnancy recurs about 1 to 2 percent of the time.

Signs of a molar pregnancy include persistent nausea and vomiting, bleeding occurring at about the twelfth week of pregnancy or earlier, a uterus larger than expected for the dates of the pregnancy, and absence of a fetal heartbeat or fetal activity, even though the uterine size suggests that the fetal heart should be heard and the woman should feel movement. A characteristic sign of a molar pregnancy is the development of pregnancy-induced hypertension or preeclampsia in the first half of pregnancy. This is ordinarily a condition of the second half of pregnancy, usually not occurring before 24 weeks gestation. It is described later in this chapter, under the heading "Pregnancy-Induced Hypertension." Some women with molar pregnancies develop anemia.

When a woman presents with these symptoms, a blood test for human chorionic gonadotropin (hCG) is ordered along with a sonogram. The hCG levels will be unusually high in the presence of a molar pregnancy. Ultrasound identifies the characteristic grapelike mass quite accurately.

The treatment for hydatidiform mole is termination of the pregnancy, using the techniques for abortion described in Chapter 28. As this is a pregnancy loss, consider seeking support and counseling.

Although hydatidiform mole is not a life-threatening condition, in about 20 percent of cases it can progress to a malignant tumor. This is called a *gestational trophoblastic tumor*. One type of tumor is a rapidly growing malignancy called *choriocarcinoma*.

All women with a molar pregnancy should be evaluated after the pregnancy for evidence of a gestational trophoblastic tumor. The follow-up visit consists of measuring hCG levels in the blood at frequent intervals until they return to normal. Right after termination, hCG is measured at 2-week intervals. Once the levels are undetectable, which usually occurs within 3 months, they can be measured every month for 6 months and then every other month for a complete year. Pregnancy should be avoided until at least a year has elapsed without elevated hCG in blood. If the hCG levels do not regress, or if they rise after the molar pregnancy has been terminated, then further treatment is required.

Signs of disease spread should be looked for. A chest X ray is done, for example. If further childbearing is not desired, treatment may consist of a hysterectomy. If the woman wishes to preserve her reproductive capability, then chemotherapy is the treatment of choice. Chemotherapy may be needed following hysterectomy if the disease has spread. Whenever possible, gestational trophoblastic tumors should be treated by specialists experienced in their care.

PLACENTA PREVIA AND ABRUPTIO PLACENTAE (PREMATURE SEPARATION OF THE PLACENTA)

Placenta previa and abruptio placentae are conditions in which the placenta either implants in a dangerous place (*previa*) or separates from the uterus before the baby is born (*abruptio*). Either can be a danger for mother and fetus, but with prompt recognition, their consequences can be minimized with mother and child both remaining healthy.

These two conditions occur infrequently. Each happens about once in 200 pregnancies. The main symptom in both is vaginal bleeding. With placenta previa, the bleeding typically is painless.

Placenta Previa

In placenta previa, the placenta is situated low down in the uterus and part of it overlaps the mouth of the womb (the *cervix*). Imagine the uterus as a large inverted bottle. Ordinarily, the placenta implants high up inside the bottle, usually on the back of the bottle, less often on the front. With placenta previa, however, it is so low down that part, or all, of the bottle's opening is covered by it.

Late in pregnancy, preparatory to labor, the cervix expands slightly and any placental tissue that overlies it is torn loose, leaving a raw area from which the woman bleeds. The more completely the cervix is covered, the earlier in pregnancy the bleeding is likely to begin.

There are three types of placenta previa, depending on how much of the cervical opening (the *os*) the placenta covers:

- **Central or total placenta previa:** placenta covers all of the cervical opening
- **Partial placenta previa:** placenta covers only part of the cervical opening
- **Marginal placenta previa:** placenta is at the margin, or edge, of the cervical os

Among these three types of placenta previa, the most common is a marginal placenta previa. There is also a condition called a *low-lying placenta*, in which the placenta is right next to the cervical os, but doesn't actually reach it.

Placenta previa is uncommon in a first pregnancy and increasingly more common with additional gestations. As women grow older they are more likely to have a placenta previa. Placenta previa is also more common in women who have had a previous cesarean birth. Other possible risks for a placenta previa include multiple pregnancy, a prior placenta previa, a previous induced abortion, and smoking.

Every woman who bleeds in the latter half of pregnancy merits prompt attention. Near term, a small amount of bleeding associated with mucus is likely to be the bloody show of the onset of labor rather than anything of serious consequence. However, if the woman has painless bleeding late in the second trimester or anytime in the third trimester, especially without warning, a placenta previa must be suspected. Ultrasound is an extremely effective means of localizing the placenta. A vaginal examination should not be performed as this may cause a disruption in the placenta, triggering severe bleeding.

When a complete placenta previa is diagnosed, the woman usually stays in the hospital. Blood tests for anemia will be performed and the fetus will be monitored carefully as described in Chapter 17. If the fetus is not mature, an attempt will be made to postpone delivery until at least 37 weeks gestation.

When a baby dies due to placenta previa, it is almost always because of prematurity. We have therefore learned to carry such pregnancies as far as possible with bed rest, careful monitoring, and avoiding pelvic examination. Any sign of hemorrhage or fetal distress, however, will be a reason for delivery. Women with total placenta previa must have a cesarean birth, although with a partial or marginal previa, a vaginal birth may be possible.

A woman with a partial, or marginal, previa who is not bleeding actively usually will not be admitted to the hospital. If admitted with bleeding, she probably will be sent home once the bleeding has stopped, unless she has lost so much blood as to be severely anemic. She must not put anything into her vagina, including douches, medications, fingers, or a penis. She must avoid orgasm, which can cause uterine contractions that may result in bleeding. The woman should also stay on bed rest, to decrease pressure at the placental site.

Bed rest is very hard to maintain as you generally will not feel sick with a placenta previa (or other conditions for which bed rest may be prescribed—see, for example, "Pregnancy-Induced Hypertension," below, Chapter 15 on premature labor, and Chapter 23 on multiple gestation). The box that follows gives suggestions for coping with bed rest.

It is interesting to note that many placentas that obstruct the cervix early in pregnancy may no longer do so as the pregnancy progresses. This is called *placental migration*, and occurs commonly. In fact, if an early sonogram shows a low-lying placenta, there is no reason to repeat the sonogram unless bleeding occurs. If a sonogram performed because of bleeding showed a placenta previa in early pregnancy, it should be repeated to see if the previa resolves itself later in the pregnancy.

The circulating blood volume in a pregnant woman is considerably increased and she will therefore tolerate amounts of bleeding that would produce serious difficulty in a nonpregnant adult. Nevertheless, if signs of *hypovolemia* (insufficient blood in the vascular system) are present, the woman will need intravenous fluids with the possibility of blood transfusion. Remember—the mother, not the fetus, is bleeding. Fetal welfare, however, depends on the efficiency of the mother's circulation.

An occasional complication of a placenta previa is called a *placenta accreta*. In this rare condition, the placenta remains adherent to the uterine wall after delivery. This may necessitate a hysterectomy (removal of the uterus) at the time of delivery. If it isn't causing bleeding, however, it can sometimes be left in place to reabsorb into the maternal tissues over time.

Tips for Dealing with Bed Rest

1. Find out from your physician or midwife whether you are on complete bed rest, which means using a bed pan and taking bed baths, or whether you can get up to go to the bathroom (the more likely scenario) and take a shower. Find out if you can sit in a chair for part of the day. A rocking chair provides some exercise for your legs as you rock back and forth so this may be especially good for you. If you sit in a regular chair, always elevate your legs.

2. To set your mind at ease, find someone to help with household chores and childcare, if you have a child or children. This can be your partner, a relative, a friend, or someone you hire, if you can afford it. Some insurance plans will pay for a home health attendant who will help with some chores, but probably not all. Check with your health insurance company. You may need to be creative and enlist the help of several people. Do not be afraid to ask. You need and deserve help.

3. Find out whether your health insurance will pay for a nurse to visit several times a week. This is to monitor your health status, not to do household chores.

4. Don't lie flat on your back. Prop yourself up on pillows or lie on your side. Change positions frequently.

5. Do some simple exercises in bed, especially if you are on complete bed rest. These include bending and straightening your legs, circling your ankles, flexing and extending your feet and toes. Do deep breathing exercises several times a day.

6. Follow the same healthful diet as you would if you were not on bed rest (see Chapter 10).

7. Read, watch videos. Develop a hobby. If you knit, crochet, or sew by hand, make things for the baby. Make things for yourself. Make things for your partner. Learn something new that can be done in bed—embroidery, needlepoint, or macrame, for example.

8. Shop for the baby by catalog or on the internet, if you can sit up or have a laptop computer to bring into your bed. Join a chat room for pregnant women or new parents.

9. Read books about childbirth, especially if bed rest means

you will miss your childbirth education classes. Practice relaxation techniques. Have someone make a birth visualization tape for you (see Chapter 19) and listen to it frequently.

10. Try to remember that you are on bed rest because it is the best thing for your baby. And remember, too, that all pregnancies end. The bed rest won't be forever.

(Some information for this box was adapted from "When Your Doctor Orders Bed Rest," by Sherry L. M. Jimenez, RN, in *Childbirth*, A Cahners Publication, 1993.)

Abruptio Placentae

Premature separation of the placenta, also referred to by its technical name, *abruptio placentae* or placental abruption, is the disruption of a part or all of the placenta from its normal attachment in the uterus prior to the birth of the child. It is a cause of vaginal bleeding. Separation occurs in much the same way the placenta separates and delivers after birth but, since an abruption cuts the placenta off from the maternal blood supply before the baby is born and breathing, it is extraordinarily hazardous to the fetus.

In some cases of placental abruption, bleeding occurs in the space between the placenta and the uterine wall. The blood becomes trapped there and does not come through the cervix into the vagina, so that there is no visible bleeding. In such cases, pain and faintness are variable. The uterus, instead of being soft, may be tense and irritable, rigid and tender to touch. Because there is no obvious bleeding, diagnosis may not occur until a lot of blood has been lost.

Sometimes the separation and bleeding coincide with the onset of labor. The diagnosis of abruption may only be made then because there is otherwise unexplained evidence of fetal distress.

Placental abruption is less likely in a first pregnancy and more likely with increased age of the mother. It is seen more frequently among African-American women than among Caucasian or Latin-American women. The most common risk factor is high blood pressure—either chronic high blood pressure or pregnancy-induced high blood pressure. If the membranes rupture prematurely, there is a higher likelihood of an abruptio. This appears to be due to the sudden decrease in the volume of the uterus. A similar phenomenon can occur after the birth of a first twin so that abruptio is sometimes seen between the birth of the two twins. Both cigarette smoking and cocaine use are associated with abruption. A fibroid tumor of the uterus, if it is located behind the site where the placenta implants, may predispose to abruption. Having had an abruption makes one in a subsequent pregnancy more likely. Trauma to the uterus may cause abruption. A deficiency of folic acid has been suggested as a possible risk factor, but this is disputed.

The treatment of the woman thought to have a placental abruption begins with admission to the hospital. A sonogram usually is performed when there is vaginal bleeding, but may not show an abruption. Sometimes a clot behind the placenta will be apparent on sonogram, but the absence of this finding does not mean there is not an abruption.

The treatment for abruptio placentae usually is delivery. The exception to this might be in the case of an abruption in a premature fetus if the bleeding is well controlled. The mother and fetus must be carefully monitored in that instance—with delivery accomplished anytime there is renewed bleeding or signs of fetal or maternal distress. If the fetus is alive and labor is well under way, vaginal delivery may be anticipated. The mother will need intravenous fluids and on occasion may need blood transfusion. If the fetus is alive but shows evidence of distress, cesarean delivery is appropriate. If the fetus is no longer alive, a vaginal birth is preferable. It may be hastened by the appropriate use of agents to stimulate the labor (see Chapter 22).

The prognosis for the mother with abruption is quite good. The maternal mortality from this cause of hemorrhage is small, although the mother may require treatment for shock or anemia. The fetal loss is unfortunately much greater and accounts for a significant number of fetal deaths. However, with rapid diagnosis and prompt attention, a favorable outcome for both mother and baby can be anticipated.

POLYHYDRAMNIOS AND OLIGOHYDRAMNIOS (INCREASED AND DECREASED AMNIOTIC FLUID)

Polyhydramnios and *oligohydramnios* refer to increased and reduced amounts of amniotic fluid, respectively (Greek: *poly* = much; *oligo* = little). Polydramnios often is called *hydramnios*. These conditions can result from certain complications of pregnancy or might themselves cause complications. They can be suspected on abdominal examination and confirmed with sonogram.

Polyhydramnios

The uterus usually contains about a liter of fluid at 36 weeks gestation—the beginning of the ninth month. (A liter is just over a quart.) After 36 weeks, the amount of fluid decreases somewhat. In mild polyhydramnios, 2 or 3 liters are seen; in severe polyhydramnios the uterus may contain up to 15 liters of fluid. Polyhydramnios may have a sudden or gradual onset.

Polyhydramnios is present with a number of fetal malformations. Its presence prompts a sonogram to look for such conditions. The anomalies include disorders in which extra fluid leaks from the fetus, such as open neural tube defects (see Chapter 5), or where there is extra fetal urination due to defects such as those of the nervous system. Polyhydramnios also may occur in anomalies in which the fetus cannot swallow, such as a condition called *esophageal atresia*. In this condition, the esophagus, a tube in the digestive system that provides a passage from the throat to the stomach, is closed off. Excess amniotic fluid may be seen with twin pregnancies or with diabetes, for unknown reasons.

Polyhydramnios may cause a variety of obstetrical complications including malpresentation of the fetus (see Chapter 5), abruptio placentae (see above), poor uterine contractions in labor, a prolapse of the umbilical cord (see Chapter 21), and postpartum hemorrhage, which is more likely to occur whenever the uterus is overdistended.

A woman with polyhydramnios may complain of abdominal discomfort, back ache, swelling of the legs and vulva, nausea and vomiting, and difficulty breathing. On examination, the uterus will be larger than it should be for the gestational age, the uterine wall may be tense, the fetal parts difficult to feel, and the fetal heart hard or impossible to hear.

Mild polyhydramnios does not require treatment. Severe hydramnios may be treated with a slow removal of amniotic fluid via an amniocentesis. This carries a risk of premature labor, so it is something to discuss carefully with your physician. The main reason for this treatment is to relieve the mother's discomfort. Mother and fetus are carefully monitored during amniocentesis. At birth the newborn always will be examined thoroughly for anomalies.

Oligohydramnios

Like polyhydramnios, oligohydramnios may occur when there is a fetal abnormality. When the uterus measures smaller than expected for gestational age or when the examiner feels an absence of fluid, a sonogram will be performed to confirm the condition of oligohydramnios and to look for related fetal anomalies. Disorders in which the fetus cannot urinate, such as obstruction of the urinary tract or a failure of the kidneys to develop (*kidney agenesis*), result in oligohydramnios. Oligohydramnios may be present when the fetus is not growing properly or when there is an abruption of the placenta. A leak in the fetal membranes will cause oligohydramnios, but will also most often be followed shortly by labor.

Oligohydramnios early in pregnancy may cause normal fetuses to develop anomalies because of the loss of the protective effect of the fluid or because, without the fluid to act as a barrier, the membranes can adhere to the fetal parts. Oligohydramnios may result in incomplete development of the fetal lungs, called *pulmonary hypoplasia*.

Oligohydramnios may occur in a *postdates pregnancy*—one that has continued 2 or more weeks beyond the due date. In this case, it portends the possibility of fetal distress in labor as the cord is subject to undue compression without the cushioning effect of sufficient fluid. Assessment of amniotic fluid volume is an important component of late pregnancy fetal testing (see Chapter 17). In some cases of oligohydramnios, an amnioinfusion is done in labor. This is the replacement of fluid into the amniotic sac, discussed in Chapter 22. As with polyhydramnios, the newborn will be examined carefully to check for anomalies.

PREGNANCY-INDUCED HYPERTENSION (PIH OR TOXEMIA)

Toxemia of pregnancy is a very old term to describe high blood pressure or an increase in blood pressure that was elevated before pregnancy. It occurs in the latter half of pregnancy and is accompanied by protein in the urine and excess water in the tissues. The word "toxemia" is derived from Greek roots meaning poison and blood. It suggests that the condition is a kind of poisoning that arises from the pregnancy. Medical researchers have been searching for over 100 years for confirmation of such a poison. None has ever been identified, despite all sorts of studies. Abnormal amounts of some regular components appear in the blood of women with toxemia, but no new substances have been found. A host of culprits has been suspected but the evidence for any one of them is weak. Toxemia thus remains a disease of theories.

A Note on Excessive Weight Gain and Salt in PIH

For a long time it was thought that excessive weight gain and excessive intake of salt had a causal relationship to toxemia of pregnancy. Weight gain actually is not a cause but a consequence of the disease, reflecting the abnormal accumulation of water in the tissues of women with PIH. Even in the presence of acute disease, the kidneys excrete the salt that is in excess of the body's need. Salt plays no causative role in toxemia. Thus, there is no merit in limiting salt intake while pregnant. Diuretics (water pills) that cause loss of water and salt do not have a place in the treatment of PIH. They neither prevent nor cure it, and may dangerously reduce blood flow to the placenta.

Today, the most accurate terminology for what was previously called toxemia is the *hypertensive disorders of pregnancy*. Three main categories of disorders fall into this broad classification. Hypertensive disorders are those in which blood pressure is elevated. In pregnancy, these are:

1. Pregnancy-induced hypertension
2. Pregnancy-aggravated hypertension
3. Coincidental hypertension

Coincidental Hypertension

Coincidental hypertension is elevated blood pressure that existed before the pregnancy, or persists afterward, implying that the condition is not related to the pregnancy. Women with elevated blood pressure may have an increase of pregnancy complications, including abruptio placentae or poor growth of the fetus. They do not have toxemia of pregnancy or a pregnancy-related disease, although they may develop one.

Pregnancy-Induced Hypertension

Pregnancy-induced hypertension is elevated blood pressure caused by the pregnancy. Within this category are three subcategories:

1. Hypertension without protein in the urine (*proteinuria*) or swelling (*edema*), except for edema of the lower extremities—the legs, ankles, and feet—which is not considered pathological. This has also been called *transient hypertension*.
2. *Preeclampsia*—hypertension with proteinuria and/or edema. Preeclampsia may be further categorized as mild or severe.

3. *Eclampsia*—hypertension with proteinuria and/or edema and convulsions.

Pregnancy-Aggravated Hypertension

Pregnancy-aggravated hypertension is, in essence, a combination of the other two categories: preexisting hypertension that is worsened by pregnancy. The two subcategories of pregnancy-aggravated hypertension are *superimposed preeclampsia* and *superimposed eclampsia*.

Pregnancy-induced hypertension (PIH) most often occurs in women pregnant for the first time. Older women are at greater risk for pregnancy-aggravated hypertension as they are more likely to have preexisting high blood pressure. Women with twins are more likely to develop pregnancy-induced hypertension, as are women with hydatidiform mole. Although PIH is a condition of late pregnancy rarely seen before 24 weeks gestation, women with hydatidiform moles develop pregnancy-induced hypertension before 20 weeks of pregnancy.

Theories have abounded over the years regarding the cause of PIH. The disorder has been thought to be a disease of the immune system, a genetic disease, an infectious disease, and a disease of dietary deficiency. An inadequate intake of protein has been blamed, though never proven. Calcium deficiency has been implicated as a cause of PIH. Whether the deficiency is because of low intake or poor absorption is not clear. High-dose calcium supplements in the second half of pregnancy have been shown to prevent hypertension in pregnancy, although not in all studies. Researchers continue the quest to find a cause for PIH.

While the cause of PIH remains elusive, some aspects of the disease process have been uncovered. Spasm of the small blood vessels throughout the body is believed to be a prime cause of the disease manifestations. The vascular system adjusts to this vasospasm by increasing blood pressure in order to maintain blood flow to vital organs. There is then leakage of water from the vessels into the tissues and leakage of protein into the urine. This increased fluid in the body tissues leads to the edema, sometimes severe.

Because of vasospasm, women with PIH do not have the expanded blood volume seen in normal pregnancy. Blood loss at delivery is less tolerated in women with PIH because they lack this extra blood.

One potentially dangerous consequence of PIH is a decrease in the number of circulating platelets. Platelets, also called *thrombocytes*, are cells involved in blood clotting. A very low platelet count, called *thrombocytopenia*, is often a sign of severe disease.

Ultimately, PIH affects most body systems. It affects blood flow to the fetus and can result in severe fetal problems. In recent years a syndrome called *HELLP* has been identified. Some experts believe this is a description of severe preeclampsia while others consider it a separate entity. HELLP stands for Hemolysis, Elevated Liver enzymes, and Low Platelets. Hemolysis is the destruction of blood cells, elevated liver enzymes indicate a disorder of liver function, and the low platelets interfere with the ability of the blood to clot.

There does not seem to be much we can do to prevent PIH. The disease does not tend to reappear in subsequent pregnancies. Many experts believe that recurrent PIH is really a form of chronic hypertension. When PIH occurs in a woman with chronic hypertension, the hypertension persists through future pregnancies and pregnancy-aggravated hypertension remains a risk.

Pregnancy-induced hypertension is still a major complication of obstetrics, whose detection quite properly justifies all the efforts we make in prenatal care. Fortunately, the women who experience PIH rarely suffer long-term injury. The newborns, once they are delivered in good condition, do not exhibit any aftereffects.

Preeclampsia and Eclampsia

Preeclampsia and eclampsia run in families, although the exact mode of inheritance is unknown. Overall, as many as 5 percent of pregnancies may show preeclampsia. Fortunately, eclampsia is now rare. One recent textbook cited a drop in incidence in a hospital with a large obstetric population from 1 in 1,150 deliveries between 1983 and 1986 to 1 in 2,300 deliveries in 1990 and 1991. The reduced incidence of eclampsia can be attributed to widespread prenatal care, allowing for early recognition of preeclampsia with treatment that prevents it from progressing to eclampsia.

The early symptoms of preeclampsia often are silent. Women do not feel their hypertension or know they have protein in their urine. The only symptom they may notice at first is swelling, especially of the hands and the face. Sudden and unusual weight gain is also a noticeable symptom of the disease, due to the increased fluid retained by the body tissues, without any relationship to diet or fat deposits. The diagnosis usually is made at a routine prenatal visit. A blood pressure of 140/100 or higher is considered indicative of PIH, although it may not indicate preeclampsia.

Once an increase in blood pressure is identified, the urine is tested for protein and the body examined for fluid retention. Bloods for kidney and liver function usually are drawn so that they can be used as a baseline should the disease get worse. A *complete blood count* (CBC) to check for hemoglobin and hematocrit and platelets is performed. The hemoglobin and hematocrit may be elevated, indicating a condition called *hemoconcentration*, seen when the blood volume is reduced. If the woman has not been tested for diabetes and an ultrasound not yet performed, both should be done. In fact, they will likely be repeated even if they were performed previously. The ultrasound will check for fetal growth and multiple pregnancy. Additional tests to monitor the fetal condition will be set up (see Chapter 17).

The first step in treatment for preeclampsia is bed rest. A diet with adequate calories, protein, and fluid is important. If the woman has chronic hypertension, she already may be on antihypertensive medications and possibly a low-salt diet. Otherwise, the salt in her diet should not be restricted and antihypertensive medications may or may not be prescribed.

A woman with early signs of preeclampsia will return to have her blood pressure checked, usually in less than a week. If her pressure is back to normal, she needs to continue to rest and to be watched at frequent intervals. If blood pressure remains the same, with no other signs of worsening disease, the woman can continue to stay at home on bed rest with close monitoring of her condition and of the fetus. If the blood pressure increases, hospitalization becomes necessary.

While at home, if any symptoms appear that might indicate worsening disease, the woman should immediately contact her care provider. These symptoms include headache; visual disturbances such as flashing lights or spots in front of the eyes or blurred or double vision; and pain in the upper abdomen, referred to as *epigastric pain.*

Once a woman is hospitalized, her urine will be checked for protein and creatinine. These chemicals are indicators of kidney function and may signal worsening disease. The most useful values come from a 24-hour urine. This can be collected at home, but the woman must make certain to collect every bit of her urine for 24 hours. In the hospital, the woman's intake and output will be measured as a decrease in urine flow is another indicator of worsening preeclampsia. Bloods will be drawn frequently for platelets and liver and kidney function (also called *blood chemistries* or a SMAC test). The fetus will continue to be monitored frequently.

The woman hospitalized with preeclampsia will stay on bed rest, lying on her left side as much as possible. This is intended to take the weight of the pregnant uterus off the major blood vessels on the back wall of the abdominal cavity, with the immediate effect of improving blood flow to the kidneys and loss of excess body water in the form of urine. Weight and edema will be checked frequently. Reflexes in a woman's legs and arms will also be checked as increasingly brisk reflexes (as when your leg shoots out rapidly when your knee is tapped) are another indicator of worsening disease. Intravenous fluids may be part of treatment, but fluids have to be given carefully so as not to overload a circulatory system that cannot tolerate them. A tube to collect urine (a *urinary catheter*) may be placed if urine output is insufficient.

The only cure for preeclampsia is delivery. If the baby is mature and the cervix is ready, labor may be induced. If the cervix is not ready, then whether or not to attempt to induce labor will depend on the severity of the disease and evidence of fetal well-being or possible distress. Whether or not to perform a cesarean birth also will depend on the fetal and maternal well-being, the condition of the cervix, or the progress of the labor induction (see Chapter 22). These are decisions that require exquisite clinical judgment and are best made by a specialist in high-risk obstetrics or perinatal medicine, whenever possible. If necessary and feasible, the woman can be transferred to a hospital with a neonatal intensive care unit before she gives birth.

In labor, and sometimes before labor, depending on the disease severity, medications will be used to prevent eclamptic convulsions. Magnesium sulfate is the drug used most commonly for this. The exact way that magnesium sulfate prevents convulsions is not entirely understood, but the drug has been shown in experimental studies with animals to minimize electrical activity over the surface of the brain.

Magnesium crosses the placenta slowly and has effects on the fetal heart rate. It can cause reduced variability, but this does no known harm in utero. If the dosage is not watched carefully, it would be possible for the newborn to have breathing difficulties at birth, but with careful monitoring, the newborns of mothers treated with magnesium do not have problems at birth. Magnesium sulfate is administered either intravenously or as an injection (intramuscularly). It may be given both ways. If a woman gets too much magnesium sulfate, it can depress her breathing. Anybody treated with this medication, therefore, requires intensive nursing care with respirations checked carefully and frequently. Reflexes should also be monitored. If respirations or reflexes become depressed, the woman will need to be given an antidote, usually calcium gluconate.

During labor the fetus should be monitored continuously and the mother given pain medication as needed. An experienced anesthesiologist should be available, as the mother's condition increases the risks associated with any form of anesthesia. Epidural or general anesthesia may be used, each requiring watchful care (see Chapter 20).

Rarely, a woman who has appeared perfectly healthy all through pregnancy and labor may without warning have convulsions after delivery. When a woman is treated with magnesium sulfate during labor, this treatment often will be continued for 24 hours postpartum to prevent the occurrence of postpartum eclampsia.

GESTATIONAL DIABETES

Gestational diabetes is a diabetic condition that occurs during pregnancy. Although women who develop gestational diabetes are at higher risk for developing diabetes mellitus later in life, gestational diabetes will resolve after the birth.

In diabetes, the body cannot properly metabolize glucose (*simple sugar*). Blood levels of *insulin* actually increase in pregnancy. (Insulin is the hormone that metabolizes glucose.) The body, however, becomes resistant to insulin's effects. How this occurs is not entirely clear but may be an effect of pregnancy hormones: estrogen, progesterone, or human placental lactogen. The purpose of insulin resistance is quite likely to ensure an adequate supply of glucose for the fetus.

Gestational diabetes occurs in 1 to 3 percent of pregnancies in the United States. Risk factors include a family history of diabetes, obesity, age greater than 30, a history of a very large baby or a malformed or stillborn baby without apparent cause, or high blood pressure. Glucose appearing in the urine may signify gestational diabetes, but is not diagnostic.

With appropriate control of glucose levels, women with gestational diabetes do not experience fetal death more often than women without diabetes. The main problem seen in these babies is *macrosomia*—excessive growth. Because of their large size, babies born to women with gestational diabetes are more prone to injuries at birth, such as those that can occur when the shoulders are delivered with difficulty (see page 586).

Experts do not agree on whether all women should be screened routinely for gestational diabetes or whether screening should be restricted to women at risk. Those who favor screening all women point out that as many as one-third to one-half of women with gestational diabetes may be missed if screening were limited.

The screening test for gestational diabetes is called a *glucose challenge test* (GCT), or an *oral glucose challenge test* (OGCT), because the sugar is given by mouth. Women drink a solution containing 50 grams of glucose, usually in the form of a very sweet carbonated beverage. Blood is drawn 1 hour after the woman drinks the soda. The GCT is performed between 24 and 28 weeks of gestation. If you have risks for diabetes, it may be performed earlier and repeated between 24 and 28 weeks if the early test is negative.

The soda is so sweet that some women find it nauseating. You might tolerate it better if you bring a lemon and squeeze a bit of lemon juice into the drink. This won't affect test results.

If the GCT result is above a set cutoff value (usually 140 mg if the glucose is measured in the plasma portion of the blood), then a more accurate, but more difficult, diagnostic test is performed. An exception is the rare circumstance that the GCT is so high that giving more glucose would be dangerous.

The diagnostic test for gestational diabetes is called a *glucose tolerance test* (GTT) or *oral glucose tolerance test* (OGTT). In this test, 100 grams of gluocse are given to a woman to drink after she has fasted overnight for 8 to 14 hours. About 15 percent of women are estimated to have abnormal GCT values. Of these, about 15 percent are found to have gestational diabetes based on the GTT. The GTT is a 3-hour test, so you need to be prepared to spend the morning at your provider's office or in the clinic or laboratory. Bring reading material!

Blood will be drawn four times during a GTT. The first time is before you drink the glucose solution. This is called a *fasting blood sugar* (FBS). Blood is then drawn at 1 hour, 2 hours, and 3 hours after you drink the sugar solution. The FBS value should be low, and glucose values should increase at 1 and 2 hours and then decrease at 3 hours, although not usually back to the fasting level. For each of these bloods, a cutoff value is set that indicates a high level of glucose. If a woman has two or more high values, she is considered to have gestational diabetes.

The first step in treatment for gestational diabetes is a special diet. This diet is based on guidelines of the American Diabetic Association (ADA). All women with two or more abnormal values on the GTT will be given an ADA diet. Many times, women with only one abnormal value will be placed on the diet as a precautionary measure, especially if the high value was the FBS.

If you need to be placed on an ADA diet, you should meet with a dietitian, nutritionist, or nurse who specializes in the care of pregnant women with diabetes and is familiar with this diet and how to individualize it. The diet usually consists of 30 to 35 calories per kilogram of ideal body weight based on height. (A kilogram is 2.2 pounds.) The exact number of calories will depend on the time in pregnancy of diagnosis and your level of activity. The ADA diet gives you choices throughout the day from various food groups, so you can adjust it to meet your personal, family, and cultural eating patterns. In general, you will avoid a *carbohydrate load*—eating a lot of carbohydrates at one time, such as a large bagel. You will limit simple sugars or sweets.

If you are at risk for gestational diabetes, and your GCT is normal, it may be repeated at 34 weeks. The GCT may be repeated if the baby is growing larger than expected or if you develop pregnancy-induced hypertension. In one study, it was reported that 8 percent of previously negative GCTs become positive at 34 weeks gestation.

Women with diabetes will be taught to test their own blood sugar at home, usually several times a day, an hour after meals, and before eating in the morning. This determines whether the diet is working and whether there is a need for insulin. When the mother's blood sugar is well controlled, the baby grows normally. The complications of birth sometimes seen with large babies will be avoided.

The fetuses of women with diabetes will be carefully monitored in the third trimester for signs of distress. Knowing the due date is important, as most experts advise avoiding a postdates delivery with diabetes. A sonogram usually will be performed at the time of diagnosis to verify gestational age if one had not been done previously. With care and attention, gestational diabetes will not adversely affect mother or baby.

Pregnancy in women with diabetes that existed prior to the pregnancy is discussed in Chapter 16.

FETAL DEATH IN UTERO

Once in a rare while a fetus dies prior to birth, often without warning. When this occurs before 20 weeks gestation, it is called a *miscarriage*. When this occurs after the twentieth week, it is considered a fetal death in utero—a *stillbirth*.

There are several possible causes of death of the fetus, none of them common. The list includes congenital anomalies incompatible with life; severe maternal blood vessel disease resulting in marked impairment of fetal growth; severe long-standing high blood pressure; severe preeclampsia and eclampsia; in utero accidents involving the umbilical cord; and premature separation of the placenta.

Fetal death may be due to *nonimmune hydrops fetalis*. *Hydrops* is a term derived from the Greek word for water, and refers to the fact that in this condition the fetus becomes filled with fluid. There is an excess of amniotic fluid, and the mother may develop complications, including preeclampsia. Hydrops was formerly observed most commonly when Rh-negative women who had been sensitized to Rh were carrying an Rh-positive fetus. This fetus was severely affected by the anti-Rh antibodies crossing the placenta from the mother to the fetus. This complication has become rare since the introduction of RhoGAM—the anti-Rh antibody—now administered to pregnant Rh-negative women to protect them and their babies against the development of Rh sensitization. Today, hydrops fetalis is seen with maternal infections, chromosomal disorders, congenital anomalies, bleeding problems in the placenta, and as a rare complication of twin pregnancy (see Chapter 23).

Mothers with severe unregulated diabetes may experience fetal death in the latter half of pregnancy, usually as a result of a congenital anomaly associated with preexisting diabetes. Other reasons for fetal death among women with preexisting diabetes include their increased likelihood of having high blood pressure and developing pregnancy-induced or pregnancy-aggravated hypertension. Since the discovery that strict control of glucose levels both before and during pregnancy leads to improved fetal outcomes, the fetal death rate among diabetic women has been comparable to that of the general population, except for infants with anomalies. Pregnancy in women with preexisting diabetes is covered in Chapter 16, "Diseases and Operations During Pregnancy," and gestational diabetes, or *diabetes of pregnancy*, is discussed above.

Finally, fetal death may occur when pregnancy has gone several weeks or more past term. This condition is called *postterm* or *postdates pregnancy*. Postterm pregnancy occurs in up to 10 percent of pregnancies, but some apparently postterm pregnancies are actually within the normal range of pregnancy duration. The woman may have conceived later than 2 weeks after her missed menstrual period, especially if she has a history of irregular periods or more than 28 days between periods. Other so-called postdates pregnancies may reflect incorrect pregnancy dating, for reasons such as a forgotten period.

Whenever a pregnancy continues past expected term, fetal assessment tests are performed. At the first sign of fetal distress, or by a particular number of weeks past the due date (which varies among physicians and institutions), labor will be induced and the fetus delivered. Death from postmaturity thus is very rare today. Fetal assessment in late pregnancy is covered in Chapter 17 and induction of labor can be found in Chapter 22.

Clearly, all high-risk pregnancies require vigilance for signs of fetal distress. The least invasive and easiest to perform test for fetal well being is the mother's own observation of the activity of her fetus. Often called a *kick count*, this test can be done in several ways. Fetal movement can be counted for 1-hour periods several times a day at the same hour each day. It's good to pick an hour following a meal. At least four movements should be felt during this hour. If fewer than four movements are felt, then continue for another hour. If you still feel fewer than four movements, contact your physician or midwife immediately. Another way to count movements is to start when you arise in the morning. Once you reach ten movements, you can stop for the day. If you don't get to ten by bedtime, call your care provider.

Even without formal kick counts, fetal death may be presaged by the absence of fetal activity. If ignored, within a few days the pregnant woman would note a loss of weight and a decrease in the size of her breasts, a sign of fetal death observed by Hippocrates 2,400 years ago. The diagnosis can be suspected if the uterus is found to be markedly smaller than it ought to be for the known duration of pregnancy, and if there is a significant loss of maternal weight without anything else to account for weight loss. Fetal death can be confirmed by ultrasound, which shows an absence of fetal heart activity. When the fetus dies in utero, labor usually ensues naturally within 2 to 3 weeks, but may be delayed for an unpredictable duration of time.

When the cause of fetal death is a condition associated with or aggravated by pregnancy, the mother will improve thereafter. This is often the case with pregnancy-induced hypertension and the maternal effects of hydrops fetalis.

Labor After Fetal Death

The interval between the death of the fetus and the onset of labor will depend to some extent on how early in pregnancy the death has occurred. The earlier the pregnancy, the longer the interval is likely to be. Most labors ensue within 2 to 3 weeks. If labor does not begin spontaneously it can sometimes be induced. Induction of labor is discussed in Chapter 22. Chances for successful induction are greater if there already have been cervical changes such as softening, shortening, and opening. As uterine stimulant drugs are very potent, they must be used with great care. In general, waiting for labor to begin is preferable.

Of course, waiting for labor once a woman knows she has lost the baby is very difficult and trying. Parents will often search for reasons for the fetal loss. Oftentimes, there is no apparent cause. Certainly, there is no one to blame for the tragedy. Counseling may be helpful. Many hospitals have bereavement teams who are experienced in assisting parents with adjustment to the loss of a baby or fetus. Ask to speak to the bereavement counselor when you are in the hospital. Get a telephone number of somebody you can call when you feel depressed at home before or after the birth.

Decide whether or not you want an autopsy and make the arrangements before you go into labor. Be aware that an autopsy often does not provide the answers you may be looking for. Results take 6 weeks to 3 months. Find out if there will be an expense involved. Decide if you want a burial and make those arrangements as well.

We advise being awake for the birth and seeing and holding the baby after it is born. Although this may be a difficult experience, most women and families report that grieving is helped when there is a tangible object to grieve. Many parents find comfort in holding their baby, even if it is a stillbirth. Some hospitals provide you with a photograph or other memento of the baby.

Most times there is no particular reason to wait to become pregnant again after a fetal death, although we advise waiting until you have at least one menstrual period so the subsequent pregnancy can be dated accurately. Most counselors suggest waiting if you feel you will be unable to bond with a new baby before you have completed grieving for the lost child. This takes a different length of time for different women and families. For some families, however, grieving is not complete until a new pregnancy is achieved. You may need some counseling to help you in making this decision. Discuss it with your physician or midwife and ask for a referral for psychological counseling if you feel you need it. There is no reason to "tough it out" in this situation. Seeking help is quite appropriate.

Disseminated Intravascular Coagulation (DIC)

When labor is delayed for several weeks following fetal death, a woman may experience an abnormality in the ability of her blood to clot. This may also occur after a placental abruption. This problem is known as *disseminated intravascular coagulation* (DIC) or *consumptive coagulopathy*. DIC is a serious condition with a complex pathological course. Simply put, the body first develops an increased tendency for the formation of blood clots. When that happens, some of the cells and proteins in the blood that take part in clotting become used up. This withdraws from the woman's blood many of the essential elements necessary for normal clotting, setting the stage for hemorrhage. Hemorrhage can occur anywhere in the body.

When suspected, DIC can be identified by blood tests that measure the number of platelets (cells involved in blood clotting) and the amount of the protein clotting factors in the blood. After a fetal death or placental abruption, these values are checked at frequent intervals.

If DIC is present at the time of delivery there may be serious hemorrhage from the site of the placental separation. DIC is also a major complication should cesarean section be required. It therefore has to be recognized promptly. Treatment consists of administering fresh whole blood or thawed-out frozen plasma to replace the clotting factors lost in the disease process. Platelet transfusion also may be part of the treatment. DIC will not be cured, however, until its underlying cause is eliminated—and in pregnancy, this means delivery.

Sometimes, when all the facts are taken into consideration, it seems best to induce labor after fetal death, before full-blown DIC makes its appearance. As the situation is complicated and one woman is not exactly like another, it is not wise to state a blanket rule for treatment.

DANGER SIGNALS—WHEN TO NOTIFY YOUR PHYSICIAN OR MIDWIFE

The pregnant woman is a competent adult able to make decisions about her own health. She seeks professional help in order to have appropriate advice from someone she knows and trusts. You can certainly make decisions about the importance of minor injuries, transitory upper respiratory infections, short-term stomach upsets, and the like. These are things that you would ordinarily decide about if you were not pregnant, and the existence of the pregnancy certainly does not impair your judgment.

There are, however, some specific circumstances when you should consult your obstetrician, your family practitioner, or your midwife.

1. **Vaginal bleeding at any time during pregnancy.** Bleeding calls for prompt consultation and possibly examination and sonography. A small amount of pink discharge accompanied by mucus can occur late in pregnancy as the cervix begins to shorten and open; this may be associated with some uterine cramps and is entirely normal. At the other end of the spectrum is the hemorrhage associated with placenta previa or premature separation of the placenta. In such an event it might be wise for you to report

promptly to your hospital without spending time to reach your care provider.

2. **Puffiness of the face and eyes, particularly if this occurs suddenly.** Swelling of the legs and ankles without involvement of the face and hands usually signifies only an effect of gravity on the normally occurring extra water in the body. If your ankles are still swollen when you wake up in the morning, it is worth a telephone call and an inquiry.

3. **Severe headache late in pregnancy.** This may be a sign of severe PIH. The headache is usually felt in the forehead and behind the eyes and does not respond to ordinary headache medications. Because the convulsions of eclampsia are almost always preceded by headache, this could signal a serious impending problem.

4. **Dimness or blurring of vision, flashing lights before the eyes, or double vision in the second half of pregnancy.** These also may be signs of severe PIH, possibly imminent convulsions.

5. **Severe abdominal pain,** especially if it is constant, no matter where it occurs in the abdomen and no matter what the duration of pregnancy.

6. **Temperature over 100.4 degrees Fahrenheit,** especially if this is associated with chills or is persistent.

7. **Burning with urination and/or discomfort at the end of urination.**

8. **Rupture of the membranes,** which results in a gush or an uncontrollable, continuous leakage of the fluid from the vagina. The closer you are to the expected date of childbirth, the shorter the delay between rupture of the membranes and the onset of the labor. Rupture of the membranes with a known abnormal presentation of the fetus—such as breech—is a medical emergency, but rupture of the membranes at the onset of normal labor is expected. Still, any rupture should warrant a call.

9. **Beyond 26 weeks of pregnancy, the unexplained absence of fetal movements for 8 to 10 hours,** especially at the times when the fetus is ordinarily active.

10. **Reduced fetal movement.** A fetus should move at least ten times every 24 hours.

CHAPTER THIRTEEN

⊶⊷

Infertility

We hope that some women read this book before they are pregnant. We hope that you will be successful then in your efforts to become pregnant and that your pregnancy is as healthy as possible. Unfortunately, not all women are able to achieve pregnancy. Coping with infertility, both physically and psychologically, has become a part of pregnancy planning for many women and couples.

THE CHANCES OF INFERTILITY

Infertility is defined as an inability to become pregnant after 12 months of trying. This definition is somewhat narrow and doesn't necessarily reflect individual experiences. Women over age 35 or 40, for example, may worry about infertility after a much shorter time of attempting pregnancy, as short as 3 to 6 months, depending on age and other circumstances, such as history of disease like pelvic inflammatory disease or polycystic ovarian syndrome. Some women who are able to become pregnant have repeated miscarriages, essentially resulting in infertility.

Infertility is not the same as sterility. Sterility is the inability to become pregnant or, for a man, the inability to cause pregnancy in a woman. This occurs, for example, in a woman who has had a *hysterectomy* (surgical removal of the uterus). With today's infertility treatments, most women and couples who seek help for infertility eventually achieve their goal.

We cannot say exactly how many women or couples experience problems with fertility. Some couples who try to get pregnant never seek care.

Surveys usually include only married people, ignoring those couples who live together without being married and who may be trying to have a child. A reasonable estimate is that 8 to 15 percent of couples of child-bearing age have infertility problems. That is about 1 in 13 to 1 in 7 married couples in the United States. There seem to be no inherent social, economic, or racial group differences affecting fertility. Group differences seen in family size are dependent upon the use or lack of use of contraception.

EFFECT OF AGE AND FREQUENCY OF INTERCOURSE ON CONCEPTION

The consensus is that as women become older their fertility declines until it ceases at menopause. Generally, age 35 is the age at which most experts agree that a woman's fertility begins to show the effects of decline.

Little attention has been paid to the relationship of a man's age to fertility. One analysis of men up to age 64 showed no effect of aging on sperm characteristics or on a man's ability to cause a pregnancy. A study examining semen samples over a 25-year period in three regions of the United States found no decrease over that time in sperm count or quality, despite fears that environmental exposures might have adverse influences on sperm among the general population. This does not mean that individual males cannot be exposed to toxins that harm their sperm. Possible adverse exposures are shown in the box on pages 343–344.

The only other general factor, in addition to a woman's age, that seems to influence fertility is frequency of intercourse. As a rule, couples having sexual intercourse four times or more per week are far more likely to achieve pregnancy in a short time period than couples having intercourse once a week or less often. Since frequency of intercourse relates to age, the decline in fertility seen in older women may be related to changes in sexual practices as well as biological changes.

USUAL TIME REQUIRED TO BECOME PREGNANT

Any couple trying to become pregnant has only a 25 percent chance of achieving pregnancy in any menstrual cycle. More than half (57 percent) of couples will be pregnant within 3 months, about three-fourths within 6 months, and 85 percent within 1 year. By definition, the remaining 15 percent are infertile. After another year, however, approximately half of these 15 percent will be pregnant.

Most physicians and midwives advise women trying to become pregnant to have intercourse every other night (or day, of course) starting a few days after the menstrual period ends. This advice is meant to minimize the chances of missing the presence of the egg and to maximize the chances of having an adequate number of sperm (thought to decrease with daily intercourse). Recent studies have shown that pregnancy is most likely to occur if you have intercourse during the 6 days preceding *ovulation*—the release of the egg.

There are a number of ways to determine when you ovulate. Ovulation usually occurs 12 to 16 days before a menstrual period. If your periods are always every 28 days, counting from the first day of one period to the first day of the next period, then you ovulate midcycle. Midcycle is sometime between 12 and 16 days after a period begins, averaging 14 days after the period's first day. Since most women don't have exactly 28-day cycles every month, there is no surety to this "rhythm" method. Other methods give you more information.

Your basal body temperature, discussed later, is most useful for showing when ovulation has occurred, but is not as clear about showing when ovulation is about to occur. This may not be helpful in figuring out when to have intercourse to become pregnant. Some ovulation kits that test for a hormone called LH (*luteinizing hormone*) in the urine predict ovulation. These may be used successfully for timing intercourse to be most effective in achieving pregnancy. Ovulation kits can be purchased over the counter.

WHEN TO SEEK MEDICAL HELP

In general, if both partners are less than 35 years old, there is no urgency about seeking medical advice until you have been trying for at least a year without becoming pregnant. If either is above 35, you should seek help after 6 months of unsuccessful attempts. If you are in your twenties, you may want to wait a bit more than 12 months after you start trying to become pregnant before you seek the help of a physician or other care provider. Some women in their twenties wait up to 2 years and achieve pregnancy without intervention. However, once 3 or 4 years have passed, the chances of successfully becoming pregnant are reduced.

Women who know they have a problem, such as previous pelvic inflammatory disease or already-diagnosed endometriosis, may want to seek help after only a few months of trying to become pregnant. With certain conditions, such as polycystic ovarian syndrome (PCOS), you should seek help once you decide you want to become pregnant. Remember, all women should seek preconception care before trying to get pregnant (see Chapter 6) and take 0.4 mg of folic acid (400 micrograms) daily starting several months before you stop using birth control.

WHOM TO CONSULT

Treatment of infertility is a complicated field, and many family doctors have not had the training to manage it. However, your regular doctor, nurse practitioner, or midwife can begin an examination to look for simple reasons why you may not have become pregnant. This practitioner can then refer the problem as necessary to a specialist or a specialized clinic. He or she can help you determine the appropriate type of specialist to see.

Most infertility specialists are members of the American Society for Reproductive Medicine (formerly called the American Fertility Society). This organization can provide you with listings of members in or near your community. A first-rate local hospital, especially a teaching hospital, can refer an inquiring couple to qualified members of its staff. Another source of referral is the organization RESOLVE, whose membership includes individuals and couples who have faced infertility as well as professionals who treat infertility. Finally, there are fertility clinics in many cities in the United States. If you are unable to locate such a clinic in your community, you can contact the Planned Parenthood Federation of America. Various ways to contact each of these organizations can be found in the Appendix.

THE MEDICAL CONSULTATION

Ideally, both partners should participate in infertility treatment. Once you decide you have a possible infertility problem, you should both see your regular providers: your doctor, nurse practitioner, midwife. The initial part of your infertility care will be a thorough medical history. The box on pages 342–343 lists parts of your health history that influence fertility.

You should be prepared to be quite open and frank with your care provider in this interview. Many providers will ask to speak to you separately from your partner, and your partner separately from you. This is in case there is something in either of your pasts that you have not revealed to each other—perhaps a history of a sexually transmitted infection that occurred so long ago it never seemed important to discuss with your current partner. Your doctor, nurse practitioner, or midwife may realize that this could influence fertility, even though you may never even think about it anymore. You should not feel that your privacy is being intruded upon by the extensiveness of the questions asked or the intimate areas they cover.

Often, a history alone will reveal areas that are amenable to correction without any medical tests or treatments. These may be rather simple. The box on pages 343–344 lists exposures that might decrease sperm counts and the box on pages 344–345 lists self-help measures that might enhance fertility. Self-help strategies can be tried before consulting a fertility specialist. How long you wish to try on your own before having a more extensive workup will depend on how long you are willing to wait to get pregnant; how long you have already been trying; how important pregnancy is to you at any given time; what, if any, obvious problems you have that might be interfering with your fertility; and how old you are.

Treatment for infertility can be a lengthy and difficult process. One author described it as a "roller coaster" of emotions. Each month you become hopeful, and each menstrual period or negative pregnancy test deflates that hope. Both partners become subjected to extensive medical testing. People usually associate becoming pregnant with an intimate act of sexuality, but for infertile couples, conceiving may become a medical procedure. Time and sometimes enormous expense is involved.

Any couple considering entering into infertility treatment should first have an honest and open discussion. You should make certain that you both really want to proceed with the testing and treatment. Discuss alternatives such as adoption or remaining without children, or with the children you already have. Consider contacting RESOLVE, an organization of parents who have been through treatment, with varying outcomes. If your community has a local chapter, attend a meeting and talk with people who have gone through the experience. If you cannot attend a meeting, or live in an area that is remote from a RESOLVE chapter, order some of their literature. Much of it is available rather inexpensively. The address for RESOLVE is in the Appendix.

Remember, you can stop infertility treatment at any step of the way. Don't feel that you must continue beyond the point where it is comfortable or affordable for you or your family. In fact, of the women who might be helped by *assisted reproductive technologies* (ART), only about

10 percent ever actually use these technologies—by choice or because of expense. Contact your health insurance company and find out what components of infertility diagnosis and treatment will be covered.

Questions in a Medical History for Infertility

1. **General information:** age, place of birth, current residence, occupation.

2. **Chronic disorders:** diabetes, hypertension (high blood pressure), thyroid abnormalities, adrenal disorders (for example, Cushing's syndrome), liver disease, anemia, psychological problems, allergies. Medication use for chronic illnesses.

3. **Health history:** sexually transmitted infections (STIs), childhood illnesses; history of any cancer; history of any surgeries. History of sterilization operation. Exposure to in utero DES (diethylstilbestrol).

4. **Gynecologic health for the woman:** fibroids, endometriosis, pelvic infections, pelvic surgeries, known congenital anomalies (such as double or divided uterus or vagina); cystic ovaries or polycystic ovarian syndrome; any breast discharge. History of D & C, which can cause Asherman's syndrome—when the uterine walls adhere to each other.

5. **Reproductive health for the man:** any history of undescended testicles, testicular surgery, infections of the reproductive tract or previous surgeries; known varicocele (varicose vein of the scrotum).

6. **Recent health:** any recent illnesses; large weight change; symptoms of thyroid disorders such as intolerance to heat or cold, increased or decreased sweating, difficulty sleeping, diarrhea or constipation; recent severe psychological trauma. Medication usage including psychotrophic medications, pain killers. For women: recent changes in the skin, including acne and increased body hair.

7. **Menstrual history:** age of menarche (first menstrual period); length of cycles, premenstrual or menstrual symptoms; amount of flow; recent changes. Increasing pain associated with periods. Unusual bleeding between periods. Signs of menopausal changes including vaginal dryness or hot flashes (at any age). Past or current amenorrhea (lack of a period).

8. **Contraceptive history:** past or current use of birth con-

trol methods. Problems with any methods. (Depo-Provera—the shot—can result in delayed fertility after the last shot; no birth control method has a permanent effect on fertility.)

9. **General health habits:** nutrition; exercise, especially intense exercise, such as marathon training, ballet dancing; smoking, including exposure to passive smoke; alcohol or any drug use, including marijuana; use of any herbal remedies, other alternative remedies; douching; eating disorders. *For the man:* wearing of tight underwear; use of saunas, hot tubs.

10. **Occupational, military, hobby history:** any that would cause exposures to the substances listed in the box below. *For the man:* extended periods of sitting on the job (such as occur with truck driving, for example).

11. **Sexual history:** frequency of intercourse, timing of intercourse in relationship to the woman's cycle, use of lubricants, douching (after intercourse or any time); whether erection and ejaculation are achieved; whether ejaculation occurs during intercourse; whether intercourse and ejaculation occur in the vagina; any periods of abstinence, such as dictated by certain religions for certain times of the month, for example, until 7 days after the period (which for some women, depending on the length of their menstrual cycles, would mean missing the fertile time). Use of barriers to protect against sexually transmitted infections including HIV/AIDS.

12. **Reproductive history:** has either partner ever had any children, biologically, with each other or with someone else. History of infertility, tests, and treatments. History of miscarriage (spontaneous abortion), stillbirth, congenital malformations in any children. History of postpartum hemorrhage in the woman (very heavy bleeding after childbirth can lead to a problem called Sheehan's syndrome, a shutdown of the pituitary gland).

Environmental Exposures with Possible Adverse Effects on Sperm

(*Note:* Exposures may occur at your place of residence, place of work, in the military, or as part of a hobby. Not all these exposures have been proven to have effects on sperm, but any such exposure with an infertility problem warrants sperm testing. Most of the time, sperm changes are reversible with discontinuation of the exposure.)

- Halogenated hydrocarbons including: PCBs, DPCBs, dioxin, vinyl chloride, ethylene dibromide
- Aromatic hydrocarbons and organic solvents, such as acetone and methylene chloride
- Gossypol, found in cotton plants and cotton oil
- Carbon disulfide, used in the production of rayon fibers
- Ethylene glycol, used in some antifreeze preparations
- Metals: lead, cadmium, manganese, copper, mercury, nickel, chromium, cobalt, boron, and silver
- Anesthetic gases
- Smoking and passive smoking
- Alcohol
- Marijuana
- Cocaine
- Other drugs: anabolic steroids, chemotherapeutic agents; anti-hypertensives; cimetidine (Tagamet)
- Antibotics: nitrofurantoin (Macrodantin or Macrobid) and sul-fasalazine (Azulfidine)
- Heat: hot tubs or saunas
- Tight fitting clothing and prolonged sitting (for example, wearing tight jockey shorts)
- Prolonged fever
- Prolonged exposure to microwaves, used in the production of dehydrated fruits or the manufacture of rubber and plastic
- In utero exposure to DES (diethylstilbestrol)

Self-Help Strategies for Infertility

1. *For both partners:*
   Eat a well-balanced diet.
   Maintain weight as close to "ideal" as possible—neither too thin nor too heavy.
   Avoid drugs, including marijuana and other "recreational" drugs and alcohol.
   Avoid anabolic steroids.
   Avoid smoking, avoid exposure to passive smoking.

Have a complete physical examination.
Take medications for chronic illnesses as prescribed.

2. *For the woman:*
    Avoid excessive exercise (such as marathon running, professional ballet training).
    Do NOT douche—ever.
    Maintain a basal body temperature (BBT) chart (see page 354).
    Take vitamin C supplements, up to 1,000 mg (1 gram) daily.
    Avoid herbal preparations, especially those with uncertain ingredients, or made in one country and sold in another, including sage, nutmeg, apiol, black cohosh, blue cohosh, devil's claw, pennyroyal oil, rue, and ginseng.
    Limit caffeine intake to less than 500 mg daily (2 cups of brewed caffeinated coffee or 5 cups instant coffee, 10 cups of tea brewed for 3 minutes).
    Avoid drugs with caffeine such as Dexatrim, Dietec, Dristan, Excedrin, Midol, No-Doz, Triaminicin, Vanquish, Vivarin.
    Remember: take 400 micrograms (or 0.4 milligrams) folic acid daily.

3. *For the man:*
    Avoid wearing tight pants, especially jockey shorts.
    Avoid exposure to items in the table on pages 343–344.
    Take vitamin C supplements, up to 1,000 mg (1 gram) daily.
    Take vitamin E supplements, 200 mg (or IU) daily.
    Avoid ginseng.

4. *For the couple:*
    Have intercourse either every other day (or night) starting a few days after the end of the woman's menstrual cycle, or, if you can predict ovulation with a urine kit, then every 24–36 hours for the 6 days just before ovulation.
    Have intercourse in the vagina with ejaculation into the vagina.
    Don't use birth control.
    Don't use barriers for disease prevention (if you are at risk for a sexually transmitted infection, including and especially HIV/AIDS, then know you are taking a risk if you are

> trying to become pregnant and make your decision based on understanding this risk—speak to a physician, HIV counselor, or other health care provider if necessary).
>
> If you need lubrication for intercourse, use vegetable oil which does not interfere with the movement of the sperm. Avoid other lubricants such as petroleum jelly, K-Y jelly, Surgilube.

CAUSES OF INFERTILITY

Understanding the possible causes of infertility requires basic knowledge of the reproductive cycle (discussed in depth in Chapter 2). Fertility is based on the ability of the woman to release an egg (*ovulation*) and the man to ejaculate sufficient healthy sperm to fertilize the egg. The man requires not only an adequate production of sperm but an unobstructed passageway from the testes in the scrotum to the urethral opening. The sperm must be able to meet the egg (*ovum*) in the woman's unobstructed fallopian tube and fertilize it. The fertilized ovum must then travel from the tube to the uterus, and implant in a uterus that is ready to receive it. Once the fertilized ovum enters the uterus, the proper hormonal balance must exist to maintain it. Interference with any of these steps can lead to infertility.

Finally, the fertilized ovum must divide and grow properly, or it may be aborted spontaneously. Repeated miscarriage (called *spontaneous abortion*) is considered a form of infertility.

Approximately 40 percent of infertility is due to a problem in the woman. In approximately another 40 percent, a problem exists in the male that causes or contributes significantly to the infertility. Less than 5 percent of infertility is due to recurrent miscarriage. Approximately 10 percent is unexplainable, and the small percentage that remains is due to various problems relating to sexual intercourse.

Causes of Infertility in the Woman

Infertility can occur when the woman has a problem ovulating. This may occur as a direct result of a problem in her *ovaries*, the organs from which eggs are released, or it could be due to a disorder in the glands that regulate ovulation. Ovulation is regulated by the *hypothalamus*, a structure that is part of the central nervous system, located at the base of the brain. The hypothalamus secretes gonadotropin releasing hormone (GnRH) that stimulates release of hormones from the *pituitary gland*. The pituitary is a small gland attached to the base of the brain. The pituitary hormones are LH and FSH (luteinizing hormone and follicle stimulating hormone). These in turn stimulate the secretion of the hormones estrogen and progesterone from the ovaries. A central nervous system disorder or pituitary problem, such as a pituitary tumor, could thus affect fertility.

Successful ovulation requires maturation of what is called a *graafian follicle*, the egg-containing part of the ovary. It then requires rupture of the follicle with release of the egg. Following egg release (*ovulation*), the woman must secrete sufficient progesterone to sustain a pregnancy should one occur. If she cannot sustain a pregnancy once ovulation and fertilization have occurred, this may be called a *luteal phase defect*. The luteal phase is the second half of the menstrual cycle—the part following ovulation.

Infertility may occur when a woman has a defect in her tubes or uterus. Such defects could be from birth or from disease. Birth defects include a *double* (bicornuate) *uterus* or *divided* (septate) *uterus*. Diseases such as pelvic inflammatory disease or *salpingitis* (an infection in the pelvic region or in the tubes) can cause tubal damage. This may interfere with the ability of semen to reach the egg or of the fertilized egg to travel to the uterus. Endometriosis, which is the growth of uterine tissue in places other than the uterus, can lead to infertility, sometimes because the tissue causes a blockage of the tubes, sometimes for unknown reasons.

Fibroids (also called *myomas*) can interfere with uterine function. These commonly occurring tumors are benign. If they are on the outside of the uterus, they usually do not interfere with a woman's becoming pregnant, although they could press on the fallopian tubes. If they are in the uterine cavity (*submucous myomas*), or pushing into the uterine cavity from within the muscular uterine wall (*intramural* or *interstitial myomas*), they can interfere with implantation or growth of the embryo or placenta.

The immune system has recently received attention regarding infertility. There has been some question regarding whether a class of antibodies present in the woman's blood called *antiphospholipid antibodies*, which include lupus anticoagulant antibody and the anticardiolipin antibody, might contribute to recurrent miscarriage. These antibodies are directed against the woman's own system. They attack the vascular system and cause clotting in vessels in the lining of the uterus or placenta.

There may also be immune system responses that cause the mother to reject the fetus, as if it were a foreign body. These can cause miscarriage and are discussed in Chapter 14. Interestingly, unlike true foreign bodies, which are rejected because of their differences with the mother, the fetus appears to be rejected when it is too similar to the mother. This happens when mother and father share certain *antigens* (antigens provoke immune or antibody responses). These are called the *human leukocyte antigens* (HLA), a group of genes located on chromosome 6. Immune system problems are not entirely understood yet, and remain an area for further research.

When infertility occurs because of a problem in the woman, about 40 percent of the time it is an ovulatory problem. About 30 to 50 percent of the time it is a problem in the fallopian tubes. Less than 10 percent of the time it is a barrier in the cervix, such as thick cervical mucus. Although the exact incidence of endometriosis is unknown, estimates are that 25 to 35 percent of infertile women have endometriosis. This is a higher rate than among all women, but the special contribution of endometriosis to infertility is difficult to assess.

Causes of Infertility in the Man

In men, the causes of infertility usually involve disorders of the production of sperm, disorders of the quality of sperm, or obstructions in the passageway for the sperm. Other causes include a *varicocele* (varicose vein of the scrotum), or a physical abnormality such as *hypospadias*, in which the opening from the urethra is on the underside of the penis rather than its tip. Sperm can be damaged by exposures to environmental toxins: drugs; alcohol; smoking; heat, including external (hot tubs) and internal (fever); allergies; and injury to the testes from trauma, surgery, or mumps (usually if the infection was in adulthood or very severe in childhood). Specific exposures are listed in the box on pages 343–344. About one-fourth of male infertility has an unknown cause.

Causes of Infertility in Either Partner

Some infertility appears to be due to problems relating to the immune system—an antibody reaction, for example, against the sperm. Either the man or woman might have antisperm antibodies (ASA). Antisperm antibodies are found in approximately 10 percent of infertile men (and up to 70 percent of men who have had a *vasectomy*—male sterilization). They are found in approximately 5 percent of infertile women. These rates are substantially higher than among normally fertile people.

TESTS FOR INFERTILITY

A number of specific tests are available to determine or confirm the cause of infertility. If history or physical examination reveals an obvious cause, that particular cause usually is tested for first. For example, if there is a strong likelihood of a tubal blockage because of a history of repeated pelvic inflammatory disease, a test for tubal patency (*openness*) may be utilized early in the diagnostic workup. Either a *hysterosalpingogram* or *laparoscopy* is used for this purpose. If, however, there is no reason to suspect that the tubes may be blocked, these tests may be deferred until other tests have been accomplished and possibly even certain treatments have been tried.

If the history and physical examination do not point to an obvious reason for infertility, then certain basic tests usually will be done first. In the woman, testing for ovulation and for tubal patency and anatomic defects in the uterus are the tests most commonly performed. For the man, a semen analysis is basic. For the couple, a postcoital test—which examines sperm in the cervical mucus after intercourse—may be performed.

Unless the history or the physical examination shows other possible problems, treatment can be initiated based on the results of these tests. Other tests may be done later if the couple's infertility persists after routine treatment. Some tests are performed as part of a particular recommended treatment.

You may choose to see an infertility specialist immediately, although many gynecologists who do not specialize in infertility will test for ovulation and perform a semen analysis. Some may do a postcoital test. Physician assistants, nurse practitioners, and midwives may be specially trained to do these tests.

For more elaborate testing and for most treatment, a fertility specialist is the best person to see. However, even among such infertility specialists, there are subspecialists. One doctor may focus on endocrinology and be the person who tests and prescribes treatment for ovulatory problems. Another doctor may do nothing but surgical repairs. Other doctors specialize in *assisted reproductive technologies* (ART) and will be consulted only when this option is chosen—usually well along the treatment path.

Examination of the male genitals and corrective surgery for problems such as a varicocele or reparative surgery following a vasectomy will be carried out by a *urologist*—a specialist in disorders of the male reproductive and urinary systems. The urologist also may do the semen analysis. A plastic surgeon may be involved for surgery such as correction of hypospadias.

Because tests for the man are often simpler, we start by describing these. They are often done first or concurrently with tests to determine whether the woman ovulates.

Tests for the Man

The first test for the man is an examination of the sperm content of the semen. This is called a *semen analysis*. Before the test, the man should abstain from ejaculation for 2 to 5 days, depending on instructions of the practitioner performing the test. The semen specimen is collected directly into a wide-necked, dry, clean bottle or jar. The man must be careful none is lost, as the first few drops of the ejaculation contain the bulk of the sperm cells. If the first few drops are lost, normal semen may test as defective. The specimen can be collected at home either by masturbation or during sexual relations with use of a special type of condom. Once collected, the specimen is kept warm and taken within an hour to the doctor's office.

What constitutes "normal" sperm varies among experts. The following values are from the the World Health Organization:

- The semen specimen must be about half a teaspoon or more in quantity (at least 2 milliliters).
- Its pH (acidity) must be between 7.2 and 8.0.
- Under the microscope there must be 20 million or more sperm cells per milliliter (cubic centimeter).
- At least 75 percent of the sperm must be alive.
- At least 50 percent of the sperm must show a progressive type of swimming movement in the seminal fluid (called motility).
- At least 30 percent of the cells must appear normal in form (called morphology).

Some laboratories use slightly different values to denote normal, such as at least a teaspoonful of semen or at least 60 percent of sperm showing normal morphology.

If two or three examinations of the semen demonstrate a subfertile specimen, then further testing may be done. A physical examination by an experienced urologist, if not already carried out, is important. It may reveal abnormalities such as a varicocele or other anatomic defect in the male reproductive system.

If there is pus in the semen or white blood cells seen under the microscope, or a history indicates a possible sexually transmitted infection, this can interfere with sperm movement and its ability to penetrate the egg. A common cause of chronic infection is chlamydia. This infection is amenable to antibiotic therapy, although it is unreasonable to expect spectacular increases in fertility after the infection is conquered.

Blood tests can sometimes reveal hormonal problems in men that affect sperm production. Tests for thyroid hormone, pituitary gonadotropins, prolactin, and testosterone may be carried out, although their usefulness is debated. Elevated prolactin levels, for example, are rarely seen in the absence of *impotence* (an inability to get or sustain an erection long enough for ejaculation to occur). However, hormone deficiencies that are revealed may suggest possible treatments.

If sperm cells are completely absent from the semen specimen, two possibilities present themselves. Either no spermatozoa are being produced in the two testicles, or they are being produced but their exit through the penis is blocked so that they cannot appear in the ejaculated fluid. Such blockage usually occurs in the *vas deferens*, the conducting tube that conveys the sperm cells upward from the scrotum. A biopsy, the removal of a fragment of tissue from the testicle for microscopic study, will determine whether the absence of spermatozoa is due to failure of their formation or to blockage.

Failure of formation of sperm may be due to damage to the testicles from a severe case of mumps, from *cryptorchidism* (undescended or abdominal testicles), or *Klinefelter's syndrome*. The latter is a genetic disorder in which the male has three sex chromosomes—XXY. (Sex chromosome disorders are discussed in greater detail in Chapter 8.)

It is important to determine the extent of the sperm problem. Different treatments have been suggested for mild, moderate, and severe sperm problems, as well as for women whose partners do not produce any sperm. These are discussed in the treatment sections, below.

If the sperm are normal, two other tests can be performed: the post-coital test, described below, and the *sperm penetration assay* (SPA). The sperm penetration assay is based on the fact that golden hamster eggs have a unique property of being able to be fertilized by the sperm of several species, including human sperm. This can only be accomplished in the laboratory when the *zona pellucida* (or outer layer) is removed from the hamster egg. This gives the test its other name: the *zona-free hamster egg penetration assay*. The hamster is treated with hormones to achieve superovulation (as described in the section "Medical Treatment for the Woman"). The eggs are prepared and put into culture with the sperm.

This test measures either the percent of eggs penetrated by sperm or the number of sperm penetrations per egg.

An abnormal SPA does not indicate with certainty that the sperm will be unable to enter a woman's egg. In fact, what constitutes a normal SPA result is not entirely clear. Some consider any number of eggs fertilized as normal; others say the sperm should be able to fertilize at least 10 to 14 percent of the eggs. In any case, even with an abnormal SPA, sperm have been known to fertilize human eggs. However, couples may choose donor semen in cases where the SPA is abnormal and pregnancy has not been achieved.

Tests for the Couple

The Postcoital Test

Even if normal ovulation is occurring, the tubes are open, and the sperm appear healthy, pregnancy will not result unless the sperm cells can make the 4- or 5-inch journey to the midportion of the tube where fertilization takes place. The postcoital test determines whether live sperm are present at the starting line in the cervix following sexual intercourse. To prepare for the test, the woman and man must be sure not to use a barrier method of contraception out of habit.

The woman comes to the doctor's office 8 to 12 hours after intercourse. A sample of fluid from the mucus of the cervix is aspirated during a pelvic examination. This test feels about as uncomfortable as a Pap smear. The sample is placed under the microscope. Live, moving sperm should be present in the cervical mucus.

The postcoital test is carried out at about midcycle, when the mucus is at its best for sperm penetration. An abnormal test indicates a problem related to either sperm or cervical mucus. The test might be abnormal when either of the couple has antisperm antibodies, although the exact role of these antibodies in infertility is unclear. These can be tested for in the sperm or mucus, or, in the woman, the blood.

Tests for Both Partners

If the infertility problem results from recurrent miscarriages, then genetic testing of both partners is warranted. This involves a blood test for a *karyotype*—a genetic map, as described in detail in Chapter 8. Testing for sexually transmitted infections is done as well. A swab of the urethra in the man and of the cervix in the woman are done. The specimen is cultured for gonorrhea, chlamydia, and mycoplasm.

Tests for the Woman

The first test to be done on most women is a test of ovulation. The exception is when the history or physical examination points to the likelihood of another problem such as a blocked tube or endometriosis.

Tests for the Woman Who Is Not Menstruating

If a woman is not menstruating, either because she has never menstruated or has ceased menstruating, the condition is called *amenorrhea* (prefix from the Greek: *a* = not or without). We know that this woman is not ovulating, and the purpose of testing is to determine whether the woman is secreting sufficient estrogen or is lacking in both estrogen and progesterone, or whether she has a pathology such as an anatomical or chromosomal abnormality.

If the woman has never menstruated, she might have *Turner's syndrome* (XO sex chromosomes), described in Chapter 8. A karyotype, or chromosomal map, will reveal this. It requires a simple blood sample. An ultrasound may be performed to see if there are defects in her tubes, uterus, or vagina that obstruct the flow of menses. She may even be lacking one of these structures.

If the woman has previously menstruated but has stopped, then she may be given a *progesterone challenge test.* After 10 days of oral or injected progesterone, if she has what is called *withdrawal bleeding* (like menstrual bleeding), this means her body is producing a normal amount of estrogen. If she does not desire pregnancy she can take oral contraceptives or progesterone every month or two in order to have regular cycles (the progesterone in this situation doesn't work as a contraceptive method, however). This treatment prevents the uterine lining from continually building up without shedding. Such an overgrowth of tissue could lead eventually to cancer of the lining of the uterus (*endometrial cancer*). If she wishes to get pregnant, she can be given medications to induce ovulation, as described in the section "Medical Treatment for the Woman."

If the woman with amenorrhea does not bleed following the progesterone, she can be given an *estrogen-progesterone challenge test.* If she has withdrawal bleeding (again, like menstrual bleeding) after 21 days of estrogen, with progesterone added for the last 10 days, then she is lacking in both estrogen and progesterone. If she desires pregnancy, she can be given medications to stimulate ovulation; if not she can be given oral contraceptives or hormone replacement therapy. If she does not bleed after taking these hormones, then she might have an obstruction, but not one that occurred as a birth defect (since she previously had periods). She might have adhesions in the uterus, which can follow a dilation and curettage procedure (*D & C*). Her cervix might have become so rigid that it doesn't permit the outflow of blood, a condition called *cervical stenosis*, also seen following surgical procedures.

Another way to test if the ovaries are being stimulated by the pituitary gland is to measure the blood level of FSH—*follicle stimulating hormone*. If FSH is low or normal, then the ovaries are not being stimulated by the pituitary gland to develop eggs and grow follicles. This is often due to extreme weight loss and exercise and thus correctable with changes in behavior. If FSH is high, this means the pituitary is attempting to stimulate the ovaries, which are not responding. With high FSH, the woman may be perimenopausal, or if younger than age 45, have what is called *premature ovarian failure*. The treatment for this, should the woman wish to get pregnant, is to use donor eggs with in vitro fertilization (see later in the chapter for discussion of these treatment options).

Tests for Ovulation in a Woman Who Is Menstruating

For a woman who does menstruate, the oldest and least technological way of identifying ovulation is to record the daily basal body temperature (BBT). Although some specialists think this test is outdated, preferring more technologically based tests such as urine kits that measure LH or serial sonograms, this test is one you can do on your own. It is inexpensive and can be started before you seek infertility care. The temperature chart also can provide additional information about your body such as the length of each menstrual period and the lengths of your menstrual cycles (the number of days from the day you start bleeding in one period to the day you start bleeding in the next). It can alert you to abnormal bleeding. As some infertility specialists have long waits before you can get your first appointment, many women make an appointment and, in the months of waiting, begin their BBT charts.

To get an accurate BBT, you take your temperature each morning immediately upon awakening before any activity and, if possible, at the same time every day. You always use the same method. You can purchase a rectal or oral mercury thermometer that shows one-tenth of a degree (most thermometers show two-tenths of a degree). This makes it easier to read. Such thermometers are called *basal body thermometers* and often come with graph paper for charting the temperature. They are available at most drug stores. A more expensive type of thermometer is called a *tympanic thermometer*, which takes the temperature instantly in the ear. These are not approved by the Food and Drug Administration for BBT, but some studies have shown that they are good enough to show the ovulatory temperature shift. They are much more expensive than glass mercury thermometers.

Your temperature should be written down immediately, or the thermometer put in a safe place where it can be read later. Record on the chart anything that might affect temperature such as a cold, a headache for which you took aspirin, poor sleep. Mark when you have intercourse and any other symptoms that might indicate ovulation, such as slight midcycle lower abdominal pain (called *mittelschmerz*) or slight midcycle spotting.

The BBT is low during menstruation and for a week or so thereafter. It then rises at midcycle and remains at an elevated level until about 24 hours before the next period. All these temperatures are within normal limits. The increase we are referring to is as small as two-tenths of a degree above the highest of the previous six temperatures. This is called a *biphasic pattern* and is strong evidence of ovulation. Absence of the maintained temperature rise in the second half of the menstrual cycle, however, does not prove a lack of ovulation.

Sometimes the temperature patterns are not easy to read and you will require the assistance of somebody experienced in the interpretation of BBT charts. This might be your regular physician, nurse practitioner, or midwife, or you may need to consult a fertility specialist.

Along with BBT measurements, you can check the mucus of the cervix to determine whether it goes through a "watery" phase during midcycle. At midcycle, you can check by putting your fingers deep inside your vagina. When you remove them, the mucus on them will look like the white of an egg. You will be able to stretch it between your fingers without its breaking (a quality called *spinnbarkeit*). Having intercourse without a barrier method of contraception will make this test impossible as the semen in the vagina mixes with the mucus. You can check your mucus if you limit intercourse to every other night.

Recently, kits that test urine for luteinizing hormone (LH) have become popular. This pituitary hormone surges around ovulation. A urine specimen is collected and a color change on a strip placed into the urine indicates impending ovulation. These can become expensive but are relatively easy to use and interpret compared to BBT charts.

The LH surge also can be identified through a blood test.

A new device, called Cue Ovulation Predictor, works by testing saliva vaginal and cervical mucus. This device can predict ovulation up to 5 days in advance, so it can be utilized to time the most effective intercourse. It is expensive (costing several hundred dollars), but can be rented by the month (see Appendix).

Another test for ovulation is an *endometrial biopsy* in which tissue from the lining of the uterus (the *endometrium*) is sent to a laboratory for microscopic analysis. Tissue is removed gently with a small suction tube. The test is scheduled for a few days prior to menstruation.

An endometrial biopsy can be carried out in a physician's office or clinic. It may be done by a nurse practitioner, physician's assistant, or midwife. The suction tube has a diameter much smaller than an average straw. You will be in the same position as you are for a regular pelvic examination. The speculum will be inserted to visualize the cervix and the tiny catheter inserted through the cervix into the uterus.

There is some discomfort associated with an endometrial biopsy, but it lasts only a minute or less. Some women who are anxious about it can have a mild analgesic or even a mild sedative by mouth about a half hour to an hour before the test. Ask your care provider in advance for a prescription for this medication. You can take nonsteroidal antiinflammatory medication, such as ibuprofen, afterward if you have cramping. Some spotting is normal following the biopsy.

If ovulation has occurred that month, the biopsy specimen will show that the lining of the uterus is in the *secretory phase*. This means it is thick enough for the reception and implantation of a fertilized egg. This preparation for the entry of the fertilized egg takes place under the influence of the hormone progesterone, made in the corpus luteum, which is formed from the ruptured follicle after the egg is released. If ovulation has not occurred and therefore no corpus luteum is formed, the uterus omits this chapter of its story and characteristic secretory changes are absent.

A less invasive way to demonstrate the secretory phase of the menstrual cycle, which implies ovulation, is to use *serial ultrasound*. This is done either abdominally or through the vagina. The ultrasound done abdominally requires a full bladder and may therefore be more uncomfortable. The discomfort can be limited somewhat if you are able to drink fluid over several hours before the sonogram, rather than in a shorter period just before the test. The ultrasound done through the vagina uses a very small probe, about the diameter of an average tampon, and does not require a full bladder. It will be to your advantage to eat a diet of high fiber and drink lots of fluids in the days before your sonogram so your colon will not be full of stool, which may make the sono-gram difficult to read.

If an infertile woman demonstrates failure to ovulate, she can be treated with medications that will induce ovulation. Before this is done, several additional tests should be carried out to determine a possible cause for the failure to ovulate. If she demonstrates ovulation, then tests for additional causes of infertility can be performed, or the couple can stop the workup for a period of time and initiate the self-help measures outlined in the box on pages 344–346. This assumes the sperm has tested normal. The decision is best made in consultation with your physician or infertility specialist.

If ovulation is not occurring, blood tests for *prolactin* (PRL), *thyroid stimulating hormone* (TSH), and *follicle stimulating hormone* (FSH) can be done. Prolactin is a pituitary hormone and elevated levels can inter-fere with ovulation. Elevated prolactin may be associated with a benign tumor of the pituitary gland, which can be found by MRI (*magnetic reso-nance imaging*). This type of tumor usually causes a milky discharge from the breasts. If a woman has this discharge, a prolactin level will be performed earlier in the infertility workup. Some medications might also cause elevated prolactin levels and should be discontinued or changed if possible. Discuss this with your physician or other care provider before you stop any prescribed medications.

A thyroid disorder can interfere with ovulation or cause increased prolactin levels. If you have signs of hypothyroidism or hyperthyroidism, then tests of thyroid function will be done earlier in the workup. Thyroid tests will also be done earlier in the workup if a thyroid enlargement, or possible cyst or tumor, is felt on physical examination. Symptoms of underactive thyroid (*hypothyroidism*) include constipation, fatigue, intol-erance to cold, and weight gain. Symptoms of overactive thyroid (*hyper-thyroidism*) are the opposite: diarrhea, intolerance to heat, anxiety or sleeplessness, and weight loss. In addition, function of the adrenal gland and the liver should be checked.

Persistent failure to ovulate is associated in some circumstances with *polycystic ovarian syndrome* (PCOS), a complex hormonal situation that probably is due to several different factors. It is a condition often marked by multiple small cysts in the ovaries (hence its name). These derive from the failure of graafian follicles to develop and rupture normally through the surface of the ovary. Diagnosis requires a number of blood tests for various hormones, including testosterone, which is increased in this disorder. Ultrasound may or may not show multiple cysts on the ovaries.

If you do show ovulation, blood tests for progesterone might be done in the second half of the menstrual cycle, as some regularly ovulating women have what is called a *luteal phase defect*, in which the progesterone levels in the second half of the menstrual cycle are low. Progesterone is needed to make the uterine lining receptive to the fertilized ovum and permit implantation.

If the problem is recurrent miscarriage, blood may be tested for certain antibodies and the lack of other antibodies. Although the role of the immune system in infertility is not entirely understood, the identification of particular antibodies in the blood or the lack of other antibodies may signal the need to either suppress or provoke the immune system.

Some women who ovulate normally, have a normal laparoscopy (see below), and have no other pathology are still infertile. If their partner's sperm are normal, then they fall into the subgroup of couples with unexplained infertility. Even without an apparent cause, treatment may produce a pregnancy, as described later.

Tests for Tubal Patency (Openness)

The fallopian tubes must be open so that eggs can proceed down and sperm travel up to impregnate the ova. The most common cause of tubal obstruction is prior infection, although the obstruction can be due to endometriosis or scars from previous surgery. The common causes of infection are the sexually transmitted infections gonorrhea and chlamydia, if untreated early in their course. Infections following childbirth or abortion, unless they are extraordinarily severe, are less likely to have this effect.

Accurate identification of the location of tubal blockage involves two procedures: X ray and laparoscopy. The X ray of the pelvis is done while a radiopaque fluid is injected through the cervix, into the uterus and the tubes. *Radiopaque* means the fluid can be seen on an X ray—it is what is called a *contrast medium*. When the tubes are open and the fluid passes rapidly through them, it spills into the peritoneal cavity behind the uterus and produces a readily recognized picture. If the radiopaque material cannot pass through the tubes, it can be seen up to the point of obstruction.

This X-ray procedure is called a *hysterosalpingogram* (from Greek and Latin roots meaning uterus, tube, and picture), abbreviated as HSG. HSG can be performed by a specialist in *radiology* (imaging techniques) or an infertility specialist. It may be uncomfortable. You can request premedication with an analgesic medication or sedative like diazepam

(Valium). The procedure is performed in an office or clinic. Bring your partner, another family member, or a friend to accompany you home.

Hysterosalpingogram may have some curative value in itself, as the dye going through the tubes might open them. Occasionally a woman will become pregnant with no further diagnostic or therapeutic undertaking. With modern X-ray equipment the amount of radiation delivered to the pelvis is minimal and without measurable genetic hazard. The best time for the test is a few days after your period ends, to avoid inadvertent radiation of a new pregnancy.

If the tubes appear to be blocked, the next step is direct visualization of the pelvic structures by laparoscopy. Some physicians today use laparoscopy instead of HSG. When a woman has a history of pelvic inflammatory disease, many physicians avoid an HSG because of the risk of a flare-up of the infection.

Laparoscopy is a surgical procedure performed by putting a lighted scope into the abdominal cavity through a tiny incision in or just below the navel. The surgeon performing the laparoscopy can usually tell whether the tubal obstruction is due to pressure from the outside or whether the tube itself is damaged. This information greatly helps the doctor evaluate the likely benefits of corrective tubal surgery. Direct viewing of the pelvic organs through surgery is also the only way to diagnose endometriosis, another possible cause of infertility. Surgical treatment of endometriosis can also be accomplished this way, with varying results.

Among women who have had previous tubal surgery, including a previous sterilization operation, laparoscopy gives the surgeon an accurate picture of what needs to be accomplished. Diagnostic laparoscopy can be done without hospitalization under general or regional anesthesia (an *epidural*). If the procedure is done in a hospital operating room, as either same-day or overnight surgery, then often treatment can be accomplished during the same procedure.

Additional Tests for the Woman

Another test sometimes performed is a *hysteroscopy*—in which a lighted scope is placed through the cervix directly into the uterine cavity. This will reveal fibroids that are inside the uterine cavity or other pathology of the uterus. This procedure is usually done in a same-day surgery unit and may cause some cramping afterward. You can request pain medication. It may be done under general anesthesia and can be performed at the same time that the laparoscopy is done.

Most women who don't ovulate are treated by the administration of clomiphene citrate (brand name: Clomid or Serophene, also called CC).

Ovulation induction may also be an effective treatment for unexplained infertility. Some women may choose to have a *clomiphene citrate challenge test* before undertaking clomiphene therapy. This test may be recommended in women for whom there is a good possibility of having poor ovarian reserve, meaning that even with treatment, conception will be highly unlikely. Such women might include those over 40 and those who have had a previous poor response to ovarian stimulation. In this test, blood is drawn on the third day of the menstrual cycle to measure *estradiol* (a type of estrogen) and FSH levels. Clomiphene citrate is given daily on menstrual days 5 to 9. Blood is then drawn on day 10 for FSH and progesterone levels. Elevated FSH levels on days 3 and 10, elevated estradiol levels on day 3, and elevated progesterone levels on day 10 predict a poor outcome.

Women with a poor outcome on the clomiphene citrate challenge test may choose to go right to more aggressive ovulation stimulation with human menopausal gonadotropin, described later, or choose assisted reproductive technologies such as in vitro fertilization or ovum donation, or perhaps even choose adoption without further treatment. You and your partner should discuss all options with your fertility specialist, who can help you interpret test results and review your individual situation with you.

Another measure of ovarian reserve is to test blood levels of FSH and estradiol on day 3 of the menstrual cycle. FSH values above 40 (measured as a milli-unit per milliliter) indicate reduced ovarian function. Estradiol above 100 also indicates decreased ovarian function.

TREATMENT FOR INFERTILITY

Medical Treatment for the Woman

Ovulation Induction

A failure to ovulate is called *anovulation*. The first treatment for anovulation usually is clomiphene citrate. Clomiphene is an antiestrogen drug that works by tricking the hypothalamus into thinking that estrogen levels are low. The hypothalamus will then release its gonadotropin releasing hormone (GnRH), stimulating the pituitary to release FSH and LH. FSH stimulates follicle growth and LH stimulates ovulation.

Clomiphene is given initially in daily doses of 50–100 milligrams (one to two tablets) on days 3 to 7 or 5 to 9 of the menstrual cycle. In women who are not ovulating, clomiphene is given early in the cycle in order to start the maturation of the ovarian follicle in a timely fashion. In women who are ovulating, it is given early to prevent the ovary's natural tendency to choose only one follicle (the dominant follicle) to mature and rupture. The sooner it is given, the more likely it is that more than one follicle will develop. If a woman has not been having menstrual periods, they are first induced with either birth control pills or a synthetic form of progesterone (trade name: Provera). If pregnancy does not occur, the clomiphene course may be repeated. The dose may be increased.

Clomiphene is a relatively simple treatment. It is taken by mouth, is less expensive than other infertility medications, and usually has relatively few side effects. It may cause depression or anxiety, causing some women to discontinue it. Other side effects may be nausea and vomiting and hot flashes.

Clomiphene induces ovulation in about 50 to 80 percent of anovulatory women. Pregnancy rates are about half of the ovulation rates, but in any given cycle only about 10 to 15 percent of women become pregnant. So, for 40 percent of treated women to become pregnant, each woman needs to take the medication for a number of cycles. Women who get pregnant with clomiphene therapy usually do so within six treatment cycles. Success rates are similar for women with polycystic ovarian syndrome (PCOS) and women whose anovulation is due to other causes.

Although we often hear that stimulating ovulation causes multiple births, most reports put the rate of twin pregnancy with clomiphene treatment as 10 percent of births. (Without assistance, twins occur naturally in just over 1 percent of pregnancies.) Generally, this therapy does not lead to pregnancy with more than two fetuses.

Women who do not respond to clomiphene therapy within 6 to 9 months can be treated with *ovulation stimulating medications*, usually injections of human menopausal gonadotropin (hMG; trade name: Pergonal). This injection contains both FSH and LH (hormones whose levels are very high in menopausal women). The amount of Pergonal given varies from woman to woman. It is based on an estimation of how responsive their ovaries are likely to be. This is determined by a number of factors including age, hormonal blood levels (drawn on day 3 of the menstrual cycle), previous ovarian surgery, previous response to infertility medications, perhaps an ultrasonic evaluation of the number of follicles in the ovary, and whether the woman has polycystic ovarian syndrome. During treatment, the dosage of Pergonal may be adjusted up or down depending upon how the woman is responding. This is based on ultrasound evaluation of the developing ovarian follicles and hormonal blood levels.

When the follicles have reached a sufficient size, an injection of human chorionic gonadotropin (hCG; trade name: Profasi) is given to cause ovulation. Once ovulation has occurred, progesterone may be given to maintain the uterine lining.

Most couples learn to administer these drugs by injection at home. Often the partner will give the injection. It is given into the upper outer part of the buttock.

Injections are needed for 8 to 14 days per cycle. Each *ampule* (little jar) of medication costs at least fifty dollars. Women use one-half to six ampules per day during treatment. So, at the least, this treatment costs two hundred dollars a month just for the medication. Physician and laboratory fees are, of course, additional. Some health insurance company plans will pay for all of this treatment, some plans will pay for some of the treatment, and others will not pay at all. Again, we recommend checking your insurance before investing in these treatments.

Sometimes a drug containing FSH but not LH is given instead of hMG. These drugs are known as *follitropins* or *urofollitropins* (brand names: Follistim, Gonal-F, or Fertinex). Follistim can be injected subcutaneously or intramuscularly. Gonal-F and Fertinex always are injected subcutaneously. This means the injection does not need to go deeply into the muscle tissue. It is given just under the skin, similarly to the way people with diabetes inject themselves. The woman can learn to give herself these injections.

The determination of the correct medication regimen will be made by a reproductive endocrinologist or infertility specialist based on assessments of the blood levels of different hormones in the individual woman.

Although injections can be given at home, treatment with gonadotropins does require visits to the physician's office for monitoring of the follicle. This is done by serial blood values of estradiol and ultrasound measurement of the follicle diameter, 2 to 3 days a week. Monitoring is necessary because of the risk of ovarian hyperstimulation with these potent drugs. This is more likely to occur with gonadotropin treatment than with clomiphene. When this happens, the woman may have nausea, vomiting, abdominal distention, and often pain. The diagnosis is made via ultrasound. The sonogram will show enlarged ovaries and fluid in the abdominal cavity.

Ovarian hyperstimulation can lead to imbalances in the body's necessary chemicals. In its most severe form, this can cause kidney damage

and respiratory difficulties. Usually women with severe ovarian hyperstimulation are hospitalized. Extensive blood work is ordered and treatment individualized according to symptoms and results of blood work.
Neither vigorous pelvic examinations nor deep abdominal examinations
should be performed in a woman with ovarian hyperstimulation. Sometimes women with ovarian hyperstimulation are pregnant. Every effort
is made to maintain the pregnancy.

Ovulation stimulation with injectable gonadotropins is successful
90 percent of the time. Approximately 15 percent of treated women who
have no other causes of infertility besides anovulation become pregnant
each cycle. Again, success rates are similar for women with polycystic
ovarian syndrome and those without this disorder. This therapy can be
tried for 3 to 5 cycles, occasionally more. At this point, if pregnancy is not
achieved, assisted reproductive technologies are the next step. They are described later. If this is not an option, then a few more cycles may be tried.

The most recent development in ovulation induction is the injection
of gonadotropin releasing hormone (GnRH) at 60- to 90-minute intervals by electric pump. This closely mimics the normal functioning of
the *hypothalamus*, the structure that produces GnRH. This small pump
must be worn at all times, including during sleep. It is particularly effective for women who do not menstruate because their own hypothalamus is not releasing GnRH.

An advantage of the pump is that it does not cause multiple follicles
to grow. Therefore, it does not increase the risk of multiple pregnancy
and the woman's ovaries do not require monitoring to the same degree.

Women treated with medications to induce or stimulate their ovaries
may get pregnant with intercourse timed to coincide with ovulation.
Depending on the medication used, women can monitor ovulation at
home using a urine kit to test for LH or be monitored with blood work
or ultrasound performed in the physician's office. Many times, an injection of human chorionic gonadotropin (hCG) is given when the follicle
is ripe. This will cause ovulation in approximately 36 hours. Women
often call this shot the "trigger." This can help to time intercourse or
insemination.

Often, ovarian stimulation is combined with insemination. Today,
such insemination is done directly into the uterus and is called *intrauterine insemination* (IUI), discussed later under its own heading.

Multiple pregnancy can occur with ovulation stimulation, although
the risk is overplayed in the media. About 80 percent of pregnancies
achieved this way are single fetuses. Approximately 15 percent are twins
and 3 percent are triplets. One percent of these pregnancies results in

four or more fetuses. The risk of poor outcome for fetuses in multiple pregnancies is higher than the risk for pregnancies with one fetus, and the risk increases with an increased number of fetuses. A pregnancy of more than five fetuses only rarely results in a live birth, despite the publicity that has been generated recently around sextuplet and septuplet births. Such births are the rare exceptions.

Other Medical Treatments for the Woman

Another drug, bromocriptine (trade name: Parlodel), is used when a woman's prolactin level is elevated. Bromocriptine is an oral tablet taken once or twice a day. It is less expensive than some of the other treatments and very effective when prolactin is only slightly or moderately elevated.

Medications may be used to treat endometriosis. The treatment of this disease is controversial. The only complete cure consists of removal of the uterus and ovaries. Some medications, however, have been tried in an effort to help women with endometriosis conceive. These are synthetic hormones used to suppress ovulation and growth of the uterine lining for several cycles, that is, to induce a pseudomenopausal state. Once treatment is stopped, the hope is that the endometriosis will not recur and pregnancy will ensue. Success rates vary.

These hormones include danazol (Danocrine), whose chemical structure is similar to the male hormone testosterone, and GnRH agonists— hormones that work like GnRH (gonadotropin-releasing hormone). Common GnRH agonists are leuprolide acetate (Lupron) and nafarelin acetate (Synarel). GnRH is the hormone produced by the hypothalamus that controls other glands. When one of these hormones is given, it works to prevent the pituitary gland from producing FSH and LH. These hormones stimulate the ovary to produce an egg cell. When FSH and LH are not produced, the ovary is "turned off." Because of side effects, such as menopausal symptoms, these hormones are only used for short periods of time, never more than 6 months.

Sometimes estrogen therapy is used to improve the quality of cervical mucus if the postcoital test shows that the sperm cannot navigate the mucus. Intrauterine insemination may also be used for this problem.

If an endometrial biopsy shows evidence of poor quality response to ovulation, some authorities believe that taking a progesterone hormone in the latter half of the cycle will increase the secretory state of the endometrium sufficiently to support implantation of a fertilized egg.

Finally, in instances of recurring miscarriage, *immunotherapy* may be indicated. This is used when tests reveal the presence or absence of certain antibodies. Several treatments are available, depending on the problem. In women with autoimmune disease, such as systemic lupus erythematosus, or women who have antiphospholipid antibodies in their blood, corticosteroid therapy might suppress these immune responses. Anticoagulant therapy, including low-dose aspirin or heparin, might be tried as these antibodies tend to cause the vascular system to form clots, detrimental to the success of a pregnancy.

Conversely, when certain antibodies are lacking, injections of white blood cells (*leukocytes*) from either husband or donor may stimulate the formation of these antibodies. Apparently, such antibodies are needed to maintain the pregnancy, despite the fact that in most instances of rejection of foreign bodies, it is the antibodies, not their lack, that causes rejection. In pregnancy, as paradoxical as this may seem, there appears to be a benefit in some amount of antibody response to the fetus.

Medical Treatment for the Couple

Treatment for antisperm antibodies has been undertaken by having the male partner use a condom until the laboratory evidence of sensitivity disappears. The process may be hastened by suppressing the woman's immune response with corticosteroids. Studies have been done in which the sperm are concentrated and specially treated to remove the antigen— which is stimulating the formation of the antibodies. The sperm are then used for insemination.

Donor Sperm

If a woman is using donor semen because she is single, lesbian, or has a male partner with very poor quality semen, but she has no fertility problems, the semen can be injected into the vagina. Some women do this on their own, with semen received from sperm banks that make it available directly to women with supervision of a health care provider. Some women use semen donated by a friend or relative.

Receiving sperm from a reputable sperm bank helps with the legal issues involved in the procedure as the donors are screened and have signed legal consent forms. They remain anonymous to the sperm recipients. Receiving sperm from a friend, relative, or acquaintance should be considered carefully. Appropriate documents should be signed in consultation with an attorney experienced in this field.

Legal issues arise with donated eggs as well; these issues are discussed on page 372.

Donor insemination has the advantage, as compared to adoption, that the woman and her partner go through the experiences of pregnancy and delivery. The resulting child has the genetic material of one of the parents.

Sperm banks usually provide a list of characteristics of the donor so you can choose a donor with characteristics that you want or that most closely match those of your partner. You should verify that the sperm bank screens donors for genetic and infectious disorders.

Women have been known to seek donor insemination repeatedly. For the past several years, all donor sperm purchased from a sperm bank is frozen. This is so that it can be tested for HIV and retested 6 months later. All sperm should be ordered from sperm banks that follow this procedure.

Intrauterine Insemination (IUI)

The placement of sperm directly into the uterus is called *intrauterine insemination* (IUI). IUI can be used when the problem is low numbers of sperm in the semen or poor sperm quality. It can be used when there is poor cervical mucus or when either the woman or man has antibodies to sperm. It is often recommended following a poor postcoital test. It can be used in cases of mild endometriosis or unexplained infertility. IUI can be used with donor semen when the male partner has a genetic abnormality, very poor sperm mobility, very few sperm, or a complete lack of sperm (*azoospermia*). It is used frequently with ovulation induction or stimulation.

Before IUI, the ovary is stimulated to produce multiple eggs. Ovulation is determined by any of a variety of techniques including basal body temperature, LH surge shown by a urine or blood test, or ultrasound. After not ejaculating for 2 to 5 days, the man provides a semen specimen through masturbation. After sperm washing and separation, the specimen is placed into a small catheter and the sperm deposited through the cervix into the uterine cavity. From there, the sperm swim around and, if fertilization occurs, it will take place in the fallopian tube—the usual site. The woman will, of course, be in position for a pelvic examination with a speculum used to visualize the cervix. Anesthesia is not required, but since the uterine cavity is entered, cramping may occur. The woman will usually lie down for about 10 to 20 minutes following the insemination.

In cases of poor sperm production, and often when the woman is taking medications for ovulation induction, the sperm will be prepared with various techniques in advance to improve their shape and motion. The best sperm will be concentrated in a solution. If bacteria or pus had been present in the semen, it will be removed.

Pregnancy rates with IUI depend on the quality of sperm, the age of the woman, the cause of the infertility, and how long the couple has been infertile. With very poor quality sperm, IUI generally is ineffective. It cannot be used if the woman has blocked tubes or severe endometriosis. It can be used in most other instances of infertility. Pregnancy rates vary from 3 to 15 percent per cycle. They are higher when injectable gonadotropins are used for ovarian stimulation compared to clomiphene, as injectables stimulate the maturation of more follicles and the release of a greater number of eggs. After four to six cycles of IUI, the success rate tapers off considerably and most experts do not recommend continuing it beyond six attempts.

The fetal outcomes from inseminated pregnancies do not differ from those of pregnancies achieved without intervention.

Surgical Treatment for the Woman

Surgery may be performed when the tubes are blocked, when uterine fibroids interfere with implantation, and sometimes with endometriosis. Outcome of surgery is quite variable and depends on the extent of the problem.

Treatment for Tubal Blockage

If the outer end of the fallopian tube is scarred closed but the remainder of the tube is normal, delicate surgery can be done, usually with an operating microscope, to open this up. The microscope facilitates identification of the layers of the tube, so that they can be accurately sewn to one another. If there are areas of obstruction along the length of the tube, they can be excised and the tube brought together again. The most difficult problems are encountered when the obstruction is in the very narrow portion of the tube as it passes through the uterine wall.

Efforts to reestablish *patency* (openness) of the fallopian tubes have a success rate well above 50 percent in instances where the damage is mild. Patency is reestablished in no more than 15 to 30 percent of women with severe tubal damage. Unfortunately, in such reconstructed tubes, the rate of ectopic pregnancy is increased (see Chapter 12).

If the woman has had her tubes tied (*tubal ligation*) as a birth control measure, surgery can reestablish tubal patency and in many cases reestablish fertility. The great majority of women who have had tubal ligations have no hormonal problem. If the sterilization was done by applying clips to the tubes, the success rate of rejoining (*tubal reanastomosis*) is higher than if the tubes were burned. The length of the remaining tube is an important criterion in determining the success of the surgery and this cannot always be ascertained until the time of the surgery. The older the woman, and the longer the time that has elapsed since the sterilization, the less chance of success. Success rates range from 45 to 86 percent in various studies.

Tubal surgery, including reversal of previous sterilization procedures, may require hospitalization for up to 3 days. The surgery usually is done through a *laparotomy*, an abdominal incision. On occasion, a surgeon will try to repair tubes with a laparoscopy. This generally involves two small incisions above the pubic hair line along with the incision in or near the navel. Women usually will need several weeks to recuperate from the operation.

Some women will choose in vitro fertilization (IVF) rather than tubal surgery. One unfortunate consideration may be whether health insurance will pay for one procedure and not the other. With tubal reversal procedures pregnancy presumably can be achieved in the old-fashioned way—through sexual intercourse. With IVF, ovarian stimulation with medication is required, followed by procedures, described later, to retrieve the egg and then to transfer the embryo back into the body. Each of these choices has advantages and disadvantages to consider.

Surgical removal of fibroid tumors of the uterus that distort the endometrial cavity and are associated with either inability to become pregnant or repeated miscarriage results in a high success rate in women who are otherwise without a problem. Surgery can be accomplished through an abdominal incision or a hysteroscopy, depending on where the fibroids are located and the skill, experience, and preference of the surgeon. Surgery to remove the abnormal growth of uterine tissue that occurs with endometriosis has variable success. This often is accomplished via laparoscopy.

Medical Treatment for the Man

A wide range of hormonal therapies has been undertaken when a man has subfertile sperm. Some of the same medications used in women, including gonadotropin releasing hormone, clomiphene citrate, and human chorionic gonadotropin, have been tried to increase sperm counts. None, however, seem to be particularly effective.

Close-fitting jockey shorts, which may raise the temperature in the scrotum, thus destroying sperm, should be abandoned where there is infertility. Discontinuing exposures as noted in the table on pages 343–344 may be effective, whenever possible.

Surgical Treatment for the Man

If sperm cells are being formed but there is obstruction in the passageway from the scrotum to the urethra, a bypass operation around the point of blockage may be successful.

Very infrequently, the opening to the urethra, the excretory tube leading through the penis, is not on its tip, but at the base of the penis (*hypospadias*). Semen is ejaculated outside the vagina. A plastic surgeon can close the defect. This allows the semen to exit from the tip of the penis into the vagina.

If a male with a poor semen specimen has a large *varicocele* (scrotal varicose vein), this condition can be eliminated surgically. Success rates vary.

If the testicles are retained in the abdomen, either hormonal or surgical correction can be successfully accomplished, but this must be carried out before puberty.

More than 50 percent of men who have been sterilized by *vasectomy* (a tie or ligature placed around the vas deferens on each side and a small segment removed) are able to initiate a pregnancy after corrective surgery. Success rates are best within the first 10 years after the vasectomy has been performed.

Another option for pregnancy after vasectomy or with anatomical defects is to aspirate sperm with a needle from the testicle or *epididymis* (the part of the passageway for sperm adjoining the testes). This procedure is called TESA—Testicular/Epididymal Sperm Aspiration. The aspiration is carried out with sedation and local anesthesia. Usually, there are not enough sperm retrieved with this procedure to perform an intrauterine insemination, and in vitro fertilization with ovarian stimulation and intracytoplasmic sperm injection (see later) is done.

ASSISTED REPRODUCTIVE TECHNOLOGIES (ART)

Until the end of the twentieth century, a woman who had lost both her tubes due to infection, tumors, or ectopic pregnancies had no possibility of becoming pregnant. Women with endometriosis or unexplained infertility often had extremely poor chances of becoming pregnant. To-day, a variety of assisted reproductive technologies have enabled women who, only 3 decades ago, could never become pregnant to do so. This is a remarkable achievement, although even with the most elegant and so-phisticated techniques, not all women are able to achieve pregnancy. There are couples who invest a tremendous amount of time and money into their attempt to become pregnant, only to be disappointed.

Each woman and each couple facing infertility should become as knowledgeable as possible about the options available to them. They should try to be realistic about their chances of success and how much effort—in terms of time and money—they want or are able to invest in this endeavor. Unfortunately, the most up-to-date approaches may be available only in large cities with major medical centers, or in a few cen-ters located in smaller cities or towns. Because infertility is not covered by all health insurance policies, the technologies are inequitably avail-able according to the income and resources of couples. The extent to which a woman can devote several days a month to a treatment span of several months is another issue. Even couples with the financial re-sources to invest in ART may not have the resources in terms of time.

Success of assisted reproductive technologies (ART) varies according to the personal characteristics of the man and woman involved. For some couples, success will require using either donor semen or donor eggs. The offspring produced thus will be genetically related to only one member of the couple. If donor eggs are utilized, the woman who car-ries the pregnancy, while not genetically related to the offspring, will have a biological relationship to the child. And, despite a lack of genetic or biological relationship, both partners will experience pregnancy, la-bor, and the birth of the child. Potential parents should know that in the event pregnancy is impossible, the lack of a biological relationship to an adopted child in no way precludes a strong and loving relationship.

In Vitro Fertilization (IVF)

In vitro fertilization is the most popularized of the assisted reproductive technologies. The birth of the first so-called test tube baby in England, in July, 1978, made worldwide headlines. Since then, thousands of ba-bies have been born following in vitro fertilization (IVF). The technique has become an accepted part of reproductive care.

In vitro literally means "in glass," referring to the fact that the egg is fertilized in a laboratory, outside of the woman's body. This allows the egg to meet the sperm without the need for the sperm to travel through cervical mucus that might be too thick or through tubes that might be full of scar tissue. It gives a chance to sperm that are poor swimmers or misshapen. IVF even allows the sperm to meet the egg where there are missing structures—a birth defect, for example, that caused a man to be born without a vas deferens to transport sperm to the urethra. It allows a pregnancy when a woman cannot ovulate normally and when a man has too few sperm.

IVF cannot be used when the infertility problem is uterine, such as occurs when adhesions form following a D & C (*Asherman's syndrome*). It is appropriate for women with blocked fallopian tubes and is an alternative to reversal surgery for women who have had tubal ligation. IVF can be used when a woman has severe endometriosis.

It is appropriate for women whose partners have such a low sperm count or low sperm motility that insemination is considered impossible. It is used for women aged 40 and over, and women with poor egg quality. In the latter case, donor eggs might be combined with IVF.

How is IVF done? Regardless of whether a woman is ovulating on her own or not, her ovaries need to be stimulated so that multiple eggs are produced. This is called COH—*controlled ovarian hyperstimulation*. First, the woman will receive drugs called *gonadotropin-releasing hormone agonists* (GnRH-agonists) or others that have the same effect— suppression of the woman's pituitary gland. This prevents the pituitary from stimulating ovulation. These drugs are followed by FSH (follicle stimulating hormone), or hMG (human menopausal gonadotropin). This causes follicles in the ovary to grow.

These medications are given by injection and the woman usually learns to give the injections herself or with the help of her partner, as they need to be given daily for several weeks. GnRH is injected *subcutaneously*, just under the skin, while hMG is given deep into the muscle. FSH may be given subcutaneously or into the muscle, depending on the specific brand used.

Once FSH or hMG is given, blood tests and ultrasound are done every 1 to 3 days to monitor the development of the follicles in the ovary. These follicles contain the eggs. When there are enough follicles of sufficient size, hCG (human chorionic gonadotropin) is given, also by injection into the muscle. Eggs are retrieved about 34 to 36 hours after the hCG is injected.

As many eggs are retrieved as possible; not all will become fertilized. Eggs are retrieved via a long needle passed through the vagina. Strong pain killers are usually used for this procedure, which takes about 10 to 15 minutes. The woman will be observed for a few hours after the retrieval.

Sperm is mixed with the eggs about 4 hours later. Eggs that become fertilized are transferred to an incubator before they are transferred into the uterus.

Following egg retrieval, progesterone is given, either by intramuscular injection or as a vaginal suppository. This maintains the uterine lining. In most procedures, the embryos are transferred to the uterus 3 days following retrieval.

Embryo transfer (ET) also is accomplished through the vagina and cervix. Two to five embryos are put into a *catheter* (small tube). This is introduced through the cervix into the uterus and the embryos literally are squirted out of the catheter.

About 10 days after the embryo transfer, blood is drawn for a pregnancy test.

For women with *low ovarian reserve*—few viable eggs in the ovary— donor eggs are used. Use of donor eggs is recommended for women in their forties (or older), women whose natural FSH levels are high, and women who do not respond to ovarian stimulation.

The donor's ovaries are stimulated as described above and her eggs are retrieved. They are then fertilized with sperm.

The woman who will receive the fertilized eggs—called the *recipient*—is given medications to suppress her menstrual cycle and to make her uterine lining receptive to the fertilized eggs. Egg donors generally are reimbursed for their services, although the donor may be a friend, family member, or volunteer who gives her egg as a gift. Success of this procedure seems to be increased if the egg donor has had a successful pregnancy herself.

Like sperm donors, egg donors should be screened carefully for infectious diseases that could be transmitted via the procedure. Sometimes donors are screened for carrier status for genetic disorders such as cystic fibrosis or Tay-Sachs disease (see Chapter 8). Other times, a good medical and family history is all the screening done. The parents choose a donor based on a supplied description of physical characteristics.

The egg donor, recipient, and recipient's partner should all sign consent forms regarding this procedure. Most experts advise anonymity for the egg donor, as they do for sperm donors. Of course, if the donor is a family member or friend, this is not possible. Legal issues do sometimes come up regarding maternity and paternity in these cases. Questions might arise, for example, when the child born has a birth defect, although not all defects can be anticipated. The recipient couple must be aware of this possibility, which could occur just as well with their own sperm or egg cells.

New Techniques Combined with IVF

Several procedures have been added recently to the techniques used in IVF. One is the freezing of retrieved eggs, sperm, and embryos. This is also called *cryopreservation*. Today all donor sperm is frozen in sperm banks, unless a woman or couple receive fresh sperm from a friend or relative. Cryopreservation of sperm also has been used in special circumstances—for example, when a man is about to have chemotherapy for cancer treatment and is expected to become sterile secondary to the treatment. Cryopreservation of embryos has been used to reduce the number of invasive procedures needed for ovulation stimulation and egg retrieval. The cryopreservation of eggs is still new and experimental.

When the sperm quality is poor, a technique called *intracytoplasmic sperm injection* or ICSI can be tried. In this technique, a single sperm is injected directly into an egg cell. Because poor quality sperm may be due to a genetic problem, the man should first have genetic testing, including a karyotype. Results take several weeks, so these tests should be done well in advance of the woman's beginning hormonal treatment.

Some speculation has arisen that undetected genetic disorders might be passed onto a child conceived via ICSI. To date, no such disorders have been seen, but the possibility exists that future defects will be noted, such as abnormal sexual development or infertility in these children. Knowing this small risk is part of the decision-making process when choosing ICSI over donor sperm.

Assisted hatching is a technique used in circumstances such as when the woman is over age 37, when her egg quality is known to be poor, when the embryos show slow rates of cell division, or after failed IVF cycles. It may also be used when frozen embryos are thawed before they are transferred into the uterus. The purpose of this technique is to make implantation into the uterine lining more successful by helping the embryo emerge from its shell or cover (called the *zona pellucida*). Several techniques may be used to actually make a cut into the zona. The embryo cover can be slit open with a long glass needle. This is called *mechanical hatching*. The zona can be opened with an acid solution. This is called *chemical hatching*. The zona also may be opened with a laser, called *laser hatching*. Pregnancy rates can be increased with embryo hatching, but the danger exists that the embryo can be damaged by the procedure.

Another recent innovation in ART is *preimplantation genetic diagnosis*. This is used to test either retrieved ova or cultured embryos for genetic diseases, as described in Chapter 8. The advantage of this is that it avoids prenatal diagnosis later in pregnancy, which may necessitate abortion should the baby prove defective and the parents not want to carry it. Preimplantation diagnosis allows couples to avoid an abortion procedure. There is a small chance of damaging an embryo during biopsy of its cells to obtain the specimen for preimplantation diagnosis. As the technique is new, there remains a chance for misdiagnosis. After a negative result, couples are counseled to undergo regular prenatal diagnostic procedures as described in Chapter 8 should they want a more definitive diagnosis.

Some centers are trying different methods of embryo transfer. One new method of transfer is *blastocyst transfer*. In blastocyst transfer, the embryo is cultured in the laboratory for at least 5 days, until it reaches the stage known as a blastocyst. The advantage is that when a blastocyst is transferred to the uterus, it is at the point in its development when it would normally enter the uterus from the tubes.

Another rationale behind blastocyst transfer is that fewer embryos need to be transferred because their capacity for continued growth can be better assessed. This would decrease the likelihood of multiple pregnancies occurring with IVF. However, it is also possible that the embryos, if left in culture for 5 days, will be lost. In the early days of IVF, it was not possible to maintain embryos in in vitro cultures for 5 days. Today, new culture media have made this more possible, but not guaranteed. This technology is still in its experimental stages and its success remains to be determined.

Two other transfer procedures have been utilized in ART: GIFT and ZIFT. GIFT stands for *Gamete Intrafallopian Transfer* and ZIFT for *Zygote Intrafallopian Transfer*. These are procedures that were developed to improve the rate of successfully implanted pregnancies by transferring into the fallopian tubes, rather than the uterus, as fertilization naturally takes place in the tubes. The thought was that by more closely replicating what happens naturally, success rates would be improved.

In GIFT a laparoscope is used to guide the transfer of unfertilized eggs and sperm (gametes or sex cells) into the fallopian tubes through small incisions in the abdomen. In ZIFT, a fertilized egg is transferred via laparoscope into the tubes. A zygote is the fertilized ovum before it reaches the stage of being an embryo, so this transfer is done right after fertilization. There are two distinct disadvantages to GIFT and ZIFT. One is that they require open and working tubes, limiting their use. Another is that they require abdominal incisions. As IVF has improved, the use of GIFT and ZIFT has decreased because of these disadvantages compared to IVF.

ART has also been used to collect eggs from a woman whose uterus had been removed. After IVF, the ova were transferred to the uterus of her sister, who had previously delivered healthy children. The baby thus produced was genetically the child of the donor of the eggs and her husband.

How Successful Is ART?

Several questions naturally come to mind to couples considering IVF. How successful is the procedure? How does one choose an appropriate facility for the procedure?

To help prospective parents assess IVF centers and determine whether they want to risk a time-consuming and expensive procedure, the Centers for Disease Control and Prevention monitors and publishes overall national success rates, and rates for individual IVF centers affiliated with its monitoring program. A good first question, then, is whether or not a center is part of the CDC's monitoring program.

IVF Rates of Success

In evaluating success rates, it is important to understand how the rates are presented. Pregnancy rate is not a measure of success because the pregnancy may miscarry. Live births is the measure of success. Couples should evaluate numbers of pregnancies per cycle, not per embryo transfer. There may be cycles without any transfer, but the couple still has undergone various procedures up to that point. Realize, however, that success rates may look better in a clinic that has a strict protocol for accepting women and couples into its program. Another clinic may have a lower success rate but may accept women who are less likely to have successful IVF procedures. Inquire, then, about criteria for acceptance into a center's program as part of your overall evaluation of the center. If you know your chances of success are limited, but wish to proceed with IVF, then you must find a center that is willing to work with you, despite the expected difficulties.

The CDC publishes detailed ART results by age of the woman and according to whether the embryos used were fresh or frozen (see figures below) and whether the eggs were from the woman or a donor. These detailed results are available on the CDC's website at www.cdc.gov/nccdphp/drh/art.htm. The numbers presented here are of live births per one hundred cycles for fresh embryos from nondonor eggs in 1999:

Age ≤35:   32.2
Age 35–37:   26.2
Age 38–40:   18.5
Age 41–42:   9.7
Age ≥42:   5

When frozen embryos were used from nondonor eggs, the rates were somewhat lower than the above numbers. The rates for ART with donor eggs were somewhat higher, especially in the older age groups. Donor eggs are typically from women in their twenties and early thirties. While the success rates using frozen embryos are somewhat lower, cycles in which frozen embryos are used involve fewer invasive procedures and are less expensive. The woman need not go through repeated ovarian stimulation or egg retrieval.

The CDC also has published the numbers of twin, triplet, and total multiple births per one hundred ART pregnancies. In 1999 these were:

Twin gestations:
Age ≤35:   32.6
Age 35–37:   28.6
Age 38–40:   22.7
Age 41–42:   14.0
Age ≥42:   unavailable

Triplet or more gestations:
Age ≤35:   9.4
Age 35–37:   8.6
Age 38–40:   6.6
Age 41–42:   2.6
Age ≥42:   unavailable

Total multiple live births:
Age ≤35:   41.0
Age 35–37:   37.5
Age 38–40:   28.6
Age 41–42:   14.4
Age ≥42:   unavailable

Overall, in 1999, 40.9 percent of cycles of ART produced a pregnancy and 14.8 produced a single live birth, while 10.1 percent produced a multiple birth—for a total live birth rate of 24.9 percent.

Sixteen percent of pregnancies had an adverse outcome—an ectopic pregnancy, miscarriage, induced abortion, or stillbirth.

The above statistics are actually for all forms of ART, including GIFT and ZIFT, not just IVF.

Women who conceive with multiple fetuses may consider a *fetal reduction procedure*. This is sometimes called *selective reduction* or *selective abortion*, but in the case of ART either of these is usually a misnomer. Selective reduction or abortion is the procedure of aborting one or more fetuses after prenatal diagnosis shows that the pregnancy consists of one or more fetuses with a disease or defect and one or more without such a problem. In these cases, the fetus to abort is "selected."

In procedures following ART, one or more of the fetuses are aborted at about 9 to 11 weeks gestation, but generally not selected by genetic study. Either the smallest fetus or the one lying lowest in the uterus is chosen for abortion. This usually is accomplished with an injection of potassium chloride, using a thin needle passed through the mother's abdomen, into the chest of the fetus, causing death. The procedure is done under ultrasound guidance. A reduction procedure involving suction through the mother's cervix is another possibility.

Fetal reduction is used to reduce quadruplets and multiple pregnancies of higher order. They are usually made into twin gestations. It has been used to reduce triplets to twins, but this hasn't been shown to improve survival or reduce illness for the newborns.

Although many fetal reduction procedures are performed safely, the procedure carries some risk. Risks include miscarriage of the remaining fetus or fetuses; a genetic disease or defect in the remaining fetus (not caused by the procedure, but a reality that will have the parents questioning whether they aborted a healthy fetus in place of one with a problem); and maternal infection or hemorrhage. There is also a small possibility of causing damage, but not death, to the fetus injected with the potassium solution.

Fetal reduction procedures raise various ethical issues for many people, but the alternative is a high likelihood of losing all the fetuses, or having newborns with multiple health problems. For many women and couples, contemplating aborting a fetus or more than one fetus after months, even years, of trying to achieve pregnancy presents not only ethical issues, but a huge personal dilemma. This is an individual and private decision to be made by the woman and her partner, with the consultation of their physician, family, friends, a religious advisor, and other people whose opinions they respect and trust.

SURROGATE MOTHERHOOD

Some normally fertile women have agreed to be inseminated by fertile men whose partners for one reason or another are unable to conceive. They have had a hysterectomy and *oophorectomy* (removal of the uterus and ovaries), for example, or have an anatomical anomaly such as a congenital absence of the uterus and vagina. These women cannot have ART. The recipient mother agrees to go through pregnancy and then to turn the baby over for adoption by the couple.

The legal and ethical status of this is very unclear. For example, who is responsible for the care of a defective child born from such an arrangement, however unlikely such an event might be? And how can an agreement of the sort described above be enforced if the woman carrying the baby, or the one whom she is carrying it for, changes her mind? Such cases have been reported in the news media in recent years, and many issues remain unresolved.

The Future of ART

We have all heard of the cloning of animals, the creation of a new life from the genetic material of one being, not two. We have heard of organ transplants, which might allow uteri, tubes, or ovaries to be transferred from one woman to another. We have heard of instances of 60-year-old women becoming pregnant with ART.

Assisted reproductive technologies create many possibilities, limited perhaps only by the human imagination. Some of these present greater challenges in the arenas of ethics and law than they do in the fields of biology and technology. No legal or ethical group in the United States, for example, currently supports research in the cloning of human beings. Expansion of technology often precedes expansion of the ability of human beings to determine the ethics of situations created by the technological advancements. If the new century brings as rapid technological and scientific achievement as we have seen in the second half of the past century, the questions raised will allow ethicists and legal experts to ponder for years to come. We trust the ethics-seeking component of technological advancement never will be abandoned.

A MESSAGE TO WOMEN AND COUPLES FACING INFERTILITY

If you are one of the couples who have unsuccessfully been trying to establish a pregnancy for a year or two, what are your chances? Three decades ago the likelihood of your having a baby was perhaps in the neighborhood of 25 percent. Now it is much greater than 50 percent. You do not have to greet infertility with inaction and guilt. You can seek skilled medical assistance to help you exhaust all possible avenues of having a baby. If these fail, or you are unable or unwilling to use all available technology, you may adopt one or more children or simply continue in a strong and loving relationship with your partner, if you are so blessed.

We highly recommend contacting RESOLVE (see Appendix). Its information and resources undoubtedly will be of value to you. You may wish to join one of its support groups, or simply read its printed or online material. This organization was founded in 1974 by people who faced the same problems, decisions, and emotional turmoil you are facing. It is a wonderful resource for support.

CHAPTER FOURTEEN

❧

Miscarriage
(Spontaneous Abortion)

Parents use the term miscarriage to describe an early pregnancy loss. The medical term for such a loss is *spontaneous abortion*. It is defined as a termination of pregnancy before the twentieth week or when the fetus weighs less than 500 grams (about 1.1 pounds). More than 80 percent of such losses occur in the first trimester or first 12 weeks of pregnancy. The majority of these take place between the ninth and the eleventh week. Only one in four pregnancy losses occurs between the twelfth and twenty-sixth week.

We will use the term miscarriage in this chapter. The medical terminology causes confusion between this event, neither planned nor chosen, and induced abortion, a termination of pregnancy by choice.

Most times, a miscarriage is nature's way of seeing to it that newborns are born healthy. In more than half of miscarriages, there is a problem with the egg, the sperm, or the developing embryo.

Many more eggs are fertilized than pregnancies are achieved. Some of these ova undergo a few cell divisions in the fallopian tube and develop no further. Some proceed to a many-celled stage, but fail to implant in the uterus. Some implant close to a blood vessel in the lining of the uterus and cause a hemorrhage, which expels them. All these events take place before a woman misses a menstrual period. In the past, women had no way of knowing that an egg had been fertilized in such a cycle.

Today, with pregnancy tests that detect the pregnancy hormone hCG (human chorionic gonadotropin) in the mother's blood about the fifth or sixth day after fertilization, or about the twentieth day of a normal cycle, more women are aware that this event has taken place, even when no other sign of pregnancy is present. This often is referred to as a *chemical pregnancy*, but in fact, these fertilized ova are not yet pregnancies. They are lost quite frequently. The woman experiences a regular menstrual period. It may be heavier than normal, but not necessarily.

Of the eggs that implant more successfully and therefore cause a delay in your period and symptoms that you recognize as pregnancy, approximately 10 to 15 percent are subsequently lost. These are what are known ordinarily as miscarriages.

WHAT INFLUENCES MISCARRIAGE?

The risk of miscarriage increases with increased age of the mother and with increased numbers of pregnancies. A woman in her early twenties having a first baby is less likely to have a miscarriage than a woman in her late thirties having her fourth baby. An increase in age of the father also seems to cause an increase in the likelihood of having a miscarriage. Pregnancies that are conceived within 3 months of a live birth have a greater chance of miscarrying.

Specific Causes of Miscarriage

Abnormalities of chromosome number and, less commonly, chromosome structure account for more than half of all miscarriages. A detailed discussion of chromosomal abnormalities is in Chapter 8. Because the risk of having an abnormal ovum increases with age, this is one reason why the rate of miscarriage increases with the age of the woman.

Some chromosomal abnormalities are incompatible with life, such as tripling of the larger chromosomes. They almost always result in a miscarriage. Others, such as tripling of chromosome 13, called *trisomy 13*, sometimes result in a live birth, but have an increased chance of miscarrying. If such a pregnancy does go to term, the babies born have serious problems.

When a miscarriage is caused by a chromosomal abnormality, 60 percent of the time it is a trisomy. Twenty percent of the time it is a lack of the Y sex chromosome. This condition, denoted as 45X or 45XO, is called *Turner's syndrome* and 99 percent of the time it causes a miscarriage. (The 1 percent of babies born with Turner's syndrome live normal lives, although they need hormonal treatment and are not able to reproduce.) About 15 percent of chromosomal abnormalities in miscarriages involve more than three chromosomes. This is called *polyploidy*. The remaining 5 percent of miscarried anomalies are abnormalities of chromosome structure such as a *translocation*. In the healthy parents, the translocation is balanced. This means a part of one chromosome has moved to another chromosome. There is no change in the total amount of chromosomal material. When a sex cell with a balanced translocation divides, however, chromosomal material may be lost or gained, causing an abnormality of development.

Maternal disease occasionally causes miscarriage. Unregulated diabetes increases the risk for miscarriage, although diabetes in which the mother's blood sugar levels are well controlled does not lead to miscarriage. Some experts report *hypothyroid*, or underactive thyroid disease, to be associated with miscarriage, although not all agree. Treatment of the thyroid disorder should resolve the problem. *Celiac disease* is another illness possibly associated with miscarriage if untreated. Treatment for this intestinal malabsorption syndrome consists of a gluten-free diet. (Gluten is a protein found in some grains and vegetables.)

Women with *systemic lupus erythematosus* have an increased risk of miscarriage. This might be due to the presence of lupus anticoagulant antibody. Experts do not agree on the role antibodies play in miscarriage. In addition to the lupus anticoagulant antibody, antibodies of concern are the antisperm antibodies and antiphospholipid antibodies. The lupus anticoagulant antibody is included in the antiphospholipid antibody group, as is the anticardiolipin antibody. These can be tested for in blood. In this type of antibody response, called an *autoimmune response* (Greek: *autos* = self), the mother's antibodies are directed against herself.

There may be other causes of miscarriage related to the mother's immune system. These are complex mechanisms, that are not completely understood. In a healthy pregnancy, although the fetus is a "transplant" into the mother's body, certain responses of the mother's immune system prevent rejection of the fetus. When these mechanisms are disturbed, the woman's body seems to treat the fetus as if it were a true foreign body. This is thought to occur somewhat paradoxically when the fetus and mother are too much alike in terms of certain antigens (antigens are substances that cause antibody formation). Apparently, to prevent rejection, the mother needs to recognize the fetus as somewhat foreign to her. Certain antibodies need to form. If a type of antigen called *human leukocyte antigen* (HLA) is too similar in mother and fetus, the mother "rejects" the fetus. This occurs when the mother and father share similar antigens, which the fetus inherits. Rejection also may occur when the mother lacks certain antibodies, such as *antipaternal cyto-toxic antibodies.*

Severe malnutrition increases the possibility of miscarriage but the developing embryo is not miscarried when the mother is poorly nourished or lacks a particular nutrient. Smoking increases the rate of miscarriage. If a woman smokes more than fourteen cigarettes a day (three-fourths of a pack), she doubles her risk of miscarrying. In one study, as few as five cigarettes a day increased the possibility of miscarriage. Alcohol, even drinking twice a week, contributes to miscarriage. One study reported double the rate of miscarriage in women who drank twice a week and triple the rate in women who drank daily compared with women who did not drink.

Cocaine has been named as a cause of miscarriage. The evidence for this is not strong, but, of course, this drug can cause other serious pregnancy complications and should not be used in pregnancy.

There is no consistent evidence that caffeine intake increases miscarriage, although some studies have suggested that it does. A prudent approach is to limit caffeine to two cups per day of brewed coffee, five cups of instant coffee, or up to ten cups of tea brewed for 3 minutes. One interesting study found that drinking coffee and tea increased the risk of miscarriage, but drinking the equivalent amount of caffeine in soda did not. Perhaps there are components other than caffeine in tea and coffee that could be the culprits in causing miscarriage, if there are such culprits.

Environmental exposures that can cause miscarriage include arsenic, lead, formaldehyde, benzene, and ethylene oxide. Organic solvents, such as gasoline, lighter fluid, spot removers, aerosol sprays, and paints, can lead to miscarriage. Women who operate dry-cleaning machines have a risk of miscarriage. Some research indicates a possible link of miscarriage with working with superconductors found in the computer chip-making industry. Occupational pesticides might increase miscarriage rate. If you have a miscarriage, particularly repeated miscarriages, and think you may have been exposed to one of these toxic chemicals, you should discuss this with your employer or contact your local department of health, or the local office of the Occupational Safety and Health Administration (OSHA). Exposures in men who father children may also play a role in miscarriage. These include lead and mercury, discussed in detail in Chapter 5, and pesticides.

Electromagnetic fields, such as those emitted from video display terminals and television screens, have not been found to cause miscarriage, although there have been conflicting reports about the possible adverse effects of electric blankets. Since there is no need, really, to use an electric blanket, these are best avoided in the early months of pregnancy and the pregnancy planning stage.

Some studies have found an association between miscarriage and drinking more than five glasses of tap water from chlorinated water supplies. In 1998, an expert panel in Canada reviewed these studies and concluded that the evidence is not strong enough to prove this association, but that it warrants further investigation. *Chlorination* is used to destroy disease-causing bacteria that might otherwise exist in water supplies. There have been a few reports of miscarriage associated with well water contaminated with chemicals called *nitrates*.

Some people recommend that pregnant women use water filters or drink bottled water, although the purity of bottled water may be hard to confirm. You can contact your local department of health to get information about chlorination of the water supply in your community, as well as its lead levels.

In very high doses, radiation can cause miscarriage. This is higher than the amount of radiation in diagnostic use of X ray, but women who need x-ray therapy must seriously discuss with their physicians the likelihood of the treatment causing a miscarriage. They, together with their physicians and family members, must weigh carefully the risk of losing their pregnancy versus the risk of delaying necessary treatment. (Used between 10 and 27 weeks of pregnancy, X rays also may be teratogenic, causing birth defects; this is discussed in Chapter 5.)

A number of studies have looked at the effect of various types of work on pregnancy outcome. There is no proven association between any specific work factors and miscarriage, but shift work, long working hours, standing for hours at a time, and heavy work have all been implicated as possible contributors to miscarriage. Most physicians and midwives do not advise women to change their work when they become pregnant (except where a clearly dangerous exposure exists), but if miscarriage is recurrent (see the discussion later) and no other causes are found, you might consider adjusting such work factors, to the extent possible.

Uterine defects may cause miscarriage. These include defects in the body of the uterus and in the cervix or neck of the uterus. Some abnormalities of the uterus result from the fact that it arises in the embryo from a pair of tubes, the *Müllerian ducts*, which later fuse together. They may fail to combine properly, or one duct may fail to develop. This results in a uterus with an inadequate cavity (*uterine dysgenesis*), which may reject the fetus long before it has become large enough to survive.

Incomplete fusion of the two ducts produces an abnormal uterine cavity (*septate* or *bicornuate uterus*) or even complete doubling of the uterine body and cervix (*uterus didelphys*). Defects similar to these, such as a T-shaped uterus, may have been caused by DES (diethylstilbestrol) exposure of the woman when she was a fetus.

Fibroid tumors of the uterus, also called *myomas* or *leiomyomas*, may sometimes cause a distortion of the uterine cavity and interefere with the growth of the embryo. This happens when the fibroid is on the inside of the uterine lining (*submucous myoma*) or inside the muscle, but causing the muscle to push into the uterine lining (*interstitial* or *intramural myoma*). Most fibroids, however, do not interfere with pregnancy.

Sometimes uterine or cervical defects may result from prior conditions or surgical procedures. Severe postpartum bleeding in a previous pregnancy, for example, could have caused Asherman's syndrome, in which the uterine walls adhere to each other. Implantation cannot occur. In women who have had surgery of the cervix, sometimes a condition called *incompetent cervix* or *incompetent cervical syndrome* results. When this happens, the cervix opens, without labor or warning, before the baby is old enough to survive on its own. Miscarriages due to cervical incompetence are somewhat unique in that they occur in the second trimester and are without pain.

Another possible cause of miscarriage is an infection in the uterus. *Ureaplasma urealyticum* has received the most attention as an offending organism in spontaneous abortion. Others are *Chlamydia trachomatis* and *Mycoplasma hominis*. These can all be transmitted sexually.

On very rare occasions, a miscarriage may be due to trauma to the mother's abdomen. When this occurs, the miscarriage is likely to follow the trauma within several weeks.

An interesting recent study found that women who exercised had a lowered chance of miscarrying than women who did not.

We still do not know all the reasons for miscarriage and cannot identify them all even with the best technologies available at the moment.

Causes of Recurrent Miscarriage

Some of the conditions just discussed will cause repeated or recurrent miscarriage, also called *habitual miscarriage*. Miscarriage is defined as recurrent if it happens three or more times in a row. If a term pregnancy or a pregnancy that resulted in the birth of a viable newborn ensued between miscarriages, they are not considered habitual.

Most chromosomal abnormalities seen in miscarriage are not inherited abnormalities, but occur as a result of a defect in the cell division that formed the particular egg or sperm. For this reason, most miscarriages are isolated events that will not recur. In some cases, however, the defect is an inherited disorder. This is likely when the abnormality of the chromosomes is an abnormality of structure, rather than an abnormality of number. Abnormalities of chromosomal structure are rare compared to abnormalities of chromosomal number. Of the miscarriages that are due to chromosomal abnormalities, at least 95 percent are due to abnormalities of chromosome number. About 25 percent of recurrent abortions are due to chromosomal abnormalities.

Anatomical uterine defects or cervical incompetence will result in recurrent or habitual miscarriage.

Since most women who have a miscarriage do not have a repeat miscarriage, most times the cause of the miscarriage is never discovered. If the woman is able to save the material that she expels from the vagina, or if the physician performs a dilation and curettage or suction procedure to empty the uterus, these products of conception can be sent to the laboratory for analysis of chromosomes and culture for infection. However, this is a time-consuming and expensive examination. It may not be covered by health insurance. In most instances, after a single miscarriage, analysis doesn't provide information that will help you determine treatment or prevention for the future.

When a woman has three or more miscarriages, then testing for each of the possible causes is worthwhile. In this case it is helpful to send the products of conception to a laboratory for analysis. This may mean placing the blood and tissues passed into a jar to bring to your physician or midwife.

Depending on the result, or if the fetal or placental material is not available for study, a karyotype or genetic map of the parents might be useful. If the fetus shows a defect in chromosome structure, then a karyotype might reveal a balanced translocation, for example, in one of the parents.

Other tests include a *sonogram* to rule out a uterine or cervical anomaly, *blood tests* of the mother to look for certain antibodies or their lack, *hormonal studies* to see if there is a progesterone deficiency in the second half of the menstrual cycle, and testing for specific maternal diseases.

On a reassuring note, even with three miscarriages, the likelihood for any given woman is that her next pregnancy will be successful.

WHAT HAPPENS
DURING A MISCARRIAGE?

Miscarriage in early pregnancy usually begins with bleeding. Cramping may or may not accompany the bleeding. Bleeding in early pregnancy falls into one of four categories (here we will use the medical terminology): threatened abortion; inevitable abortion; incomplete abortion; and missed abortion. This is assuming that the pregnancy is not an *ectopic pregnancy*—a pregnancy outside of the uterus, discussed in Chapter 12.

A *threatened abortion* is any bleeding in early pregnancy. A woman may also have cramping, often feeling like menstrual cramps, or aches in the lower back. Up to 20 or 25 percent of pregnancies have bleeding in the first trimester; there is at least a 50 percent chance of keeping the pregnancy even with early bleeding.

Slight bleeding around the time of the missed period is normal. There may be a bit of blood at the time of implantation—well before you are aware of any pregnancy. If the cervix is at all irritated, it might bleed, especially after intercourse. And then there is bleeding for which there is no explanation, but which does not end in miscarriage. Usually, if the pregnancy will be maintained, there is no cramping.

Anytime you have bleeding in pregnancy, you should contact your physician or midwife. Most important, they will make sure you do not have an ectopic pregnancy. Your physician or midwife will do a pelvic examination with a speculum to look for any obvious bleeding. He or she will look for any signs of an infection or inflammation of the cervix. An examination with the care provider's fingers (a *bimanual examination*) will be performed to check the size of the uterus and for enlargements or unusual tenderness in the area of the fallopian tubes. The care provider also will check whether the cervix is open (*dilated*) or thin (*effaced*) and if the membranes are bulging through the cervix or if there is amniotic fluid in the vagina or leaking through the cervix. Cervical opening or rupture of the membranes makes this an inevitable abortion, rather than a threatened abortion.

Before an abortion is said to be inevitable, however, you will have an ultrasound. Ultrasound will determine if the pregnancy is in the uterus, which is detectable at about 34 days (almost 5 weeks) after the first day of the last menstrual period. If you are at least 7 weeks (49 days) from your last menstrual period, the fetal heartbeat should be seen on ultrasound.

If the pregnancy is in the uterus, bloods may be drawn to see if hCG is at the level where it should be for the gestational age. Blood will then be rechecked to see if it is increasing appropriately. In the first weeks of pregnancy, hCG should increase by 66 percent in 48 hours and double in 72 hours. A progesterone value might be drawn as well. A value less than 5 (nanograms per milliliter) is evidence of fetal death, in the uterus or outside it.

When ultrasound shows a living fetus or fetal sac appropriate for the gestational age, whether or not blood work is done, the pregnancy is still viable. You should discuss with your midwife or physician whether blood work will be helpful in determining the possibility of a continuing pregnancy. A repeat ultrasound may be scheduled if bleeding continues or the uterus doesn't grow properly.

TREATMENT FOR MISCARRIAGE

Women used to be advised to rest in bed anytime they had bleeding in pregnancy. Physical exertion, however, really has no relationship to miscarriage. In a normal pregnancy, the embryo is solidly implanted. You can't shake a good fertilized human ovum loose from the uterus any more than you can shake an unripe apple loose from the apple tree. Nature sometimes makes mistakes, but normal seed and its fruits are guarded jealously.

Since most miscarriages are a consequence of an untreatable defect in the embryo or the placenta, the woman cannot prevent this from happening. The exception is recurrent miscarriage, for which treatment may be possible, often in advance of the next pregnancy.

While bed rest does not help preserve early pregnancy when there is a threatened abortion, pelvic rest is advised, although there is no real scientific evidence to show that this helps. Pelvic rest means you should not have sexual intercourse or put anything else in your vagina, such as the nozzle of a douche. Orgasm should be avoided as well, as orgasm causes uterine contractions.

If you have bleeding and the pregnancy is still viable, report to your midwife or physician any increased bleeding, cramping, or low back ache, or passage of fluid from the vagina. If there is cramping or pain, the likelihood of a continuing pregnancy is reduced.

If pelvic examination findings reveal an open cervix or rupture of the membranes, especially if the bleeding is moderate to heavy and you are experiencing pain or cramping, the miscarriage is no longer threatened, but inevitable. When the ultrasound reveals with certainty that the fetus has died, this may be a missed abortion. A missed abortion is one in which the fetus is no longer alive, but the miscarriage is delayed. It may be delayed for several weeks or longer.

In most instances of inevitable or missed abortion, the body will be able to work well enough to end the pregnancy safely so that intervention is not necessary. Most studies of watchful waiting, what is called *expectant management*, compared to vacuum aspiration or dilation and curettage (D & C) to empty the uterus, show no difference in terms of bleeding, infection, or other complications. Watchful waiting can only be used when bleeding is of a reasonable amount, when the woman is not anemic (so she can tolerate some possible extra bleeding), when pain is not intolerable, and when there are no signs of infection or hidden hemorrhage, including fever or changes in blood pressure or heart rate.

Complications

Whenever a woman with an inevitable or missed abortion is sent home, she must be careful to call her care provider immediately should she have excessive bleeding or fever and chills. Excessive bleeding usually means soaking through a regular sanitary napkin in an hour or less or passing clots larger than the size of a half-dollar. You should take your temperature several times a day (every 4 hours when awake is standard advice) and anytime you feel chills or ill. If your fever exceeds 100°F (37.8° centigrade), you should contact your physician or midwife as this may indicate infection.

If the miscarriage does not occur within 4 or 5 weeks or more, a missed abortion can lead to *disseminated intravascular coagulation* or DIC. This also can occur with a retained fetus later in the pregnancy and is discussed in Chapter 12. In this condition, the body essentially uses up the proteins that help with blood clotting. The result is bleeding, sometimes throughout the body. This usually doesn't happen until the fetus has been retained for more than a month, while miscarriage usually takes place within a few weeks after the fetus dies. However, to make sure that your clotting mechanisms are functioning, once a missed abortion is diagnosed, your physician (or midwife, in consultation with a physician) usually will draw several blood specimens over time for clotting studies. If these become abnormal, then intervention to end the pregnancy is needed.

Stages of a Missed Abortion

With a missed abortion, you may have bleeding, with or without cramping or pain. You first may notice, however, that the symptoms that tell you you are pregnant start to regress. Your breasts may stop being tender (although sometimes they do anyway at the end of the first trimester). They may get smaller. You may lose a few pounds and just stop feeling pregnant, even though you don't get a period. You may have heard that the second trimester is a relatively quiet trimester in terms of how the pregnancy feels, and may think you are entering that stage, even if a bit early.

Depending upon how many weeks pregnant you are, your physician or midwife may find at your regularly scheduled examination that your uterus is smaller than it should be for the expected gestational age, or that it hasn't grown. However, the uterus cannot be felt through the abdomen until about 12 weeks of pregnancy. If you are only 10 weeks or so when you have a missed abortion, and you had a pelvic examination at your previous visit at 6 weeks, then your physician or midwife wouldn't ordinarily do another pelvic examination to feel the size of the uterus—unless you are bleeding or report that you no longer feel pregnant. As there are many reasons for weight loss early in pregnancy, this alone wouldn't necessarily cause your physician or midwife to consider doing an internal examination. For this reason, even your care provider may miss a missed abortion for at least one prenatal visit. Or, you may not have a visit planned when you first feel these changes.

A week or so later, perhaps 10 or 11 weeks following the last menstrual period, you may notice a small amount of brownish stain on the toilet tissue after urinating. There is no pain or at worst a slight sensation deep in the pelvis, which is reminiscent of the sensation just prior to menstrual flow. This minimal brownish red discoloration from the vagina may reappear each time you urinate and a small amount may leak out with ordinary activity. Overnight nothing is noted but first thing in the morning some more of this discolored blood comes out of the vagina. In fact, this bloody discharge from the uterus does not cease overnight, but when you lie down, the blood pools in the vagina. When you get up in the morning it comes out from the effect of gravity.

The early staining may be followed by an increase in the sensation of impending menses. This is succeeded by cramps, which gradually increase in intensity, with the same kind of crescendo that occurs in normal labor. At the same time, bleeding tends to increase and the blood becomes a brighter red. The bleeding may be so rapid that clots form. Eventually, when the cramps reach their peak, you may experience an urge to urinate or move your bowels. On attempting to do so, you may pass a mass of blood and tissue, ranging anywhere from the size of a plum to a moderate size peach. The outside appearance of this mass is clearly firmer and shaggier than that of a blood clot. The cramps stop and bleeding slows down to a volume typical of a menstrual period.

If the tissue is examined, it turns out to be a compact mass of placenta within which there may be a small sac containing a degenerated fetus or, in some instances, no fetus at all. If the bleeding uneventfully reverts to the average for the ordinary menstrual period, there is no need for treatment. If this is your third miscarriage, you should salvage the blood and tissue that you pass and carry it in a jar to your provider's office to be sent to the laboratory for analysis for genetic abnormalities and infection.

As the cramps with miscarriage can be painful and it may take hours for the miscarriage to be over, you may want to call your physician or midwife, who can prescribe pain medication.

Medically Managed Miscarriage

Some physicians have begun to use medications for missed abortions rather than watchful waiting or surgical procedures. The usual medications are misoprostol and mifepristone, possibly in combination. *Mifepristone* (commonly known as RU 486) is an antiprogesterone. Progesterone is necessary to maintain the uterine lining. *Misoprostol* is a synthetic prostaglandin-type drug. Prostaglandins cause uterine contractions; they can be used in labor inductions. These, and similar medications, are used for induced abortion. They are discussed in Chapter 28.

To date, research on the use of these medications has shown varying results. In one analysis of all the published reports on various ways to treat miscarriage, watchful waiting and surgical treatment by D & C showed excellent results in terms of ending the pregnancy without undue bleeding or infection. Medical management showed about a 50 percent rate of effectively ending the pregnancy without surgical intervention.

If your physician recommends medical treatment, discuss this with him or her. There may be a good reason for this recommendation and experience over time with these treatments may bring better results.

In general, most women with threatened, inevitable, or missed abortions can be watched at home. Signs of infection or increased bleeding indicate the need to help the body complete the miscarriage.

If you experience very heavy bleeding, especially after 10 weeks of pregnancy, you may have an incomplete abortion. In an incomplete abortion, the fetus is expelled from the uterus, but the placenta remains inside. Severe blood loss and infection are possible.

When miscarriage is incomplete, nature needs some assistance to empty the uterus. This usually is accomplished by a suction aspiration procedure, although sometimes a *curettage*, which utilizes a sharper instrument to scrape the lining of the uterus, may be performed. Suction is created with the introduction of a hollow, semirigid plastic tube (*catheter*) into the uterine cavity. Under these circumstances nature ordinarily has *dilated* (opened) the cervix so that dilation by the physician is unnecessary. Once this catheter is in place, it is connected to a vacuum device that creates negative pressure. Since the placenta is only loosely attached to the uterine wall, its loose fragments are sucked easily into the tubing, completing the miscarriage. Suction aspiration does not require hospitalization, but since there may be considerable bleeding, it is often done at the hospital, usually in a same-day surgery unit.

Miscarriage and Emotion

Waiting at home, worrying about whether you will lose your pregnancy, or knowing that your fetus has died and waiting for the miscarriage to occur, can be an intensely stressful experience. Remember, at least half of all threatened abortions never become actual miscarriages. There is an excellent chance that your pregnancy will continue. Once miscarriage is inevitable, or once you know that the fetus has died, try to keep in mind that there usually is a purpose for this occurrence. For many women, of course, this is scant comfort. Time is needed, during which you will go through the many stages of grieving—disbelief and denial, anger, and finally acceptance.

With a missed abortion, your understandable desire to end the ordeal may cause you to ask your physician to intervene. While this is not an inappropriate way of treating a missed abortion, anytime the uterus is entered with an instrument, the possibility of a complication, however rare, exists. The best choice is to let nature take its course—unless your body gives signs that it is developing a complication or the pregnancy goes on for an extended period, although there is no hard and fast rule about what constitutes an extended period.

TREATMENTS FOR
RECURRENT MISCARRIAGE

The treatment for recurrent miscarriage is based on the reason for the recurrences, if one can be found. If there is a genetic problem, a genetics counselor will help you understand your chances of having a successful and genetically normal pregnancy. You may decide to seek sperm or egg donation, discussed in Chapter 13. If there is infection, antibiotic treatment of both partners before the next pregnancy may be helpful.

If antibodies are found, including antiphospholipid antibodies or antisperm antibodies, discussed in Chapter 13, treatments may involve corticosteroid drugs to suppress the immune system or anticoagulant therapy during early pregnancy. The reason for the anticoagulants is that these antibodies seem to target the vascular system, causing clotting in the region of placental attachment. Anticoagulant therapy may include low-dose aspirin or heparin, a more potent anticoagulant (sometimes called a *blood thinner*). Heparin usually is given intravenously. Women taking heparin generally get what is called a "hep lock," a small plastic tube or catheter placed into a vein in their hand through which the medication can be injected easily. Heparin can also be given as an injection deep into the tissues under the skin, but not directly into muscle. Immune system treatment, including anticoagulation, is controversial as the role of these antibodies in causing miscarriage is still unclear and the effects of treatment unproven.

When there is thought to be a maternal rejection of the fetus, efforts may be made to induce the mother's immune system to develop the normal responses to the father's antigens or those antigens inherited by the fetus. This may be accomplished through an injection of the father's *leukocytes* (white blood cells), allowing the mother to develop antibodies she is otherwise lacking. Donor leukocytes or blood have also been used, but the possibility of introducing infection, even HIV, exists with this therapy. Of course, this chance is minimized with the screening tests that are always done today.

Since the immune system response as a cause of miscarriage remains unproven, so the treatment remains unproven. Reports of success sometimes fail to compare the treated group with an untreated group, or a group receiving a sham treatment (a *placebo*). Since the majority of women even with three miscarriages will have a successful pregnancy, it is difficult, without a comparison group, to know for sure whether the treatment is effective or simply appears effective by chance.

If there is a defect in the uterus, this may or may not be correctable by surgery. Surgical removal of fibroids may help if that has been determined to be the cause of the recurrent miscarriages. This can be done through an abdominal incision or through the vagina using an instrument called a *hysteroscope*. How the surgery is done will depend on the location and size of the fibroids and the preference of the surgeon.

Of course, smoking, drinking, and drug use should be discontinued if there is a history of recurrent miscarriage. Caffeine use, if heavy, should be cut back. Toxic exposures should be avoided. You might consider reducing working hours, workload, or prolonged standing on the job.

An incompetent cervix involves the use of a *suture* (or stitch) in the cervix to hold it closed during the ensuing pregnancy.

Incompetent Cervical Syndrome

The incompetent cervical syndrome can be diagnosed in a number of ways. It is almost never diagnosed in a first pregnancy until the miscarriage has occurred. Sometimes if a woman has undergone a surgical procedure on the cervix, the possibility might be considered. Vaginal examinations to check whether the cervix is thinning or opening might be performed every 1 to 2 weeks starting in the early part of the second trimester. Alternatively, transvaginal ultrasound can determine the status of the cervix during pregnancy.

When a woman has experienced a second-trimester miscarriage characterized by painless bleeding one or more times, cervical incompetence syndrome becomes the likely suspect.

Cerclage

Once cervical incompetence is diagnosed your care provider will likely recommend a procedure known as cerclage (French: *cerclage* = an encircling). In this procedure, a suture or "stitch" is placed around the cervix to hold it closed for the duration of the pregnancy. There are two options for deciding when a cerclage should be performed. In the first, you can be watched very carefully with vaginal examinations and/or transvaginal ultrasound starting at about 14 weeks of pregnancy. At the first sign of cervical change, you can have the suture placed around the cervix to hold it closed. Or, the suture can be placed without any signs of change, usually after 14 weeks and before 20 weeks of gestation. After 20 weeks, there is an increased risk that placement of the suture itself will cause preterm labor or rupture of the membranes.

Before a suture is placed, ultrasound usually is performed to ascer tain a live fetus without major identifiable anomalies. If any infections are present, they should be treated. Cultures for infection should have been taken previously. Vaginal intercourse is avoided 1 week prior to suture insertion (if the procedure is planned in advance) and 1 week afterward. If a woman has a Pap smear showing abnormal cells, the physician may decide not to place the suture. If a suture cannot be placed, bed rest and pelvic rest will be prescribed until the fetus has reached a gestational age at which it is mature enough to survive outside the uterus, although the value of these precautions is unproven.

Three types of procedures are available to keep the cervix closed, named after the surgeons who developed them. The ones most used today are the McDonald and the modified Shirodkar procedures. The complete or original Shirodkar procedure is complex and meant to keep the cervix closed permanently—women who had these procedures had cesarean births. Today, the *McDonald procedure* is used most often and the *modified Shirodkar* used if the McDonald failed in a previous pregnancy.

The cerclage procedure is difficult to perform if there is cervical dilation or if the membranes are starting to protrude through the cervix. It can be tried in these circumstances but is not as successful as when performed before cervical changes. Of course, when the procedure is done before cervical change occurs, the high success rate may be due to the fact that some of the sutured cervixes would never have opened anyway. This is difficult to measure.

With these two procedures, the suture is removed either at the start of labor or at about 38 weeks gestation to allow for vaginal delivery. Following placement of the suture, if at any time miscarriage or premature delivery becomes apparent, the suture must be removed quickly. It must be removed if there are signs of infection such as fever, uterine pain, or an increased heart rate in the mother or fetus.

INTERVAL BETWEEN MISCARRIAGE AND ANOTHER PREGNANCY

How long to wait before getting pregnant again is a common and reasonable question after miscarriage. There is no consensus on this subject. From the physiological standpoint, if the pregnancy has miscarried completely and the uterus is empty, the mother's ovaries will return promptly to normal function. While the lining of the uterus remains unhealed, it will be inhospitable to the implantation of any ovum that might be fertilized in the next period and pregnancy will not take place.

If the uterine healing is complete, then a newly fertilized egg can implant without any difficulty. Ovulation can occur as quickly as 2 weeks after the miscarriage. Waiting for one period allows for easier dating of your next pregnancy. Some physicians and midwives recommend using a method of birth control until after this one period.

From the psychological perspective, you and your partner may need time to resolve your grief. Or you may have a strong need to have a successful pregnancy as quickly as possible.

Grieving after a miscarriage is a normal response. Counseling may be beneficial and should be sought as necessary. You can speak first to your physician or midwife, who can help you examine your feelings and refer you for expert counseling if you are finding adjustment to the loss especially difficult. Although most miscarriages take place at home with a follow-up examination at your physician's or midwife's office, your care provider may be able to refer you to the bereavement group at the hospital with which he or she is affiliated. You may wish, for example, to join a support group of parents who have had similar losses. The bereavement team in the hospital may know of an appropriate group.

FOLLOW-UP AFTER MISCARRIAGE

Today women should never die from spontaneous abortion. When they do, which is rare, it is almost always under the circumstance of great neglect. Blood loss from this condition can be severe, but it is readily treated. Uterine infection, an uncommon occurrence, is treatable by antibiotics and by completely emptying the uterine cavity.

Once you have passed what appears to be blood and tissue, you should have a visit with your physician or midwife. You will have a pelvic examination to make sure the uterus is back to its nonpregnant size, feels firm, and that the cervix is closed. If the uterus is still large or softened, or the cervix is a bit open, you will most likely have an ultrasound to see if the uterus is empty. If it is not, there may be a need for a physician to empty the uterus with the suction tube described on page 392. If you are not bleeding actively, but there is a question as to whether the miscarriage is complete, you can have blood drawn for hCG, perhaps on a few occasions, to ascertain nonpregnant values, or values dropping toward nonpregnant values.

If at any time in the weeks following a miscarriage you experience bleeding heavier than a normal menstrual period, fever, chills, foul smelling vaginal discharge, or abdominal pain, call your physician or midwife.

You can ovulate within 2 weeks after a miscarriage. Vaginal intercourse should wait about 1 to 2 weeks or until bleeding has stopped. Unless you want to get pregnant immediately, use birth control. Any birth control method can be used, although you should wait at least 2 weeks or until bleeding has stopped to use a diaphragm or cervical cap. These should be refit at this time. Read Chapter 27 for a complete discussion of available birth control methods.

A SUCCESSFUL NEXT PREGNANCY

What are your chances of having a successful pregnancy if you have previously had a miscarriage? If you have miscarried just once your chances are as good as if you had never been pregnant before. This is true in the absence of any efforts at treatment. If you have miscarried twice in a row, there may be something going on, however unusual. You and your physician may want to initiate investigation and possible correction before you become pregnant again. This is particularly true if you have never had a successful pregnancy. However, if you should become pregnant without testing, the chance for a successful pregnancy following two prior spontaneous abortions is only slightly decreased as compared with that for a woman who has never miscarried. After three consecutive prior miscarriages, the odds in favor of success go down a little further. Nevertheless, most women who have a miscarriage have a successful subsequent pregnancy without treatment.

CHAPTER FIFTEEN

~

Preterm Labor and Birth

Preterm birth remains a major cause of newborn and infant illness and death. If its causes were better understood and prevention or treatment more effective, fewer babies would die every year. For a pregnant woman, prevention of preterm birth requires knowing the early signs of impending labor and seeking prompt care should any occur.

There is no exact physical or physiologic point at which a fetus ceases to be premature and becomes mature, no matter how precisely the pregnancy is dated. All the changes that occur are gradual, especially in the latter two-thirds of the third trimester. There are no great leaps forward in baby behavior from one day to the next. In general, however, 37 weeks completed gestation is considered mature. Any labor occurring before 37 weeks is considered preterm labor and any baby born before 37 weeks is considered preterm.

Today, a distinction is made between *premature* babies and *preterm* babies. "Maturity" refers to how well the baby is able to function outside the womb, with the most emphasis on the respiratory system, as breathing is a crucial function the baby must assume. A baby whose lungs cannot function is "premature." A "preterm" baby is one whose gestational age is less than 37 completed weeks gestation. Some "preterm" babies may not be "premature" from the perspective of their ability to breathe.

Acknowledging the difficulty in precisely dating a pregnancy, particularly prior to ultrasound, experts in the early part of the twentieth century suggested defining prematurity by weight, not gestational age. Any baby weighing less than 2,500 grams (2.5 kilograms), or approximately 5½ pounds, was considered premature. However, using weight imposes its own imprecision, as weight varies greatly with many other factors. We now make a distinction between birth weight and gestational age.

A baby's birth weight may be said to be *appropriate for gestational age* (AGA) or *small for gestational age* (SGA). Small babies may be small because they are preterm or small because they are "growth retarded," or "growth restricted." A baby may be both preterm and small for gestational age.

If two babies are the same birth weight, but one is born at 33 weeks and is the appropriate weight for this gestational age and the other is a growth restricted baby born at 38 weeks, in general, the older infant will have an easier time adapting to life outside the uterus. If a baby is large, but born early, it may still have the problems that accompany early birth. The baby who will have the most trouble is the one who is both premature and small for gestational age.

Prior to delivery, when the baby can physically be examined to determine its gestational age, the date of the first day of the last menstrual period is the best single piece of information regarding the duration of the pregnancy. When a woman does not remember this date, when she has irregular periods or gets pregnant after discontinuing a birth control method that made her periods stop, such as Depo-Provera (the "shot"), an ultrasound determines the duration of pregnancy. Ultrasound may also be relied upon when the uterine size does not match the dates. The ultrasound may need to be repeated to ascertain if the difference in uterine size and menstrual dates (called a *size-dates discrepancy*) is due to the baby growing excessively or not growing adequately, or if in fact the baby is growing as expected, just older or younger than the dates suggest. Serial ultrasounds, done several weeks apart, can measure the fetus's rate of growth. Proper growth may also be determined by using a variety of ultrasound measurements to assess the relationship of the size of the head, for example, to the size of the abdomen. If there is a big discrepancy between these two, the baby may be growing improperly.

Although 37 weeks gestation is considered mature, a fetus can reach maturity as early as 35 weeks. This does not mean that younger or smaller babies cannot survive. Today, they frequently do. With neonatal intensive care, highly sophisticated equipment for assisting babies to breathe, a recently developed medication called *surfactant*, which helps the lungs stay expanded, and round-the-clock attention by expert staff, premature babies have a better chance of survival than they did a few decades ago. Newborns can survive with birth weights as low as

500 grams (just over one pound) and a gestational age of about 23 or 24 weeks. Such tiny infants, however, often have developmental problems in childhood.

Most of the difficulty in functioning among preterm babies is seen in babies less than 34 weeks gestational age. Government statistics today make a distinction between *moderately preterm* births (32 to 36 weeks) and *very preterm* births (less than 32 weeks completed gestation). Distinctions are also made among *low birth weight* (less than 2,500 grams or 5½ pounds), *very low birth weight* (1,500 grams or less, approximately 3⅓ pounds), and *extremely low birth weight* (1,000 grams or less, approximately 2¼ pounds).

In 1998, the overall percentage of premature births in the U.S. was 11.6. This rate has been on the rise. In 1990, it was 10.6 percent; in 1981, 9.4 percent. Most of the increase in 1998 was in the moderately preterm group—babies born between 32 and 36 weeks gestation.

One major reason that preterm births are rising is that multiple births have become more common. Pregnancies with more than one baby are more likely to end prematurely than are pregnancies with only one baby (called *singleton pregnancies*). Multiple birth babies are also more likely to be low birth weight.

Two trends account for the recent increase in multiple births. One is the greater number of births to women in their thirties, who are naturally more likely to have a multiple birth than younger women. The other is the proliferation of fertility treatments, some of which result in multiple fetuses (see Chapter 13). About 80 percent of births of triplets or more were due to fertility treatment in 1996 and 1997. In 2000, 18 percent of births to women aged 45 to 49 years was a twin, triplet, or higher order multiple birth. In 1999, one out of every 3 births to women aged 50 or older was a twin or triplet or higher-order multiple birth.

We cannot discuss the rate of prematurity in the United States without noting the difference between the rate for Caucasian women (10.2 percent) and for African-American women (17.6 percent). A small part of this difference is due to the slightly more common occurrence of multiple births among African-American women. Socioeconomic background (poverty, inadequate nutrition, and lack of access to health care) accounts for another part of the difference. Even among African-Americans who have achieved a high socioeconomic status, however, there is a difference in the preterm birth rates compared with Caucasians. We can only reflect that racial inequalities in this country continue to have effects even when aspects of inequity are overcome.

CAUSES OF PREMATURE LABOR

Unfortunately, we know very little about the cause of most instances of preterm labor. Occasionally it is due to an abnormality of the uterine body or cervix. These are discussed in Chapter 14, as these abnormalities also may cause spontaneous abortion or miscarriage. Miscarriage is different from preterm birth in that a miscarried fetus cannot survive. Today, 24 weeks gestation is the usual cutoff used to distinguish preterm from miscarried babies.

One of the most likely causes of preterm labor is an infection in the uterus. This is called *chorioamnionitis*—an inflammation of the chorion and amnion, or the two membranes surrounding the fetus. Infection also may be a cause of *rupture of the membranes*—the bag of waters breaking. Preterm rupture of the membranes often leads to preterm labor.

Although infection is thought to be an important cause of preterm rupture of the membranes and preterm labor, the specific infectious organisms involved have not been identified conclusively. *Bacterial vaginosis,* a rather common condition in which the usual "flora" of the vagina is disturbed, is a possible cause. This may involve the organism *Mycoplasma hominis,* frequently found with premature rupture of the membranes. *Chlamydia trachomatis,* the most common sexually transmitted organism in the United States today, also may be involved in preterm birth and preterm rupture of the membranes, but studies do not prove this association.

Group B streptococcus is an organism possibly associated with preterm labor. It is also a major cause of severe newborn infection. It does not always cause any unusual symptoms in a woman, although it may cause urinary tract or uterine infection during pregnancy or after birth. The Centers for Disease Control and Prevention, in collaboration with the American College of Obstetricians and Gynecologists and the American Academy of Pediatrics, have developed specific guidelines for testing and treatment for Group B "strep" in pregnancy. These guidelines are in the box on pages 402–404.

Treatment of Group B strep (GBS) in labor is intended to prevent the consequences of GBS disease in newborns. As GBS is one possible cause of preterm labor, treatment is recommended for any woman in labor or with ruptured membranes before 37 weeks gestation, unless a culture from her vagina and rectum taken at 35 to 36 weeks gestation is available and shows no GBS. If a prior culture is unavailable, then a culture can be taken at the time the woman sees her care provider or comes to the hospital. Antibiotics (usually penicillin) are started. If the culture is negative, the medication can be stopped. If the culture is positive, antibiotics are continued until and through labor. If delivery does not occur within 4 weeks, the culture should be repeated.

A urinary tract infection might lead to preterm labor if untreated.

Guidelines for Prevention of Group B Streptococcal (GBS) Disease in Newborns (2002)

All women should be screened for colonization with GBS from the vagina and rectum at 35 to 37 weeks gestation. A swab from the vagina and rectum is sent to the laboratory for culture. The only exceptions to this are women who have already demonstrated GBS in their urine during the current pregnancy or women who had a previous infant with invasive GBS disease.

Prophylaxis during labor (preventive treatment with an antibiotic) is recommended in the following situations:
  • Previous child with invasive GBS disease
  • GBS in the urine culture during this pregnancy
  • Positive GBS screening culture during the current pregnancy, unless a planned cesarean delivery is performed, before the woman goes into labor and before her membranes have ruptured
  • If the GBS status is not known because the culture wasn't done or is incomplete (was done too recently for the colonization to be documented) or if the results are unknown for any other reason *and* any of the following circumstances exist:
    • Delivery before 37 weeks gestation
    • The membranes have been ruptured for 18 hours or longer (even at greater than 37 weeks gestation)
    • A temperature develops in labor of 100.4° F or greater (38.0° C or greater) (this may require a different antibiotic therapy)

Prophylaxis during labor (preventive treatment with an antibiotic) is *not* recommended in the following situations:
  • Previous pregnancy with a positive GBS screening culture (unless a culture was also positive during this pregnancy)
  • Planned cesarean delivery performed in the absence of labor or rupture of membranes (regardless of whether the GBS culture is positive or negative)

- Negative vaginal and rectal GBS screening culture in late pregnancy during the current pregnancy

Antibiotics are given during labor through an intravenous line. A usual dosage schedule is penicillin G 5 million units for the first dose, then 2.5 million units every 4 hours until delivery. If a woman is known to be penicillin allergic, Cefazolin may be given if she is not considered to be at high risk for serious reaction (anaphylaxis). If she is at high risk for an anaphylactic reaction, then clindamycin or erythromycin may be used. All medications are given intravenously.

If the culture shows the organism to be resistant to these medications, then a very strong antibiotic is used, called vancomycin.

Two risks exist with this treatment: 1) some women may have a potentially dangerous allergic reaction to penicillin, and 2) the development of resistant organisms is possible with widespread treatment.

New Approaches

Currently, researchers are investigating two other approaches: the development of a vaccine against group B strep and the development of a rapid, easily available, and accurate screening test that could be performed in labor with immediate results. A screening test would identify the women who carry GBS at the time of delivery and reduce the overall number of women receiving treatment. Screening tests are currently available but not considered accurate enough to determine treatment to prevent newborn GBS infection.

Informed Consent

To allow for informed consent, women should know the following:

- Approximately 1 in 200 newborns born to a mother colonized with GBS will develop GBS disease early in the newborn period.
- The risk of a newborn's acquiring GBS from a mother who tests positive for the organism is 29 times higher than the risk for a newborn whose mother had a negative prenatal culture.
- The risk of a newborn's acquiring GBS in a labor that is preterm or complicated by long duration of membrane rupture or fever is 7 times higher than the risk for newborns born without these labor complications.
- Five to 20 percent of newborns infected with GBS will die.

- The treated woman's risk of a mild allergic reaction to penicillin is 1 in 10.
- The treated woman's risk of a serious allergic reaction to penicillin is 1 in 10,000.
- The risk of dying from an allergic reaction to penicillin is 1 in 100,000 treated women.
- Treatment for GBS before labor is not effective in preventing newborn GBS disease.

Any condition that causes the uterus to be *overdistended* (unusually large) may result in preterm labor. These conditions include hydramnios (see Chapter 12) and multiple pregnancy. Among multiples, quadruplets deliver earlier than triplets, triplets deliver earlier than twins. Placental problems, described in Chapter 12, may also cause preterm labor.

A pregnancy that occurs with an intrauterine device (IUD) in place has an increased chance of ending in preterm labor. If you have an IUD and become pregnant, you should have the IUD removed if you want to keep the pregnancy. Sometimes, however, the IUD strings have moved up into the cervical canal and removing the device would be dangerous to the pregnancy. While a retained IUD increases the chances of preterm birth, it does not cause anomalies in the fetus.

A recent review of studies on work and pregnancy found a number of work-related risks for preterm labor. These include heavy and/or repetitive lifting or carrying loads; manual labor; physical exertion; prolonged standing; shift work; and work fatigue.

Substance abuse, including cigarettes, drugs, or alcohol, may lead to preterm labor. Because more than 10 percent of pregnant women smoke, tobacco use is responsible for a large number of preterm births. Young adolescent mothers are more likely to deliver preterm and women living in poverty have a greater chance of having a preterm birth. Poor weight gain during pregnancy and some severe diseases of the mother can contribute to preterm labor.

Women who have had a preterm birth have an increased chance for another preterm birth. This does not explain the cause for preterm birth, but is a major risk factor.

SYMPTOMS OF PREMATURE LABOR

Any of the symptoms highlighted in the box below may or may not be indicative of preterm labor. If any of these symtoms occur before you are 37 weeks pregnant, the safest route is to consider that you might possibly be in preterm labor and notify your physician or midwife without delay.

Warning Signs for Premature Labor:

When to Call Your Physician or Midwife
- Painful menstrual-like cramps
- Dull ache in the lower back (If you have had a dull backache throughout the pregnancy, then this symptom is only a danger sign if it is different from the backache you've had before.)
- Pain or pressure above the pubic bone (in the area of the pubic hair)
- Sensation of pressure or heaviness in the pelvic region
- Increase in vaginal secretions, including loss of the mucous plug
- Change in the type of vaginal secretion (for example, from thick to thin or watery)
- Bloody discharge from the vagina
- Diarrhea
- Uterine contractions occurring 10 minutes apart or more frequently for more than 1 hour, even if they are not painful (a contraction is palpated when the top of your uterus—the fundus—gets hard, softens, and hardens again). If these disappear when you lie down, they are probably not labor.
- Symptoms of urinary tract infection—pain or burning on urination, especially at the end of urination; urgency—an unusually strong feel of the need to urinate, especially if you actually urinate very small amounts; frequency—needing to urinate very often (although this may be difficult for pregnant women to differentiate from the usual increased frequency of late pregnancy).
- Any leakage of fluid from the vagina. This can be a big gush or a continuous dripping of watery fluid. This may indicate rupture of the membranes.

These symptoms may be seen with a number of other conditions. False labor, a vaginal infection, a urinary tract infection, round ligament pain, or growing uterine fibroids may each cause one or more of these symptoms. As a vaginal or urinary tract infection can lead to rupture of the membranes or preterm labor, these need to be diagnosed and treated.

If you have any question about whether or not what you are feeling fits the description of preterm labor, it's better to call your physician or midwife than to risk having a dangerous condition ignored. Physicians and midwives are quite used to getting phone calls that turn out to be false alarms and prefer to have this happen than to wait until it's too late to prevent a premature birth.

PREVENTION OF PRETERM LABOR

The causes of preterm labor are not entirely understood and, so far, its prevention eludes medical science. Obvious preventive measures include the elimination of the risks noted earlier. Avoid smoking, drinking, and recreational drug use. Report signs of urinary tract or vaginal infections to your physician or midwife so they can be treated promptly. Let your physician or midwife know if you have had a prior preterm birth.

If your work involves heavy physical labor, rotating or night shifts, long periods of standing, or makes you excessively tired, consider changing or reducing your workload. Unfortunately, women in the United States are not uniformly guaranteed paid maternity leave.

As sexually transmitted infections may be implicated in premature rupture of the membranes and preterm labor, you should use a condom if you are at risk for such an infection. Being at risk means that either you or your partner has more than one sexual partner. If you have any doubt about whether this is the case for your partner, or you have had a preterm birth, you should use condoms. In fact, because semen contains *prostaglandins*—body chemicals that cause uterine contractions—use of a condom from midpregnancy to 37 weeks gestation is a good idea for any woman who has had a previous preterm birth. The condoms provide a barrier between your body and your partner's semen.

If you have a history of preterm labor or signs of preterm labor, avoid nipple or breast stimulation in the third trimester, before 37 weeks gestation, as this initiates uterine contractions. Abstain from orgasm if there is any question of threatened preterm labor, as it can lead to contractions.

There is some evidence, although not conclusive, that calcium supplementation may help prevent preterm labor. Routine calcium supplementation is not currently advised in pregnancy, but you should certainly maintain an adequate dietary intake of calcium sources (see Chapter 10). Except for sometimes causing constipation, a calcium supplement is not dangerous in pregnancy. If you have had a preterm birth, discuss with your physician or midwife whether or not they advise calcium supplementation as a possible preventive measure.

In the 1980s, some promising studies showed that preterm birth might be prevented with frequent prenatal visits and vaginal examinations for women at risk for preterm labor. A number of "Prevention of Preterm" birth programs were funded by various governmental and private agencies. Unfortunately, these did not demonstrate that such measures were uniformly valuable in preventing preterm birth. Whether or not to do weekly or biweekly vaginal examinations or ultrasounds to check the cervix in the third trimester for women with a previous preterm birth remains controversial.

Researchers have tried to find biochemical markers in the blood, saliva, or vaginal secretions of a pregnant woman that might predict a preterm birth. One such chemical is *fetal fibronectin*. This can be detected in vaginal secretions. Unfortunately, while the absence of fetal fibronectin seems to be very predictive that preterm labor will not occur, its presence does not necessarily signal impending preterm labor. To date, it is not useful as a test for preterm labor. The benefit of testing for *estriol* in a pregnant woman's saliva is also being investigated. Estriol is a hormone produced from chemicals secreted by the fetus's adrenal gland and liver. Maternal estriol levels show a steep rise approximately three weeks before delivery—term or preterm. This hormone can be detected in the mother's saliva. Saliva testing for women at high risk for a preterm birth might prove to be of predictive value, but then the question of what treatment to implement must be considered.

Some companies have marketed home uterine monitors in an effort to pick up uterine contractions before a woman might feel them. The American College of Obstetricians and Gynecologists has stated, "It is not clearly demonstrated that this expensive and burdensome system can be used to actually affect the rate of preterm delivery." Women who have had previous preterm labors can use their own hands to palpate the top of their uterus one hour each day in the third trimester to feel for contractions that they do not perceive.

TREATMENT OF PRETERM LABOR

The goal of treatment of preterm labor is the prevention of preterm birth. The initial step in the treatment of preterm labor is to determine that the symptoms exhibited are labor. Sometimes this is easier said than done.

Diagnosis of Preterm Labor

A pregnant woman may become aware of uterine contractions by 24 weeks of pregnancy. These contractions are normal. They are called *Braxton-Hicks contractions*. On occasion, Braxton-Hicks contractions are rather severe. In addition, the cervix often shortens and occasionally dilates during the early part of the third trimester. If these two events combine in a single woman, deciding whether or not she is in early labor may be extraordinarily difficult. If in fact she is not, any treatment or none at all will appear equally successful. Evaluating the treatment thus is very difficult, as the measure of success is that nothing has happened. Often, we cannot be sure that there was ever a condition that required treatment.

Despite the inexact nature of diagnosis, certain steps usually are taken when a woman complains of any of the symptoms in the box on page 405 at any time between 23 and 37 weeks of pregnancy. (There is some disagreement regarding when to initiate treatment, although generally before 23 or 24 weeks, survival of the preterm infant is unlikely. Delivery at that time is considered a miscarriage, not a preterm birth. After 37 weeks, there is no worry about prematurity of the baby.)

If you have any of the symptoms noted in the box, call your physician or midwife or go to the hospital where you will have your baby (or your "back-up" hospital if you had planned a home or birth center birth). The physicians and midwives in the practice or clinic where you have your prenatal care will have given you instructions on how to contact somebody in case of an emergency or whether to go to the hospital's labor unit or emergency room. Signs of preterm labor can be considered an emergency.

You will most likely be advised to meet your physician or midwife at the office or hospital. First, you will have an abdominal examination to determine if the examiner can feel any contractions and to estimate the size and position of the baby. You may be placed on a fetal monitor so that a recording of contractions can be made, although this is not always necessary. The straps placed around your abdomen may be irritating to the uterus and increase the contractions, if there are any. Usually, a recording of the fetal heart tones will be made.

An examination of the cervix with a speculum may be done next. If there is any question about whether or not the membranes have ruptured, this examination will be carried out under sterile conditions. The physician or midwife will look to see any signs of cervical opening and will check to see if the membranes are ruptured. There are a variety of ways to do that. Sometimes, there is an obvious pooling of fluid in the vagina. Other times, a sterile swab can be placed into the vagina. The secretions picked up by the swab are looked at under a microscope. When amniotic fluid dries on a slide, it forms a characteristic pattern that resembles a fern. This is called *ferning*, and indicates that the membranes have ruptured. A type of litmus paper, called *nitrazine paper*, may be placed on the discharge. If the yellow paper turns blue, this shows an alkaline pH. Since the vagina is acidic, the alkalinity often is due to amniotic fluid and means that the membranes have ruptured. A number of other secretions are alkaline, however, such as blood, the vaginal discharge of certain infections, and even cervical mucus. This test, then, is not completely reliable.

During this sterile speculum examination, vaginal or cervical cultures for organisms including group B strep, gonorrhea, and chlamydia may be taken. This feels no different from a Pap smear.

If the membranes are ruptured, the physician or midwife should refrain from doing a *bimanual examination*—an examination with his or her fingers. When the protective membranes are torn, vaginal examinations increase the risk of infection—a danger for both mother and baby. Usually, once an examination is done, the delivery needs to occur within 24 hours. Avoiding examinations minimizes the possibility of infection and allows for more flexibility in handling the situation. This is especially important if you have ruptured membranes without signs of labor.

If the membranes have not ruptured (said to be *intact*), then a *bimanual* or *digital* (finger) *examination* allows the physician or midwife to check with more accuracy whether the cervix is *effaced* (thinned) or *dilated* (opened). Ultrasound is an alternative way of checking, used in some medical centers. If the cervix is thick and closed or just a bit open or thinned, most likely you will be observed for several hours, lying in bed on your side, and reexamined. If there is cervical change, then the diagnosis of preterm labor is made. If there is no cervical change, then you will continue to be watched or sent home, depending on whether contractions are still present. Contractions consistent with preterm labor are 5 to 8 minutes apart, or occur at a rate of 4 in 20 minutes or 8 in 60 minutes.

If the cervix is open to at least 2 centimeters (a bit more than the width of the average finger), or 80 percent or more effaced, and contractions are occurring, then the diagnosis may be made without waiting to see if the cervix changes. Under these circumstances, if treatment is delayed, the opportunity to stop the labor may be missed.

If your physician or midwife determines that you are not in preterm labor, or you become aware that your contractions have stopped, you will most likely go home with instructions to rest, to refrain from heavy work, including housework and lifting of toddlers, and to avoid vaginal intercourse, nipple or breast stimulation, and orgasm until all signs of possible preterm labor are gone or you have reached 37 weeks gestation.

If your physician or midwife determines that you are in preterm labor, then an attempt usually will be made to stop the labor if you are less than 4 centimeters dilated and less than 34 weeks gestation. After 34 weeks gestation, most babies will survive and the risks of treatment usually render such treatment inadvisable. Other reasons for not treating preterm labor are:

- Dilation of 5 centimeters or more
- Fetal death or an anomaly known to be incompatible with life (both of which may predispose to preterm labor)
- Fetal distress or growth restriction (meaning that the baby may do better outside the uterus, despite being premature)
- Maternal bleeding
- Maternal preeclampsia or eclampsia (see Chapter 12)
- Abruptio placentae (see Chapter 12)
- Chorioamnionitis (infection of the membranes)

Specific Treatments of Preterm Labor

With Intact Membranes

There is no completely safe drug that will predictably and reliably turn off true preterm labor. Besides the uncertain value of the medications in stopping preterm labor, they all carry risks to the mother or the fetus or both. They must be used only with close observation. If a woman clearly has a vaginal or urinary tract infection, that condition is treated, although once labor has begun, antibiotic therapy will not stop it.

Without a known cause of preterm labor, treatment is aimed at stopping the contractions, rather than alleviating the cause. This is sometimes effective, although studies have shown that most treatments postpone birth for only 48 hours. This is enough time, however, to give the mother a medication that many experts believe speeds up maturation of the fetal lungs, helping to increase survival. It is also sufficient time to transfer the pregnant woman to a hospital that has a neonatal intensive care unit (NICU), called a *tertiary care center* or a *Level III hospital*. This is preferable to transferring a premature infant after birth, which poses more risks for the newborn and separates the mother and baby.

PROMOTING FETAL LUNG MATURITY   A corticosteroid drug called *betamethasone* or *dexamethasone* is given to the mother to promote fetal lung maturity. This drug is thought to cause the fetal lung to produce *surfactant*—a chemical that keeps the lungs expanded after each breath. In *respiratory distress syndrome* (previously called *hyaline membrane disease*), the lungs of the premature newborn collapse after each breath, making each breath as difficult as the first. This is a major cause of death in premature infants. Surfactant appears in the fetal lung in the second trimester, but may not be present in sufficient quantity to be effective before 34 weeks of pregnancy.

In 1995, the National Institutes of Health (NIH) hailed the use of corticosteroids as a major breakthrough in care for preterm newborns. Since this report, the therapy has been used widely in preterm labor. Recent studies, however, have not consistently supported its value.

For corticosteroids to be beneficial in causing lung maturity, there must be a delay of at least 24 hours between treatment and birth. If birth is delayed for 7 days, their effectiveness is unclear.

Standard regimens for administering the medication vary. One major obstetrical text reports the use of two doses of 12 mg betamethasone, injected into the muscle, 24 hours apart, or 12 hours apart if labor seems likely to occur before 48 hours have passed. Another major text reports use of 5 mg of dexamethasone every 12 hours for four doses. The therapy may be repeated every 7 days until 34 weeks gestation, although some controversy exists about whether repeated courses of steroid treatment might impair brain or immune system development in the fetus. More research is needed in this area.

STOPPING LABOR   Various drugs have been used to stop preterm labor, including beta-adrenergic receptor agonists, magnesium sulfate, prostaglandin inhibitors, calcium channel blocking agents, and oxytocin inhibitors. Each of these is briefly discussed here. The act of stopping uterine contractions is called *tocolysis* (Greek: *tocos* = birth; *lysis* = dissolution). Women with medical diseases may not be able to use some or any of these drugs as they aggravate certain conditions.

Beta-Adrenergic Receptor Agonists. A group of cells called *adrenergic receptors* are found on the surface of smooth muscle cells. An *agonist* is a drug or other substance that can combine with the receptor cells. In the uterine muscle, stimulation of the beta-adrenergic receptors by an agonist causes the receptors to inhibit uterine contractions. Two beta-adrenergic agonists used to stop preterm contractions are ritodrine and terbutaline, although only ritodrine is approved for this use by the Food and Drug Administration.

Studies have found that these medications, given intravenously, stop labor for a day or two, at most. While this doesn't give the fetus much time to grow, it may allow for the adminstration of corticosteroids or maternal transfer.

Since beta-adrenergic receptors are found in smooth muscle cells all over the body, these drugs affect many body systems. This limits their use. They can cause heart and lung problems, as serious as rapid or irregular heartbeat, decreased blood pressure, chest pain, and *pulmonary edema* (fluid in the lungs). They cause changes in body chemistry, including increased blood sugar, decreased blood potassium, and increased blood insulin levels. They cause less serious but quite unpleasant side effects such as vomiting, headaches, fever, and hallucinations. They may cause anxiety in the woman.

Women receiving ritodrine or terbutaline must be hospitalized and watched with extreme care. Women with poorly controlled diabetes or poorly controlled high blood pressure should not be given beta-adrenergic agonists.

Magnesium Sulfate. Another medication used in the effort to stop preterm labor is magnesium sulfate, usually given intravenously. Studies show its effects on labor to vary from none to stopping labor for the same duration as ritodrine. Magnesium can depress maternal respiration, although this effect is rare. A woman must be closely observed while the drug is being given. Magnesium therapy may also cause nausea and vomiting, decreased blood pressure, and headache. Magnesium eventually crosses the placenta and may affect newborn respirations as well.

Magnesium sulfate cannot be used in women with kidney failure, low blood calcium levels, or a disease called *myasthenia gravis* (characterized by severe muscle weakness).

Prostaglandin Inhibitors. Prostaglandins are a group of body chemicals involved in normal uterine contractions. Prostaglandins can be given to induce labor. Conversely, prostaglandin inhibitors can be used to stop labor. These inhibitors work by either reducing the formation of prostaglandins or blocking their action. Indomethacin is an example of a prostaglandin inhibitor that has been used to arrest labor.

Research studies have found prostaglandin inhibitors more effective than beta-agonists for delaying labor up to 48 hours, with fewer maternal side effects. Prostaglandin inhibitors, however, are associated with severe adverse effects on the fetus, including cardiac defects and brain hemorrhage. They can also cause bleeding in the mother. The use of these drugs for stopping labor is still under investigation.

Indomethacin cannot be used with maternal asthma, coronary artery disease, gastrointestinal bleeding, kidney failure, and oligohydramnios. Suspected heart or kidney abnormalities in the fetus also preclude its use.

Calcium Channel Blocking Agents. Reducing calcium levels in muscle cells reduces muscle contraction. Calcium channel blockers stop the entry of calcium into cells. (These drugs are used to treat high blood pressure because they relax the muscles in blood vessels.) An example of a calcium channel blocker that has been used to stop preterm labor is nifedipine.

Studies have shown that nifedipine can postpone delivery by 3 days—a greater delay than that seen with ritodrine. Maternal side effects are less than with ritodrine. The effect of this drug on the fetus, however, has not been studied extensively. Because it relaxes the muscles in blood vessels, it could lead to decreased blood pressure in the mother. This, in turn, could lead to decreased blood flow to the placenta. The extent to which this occurs warrants further study.

Nifedipine should not be used with magnesium sulfate as it enhances the effect of magnesium, leading to serious lung and heart problems. Women with liver disease cannot use nifedipine.

Oxytocin Inhibitors. Atosiban is a type of drug currently under development. It works by inhibiting *oxytocin*, a chemical responsible for uterine contractions. Its use has been limited but it may prove to be beneficial in the future.

The search for safer and more predictable drugs continues. It is difficult to slow down or speed up the uterus without affecting other body systems. The best drug would be one that limits its effects to the uterine muscle. Such a substance has not been identified.

With Premature Rupture of the Membranes

Premature rupture of the membranes (PROM) occurs as an uncontrollable gush or leakage of fluid. By definition, PROM is rupture of the membrane that occurs more than 12 hours before the onset of labor. If this occurs before 37 weeks gestation, it may be called *preterm premature rupture of the membranes* (PPROM).

In the past, due to concern that prolonged rupture of membranes would lead to maternal and fetal infection, babies were all delivered shortly after rupture, regardless of gestational age. Research has not shown this to be beneficial to mother or baby.

Today, one of two care paths generally is followed when a woman has PPROM without labor:

1. Nothing is done except to wait for labor with monitoring of maternal temperature and avoidance of all vaginal examinations.
2. Corticosteroid therapy is initiated, with or without medications to try to stop labor.

Delivery is only induced in the presence of maternal fever, indicating infection. Most women with PPROM will be in labor, either immediately or within 2 days.

Women with ruptured membranes before 37 weeks usually are admitted to the hospital for observation. The woman may be discharged home before the baby is born if the leakage of fluid stops and certain other conditions exist. The baby should be in the vertex or head down position; there must be no sign of infection; the woman must be able to rest and avoid vaginal intercourse at home; the woman or somebody in her family must be able to read a thermometer; the woman must be able to return for prenatal care visits at least weekly. This is a decision to be made individually for each woman.

Delivery of Premature Infants

Several decades ago, some experts proposed that elimination of the stresses of labor by delivering all preterm babies by cesarean would increase the newborn survival rate. The rationale was that reduced stress on the infant's head would reduce the possibility of bleeding into the skull. This complication, called *intraventricular hemorrhage*, is another major cause of death in premature newborns. The best evidence now shows that cesarean delivery does not prevent ventricular hemorrhage. The best currently available evidence does not support performing a cesarean if the only reason for the surgery is a premature infant. Of course, there are times when cesarean is performed for the same reasons as it is in mature babies.

Episiotomy is another procedure that has been advocated as a way of reducing stress on the skull of the immature fetus. Studies are not available to demonstrate whether this is beneficial. The resistance of the perineal muscles, through which the infant passes just as it leaves the vagina and which are cut with an episiotomy, is less than the resistance of the cervix and the vaginal muscles through which the infant has already passed. Despite a lack of definitive evidence, some experts recommend episiotomy for the delivery of preterm infants. Others recommend it only when there is resistance in these muscles, rarely seen except in women having a first baby. This is an area worth further research.

Most important for the premature baby is the presence at the birth of personnel skilled in resuscitation and care of premature infants. Whenever possible, the delivery should take place in a hospital with a neonatal intensive care unit and with constant attendance of physicians, nurse practitioners, and nurses who are knowledgeable in caring for these tiny infants. A staff member, or team of staff members, should be present in the delivery room whenever a premature baby is born, ready to provide expert care from the moment of birth.

CHAPTER SIXTEEN

※

Diseases and Operations During Pregnancy

Serious disease in childbirth is rare. There is no illness, however, to which a pregnant woman is immune unless it is a menstrual disorder. There is no complaint that a pregnant woman may not experience, with the exception of infertility. Most pregnant women are young and healthy. Still, it would take an encyclopedia to consider in detail all the possible deviations from normal health, their effects on pregnancy, and, in turn, the influence of pregnancy on the ordinary course of every disease. This book is not an encyclopedia, but within its confines we can discuss briefly some of the common major health problems as they occur in a pregnant woman.

GENERAL GUIDELINES FOR PREGNANT WOMEN WITH AN ILLNESS

Today, because of advances in disease prevention, diagnosis, and treatment, women who in the past would not have become pregnant, would have had a very difficult pregnancy, or perhaps would not even have survived to adulthood are having successful pregnancies. Their disease neither interferes with fertility nor with the healthy development of the fetus. Pregnancy may or may not have an effect on the disease, but not to the extent that the illness becomes a major risk to health or life.

If you have a disease when you become pregnant, or develop one during your pregnancy, there are certain guidelines to follow to stay healthy and protect your fetus.

• Use effective contraception (see Chapter 27) until you are sure you want to be pregnant so that you can plan your pregnancy. Discuss in advance with your physician or nurse practitioner the effects of pregnancy on your illness and the effects of your illness on pregnancy. With the guidance of your care provider, you can change medications or reduce drug dosages as necessary before pregnancy. Remember, the earliest weeks of a pregnancy are the time the fetus is most vulnerable to adverse effects of drugs.

• If you do have an unplanned pregnancy, do not discontinue your medications or change any of your treatment regimens without consulting your physician. An untreated illness can be more damaging to a fetus than its treatment.

• Seek early and consistent prenatal care.

• Let your usual physician or nurse practitioner know you are pregnant or planning a pregnancy so he or she can talk to your obstetrician or midwife about your care during your pregnancy. (Usually women with an illness will be under the care of an obstetrician, but if you have a treated illness that does not preclude a normal pregnancy, you often can be cared for by a midwife if you so choose. Either your obstetrician or midwife should be in contact with your medical care provider.)

• Anytime you see a physician or other health care provider for care for your illness, be sure to mention that you are pregnant.

• Be sure to tell your obstetrician or midwife about your illness and all treatments you require.

SEXUALLY TRANSMITTED INFECTIONS (STIs)

When this book was first written, sexually transmitted infections were called *venereal disease* (VD). Later they were renamed *sexually transmitted diseases* (STDs). Most recently their name has changed to sexually transmitted infections (STIs). Today, more than twenty infections are known to be sexually transmitted. Some of these are of particular importance in pregnancy because they may adversely affect the fetus through the placenta or infect the newborn as it passes through an infected birth canal. Some STIs may also increase the likelihood of premature rupture of the membranes or premature labor. Research is still needed to clarify which organisms are related to these events.

In general, any pregnant woman who is not in a mutually monogamous relationship throughout pregnancy (that is, neither she nor her partner has other sexual partners) should use condoms for sexual relations, even though they are not needed to protect you from pregnancy. They provide protection against STIs.

Whenever you are treated for a sexually transmitted infection, your partner (or partners) must be treated. If you resume intercourse before he or she is treated, you are likely to be reinfected, with the same consequences for the pregnancy or the fetus or newborn as if you had not been treated.

Herpes Genitalis

Herpes genitalis is one of the more common sexually transmitted infections. Although the herpes virus causes only local symptoms in an adult, it can cause a serious infection throughout the body of a fetus or newborn.

Many people acquire herpes infections in childhood, often without obvious symptoms. The common "cold sore" is a herpes infection. Adults can acquire herpes from kissing, oral sex, and genital sexual contact. Once the virus enters the body, it remains there, living in cells of the nervous system, hiding from the body's immune system. Outbreaks of the virus, during which a person has a painful blister, may occur frequently or infrequently. They often follow times of stress, including fatigue, heat exposure, and emotional upheaval.

Women known to have herpes rarely pass the virus on to their fetus. This appears related to the mother's formation of antibodies to the herpes virus. The antibodies cross the placenta into the baby's circulation and give it some immunity to the disease.

Women who acquire herpes for the first time during pregnancy are most likely to pass it to the fetus at birth, or before birth, through the placenta. Any woman, however, who has an active herpes blister in the birth canal may pass the virus to the newborn as it comes through the birth canal. When a blister is present, a cesarean birth usually is performed to prevent the baby from coming into contact with the virus. A cesarean birth is also recommended if a woman with recurrent herpes infection has *prodromal symptoms* at the start of labor. These are symptoms that she recognizes as signaling an imminent herpes outbreak.

If you know you have genital herpes, tell your physician or midwife early in your pregnancy. Be alert to symptoms that occur late in pregnancy. If you have never been diagnosed with herpes, but have a history of outbreaks of painful blisters in the vaginal area that last for 2 to 5 days and are often preceded by a *prodrome*—a tingling or itching sensation in the area where the blister erupts—you may have herpes. In that case, tell your physician or midwife and try to be seen anytime you have an outbreak so a culture can be taken of the blister to see if it grows the herpes virus. If you have never had such an outbreak, but develop these symptoms, especially if they are severe, with blisters covering a large part of the vaginal area and causing intense pain, see your physician or midwife immediately so you can be diagnosed. An antiviral drug (acyclovir) may be given. Some practitioners will give acyclovir preventively from 36 weeks until delivery. The medication may also be prescribed if you have what is known as a *primary infection* in pregnancy—the first outbreak of herpes, which can be passed to the fetus through the placenta. This drug may prevent abnormalities in the fetus.

To protect an infant from infection after birth, wash your hands carefully with soap and water anytime you use the bathroom or touch your genitals. Women with herpes can certainly breast-feed. If you (or anyone else who comes in contact with the baby) has oral herpes (a cold sore on the lips), you must avoid kissing the baby until the blister is completely healed. Do not touch the blister and then touch the baby without washing hands first.

Gonorrhea

Gonorrhea is another relatively common STI. Gonorrhea is caused by a bacteria that can be passed from an infected mother to the baby as it comes through the birth canal. The baby's eyes are particularly susceptible to infection. *Gonococcal conjunctivitis*—infection under the eyelids and in the cornea—can result in visual loss.

In most women, gonorrhea has no immediate symptoms. Therefore, testing of pregnant women is recommended. A specimen for testing is taken from the cervix with a cotton-tipped swab during a regular pelvic examination. Testing is recommended early in pregnancy, usually at the first prenatal visit. In women at high risk for STIs, testing is repeated later in the pregnancy, usually at 32 or 36 weeks, or anytime you think you or your partner may have become infected. The man with gonorrhea usually has a discharge from the penis or pain with urination.

Gonorrhea is treated by an antibiotic effective against the strain of gonorrhea causing the infection. This is determined by testing the specimen obtained through the cervical swab. Most commonly, ceftriaxone

(Rocephin) is given as a one-time injection. Spectinomycin and erythromycin are used in the case of an allergy to ceftriaxone (or to similar antibiotics—called *cephalosporins*).

The preventive treatment for the newborn consists of instillation of antibiotics under the eyelids. Further discussion of preventive treatment is in Chapter 24.

Chlamydia Trachomatis

Infection with the organism *Chlamydia trachomatis* is the most common STI today. This organism also may cause a type of conjunctivitis in the baby—usually not occurring until the second week of life, as compared with the rapidly occurring conjunctivitis that results from gonorrhea. Chlamydia also can cause pneumonia in the newborn.

Like gonorrhea, chlamydial infections in women are usually without symptoms, so testing is recommended during pregnancy, especially for women at risk for STIs. Pregnant women are treated with amoxicillin, erythromycin, or azithromycin (Zithromax). Azithromycin is a one-time treatment and therefore easy to comply with, although there is less experience with its use in pregnancy than with the other medications. Today, preventive treatments of the newborn's eyes that are effective against both gonorrhea and chlamydia are used most commonly.

Syphilis

Syphilis has long been recognized as a sexually transmitted infection. In past years, laws were enacted making blood testing for syphilis mandatory for marriage and during pregnancy. Many of these laws have been rescinded as the disease has become less common. However, women still become infected and can pass syphilis through the placenta to the fetus. Most women have their blood tested for syphilis early in pregnancy. Women at risk for STIs are retested later in pregnancy.

Syphilis is an unusual disease that goes through four distinct stages. In the first stage, an infected person develops a firm, usually painless, sore on the genitals. This is called a *chancre*. The chancre can be tested to see if it contains the syphilis organisms. The chancre denotes the stage of primary syphilis. Primary syphilis is very contagious.

The chancre will heal without any treatment. The syphilis diagnosis may be missed, especially if the chancre was on the cervix. Within a few weeks or months, the disease enters its secondary stage. During secondary syphilis, an infected person may develop flulike symptoms. A rash may appear on the skin or mucous membranes (the mouth, for example). The palms of the hands or soles of the feet are common places for the rash. A genital rash, called *condylomata lata*, may develop. Hair may be lost in patches.

Secondary syphilis is also contagious. During this time, antibodies form in the blood, allowing the disease to be diagnosed by the syphilis blood test (called a *serologic test*). This test may be positive, however, in the presence of conditions other than syphilis. Even pregnancy itself may occasionally make the test positive. Therefore, if a syphilis test is positive, a second test is done. Known as the *fluorescent treponema antibody test* (FTA), this is positive only when you actually have syphilis. *Treponema* is the organism that causes syphilis.

Again, without treatment, the symptoms of secondary syphilis heal themselves. This usually occurs within 2 to 10 weeks. The disease then enters a latency phase. Early latency is defined as the first year following infection and late latency as the period following early latency until symptoms of tertiary syphilis appear. You will not have symptoms in the latent stage of syphilis, but the disease is contagious for several years after its acquisition. It can be passed to the fetus for at least 8 years after infection in the mother. The tertiary stage can occur within 1 to 2 years after a person becomes infected, or 30 to 40 years later. Tertiary syphilis is a potentially fatal disease that attacks many of the body's organs.

Women can pass syphilis to their fetuses during pregnancy if their disease is untreated. When a fetus is infected in the uterus, the disease is called congenital syphilis and is very serious. Untreated disease can result in premature labor and even stillbirth. However, penicillin readily treats maternal, fetal, and newborn infection. If you are allergic to penicillin, the Centers for Disease Control and Prevention recommend that you be desensitized to penicillin, as it has the best treatment results among the medications that are safe for the fetus. Sometimes skin testing can be performed to see if your penicillin allergy still exists, but complete testing is not universally available. Desensitization is performed in the hospital and usually takes about 4 hours. Penicillin can then be given safely.

Depending on the stage of the disease, a woman will receive one to three antibiotic injections at weekly intervals. If it is not possible to determine disease stage or how long the woman has been infected, she will receive three courses of antibiotic treatment. In pregnancy, serologic testing for syphilis is repeated approximately 1 month following treatment to check for its effectiveness.

Trichomoniasis Vaginalis (Trichomonas)

Trichomoniasis (commonly called *trich*) is a common vaginal infection. Trich causes itching, a yellow or grayish discharge, and a foul or fishy odor. Occasionally, a woman may not have symptoms, but the trichomonads are found under the microscope. Trichomoniasis is not usually dangerous for the fetus or newborn, but the trichomonad is one of the organisms that might have a relationship to premature labor or premature rupture of the membranes.

Trichomoniasis is treated with an antibiotic called metronidazole (Flagyl). Dosages are either 250 mg by mouth 3 times a day for 7 days, or 2 grams (2000 mg) by mouth at one time. Metronidazole is given after the first trimester. If sexual partners are not also treated, the rate of recurrence is high.

Human Papilloma Virus (HPV)

Human Papilloma Virus or HPV is a common virus that has many strains. Several strains cause warts of the genital area—called *condylomata acuminata*. These warts have a characteristic cauliflower-like appearance and can be diagnosed simply by inspection, although a blood test for syphilis should be performed to make sure the warts are not condylomata lata of secondary syphilis. Sometimes the warts are on the cervix and are microscopic. These usually are discovered on a Pap smear and their diagnosis is confirmed by a procedure called a *colposcopy* (in which the cervix is viewed with a microscope).

Some types of HPV, especially those causing microscopic warts, have been implicated as a causative factor in cervical cancer, so women infected with the virus should be sure to have annual Pap smears. Pregnancy hormones may cause the warts to grow rapidly and become quite large. They may not be as responsive to treatment as they are when an infected woman is not pregnant. Even without treatment, they will recede following delivery. However, if untreated, they may become so large as to obstruct birth. This may necessitate a cesarean delivery. The warts may also cause discomfort. Rapidly growing or uncomfortable warts may be treated with topical applications of trichloroacetic acid, repeated one to three times a week, depending on the strength of the solution. The warts also can be removed with laser treatment or *cryotherapy* (freezing). Keeping the area clean and dry may help with discomfort.

Some children born to women infected with HPV will eventually develop *laryngeal papillomatosis*—benign tumors in the larynx or vocal cords. Neither treatment nor cesarean reduces the possibility of this transmission, as it appears to occur through the placenta. Fortunately, few children become infected.

Hepatitis B and C

Hepatitis is an infection of the liver caused by a number of viruses. Among these, hepatitis B and C can be transmitted through blood exposure, shared needles, or unprotected sex. A baby born to an infected mother may be infected.

Risks for hepatitis, in addition to having unprotected sex with somebody who is infected, are:

• Having received blood from a donor who later tested positive for hepatitis C (you should be contacted in this instance)
• Having ever injected illegal drugs, even if you experimented a few times many years ago
• Having received a blood transfusion or solid organ transplant before July, 1992
• Having received a blood product for clotting problems produced before 1987
• Having ever been on long-term kidney dialysis
• Having evidence of liver disease, such as abnormal tests of liver function

You may not know you are infected with hepatitis, or that you have been infected in the past. Approximately one-third of all people with hepatitis have no apparent illness. Some have obvious symptoms such as *jaundice* (yellow skin and eyes), but others have vague symptoms such as fatigue, loss of appetite, nausea and vomiting, and stomach pain. These eventually go away without treatment.

In most people, acute hepatitis B infection lasts a few months. The virus then leaves their body, although *antibodies* (infection-fighting cells) remain. Approximately 10 percent of adults infected with hepatitis B will carry the virus for life. These persons are said to have chronic infection or to be carriers. Ninety percent of babies born to women who have an acute infection during pregnancy or to women who are carriers of the hepatitis B virus will become infected in late pregnancy or during birth. Without treatment, approximately 25 percent of these babies will eventually develop serious liver damage (called *cirrhosis*) or cancer of the liver.

Because of the large risk of infection passing from mother to baby, and the success of early treatment, many physicians and midwives routinely test all pregnant women for hepatitis B (see Chapter 7).

Treatment will prevent acute infection and its consequences in approximately 95 percent of babies exposed during pregnancy or birth to hepatitis B. Treatment consists of a series of injections of hepatitis B vaccine—at birth, at 1 to 2 months of age, and again at 6 months of age. Hepatitis B immune globulin (H-BIG) is given with the first vaccination. Several months after the last vaccination, the baby will have a blood test to make sure that he or she is making antibodies to hepatitis. Babies who test positive for these antibodies do not develop infection.

Hepatitis C is another form of sexually transmitted virus that will cause serious liver problems. Only women with risks are tested for hepatitis C infection as only about 6 percent of babies born to women infected with hepatitis C or to carriers of this virus will be infected.

Babies born to mothers who carry this virus should have blood tests for the virus and for antibodies at 6 to 8 weeks after birth, and at 6 and 18 months of age. This allows for diagnosis of infants infected right after birth as well as those in whom infection does not show up for many months. Treatments for hepatitis C are available.

Neither hepatitis B nor C is passed through breast milk. Most experts agree that mothers who have either virus in their blood can safely breast-feed; however, there is some controversy concerning hepatitis C and breast-feeding. Discuss this with your obstetrical and pediatric care providers.

Human Immunodeficiency Virus (HIV)/ Acquired Immunodeficiency Syndrome (AIDS)

The human immunodeficiency virus (HIV) and the syndrome it causes, acquired immunodeficiency syndrome (AIDS), were identified in 1981. In a remarkably short span of time, HIV has been transformed from an untreatable infection, quickly leading to AIDS, to a treatable, long-term condition. Progression to AIDS has slowed and many individuals live with HIV infection for years. Still, the disease carries a significant rate of death and prevention remains the key to conquering it.

An important part of prevention is preventing transmission of the virus from mother to fetus or newborn. Fortunately, passage from mother to fetus has declined dramatically. Treatment in pregnancy, during labor, and in the immediate newborn period has reduced the transmission of disease to the newborn from about 25 percent to 8 percent (1 in 12 babies).

Many states now mandate that all pregnant women be counseled about HIV and offered testing. The Institute of Medicine, The American Academy of Pediatrics, and The American College of Obstetricians and Gynecologists recommend routine prenatal testing, with the mother retaining the right to refuse to be tested.

Since pregnancy means having had unprotected intercourse, then all pregnant women have some risk for HIV. Certain current or past behaviors increase the risk for acquiring HIV. These are:

• Intravenous drug use (or exposure to needles for other nonmedical reasons)
• Exposure to drug transfusions or treatment with blood products between 1977 and 1985
• Exchanging sex for money
• Having another STI or a history of an STI
• Coming from a country where HIV/AIDS is especially common among heterosexual individuals
• Having or having had a partner who is HIV-positive, who has used intravenous drugs, is bisexual or has had homosexual experiences, has hemophilia, was exposed to drug transfusions or treatment with blood products between 1977 and 1985, or has been incarcerated (in jail)
• Having multiple partners
• Having had a partner whose risk behaviors are unknown

The test for HIV is an indirect test that examines the blood for antibodies to the virus. These are viral-fighting agents specific to HIV. Two tests are performed. One is very sensitive, the other more specific. A sensitive test will not miss many people with antibodies, but may show false positives. A *false positive test* indicates that a person has antibodies when in fact the person doesn't have the disease. When this sensitive test, called the *ELISA test*, is positive, it is repeated. If it remains positive, a more specific test, called a *Western blot test*, is performed. A more specific test is less likely to show false positives. Few, if any, Western blot tests are positive when there is no disease. Anybody with a positive Western blot test is therefore considered infected with HIV.

Because the HIV test relies on the development of antibodies, the test may not be positive for up to 6 months after viral exposure. A negative test should be repeated 6 months after the last possible exposure. If risk behaviors continue, testing should be repeated every 6 months.

Tests performed by private practitioners and most health centers are confidential; results are not revealed without your consent. However, all states offer *anonymous testing*—testing that is conducted solely by number. Each state has a toll-free hotline listed in the phone book to call for information about anonymous testing. A national toll-free AIDS Hotline— 800-342-AIDS—also will provide you with your individual state hotline number.

In 1994, a study conducted by the National Institutes of Health (NIH) found that when HIV-positive women were treated with zidovudine (AZT, ZDV, or Retrovir) during pregnancy and labor and their babies treated at birth, transmission of the virus to babies decreased by two-thirds. (This study is known as ACTG 076—AIDS Clinical Trials Group 076.) Unless you are already on a treatment regimen for HIV/AIDS, the pregnancy treatment usually will begin after the first 3 months of pregnancy so that the baby is not exposed to the medication during the crucial period of organ development. If you are taking medications and become pregnant, your health care provider will discuss with you the pros and cons of continuing or stopping treatment for the initial 3 months of pregnancy. During labor, AZT is given to the mother intravenously. The baby begins AZT treatment within the first 8 to 12 hours after birth and continues for 6 weeks. The AZT is usually given as a syrup, although it can be given intravenously in babies who cannot tolerate oral feedings (such as the very premature).

To date, the only significant side effect in newborns exposed to HIV treatment in utero and after birth has been mild anemia in some of the treated babies that resolved when the treatment was stopped. Treated babies have been followed for up to 6 years without apparent abnormal development. Whether these children will manifest problems as they reach adulthood is still unknown.

Because all babies born to HIV-positive women will show antibodies to the virus at birth, all babies must be treated. Those who have antibodies only because the mother has passed her antibodies to them through the placenta cannot be differentiated for 6 to 18 months from those whose antibodies reflect true infection with the HIV virus. Today, blood tests are available which can demonstrate tiny amounts of the HIV virus in an infant's blood. These can detect HIV infection within 2 to 3 months after birth, but treatment is recommended to begin immediately, before detection is possible.

A pregnant woman may already be in treatment with AZT or other HIV-fighting drugs. If her current drug regimen does not include AZT, it should be added to her treatment regimen when she becomes pregnant. The effect of most other anti-HIV drugs on babies is not known, but they may be beneficial to the mother's health. (In developing countries, a single dose of nevirapine (Viramune) may be given to the mother in labor and to the newborn after birth. One study showed a 50 percent reduction in transmission with this treatment. Although not quite as effective as AZT, the nevirapine regimen is easier to administer and less expensive.) Tests for viral load and CD4 T cells (infection-fighting cells) are done periodically in pregnancy to evaluate the status of the infected woman's disease. Women who have high viral loads and/or low CD4 T cells are more likely to pass the disease onto their babies, but treatment to prevent transmission to the baby is recommended regardless of these values. Additional treatment for the mother may be determined according to the results of these tests, however. Specific symptoms and the presence of other infectious diseases may also signal the need for additional treatment.

If a woman is known to be HIV-positive, procedures that might increase the exposure of the fetus to the mother's blood should be avoided. These include amniocentesis, fetal scalp blood sampling in labor, and artificial rupture of the membranes.

In 1998, a study conducted in France showed that a planned cesarean birth before labor may reduce the likelihood of transmitting the virus to the baby even further, to 1 to 2 percent of exposed babies. This is still under study.

HIV also can be transmitted through breast milk. The National Institutes of Health estimate a 10 to 14 percent chance of infecting an infant through breast-feeding. If you know you are HIV positive, breast-feeding is not the wisest choice as infant formulas are available that provide adequate nutrition. In countries where formula is not available or where water is impure, breast-feeding may still be a better feeding method even for HIV-infected women.

Of course, women infected with HIV should practice other healthful behaviors including getting early and regular prenatal care, following good nutritional guidelines (see Chapter 10), and avoiding smoking and alcohol and drug use. Treatment programs for substance use may be helpful and you should talk to your physician or midwife if you have such a problem.

OTHER INFECTIOUS DISEASES

Vaginitis/Vaginosis

Along with trichomoniasis, discussed above because it is sexually trans-mitted, *bacterial vaginosis* (BV) and *candidiasis* (yeast infection) are the typical vaginal infections. The symptoms and course of these infections do not differ in pregnant and non-pregnant women. However, pregnant women are somewhat more susceptible to yeast infections. These are characterized by a cottage-cheesy discharge and severe itching. A rash may develop from scratching. Diagnosis is made by taking a specimen of vaginal secretions with a cotton swab, placing the vaginal secretions onto a slide, and examining them under a microscope.

Yeast infections are not transmitted to the fetus via the placenta. The baby can develop a yeast infection of its mouth if it is born through a yeast-infected birth canal. This newborn infection is called *thrush* and is treatable, but may make early nursing difficult.

Yeast infections can be treated readily with vaginal creams or tablets. Some experts recommend a 7-day course of treatment during preg-nancy. Oral treatment with fluconazole (Diflucan) is not recommended in pregnancy.

Keeping the vaginal area dry (wearing all-cotton underwear and changing out of wet bathing suits quickly, for example) and going easy on sweets may help prevent yeast infections.

Bacterial vaginosis is called vaginosis because it does not cause in-flammation of the vagina. It is caused by a disturbance in the usual bac-terial environment of the vagina. It may have no symptoms or be characterized by a milky discharge and a fishy odor. The odor may be es-pecially noticeable after sexual intercourse, although BV is not sexually transmitted. BV is associated with premature rupture of membranes and premature labor and birth. The same organisms present in BV are fre-quently present in postpartum infection. BV can be diagnosed by look-ing at a smear of vaginal secretions under the microscope. Such testing is recommended even without symptoms in women who have previously had a premature baby.

BV can be treated in pregnancy with metronidazole (Flagyl or Proto-stat) taken orally at a dose of 250 mg three times daily for 7 days or 2 grams in a single dose. Clindamycin can also be taken orally at a dose of 300 mg twice a day for 7 days. Both medications are available for vaginal treatment. Metronidazole gel can be used during pregnancy. An applicatorful of gel is applied to the vagina once or twice a day for

5 days. Clindamycin vaginal cream, however, has been associated with preterm deliveries and should not be used in pregnancy.

Rubella

The virus of rubella (*German measles*) formerly caused a great deal of fetal injury but the availability since 1969 of an effective and safe vaccine has almost eradicated the problem. Rubella in adults, pregnant or not, is a relatively mild disease associated with low fever and discomfort, a light rash that tends to be slightly itchy, and enlarged lymph nodes, particularly at the back of the head and behind the ears. Discomfort may last up to 3 days.

For the fetus, who can become infected because the virus readily crosses the placenta, the impact of rubella is much more severe. If rubella occurs early in pregnancy the infant may have eye cataracts, deafness, heart defects, and hernias. The likelihood that one or more defects will occur has been variously estimated but is probably about 25 percent in women who have had rubella in the first 8 to 10 weeks of pregnancy. Some problems caused by rubella, such as blood and liver abnormalities, resolve without treatment. Others can be corrected or improved with surgery. Still others require extensive care throughout life. Some women infected with rubella in the first trimester may miscarry and others may choose to have an abortion.

When rubella occurs in the second trimester, congenital anomalies do not ensue, because the fetus already is fully formed, but the fetus can acquire the disease, and the baby may be born with congenital rubella. These active infections in the second trimester are not treatable in the mother, the fetus, or the newborn. Many such babies are small for gestational age and at least half of them become seriously ill sometime in the first year of life. They also can transmit rubella to nonimmune persons with whom they come in contact. About 20 percent of the fetuses infected with the German measles virus develop diabetes later in life.

Routine prenatal blood testing includes a test for immunity to rubella. Pregnant women who are not immune should avoid contact with anyone who has a rash of unknown cause. Any nonimmune woman should have a blood test for antibodies to the virus if she develops a mild illness with a rash. Development of antibodies in a previously nonimmune woman means that she was likely infected with the virus.

Women who are not immune to rubella should be vaccinated at least 1 month before planning a pregnancy, or immediately after a pregnancy, if they did not know they were not immune until they were tested in pregnancy. Breast-feeding is not a reason to avoid vaccination. Although the Centers for Disease Control and Prevention and most practitioners recommend the 1-month waiting period between vaccination and pregnancy, babies born to women inadvertently vaccinated during pregnancy or shortly before a conception have not shown birth defects like the ones caused by rubella. Still, the waiting period is advised for absolute safety.

Other Viral Diseases

The other relatively common viral diseases, such as influenza (the flu), measles, and mumps, ordinarily do not have any effect on the fetus and have no more effect on a pregnant woman than on a nonpregnant adult. Some infectious diseases, however, can cross the placenta and cause illness in the fetus and newborn—often more serious than the illness seen in the pregnant woman. Sometimes, in fact, the woman may not become ill at all, but can pass infectious organisms onto her baby.

Chicken Pox

The chicken pox virus (*varicella*) is capable of crossing the placenta and infecting the fetus in utero. Chicken pox may cause fetal anomalies in about 20 percent of fetuses exposed in the first few months of pregnancy. These might affect the eyes, skin, brain, limbs, urinary tract, and the genitals. In the second half of pregnancy, this virus does not have teratogenic effects. If a mother passes the chicken pox virus to her fetus shortly before birth, however, or during the birth process, the newborn can develop a serious form of the disease.

Most adult women are immune to chicken pox as the virus is so common in childhood. If you know you had chicken pox as a child, you can consider yourself immune. If you are not certain, you can have your immunity tested, preferably before becoming pregnant. A vaccine known to be effective for up to 10 years is available and you can talk to your physician or other health care provider about being vaccinated before you become pregnant. If you are exposed to chicken pox in pregnancy and are not immune, you can receive an injection of *varicella zoster immune globulin* (VZIG). This immune globulin is made from the plasma of healthy volunteer blood donors who have high levels of antibody to the virus. Call your physician or midwife immediately if somebody you are with develops chicken pox unless you are certain you have had chicken pox. Your immunity can be tested and you can receive ZVIG if necessary. The virus is contagious 1 to 2 days before the rash appears. If you have any questions about your immunity to chicken pox, avoid contact with anybody with an itchy rash.

Cytomegalovirus (CMV)

The most common viral disease affecting the fetus is cytomegalovirus or CMV. CMV causes only mild symptoms, if any, when acquired during childhood or later in life. The virus remains in the body but infected children and adults suffer no health problems unless their immune system becomes suppressed due to medications or diseases such as AIDS.

CMV belongs to the herpes virus group and, like herpes genitalis, it can cause serious disease in newborns who acquired the virus while in the uterus. Most newborns survive this disease, but the majority develop problems in the first few years of life. These include hearing and vision loss, and possibly mental retardation. The only time this happens is when a woman becomes infected for the first time with CMV during pregnancy. This occurs in 1 to 3 percent of pregnancies. Only about one-third of these newborns will become infected, and only 10 to 15 percent of those will show symptoms at the time of birth. Among the newborns without symptoms at birth, 5 to 10 percent will have later problems with hearing, coordination, or mental development. Overall, affected babies represent a very small percentage of all newborns, but in actual numbers, more than a thousand newborns and infants will show varying degrees of impairment from CMV every year.

It is now not considered feasible to screen all pregnant women for CMV, partly because we do not have effective treatment. However, the greatest risk for acquiring this infection comes from women who care for small children—in hospitals, at day care centers, or at home. This includes mothers of infants and toddlers. The most important preventive measure is handwashing with soap and water after contact with diapers or oral secretions. If you develop an illness with mononucleosis-type symptoms (fever, sore throat, and swollen lymph nodes that last for 1 to 4 weeks) during pregnancy, you should tell your physician or midwife and be tested for CMV antibodies. A blood test at the beginning of the illness and another 2 weeks later that shows increasing antibody levels indicates that you have had the infection.

CMV also can be transmitted through breast milk, but infections transmitted this way do not cause significant illness in the newborn. The benefits of breast-feeding clearly outweigh any possible risks of infection.

Human Parovirus B19 (Fifth Disease)

Human parovirus B19 was identified in 1975. It causes a disease called *erythema infectiosum* (EI), more commonly known as Fifth disease. Animals get paroviruses, but these cannot be transmitted to humans, so you cannot catch parovirus B19 from your pet. About 50 percent of pregnant women have been exposed previously to parovirus B19 and are immune.

Of those infected with B19, up to 20 percent have no symptoms. Most others have a mild illness with a facial rash looking like a slapped cheek, and a lacy rash on the trunk, arms, and legs. Sunlight, changes in temperature, and emotional stress may cause the rash to recur over several weeks. Often, mild symptoms occur 1 to 4 days before the rash appears. In adults, joint pain, weakness, or inflammation may be the only symptoms of EI. When a woman is infected between 10 and 20 weeks of pregnancy, there is a small possibility (probably less than 5 percent) of fetal loss. Although some animal paroviruses are teratogens, most evidence does not support such an effect for human parovirus B19. However, it can be a cause of a serious or even life-threatening form of fetal anemia.

Lyme Disease

Lyme disease is a bacterial infection passed by tick bites. Rarely, it can be passed to the fetus and even cause stillbirth. Pregnant women do not have an increased susceptibility to the illness. Antibiotic treatment can be initiated during pregnancy if necessary and is effective.

Lyme disease symptoms include a small reddened mark that looks like an insect bite with a characteristic clear center like a bull's-eye; fever; fatigue; headache; muscle and joint pain (even occurring years later); and swollen lymph nodes. Lyme disease is most prevalent in the Northeast, from Massachusetts to Maryland, the north-central states, especially Wisconsin and Minnesota, and the West Coast, particularly northwest California.

If you live in these areas, try to avoid wooded, bushy, or overgrown grassy areas, particularly in the spring and summer. If you do walk in such an area, protect yourself by wearing long sleeves and long pants. Tuck your pants into your socks. Use insect repellent on your skin— following the precautions noted in the section on malaria—and permethrin on clothing (see page 435). The tick must adhere to the skin for about 36 hours before it can pass the infection on to you, so check yourself nightly for ticks. If you find a tick, remove it with a fine tweezer and apply antiseptic (and nothing else) to the area. Don't worry if the tick's mouth remains on your skin; the infection is not passed through its mouth.

A vaccine against Lyme disease has been developed recently. The Centers for Disease Control and Prevention recommend it only for people living in high-risk areas, or those who travel to such areas, especially hikers and campers. The safety of the vaccine in pregnancy has not been established, so it is not recommended for pregnant women. The company that manufactures the vaccine, SmithKline Beecham, has established a registry for pregnant recipients of the vaccine so possible effects can be monitored. If you inadvertently receive a Lyme disease vaccine while you are pregnant, have your physician or midwife contact this registry at 800-366-8900, ext. 5231.

Listeriosis

Listeriosis is a foodborne illness to which pregnant women are extra prone. They are about twenty times more likely than other healthy adults to get listeriosis. The newborn suffers the effects of the disease, not the pregnant woman.

Listeriosis is caused by *listeria monocytogenes*, found in soil and water. Raw foods, meats, and dairy products can contain the bacteria. The following guidelines from the CDC will help prevent listeriosis:

- Thoroughly cook meat and poultry.
- Thoroughly wash raw vegetables before eating.
- When storing foods, keep uncooked meats away from vegetables and from cooked and ready-to-eat foods.
- Avoid unpasteurized milk and its products.
- Thoroughly wash hands, knives, cutting boards, and countertops after handling uncooked foods; use hot soapy water.
- Avoid soft cheeses such as Brie, Camembert, feta, blue-veined and Mexican-style cheese. (Hard cheeses, processed cheese, cream, cottage cheese, and yogurt are fine to eat.)
- Cook leftovers or ready-to-eat foods such as hot dogs until steaming hot.
- You may want to avoid foods from deli counters (although the risk of listeriosis from these is low), or thoroughly reheat cold cuts before eating.

Tuberculosis

Before the age of antibiotics, tuberculosis (TB) was the major cause of death in the United States. TB is a bacterial disease that can attack any body organ, but usually chooses the lungs. From the 1940s, when anti-tuberculosis medications were discovered, until the mid-1980s, TB declined, almost to the point of disappearance. Since 1984, however, it has again been on the rise.

The tuberculosis bacteria gets into the lungs by ordinary breathing. Most people who become infected are not sick. Disease, however, can develop at any time. For this reason, anybody testing positive for tuberculosis should receive preventive treatment. In pregnancy, this treatment may be postponed until the postpartum period if there are no symptoms of disease and a chest X ray (performed after 20 weeks of pregnancy to minimize effects on the fetus) shows no disease. Active infection, however, must be treated. Medication is taken for 6 months to 1 year.

To test for TB exposure, a small amount of fluid, called *tuberculin*, is injected just under the skin of the inner forearm. You may have redness or swelling at the area of the injection. Two to three days later, a health care worker will measure the area of swelling to see if the test is positive.

If you come from a country where BCG vaccine is given against tuberculosis, your test may be harder to interpret. This vaccine is not used frequently in the United States because its effectiveness is questionable and it can confuse the diagnosis of the disease. You may have a positive skin test just from the vaccine. However, you cannot assume that the vaccine is to blame. In certain circumstances, a positive test will be considered indication of infection, not immunity. These include showing a very large area of reaction, having received the vaccine many years previously, having recent exposure to someone with TB, or coming from a country where the infection is common. TB is common in most countries in Latin America, the Caribbean, Africa, and Asia (except for Japan).

Although some physicians and midwives routinely test all pregnant women for TB, the recommendation is to test women in high-risk groups. In addition to being common in certain countries, TB is most common in the United States in people who live in homeless shelters, are in jail or prison, live in migrant farm camps, or live in some nursing homes. Other risk groups include people with HIV, close contacts of people known to have TB, medically underserved populations, and drug or alcohol users.

Symptoms of TB include a cough with a small amount of *sputum* (the substance you cough up) or blood, a low-grade fever, and weight loss. Tests for active TB include a chest X ray and a test of sputum.

Malaria

Malaria is spread by the bite of an infected mosquito. It is quite common in many parts of the world. The CDC recommends postponing travel to malaria-risk areas until after pregnancy, if at all possible. If such travel must be taken, the CDC recommends taking antimalarial drugs and measures to prevent mosquito bites. The antimalarial drugs chloroquine and mefloquine appear to be safe during pregnancy. Pregnant women should not take doxycycline or proguanil (Malarone). The drug to be prescribed depends on where you are traveling. Antimalarials can be taken during breast-feeding, but the amount of drug passed through the breast milk is not enough to protect the infant. The infant will need its own preventive treatment.

When traveling to a malaria-risk area, wear long-sleeved shirts and long pants. Apply insect repellent to any exposed skin, especially between dusk and dawn. Use repellents containing a 30 to 35 percent concentration of DEET (diethyltoluamide topical). Wash them off when inside. Avoid getting the repellent into your eyes or breathing it in. Don't use it on wounds or open skin.

It's best to sleep in well-screened, air-conditioned rooms. If you cannot arrange this, use a pyrethroid-containing flying-insect spray at night. Sleep under mosquito netting. Treat the netting with permethrin liquid or spray.

See a health care provider with experience in prescribing antimalarial medication 4 to 6 weeks before your scheduled travel. Remember to report that you are pregnant. The CDC provides three sources of information about malaria:

1. Toll-free Voice Information Service. 1-877-FYI-TRIP
2. Toll-free Fax Information Service. Call 1-888-232-3299. Follow the instructions. Request document 000005 for information about the available travel faxes.
3. The CDC Travelers' Health Website.

Parasites

Parasites do not ordinarily cross the placenta. An exception is the microscopic protozoon, *Toxoplasmi gondii,* that causes toxoplasmosis. If a woman is exposed for the first time to this parasite during pregnancy, she can pass the disease onto the fetus. The fetus can become seriously ill, even if the mother's illness is mild or barely noticed.

Toxoplasmosis is spread in two ways other than through the placenta. One is by eating raw or undercooked meat from an animal that has had the disease, or handling such meat prior to cooking. The other is through a household cat, which sheds a form of the parasite in its feces. When these dry out, the toxoplasma egg cells (*oocysts*) can be inhaled by people handling the cat litter. The oocysts are shed by the cat only during the initial phases of infection and are generally acquired when the cat eats infected small animals while out foraging. Toxoplasmosis does not occur in cats who have always lived indoors, were not born to mothers with the disease, and have not been exposed in close quarters to other cats who have the infection.

Acute toxoplasmosis in an adult is marked by flulike symptoms of fatigue and aching muscles. It has no particular characteristics that would make the diagnosis easy without laboratory tests. The disease cannot be confirmed unless the mother had a blood test for toxoplasmosis early in the pregnancy and was found not to have toxoplasma antibodies. A subsequent test with a high antibody value is presumed to be evidence of the disease. If the woman did not have a blood test before possible exposure, then presumption of recent infection is based on a high or moderate level of antibody and the presence of a specific antibody called IgG (which eventually goes away). If the only antibody present is IgM (which persists), this usually means the infection occurred longer than 3 to 6 months previously. Infection occurring before pregnancy will not affect the fetus or newborn.

Toxoplasmosis normally is treated with the antibiotic spiramycin or with pyrimethamine combined with a sulfa drug. However, since pyrimethamine may cause congenital anomalies if the woman is in the first trimester of pregnancy, treatment at that stage must be with sulfa drugs only. Appropriate treatment reduces fetal infection by 50 percent.

In babies, the *Toxoplasma* organisms infect the brain and produce a rather serious illness. In a slightly less severe form, these organisms may involve the eyes and eventually cause partial loss of vision. If the mother is diagnosed as having toxoplasmosis during pregnancy, many experts advise starting preventive treatment of the newborn at birth, rather than waiting to see whether the baby has been infected or not.

Guidelines for prevention of toxoplasmosis are outlined in Chapter 5.

Urinary Tract Infection (UTI) and Pyelonephritis

The urinary tract is divided into two parts, the upper and lower tracts. The *upper tract* consists of the kidneys and the *ureters*—the tubes leading from the kidneys, where urine is made, to the bladder, where urine is stored. The lower tract consists of the bladder and the *urethra*, the tube that carries urine from the bladder out of the body. In women, the urethral opening is just above the vaginal opening.

The urinary tract undergoes a number of changes during pregnancy. The kidneys enlarge. The ureters open or dilate. These changes result from both hormonal and mechanical influences. As the uterus enlarges, it puts pressure on the ureters. These changes make the pregnant woman more prone to urinary tract infections. Urinary tract infections (UTIs) in pregnant women are more likely to move into the kidneys and to be serious.

A pregnant woman with a UTI may have the usual symptoms, or no symptoms. The usual symptoms are feelings of an intense need to urinate (*urgency*), urinating often (*frequency*), and pain with urination (*dysuria*). The pain sensation is usually burning and most often occurs at the end of urinating. Urgency and especially frequency may be hard to distinguish from the ordinary increased urination of pregnancy. However, if these symptoms seem unusual and if there is pain with urination, you should call your physician or midwife. These infections need prompt treatment in pregnancy to prevent their moving upward into the kidneys. When there is an infection without symptoms, it is called *asymptomatic bacteriuria*. This is found by examining a urine sample. In nonpregnant women, asymptomatic bacteriuria does not lead to symptomatic infections and does not require treatment, but in pregnancy, either symptomatic or asymptomatic lower tract infection can lead to serious upper tract or kidney infection.

Kidney infection is called *pyelonephritis*. Women with pyelonephritis usually are quite ill. Symptoms include fever and chills and aching pain in the lower back, on one side or both. You may have a loss of appetite, nausea, and vomiting. On physical examination, you will experience pain when the examiner presses on one or both sides of your back in the area called the *costovertebral angle* (Latin: *costa* = rib) or CVA—the place where the lowest ribs meet the vertebrae. This is the region of the kidneys. Often this pain (called CVA tenderness) is severe.

A urinary tract infection confined to the lower urinary tract (called *cystitis* or *urethritis*) is treated with oral antibiotics. These may be given as a one-time dose, for 3 days, or for up to 10 days. A number of antibiotics may be used in pregnancy such as ampicillin, amoxicillin, or macrofurantoin (brand names: Macrodantin or Macrobid). Classes of drugs called sulfonamides or cephalosporins also may be used.

The appropriate antibiotics can be determined by a test of the urine called a *culture and sensitivity* (or C&S). You will be asked to give a clean catch or midstream urine specimen. This means you clean your vaginal and urethral area from front to back before urinating, urinate the first few drops into the toilet, and then urinate the rest into a sterile specimen cup. This is sent to the laboratory to see what infectious organism grows, usually over a period of 48 hours. The organism is then tested to see which antibiotics are effective against it. Most often in pregnancy treatment is begun based on symptoms or the presence of bacteria on a simple urine specimen looked at before the culture has time to grow. A common antibiotic will be prescribed. If you don't get better, the treatment may be changed based on the results of the culture and sensitivity.

Pyelonephritis requires hospitalization with fluids and antibiotics given intravenously. You may then take oral antibiotics for up to 10 days. If urinary infection recurs in pregnancy, some practitioners prescribe preventive antibiotics—usually nitrofurantoin, 100 mg, taken daily at bedtime for the entire pregnancy.

Self-help measures to prevent and help treat urinary tract infections are the same in pregnancy as any other time. Drink lots of fluids, especially water. Try to have six to eight glasses a day throughout pregnancy. You can carry a water bottle and sip all day. Cranberry juice is good to drink as it makes the urine acidic, which increases its resistance to bacteria. Vitamin C also increases the urine's acidity. You can take 1,000 mg of this vitamin a day safely. As UTIs usually are caused by germs that live in the rectum, always wipe yourself from front to back after you use the toilet so you don't bring these germs forward to the urethral opening. During sex, your partner should avoid touching the vaginal and urethral areas with any part of his body that has touched your anal area, without first washing. Urinate after sex.

CHRONIC ILLNESS

Diabetes

Insulin is the hormone produced by the body to metabolize or help the body utilize its intake of sugar or glucose. Because the fetus needs a lot of glucose during pregnancy, the hormones produced by the placenta have an anti-insulin effect. This allows a large amount of glucose to pass through the placenta to the fetus. Generally, despite this anti-insulin effect, pregnant women have normal blood sugar levels because so much glucose goes to the fetus. However, in some women, the anti-insulin effect of pregnancy causes an elevated blood sugar level. These women develop what is called *gestational diabetes.*

Gestational diabetes generally is a milder condition than preexisting diabetes. Before the introduction of insulin in 1922, women with preexisting diabetes rarely became pregnant. When they did, the outcome was frequently catastrophic for both mother and baby. With the use of insulin, diabetic women have become normally fertile and the threat to the life of mother and fetus has virtually vanished. Today, self-monitoring of glucose blood levels has also reduced the need for prolonged hospitalization to regulate blood sugar levels.

When diabetes is not well controlled, however, the disease leads to a small but significant increase in the rate of congenital anomalies. The excess sugar present in the mother's blood crosses through the placenta so that as the mother's blood sugar rises, the blood sugar of the fetus goes up, too. The cells in the fetus's pancreas that are responsible for regulating blood sugar then produce extra insulin, which also functions as a growth hormone in the fetus. Consequently, when the mother's blood sugar is constantly elevated, the fetus tends to become very large. This size may hinder normal birth. Furthermore, efforts of the mother and baby to regulate their blood sugar create a metabolic stress that alters a number of the baby's other chemical systems, sometimes severely.

Screening for Diabetes

There are two schools of thought about screening for diabetes in pregnancy. Screening means performing a relatively simple test to decide which women need a more extensive and accurate test to actually diagnose the disease. Some care providers and the American College of Obstetricians and Gynecologists recommend screening tests only for women who have an increased risk of developing gestational diabetes. These include all women over the age of 30 and women who have or have had:

- A baby over 9 pounds at birth
- A previous stillbirth or premature baby for which the cause was unknown
- A previous baby with birth defects for which the cause was unknown

- Five or more previous births
- Obesity
- Gestational diabetes in a previous pregnancy
- Close family members with diabetes
- Sugar in the urine at a high level or at several visits during pre-natal care. (In some pregnant women, the increased flow of blood through the kidneys results in leakage of sugar even though the blood sugar is normal. These women do not have diabetes, but only a blood test will ascertain this.)

Many physicians and midwives prefer to do screening tests on all pregnant women. This is the recommendation of the American Diabetes Association. The screening and diagnostic tests for diabetes in pregnancy are discussed in detail in Chapter 12. Preexisting diabetes, of course, will have been diagnosed before your pregnancy. Someone with known diabetes is never given extra glucose as a test.

Care of the Woman with Diabetes

Complications of diabetes for both mother and baby can be avoided if the pregnant woman's blood sugar is monitored by frequent tests and kept within normal limits. The woman can take small samples of her own blood from her fingertip and test them at home to find out the range of her blood sugar. This is a simple test, but a few women find it difficult to perform. Today, products are available that test the blood sugar without a finger prick. You can ask your physician or office nurse about these. Occasionally, a woman needs to be admitted to the hospital for a short while and have testing performed by hospital staff. The goal is to maintain blood sugar at normal values by diet and, when necessary, the administration of insulin.

If you have preexisting diabetes, your dietary or insulin requirements—or both—may change in pregnancy. If you are diagnosed with diabetes during pregnancy, the first effort will be to try to control your blood sugar with dietary changes. In either case, you will likely be referred to a dietitian, nutritionist, or nurse who specializes in the care of pregnant diabetic women. You will be given instructions on what foods to avoid, what foods to eat, how much to eat, and how to divide the types of food you can eat into meals and snacks. This diet will be individualized for you. Its calorie count will be based on how pregnant you are, how active you are, and either your prepregnant weight if that was within a normal range, or your desirable weight if you were underweight or overweight. This diet should not be difficult to follow as it allows you many food choices within specified food groups, but it does require planning and effort. Of course, you must avoid most sweets. You will be taught how to check your blood sugar at various times during the day and, if necessary, how to give yourself injections of insulin. Oral medications for diabetes are not used in pregnancy.

In years past, the threat of stillbirth was thought to be so serious that babies of women with diabetes were delivered as soon as they were mature enough to survive without serious respiratory problems. Today, however, the trend is to begin fetal monitoring by the *nonstress test* (NST) and *biophysical profile* (described in Chapter 17) as the woman nears full term, and to continue frequent determinations of blood sugar. If these tests are normal, the baby need not be delivered early.

Exactly when to begin testing of the fetus will vary among physicians and may depend on whether or not the woman has other complications, such as *pregnancy-induced hypertension* (high blood pressure). Pregnancy complications are somewhat more likely to occur with diabetes. When to begin testing will also depend on how the fetus is growing. Certainly, you can start to count the baby's movements from the beginning of the third trimester of pregnancy.

There are a number of ways to count fetal movements. Both large and small movements are included in a movement count. You can pick an hour during which the fetus is usually active. For many women, this is in the evening. Count for an hour. If you feel fewer than four movements in that hour, count for another hour. If you still feel fewer than four movements in the second hour, call your physician or midwife right away. Another way to count is called the Cardiff Count-to-Ten method. From the time you wake in the morning, start counting all fetal movements. You can stop when you get to ten. Call your physician or midwife if you feel fewer than ten movements during the course of the day (about 12 hours) or if, over time, it takes longer and longer for you to get to ten movements.

In previous decades, a great majority of women with diabetes had their babies delivered by cesarean. With the improvements in testing and treatment, very large infants are encountered less often. The cesarean delivery rate among women with diabetes, however, is still somewhat higher than that in women without diabetes, but cesarean birth is not routine.

Appropriate care of the woman with diabetes in the first few days after delivery can be difficult if there are rapid, wide, or unpredictable changes in her sugar metabolism. If you have gestational diabetes, usually your blood sugar will return to normal right after birth and you require no further care other than follow-up during your lifetime, as women with gestational diabetes have an increased likelihood of developing diabetes as they age. The infant of the mother with diabetes also requires meticulous care by experienced pediatricians.

Hypertension (High Blood Pressure)

Hypertension, or high blood pressure, is another reason for concern in pregnancy. Since hypertension is usually of unknown cause, its impact on pregnancy is difficult to predict in an individual case. Some women with high blood pressure go through pregnancy without any change in their blood pressure and without any sign of hypertension affecting the pregnancy, while in others blood pressure worsens. Protein may appear in the urine. This is called *superimposed toxemia* or *superimposed preeclampsia*. This problem may require prompt delivery if medications fail to bring the blood pressure into a safe range. In general, the woman with hypertension experiences a lowering of blood pressure in the second trimester of pregnancy, as does the woman without high blood pressure. As the pregnancy approaches term, blood pressure tends to return to its prepregnancy level. Women with elevated blood pressure may produce small babies with small placentas.

The woman with hypertension who is on long-term medications designed to lower blood pressure should continue these medicines during pregnancy. If blood pressure becomes difficult to control, the dose of medicine must be increased.

Most antihypertensive medication has no known adverse effect on the fetus. However, medications falling into the category of *angiotensin-converting enzyme inhibitors* (ACE inhibitors) should be avoided because they can cause kidney abnormalities in the fetus. Captopril (Capoten) and enalapril (Vasotee) are examples of ACE inhibitors. Many alternative antihypertensive agents are available.

Diuretics or "water pills" used to be prescribed extensively in pregnancy. In excessive doses they can lower the maternal blood volume enough to interfere with blood flow to the placenta. Therefore, diuretics should not be used in the routine treatment of high blood pressure.

Complications of hypertension such as stroke and heart enlargement are no more common during pregnancy than they are otherwise.

Heart Disease

In past years, a substantial number of young women entered pregnancy with defects of the heart valves due to *rheumatic fever*, a consequence of a strep infection. Since antibiotic treatment has been used extensively for strep infections, there has been a tremendous reduction in heart disease due to rheumatic fever. Where medical treatment has not sufficed, surgery has done much to make heart function in women with valvular heart disease close to normal. Women with artificial heart valves usually tolerate pregnancy well.

Some women who have had heart valve replacements need to take blood thinning medication (anticoagulants). Many women take warfarin (brand name: Coumadin) because it can be given by mouth. Warfarin may have adverse effects on the fetus, especially in the first 6 to 12 weeks of pregnancy. Heparin is an alternative, but must be given intravenously or by subcutaneous injection and may not be quite as effective in pregnancy in preventing blood clots. Some physicians will use heparin throughout pregnancy, others only in the first trimester, switching back to warfarin after this crucial period of organ development. If you are on anticoagulant treatment, discuss this before pregnancy with your physician. Anticoagulation must be stopped before delivery to avoid extra bleeding during the birth. It can be started within 6 hours after vaginal delivery and 24 hours after cesarean birth.

Since infants born with heart and related problems are now surviving childhood, there has been an emergence of pregnant women who have *congenital heart disease*—heart defects present from birth.

Most women with congenital heart disease do fine in pregnancy and so do their fetuses. The blood volume ordinarily expands during pregnancy, and the heart rate increases. These changes place an added load on the heart. Women who are in good health, however, ordinarily will handle pregnancy well. There are only a few rare conditions in which the risk is so great that pregnancy usually is not advised. These conditions are:

- Pulmonary vascular obstructive disease or pulmonary hypertension, which may be from a condition called *Eisenmenger syndrome*, or due to other causes
- Severe stenosis (constriction or narrowing) of the aorta (the aorta is the main artery leading from the heart)
- Marfan syndrome with pathology of the aorta

Women with congenital heart defects may have a chance of passing these onto their fetuses. If you have such a condition, you should consider seeking genetic counseling before undertaking a pregnancy, although the risk, while higher than the risk in the general population, is still not great for most conditions. Prenatal diagnosis (see Chapter 8) may be helpful in identifying some of these problems in the fetus.

In some instances, women with heart disease may need to reduce activities as they approach full term. This is especially true if a woman experiences symptoms categorized as *New York Heart Association Class III* or *IV*. Class III symptoms are fatigue, heart palpitations, difficulty breathing, or pain with less than ordinary activity. Class IV symptoms are the same, but they occur either at rest or with any physical activity. (Classes I and II are described as no symptoms with activity and slight symptoms with ordinary activities, respectively. Women whose problems fall into those categories usually are not affected by pregnancy.)

In general, the future for most women with heart disease is not changed by a pregnancy. Women with heart disease should have their babies in a major medical center if possible. They should have careful postpartum monitoring, as symptoms may develop during that time. The heart undergoes rapid changes as the body reverts back to a non-pregnant state.

Some heart conditions make a person more susceptible to the development of a bacterial infection within the tissues of the heart called *endocarditis* (Greek: *endon* = within; *kardia* = heart; *itis* = inflammation). These conditions include artificial heart valves and congenital heart defects such as *patent ductus arteriosus* and *ventricular septal defect* (persistence of the shunts that are normal during fetal life but ordinarily close at birth). The American Heart Association recommends *prophylactic* (preventive) antibiotic therapy for individuals with such conditions when they undergo medical procedures considered high risk for the development of bacterial endocarditis. Neither vaginal nor cesarean birth is considered a high-risk procedure but some complications are high risk. These include prolonged rupture of the membranes, manual removal of the placenta, and fourth-degree *perineal lacerations* (tears into the rectum). Because antibiotic prophylaxis is recommended 30 to 60 minutes before a high-risk procedure, and some of these complications cannot be predicted (such as a fourth-degree laceration or the need to do a manual removal of the placenta), the American College of Obstetricians and Gynecologists suggests all women with high-risk heart problems receive antibiotics before delivery. Again, discuss this with your obstetrician. He or she might want to further discuss this with your *cardiologist* (heart specialist).

The development of heart disease in pregnancy is rare. Because of changes in hormones and increased blood volume, many women have some shortness of breath in pregnancy and find it easier to breathe if their head is elevated, rather than flat. However, if you have severe or worsening breathing difficulties, cannot breathe when you are lying down, have fainting or dizziness, have chest pain with activity or with emotional stress, or cough up blood, check this out with your physician or midwife. Most diagnostic tests for heart problems are safe in pregnancy and many therapeutic procedures and medications also are considered safe. Most pregnant women, of course, are young and in good health and these problems do not arise.

If a woman develops a very rare condition called *peripartum cardiomyopathy* during pregnancy or in the postpartum period, meaning she has heart failure not due to a known condition, she has a high chance of having a recurrence in a subsequent pregnancy, especially if dysfunction continues after delivery or if the heart remains enlarged. Before undertaking another pregnancy, she should discuss her condition with her cardiologist.

Allergies

Women with allergies may continue to suffer during pregnancy. Studies of the use of *antihistamines*—the major category of medications used to treat allergies—have not shown adverse effects on the fetus. Check with your physician or midwife before using over-the-counter medications, however.

Some women experience *itching* (*pruritus*) during pregnancy. Although this can be associated with a liver problem, it may occur for no apparent reason. *Topical* (skin) treatment, such as emollients added to the bath, moisturizing creams, or powders such as corn starch can be tried. If these do not work, antihistamines can be used. One study found that aspirin is effective for itching when there is no rash present. Before using nontopical medications, consult your physician or midwife.

Asthma

Women with asthma may fall with equal likeliness into one of three categories during pregnancy—those whose asthma improves, those whose asthma worsens, and those whose asthma neither improves nor worsens. In general, asthma has no effect on the pregnancy, although some studies have shown an increased chance of having a preterm or small baby, and of developing hypertension and infection of the amniotic cavity. However, these problems usually occur only when the asthma is poorly controlled. With appropriate treatment, adverse effects are infrequent.

The treatment of asthma in the pregnant woman is the same as it is in the woman who is not pregnant. Drugs used to treat asthma—including steroids, inhaled or taken orally—are not considered harmful in pregnancy. Do not stop taking any medications that you need for your asthma. The worst thing for a fetus is a mother who cannot breathe.

You may need to use your regular inhaler throughout labor. If you take medications by mouth, these may be given by injection during labor as they will not be absorbed orally. Any form of pain relief can be used in labor, except during an acute asthmatic attack. In that rare case, opiates (see Chapter 20) should not be used. If you need a cesarean section, epidural anesthesia is preferable to general anesthesia. Breast-feeding may the reduce of risk of asthma in your baby and asthma medications do not preclude nursing.

Seizure Disorders (Epilepsy)

If you have a seizure disorder such as epilepsy, the single most important thing for you and your baby during pregnancy is that your disease be controlled.

Anticonvulsants, such as Dilantin (phenytoin) and barbiturates (phenobarbital, for example), are used to control epilepsy and other seizure disorders. A number of fetal abnormalities have been associated with these drugs, but some of the problems may be related more to the disorder than to the drugs.

If at all possible, anticonvulsant doses should be reduced in pregnancy. Some anticonvulsants are more potentially dangerous to the fetus than others. Whenever possible these medications should be changed before pregnancy begins. Valproic acid (Depakene, Depakote) and trimetha-dione (Tridione) can cause fetal damage and should be avoided.

Women taking antiseizure medications should never try to adjust dosages or switch medications without the supervision of their physician, as seizures are dangerous for the fetus and the pregnant woman. It is better to be on medication, even with a risk, than to have a seizure in pregnancy. The neurologist or physician who manages your seizure disorder should work in collaboration with the obstetrician caring for your pregnancy.

Although anticonvulsant medications pass through the breast milk, breast-feeding is still considered beneficial.

Thyroid Disorders—Hypothyroid and Hyperthyroid

The thyroid gland controls the body's metabolism. The thyroid may dysfunction in either of two ways. The gland may not produce enough of its hormone. This is called *hypothyroidism* (Greek: *hypo* = under). Alternatively, the gland may produce too much of its hormone. This is called *hyperthyroidism* (Greek: *hyper* = above or excessive). A type of hyperthyroidism is called *Graves' disease*.

Women with untreated thyroid disease may have trouble becoming pregnant. Correcting their disorder usually restores fertility. During pregnancy, hypothyroid disease may be associated with miscarriage or developmental problems in the fetus, especially neurological development. Hyperthyroidism may be associated with miscarriage, low birth weight, or prematurity in the newborn. Therefore, like the woman with asthma and epilepsy, the most important consideration for the pregnant woman with a thyroid disease is that her thyroid function be controlled. Doses of medication may need adjustment during pregnancy, so careful surveillance is important. Problems can be avoided when thyroid function is maintained as close to normal as possible (a state called *euthyroid*—Greek: *eu* = well).

In hypothyroidism, a synthetic form of thyroid hormone is given (thryoxine or brand name: Synthroid). In hyperthyroidism, medications are given to suppress the thyroid. Among the available medication, propylthiouracil (PTU) is recommended in pregnancy and breast-feeding. Hyperthyroidism also may be treated by surgery or radioactive iodine. If necessary, surgery is considered safe in the second trimester. Radioactive iodine, however, should not be used during pregnancy. If such treatment is inadvertently administered in pregnancy, it may have an adverse effect on the fetus.

Tell your physician or midwife if you experience symptoms of thyroid dysfunction before or during pregnancy. Symptoms include large changes in appetite or weight, changes in tolerance to heat or cold, increased perspiration or dry skin, constipation or diarrhea, heart palpitations, excessive energy or nervousness, insomnia or unusual fatigue. Of course, many of these are similar to the normal changes of pregnancy so new onset disease may be missed in pregnancy.

Let your physician or midwife know if you have a family history of thyroid dysfunction. You may then be tested before pregnancy or early in pregnancy. Thyroid dysfunction is diagnosed with a number of blood tests that measure thyroid hormones and the hormone that stimulates the thyroid to produce thyroid hormone. Your physician or midwife may also order thyroid function tests if your thyroid feels enlarged during physical examination or if you appear on examination to have other signs of thyroid disorder. Thyroid function should also be evaluated if you develop excessive vomiting of pregnancy, called *hyperemesis gravidarum* (see Chapter 12).

Some women develop *postpartum thyroid disease* (PPTD) in the first 6 months following birth. This is most often short term, but some women with hypothyroidism in the postpartum period will have persistent hypothyroidism or develop thyroid problems later in life.

Systemic Lupus Erythematosis (SLE)

Systemic lupus erythematosis (SLE) is an autoimmune disease that tends to occur in young women. SLE is characterized by periods of remission and exacerbation. Exacerbations also are called *flares*. With improved treatments, today many women live with SLE in remission for years. Women with SLE are fertile, although menstrual irregularities with some anovulatory cycles may occur during active disease and with high-dose corticosteroid treatment. One of the drugs used in treatment, cyclophosphamide, also may reduce fertility. Most women with SLE, however, can become pregnant and many do.

Whether there is an increase in flare-ups of lupus during pregnancy is not certain. Studies show different results. However, women with SLE should be followed closely. Flares during pregnancy tend to be mild. The main symptoms are arthritis and skin problems. Some women may have fatigue, fever, and blood problems. Involvement of the kidney and central nervous system may occur. Disease flares during pregnancy are associated with active disease at the time of conception. The longer a woman with SLE is in remission at the time of conception, the more likely it is that she will not experience an exacerbation of her disease during pregnancy. Timing of pregnancy, then, is important for women with SLE. At least 6 months of remission is recommended before a planned pregnancy.

Women with SLE have an increase of some pregnancy complications, including pregnancy-induced hypertension and kidney problems. Their infants are more likely to be premature or growth restricted. There is an increase in the number of miscarriages. Miscarriage occurs most frequently in women having certain antibodies, the anticardiolipin antibody and lupus anticoagulant (together called the *antiphospholipid antibodies*). About one-third to one-half of women with SLE have these antibodies, which can be detected on blood tests. Using blood thinners such as baby aspirin and heparin may improve pregnancy outcome. This is an issue to discuss with your physician.

Two other types of specific antibodies called *anti-Ro* (SSA) and *anti-La* (SSB) are associated with certain symptoms in newborns. Babies born to women with SLE who have either of these two antibodies may have *neonatal lupus erythematosus* (NLE) *syndrome*. This is marked by congenital heart block, skin lesions, and possible liver involvement. Most of the time these symptoms are mild and will improve without treatment, with the exception of heart block. However, even in women with SSA or SSB antibodies, the risk of NLE is still small, averaging about 7 percent of their newborns. Women with SLE can be checked for these two antibodies before pregnancy. Heart block can be diagnosed in the fetus between 16 and 24 weeks of gestation by fetal *echocardiography* (sonography of the heart). This procedure is best performed by a specialist, not a general sonographer. The mother can be treated with dexamethasone (a corticosteroid) if echocardiograms performed at intervals during pregnancy show the fetus is developing heart failure.

A discussion of the various types of medications used in the treatment of SLE is beyond the scope of this book. However, the following guidelines should be adhered to in pregnancy:

• Avoid high doses of aspirin and nonsteroidal anti-inflammatory drugs (such as ibuprofen) in the last few weeks of pregnancy.
• Corticosteroids and hydroxychloroquine (an antimalarial drug used to treat SLE) have not shown *teratogenic* (causes fetal malformations) effects, but cyclophosphamide should be avoided as it is teratogenic.
• When intense therapy is needed, the *cytotoxic* (cell-killing) drugs azathioprine and cyclosporin A may be considered. (Cytotoxic drugs are used in cancer treatment.)

The following guidelines exist for breast-feeding in women being treated for SLE:

• Aspirin should be used carefully, with large doses avoided.
• The nonsteroidal anti-inflammatory drugs ibuprofen, indomethacin, and naproxen are considered safe during breast-feeding, but should be used cautiously.
• The corticosteroids prednisone and prednisolone are considered compatible with breast-feeding. Some clinicians recommend waiting 4 hours before nursing if the dose of prednisone is greater

than 20 mg/day. There is no information on dexamethasone or
betamethasone in breast-feeding.
• Cyclophosphamide should not be taken if you are breast-feeding.
If you must take this medication, do not breast-feed. Other cyto-
toxic drugs, including azathioprine, cyclosporin A, and methotrexate, are also to be avoided during breast-feeding.

Although SLE flares may be seen in the postpartum period, there is
no data regarding the relationship of these flares to breast-feeding, if
any. Unless you must rely on medications that are not safe during breast-
feeding, this remains the preferred method of infant feeding.

Cystic Fibrosis

Like women with congenital heart disease, women with the genetic disorder cystic fibrosis are increasingly reaching reproductive age in good
health. Those women whose disease is well controlled generally tolerate
pregnancy well. Those who are severely affected, particularly with *pulmonary* (lung) complications, have increased respiratory difficulty as pregnancy proceeds. Any woman with cystic fibrosis should discuss with her
physician how likely a pregnancy is to be detrimental to her health.

During pregnancy, women with cystic fibrosis should be monitored
for lung function, infection, gestational diabetes, and heart problems.
Women must continue treatments they were on prior to pregnancy. As
cystic fibrosis is a genetic disorder, a woman with the disease will pass
the gene for the disease on to her fetus. As the disease is a recessive trait,
a person must inherit two genes—one from each parent—to have the
disease. Therefore, the partner of any woman with cystic fibrosis should
be tested to see if he is a carrier of the gene. Testing ideally should be
carried out before pregnancy, or in its early stages. Genetic testing for
cystic fibrosis is discussed in greater detail on pages 208–210. Cystic fibrosis can be diagnosed in the fetus by amniocentesis.

Inflammatory Bowel Disease

Inflammatory bowel disease, which refers to forms of *intestinal inflammation*, including ulcerative colitis and Crohn's disease, may be encountered in women of childbearing age. These diseases are characterized by
times of quiescence and times of exacerbation. How active they are in
pregnancy usually depends on how active they are at the time the woman

becomes pregnant. Diagnostic testing and treatment during pregnancy are the same as would be appropriate for the nonpregnant woman.

Blood Diseases

Various abnormalities of the blood system present some health problems in pregnancy. *Anemia,* a reduction in the amount of hemoglobin in the blood, is a common problem. Hemoglobin is the oxygen-carrying component of the red blood cells, so it is important for the fetus that the mother's hemoglobin remains in a normal range. Pregnancies complicated by anemia show an increase in low birth weight and prematurity.

Nutritional Deficiency Anemia

The most common type of anemia is caused by a nutritional deficiency, usually iron or folic acid (a B vitamin). These deficiencies can be diagnosed with routine blood testing, performed early in pregnancy. Low values of hemoglobin or of the *hematocrit* (a measure of the percentage of cellular material in blood) indicate anemia. When the red blood cells are small and pale, you usually are deficient in iron, although in the early stages of anemia, the cells may be normal size and color. If the red blood cells grow extra large, then you usually are deficient in folic acid. This is a form of *megaloblastic anemia* (Greek: *mega* = great or large; *blastos* = germ—refers to a cell).

Both iron and folic acid deficiency anemia can be treated with food and supplementation. Foods rich in these nutrients are listed in Chapter 10. All women should take folic acid while trying to conceive and in the early weeks of pregnancy to prevent a fetal anomaly called a *neural tube defect.* The usual dose is 0.04 mg daily, although if you have had a previous baby with a neural tube defect, then the recommended dose is 4.0 mg daily. With megaloblastic anemia, 1 mg of folic acid may be prescribed daily. Iron supplementation is 30 to 60 mg of elemental iron, usually available in a 300 to 350 mg pill.

Other Anemias

Other causes of anemia are less common. A vitamin B_{12} deficiency is called *pernicious anemia.* Pernicious anemia is rarely discovered in pregnancy as it usually presents symptoms earlier in life. Also, if untreated, pernicious anemia may interfere with fertility. Other causes of anemia include a deficiency of the enzyme glucose-6-phosphate dehydrogenase (G6PD), sickle-cell disease, and thalassemia. With G6PD deficiency, most frequently occurring in African-American women, red blood cells are destroyed in the presence of infection or when certain oxidant drugs are used. Such drugs include some antibiotics and even some vitamin supplements. A test for this deficiency may be carried out when you have *anemia* (hemoglobin less than 10) that is not responsive to iron or folic acid treatment.

Sickle-cell disease is a condition in which the molecules of hemoglobin acquire an abnormal shape when their oxygen is released to the tissues. The ability of these misshapen cells to transport oxygen is diminished. Severe anemia may result. Persons who suffer from sickle-cell anemia experience episodes of intense pain, called *sickle-cell crises*, with varying degrees of frequency. In a pregnant woman, pain of sickle-cell disease must be differentiated from pain of a pregnancy complication such as ectopic pregnancy or premature labor.

Sickle-cell disease seems to worsen during pregnancy, with more frequent crises. Urinary tract problems including bladder and kidney infection are more common in women with sickle-cell anemia. There is an increased risk for gestational hypertension. Infants are more likely to be growth restricted or born prematurely. The effect on the baby is related to the severity of the disease.

A controversy regarding sickle-cell treatment in pregnancy is whether to use blood transfusion as a preventive measure. The purpose of transfusion is to replace sickle cells with normal red blood cells and maintain normal or close-to-normal levels of hemoglobin. Transfusions, however, carry risks. Some practitioners will use transfusion only during periods of crisis. This is an issue to discuss with your obstetrician. Supplementation with iron also is controversial, but folic acid supplementation is helpful in promoting production of red blood cells. Fortunately, virtually every adult woman who has sickle-cell disease is aware of it and therefore can participate in making careful plans for her care before and during the pregnancy.

Sickle-cell anemia is an inherited disease. Because the inheritance of the disorder also confers protection against malaria, the disease is seen where malaria is endemic—among people from Africa and the Mediterranean, and their descendants. If a person inherits the gene for the disease from one parent, then she has what is called *sickle-cell trait*. This is also called *hemoglobin AS*—for normal hemoglobin (hemoglobin A) combined with sickle hemoglobin (hemoglobin S). Women with sickle-cell trait rarely have symptoms, but in pregnancy are more prone to urinary tract infections. They may not show symptoms but may have *asymptomatic bacteriuria*—bacteria in the urine that doesn't cause pain or other symptoms. In pregnancy, this can lead to a kidney infection called *pyelonephritis*. Therefore, their urine should be tested for bacteria at intervals throughout pregnancy.

All women with sickle-cell disease will pass a gene for the disease to their newborns. If the father also has sickle-cell anemia, then the infant will also have the disease. If the father has sickle-cell trait, the infant has a 50 percent chance of inheriting the disease. If the father has no gene for sickle-cell disease, then the infant cannot inherit the disease. All newborns of women with sickle-cell disease who do not inherit the disease will have sickle-cell trait. This is discussed in detail in Chapter 8.

Other inherited disorders of hemoglobin are the *thalassemias*. The thalassemias occur in persons from the Mediterranean region: Italians, Greeks, and Africans. The two main types of thalassemia are *alpha-thalassemia* (α-thalassemia) and *beta-thalassemia* (β-thalassemia). Each of these has a number of forms, and minor, intermediate, and major variations. β-thalassemia major is commonly known as *Cooley's anemia*. If the fetus inherits the gene for β-thalassemia from both parents, it usually dies in utero or shortly after birth, although recently fetal treatments, including blood transfusions, have been tried in an attempt to save these fetuses. In the future, stem cell transplants may provide effective fetal treatment.

Women with thalassemia minor may have mild or moderate anemia, but pregnancy usually proceeds normally. Women with β-thalassemia major are often infertile, although occasionally pregnancy does occur. Iron supplementation in pregnancy will cause iron overload, with heart failure possibly resulting. Folic acid should be supplemented, but not iron. Blood transfusions may be necessary for these women.

Sickle-cell disease and thalassemia can be diagnosed in the fetus via amniocentesis or chorionic villus sampling (see Chapter 8).

Thrombocytopenia Purpura

A disease with the lengthy name thrombocytopenia purpura occasionally occurs in pregnancy. This name derives from a series of Latin and Greek terms that mean that the person develops bleeding under the skin (*purpura*, from which comes the adjective purple), due to a shortage of *thrombocytes* (or platelets) in the circulating blood (thrombocytopenia: the blood cell *(cyte)* which assists in clotting *(thrombo)* and *penia*, a shortage).

In the most common form of thrombocytopenia purpura, called *immune thrombocytopenia purpura* (ITP), the disease is due to a circulating antibody, which the mother unfortunately forms against her own platelets. This substance may cross the placenta; thus the fetus of the mother with thrombocytopenia may have the same problem. ITP occurs three times more commonly in women than men, and usually occurs before the age of 30.

Miscarriage may occur in 5 to 35 percent of pregnancies in women with ITP. Treatment before pregnancy with corticosteroids, immunoglobulins, blood platelet transfusions, and occasionally *splenectomy* (removal of the spleen, where the antibodies are made) can cause the disease to go into remission. Ideally, pregnancy will occur when the disease is in remission and treatment during pregnancy will not be necessary.

Controversy exists as to whether or not babies born to women with ITP need to be delivered by cesarean to protect the babies from bleeding during vaginal birth. Tests of fetal blood samples retrieved through the umbilical cord under ultrasound guidance can determine whether the fetus has a low platelet count. Such testing is available only in certain medical centers. Precisely how to deal with the management of delivery in a woman with thrombocytopenia has to be left to the obstetrician, assisted by a skilled *hematologist* (a physician who specializes in diseases of the blood). Although the woman suffering from ITP has a clotting disorder, the control of postpartum hemorrhage is through contraction of the muscle of the uterus (the *myometrium*) so usually she will not have undue bleeding following delivery. However, postpartum hemorrhage may occur from bleeding from episiotomy or lacerations. Careful birthing techniques should be employed to minimize these occurrences.

VENOUS THROMBOSIS

Pregnancy increases the chance of developing a venous thrombosis—a blood clot in a vein. This blood clot becomes a threat to life when it breaks off and travels to the lungs, causing a blood clot in the lung (*pulmonary embolism*). Venous thrombosis may also occur in the postpartum period, although because women now get out of bed soon after birth, the likelihood of having a postpartum thrombosis has been reduced dramatically.

There are two types of venous thrombosis: superficial and deep. Superficial thrombosis often is seen with varicose veins. It may follow a *thrombophlebitis*—an inflammation in a vein. *Thrombophlebitis* or superficial thrombosis can be treated with rest (leg elevation), elastic stockings, and pain medication if necessary. It does not lead to a pulmonary embolism. Deep vein thrombosis is more serious. It presents with severe pain, swelling, and warmth in the leg or thigh. Sometimes, however, the leg may be cool and pale. Noninvasive methods to diagnose deep vein thrombosis are now available and include ultrasound and *magnetic resonance imaging* (MRI). Deep vein thrombosis is treated with anticoagulants, usually heparin. A pulmonary embolism causes chest discomfort and breathlessness. It may be accompanied by severe anxiety. Pulmonary embolism is a life-threatening disorder that requires prompt hospitalization for diagnosis and treatment.

CANCER

Although pregnant women are not likely to have cancer, this disease is seen in about 1 in 5,000 pregnant women. The most common types are cancers of the genital tract (the cervix, for example), the breast, and malignant melanoma. *Lymphomas* (cancers of the lymphatic system) and *cancers of the blood* (such as leukemia) are also seen in pregnant women.

Most procedures to diagnose cancer and to determine its stage can be carried out during pregnancy. These procedures include surgical biopsy, x-ray imaging, and magnetic resonance imaging (MRI). When feasible, MRI is preferable to X ray as it does not utilize potentially dangerous ionizing radiation.

Cancer is treated by surgery, radiation, chemotherapy, or a combination of these. Their safety in pregnancy needs to be discussed with a cancer specialist (*oncologist*).

Of course, a diagnosis of cancer always causes emotional upheaval. You will need all the support you can muster. Accept help. A team of medical and nursing specialists will be involved in your care. You may want to seek consultation with a psychiatric social worker, a psychologist, or a psychiatrist as counseling is usually beneficial. Ask your care providers for a referral to a support group.

TRAUMA AND
SURGICAL COMPLICATIONS

In general, the management of acute surgical emergencies, such as after an automobile accident, involves caring for the injuries caused by the accident and ignoring the pregnancy, except to determine by ultrasound whether the fetus has survived the accident. A leg broken in a skiing accident or a fall down stairs is no threat to the fetus. In rare instances, violent trauma such as can be incurred in automobile accidents may cause serious damage to the fetus without injury to the same degree in the mother. The use of seat belts has reduced greatly the injuries sustained in automobile accidents. In pregnancy, make sure the seat belt goes under the uterus.

Pregnant women can be the victims of domestic or other violence. A gunshot or knife wound to the uterus may harm the fetus. These types of injuries must be dealt with on an individual basis.

When a disease, such as appendicitis, requires surgery, the surgery must be done. The fetus usually is not harmed by the surgery or the anesthesia.

Elective surgical treatment for conditions such as hemorrhoids, varicose veins, and cosmetic purposes is better postponed until the pregnancy is completed. There is no need to be subjected to such operative risk.

Pregnancy today is occasionally seen in women who have had organ transplants. Among women who have undergone heart transplants, those who are *New York Heart Association functional Class I* will best tolerate pregnancy. This means they have no symptoms of heart disease. A careful examination by a cardiologist or transplant physician prior to pregnancy should be done, with an effort made to assess the risk of pregnancy to the mother. Careful heart monitoring should continue throughout pregnancy. The immunosuppressive medications used after transplant must be continued and monitored throughout pregnancy. Breast-feeding is not recommended for women taking these medications.

Similarly, women who have had kidney transplants should have their kidney function assessed before undertaking a pregnancy. They should be in good health without high blood pressure, protein in the urine, or evidence of rejection of the transplant. Kidney function tests should be normal. Experience shows that it is best to wait at least 2 years following the transplant before becoming pregnant.

DENTAL PROBLEMS

Dental care can certainly be given at any time during pregnancy with complete safety. The local anesthetic agents used by dentists are safe. Make sure you tell the dentist that you are pregnant. If you are planning to become pregnant, have your regular dental checkup with X rays before you stop using birth control.

PSYCHIATRIC ILLNESS

Pregnancy is a time of stress for many women. A pregnant woman often suspects, or is made to feel, that whatever she may do or think will adversely affect the pregnancy's outcome. In a first pregnancy, she may uneasily anticipate the nondangerous but numerous discomforts she may suffer, or feel anxiety about labor and birth. She may be concerned about her adequacy as a mother. She may worry that the arrival of another person in the family will disrupt established emotional ties. The catalog is familiar and lengthy. In a second or later pregnancy, these concerns may still be on her mind and she may further worry about the response of her child or children to the new arrival.

Not surprisingly, pregnancy may be marked by swings of emotion, from outright sorrow to ambivalence to euphoria. In the first trimester, feelings may be aggravated by nausea, which actually may be a sign of a well-functioning placenta and a good pregnancy.

Psychiatric illnesses such as schizophrenia and depression are not materially changed in pregnancy. The treatment of these major illnesses in pregnancy is, again, the same as it would be in the nonpregnant woman. Lithium, a drug used to treat manic-depression, also called *bipolar disease*, may be teratogenic. Its use is not advised in pregnancy. As with many treatments, however, the benefits must be measured against the possible risk—always in consultation with your psychiatrist and obstetrician or midwife.

The pregnant woman can and should turn to her support systems for help when and how she needs it. The most obvious resource is her partner. She may choose to confide in the women in her family: mother, sisters, mother-in-law, and sisters-in-law. Friends can be invaluable. Her care provider, whether physician or midwife, comes next on the list. A book such as this (and there are many to choose from) can be reassuring. Childbirth education classes may offer support. Helping professionals such as social workers, psychologists, and psychiatrists may be involved when necessary.

Sometime after giving birth, many women experience a mild depression, known as the *postpartum blues*. This is characterized by periods of sadness and weepiness. It usually occurs a few days after birth but does not persist. Some have proposed a hormonal basis for these blues, although the fact that they do not seem to be experienced universally argues against this theory.

A more serious form of postpartum problem is true *postpartum depression*, characterized by longer and more intense feelings. This is most likely to occur in women with a history of depression. It can be treated with individual and group support, therapy, and, if necessary, antidepressant medication. You can breast-feed if you take the most commonly used antidepressants, the *selective serotonin reuptake inhibitor*s (SSRIs) such as fluoxetine (Prozac), sertraline (Zoloft), and paruxetine (Paxil). If you have a history of depression, speak to your physician or midwife in advance. If you think you have postpartum depression, do not hesitate to seek help. If the "blues" continues beyond a week or 2 following delivery, you may be suffering from depression. Don't wait until your 6-week checkup if you feel you are having difficulty coping. And certainly don't ignore the symptoms or stuff them deeper inside yourself.

An even more serious form of postpartum emotional disorder is *postpartum psychosis*. Again, this usually is seen in women with a history of psychological problems or a previous episode of postpartum psychosis. Psychosis is defined as a break with reality and help is needed immediately in this circumstance, particularly if you have thoughts of hurting yourself or your child.

Stay Calm!

Although women with medical illness may be concerned about their health and the health of their newborns, the take-home message of this chapter should be that even pregnancies complicated by medical illness usually proceed without problems. With appropriate care, the mother and baby do fine. Most important is continuing necessary therapies and receiving close and attentive care throughout the pregnancy and during the postpartum period.

CHAPTER SEVENTEEN

Late Fetal Assessment

In its earliest days, the purpose of prenatal care was primarily to ensure the health of the mother. Visits to the doctor were to assess her blood pressure and detect preeclampsia of pregnancy in its mild stage. Concern for the fetus came later in the history of prenatal care. As pregnancies became healthier for women and the ability to monitor the fetus increased, physicians and midwives increasingly focused on the well-being of the fetus. Today, the goal of every pregnancy is a healthy mother and a healthy baby.

Some components of fetal assessment involve technology, but monitoring can be accomplished through the mother's observations of the fetus's movements and the use of a simple instrument called a *fetoscope* to listen to the fetal heart. All fetuses are assessed throughout pregnancy, more frequently late in the pregnancy. Technological types of prenatal evaluation are used in high-risk pregnancies. This chapter focuses on this type of assessment.

In general, late antepartum fetal assessment is begun between 26 and 34 weeks for pregnancies complicated by medical illness or obstetrical problems. The timing of initiation depends on what complication exists, when it presents itself, and how severe it is. In a pregnancy that has been normal all along, but persists past its due date, for example, technological fetal monitoring may not begin until 41 or 42 weeks gestation.

The type of assessment also depends on the particular complication and its severity. If the baby appears to be growing poorly, its growth will be charted by repeated ultrasound and its well-being checked by electronic fetal heart rate testing. In a baby affected by Rh sensitization, the severity of anemia caused by damage to the baby's red blood cells may be assessed by tests of amniotic fluid or fetal blood. In diabetes, the mother's blood sugar is watched carefully and the fetus's heart rate monitored frequently. Ultrasound may be used to measure the fetal growth.

In addition to testing for fetal well-being, fetal lung maturity can be evaluated. This evaluation is used when determining whether the fetus will do better inside or outside the uterus, such as when the fetus is growth restricted or the mother has severe pregnancy-induced hypertension. Chemicals in the amniotic fluid may reveal how well the newborn's lungs will respond to breathing efforts.

Fetal assessment is not an exact science. Experts do not agree on which test is best. The time to begin monitoring is not set precisely, and the schedule of repeat testing may vary among physicians or according to the reason for the testing. In general, tests for fetal well-being are repeated weekly. However, testing may be repeated twice a week or more frequently in certain very high risk situations. The frequency of testing is at the discretion of your physician or consulting specialist, or set by the policies of the institution where you will have your baby.

The first two methods of assessment described below—fetal movement counts and the auscultated acceleration test—are performed without technological equipment. They can be used in any pregnancy and in conjunction with electronic testing in pregnancies with complications. The most common reasons for technological fetal monitoring are diabetes or high blood pressure, either pre-existing or occurring during pregnancy; intrauterine growth restriction; Rh disease; pregnancy continuing past its due date (postdatism); and a previous stillbirth.

TESTS OF FETAL WELL-BEING

Fetal Movement Counts

Healthy fetuses are active in the uterus. They move most of the day, with only brief periods of inactivity. They stretch, kick, and somersault. Mothers usually feel about 70 to 80 percent of these movements. Fetuses also make fine movements like grasping their hands and sucking, although these movements are not perceived by the mother.

In the early 1970s, research revealed that fetal movement signifies fetal well-being. An article appeared in a major obstetrical journal in 1973 reporting on seven pregnancies in which decreased fetal activity was followed by fetal death. Of course, a decrease in fetal movement does not always mean that the fetus is in trouble. A normal decrease in movement may be seen toward the end of pregnancy as the fetus simply has less room to move around. Extra fluid (*polyhydramnios*, described in Chapter 12) may make it difficult for the pregnant woman to feel fetal movements. To be safe, if the fetal movements are decreased enough for you to notice a difference, you should contact your midwife or physician immediately.

When there is a decrease in fetal movements, additional testing will be carried out. Usually, the fetus is not in danger, but when a problem is detected, early intervention such as induction of labor can save the baby.

Women who have complications should begin formal fetal movement counting at about 28 weeks of pregnancy. Counting should be performed daily. It is a simple and completely noninvasive way for you to monitor the well-being of your own fetus.

Fetal movements can be counted in a number of easy ways. Some physicians or midwives will advise you to count while lying on your left side for up to 60 minutes, two or three times daily. Fewer than four movements in an hour is the signal to contact your physician or midwife. Another way to count fetal movements is to begin when you wake up in the morning. Without changing your normal routine, you should count at least ten movements by the time 12 hours have passed. Women who use this method usually report that they reach ten movements in a short time—in one study the average counting time was about 3 hours.

Whether you use a formal counting system or just pay attention to the fetus's movements, a perceived decrease should be reported immediately. An absence of movement over the course of a day is a particular cause for concern.

Tests of the Fetal Heart Rate

Auscultated Acceleration Test

A test of the fetal heart performed without electronic equipment or invasive procedures was described in the *Journal of Nurse-Midwifery* in 1986. Called the *auscultated acceleration test* (AAT), this procedure uses only a fetoscope to *auscultate* (listen to) the fetal heart rate. Although firm conclusions require further research about this test, its results appear to be equivalent to the results of the NST, described later.

In the AAT, the fetal heart is listened to with a *fetoscope* (similar to a stethoscope) for 6 minutes. The listener counts the fetal heart for 5 seconds, stops counting for 5 seconds, then repeats the cycle for the 6-minute time frame. The fetal heart rate is charted on a graph. Accelerations are present when a 5-second counting period shows an increase of two beats (e.g., the 5-second heart rate was 10 and rose to 12). In this test, one acceleration is considered to show reactivity. A reactive test is the desired result, indicating fetal well-being. It means that a functioning, well-oxygenated nervous system is able to send signals to a responsive cardiovascular system.

The AAT, combined with fetal movement counting, has been proposed as a way of monitoring the well-being of fetuses in pregnancies that do not have risk factors, as risk factors warrant the use of more technologically based fetal monitoring techniques.

The Contraction Stress Test

The first prenatal fetal heart rate test was the contraction stress test (CST). When the hormone oxytocin is used to bring on contractions, it is called an *oxytocin challenge test* (OCT). The CST or OCT was widely used in the early to mid-1970s. Based on the observation that blood flow to the placenta is reduced during a uterine contraction, its goal is to evaluate the fetus's ability to withstand this stress. In labor, decreases in the fetal heart rate that begin after the start of a contraction are considered a sign that the fetus cannot tolerate the decreased blood flow of the contraction. These decreases are called *late decelerations*. When repetitive, they indicate a condition called *utero-placental insufficiency*.

The idea behind the contraction stress test was that the fetus would be "challenged" with contractions—for a short period so that labor would not be induced—to see if its heart demonstrated decreases or decelerations. The fetus with a positive test usually would need to be delivered.

HOW THE CONTRACTION STRESS TEST IS PERFORMED   A contraction stress test generally is conducted in the labor and delivery unit in the hospital or in a special antepartum fetal evaluation area. You usually will lie on your left side. Two fetal monitor belts will be placed around your abdomen. One picks up uterine contractions and the other picks up fetal heart tones. Both the contractions and the fetal heart register on graph paper. The heart tones form a line at the top and the contractions form a wavelike pattern at the bottom of the graph. In this way the fetal heart can be matched against the contractions to determine the significance of any decelerations.

When the stress test was first developed, contractions were induced with oxytocin (usual brand name: Pitocin). This is the same hormone often used to induce labor (discussed in Chapter 22). Oxytocin is given through an intravenous line so that the dosage can be carefully controlled. Before the medication is started, a baseline fetal heart rate is recorded for about 10 to 20 minutes.

The criteria for an adequate contraction stress test are three contractions in 10 minutes of moderate intensity lasting 40 to 60 seconds. This is considered the approximate stress that the fetus experiences during labor. Contractions may be present without any oxytocin. When oxytocin is used, it may take an hour or longer to induce enough contractions for an adequate test.

THE NIPPLE STIMULATION CONTRACTION STRESS TEST   Today, nipple stimulation often is used to induce a natural surge of oxytocin (as occurs during nursing). A warm moist towel may be applied to each breast for 5 minutes. If this does not produce an adequate number of contractions, you may be asked to massage one nipple for 15 minutes or to stroke one breast through your clothing with your fingers for 2 minutes, rest for 5 minutes, and repeat the cycle until adequate contractions are achieved. In one study, contractions occurred in an average of three cycles.

A nipple stimulation CST usually induces contractions more quickly than an OCT. It does not require an intravenous line.

HOW THE CONTRACTION STRESS TEST IS INTERPRETED   The possible interpretations of contraction stress testing are:

- Negative
- Positive
- Suspicious or Equivocal
- Hyperstimulation
- Unsatisfactory

Negative. A negative CST is the desired result. It means no late decelerations are present with an adequate number of contractions. Most contraction stress tests are negative. A negative CST is believed to indicate that the placenta is functioning well and that fetal well-being is reasonably assured for one week. In situations of very high risk, however, the CST may be repeated more often than weekly.

Positive. A positive CST is defined as one in which late decelerations are seen with the majority of contractions, even if there are fewer than 3 contractions in 10 minutes. A positive CST usually is followed by delivery of the infant—either by induction of labor with continuous monitoring (see Chapter 22) or cesarean delivery.

Unfortunately, the CST is not a perfect test. There can be "false positive" results: the test shows decelerations, but in fact the fetus is not in danger. There is no current solution to this inherent problem. The decision whether or not to induce labor is based on the clinical judgment of your doctor.

Decelerations other than late decelerations—for example, those occurring between contractions (called *variable decelerations*)—require further evaluation. Usually, the amniotic fluid volume is measured (see page 467). Variable decelerations indicate that the umbilical cord is being compressed. Compression is more likely to occur and to be dangerous to the fetus if the amniotic fluid is decreased.

Suspicious or Equivocal. A suspicious CST means that there are some late decelerations, but they are not consistent. They occur with less than the majority of contractions. Some experts use the term *equivocal* to refer to a CST that cannot be interpreted. For example, the monitor tracing might show several 10-minute phases (called *windows*), each with three contractions, and each with one or two late decelerations. If any one window has three late decelerations, the CST would be considered positive. If any one window is without decelerations, and there is no positive window, the CST would be considered negative. In the case where there are inconsistent late decelerations, without either a positive or negative window, the test is less clear. A suspicious or equivocal CST requires repeating, generally in 24 hours.

Hyperstimulation. A CST shows hyperstimulation when contractions occur too frequently (5 or more in 10 minutes) or last too long (90 or more seconds). A hyperstimulated test may be considered negative if no decelerations occur. If decelerations do occur, however, the test is invalid. An invalid CST should be repeated in 24 hours.

Unsatisfactory. An unsatisfactory CST is one in which the fetal heart rate tracing cannot be read or 3 contractions in 10 minutes cannot be achieved. An unsatisfactory CST should be repeated in 24 hours.

Fortunately, there are extremely few "false negative" CSTs. A *false negative* would mean that the test appears to show fetal well-being, but the fetus is actually in danger.

The Nonstress Test

Today, the nonstress test (NST) is the most widely used test of fetal well-being. Like the auscultated acceleration test, the NST is based on the principle that a fetus with a well-functioning nervous system shows accelerations in its heart beat. These accelerations occur in response to movement, contractions, or stimulation (such as noise).

HOW THE NONSTRESS TEST IS PERFORMED The NST can be performed in the office, clinic, or outpatient area of a hospital. It usually takes only 10 to 15 minutes. The NST is less likely to show equivocal results than the CST. You sit in a reclining chair or lie on your left side. The fetal monitor belts are placed around your abdomen, as they are in a CST. You may be shown how to use the monitor to mark the tracing when the fetus moves. Fetal movement is itself an indicator of well-being.

When the NST is complete, a midwife or physician will read the monitor tracing to see if there are accelerations of the fetal heart. In very high risk pregnancies, the NST usually is performed once or twice a week.

HOW THE NONSTRESS TEST IS INTERPRETED · A nonstress test is interpreted as:

• Reactive
• Nonreactive
• Inconclusive

Reactive. A reactive NST is the desired result. Sometimes we say the fetal heart shows reactivity. The definition of a reactive NST has varied over time and in different places, but the American College of Obstetricians and Gynecologists recommends defining reactivity by at least two accelerations of the fetal heart rate, each at least fifteen beats above the baseline rate and lasting 15 seconds. This should occur within 20 minutes of monitoring. The NST can be considered reactive even if fetal movements are not recorded.

Nonreactive. A nonreactive NST occurs when accelerations meeting the above definition do not occur. This may simply mean the fetus is sleeping. If the test is prolonged to 40 minutes or more, the heart rate often will become reactive. Sometimes, attempts are made to arouse the fetus (see "Vibroacoustic Stimulation" below). A true nonreactive NST is followed by other testing, usually a contraction stress test (described earlier) and biophysical profile (described later).

Nonstress tests have a very low *false positive* (or falsely nonreactive) rate. Nonreactivity may be seen if the test is performed before 28 weeks of pregnancy and even sometimes between 28 and 32 weeks. Nonreactivity may also be due to maternal smoking or the use of certain medications or drugs.

Sometimes the NST shows decelerations of the fetal heart rate or a prolonged decrease in the rate (called *bradycardia*). These findings also require further testing.

Inconclusive. An inconclusive NST occurs occasionally when the fetal heart cannot be recorded adequately. This may happen when the mother is very obese or the pregnancy is complicated by excess amniotic fluid (*polyhydramnios*). The NST may be inconclusive when there are so many fluctuations in the heart rate that a baseline rate cannot be determined. A biophysical profile or a contraction stress test can be performed when the NST is inconclusive.

VIBROACOUSTIC STIMULATION   The fetal heart beat will be nonreactive when the fetus is asleep. After about 40 minutes of a nonreactive NST, the fetus can be awakened with stimulation. The usual source of stimulation is called *vibroacoustic stimulation* (VAS). VAS is provided by an *artificial larynx* or voice box—the small apparatus that people whose voice boxes have been removed hold up to their throats to create speech. This device causes both vibrations and noise. It is held for about three seconds at the mother's abdomen above the fetal head. Whether the vibrations or the noise arouses the fetus is not known. The stimulation is repeated every minute up to three times before the NST is read as nonreactive.

You might wonder whether the sound or vibrations can harm the ear of the fetus. A few studies have shown that the amniotic fluid reduces both the vibrations felt and the sound heard by the fetus. Several researchers found no hearing loss in children studied up to 4 years after they received VAS. Current research is investigating the use of lesser degrees of vibration and sound, including the mother's voice, as a stimulus for the fetus.

Biophysical Profile

In 1980, Dr. Frank Manning and his colleagues proposed that a comprehensive evaluation of the fetus could give more valuable results than those given by any one test. In the *American Journal of Obstetrics and Gynecology*, this group of researchers advocated examining "the fetus, its activities, and its environment" to accurately differentiate "fetal health from disease states." They developed the biophysical profile (BPP), a test of five areas utilizing real-time ultrasonography. *Real-time ultrasonography*, discussed in Chapter 8, shows the fetus in motion.

The five components of the BPP are:

- Fetal breathing movements
- Fetal body movements
- Fetal tone (extent to which the arms and legs are flexed or bent)
- Fetal heart rate reactivity (the NST)
- Amniotic fluid volume (AFV)

The BPP is reported as a numerical value from 0 to 10. The table below shows the normal and abnormal values for each of these areas. Each area can receive a score of 2 (normal) or 0 (abnormal).

SCORING OF THE BIOPHYSICAL PROFILE		
Biophysical Component	Score 2 (Normal)	Score 0 (Abnormal)
Fetal breathing movements	At least 30 seconds of sustained breathing in 30 minutes	Less than 30 seconds of breathing movements in 30 minutes
Fetal movements	Three or more body movements in 30 minutes	Less than 3 movements in 30 minutes
Fetal tone	At least one motion of a hand, arm, or leg going from flexed to extended and flexed again (such as opening and closing of the hand or extending and bending of the knee or elbow)	Fetal limbs remain partially or fully extended, do not flex with movement, or absence of fetal movement
Fetal reactivity (nonstress test)	Two or more accelerations of the fetal heart of at least 15 beats above the baseline rate and lasting at least 15 seconds in 20 minutes	Fewer than 2 accelerations or accelerations lasting less than 15 seconds in 20 minutes
Amniotic fluid volume	At least one area (pocket) of amniotic fluid of 1 centimeter (approximately ⅖ of an inch) in two perpendicular directions	Either no pockets of amniotic fluid or a pocket smaller than 1 cm in two perpendicular directions

HOW THE BIOPHYSICAL PROFILE IS INTERPRETED   **Reassuring Scores.** A total BPP score of 8 or higher is reassuring. The test then is repeated once a week or more often, depending on the seriousness of the complication for which it was performed. However, if the amniotic fluid is reduced with a score of 8 (or less), then the recommendation usually is to deliver the baby.

Equivocal Scores. A BPP score of 6 is considered an equivocal score. At this score, the recommendation for action varies according to the gestational age of the fetus (unless the amniotic fluid is reduced). Except for amniotic fluid volume, only the score—not the specific criteria—is considered. If the pregnancy is greater than 36 weeks, the recommendation is to deliver the baby if the cervix is what is called *favorable* to induce labor (see Chapter 22). If the cervix is "unfavorable" or the pregnancy is less than 36 weeks, then the test is repeated in 24 hours. At that time, if the BPP score is greater than 6, the woman can continue to be observed with frequent reassessment. If the score is less than 6, then the recommendation is to induce labor to deliver the baby.

Nonreassuring Scores. When the BPP score is 4, the test is repeated the same day. If the repeat BPP is less than 6, the baby should be delivered. If the first score is 0 to 2, the recommendation is to deliver the baby regardless of any other circumstances.

False Positive and False Negative Results

False positive or falsely nonreassuring results can occur with the BPP. With a very low score, this is quite unlikely. A score of 6, however, would be falsely positive in as many as 75 percent of BPPs. For this reason, the recommendation at this score is to repeat testing. Fortunately, false negative results—which mean that babies with problems are missed—occur very rarely.

The Modified Biophysical Profile

The biophysical profile is a rather extensive evaluation. It must be administered by personnel with training in ultrasonic examination of the fetus. Since the NST and the amniotic fluid volume are the most important components of the BPP, an alternative test is the *modified BPP*—using just these two parts of the assessment. The modified BPP is highly reliable.

In the modified BPP, the NST is performed in the usual way, sometimes with vibroacoustic stimulation, and the amniotic fluid volume is calculated using ultrasound. The fluid is measured in four quadrants of the uterus: the left upper and lower areas, and the right upper and lower areas. The depth of the largest pocket of fluid in each quadrant is recorded and the four measurements are added. Their sum should equal 5 centimeters (2 inches) or more. This is called the *amniotic fluid index* (AFI). If either the NST is nonreactive or the AFI less than 5 centimeters, a full biophysical profile may be performed, or the baby may be delivered.

Doppler Velocimetry

Doppler velocimetry or *continuous wave Doppler ultrasound* is a technique that measures the velocity or speed with which blood flows through vessels. The technique is named after Johann Christian Doppler, a nineteenth-century Austrian physicist. Doppler ultrasound studies are based on his observation that the pitch of a source of sound (in this case moving red blood cells) appears to vary with its speed. The echoes picked up by ultrasound thus change with the speed of the movement of the object being imaged. This is called the *Doppler shift*. In pregnancy, blood flow through the arteries that bring blood to the placenta can be examined with Doppler studies.

The speed of blood flow can be measured directly or indirectly. The direct technique involves measuring the diameter of the involved blood vessels. However, there are many technical difficulties involved with the direct technique. As a result, it has a high error rate. It also requires more expensive equipment. Indirect measurement or *waveform analysis* is used more often. Waveform analysis provides a ratio between the blood velocity when the fetal heart is beating (*systole*) and when it is not (*diastole*). This is called the S-D (*systole-diastole*) ratio. (A variation of this ratio called the *resistance index* or *Pourcelot ratio* can also be used.) The ratio is increased when the resting (*diastolic*) flow decreases. This diastolic decrease indicates narrowed blood vessels, so a high ratio may be a sign of a fetus in trouble. By 26 weeks gestation, the ratio in the uterine artery should be less than 2.6 and by 30 weeks gestation, the S-D ratio should be below 3 in the umbilical artery.

Sometimes abnormal Doppler studies are associated with fetal abnormalities, possibly those incompatible with life. An abnormal study may warrant further evaluation of the fetus, so that intervention such as cesarean birth is not initiated for a fetus that will not survive outside the uterus.

Doppler studies generally are performed when the fetus is not growing well or in pregnancies complicated by conditions that can interfere with placental blood flow and fetal growth. These conditions include high blood pressure and certain diseases of the cardiovascular system. Doppler velocimetry usually is available in only large medical centers. Its usefulness is debated; many experts do not believe that it provides better information than that obtained via NST and BPP. The equipment for Doppler studies is expensive and the procedure requires skilled practitioners to perform and interpret it accurately. In the future, as the technique becomes perfected, Doppler velocimetry may become more commonly used.

MEASURES OF FETAL LUNG MATURITY

Sometimes when pregnancy complications such as preeclampsia or preterm premature rupture of the membranes occur prior to term, continuing the pregnancy may pose more risks to the mother and fetus than delivering even a small baby. A major consideration in deciding whether to recommend delivery is how well the newborn will be able to breathe on its own. Testing for certain chemicals in the amniotic fluid, their relative amounts, and their ability to do their job can reveal whether the lungs are mature enough to function.

Lung expansion, which must occur every time the newborn takes a breath, requires the presence of a chemical called *surfactant*. Surfactant is released into the amniotic fluid with fetal breathing movements. The main components of surfactant are various chemicals called *phospholipids*. These include lecithin, phosphatidylglycerol (PG), phosphatidylinositol (PI), phosphatidylserine (PS), phosphatidylethanolamine (PE), sphingomyelin, and lysolecithin. Of these, lecithin is the most abundant, followed by PG.

Testing for these chemicals requires an amniocentesis, except when the membranes have ruptured and amniotic fluid can be obtained from the vagina. If the vaginal fluid is contaminated with blood or vaginal secretions, however, some of the tests noted below will be inaccurate.

Amniocentesis in late pregnancy is performed similarly to the way it is performed earlier, described in Chapter 8. It is, of course, accomplished under ultrasonic guidance. Once a sample of amniotic fluid is obtained, it can be tested in various ways to assess for these chemicals or how well they are functioning.

L/S Ratio

The most commonly used test of lung maturity is the lecithin-to-sphingomyelin ratio (L/S ratio). At 35 weeks gestation, amniotic fluid lecithin increases while sphingomyelin decreases or remains at a steady level. The absolute amount of lecithin may fluctuate according to the volume of amniotic fluid, but the ratio of the two chemicals is less subject to variation. Once the ratio reaches 2:1 (usually referred to as "2"), the newborn's lungs almost always have sufficient surfactant to function.

Below this ratio, the risk of the baby's developing respiratory distress syndrome (RDS) increases. When a woman has diabetes, the L/S ratio must reach 3.5 for fetal lung maturity to be reasonably assured.

PG Assay

Amniotic fluid measurement of PG is a simpler test to perform. While an L/S ratio takes approximately 1 hour, an assay of PG can be completed in 20 to 30 minutes. It also requires much less amniotic fluid (1.5 milliliters compared to 5 milliliters—or about 1/20 of an ounce compared to about 1/6 of an ounce). If PG is present in the amniotic fluid, the newborn's risk for respiratory distress syndrome is very low. If PG is absent, however, the infant will not necessarily have breathing difficulties. Therefore, further testing may be appropriate if the PG assay is negative. Because PG can be measured in the presence of blood or vaginal secretions, this is a particularly good test to use when the membranes are ruptured because it may avoid an amniocentesis.

Fetal Lung Profile

Sometimes a fetal lung "profile" is performed. This profile includes the L/S ratio as well as measurement of both PG and PI.

Fluorescent Polarization

A relatively expensive, but rapid and easily performed test involves the use of a fluorescent dye. The dye is mixed with amniotic fluid. When the phospholipids that constitute surfactant are present, the dye is absorbed into them. A measurement called *fluorescent polarization* is taken 30 minutes after the dye is added to the fluid. This uses a highly specialized instrument called a *microviscosimeter*. The fluorescent polarization value decreases as surfactant increases.

Surfactant to Albumin Ratio

The ratio of surfactant to the protein albumin also can be examined. This requires an instrument called a *TDx analyzer*, so the test is often called TDx-FLM (TDx-Fetal Lung Maturity). The TDx-FLM requires very little amniotic fluid and is performed rapidly—in less than 1 hour. Ratios of 50 to 70 milligrams of surfactant per gram of albumin are considered indicative of mature fetal lungs.

Tests of Surfactant Function

Several tests of surfactant function can be performed easily. The most common is the *shake test*. The shake test does not require expensive equipment or even sending the fluid specimen to a laboratory. It is based on the ability of surfactant to form foam in the presence of the chemical ethanol. Foam will only be formed if the fluid contains an adequate amount of lecithin. A complete ring of bubbles means the infant probably will not have RDS. A negative shake test, however, does not necessarily mean that the fetal lungs are immature.

A variation of the shake test is called the *foam stability index* (FSI). An FSI value of 47 or higher means RDS is unlikely in the newborn. Yet another variation is called the *tap test*. In this test the amniotic fluid is mixed with hydrochloric acid and ether in a test tube. The tube is then tapped three or four times, forming bubbles. If the bubbles rise from the bottom layer of the fluid to the surface and then break down, this indicates lung maturity. If the bubbles are stable or break down slowly, the lungs probably are immature. Unfortunately, these various tests of surfactant function are less reliable when the pregnancy is complicated by conditions such as diabetes or intrauterine growth restriction (IUGR).

Amniotic Fluid Inspection

Another way to assess for fetal lung maturity is visual inspection of the fluid. Fluid from an immature fetus is clear. As the pregnancy nears term, the fluid becomes cloudier and more difficult to see through. The *optical density* (OD) of the fluid can be measured. This relates to the fluid's absorbance of light at a particular wavelength. Measurement of OD requires a relatively inexpensive machine called a *spectrophotometer* and is performed rapidly. OD increases as the lungs mature. An OD value of 0.15 or greater indicates mature lungs, although in women with diabetes the value should be 0.2 or greater. If the fluid contains blood, vaginal secretions, or meconium the test is invalid. (*Meconium* is the content of the fetal bowels, which sometimes is secreted into the fluid.)

Lamellar Body Count

In another comparably simple test, the fluid is inspected under the microscope to look for a type of cell called a *lamellar body*. As these cells store surfactant, their presence indicates lung maturity. A standard technique for performing a lamellar body count needs to be developed in each institution, with appropriate values set for fetal lung maturity. Cut-off values that predict lung maturity have been suggested at 35,000 to 46,000. Blood or other contaminants in the fluid do not affect this test.

Placental Grading

Because amniocentesis occasionally leads to a complication, attempts have been made to infer fetal maturity from the appearance of the placenta viewed by ultrasound. Progressive changes in the placenta have been described, and grades of one to four assigned. A grade of three indicates maturity. Many mature fetuses, however, do not have grade three placentas. Furthermore, the placenta may show maturity in one section and not in others. Finally, when the pregnancy is complicated by IUGR, high blood pressure, diabetes, or Rh sensitization, placental grading is not a reliable gauge of lung maturity. Although the placenta may be graded as part of an ultrasound assessment, this test is not used solely to make decisions about whether the fetus is mature.

Fetal Measurements

An attempt also has been made to equate certain fetal measurements, taken easily by ultrasound, with maturity. In general, in an uncomplicated pregnancy, a *fetal biparietal diameter* (BPD) of 9.2 centimeters means that the lungs are mature. The BPD is the widest diameter of the fetal head and is used early in pregnancy to ascertain fetal age. Later in pregnancy it shows greater variation at any given week of gestation and so becomes less reliable to determine age of the fetus. Yet, a BPD of 9.2 is almost never seen in a fetus before term. Term fetuses, however, may have smaller diameters.

LATE FETAL ASSESSMENT IN A FETUS WITH RH SENSITIZATION

Another form of fetal assessment is specific to those now-rare instances where the mother's antibodies to the Rh factor have crossed the placenta to attack the red blood cells of the baby. This occurs when the baby is Rh positive and the mother is Rh negative. If fetal blood gets into the mother's circulation, she makes antibodies to the fetus's Rh factor, which is foreign to her body. When the fetus has been exposed to these antibodies, the condition is called Rh sensitization or *isoimmunization*. This is seen so rarely today because preventive treatment is available and routinely used. Sensitization might be seen in a women whose previous deliveries occurred without prenatal or labor care, such as a woman from a developing country. Maternal blood is tested early in prenatal care (or during the preconception visit described in Chapter 6) for Rh and other antibodies that might prove harmful to the baby. This is called an *indirect Coombs test*. Usually, these antibodies have formed in a previous pregnancy, often after delivery.

Rh-sensitized babies may develop *hemolytic disease* (Greek: *aima* = blood; *lysis* = dissolution). In this disease, severe *anemia* (low blood count) occurs in the fetus because of the *hemolysis* or destruction of its red blood cells by the mother's antibodies that cross the placenta. The illness may be serious, even fatal.

Several tests are performed to evaluate the extent of disease in the fetus and the need for intervention. Interventions might include intrauterine blood transfusion or delivery to allow for blood transfusion after birth.

The need for fetal testing is determined by tests of the mother's blood during pregnancy. If the mother's blood contains antibodies, then an *antibody titer* is measured at frequent intervals. This is an indirect measure of the amount of antibody in the mother's blood. Titers are reported in ratios. If the titer is low (1:8 or lower), then the fetus is not in danger. If the titer is higher than 1:8, testing of the fetus is advised.

Tests can be carried out to determine the seriousness of the fetal anemia and a resulting condition called *hydrops fetalis*. Hydrops fetalis is marked by gross swelling (*edema*) of the fetus and organ damage. This condition can be visualized with ultrasound. Anemia can be inferred from studies of amniotic fluid obtained via amniocentesis or tested for directly in fetal blood obtained via *cordocentesis* (also called *percutaneous umbilical blood sampling*—or PUBS). These procedures are described in Chapter 8. The techniques for obtaining the samples are similar whether the procedure is performed early or late in pregnancy. Briefly, an amniocentesis involves entering the uterus through a needle puncture of the membranes and withdrawing a small amount of amniotic fluid with the needle. This is done through the mother's abdomen. A cordocentesis involves the same puncture of the abdomen and membranes, but in this case fetal blood is withdrawn from the umbilical cord blood vessels. Both procedures are guided by ultrasound.

When amniotic fluid is obtained, its *optical density* (OD) is measured. This varies with the amount of *bilirubin* pigment in the fluid. Bilirubin is a chemical released when red blood cells are destroyed. OD measurement is begun at about 24 to 26 weeks gestation, or anytime thereafter if the mother's antibody titer rises to an unsafe level. The test is repeated at 1- to 3-week intervals. Values are plotted on a graph that shows a specific zone into which the OD falls: zone 1, 2, and 3, or mild, moderate, and severe. Transfusion or delivery is the usual course when the fluid exhibits zone 3 OD values. Values in zone 2 require either repeat amniocentesis or direct fetal blood sampling.

Some physicians no longer perform amniocentesis to evaluate Rh disease, but routinely test the fetal blood, obtained via cordocentesis. This may be most appropriate in women who previously have had an infant with severe Rh disease, as antibodies do not disappear between pregnancies. The extent to which a physician uses cordocentesis varies with experience. The technique, however, has more risks than amniocentesis, including the possibility of increasing the degree of isoimmunization, through inadvertent blood transfer from fetus to mother.

Fortunately, preventive treatment for Rh isoimmunization exists. The antibodies are given to the mother before her own body manufactures them. These injected antibodies are short lived and do not harm the fetus. The mother's lifelong reaction of creating her own antibodies never occurs. The antibody injections, called RhoGAM, are given shortly after the birth and routinely at about 28 weeks gestation. They are also given anytime there is a procedure that might cause any amount of fetal blood to pass into the mother's circulation, such as amniocentesis.

A Final Word

Ultimately, when a fetal test shows a possible problem, a recommendation on what to do is made by the physician caring for you. If your care has been with a midwife, the midwife will consult with a physician or you will have a visit with a physician at the time a problem is identified. In many cases, your midwife or regular obstetrician will consult a *perinatologist*, a physician who specializes in problems of the fetus and newborn (Greek: *peri* = around; Latin: *natus* = birth).

The decision-making process is based on the *entire clinical picture*. This includes assessing not just the results of a specific fetal test, but considering the reason the test was performed and any other medical or obstetrical conditions that exist. Whether to recommend delivery or waiting, whether to recommend induction of labor or a cesarean birth, requires clinical judgment—judgment that comes from education and experience. The reasons for the recommendation should be explained fully to you, in terms you understand, and you must be given the opportunity to ask any and all questions you have. Never consider your concerns inappropriate or silly!

Fortunately, in the overwhelming majority of cases, the baby will be just fine. If induction or cesarean is the choice and the baby is healthy, remember that this doesn't mean the delivery wasn't necessary. It means it was accomplished before the baby was harmed.

CHAPTER EIGHTEEN

Labor

In today's age of information, only a rare woman living in the developed world could be like the newly delivered mother described by Grantly Dick-Read in the early part of the twentieth century. After attending this woman's birth at home, Dr. Dick-Read noted how easily she seemed to cope with labor. When he asked her about this, she replied, "Labor wasn't supposed to hurt, was it?"

Dr. Dick-Read used this woman's answer to pioneer education for childbirth. He developed a program based on helping break what he called the "fear-tension-pain syndrome." He believed that the fear of labor leads to tension, tension that greatly contributes to pain.

Today, women, even young girls, hear that labor is almost always painful. What should be remembered is that for every human being who has ever inhabited the earth, a woman was pregnant, and with a few exceptions, that woman experienced labor. Labor is painful, but with support and sometimes the assistance of medications, labor can be comfortable, certainly tolerable. Of course, until it is experienced, how it will feel remains a mystery. We hope it is not a mystery to be unduly feared.

LABOR PAIN

A woman pregnant for the first time often wonders how she will know that labor is beginning. Will she distinguish the pains of childbirth from intestinal cramps or a backache? Will she distinguish real labor from the Braxton-Hicks contractions of pregnancy?

The throes of labor are unique in several ways. First, the pains are never constant; they come and go. Actually, in labor, more time is spent between pains than in pain. Think of each labor pain like a scale that makes a leisurely ascent to its high tone and is held aloft for a few beats before the descending notes. Each contraction rises in *slow crescendo*, remains *fortissimo* for a brief period, and closes in moderate *diminuendo*. The transcription of a labor pain into music might be:

Susan Peterson, a reader of a previous edition of this book, suggested that a major scale does not convey the "grinding and twisting" sensation of a labor pain. For musically literate readers she offered this transcription as "a probably more accurate and certainly more contemporary idiom":

Labor Pain for Two Oboes

For those less musically minded, a wave provides a visual image of a contraction. Each wave builds up slowly, reaches an awesome height somewhere before it hits the shore, then disappears forever. Each is followed closely by another. Ina May Gaskin, in a well-known book for midwives, *Spiritual Midwifery*, calls the feelings of labor "rushes."

Another distinctive quality of labor is that its pains are always associated with a muscular contraction of the uterus that can be palpated or felt with the hand. If you feel the top of your abdomen during the height of a labor pain, you will notice a large, firm mass, difficult or impossible to indent. This becomes less hard and easier to indent once the pain is over. The uterus is literally flexing and resting its muscle.

A further characteristic of labor is its rhythmic nature, its waves recurring at somewhat fixed intervals. As labor progresses, the interval from the beginning of one pain to the beginning of the next is gradually shortened from 15 or 20 minutes to 2 or 3 minutes. This is called the *frequency of the contractions*. In addition, the total length of an individual pain increases from less than half a minute at labor's start to a full minute or more toward its end. This is called the *duration of the contractions*.

Along with these increases in frequency and duration, contractions increase in *intensity*—they get harder, stronger, and more painful as labor progresses. These progressive changes, as difficult as they can be at times to tolerate, are good signs—without them, only rarely will labor do its job. Many women compare labor pains to powerful, intense, perhaps exaggerated, menstrual cramps.

Finally, true labor is ordinarily accompanied by a pinkish vaginal discharge, called *show*. Show is blood-tinged mucus dislodged from the cervix as it opens or dilates. Sometimes this normal show, which is to be distinguished from *abnormal bleeding* (frank red blood without mucus), anticipates the onset of labor by a day or two.

FALSE LABOR

True labor may be preceded by one or more bouts of false labor. In false labor the cervix does not dilate and the baby does not descend or move downward toward the birth canal. Despite this, the pains of false labor are real and can be uncomfortable and exhausting. Often false labor contractions will subside if you walk, whereas real labor contractions may increase with walking.

If this is not your first experience with labor, you may make the distinction between true and false labor. If you previously have had a very rapid labor, caution dictates that you report the onset of any contractions to your physician or midwife.

If you find you are having many episodes of false labor, losing sleep, and becoming overly fatigued, try some simple remedies to help you rest and sleep: a warm tub bath (with assistance), soothing music, heated milk, a back rub, use of pillows under all your joints. As false labor comes and goes, try to rest or sleep when you can during pain-free periods.

Even though false labor doesn't accomplish the tasks of labor, take comfort in knowing that it does signal that labor is fast approaching. False labor also can help prepare or "ripen" the cervix by making it softer and perhaps thinner.

BACK LABOR

Back labor describes the discomfort of uterine contractions felt mostly over the lower back. The discomfort of both false and true labor may be focused in this area. Sometimes labor pains occur first in the small of the back and after a few hours migrate down the flanks to the lower abdomen.

Back labor is usually, though not always, caused by the baby's head pressing on the mother's back when the fetus is positioned in the pelvis so that it faces the front of the mother rather than her back. This position is a variation of the more usual backward facing fetal position. It is not a problem, but it puts extra pressure on the mother's back. It is called the *occiput posterior position*, or OP. The *occipital bone* is the bone in the back of the baby's head. It is the landmark used to describe the position of the fetal head. When the baby's face is toward the front of the mother's body, the occipital bone is toward the mother's back, hence the term *occiput posterior* (posterior means back).

Labor may be prolonged somewhat with a posterior position of the head. This is expected and normal. Either the dilating or pushing stage of labor, or both, can be extended. Often, the baby will turn or rotate 180 degrees to be born in the more commonly seen position, facing the mother's back (occiput anterior, OA). In about 5 percent of births, the baby will be born in the direct OP position. We sometimes say such babies are born "sunny side up" as their face looks upward if the mother is on her back.

Comforts for back labor include position changes to relieve some of the pressure, use of cold or heat, and massage. These are discussed further in Chapter 20.

THE CAUSE OF LABOR
REMAINS UNKNOWN

What causes labor to begin? Why does it start approximately 280 days after the first day of the last menstrual period? These seem like simple questions. Yet, no one can answer them. We know that contractions of the uterus occur irregularly throughout pregnancy, beginning at about 6 weeks. These are called Braxton-Hicks contractions, after John Braxton Hicks who first described them in 1872. Suddenly, inexplicably, these painless contractions become regular and painful: labor has begun.

Researchers have proposed several theories to explain why labor begins when it does. None is proven. We know that the hormone *oxytocin* and the group of chemicals called *prostaglandins* are involved in the process of labor, but what initially stimulates their increased release remains an enigma. One theory is that the fetus itself sends a signal that it is ready to be born, perhaps by secreting a hormone or other chemical into the circulation. This in turn triggers the release of chemicals that cause uterine contractions. Support for this theory comes from pregnancies in which the fetus has a severe brain or hormonal disorder. Such pregnancies have been reported to extend past term or show a dysfunctional pattern of labor. In some pregnancies with these problems, however, labor starts on time and proceeds normally. Furthermore, no such fetal chemical has been identified.

The quest to understand the onset of human labor is ongoing. The hope of scientists involved in this endeavor is that such an understanding will lead to improved ways of preventing premature labor.

THE ONSET OF LABOR

Some labors take a slow, almost leisurely, start that allows ample time for personal business such as arranging care for older children. Other labors begin like a violent storm sweeping across the landscape, the contractions resembling the rolling thunder of the approaching clouds. One cannot predict with any certainty which labors will be lengthy and which rapid, but in most cases the woman having her first baby will have a slower start and a longer labor.

Among the things we do not recommend, when you suspect that labor has begun, is timing each contraction. It can be futile and frustrating to sit for several hours with a clock, a pencil, and paper writing down the intervals between "labor pains" that turn out to be false labor or part of what is known as the *latent phase*. It is much better to seek some sort of diverting activity that will occupy your mind until labor becomes unmistakable, or until you feel you should consult someone to find out if you are really in labor or not. A walk, a movie, television, a shower, a tub bath (if you have help) may distract or relax you, or both.

Unless you've previously had a very rapid labor, you can wait until contractions are uncomfortable and occur at approximately 5-minute intervals before you call your physician or midwife. You also may want to call if you are unable to sleep or if you feel like you cannot cope, even if the contractions are not yet close together. Don't let the time of day or night deter you from calling. Your care providers will have told you how to contact them, and they are accustomed to having these crucial events happen at any hour. It is better to resolve doubts by calling when you feel the need than to wait nervously. On occasion, with a rapid onset of labor contractions, it may be wise to proceed directly to the hospital or birth center. If you have a cell phone, you can call while traveling. A birth center, however, may only open when somebody has called in advance; so if you plan to have your baby at a birth center, make certain you know the procedures in advance. You may not have the option of going without calling first.

When deciding how soon to call your physician or midwife, or whether to go straight to the birth center or hospital, also consider the time of year and the weather. If you know that a severe snowstorm is on the way, and you are delivering in a hospital or birth center that is not just around the corner, leave earlier rather than later. In an urban area you may have to allow for congested traffic conditions. Baby-sitting arrangements for your older children can create last-minute problems. If absolutely necessary, take the children along with you. You can call your prearranged child care person from the birth center or hospital or somebody there can arrange for emergency child care.

A definite decision about whether labor is present may be based on vaginal exams done several hours apart. This will depend on how dilated your cervix is at the first vaginal examination. If it is at least 4 centimeters dilated, you are usually in labor. If it is less, your physician or midwife may ask you to walk around for an hour or two and then recheck your cervix. If it hasn't changed, you may not be admitted to the birth center or hospital, but given instructions on how to decide when to return (for example, stronger, more regular contractions, rupture of the membranes, increased bloody show).

For many years, women have been advised not to eat or drink after labor started because of the fear that they could aspirate (breathe in) stomach contents if they had to have general anesthesia later in labor. Recent research has shown that this precaution is unnecessary. The arguments on both sides of this debate are outlined in Chapter 20. In early labor, eating is beneficial. Choose light foods and, most important, drink plenty of fluids. Light food choices include tea with sugar, clear broth, fruit juice, lightly cooked eggs, toast, plain crackers, and cooked fruits, although some women prefer higher calorie snacks and drinks such as athletic beverages.

Sexual intercourse at the onset of labor is a custom in a number of cultures. In some it is considered to aid in lubricating the vagina and in others it is thought to accelerate labor. There may be a physiological basis for these beliefs, since we now know that orgasm causes release of oxytocin, which stimulates uterine activity. Semen also contains *prostaglandins*, chemicals that stimulate uterine contractions and are involved in the thinning of the cervix. However, if the membranes are ruptured, intercourse can increase the possibility of infection during and after labor. For the same reason, douching at the onset of labor is unwise.

Rupture of the Membranes

About one time in ten, labor heralds its appearance by spontaneous rupture of the membranes. This is also referred to as the bag of waters breaking. Rupture of membranes is painless as the membranes are fetal tissues and have no nerves in them.

Rupture of the membranes may be preceded by contractions of which the woman is aware, but it may occur without advance notice. When rupture of the membranes is followed by forceful and uncomfortable uterine contractions, the diagnosis of labor is quite certain.

The membranes can rupture with a sudden big gush of fluid from the vagina or a small but continuous trickle of fluid. This discharge is not likely to be confused with the ordinary increased vaginal secretions of late pregnancy because the fluid is clear and watery. However, if you have been leaking urine when coughing in the last few months of pregnancy, you may not realize that this is different. The smell of amniotic fluid is distinct from the odor of urine, but with a trickle of fluid, this may be hard to discern.

If you think your membranes have ruptured, call your physician or midwife. Your care provider may ask you to come in to be checked. Because of the risk of infection, only a sterile vaginal examination with a sterile speculum should be done.

Physicians and midwives have several ways of telling whether your membranes have ruptured. On speculum examination, they may be able to see a pool of fluid in the vagina or fluid leaking from the cervix. They may ask you to grunt or bear down; if this causes a seepage of fluid from the cervix, it clearly demonstrates that the membranes have ruptured. Amniotic fluid often contains flecks of *vernix caseosa*, the white, creamy substance that covers the fetus's skin.

If visualization cannot confirm membrane rupture, the fluid can be tested for its pH with a strip of pH testing paper (usually nitrazine paper). Amniotic fluid has a higher pH than vaginal secretions, meaning it is more alkaline (less acidic). This causes the nitrazine paper to turn from yellow to a blue-green or dark blue. A sterile cotton swab can be placed into the vaginal fluid and then touched to the nitrazine paper. This test is not foolproof as other fluids such as blood, which could be present in show, or even cervical mucus, demonstrate the same color changes on the pH paper.

Amniotic fluid also contains more *sodium chloride* (salt) than urine, so that when it dries it exhibits a phenomenon called *ferning*, a picturesque term describing the microscopic appearance of the salt crystals that form in the drying process. A small amount of fluid from the cotton swab can be placed onto a slide. Viewing this slide under the microscope will reveal whether or not the ferning pattern is present.

Rupture of the membranes is called *premature* when it happens before labor begins. When this occurs near term, labor usually follows within 24 hours, and almost always within 72 hours. Typically, the earlier in pregnancy the membranes rupture, the longer the interval between rupture and labor. More discussion of premature rupture of membranes is in Chapter 15.

When to Call Your Physician or Midwife About Your Labor

- Your membranes rupture (your bag of waters breaks)
- You have strong (painful) contractions lasting at least 30 to 40 seconds and occurring approximately every 5 minutes for at least 1 hour UNLESS

  You have previously had a very rapid labor
  You are unable to tolerate the contractions you are having
  You live very far from the birth center/hospital or your home birth attendant lives far from you
  The weather is ominous or there is heavy traffic and you expect your trip to take extra time

- In the above circumstances, call as soon as contractions start or whenever they become intolerable

---

WHEN DOES LABOR OCCUR?

The Time of Day

A part of the mythological depiction of birth in the United States today involves the mad dash to the hospital—made more dramatic when it happens in the middle of the night. In fact, few births occur rapidly enough to necessitate such dashing and many births occur throughout the day. The author of the previous edition of this book, Irwin Kaiser, and his colleague studied over 600,000 spontaneous births and found that the highest rate of delivery did, in fact, occur between 4 and 5 in the morning. The lowest rate was between 4 and 7 P.M. A more recent study of over 200,000 spontaneous vaginal births that took place from 1989 to 1995 had different findings. In this study, births peaked between 11 A.M. and 1 P.M. with a lesser peak between 11 P.M. and 1 A.M.

How Many Labor Pains Are Required?

"How many pains make a baby?" is one way the lay person might pose a serious scientific query. As can be surmised, there is extraordinary variation, just like the number of strokes in a tennis match. According to one Swiss study, first labors required an average of 135 contractions and subsequent labors, 68.

THE FORCES INVOLVED IN LABOR AND BIRTH

Imagine the baby safely encased in a large, gourd-shaped, elastic bottle, the muscular uterus. This "bottle" lies upside down within the mother's abdomen, its bottom under her ribs, and its neck deep in her pelvis, surrounded by a circle of bones. The neck of the uterus/bottle—the *cervix*—is nearly an inch long (2 centimeters) when labor begins, and it is almost closed. Before a full-term baby can leave the uterus, the neck must be thinned out completely and stretched to a diameter of 4 inches (10 centimeters). This allows the baby to pass from the uterus into the narrow but expandable, 5-inch-long corridor—the *vagina* or *birth canal*—that leads to the outside world.

Another image that will help you visualize the cervix thinning and opening is the turtleneck sweater. As the sweater is pulled over your head, first the long neck disappears, then it stretches over your head. The shortening of the neck is called *effacement*, from the French *effacer*, to remove the face. The opening of the neck is called *dilation* (or *dilatation*).

The power that effaces and dilates the cervix and propels the child through the birth canal is mainly the force generated by the contractions of the muscular uterus. The largest muscle of the body, far stronger than the powerful biceps of a heavyweight weight lifter, the uterus forms a complete protective casing about the child except for the small opening at the cervix. When the muscle fibers contract, the pressure within the uterus is greatly increased—the process is like compressing a water-filled rubber bulb—and this increased pressure is transmitted to the cervix.

The force of labor pains is directed against the cervix in two ways. The uterus has two separate inner linings, the *membranes*. These contain the child and the amniotic fluid. During a contraction, both the baby and its surrounding fluid are put under 30 pounds of pressure in all directions. When the membranes are intact, this force pushes the fluid against the cervix. When the membranes are ruptured, the baby is pushed against the cervix. Through pressure exerted either by the fluid or the baby, the cervix is made to open or dilate, pushed open from within. In addition to this pressure from within, the neck of the bottle is shortened and pulled open by the contractions of the muscle fibers of the lower portion of the uterus, to which the muscle fibers of the cervix are attached.

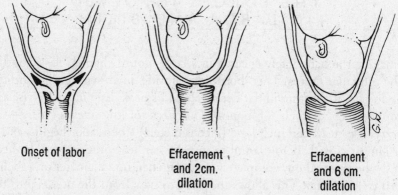

Onset of labor   Effacement and 2cm. dilation   Effacement and 6 cm. dilation

From left to right, the changes in the mother's cervix late in pregnancy. The fetus is head down, and the cervix thick and closed. In the illustration on the right the cervix is open, and the membranes are pushing down into the opening.

In some women these changes do not take place until labor has begun. In others they may have occurred even before the first noteworthy contraction.

HOW LABOR PROGRESSES

There are two criteria for progress in labor, closely related to each other. One is the *state* of the cervix. The other is the level or *station* of the presenting part (the head or the breech) of the fetus.

Not all cervixes are perfectly circular, but they are idealized as such for description of their diameter. The opening of the cervix is measured in centimeters (cm). There are 2½ centimeters to an inch. Sometimes the cervix is measured in fingerbreadths, although this is less accurate. The width of a finger is approximately 1½ cm, but naturally this varies with the size of the examiner's finger.

The extent of cervical *effacement* (thinning) can be expressed in two ways. Some examiners describe the length of the cervical canal in centimeters, whereas others express it as a percentage of the cervical canal's starting length of approximately 2 centimeters. If the cervix is 1 centimeter long, it may be described as being 50 percent effaced. Most often, when a cervix has dilated beyond 4 or 5 centimeters, it is completely effaced, which is another way of saying that it has no measurable length.

For first labors, the cervix is very much shortened and thinned out before it starts to dilate. With later babies, as the cervix has already gone through the process, effacement and dilation may take place simultaneously.

The level, or station, of the presenting part of the fetus is measured in relation to the mother's pelvis, the circle of bones through which the baby must pass to be born. The point of reference for station is an imaginary line drawn between a pair of pelvic bony structures, the *ischial spines*. They jut into the pelvis from each of its sides. This imaginary line is important because it is the narrowest part of the pelvis through which the fetus must pass.

You will hear physicians and midwives using terms such as "minus 1" or "plus 3." Decoded, these terms mean, respectively, that the presenting part is 1 centimeter above the imaginary line joining the pelvic spines or 3 centimeters below this level. Before the presenting part of the fetus reaches the level of these small bony prominences, we say the baby is *floating*. This might be said to be minus 4 or higher station. When the baby's presenting part begins to descend into the pelvis, we say it is *dipping*. A baby that is dipping may still move upward. When the presenting part of the fetus reaches the level of the pelvic spines, we say the baby is at 0 (zero) station or *engaged*. Engagement usually happens before labor starts in first pregnancies but may not happen until labor in later pregnancies.

When the baby comes down to about 4 centimeters (plus 4) below the level of the spines, the head or breech presses on the pelvic floor. The pelvic floor consists of a group of muscles attached to the pelvic bones. These muscles, arranged in a sling-like fashion, support the pelvic organs. Pressure on the muscles creates an urge to push, adding to the force of uterine contractions. Soon thereafter, the birth of the presenting part occurs.

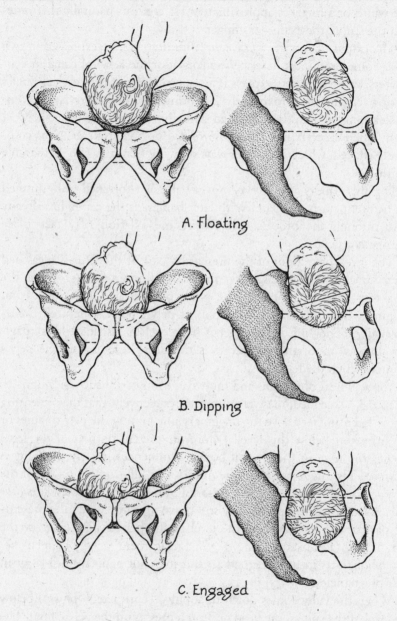

A. Floating

B. Dipping

C. Engaged

The First Stage of Labor: Effacement and Dilatation

The effacement and dilatation stage of labor is called the *first stage*. This stage of labor has been divided, somewhat arbitrarily, into several parts or phases. The first stage of labor, in reality, is a continuous process, without clear demarcations into parts. The distinctions have been made to help physicians, midwives, nurses, laboring women, and their support persons understand the course of a given labor and make decisions such as when admission into the hospital or birthing center is appropriate, if and when to assist the progress of labor with various interventions, and if and when to provide pain medication.

The first phase of the first stage of labor is the *latent phase*. Contractions are mild, spaced rather far apart, usually irregular, and last about half a minute or a bit more or less. The cervix softens, effaces or becomes shorter, and begins to dilate.

The second phase of the first stage of labor is the *active phase*. Contractions are more frequent, more regular, longer, and stronger. The cervix dilates more rapidly during the active phase of labor.

Obstetric and midwifery texts divide the active phase of the first stage of labor into three separate parts:

• Acceleration: the beginning of the active phase
• Maximum slope: the phase of rapid cervical dilation
• Deceleration: the very end of the first stage of labor. When the rate of dilation levels off

Childbirth educators call the last part of the first stage of labor *transition*. Contractions during this time are very frequent and very strong. They last a minute or even longer. The cervix dilates to 10 centimeters or *complete dilatation* during the transition phase. Transition is usually the most difficult phase to tolerate, but is the shortest.

During the last part of the stage of cervical dilatation, a number of obvious signs are seen in the laboring woman. If the membranes haven't yet ruptured, they may do so at this time. Other signs include an increase in bloody show; increased feelings of discomfort and restlessness; increased abdominal tenderness; a desire not to be touched; loss of modesty; frustration; exasperation; apprehension; irritability; shivering; chattering teeth; perspiration; burping; thirst; loss of appetite; nausea and sometimes vomiting; cramps in the calves, buttocks, thighs; curling toes; and, finally, grunting, rectal bulging, and an urge to push, which may feel at first like the need to have a bowel movement.

The Second Stage of Labor: Birth

When the cervix is fully dilated, the force of the uterine contractions is directed toward moving the baby through the birth canal. In this stage of labor, called the second stage, the force of the uterine contractions is greatly augmented by involuntary contractions of the woman's abdominal muscles, to which are added her own bearing-down efforts.

The second stage of labor, also called the *expulsive* or *birth stage*, is timed from the complete disappearance of the cervix as a separate structure to the actual birth of the baby. The birth process is discussed in greater detail in Chapter 19.

The Third Stage of Labor: The Placenta

The third stage of labor, also called the *placental stage*, is the time from the birth of the baby to the delivery of the placenta or afterbirth.

Although there is great relief following the birth of the baby, contractions do not stop. They are not as painful as before, as much less force is needed to deliver the placenta. They also occur less frequently—perhaps every 4 to 5 minutes rather than every 2 to 3 minutes. Your physician or midwife will pay close attention to the signals that the placenta has separated from the uterine wall. This may happen as quickly as 2 minutes after the birth of the baby, or may not occur for half an hour after the baby's birth.

The signs of separation of the placenta include a trickle or gush of blood, a rise of the uterus in the abdomen, a change in the shape of the uterus, so that it becomes more round or globular looking, and a lengthening of the umbilical cord, which is visible at the entrance to the vagina. Once your physician or midwife sees a sign that the placenta has separated, he or she may ask you to bear down once more for the placenta. In the absence of bleeding, there is no particular hurry about the delivery of the placenta.

You probably will not pay much attention to the placental delivery once the baby is born. Today, many physicians and midwives immediately place the healthy newborn on your abdomen. You can put the baby to the breast right after it is born. This is a good time to begin nursing as the baby has an alert period following birth. Shortly afterward, it will fall asleep. You probably will too. Skin-to-skin contact between mother and baby is also an excellent way to keep the baby warm, especially in the hospital where the delivery room is kept somewhat chilly to help prevent the spread of bacteria. A nurse or birth assistant can assist you in breast-feeding.

An interesting study in Sweden showed that newborns given uninterrupted contact with their mothers actually make crawling movements toward the breast about 20 minutes after birth. Within an average of less than 1 hour, most of the newborns in this study were nursing correctly. This is an advantage of early contact between mother and baby.

Immediate nursing, or any kind of nipple stimulation, is also valuable because it causes the release of oxytocin. Oxytocin stimulates secretion of milk in response to suckling of the baby, or what it perceives to be suckling. An extra benefit is that oxytocin also causes contractions of the uterus, helping in the delivery of the placenta, and in easing postpartum bleeding.

The Fourth Stage of Labor: Recovery

Some physicians and midwives refer to the 1-hour period following birth of the placenta as the fourth stage of labor. Technically, labor is over with the birth of the placenta, but this designation has been made because it is an important time for physicians, midwives, and nurses to be aware of the mother's condition and to make sure she is on the way to postpartum recovery (Latin: *post* = after; *partus* = birth). The postpartum period is covered in Chapter 25.

THE LENGTH OF LABOR

Obstetrical science today is quite concerned with the length of labor. Birth attendants expend a lot of effort judging whether each of the three stages of labor is normal in length. While there is a greater likelihood that either the mother or the fetus will have difficulty tolerating labor as it becomes longer, length of labor is extremely variable and a labor outside the accepted norms may pose no danger to mother or fetus. Although there are identifiable stages and phases that allow us to describe labor, there are as many variations—from slight to great—as there are women having babies. In fact, any one woman may experience very different labors for each of her pregnancies, or her labors may be remarkably similar. This may be influenced by how far apart the labors are: second and third labors, for example, are usually shorter than the first, but not if a great number of years has elapsed from one labor to the next. (What constitutes a "great number" may vary from woman to woman. Some women may have a shorter second labor even if it is 10 years since their previous child was born; others may have a labor similar to a first labor after only 5 years.)

The woman anticipating labor may be terrified by stories of 2-day or 3-day labors, but should be aware that in such labors, it is usually the latent phase that is prolonged. In this phase, contractions are mild, frequently irregular, and spaced apart. There is a lot of time to rest—as long as you remember to do so. An extremely rapid labor, while sounding enviable to a woman who has had a long labor or to a woman who has never experienced labor, may be as difficult to tolerate as a long labor. The pains often begin tumultuously and don't let up until the baby is born. Blissfully short may not be blissfully easy. The exception to this is the rare, but not unheard of, woman who delivers her baby with little warning. A few perceived contractions are all she needs.

A dilemma in any study examining the length of labor is when to begin counting. Perception varies from one woman to another as to when she believes that labor has begun. Some women come to the hospital or birth center asking to be told whether they really are in labor, only to be found far advanced in the first stage, even within an hour or less of delivery. Other women are certain they are in labor because they have been conscientiously timing what they feel as hard contractions for a number of hours. To their disappointment, when they arrive at the hospital or birth center, or when their birth attendant arrives at their home, they show no objective evidence of labor—no cervical change. Their contractions may even stop and they may not deliver for a few days. These examples are the extreme ends of a continuum of normal experiences in labor.

The best information on the start of labor would be based entirely on careful study of women by pelvic examination before and after they believe they began labor. Of course, this would be an unrealistic and indeed impossible study to carry out. Since women do not need exams early in labor, and a pelvic examination is an uncomfortable and invasive procedure, this would not even be considered an ethical study. In fact, once the membranes have ruptured, pelvic exams increase the risk for infection. At best, then, any study of the length of labor is flawed.

Much of what we believe about the length of labor has come from the work of Emanuel Friedman, an obstetrician whose extensive study of labors began in the 1950s. Physicians and midwives often plot a woman's progress in labor on a graph called the Friedman graph. They compare the labor to the norms established by Dr. Friedman and use this comparison to help decide whether the labor is proceeding normally or needs some assistance. We repeat that, of course, the length of labor is only one way to judge its normalcy.

Although Friedman's data are based on the way labors were managed over 50 years ago, and much has changed since then, his study of length of labor remains the most comprehesive and therefore is still cited and used by many of today's obstetrical care providers. However, most do not adhere rigidly to Friedman's norms.

Based on Friedman's work, the values on the table below are considered normal in labor. The table shows the maximum and *mean*—average—values for each stage of labor. A distinction is made between nulliparous women and multiparous women. A *nulliparous* woman is a woman who has never had a baby of a gestational age advanced enough to survive. (We say such a newborn is *viable*.) A *multiparous* woman is a woman who has had at least one baby. A *multigravida* has had at least one pregnancy. Commonly, labor in a nullipara is longer than labor in a multipara.

(As an aside, you may hear physicians, midwives, and obstetrical nurses using the term *primipara* or *primip* to refer to a woman who "is having her first baby." In fact, primipara means a woman who has had one baby. A *primigravida* is a woman pregnant for the first time, but a woman may have been pregnant without ever having had a baby. She would thus not be a primigravida, but would enter labor as if she were. The more accurate term to describe a woman having her first labor is *nullipara*, but this term is used less often. These terms all come from the Latin: *nullus* = none; *primus* = first; *multus* = many; *gravida* = pregnant; *parere* = to bear offspring.)

The maximum number of hours for each stage of labor reflects what Friedman considered the longest normal time period. The maximum number of hours is actually not the longest that occurs—it is defined as the longest number of hours for 95 percent of all women. This means that 5 percent of really long labors have been excluded from the range of normal. This is somewhat arbitrary as there may be no problem in labor for the mother or fetus in these 5 percent of labors. The mean is the average number of hours. The mean is unfairly influenced by labors that are many hours, so the mean is longer than most women actually experience.

LABOR IN A NULLIPARA (WOMAN HAVING HER FIRST BABY)		
	Maximum (hours)	Mean (hours)
First stage:		
Total	28.5	13.3
Latent phase	20	8.6
Active phase	12	5.8
Second stage:	2.5	.95 (57 min.)

LABOR IN A MULTIPARA (WOMAN HAVING A SECOND OR LATER BABY)		
	Maximum (hours)	Mean (hours)
First stage:		
Total	20	7.5
Latent phase	14	5.3
Active phase	6	2.5
Second stage:	.83 (50 min.)	.30 (18 min.)

In a study published in *The Journal of Perinatology* in 1999 of more than 2,000 births to women without obstetrical risk factors who were cared for by nurse-midwives, norms for the active stage of labor were longer than those documented by Friedman. The study was conducted by Leah Albers, a well-known midwife and researcher.

Dr. Albers did not include the latent phase of labor in the analysis of the length of first stage labor. She looked only at the active phase, defining it as 4 centimeters to full dilatation. She found that the maximum length of the active stage of the first stage of labor was 5.5 hours longer in a nullipara than Friedman found (17.5 hours) and 7.8 hours longer in a multipara (13.8 hours). The average or mean lengths were 2 and 3 hours longer than Friedman found (7.7 hours and 5.6 hours for primiparas and multiparas, respectively). The length of the second stage of labor in this study was equivalent to its length in Friedman's studies.

In reality, there is no absolute way to determine when the latent phase of labor ends and the active phase begins. In some labors, contractions become stronger, harder, and more frequent at about 3 centimeters of cervical dilatation. In other labors, an active contraction pattern may not be seen until the cervix has dilated to about 5 centimeters. Neither of these is abnormal or in itself a cause for concern.

During labor, the physician or midwife will evaluate progress. Friedman reports that nulliparous women should dilate at a rate of at least 1.2 centimeters per hour in the active phase of labor and that multiparous women should dilate at a rate of at least 1.5 centimeters per hour in the active phase of labor. Sometimes, however, dilatation proceeds more slowly. In that case, fetal descent might be used to determine appropriate progress of labor. Descent is movement downward in the pelvis, toward the birth canal. Friedman believed that the fetuses of nulliparous women should descend 1 centimeter per hour and the fetuses of multiparous women should descend 2 centimeters per hour. Descent, however, especially in multiparous women, may not take place until the cervix is nearly fully dilated.

In actual practice, women are not examined every hour. Vaginal examinations in labor can be uncomfortable and are invasive. With ruptured membranes, they must be limited to decrease the possibility of infection. During the latent phase, vaginal examinations are usually unnecessary. During the active phase, the frequency of examination will depend on the mother's behavior, her need for pain relief, her feeling that she needs to push, possible evidence of fetal distress, or whether her labor seems unusually prolonged. Labors that are induced may require more frequent examination, but not if the membranes are ruptured. This is discussed in Chapter 22.

Recent studies of second stage labor among thousands of births have found that prolonging this stage, even up to 6 or more hours, is not related to poorer infant outcomes, as long as the fetal heart rate pattern is reassuring. However, there is a reduced likelihood of a vaginal delivery if the second stage continues beyond 3 hours.

We urge you not to have preconceived expectations about how your labor will proceed. There may be periods of more rapid, or less rapid, dilatation. There may be periods of no dilatation during which downward movement of the baby occurs. There may be periods, such as when a woman first arrives at the hospital or birth center, when labor slows down. It will pick up a short while later. The latent stage of labor, in particular, is very varied, and most difficult to assess accurately as it is usually based on the mother's reporting of contractions, not vaginal examinations.

Women who express disappointment with their labors often have unrealistic expectations, such as the woman who assumed her labor would be like her sister's labors, which were all under 3 hours. For this woman, a normal 8-hour labor felt unduly long. She arrived at the hospital thinking she was ready to deliver after only 2 hours of contractions, and was crushed to discover that she was only 3 centimeters dilated. In fact, 3 centimeters in a nullipara after only 2 hours of contractions is very rapid progress. Labor is one part of life that can be neither predicted nor controlled.

Chapter 20 discusses the care you will receive during labor. It includes a detailed description of ways of increasing your comfort in labor.

CHAPTER NINETEEN

⸺⸙⸺

Birth

Birth is one of the events in human life that words fail to capture. No amount of description can convey the emotional quality of the experience. In video or film, the tendency is to concentrate on the blood and bodily secretions involved. In reality, these easily move to the background and all attention is on the profoundly human reactions to this life-changing moment.

Imagine a scene into which a new person has suddenly entered. There was no knock at the door. No one said, "Come in." The person is unknown to everyone in the room, yet there is no need for introductions. The newcomer instantly is an intrinsic part of the room, of the family there. He or she, without speaking a word, becomes everyone's focus. Of course, the midwife or physician performing the birth must continue to give careful attention to the mother, to watch her for bleeding, and to be prepared to catch the placenta as it is born.

THE SECOND STAGE OF LABOR

The second stage of labor is defined from full cervical dilatation to the birth of the baby. It includes the pushing stage and the long-awaited arrival of the newborn.

What is accomplished during the second stage? For one thing, the baby's head descends deeper into the pelvis. If the bony pelvic passage is narrow, the baby's head molds. The fetal skull is made up of five separate plates of bone with soft tissue between them. (See the illustration.) Each area of soft tissue is called a *suture* or *suture line*. The places where the

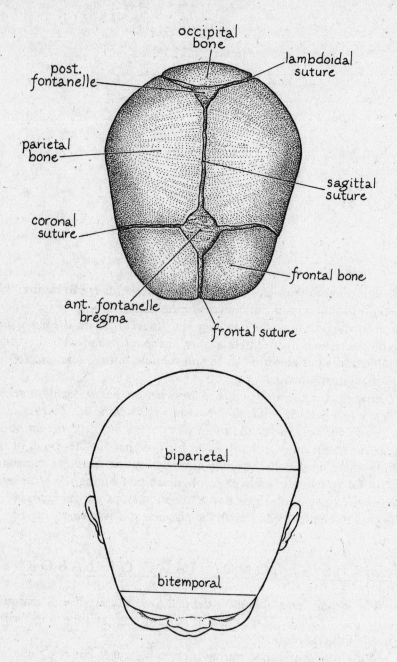

Baby's head.

front to back and sideways sutures meet are called *fontanelles*. There is a large diamond-shaped fontanelle in front, known as the *anterior fonta-*

nelle, and a smaller triangular-shaped one in back, known as the *posterior fontanelle*. Commonly, these are called the *soft spots*. This pliable, nonbony tissue provides room between the bones, allowing them to shift, even overlap, during labor. The baby's head is thus able to accommodate to the space available in the mother's birth canal. When molding has been extensive, the baby is born with a cone-shaped head. This is not an abnormality and the round shape returns within a few days.

Rotation of the baby's head (or *vertex*) is the second major feature of the second stage. The baby's head usually enters the lower pelvis in an oblique or diagonal position, that is, with the back of the baby's head, the *occiput*, partly to the right or left. At birth, the baby's head usually emerges looking directly toward the mother's back. If she is lying on her back the baby then faces the floor as it is born. This is known as the *occiput anterior* (OA) position because the back of the baby's head (occiput) faces the front part (anterior) of the mother's body. When the fetus is *vertex* or head-first, the occiput is the landmark used to describe the relationship of the fetal position to the mother's body.

If you consider the entrance to the vagina as the face of a clock, an occiput anterior has the back of the fetus's head pointing to 12 o'clock and the fetus's face toward 6 o'clock. With a left occiput anterior (abbreviated as LOA), the back of the baby's head points to between 1 and 2 o'clock on the clock face. For right occiput anterior (ROA), the back of the baby's head is pointing to between 10 and 11 o'clock. LOA and ROA are *oblique positions*.

The reason for the rotation of the baby's head is to allow it to fit through the pelvic bones, which encircle the uterus. As the baby enters the pelvis, which usually happens before labor, it must pass through what is called the *pelvic inlet*. The widest part of the pelvic inlet is its sideways—or *transverse*—measurement. The widest part of the baby's head is its front-to-back measurement. If the baby were facing front or back, it might not fit through this pelvic entrance. When the baby engages, or reaches the part of the pelvis called the *ischial spines*, the dimensions of the pelvis change so that its front-to-back measurement is wider than its side-to-side measurement. This is true of the *pelvic outlet* as well—the last part of the pelvic bones through which the fetus must travel. The fetal head must turn to accommodate this change in the shape of the pelvis. It must face front to back to leave the pelvis.

These fetal adaptations to the maternal pelvis were first described in the 1700s by William Smellie. They are called the *mechanisms of labor*. That almost all fetuses accomplish these mechanisms without difficulty is a truly remarkable part of birth.

The Mechanisms of Labor

The mechanisms of labor, or the steps in the birth process for the fetus, are listed in the box below. They are written as discrete steps, but they can occur simultaneously, and descent continues throughout the process.

The Mechanisms of Labor

- **Descent:** downward movement of the fetus. This occurs before and during labor. Some descent occurs during the first stage. Most occurs during the second stage.
- **Flexion:** bending of the fetal head so that the chin rests on the chest. This reduces the length of the diameter of the head that must pass through the pelvis. Without flexion, the head would have difficulty fitting through the pelvic bones. The fetal head is usually flexed well before labor begins, but flexion becomes more pronounced as the fetus descends.
- **Internal rotation:** turning of the fetal head that occurs when it moves through the pelvis. Internal rotation must occur because the shape of the pelvis changes. Usually, the rotation is from the tranverse (e.g., left occiput transverse or LOT) or oblique (e.g., left occiput anterior or LOA) to the direct occiput anterior position (OA).
- **Extension:** the means by which the head is actually born. The back of the head emerges first. The neck then extends and the head pivots around the pubic bones. The succession of birth (from the OA position) is the forehead, nose, mouth, and chin.
- **Restitution:** turning of the head 45 degrees back to its previous left or right position (OA back to LOA or ROA). This is done because when the head rotates, the shoulders do not. As the head is born, the neck is twisted. Once restitution is accomplished, the head and shoulders are again properly aligned.
- **External rotation:** turning of the head another 45 degrees to a sideways or transverse position. This is actually the outward sign of internal rotation of the shoulders. Since the shoulders are perpendicular to the head, the head must be turned sideways so that the shoulders become front to back. This allows the shoulders to fit through the pelvic outlet.
- **Lateral flexion:** birthing of the shoulders. The top (or anterior) shoulder pivots under the pubic bone to be born. The

posterior (or bottom) shoulder is born as the baby's body flexes sideways. This allows the shoulder to slide over the perineum (the area just below the vagina, also called the pelvic floor).

- **Birth of the body:** Once the head and shoulders are born, the body slides out without difficulty.

The combined forces of uterine contractions, resistance of the muscles of the pelvic floor, and the mother's bearing down push the baby's head to OA. If the baby has started its descent through the vagina in LOA, the rotation to OA is counterclockwise and, conversely, moving from ROA to OA, the rotation is clockwise.

Not every baby delivers in occiput anterior. A baby can, on occasion, deliver in an oblique position. This can only happen if the mother has a roomy pelvis. It is not rare for the baby to deliver in the occiput posterior (OP) position. If the mother is on her back the baby emerges looking up at the ceiling. The second stage with an OP ordinarily takes longer, particularly with first babies. This is because in the OP position, a wider part of the baby's head must move through the pelvis.

Pushing

Just when the intensity of uterine contractions in the transition period seems unbearable, they often slow down and change in quality. The change may be subtle, but it is usually unmistakable. Suddenly, the focus of pain moves from the abdomen to the *perineum*, the technical name of the muscles and connective tissue referred to as the *pelvic floor*. The perineal muscles are attached to the arch formed by the pubic bones. These muscles surround the opening of the vagina. With each contraction, the woman feels the urge to bear down. She may actually start to do this, perhaps unconsciously, perhaps with conscious knowledge but involuntary physical force.

The urge to bear down or push is remarkably similar to the sensation that all of us have when we are about to have a bowel movement. Many times it is more like the sensation we have when we need to have a bowel movement, but constipation holds back the actual movement. Toilet training taught us long ago to restrain the bearing-down impulse for social acceptability, but we also know from experience that there are times when the urge is beyond control. For most women, this is what happens in the second stage of labor.

The force of uterine contractions is sufficient to push the baby's head into the vagina but not enough to push it out though the connective tissue and muscular sling around the entrance to the vagina. The urge to push is a reflex stimulated by the stretching of the vagina and the front or upper wall of the rectum as well as the pressure of the fetus on the pelvic floor muscles. The urge occurs with the peak of the uterine contraction. In bearing down, the laboring woman contracts the muscles of her abdominal wall, and makes every effort to push the baby out through the vaginal opening.

The physician or midwife watching and evaluating your labor may examine you when you begin to feel the need to push or when, in active labor, you complain of needing to move your bowels. This exam is to ascertain that, in fact, your cervix is fully dilated. Some women feel the urge once the fetus has moved down in the pelvis and is pressing on the posterior (back) vaginal wall. This may happen before the cervix has opened completely, but it can be somewhat irritating to push against the cervix before it is completely dilated.

With epidural anesthesia, the urge to push may be muted, or even eliminated. This depends on the extent of the anesthesia produced by the block. Pushing can be accomplished without a strong physical urge, but usually requires some coaching, unless the epidural is allowed to wear off or made weaker.

With a first baby the duration of bearing down is often between half an hour and 1 hour, although it may last up to 2 hours, even longer. If contractions occur approximately every 3 minutes, the whole process takes between ten and forty effective contractions. The pushing stage is usually much shorter in a woman having a second or later baby.

Pushing—Doing What Comes Naturally!

When childbirth education classes became popular around the 1970s, their curriculum included a class or part of a class on pushing. Women were taught a very active pushing technique—the purpose of which was to shorten the second stage of labor. This was believed beneficial to the mother and baby. During that era, many physicians would intervene if the second stage was not completed within a set time limit, usually about 2 hours. After the woman pushed for this length of time, forceps or a vacuum extractor would be used to deliver the baby. In this scenario, active pushing made sense. The goal was to have as short a second stage as possible.

With active pushing, women were positioned with their heads raised, their arms pulling their legs up to their chests, their chins down. They were taught to hold their breath as soon as they felt the urge to push and to sustain each push, with breath held, for as long as possible. Many a labor room would resound with cheers. "Push, push, push," you'd hear if you walked by. Or somebody would be counting one to ten, to make sure the woman held her breath for 10 seconds.

While this kind of pushing certainly works, it can reduce the fetal oxygen supply. It also exhausts the mother. It makes her red in the face, sometimes bursting the small capillaries in her eyes, even in her facial skin.

Today, many physicians, nurses, midwives, and childbirth educators have moved away from encouraging women to push as hard and as long as possible. They are encouraging a more natural form of pushing, based on the body's own signals. These work quite well, except perhaps in the presence of epidural anesthesia.

More physiologic pushing allows the body to be the guide. Pushing doesn't necessarily start as soon as the examiner finds the cervix to be 10 centimeters, but waits until the woman feels the urge. The fetus will continue to descend without strong maternal efforts. The woman's work is needed mainly for the last part of descent.

Once the laboring woman feels the urge to push, she is encouraged to grunt with pushes, and take shorter, repetitive pushes with each contraction. This allows a greater blood flow through the placenta and conserves energy. It may take more time to push the baby out in this manner, but as long as the institution in which you are delivering does not have rigidly set time limits on the second stage of labor, this method works beautifully.

With physiologic pushing, the mother may assume any position that is comfortable. She may sit at a 45-degree angle, holding her legs toward her chest, if this feels good. She may kneel on her hands and knees, which is especially beneficial for a fetus in the posterior position. It will be more comfortable and will assist the fetus in its rotation. She can rest on her knees and hold onto the back of the bed. She can stand at the side of the bed, holding it for support, or hold onto her partner. If her leg muscles are strong enough, she can squat (remember, when women delivered in this position they also did a lot of their everyday work in this position). Side lying works well too, although you will need somebody— your partner, a doula, or the nurse or midwife working with you—to hold and support your upper leg. If your baby is posterior, the nurse or midwife may ask you to lie on one side or the other to assist in its rotation to an anterior position, which is somewhat easier for birth.

You may find that it is more comfortable for you to change positions during the pushing stage as the fetus descends. This is fine too, as long as the people working with you are flexible. If you need continuous electronic fetal monitoring, as described in the previous chapter, then your positions for pushing will be limited by the need to maintain a good fetal heart rate tracing. This may only be obtained if you are lying or sitting in bed. If you have epidural anesthesia you may also be limited to a side-lying or semi-upright position in bed.

Positions for Birthing

Just as you may be comfortable pushing in one position or another, so you may find that your body wants to assume a particular position for birth. The extent to which this is possible varies greatly. Institutional policy may dictate a particular position for birth, or at least require that you be in bed or on a delivery table. Some hospitals use special beds; see page 509. If a delivery table is used, you will be on your back, usually with legs in leg holders or stirrups. Few institutions continue to use straps on the leg holders. Tying down your wrists, thankfully, has been relegated to the past.

Your physician or midwife may be comfortable assisting your delivery only in one position, usually with you on your back, with head propped up and legs either in the stirrups or held against your chest. The side-lying position, which requires an assistant to hold your upper leg, is often preferred by midwives. It gives the birth attendant a good view of the birth, facilitating assessment of the perineum for its stretchability. When the birthing woman is on her side or in the hands and knees position, the bones of the pelvis move slightly so that there is more room for the baby to pass through them. These may be favorable positions for the woman who is carrying a large baby.

Discuss in advance with your physician or midwife whether or not she or he prefers a particular position for the delivery and whether there are any policies about this in the hospital. Home birth attendants generally are flexible about positioning, as is the staff at a birthing center.

The Birth of the Head

Shortly before the baby's head is born, it can be seen through the vaginal lips with pushing, but retreats back between contractions. With each push, more and more of the head becomes visible. Finally, the head *crowns*, does not recede again between contractions. As the head descends further and the vaginal opening enlarges with each bearing-down effort, more and more of the scalp is seen.

The head, in the OA position, flexed, with the chin on the baby's chest, begins to extend, as if the baby were trying to look up. The forehead comes over the perineum next. The extension continues with each push—the eyebrows are born, then the eyes and nose, and finally the mouth and chin. The greatest vaginal stretching is now over and the mother can take a brief breather as the head, released from the vagina, turns back to its earlier sideways position.

Up until crowning, you have been helped to push vigorously with contractions. Now, your physician or midwife wants to guide the head out of the birth canal, slowly and gently so your perineum will not tear or your episiotomy, if one was cut, will not extend. (See later.) You may be asked to stop pushing. Listen carefully to the directions given. Try to listen only to the midwife or physician or who is actually conducting the birth. Sometimes your support team or an overzealous nurse will tell you to push when actually the birth attendant would prefer that you not push.

The midwife or physician will place his or her hands on the baby's head and apply some counterpressure so that the head does not "pop." You may be asked for a gentle push with a contraction or a harder push between contractions. It is the birth attendant's decision whether to try to deliver the baby's head with or between a contraction. Sometimes, the head comes down easily; other times, it needs more help from your pushing. Some women grunt or even laugh and that pushes the baby out gently and slowly. Try, as much as possible, to focus on the directions your physician or midwife gives you.

It may be difficult to refrain from pushing when you feel the urge. Breathing rapidly may help at this time. All you can do is your best!

You usually will have a few moments or so after the head is born and before the next contraction. At this time, the physician or midwife who is attending your birth will wipe the baby's head as it loses a lot of body heat from its wet head. The attendant will check with his or her fingers to see if the baby's cord is around its neck. This is a quick and painless check.

If the cord is around the neck, several options are available. If it is extremely tight, the attendant will have to cut it, which means the rest of the birth will take place quickly as the baby has lost its oxygen supply. Most physicians and midwives prefer not to cut the cord, and if it is loose, as it usually is, it can be looped around the head. If it is not quite loose enough to fit over the head, but a finger can be placed between the cord and the neck, the physician or midwife often will choose to deliver the baby through the cord rather than cutting it. It can be slipped over

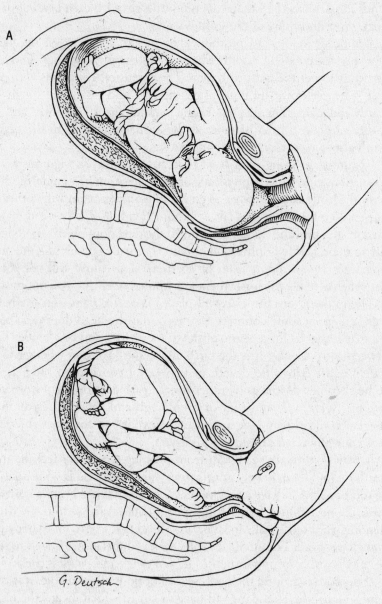

The second stage of labor. The mother is on her back, with her head to the left and her left leg in a raised position. The right half of the mother's body is transparent. The fetal head in A is well into the pelvis. The cervix is so thinned out and opened that it is continuous with the vagina, which is also opening. In B the largest part of the baby's head has been born, although its nose and mouth are not yet beyond the vagina.

the shoulders as the baby's body is born. If it is a bit too tight for this, the person delivering the baby can use a special technique called a *somersault maneuver*, which allows the baby to be born without the cord tightening around its neck. The cord can then be unwrapped. Exactly how to deliver the shoulders and body of a baby with a cord around the neck is a decision made quickly at the time of the birth, based on the preference and experience of the physician or midwife.

The pressure in the vagina on the baby's chest at this time usually squeezes some amniotic fluid out through the nose. Babies are ordinarily quite alert at this point. If meconium has been present in the amniotic fluid, efforts are made promptly to suck the meconium-laden material out of the baby's nose and throat. More discussion of meconium is in Chapters 21 and 22.

Even without meconium, many birth attendants will use a small bulb syringe for suctioning of the baby's mouth and nose after delivery of the head, assuming there is time before the next contraction. They may also use the bulb syringe to suction after the baby is born fully. Whether or not this is necessary is a source of some controversy. Most healthy babies are able to deal with the secretions that come into their throats from their lungs. Some staunch advocates of noninterventionist birth criticize suctioning as invasive, causing discomfort to the newborn. Suctioning can be quite gentle, however, need not be deep, and may help some babies breathe more easily.

The Birth of the Shoulders

Once the head is born, you will usually be asked to stop pushing until the next contraction occurs. During this time, the baby's head will restitute and externally rotate, as described in the box on pages 500–501. The midwife or physician may check to see that the shoulders are in the direct up-and-down (*anterior-posterior*) position before asking you to gently push again. Again, the shoulders may be delivered with a contraction or between contractions, depending on how easily they are coming and when they reach the proper position. The physician or midwife will help guide the shoulders out, first the top shoulder, then the bottom one, with their hands carefully on the baby's face. Once the shoulders are born, the body glides out with ease. This completes the second stage of labor.

Baby to Mom

More and more midwives and physicians have adopted the practice of handing the baby directly to the mother, laying it gently on her bare chest and placing a towel over it. There are studies indicating that if the baby is immediately placed in skin-to-skin contact with the mother, its loss of body temperature in the first half hour after birth is minimal. Skin-to-skin contact preserves heat better than wrapping the baby in towels or placing him or her in the air under an infrared warmer. Heat loss is further reduced if a stocking cap is placed on the baby's head. Many facilities supply such caps. Alternately, a warm towel can be used to cover the baby's head.

A healthy baby lying on the mother's chest, directly next to her heartbeat and in contact with her warm skin, remains quite tranquil. It will cry substantially less than babies who are tickled, rubbed, dried off, or otherwise stimulated. The baby will generally look around in the room and slowly but steadily start breathing. It will become pink more slowly than a stimulated newborn. The mother can nurse the baby at this time. A fair proportion of newborns will take to the breast and its colostrum with considerable vigor.

The Room for Birth

At home or in a birthing center, the labor, birth, and postpartum care takes place in the same room, the same bed. In hospitals, women traditionally have been transferred from the labor room to a delivery room for birth. After her labor bed is pushed to the delivery room, the woman has to move, in the midst of the pushing stage, from the bed to a narrow delivery table with a thin mattress. This move requires a delicate sense of timing on the part of nurses, midwives, or physicians so that the laboring woman is transferred neither too early nor too late.

Today, all out-of-hospital and in-hospital birthing centers as well as many regular hospital labor units have LDRs or LDRPs—*labor-delivery-recovery rooms* or *labor-delivery-recovery-postpartum rooms*. This means women give birth in the same room in which they have labored. An instrument table is ready in these rooms with items such as clamps for the cord, scissors with which to cut it, other scissors for a possible episiotomy, needle holders for repair of the episiotomy or laceration, syringes for drawing blood samples from the umbilical cord, and a variety of basins and towels. Women stay in the same bed for at least the first hour after birth. This hour is considered the *period of recovery* and is frequently called the *fourth stage of labor*. In the LDRP, the woman stays in the same room and bed for her entire stay—usually 12 to 48 hours.

A fully equipped delivery room is saved for those instances in which there is doubt about the normality of the delivery or if there is a likelihood that forceps or a vacuum extractor will be needed. If the baby needs resuscitation and this equipment is available only in the delivery room, the mother can often stay in the labor bed, which is wheeled to the delivery room.

Some birthing centers, in and out of the hospital, have rooms with beautiful wallpaper and furniture. There might be, for instance, a wooden rocking chair and cradle. The rooms may have special beds that can be converted into quasi-delivery tables with stirrups. This actually negates one of the values of delivering in a labor bed—that the bed does not get broken, your legs are not in stirrups, and the baby can be placed right on the bed at birth and then handed to you. Breaking the bed and using stirrups is convenient, however, for sewing should you need any stitches.

Neither the external appearance of a room nor an expensive bed makes a birth more natural or comfortable. The philosophy and attitudes of the personnel involved are far more important. When they are committed to birth as a normal, family experience, any room, no matter how small or large, how decorated or not, can be a warm and comforting place for a birth. Any bed will do. If the personnel are not invested in the philosophy that the human experience of birth is paramount, then the most highly decorated birthing rooms can be turned into sterile-feeling rooms, with every piece of electronic equipment moved in and all kinds of interventions employed—whether or not they are needed.

Although strict sterile technique is not used for deliveries in most birthing rooms or at home, in the delivery room sterility is usually maintained, as much as possible. An antibacterial cleansing solution is washed or sprayed over the area around the entrance to the vagina. These solutions are often cold. After this preparation, sterile drapes are placed over the legs, under the buttocks and over the abdomen so that only the skin around the entrance to the vagina is exposed. Even in LDRs, however, staff in hospitals and birthing centers today commonly practice what is known as *universal precautions* or *standard precautions*. This means that anybody working with blood or other bodily secretions protects his or her own body from the secretion. Therefore, many physicians and midwives will wear protective gear—gloves, gowns, masks, and goggles—during a birth. This is in case the mother is HIV-positive, perhaps even unbeknownst to her. This protection is called universal or standard because it applies to everyone. Universality prevents discrimination against persons who are known to be HIV-positive.

Wherever you deliver, if you are awake and alert, you can participate in your birth. You can, for example, reach down and feel the baby's head as it begins to crown. You can feel its progress as more and more of the head comes down with contractions. Since the only contamination that comes from this is with your own bacteria there is no reason to believe that this has anything to do with subsequent newborn infection. Sometimes, a woman will choose to watch the birth through a mirror, but this can be difficult in some birthing positions, and perhaps distracting.

Forceps deliveries, vacuum extractions, and cesarean births, of course, are performed in operating rooms under full sterile conditions (see Chapter 22).

Your Partner and Other Support Persons at Birth

For at least 40 years the baby's father has been welcome in the delivery room if the mother wishes him present. Today, lesbian partners are welcome as well. The experience of being present at the birth of one's own child is extraordinary. Whether or not you will be able to have other persons with you will depend on the policy of the facility where you deliver. Usually, birthing centers are quite flexible about who may be present—the limiting factor generally is your choice. Of course, at home, you make the policies.

On an extremely rare occasion, a partner or support person may become somewhat faint and require some assistance. Some partners or other support persons take photos or make videos, occasionally using elaborate equipment. The disadvantage of being behind the camera is that it takes the support person away from the birth and prevents him or her from providing needed support. Some hospitals prohibit video cameras from the delivery room, fearing their use as evidence should a lawsuit ensue. Of course, few births lead to lawsuits and if they do, one would hope that the video record would work in favor of the obstetrical staff, not against it. We do live in an age in which some practices unfortunately are dictated by the fear of legal action.

Siblings at Birth

Chapter 7 discussed having your other children with you during labor and birth. You will need to know the policy of the facility where you will deliver. You should also make certain your physician or midwife is comfortable with your decision. Find out in advance whether there is a possibility that a child will be made to feel unwelcome by any of the staff. Nobody appreciates surprises and you certainly don't want your child or children to be disappointed or hurt by anyone's reaction to their presence. We suggest you:

- **Individualize this decision.** Assess the age, maturity, usual behavior, and desire of your children before you decide to have them present for labor or birth.
- **Bring the child** or children to a special childbirth education class for siblings.
- **Have a care giver available** for the child or children. This person must be present throughout labor and birth (or you can use more than one person for relief). His or her only job should be attentiveness to the needs of the children. Neither you nor your support person or persons should feel responsible for any children during labor or birth.
- **Make sure your child or children understand** in advance that you have no expectations for them. They need not stay for the birth if they choose not to. You will not be disappointed with any choice they make. If they leave the room at the time of the birth, you can have them return right afterward so they can bond with their new sibling.

Leboyer Birth

In 1976, Frederick Leboyer, a French obstetrician, published *Birth Without Violence.* This slim volume created quite a stir in the obstetrics community. Leboyer's focus was on the psychological needs of the newborn which, he believed, could be best facilitated by altering dramatically the way births were performed. He advocated several specific changes:

- Dimming the lights for birth and after the birth
- Conducting the birth in silence or with only muted speech
- Keeping hands off the baby's head during birth
- Placing the baby on the mother's abdomen for a short while, waiting until the umbilical cord has stopped pulsating before cutting it
- Massaging the baby

He suggested placing the baby for a brief period into a warm bath, after which placing it on a warmed diaper and wrapping it in warm blankets, without its hands being restrained.

Advocates of a "Leboyer birth" believe that it eases the transition from the womb to the world, makes the baby happier, even brings a smile to the baby's face. Often the baby's father will do the Leboyer bath, increasing his overall involvement in the birth. Criticism of the Leboyer method is that it takes the baby away from the mother. Facilitating uninterrupted contact between mother and baby following birth is an equally baby-centered approach, allowing the infant to initiate bonding and breast-feeding as early as possible.

Water Birth

In recent years, there has been a movement for women to have their babies underwater. In a water birth, the mother is in a warm tub or pool. She is submerged at least from the waist down. The baby is born into the water. No part of the baby's body feels the air as it emerges.

Water birth has many of the same advantages as Leboyer birth. As the baby has been floating in an environment of water, being born into a similar environment might indeed be less stressful. Those who argue for water birth show photographs of babies smiling in the water. The mothers, too, are relaxed and feel less pain in warm water. A comfortable position for pushing can be assumed easily in water. Advocates say there is less tissue trauma to the mother and therefore less tearing of the vagina and perineum when the birth occurs in water.

The baby born into a tub of water will not drown as it will not attempt to breathe until it leaves the water. Therefore, the cord must not be cut while the baby is submerged. This way, the baby will continue to get oxygen through the cord blood. The baby must be taken out of the water immediately once the cord stops pulsating, so it can make the necessary adaptations for an existence in air. In general, the baby is taken out of the water once it is born fully, and given to the mother, just as it is in a bed delivery. This prevents the possibility that the cord will stop delivering oxygen while the baby is still in the water. The mother may continue to sit in the tub, holding the baby with its head above the water.

Whether or not a hospital will allow a water birth and whether it has facilities for this type of birth are important to find out in advance, if you are interested in having a water birth. You must also speak to your practitioner, as not all practitioners will conduct underwater births. Water birth is more likely to be practiced in a birthing center, or at home. Some birthing centers will allow you to bring your own portable tub or pool for a water birth. At home, you can use your own tub, or rent a larger tub or pool for several weeks around the time of your expected due date.

Organizations supporting water birth are listed in the Appendix. They can make referrals to companies that rent tubs or pools.

Episiotomy

Since the early part of the twentieth century, episiotomy has been a routine surgical procedure used in normal spontaneous vaginal deliveries. By the later part of the century, this surgical cut had become so commonplace that it was seen in the majority of vaginal deliveries. The rationales for cutting an episiotomy were that it prevented an irregular tear in the vagina and perineum and that it would preserve the muscular strength of the pelvic floor. In theory, episiotomy would help with healing and prevent women from having problems as they aged like *urinary incontinence* (involuntary loss of urine) or *uterine prolapse* (descent of the uterus due to muscle weakness, sometimes into the vagina or even through it).

Episiotomy is a cut in the vagina and perineum. It is performed when the birth is *imminent*—when it will occur within a few contractions. Because there is natural anesthesia to the perineal tissues as they are stretched for birth, the episiotomy can be cut at the height of a contraction without anesthesia. Most often, however, local anesthesia is injected into the area, similar to the way it is injected into the mouth for dental work. Alternatively, a *nerve block* can be used. This is called a *pudendal block* because the pudendal nerve innervates the vaginal and perineal areas. These forms of anesthesia are discussed in a later section of this chapter.

The research that has been done on episiotomy has not supported its purported advantages. Pelvic floor relaxation, in fact, seems to occur more frequently with episiotomy than it does without episiotomy. Nor does episiotomy reduce the trauma to the muscles and tissues of the vagina and perineum. Lacerations or tears into the rectum occur more frequently when an episiotomy is cut than when it is not.

Although an episiotomy is a straight cut made with a scissors, many practitioners find that if they do not cut an episiotomy and a laceration results, it is less deep or extensive than the cut made with the scissors. An episiotomy is cut into several layers of tissue—the *mucus membrane* (or mucosa) of the vagina, the *fascia* or tissue that is under the mucosa, the skin of the perineum, two underneath sections called the *subcutaneous* and *subcuticular layers* (Latin: *sub* = under; *cutis* = skin); as well as a layer of deep muscles. Most tears are much less likely than an episiotomy to extend into the deep muscles. Even though a tear may be more jagged at its edges, the tissues of the vagina and perineum are not difficult to repair.

An episiotomy may have other side effects. If it is cut too early, it may cause undue blood loss. It is extremely uncomfortable during the healing process. A *mediolateral episiotomy*—one that extends diagonally from the vaginal opening—is especially painful and takes a long time to heal as it cuts right through the belly of the muscle, which is the muscle's strongest part. A mediolateral episiotomy is less likely to result in an extension into the anus or rectum, but is more difficult to repair and more often leads to future problems such as pain with intercourse. It may be the episiotomy of choice for some practitioners for a forceps delivery or in anticipation of *shoulder dystocia*—difficulty delivering the shoulders—but many practitioners do not use mediolateral episiotomies at all.

Today, many practitioners do not routinely cut episiotomies. They will cut them when there is a need. Some physicians and midwives believe a need exists when the tissues of the vagina and perineum appear to be stretching with difficulty or seem ready to tear. These practitioners prefer cutting an episiotomy to risking a tear. A tear is imminent when marks similar to stretch marks are noted on the perineum. Other physicians and midwives allow tears to occur, using techniques to try to prevent them or keep them to a minimum.

Perineal preserving techniques include use of warm water or oil compresses or massage during the pushing stage and support of the perineum with the birth of the head. Support means that one hand, which is not assisting with the delivery, be used to push the stretched tissues toward each other, causing the perineal tautness to relax a bit. Whether this actually helps is not proven. Other practitioners believe in a hands-off approach. Their feeling is that any touch to the perineum weakens the integrity of its tissues and increases the likelihood of a tear. The best way to maintain an *intact perineum*—one that doesn't tear—is not universally agreed upon. These issues are sorely in need of research.

Your physician, midwife, or childbirth educator may instruct you to practice *perineal massage* during the last weeks of pregnancy. You can do this yourself or ask your partner to do it for you. You use your thumb or fingers. With some vitamin E oil (taken directly from a vitamin tablet, pricked with a pin) or other oil, the tissues are gently stretched. The massage is directed downward at the vaginal entrance with a side-to-side motion for several minutes each night. Again, the extent to which this actually preserves the integrity of the perineum is unknown.

There are some reasons to cut an episiotomy other than prevention of a tear. If the fetus is showing signs of distress, such as a slowed heartbeat, and is almost delivered, an episiotomy often can speed the birth by several contractions and may thus be beneficial to the newborn. If the baby is large and the physician or midwife is concerned about shoulder dystocia (see Chapter 21), having cut an episiotomy gives the birth attendant more room to manipulate the fetus and correct the problem. An episiotomy can be cut at the time the shoulder dystocia is recognized, but it is more difficult to cut at that point because the head has already delivered. Some practitioners will cut a mediolateral or diagonal episiotomy for shoulder dystocia. This gives the birth attendant more room to manipulate the fetus to deliver the shoulders. Other practitioners will risk an extension into the anus or rectum, called a third-degree or fourth-degree tear, believing that the mucus membranes of the anus and rectum heal more readily than the belly of the muscle that is cut with a mediolateral episiotomy.

A frequently cited reason for episiotomy is to prevent trauma to the fetal head when the baby is premature. In a review of the research on episiotomy, published in 1995, Robert J. Woolley found no evidence of this preventive effect. In fact, Dr. Woolley found no conclusive research evidence to justify cutting an episiotomy to protect the fetus in any situation.

Discussing the subject of episiotomy with your care provider in advance of the birth is always a good idea. Find out whether or not your physician or midwife believes in routine episiotomies or will make the decision based on an evaluation of the situation at the time of birth. If they will cut only when needed, find out what situations they consider to represent *need*—the possibility of a tear or only fetal indications as noted above. If they do use episiotomy liberally, find out if they cut *median* (straight down) or *mediolateral* (diagonal) episiotomies and why. You should be comfortable with the philosophy and practice of the physician or midwife you have chosen.

Anesthesia for Vaginal Birth

A normal vaginal birth does not require an anesthetic for the safety of either the mother or the fetus. The final passage of the baby through the vagina, a structure that readily expands to accommodate it, is not the cause of second stage pain. As the presenting part descends through the pelvis, the tissues and muscles composing the pelvic floor are stretched, producing a tearing sensation and sometimes actual tears. This is most striking in first deliveries, but may recur in later births, especially if the mother has had an episiotomy or repair of a tear in the past. For some women, the stretching is frightening and extremely painful. Other women, however, find pushing a relief after the pains of contractions.

The area at the entrance to the vagina can be anesthetized readily by nerve-blocking agents injected locally. These can either be placed in the tissues of the perineum or injected along the side of the pelvis at the point where the nerves that serve this area pass. The latter technique is called a *pudendal block* because the anesthetic agent is placed in the vicinity of the pudendal nerve. This nerve and its branches supply the entire vaginal, vulvar, rectal, and perineal areas. With a pudendal block, the injection is made from within the vagina.

When either a local or a pudendal block is put in place, there is a loss of local pain sensation but usually no loss of the normal bearing-down reflex. Neither technique has any effect on the contractions. Neither provides relief for the pain of contractions.

Local anesthesia is used for cutting an episiotomy or repairing the cut or a tear. The pudendal block can be used for cutting and repairing. It also may help those few women who find pushing difficult to bear. A pudendal block can be used for deliveries done with forceps or a vacuum extractor.

When anesthesia is used to cut an episiotomy, the anesthesia is injected before the baby's birth. Local anesthesia is injected during a contraction when the tissues are most thinned out by the pressure of the fetus. Pudendal anesthesia is injected between contractions, when the physician or midwife has the most room to put hands and a needle into the vagina to reach the pudendal nerve.

Although a pudendal block has two major advantages—it anesthetizes a large area and does not cause tissue swelling—it is more difficult to administer and takes more time. A local can be administered when the baby's head is lower down in the pelvis, so if the physician or midwife decides just before the birth to cut an episiotomy, he or she usually will choose local anesthesia.

You ordinarily will feel some pressure during the administration of a pudendal block and a pin prick at the time of injection of a local anesthetic. The anesthetic itself may cause some burning as it is injected, but soon afterward you will be numb.

On occasion, a pudendal block will be ineffective and local anesthesia will be needed as well. A few minutes after the pudendal block is administered, your physician or midwife will test the area for numbness and may ask if you feel certain sensations. If you do, the local may then be injected. As long as the physician or midwife has not used an excessive amount of local anesthetic in the pudendal block, you can have a local anesthetic infused safely.

Care is taken with either technique not to inject the medication into a blood vessel as this will cause a severe reaction, including difficulty breathing and convulsions. If this occurs, you first feel light-headed, dizzy, ringing in the ears, a metallic taste, or numbness in the tongue and mouth. Let your physician or midwife know if you have any of these feelings. An allergic reaction also is possible. Since the local nerve-blocking agents are similar to those used in the dentist's office, tell your midwife or physician if you have ever had an allergic reaction to novocaine. Usually, 1 percent lidocaine (brand name, Xylocaine) is used for local or pudendal anesthesia. It is a quick-acting local anesthetic, but its duration of action is relatively short, so the numbness will not last past the birth and time of repair.

When these medications are given before the birth, they can reach the fetus. In the small doses that are used, they almost never cause fetal problems. There may be fetal distress if the medication inadvertently gets directly into the mother's blood vessels or if too much is given in error.

If you have had epidural anesthesia for labor, this will provide pain relief for an episiotomy, if necessary, and repair. You will not need local or pudendal anesthesia.

Cord Clamping

The issue of cord clamping has entered the area of obstetrical controversy in recent years. Some people believe in clamping the cord almost immediately after birth. Other physicians and midwives wait a few minutes and still others wait until the cord stops pulsating before cutting it. The best time for cord clamping is an unresolved issue, although the newest research suggests that there are more benefits than drawbacks to delayed cord clamping.

Allowing the cord to stop pulsating before it is cut gives the baby extra blood from the placenta. One advantage of extra blood is prevention of anemia, with more red blood cells going to the vital organs of the baby. A recent study has shown that delayed cord clamping may be beneficial for premature babies by helping in the adaptation of their heart and lungs to life outside the uterus. The main disadvantage of this extra blood for both full-term and preterm babies is that it increases the number of red blood cells that are naturally destroyed, burdening the baby's immature liver. This can lead to *hyperbilirubinemia*—a potentially dangerous excess of bilirubin in the blood. Bilirubin is the chemical released when the red blood cells are destroyed. With an immature liver, it cannot be cleared properly from the body. Its buildup, if allowed to continue, ultimately can cause brain damage. Another potentially dangerous consequence of delayed cord clamping is *polycythemia*—the condition of having too many blood cells (Greek: *polys* = many; *kytos* = a hollow; *haima* = blood). Unfortunately, it isn't possible to tell which babies will benefit from the extra blood and which will have difficulty handling it.

Early cord clamping is often done when a baby needs resuscitation. Clamping the cord allows the baby to be given to the pediatrician or neonatal nurse practitioner for whatever measures are necessary when the baby is premature, has difficulty breathing at birth, or has thick meconium. Another reason is to collect cord blood for *cord blood analysis*, routinely done in most births, or *cord blood banking* (see below). If indeed further research reveals that delayed cord clamping is truly advantageous, then perhaps ways to perform resuscitative efforts before the cord is clamped should be investigated. Cord blood can be collected even with delayed cord clamping, although it may be more difficult to obtain.

When the cord is cut, two clamps are placed on the cord. The cord is cut between them. The clamps prevent the cord from bleeding when it is cut. The cut separates the baby from the placenta, from the mother. It is a very important symbolic gesture and today many cords are cut by the father of the baby or the mother's significant other. The clamps generally are placed by the physician or midwife, who will hand the scissors to the person who is to cut the cord. It is a simple cut, hurting neither mother nor baby as the cord has no nerve endings. To the baby's father or other member of the family or mother's community, cutting the cord can be an unforgettable ritual and bond.

The clamp on the cord, usually a plastic disposable one, is removed with a special clamp remover when the baby is a few days old. The cord itself will dry up and fall off on about the fourth or fifth day of life. The cord needs no care, unless you notice discharge with pus or an odor. Using a little hydrogen peroxide on any discharge or secretion almost always will clear up the problem. Some people prefer to use the herb goldenseal. If discharge or odor persists, a phone call to your pediatrician or the baby's care provider is in order.

Cord Blood Banking

Storing blood from the umbilical cord for possible use in the treatment of certain diseases has gained recent popularity. Cord blood contains special cells that are not found in adult blood. These are called *stem cells* and are the same as those in bone marrow. The job of these cells is to make new blood and immune system cells. Bone marrow transplant is used in the treatment of leukemia and other cancers, certain immune disorders, and some genetic diseases. Since 1988, cord blood cells have been used instead of bone marrow in transplants. The advantages of cord blood over bone marrow are that it is readily available, especially for persons from ethnic minorities for whom bone marrow donors have been difficult to locate; there is less risk of infection developing; and fewer side effects occur.

Cord blood banking is a relatively simple procedure. It does not hurt the newborn in any way. It involves collecting the blood from the umbilical cord and shipping it to a special laboratory where it is tested, processed, and banked. It is not known exactly how long the cells will last, but with proper freezing, they could last for at least 10 years, maybe indefinitely.

Cord blood may be used to treat diseases in a relative of the newborn. If a child has one of these diseases, there is a 1 in 4 chance that his or her newborn sibling will have compatible cells. In such families, cord blood can be privately banked and utilized for the ill child. In some situations, the cells might be used to treat the newborn himself or herself. Estimates of the child needing to use his or her own cord blood run from 1 in 1,000 to 1 in 200,000. Even if the child were to develop a disease for which cord blood might be a treatment, the disease could be in the cord blood, making the cells unusable for treatment.

In families without a known member with leukemia or another disease amenable to this treatment, the likelihood that someday a family member would develop such a disease is probably no more than 1 in 10,000. If there is a family history of childhood leukemia or other diseases for which cord blood might be used, the possibility that the infant's cord blood would be needed someday for a family member is increased, but still not great. Parents with neither a relative requiring treatment nor a family history of a disease treatable by transplant should consider the remoteness of the possibility that their baby's cells will be needed in their own family and decide whether this justifies the financial expense. Private cord blood banking usually carries a one-time cost as well as a yearly storage fee.

Some parents choose to donate cord blood. When cord blood is donated, you are asked to give up rights to the blood. Donated cord blood can be used to treat anybody for whom it is compatible. The American Academy of Pediatrics recommends donating cord blood unless there is a family member with a "current or potential need" for a stem cell transplant. It has been suggested that families maintain contact with the blood bank should a family member develop a treatable condition. There is no fee to donate cord blood. Discuss this with your physician or midwife in advance of the birth as the banking must be planned.

AFTER THE BABY IS BORN

Evaluation of the Infant's Condition at Birth

A fetus inside the uterus is actually blue when it is in what could be called the pink of condition. Although the delivery of oxygen to the fetus's tissues is adequate, the amount of oxygen in each red blood cell is low and the blood therefore looks dark. Oxygen is delivered in a great number of separate containers (the red blood cells), of which the fetus has an abundance. Each is only about two-thirds full. This explains why it is normal for a baby to have a blue color at birth. *Fetal pallor* (paleness), however, is a danger sign, because it indicates failure of the circulation or a loss of blood.

A scoring system that nicely describes the condition of the newborn was developed in the 1950s by Dr. Virginia Apgar, an anesthesiologist at Columbia Presbyterian Hospital in New York. One of the elements in the Apgar score is the color of the baby. Newborns are always blue at one minute after birth, and many are still blue at 5 minutes if they are handled gently. Color in Dr. Apgar's system, therefore, does not correlate very well with the baby's actual condition.

APGAR SCORING SYSTEM			
Score	0	I	2
Heart Rate	Absent	Below 100/minute	Over 100/minute
Respiratory Rate	Absent	Slow, irregular	Good, crying
Muscle tone	Flaccid	Some flexion of extremities or movement	Active motion, well flexed
Cry (Reflex Irritability)	Absent	Grimace	Vigorous cry
Color	Deep blue, pale	Body pink, extremities blue	Pink all over

The baby is observed and the Apgar score at 1 minute and 5 minutes of age are recorded by the physician, midwife, or nurse. A score of 3 or less indicates that the baby is in poor condition with its life in jeopardy. Resuscitation must be immediate. A score of 7, 8, 9, or 10 indicates that the baby is in excellent condition. If the baby's 5-minute Apgar score is low, a 10-minute Apgar score may be recorded as well.

Babies who have very low 1-minute Apgars but who are given prompt attention and have normal Apgars at 5 minutes seldom show evidence of any damage later in life. In the absence of a complication such as low birth weight, low Apgar scores, while they indicate the need for immediate resuscitation, are not strongly correlated with future neurological damage.

In today's highly competitive world, where toddler tutoring for admission to kindergarten is advertised in parenting magazines, some anxious parents view the Apgar score as the child's first standardized test. It is really only an indication of whether or not the newborn needs immediate help and should not be overinterpreted. Nobody has ever been denied admission to an Ivy League college because of Apgar score!

If the newborn needs resuscitation, this is done by the most experienced person present. Prudent management calls for anticipation of difficulty by having trained people on hand who can give the baby skilled care as early as possible.

Modern delivery rooms are equipped with suction devices to assist in sucking mucus, amniotic fluid, and meconium from the newborn's nose, throat, larynx, and trachea. Oxygen is available for continuous or interrupted administration under positive pressure. Tubes to be passed down into the baby's trachea are on hand in the event it becomes necessary to intubate for resuscitation. The baby is placed where it can be kept warm. This can be done with overhead heaters that radiate heat down toward the baby without interfering with the work of the medical personnel doing the emergency care.

If there is reason to think that the administration of narcotics (such as meperidine or Demerol) to the mother during labor plays a role in depressing a newborn baby's ability to breathe, the child can be given naloxone (trade name: Narcan), a narcotic antagonist. Vigorous slapping, immersing the baby in ice water, dangling it by the feet, and similar measures are no particular help, and may be harmful. Patience, imperturbability, and gentleness will resuscitate more babies than all the strenuous methods combined. Of course, few babies need any of this assistance.

Tending to the Baby

As soon as the baby is born, it can be given to the mother, who can survey it and satisfy herself that it is normal. Most mothers will react similarly when they receive their new babies. They will hold the baby *en face*—which is exactly what it sounds like: a position in which mother and baby are gazing into each other's faces. Mothers naturally will explore the baby's body.

Right after this, the professionals make their own inspection for abnormalities not immediately visible to the untrained eye. It is rare, however, to find any such problem in babies who act normally in the newborn period. At some later time, in a hospital, the newborn is taken to the nursery. There the baby has an extensive, meticulous examination by a member of the pediatric staff. In the overwhelming proportion of cases the baby gets a completely clean bill of health. This is promptly communicated to the mother.

In some hospitals, the baby is kept at the mother's bedside. This is called *rooming-in*. Some facilities have 24-hour complete rooming-in. Babies born in these hospitals may never see the newborn nursery. The physical examination is performed right at the mother's bedside. Other hospitals have more limited rooming-in. In some hospitals, the baby will visit the newborn nursery at least once after birth for its physical examination and to be admitted as a "patient." The baby's father or the mother's support person or partner may be able to accompany the baby on this trip and be present for the physical examination. Check out in advance what the routine is and be sure you are comfortable with it. Some prospective parents choose a physician or midwife based on the policies regarding newborn care at the hospital with which the practitioner is affiliated. In a birthing center or at home, mother and baby are rarely separated. All care is done at the bedside.

If you have a home or birthing center birth, you will need to have a pediatrician, family doctor, or pediatric nurse practitioner who will see your newborn within a few days after birth. A few practitioners still make home visits, but most likely you will bring the infant to their office. Chapter 24 discusses the newborn in greater detail.

Treatment of the Eyes

A small amount of antibiotic solution or ointment ordinarily is put into each eye of the baby. It is a preventive against infections, such as gonorrhea or chlamydia, that are acquired during passage through the vagina. Each of these is a sexually transmitted infection (STI). State law requires this medication be given to all newborns. If parents do not wish their newborn to receive the medication, they must sign a statement waiving the treatment. If you request that medication not be given, you must be sure that you have tested negative for these STIs in pregnancy and that neither you nor your partner has risks for these infections. This means you should both be sexually monogamous. You must also check whether the law in your state allows for you to refuse the medication.

Erythromycin ointment is the most commonly chosen medication for preventive treatment of the newborn's eyes. *Tetracycline ointment* or silver nitrate drops are also effective treatments. Silver nitrate was the earliest medication used, but because it can be irritating to the eyes, the ointments are used more frequently today. These ointments work quite well against infection caused by gonorrhea, but less well against infection caused by chlamydia. Unfortunately, if the medication is given right after birth, it might interfere somewhat with infant-mother bonding. If treatment is deferred for an hour or so, the initial bonding period proceeds without interruption. As babies are alert right after birth, and can see their immediate environment, but will fall asleep shortly afterward, it makes sense to postpone the eye treatment until right before the expected sleep period.

Vitamin K

Another preventive treatment given within 1 hour after birth is vitamin K. Vitamin K is necessary for proper blood clotting. It is made from bacteria in the colon. Babies are born without these bacteria so they cannot make the vitamin K.

A small number of newborns will develop a serious bleeding disorder if they do not receive vitamin K. This disease, *hemorrhagic disease of the newborn* or HDN, can be mild or serious. In its serious form, it can result in bleeding into the brain, causing permanent brain damage or even death. Although certain risk factors for developing HDN can be identified, these do not account for all cases. Risks include use of certain medications by the mother, antibiotic use in the newborn, prematurity, and low birth weight. The implicated maternal medications are *anticonvulsants* (to treat epilepsy or other seizure disorders); *anticoagulants* (blood thinners such as Coumadin); and *antituberculosis* medicines.

Vitamin K is given to all newborns as it is not possible to know which ones will develop HDN. The vitamin usually is given as an injection into the muscle in the baby's thigh.

Giving an injection to a newborn is objectionable to some parents. These parents are concerned about the pain inflicted. Other objections to intramuscular vitamin K have been raised as well. In the early 1990s, a study reported that injectable vitamin K was associated with the development of leukemia in childhood. This study looked at women who delivered in 1970 in Great Britain. Several later studies examined the same issue and most did not support the finding of this increased risk for leukemia. Another issue is that large doses of the vitamin may be associated with newborn hyperbilirubinemia. This problem is not seen, however, with the 1 mg dose usually given.

Because of the issues surrounding the intramuscular use of vitamin K, researchers have investigated the possibility of giving vitamin K by mouth. Unfortunately, oral vitamin K does not seem to work as well. There is always the question with a newborn of whether or not he or she has received an adequate oral dose. The oral dose may not be well absorbed. The effects of oral vitamin K do not last as long as those of the intramuscular preparation.

There are several types of HDN, differentiated in part by when they appear. Early HDN appears within the first 24 hours of life. Classical HDN shows up at 2 to 5 days, and late HDN is seen anytime between 1 and 12 weeks of life. Intramuscular vitamin K protects against each of these types of HDN, but oral vitamin K is only protective against all three types of HDN if it is given in several repeated doses. The first dose is given at birth, the second between 3 and 5 days after birth, and the last dose given in the fourth week of life. If the baby is formula fed, the last dose may be omitted as formula-fed babies rarely develop late HDN.

Since all babies are now treated routinely with vitamin K, the number of cases that would occur without treatment is not completely known. In the 1950s, before the preventive treatment was used, approximately 4 per 1,000 babies developed HDN if they were fully breast-fed. Late HDN would occur in 1 in 17,000 babies without preventive treatment. A single intramuscular dose of 1 mg of vitamin K lowers the number of cases of late HDN to 1 in 400,000. A single oral dose at birth lowers the number of cases of late HDN to about 1 in 25,000 to 1 in 70,000 babies. Repeated oral doses may be close in effectiveness to the single intramuscular dose.

All babies with risk factors should receive the intramuscular dose of vitamin K at birth. The American Academy of Pediatrics recommends an intramuscular dose of 0.5 to 1 mg for all newborns—those with risks for HDN and those without risks—depending on newborn weight. This is standard in most hospitals and birthing centers. In fact, most states have laws mandating an injection of vitamin K within an hour of birth. If you have concerns about your baby receiving an injection, this is something to discuss with your physician or midwife. Your newborn may be able to receive an oral dose, but the law may not allow you to refuse the treatment completely.

Identification of the Newborn

Before the newborn leaves the delivery room in most hospitals, it is footprinted with washable ink. The footprints are placed on the same sheet of paper as the mother's thumb print. An extra copy of the footprint sheet can be made as a keepsake for parents.

An identifying band is placed on the mother's wrist and a duplicate of the band is placed around the baby's ankle. Another copy of the same band may be attached to the mother's chart.

Some hospitals have infant LoJack systems. An identifying bracelet is placed on the newborn's ankle. If this is removed improperly or tampered with, or if the baby is taken through an exit door, an alarm will go off. In addition, many hospitals have security cameras at all doorways.

THE THIRD STAGE OF LABOR: BIRTH OF THE PLACENTA

After the baby is born, the placenta must be delivered. Before birth, it is attached firmly to the uterus over an area about eight inches in diameter. At the end of the second stage of labor, the elastic uterus retracts and becomes much smaller, since it is no longer ballooned out by the fetus. After resting for a few minutes following its strenuous work, the uterus begins to contract again. The placenta, by contrast, is spongy noncontractible tissue. With the contractions of the emptied uterus, the size of the area to which the placenta is attached diminishes rapidly. Since the placenta cannot contract nor reduce in size, it is forced to buckle away from the shrinking uterine wall. With additional contractions, the uterus squeezes the free placenta downward into the vagina.

Once the placenta has separated, the mother is able to push it out of her vagina simply by further bearing down. You shouldn't push, however, until your physician or midwife has ascertained that the placenta is separated completely from the uterus. Signs of separation include a sudden gush of blood, a change in the shape of the uterus, or a lengthening of the cord. The physician or midwife may press in a upward motion on the uterus to see if the cord retracts. *Retraction* means the placenta is not separated or incompletely separated.

There is no need to hurry the birth of the placenta in the absence of bleeding. When your physician or midwife is certain that the placenta is ready to be born, she or he will ask you to bear down. At the same time, the physician or midwife will *guard* the uterus—place a hand on the abdomen against the lower uterine wall. This prevents the uterus from *inverting*—or turning inside out. Your attendant may also assist your bearing down effort with gentle traction on the umbilical cord. The natural birth of the placenta is quite painless.

If the placenta takes longer than usual to separate, a number of natural measures can be tried to assist in the separation. You can nurse the baby. This releases oxytocin, which also stimulates uterine contractions. If you are not planning to nurse your baby, or the baby needs some help from a pediatrician, you can rub your nipples. This has the same effect. Sometimes changing your position helps. You can even try walking, if you feel up to it and the place where you are delivering will allow you to get out of bed during the third stage.

Shortly after the birth of the placenta, the physician or midwife will examine it carefully to see that it delivered completely. A placenta is formed by the fusion of twenty or so pieces called *cotyledons*. Each is actually a small placenta, a complete circulatory unit. The placenta is like a mosaic of smooth, even tiles, crowded compactly together. If the mosaic is complete the placenta most likely has been born intact. If one or more of the cotyledons is missing, it may be necessary to perform a manual exploration of the uterus to see if there are any pieces left inside. This is done with the fingers, wearing long sterile gloves, called *gauntlet gloves*. The bladder must be empty. Usually, after a manual exploration or placental removal, you are treated with antibiotics to prevent infection and with oxytocin to help the uterus contract. Manual removal is uncomfortable. If you are not actively bleeding, you can receive pain medication to make the procedure more tolerable. If it is an emergency (see Chapter 21), then it may have to be done before you can receive adequate medication. This is a painful, but lifesaving, procedure.

At the site where the placenta was attached, pencil-thick blood vessels are torn across. Women do not ordinarily bleed from this wound because the uterus is specifically constructed to meet the situation. Its muscle fibers run *crisscross*, that is, they interlace with the blood vessels running in the spaces between. It is like fitting the fingers of one hand between the fingers of the other. When the fingers are loosely fitted and held before the window, light comes through the web; but if they are tightly fitted, not even the tiniest beam filters past. In the same way as the light, the blood vessels of the placental site are shut off, the walls of the vessels squeezed together by the tightly contracted, interwoven muscle bundles surrounding them on all sides.

To prevent bleeding, the uterus must remain firmly contracted after the birth of the placenta. If the uterus does not contract well, it can be helped by gentle external massage. Nursing the baby, which results in the release of oxytocin from the pituitary, will assist in uterine contraction. If, after these measures, the uterus continues to relax and bleed, the woman can be given either oxytocin or ergonovine. The latter drug has been synthesized in the laboratory in the form of methylergonovine (Methergine). Either of these drugs, given into intravenous fluids or injected into a muscle, stimulates powerful uterine contraction often uncomfortable or painful. Methergine cannot be given with increased blood pressure, so a nurse always will check your pressure before this drug is given.

In addition to these drugs, a prostaglandin compound, 15-methyl prostaglandin, also produces well-sustained uterine contractions and can stem a serious hemorrhage.

The blood loss at delivery may be virtually nil but can be as much as several quarts. Since women have a markedly expanded blood volume at term, they often can tolerate a blood loss of over a quart (about 1,000 cc) without suffering much more than an increase in pulse rate. So massive a sudden blood loss would throw a nonpregnant adult into shock. However, when blood loss after childbirth is more than this and the volume amounts to a hemorrhage, the attendants have to take steps to stop the bleeding. These are discussed in Chapters 21 and 25. Postpartum hemorrhage has considerably decreased, largely because we are no longer anesthetizing women for delivery with drugs like ether and chloroform, which cause relaxation of the uterus and thereby weaken the contractions that would stop the bleeding.

Repair of the Vagina and the Perineum

Repair of an episiotomy or a perineal laceration can be carried out either in the delivery room or in the labor bed. This is done with fine absorbable sutures, composed either of catgut or of synthetics. The sutures are all buried in the tissues and there is no need to remove them. They are absorbed over a short time with little or no residual scarring. If you look at your perineum with a mirror as soon as 24 hours after the birth, you will be pleased to see only a thin line where you have had stitches.

Most physicians and midwives sew episiotomies with continuous lengths of suture material that comes already attached to the needle and need not be threaded through an eye. The repair is made at more than one level of tissue; how often the needle goes in and out depends upon the length and depth of the laceration or episiotomy. The number of "bites" taken with the needle generally is not counted. You usually won't be able to get an exact answer to the question, "How many stitches did I have?"

THE FOURTH STAGE OF LABOR: IMMEDIATE POSTDELIVERY CARE OF THE MOTHER

The mother who has delivered with local or pudendal block anesthesia or with no anesthetic can go immediately to the recovery room, accompanied by the baby and the mother's partner. Nowadays, if she delivered in the labor room, she may well remain there for recovery and even her entire postpartum stay.

Women who deliver without having received any pain relief medication may experience shaking chills. They start several minutes after delivery and may last for as much as half an hour. We do not know their cause. We do know that they are harmless, although very unsettling. The best guess is that, since the fetus is a heat producer, the mother reacts to losing that source of heat much as she would the removal of an electric blanket in a chilly room. Warm blankets are the ideal treatment for postpartum chills.

During the first hours after birth, staff check the mother's pulse and blood pressure frequently and observe her carefully for evidence of bleeding. The most significant immediate danger to a newly delivered woman is hemorrhage. Nine times out of ten this bleeding is from the uterus and is due to its failure to continue to contract adequately. After a difficult delivery, there may be unrecognized lacerations. If bleeding continues despite the fact that the uterus remains firm, further investigation must be undertaken promptly to find out whether such a laceration is present. The relaxed uterus, as mentioned above, can be treated medically; lacerations require meticulous surgical repair.

The length of time the mother is kept under observation in the recovery room depends upon whether the labor and delivery have been uneventful and the recovery from anesthesia smooth. If an epidural anesthetic has been employed, the woman is ordinarily not transferred until any aftereffects have worn off completely. Women who have been delivered in the labor bed without anesthesia are perfectly able to be up and about within the next few minutes, and require only a brief stay in a recovery room, if at all. If you will be transferred to a postpartum unit, hospital routine may call for you to make the journey on wheels, either in a recovery-room bed or a wheelchair.

In the 1940s, all women were required to stay in bed for the first 7 days after delivery, no matter how healthy they were. After so long a stay in bed, they practically had to relearn how to walk without losing their balance. But a dramatic lesson was learned from the experience of evacuating maternity wards during air raids in World War II. These were life-threatening emergencies, and, with a need to hurry and a shortage of wheeled equipment and of personnel, hospital staffs made the decision that healthy women should walk out of the wards, so that the available equipment could be reserved for the more disabled. To everyone's surprise, those who got up and walked did better in the recovery period than did women, equally healthy, who had spent the first 7 postpartum days in bed.

The lesson has not been lost. We now take it for granted that a woman who has had a normal birth can get up and walk away from the delivery room or labor bed, without suffering any ill effects; indeed, it may be beneficial. This is not to say that you may not be tired after being in labor and may much prefer to lie down and be waited upon.

CHAPTER TWENTY

⚬⚬⚬

Care and Support
During Labor and Birth

All laboring women are entitled to care and support throughout labor. Scientific study has borne out what childbirth educators have known for years: the presence of a supportive companion has beneficial effects on labor. This chapter discusses the physical and emotional care that laboring women need. It outlines the monitoring you should expect from the obstetrical staff, whether you deliver at home, in a birthing center, or in a hospital. The latter half of the chapter is devoted to pain relief in labor.

PREPARATIONS FOR THE BIRTH

Visit in Advance

If you are delivering in a hospital you should arrange to visit it before your expected due date. If you take childbirth education classes at the hospital, a visit will be part of the series of classes. Otherwise, you will need to make special arrangements. Speak to your physician or midwife or call the hospital's obstetrics unit or the patient education department, if there is one.

If you will be driving to a hospital or birthing center, learn the route and traffic patterns. Find out where to park. Some facilities have round-the-clock parking, whereas others expect you to rely on street parking. You should investigate where the nighttime, weekend, and emergency entrances are located and get some idea of the relationship of these places to the portion of the hospital set aside for labor and delivery. In a hospital, find out whether the security personnel at the entrance will be able to help you if you arrive at an inconvenient hour. It is possible to arrive at a large hospital in the middle of the night and at first find no one who can help you.

You might want to set aside a small overnight bag or a backpack into which you have placed the comfort items that you will want to have in the hospital or birthing center after you deliver. These include toiletries, warm socks to wear during the delivery, a nightgown and robe, slippers, and one or two nursing bras. Remember, you will likely still need your maternity clothes in the early postpartum period. You might want a book or magazine although you will likely find that you have little time or energy to read. Light and easy reading material is best. You probably will want to shower and shampoo as soon as you are comfortable after delivery. You may want a hair dryer and other personal items you are accustomed to using. Check first to make sure the hospital where you will give birth allows electronic devices to be brought from home. Some hospitals now have hair dryers installed in bathrooms, like in hotels.

Some women feel more at ease with their own bed linen. Some hospitals will not make any objection to your bringing pillows, pillow cases, and sheets, which you can use while you are in labor and in your room after delivery. Others have strict policies against outside linen. Find out the policy before labor to avoid carrying unnecessary items. An extra pillow may be all that is permitted. Bed items will become soiled and therefore should be readily washable. (Hydrogen peroxide removes blood very well. Make sure you have some on hand for a home birth.) Remember, in a birthing center, you will likely go home within 12 hours and in the hospital within 48 hours after your baby's birth. Unless you have unexpected complications or a cesarean delivery, you will spend only 1 to 3 nights out of your own bed. For a home birth, you should make up your bed with two sets of sheets, separated by a plastic sheet. After you deliver, you can simply remove the top set of linen and have a clean bed. You can also put a plastic cover over the mattress. Have extra small or folded sheets available for labor or buy waterproof pads (*chucks*) to use under your bottom so that you don't need to lie on wet linen or change the entire bed when your membranes rupture or you have bloody show.

You need not bring baby clothes to the hospital or birthing center when you go into labor except perhaps for the minimal items essential to take the baby home. This includes a cotton shirt, a simple washable cotton gown, and a small washable wrapping blanket. The facility will supply diapers. You can dress the baby up considerably more than this, but additional clothing is not necessary from a health standpoint. In the winter you will want to have additional covers for the baby's first trip out into the cold world, but in the summer the baby will hardly need to be wrapped at all. If you are driving home, as most families do, you will need an approved newborn car seat. Check with your hospital to see if they have a loaner program, if you don't think you will have to purchase a car seat (as many urban residents don't often drive) or just haven't gotten one yet.

When You Arrive at the Hospital or Birthing Center

Each facility has its own admission system, with its own forms to be filled out and signed. Some hospitals immediately attach an identification bracelet to the mother and prepare a plastic card to be used for printing her name and other vital statistics on the various pages of her records. Some hospitals will have you complete preadmission paperwork and mail it in, so that you will not have to spend your time in labor filling out forms. Some of the admission bookkeeping and paperwork may be deferred until it becomes clear that you are in labor and will remain in the hospital. A clerk will then come to your bedside or interview your partner to secure the information necessary to complete the paperwork.

In most hospitals, women in labor go directly to the labor unit. In others, they must stop at the admissions office. If you arrive at the hospital in very active labor, be sure to say so immediately, emphatically, and directly to the people who greet you as you come in. Many hospitals require that laboring women be taken to the labor area in a wheelchair despite the fact that, moments earlier, they rode to the hospital in a car or a bus and walked in through the door. Allow the staff to give you a ride, however brief and unnecessary, from the entrance to the labor area. Take along with you those personal items you have brought to the hospital; remember to leave valuables, including jewelry, at home.

Of course, if you are delivering in a birthing center, the procedure will be much simpler. There will not be a separate admissions area and undoubtedly you will have fewer forms and paperwork to complete. Women delivering at home bypass the entire admission process—one of the advantages of home birth. To ease the procedure, find out as much as possible in advance of labor so you are familiar with what needs to be done.

Admission to the Labor Area

The staff on duty in the labor area will greet you when you arrive there. These are professionals who are fully accustomed to providing labor care and doing it with maximum efficiency.

The hospital or birthing center will probably have a copy of your prenatal record available to the labor and delivery staff. If you have called in before coming, and things are not too busy, the admitting personnel may already have looked at the record to get some idea of who you are and whether you have any complications. When you arrive, staff members will ask you why you think you are in labor. Your own physician or midwife may or may not be there when you arrive. This depends on their usual policy (which you can find out in advance) and the speed with which you get to the hospital after calling them. Your first contact might be with a nurse, a trained birthing assistant, a staff midwife, a physician, or a combination of personnel. The staff will need to know if you have already consulted your physician or midwife (you should have), and whether anything of note has happened to you since your last prenatal visit. If your records are not available, a detailed history will be taken.

In the hospital, once the staff has interviewed you, they will ask you to put on a gown, so you can be examined. Hospital gowns are unprepossessing in appearance, made of materials tough enough to withstand the rigors of a hospital laundry, and not designed for style, warmth, or modesty. They have short sleeves and come to about mid-thigh in length; they close with ties or tapes, which may be fastened either in front or in back. The purpose of the gown's design is solely to facilitate examination and treatment.

If you are obviously in advanced labor when you come in, someone will see you promptly, either your personal attendant, if he or she is present, or a physician or midwife on duty in the labor and delivery area. If you are delivering in a large teaching hospital, the physician may be a *resident*—a staff doctor who is 1 to 4 years out of medical school. Should you become ready to deliver before your physician or midwife can get to the hospital, the staff physician or midwife will give you the necessary assistance.

If you are not in advanced labor when you arrive, you can request that the admission examination, or at least the pelvic examination, be delayed until your physician or midwife arrives. In fact, during your prenatal care, you should check with your care provider if they have a policy about this; some midwives and physicians will always try to meet you in the admission areas while others prefer that the physician or mid-wife on duty check you to determine whether or not you are ready for admission. If you are, they will then come to the hospital.

Assuming you are not about to have the baby at the moment of your arrival, whoever examines you will begin by feeling your abdomen, to make sure that the size of the fetus corresponds with what you and the hospital record say is the expected due date, and to feel the baby's position and estimate its level of descent. The examiner will listen to the fetal heart rate. In some hospitals, a fetal monitor will be attached to make a written record of the frequency of uterine contractions and the response of the baby's heart rate. (Further discussion of the uses of fetal monitoring in labor begins on page 542.) The examiner also will take your pulse, temperature, and your blood pressure, and if you have recently had a respiratory infection or otherwise been ill, will examine your lungs to be sure they are clear. In some hospitals, a complete physical examination on admission is routine.

The next step is pelvic examination, to check whether the membranes are ruptured, to find out what the presenting part is, and to ascertain how deep (or *descended*) the presenting part is in the pelvis. The pelvic exam also will reveal the condition of the cervix—how long it is and how far it has opened. These measurements are recorded in centimeters: 2.5 to the inch. Until the cervical opening is 3 to 4 centimeters, it is hard to be certain that a woman is in labor. (Full dilation is 10 centimeters or 4 inches.)

A speculum examination may be performed on admission if there is a question of whether your membranes have ruptured. An examination with a sterile speculum rather than one with gloved fingers (called a *digital examination*) reduces the chances of introducing bacteria into the unprotected uterine cavity. If you are in very active labor on admission (or later, when your membranes rupture), you will also have the digital examination. The exam poses less of a risk for infection when you will likely deliver within a short time after the rupture.

Unless there is no time, the admission examination also will include taking a urine specimen to test for the presence of possibly abnormal chemicals, including protein, sugar, and ketones. Blood will be drawn to update prenatal laboratory work. This includes a test for syphilis, a blood count for anemia, and an identification of your blood type and *Rh factor* (negative or positive), in the rare case a transfusion should be necessary.

If you will have an *intravenous line*, a catheter or very thin plastic tube is put into the vein at the time that the blood is drawn so that administration of intravenous fluids can begin.

Intravenous—Why or Why Not?

In the best of all possible worlds, a woman's labor is sufficiently tranquil for her to maintain her fluid balance by drinking fluids such as ice chips, clear broth, fruit juice, or tea. In strong, active labor, many women are nauseated, and some vomit. Under these circumstances, a woman may need to receive intravenous fluids, because if there is inadequate intake of water, she can become dehydrated. Dehydration may slow labor or shrink a woman's blood volume, interfering with blood flow to the placenta.

In the recent past, most hospitals prohibited oral intake for women in labor, and some still do. Some allow only ice chips. When eating and especially drinking is prohibited, an intravenous line is needed. The reason for the prohibition on oral intake is the possibility that general anesthesia will be needed for a cesarean birth sometime during labor. Since this is a possibility in any labor, however remote, the prohibition has applied to every laboring woman. When general anesthesia is used, the woman may vomit up the contents of her stomach. As she loses control of her gag reflex, she can *aspirate*—breathe in the vomited material. This can lead to a serious condition called *aspiration pneumonia*.

Research has shown a number of flaws in the reasoning that led to the prohibition on oral intake. For one thing, starvation in labor does not guarantee that the stomach will be empty at the time of the administration of general anesthesia. No time interval between intake and anesthesia can guarantee an empty stomach. Furthermore, the acidity of the stomach contents are dangerous, even in the absence of food particles. Fasting does not keep the stomach contents from being acidic. Antacids can be given to women in labor in an attempt to reduce the likelihood that the stomach contents will be acidic, although this is not always a successful prevention.

Only an extremely rare woman, even among those who have general anesthesia, aspirates. The likelihood of aspiration is related to the skill of the anesthesiologist or nurse-anesthetist administering the anesthesia. With experience and expertise, aspiration becomes even more rare.

There are reasons for intravenous fluids in labor other than vomiting or fasting. If a woman has a high likelihood of needing a cesarean birth, such as the woman who has had a previous cesarean, an intravenous line may be placed so that the line need not be inserted at the time the decision is made to perform a cesarean, when other procedures become necessary (see Chapter 22). If a woman has had a previous postpartum hemorrhage, or is otherwise at risk for postpartum hemorrhage, an intravenous line will be placed. This is said to "keep the vein open," so that if bleeding occurs, an intravenous line will not have to be placed in the midst of hemorrhage, when insertion would be more difficult. Other risks for postpartum hemorrhage include having had many previous deliveries (being a *grand multipara*), having an extremely large baby or a multiple pregnancy (see Chapter 23), and having an induced or augmented labor (see Chapter 22).

If you do need an intravenous (IV) line, request that it be placed in your nondominant arm, if possible. Most medical personnel avoid placing IVs in the space where the arm bends (the inner aspect of the elbow joint), but if somebody tries that area, ask them to use another site if possible. The IV can be placed on the back of your hand, just above the back of your wrist, or in a vein on your lower forearm. Do not feel concerned or insulted if a nurse, midwife, or doctor says you have "bad veins." This just means that the IV insertion is difficult because your blood vessels are narrow or deep in your skin. These are normal variations and not anything to worry about. This is an example of medical jargon that is so commonly used, the practitioners don't realize that they may be saying something alarming to a patient.

If Your Labor Status Is Unclear

If the status of your labor is unclear, you may be advised to wait around the hospital for several hours. This usually happens if your contractions are moderate and your cervix less than 4 centimeters open. If your contractions are strong and frequent, you may be admitted even with a cervix that is only 3 centimeters or so dilated. If your cervix is more than 4 centimeters, chances are you will be admitted even if your contractions are not yet strong. If your contractions are very mild and infrequent and your cervix is only 2 or 3 centimeters, you will most likely be sent home, assuming your membranes are intact and you live within a reasonable travel distance.

If you are in the gray area in which your cervix is somewhat open and your contractions somewhat frequent and moderate, you may be "sent walking" for about 2 hours. Some hospitals and most birthing centers provide pleasant facilities for this sort of waiting. A birthing center may have an outdoor garden or indoor "living room." A few hospitals provide a "labor walk," an area of relative privacy where you can walk undisturbed. Others may expect you to go into a nearby lounge along with visitors and other laboring women. In any event, the passage of a few hours will make clear whether or not you are actually in labor. Some women note that when they get to the hospital, contractions cease and then after a pause begin again.

When You Are Definitely in Labor

When the decision is made that you are actually in labor, you will be admitted to the hospital or birthing center. Certain procedures are standard, although in recent years a number of procedures that were previously considered important have been eliminated. Almost all hospitals today have private rooms for women in labor. Your support person or persons may be asked to put on a hospital gown or a robe over his, her, or their clothes. This may be done on admission, or just before delivery. As discussed earlier in this chapter, an intravenous line may or may not be placed. An electronic fetal monitor may or may not be used, as discussed in a later section (see page 543).

For many years, it was routine to give an enema to every woman to whom it could possibly be given. As research has shown no medical value to enemas in labor, this practice has happily vanished almost completely from obstetrics. For most women, an enema simply adds one more discomfort. If enemas seemed to accelerate labor, it was probably because they usually were given shortly after admission—a time when a woman's labor would often pick up naturally. Although women frequently will expel feces during the pushing stage, this is perfectly normal and not a cause for embarrassment. Your birth attendant or a nurse will simply wipe away the feces without complaint. In fact, soiling following an enema may be messier and more difficult to clean.

If you feel strongly that you would like an enema, or if you begin labor with severe constipation, you can give yourself a small enema at home or you can request an enema at the birthing center or hospital. A soapsuds enema should not be used as it is irritating and can lead to painful cramping.

Another source of unnecessary discomfort that has been eliminated in recent years is the shaving of the pubic hair. This used to be done to all women in labor, subjecting them first to being shaved with a dry razor on sensitive skin and then to itching during the period of regrowth. Shaving carries no medical benefit to the woman to justify the disagreeable nature of the experience. If anything, shaving may increase the risk of infection as it often causes tiny nicks in the skin, creating an excellent haven for bacteria to grow.

Some hospitals encourage women to have a shower on admission. Whether to shower or not at this stage is a matter of personal taste and comfort. A warm shower may be comforting. Some in-hospital and out-of-hospital birthing centers have showers large enough for two, so your partner can shower with you. Some even have dual-head showers. Today, many of these facilities have tubs and even Jacuzzis. The flowing warm water is quite relaxing. Recent studies have shown that it is not dangerous to labor in water, even with ruptured membranes.

To Bed or Not

Women can labor in bed, sitting in a chair, or walking about, at least during the first stage of labor. The most comfortable position varies from woman to woman and may change during labor. If you prefer to lie down, you ought to turn onto your left side or prop up your head. Use the bed, if it is adjustable, or use pillows. This prevents undue pressure on the body's largest vein, the *vena cava*, which occurs when a woman late in pregnancy lies flat on her back. Such pressure can interfere with circulation to the placenta.

No position is necessary or ideal for the first stage of labor. Some women are more comfortable sitting in bed, others prefer standing and kneeling over a bed, some sit on their knees in bed, holding onto the bed frame, others choose to walk. Some research has shown that walking reduces the time of labor, although other studies have not supported this finding. No research has shown a detrimental effect of walking on labor or on maternal or fetal well-being. Most important is for you and the people working with you to find the position that is best for you. You generally can trust what your body tells you about this.

When labor is not normal, continuous fetal monitoring is considered to be of value, and for this purpose, the woman usually should be in bed as the fetal monitoring equipment in use at present produces the best records with women lying down. Today, some medical centers have newly developed electronic monitoring equipment that allows you to be up and around if your condition permits. The practicality of this equipment awaited the recent perfection of lightweight radio transmitters, which broadcast the signals created by the uterine contractions and the fetal heartbeat to equipment at a nearby nurse's station. This is called *telemetry*. There is even a telemetry model that works underwater, although this is not available in all institutions. Projections have been made of remote stations in private offices so that care providers would be able to monitor labors without actually being present. Whether this would represent an advance in care certainly is debatable.

MONITORING IN LABOR

Monitoring in labor has become almost synonymous with the use of the electronic fetal monitor. The term, in fact, has a much broader meaning. Every woman and every fetus deserve monitoring in labor. The labor itself should be monitored for its normalcy and progress. The woman should be monitored for her physical and emotional tolerance of labor. The fetus should be monitored for its response to contractions, reflected in the rate and pattern of its heart. None of these require electronic equipment. Effective and safe monitoring can be accomplished by attentive, experienced professionals with old-fashioned devices such as a thermometer, stethoscope, blood pressure cuff, watch with a second hand, and fetoscope. Electronic devices, of course, have added to our ability to gather detailed information about the fetus, but in most cases, this is unnecessary.

Monitoring the Labor

As labor goes on, your birth attendant or members of the hospital or birthing center staff will examine you from time to time to follow your progress. You may even ask them to do so, and unless there is some reason why you should not be examined at that time, they ordinarily will oblige, and tell you what they have found. The examiner will feel your abdomen to locate the baby, find its presenting part and estimate how far it has come through the birth canal. A vaginal examination gives more specific information about the fetal position and descent. It also evaluates the cervical thinning and opening (*effacement* and *dilatation*, described in the previous chapters). If you have ruptured membranes, vaginal examinations must be limited to minimize the risk of infection.

Of course, vaginal examinations are not the only way to evaluate the progress of labor. The contraction pattern tells a lot. Over the course of a labor, contractions should increase in frequency, duration, and intensity (as described in Chapter 18). This can be evaluated in a number of ways. You will feel the changes yourself and can communicate what you feel to your midwife or physician. Obstetrical staff can palpate your contractions, which means they feel them gently with their hands. Palpation can be somewhat uncomfortable, but does not need to be done with every contraction. From time to time, the birth attendant or nurse can feel a few contractions, time their interval and duration, and sense how strong they are—in the same way you might palpate someone's biceps muscle. The electronic fetal monitor can be used to assess contractions.

A pressure-sensitive belt can be strapped externally around the *fundus* (the top of the uterus), or an internal pressure catheter can be placed inside the uterus. The internal catheter can only be used if the membranes have ruptured. In some institutions use of this equipment has become so extensive that the art of palpating contractions is in danger of being lost, but many practitioners cling to manually assessing contractions as a valued part of their practice.

Another way of evaluating the progress of labor is to be attentive to the signs and symptoms that a woman's body exhibits. Certain cues tell an experienced physician, midwife, or nurse that rapid progress is being made or that the first stage is coming to a close. Cues include an increase in bloody show, spontaneous rupture of membranes, or an urge to push. Behavior also changes as labor progresses. Most women become increasingly agitated and uncomfortable. Their toes curl, they shiver and perspire, they burp, they grunt. To an obstetrical care provider, these are all good signs.

In some hospitals, policies dictate how often physicians and midwives must perform vaginal examinations. Sometimes these are performed every 2 hours. The question then arises what to do if progress is not made at a 2-hour interval. In most cases, the "treatment" would be watchful waiting, although it depends on when in labor this occurs. At the end of the first stage, for example, 2 hours is a longer time for a lack of progress than it would be earlier in labor. The expected progress of labor is outlined in Chapter 18, but as noted there, not all labors follow a set pattern. There can be times of slow and rapid progress.

During a period of watchful waiting, simple measures can be tried to help labor progress. These measures include making sure the woman does not have a full bladder, which can impede labor, and that she is well hydrated. She can be encouraged to drink, or an intravenous line can be started if one is not already in place. At the next evaluation, other interventions, such as encouraging walking or rupturing the membranes artificially, may be tried. Finally, stimulation of labor with medications may be necessary. This is discussed more fully in Chapter 22.

In many hospitals, and certainly in birthing centers and at home, vaginal examinations are not performed according to a set routine. They are done when the physician, midwife, or perhaps nurse sees a need for one. However, unless the physician or midwife will use the information gathered from the examination to help determine the care to be given, the examination probably is unnecessary.

There are a number of good reasons to do a vaginal examination:

• You may request an examination.
• You may request pain medication.
• You may request epidural anesthesia.
• You may feel an urge to push.
• Your attendant may notice that you are involuntarily pushing, which might be somewhat harmful to the cervix before full dilatation.
• You may have been in labor for several hours without noticeable signs of progress.

A vaginal examination in labor usually is performed in bed, although the initial admitting examination may be on an examining table with stirrups, especially if the examiner needs to determine whether your membranes are ruptured. For a routine check, you will be asked to separate your legs and the examiner will use a glove and antibacterial lubrication.

For centuries women labored without vaginal examinations. Although we know that advances in maternity care have contributed greatly to infant and maternal health and survival, we also know that a great deal of modern interventions are overused. There is no ideal, perfect, or universally correct number of examinations to be done in a labor. It depends on the length of the labor, its normalcy, and how you and your fetus react to it.

Monitoring the Laboring Woman

Although labor is a normal bodily process, it does create physical stress. Changes in blood pressure, metabolism, heart rate, and temperature commonly occur during labor. *Toxemia* (also called *preeclampsia* or *pregnancy-induced hypertension*, described in Chapter 12) may occur for the first time in labor. For these reasons, the laboring woman's vital signs need to be checked periodically. Vital signs include temperature, pulse, respiratory rate, and blood pressure. Usually, blood pressure is taken every hour in active labor and temperature, pulse, and respirations every 2 to 4 hours. Once the membranes have ruptured, vital signs are checked every 1 to 2 hours.

Bladder function should also be monitored. Although there is decreased sensation in the bladder during labor, the bladder can become stretched with only a small amount of urine in it because the bladder gets compressed as the fetus descends. A full bladder can impede labor progress. It can also interfere with the ability of the uterus to contract in the immediate postpartum period. Unless there is a medical reason why you should not get out of bed, you can go to the toilet to empty your bladder. Urinating is much easier if you do it in the natural position than if you attempt to balance yourself on a bedpan. The staff may want you to urinate into a container so that they can measure the amount of urine and check for ketones. Urinary ketones may be evidence of dehydration. This occurs when a laboring woman doesn't get enough fluids.

A member of the obstetrical staff should check frequently on your overall well-being, your level of fatigue, and your ability to tolerate oral food and fluids. Somebody should be available to care for you if you become nauseated or vomit. Keeping the sheets dry, helping your lips stay moist, changing your gown should it get soiled, wiping your brow, giving feedback about your progress, and helping you should you experience leg cramps are all part of labor care.

Monitoring the Fetus

The first observation that a fetus in its mother's uterus was alive and well was made early in the nineteenth century by Francois Mayor, a Swiss surgeon, who reported that he could identify fetal life by placing his ear on a pregnant woman's abdomen and hearing the fetal heartbeat. This unmistakable sound might be heard as early as 18 weeks of pregnancy in slender women.

At the beginning of the twentieth century it was already known that very rapid and very slow fetal heart rates were signs of trouble. Today, more subtle changes in fetal heart rates are known to reflect possible fetal distress. Heart rate patterns are classified according to the presumed reason for the heart rate change. More precise information about fetal well-being can be gained by measuring the amount of oxygen in the fetal blood. Technology has become available so that this can be done through a sensor, without taking an actual blood sample. This latest technology, called *fetal pulse oximetry*, has been hailed as a major breakthrough in fetal monitoring. Of course, as it is a new technology, time will tell its true value.

The Purpose of Fetal Monitoring

During contractions, the blood supply to the placenta is reduced. Although nearly all fetuses tolerate this well, it can be a stress for some. The purpose of monitoring is to identify those fetuses for whom labor causes undue stress. In general, these fetuses enter labor with some degree of stress already. This might be caused by growth restriction in utero, a postdates pregnancy, or a maternal illness.

The use of electronic fetal monitoring is only one way to monitor the fetus. The fetal heart can be *auscultated*—listened to—with a *fetoscope*, a simple instrument similar to a stethoscope. This is called *intermittent*, as opposed to continuous, *monitoring*. The American College of Obstetricians and Gynecologists recommends auscultation every 30 minutes in the first stage of labor for a woman with a low-risk pregnancy and every 15 minutes in the first stage of labor for a woman with a pregnancy at risk (if continuous electronic monitoring is not available or not used). In both low-risk and high-risk pregnancies, auscultation every 5 minutes is advised during the second or pushing stage of labor. Auscultation is best accomplished following contractions.

The fetoscope detects most fetal hearts without difficulty, although usually the mother must be on her back for the heart to be heard well. An electronic handheld *Doppler*, operating on the principle of ultrasound, can be used instead. This allows for the fetal heart to be picked up in a greater variety of positions.

There are Doppler models that can work underwater. If a woman is immersed in a tub, then, she need not get out for the fetal heart to be heard.

Finally, there is the *electronic fetal monitoring machine*. This machine can be utilized in two different ways—for external monitoring or for internal monitoring. External monitoring can be used for intermittent or continuous assessment.

The Pros and Cons of Continuous Electronic Fetal Monitoring

When electronic fetal monitoring was introduced in 1968, an assumption was made by many in the obstetrics community that it represented an advance over auscultation. It was presumed to reflect more accurately the oxygen status of the fetus, and to allow for earlier intervention to prevent problems in the newborn. Electronic monitoring became widely adopted and is now used routinely in many hospitals.

Early studies of electronic monitoring seemed to support the rationale for its use. These studies, however, were not well conducted. Later studies, which were better conducted because they compared women whose fetuses were monitored electronically to women whose fetuses received auscultation, showed that the two ways of fetal monitoring are equivalent. While electronic monitoring picked up more heart rate abnormalities, its use did not lead to better outcomes for the newborns.

Electronic monitoring is not risk free. Because it usually requires that the woman stay in bed, electronic monitoring can prolong labor. It also leads to an increased use of forceps and vacuum extractors as well as increased numbers of cesarean births. Forceps and vacuum extractions can can cause trauma to the fetus or mother. Cesarean delivery carries an increased risk of infection or other complications in the mother, as well as a very small increased risk of maternal death. The use of the *internal fetal scalp electrode* can occasionally cause a scalp abscess in the newborn. As the external monitor operates by ultrasound, the question remains whether there are adverse effects on the fetus from continuous monitoring of a long labor.

Most researchers today have concluded that continuous electronic fetal monitoring is not beneficial for *low-risk women*—women with normal pregnancies. Most physicians and midwives will use the technology when the fetus has a risk for having a reduced ability to tolerate the stress of labor, although even this use has not been demonstrated beyond question to be of value.

The fetus might be at risk when the fetus has problems such as growth restriction or Rh sensitization; in a pregnancy in which the mother has a disease such as diabetes, high blood pressure, or kidney disease; in a pregnancy that is post-term (more than 2 weeks past its due date); or in a pregnancy with a placental abnormality. When the fetus is premature, it is considered at risk. A history of previous stillbirth or neonatal death is considered a risk to the fetus. Induced or augmented labors, described in Chapter 22, warrant electronic monitoring. Continuous monitoring is used with epidural anesthesia. Multiple gestations and breech deliveries are electronically monitored. With thick meconium, electronic monitoring is used. *Meconium* is the normal contents of the fetal bowels. It is a yellow to green to brown sticky substance that may be seen in the amniotic fluid when the membranes rupture. Except for meconium passed during the second stage in a fetus in the breech position, the presence of meconium may be a sign of distress. Some hospital or provider policies require continuous electronic monitoring whenever a vaginal birth is attempted following a previous cesarean delivery.

How Electronic Monitoring Is Carried Out

The electronic fetal monitor detects and records both the fetal heart and maternal contractions. In this way, heart rate changes can be described according to their relationship to contractions. With external monitoring, two belts are placed around the laboring woman's abdomen. One belt goes around the top of the uterus, or the *fundus*, to sense and record the contractions. The other belt, usually placed lower on the abdomen, picks up, amplifies, and records the fetal heart. These belts must be strapped fairly tightly to record properly. The woman usually needs to be on her side or back (although never flat).

Many things can interfere with the accuracy of external fetal monitoring. If the mother is obese or the baby in a very posterior position, the heart tones may be difficult to pick up. If the mother moves too much, the heart tones may be lost. Interference may come from the mother's own pulse or the sounds of her bowel. Frequent repositioning of the monitor belts by the nursing staff may be quite bothersome. A more accurate, and sometimes more comfortable, though more invasive, way to pick up and record the fetal heart tones is internal electronic monitoring. The recordings of fetal heart rate are thus obtained with less "noise" than with external ultrasound. Monitoring intensity of contractions is also more accurate if done internally. The laboring woman, while still confined to bed, usually has more mobility with internal monitoring.

Internal monitoring of the fetal heart rate requires that a fine wire or spiral electrode be attached to the scalp or breech of the fetus. The contractions can be monitored with a catheter or tube that is threaded through the cervix into the uterus.

Internal monitoring is only possible if the cervix has begun to dilate and the membranes have ruptured, or if the physician or midwife ruptures them. When somebody ruptures the membranes, it is called *artificial rupture of the membranes* or AROM. If AROM is done before the head or the breech of the fetus has descended into the pelvis, it carries a risk of causing a *cord prolapse*. This occurs when the rush of fluid from the rupture brings down the umbilical cord with it. If the head or breech is down in the pelvis, it blocks the cord from coming down. Prolapse of the cord restricts the blood flow through the cord and causes severe fetal distress. Cord prolapse usually requires an emergency cesarean delivery.

Abnormalities of the Fetal Heart Rate

BASELINE CHANGES   The normal fetal heart rate is between 110 and 160 beats per minute. This is called the *baseline fetal heart rate*. In the absence of other signs of distress, a heart beat as low as 100 may be normal. The baseline rate should be within the normal range and also show variability. Variability means that the fetal heart fluctuates with each beat and over time. Fluctuations in the heart beat indicate that the fetal nervous system, which controls the heart and is sensitive to changes in the oxygen content of the fetal blood, is working well. Using a feto-scope, variability can be ascertained by counting the heartbeats for short periods of time, for example, counting for 5 seconds, pausing for 5 sec-onds, counting again for 5 seconds. With electronic monitoring, vari-ability is recorded as a line with up and down flutter.

Several changes in the baseline fetal heart rate might indicate fetal distress. These are called *nonreassuring patterns*, while normal patterns are called *reassuring*. Nonreassuring baseline patterns include a slow fetal heart rate (*bradycardia*), a rapid fetal heart rate (*tachycardia*), a decrease in variability, or an absence of variability.

An unusual pattern that may be a sign of serious fetal distress is a regular fluctuation of rate of about five to fifteen beats every 12 to 20 seconds (a *sinusoidal pattern*). This pattern appears as a smooth un-dulating line on the fetal monitor tracing. A sinusoidal pattern is often associated with severe fetal anemia, but may indicate a loss of oxygen to the fetus for other reasons such as a placental problem or narcotic medi-cation given to the mother.

Before the assumption of fetal distress is made, other causes for non-reassuring baseline changes should be considered. A loss of variability, for example, may occur when the baby falls asleep, but these periods tend to last only about half an hour. The use of sedative and narcotic drugs (see later in this chapter on page 561) can have the same effect. Tachycardia, or a rapid heart rate, can occur when the mother has a fever. Whether the fever is due to intrauterine infection or to an inci-dental infection outside the uterus, it usually is treated with antibiotics. Such treatment is not called for when the fetal tachycardia results from an abnormality of the electrical control of the fetal heart rate. In this rare case, the rate is two hundred beats per minute or higher. It is best diagnosed by *echocardiography*, a type of ultrasound. The treatment for this condition consists of giving cardiac drugs to the fetus by adminis-tering them to the mother.

PERIODIC CHANGES   Other nonreassuring signs are known as pe-riodic changes, or short-term slowing of the fetal heart. These are called *decelerations*. There are three types of decelerations—early, variable, and late—each showing a different pattern on the fetal heart rate tracing and each having a different cause and significance.

Early Decelerations. Early decelerations are not a cause for worry. They indicate compression of the fetal head, which is normal in labor, especially after the membranes have ruptured and the head is descend-ing. Early decelerations often are seen during the pushing stage of labor. They begin with the uterine contraction and end as the uterus relaxes.

Their shape on the electronic fetal monitor tracing is a mirror image of the curve of the contraction.

Variable Decelerations. Variable decelerations are markedly abrupt and unrelated in their timing to uterine contractions. Variable decelerations often occur when the umbilical cord is around the baby's neck or trunk, or caught against the bony pelvis. They may also occur when the pregnancy becomes *postdates*, meaning it goes past its due date by at least 2 weeks, and when there is reduced amniotic fluid volume. (The two conditions often go together.) If recovery is rapid and the variable deceleration is not less than seventy beats per minute, the fetus usually tolerates these types of decelerations well. If there is good variability in the fetal heart baseline, then variable decelerations are not usually an ominous sign. If variable decelerations are repetitive, prolonged, and deep, however, they may indicate fetal distress.

Late Decelerations. Late decelerations mirror the shape of the contractions, but start well after a contraction has begun and persist after the uterus has relaxed. They may be evidence of a reduced blood flow to the placenta, especially when they are repetitive. Reduced blood flow to the placenta is most likely to occur in pregnancies complicated by conditions such as pre-existing high blood pressure or pregnancy-induced hypertension. Late decelerations may be subtle, with drops in fetal heart rate of only a few beats. Subtlety does not make late decelerations less worrisome.

COMBINATION PATTERNS   Combinations of nonreassuring patterns may be observed. When there is more than one nonreassuring sign, such as baseline bradycardia with late decelerations or prolonged, repetitive variable decelerations with a lack of baseline variability, the likelihood that the patterns represent fetal distress increases.

INTERPRETATION   Nonreassuring fetal heart rate patterns are not always associated with fetal distress. Conversely, they may be associated with distress that is greater than evidenced by the pattern. Therefore, interpretation of the fetal monitoring tracing is critical. Experience is key. Additional clinical and laboratory data should be part of interpretation. For example, if a nonreassuring pattern is seen early in labor, the fetus may have more difficulty withstanding labor than if a similar pattern is seen shortly before birth.

Immediate Measures When the FHR Shows a Nonreassuring Pattern

Sometimes, simple measures can be corrective when the fetal heart rate shows a nonreassuring pattern. These steps may be taken to improve the fetus's oxygen supply, usually by increasing uterine blood flow:

• Stopping any drug that is being given to induce or stimulate labor
• Placing the mother into a side-lying position or moving her in other ways
• Correcting maternal low blood pressure if it is from epidural anesthesia (by giving intravenous fluids in a large amount)
• Giving oxygen by mask and/or nasal catheter to the mother.

Additional Ways to Monitor Fetal Well-being

The fetal heart rate pattern is only an indirect indicator of fetal oxygen supply. In most medical centers, more direct testing is available to measure the concentration of oxygen in the fetal blood or to test the fetal blood pH. The pH is an indicator of whether the fetal blood is acidotic. *Acidosis* is a result of low oxygen levels and is a dangerous condition.

Tests of the fetal blood can be carried out in either of two ways. The blood can be sampled by pricking the fetal skin, or the blood's oxygen content can be measured through a sensor placed against the fetal skin. This sensor absorbs the red light in the hemoglobin of blood as the blood pulses through fetal arteries. The technique employing the sensor is called *fetal pulse oximetry*. It provides a continuous measure of the percent of oxygen in the fetus's blood. The sensor must lie placed against the fetal temple or cheek, as hair interferes with the transmission of light.

Both means of testing fetal blood require that the cervix be dilated at least 2 centimeters and the membranes ruptured. When the fetus is high in the pelvis (above -2 station), the sensor is difficult or impossible to place.

Mothers cannot walk with the sensor in place. It sometimes needs to be repositioned as labor progresses, although recently a balloon filled with *saline* (salt water) that wedges the sensor between the uterine wall and the fetus has become available.

To obtain the small sample of fetal blood from the skin of the presenting part, a plastic cone, open at both ends and fitted with a light, is passed into the mother's vagina and pushed through the cervix up against the baby's skin. (The smaller end of the cone goes into the vagina.) This allows the examiner to visualize the baby's skin and pass a needle up to it. The skin is then pricked so that it will bleed. The shed blood is collected in a long thin tube. The blood sample is placed into a special machine, which measures its acidity, expressed in numerical form as pH. Pressure is applied to the tiny cut so it will stop bleeding.

With nonreassuring fetal heart patterns, the pH or oxygen level of the fetal blood provides additional information that helps the physician or midwife decide whether or not prompt delivery is necessary. These tests clarify whether the heart rate abnormalities are actually causing loss of oxygen to the baby and whether they are significant enough to alter the chemistry of its blood. Normal oxygen saturation values in the fetus are between 30 percent and 70 percent. Saturation levels below 30 percent mean the fetus is suffering from reduced oxygenation and may develop acidosis, a dangerous condition. The normal pH of the blood from the fetal skin is about 7.32, depending somewhat on the mother's pH. As labor progresses, this value tends to fall. If the fetal scalp pH is low normal (7.20–7.25), it will be repeated. Generally, delivery is recommended with a repeat pH of 7.2 or less.

Most often the blood tests will show that in spite of nonreassuring fetal heart rate patterns, the fetus is not in jeopardy. One company that markets a pulse oximetry machine estimates that using the equipment can reduce the number of cesareans performed due to nonreassuring fetal heart rate patterns by approximately 30 percent.

PAIN RELIEF IN LABOR AND DELIVERY

Labor, whether lengthy or brief, is hard work, as the word implies. The work of the first stage of labor is done by a very competent smooth muscle that functions well without any specific conditioning exercises. The work of the second stage of labor is augmented by voluntary muscles of the abdominal wall, and they too do an excellent job. Women who have lengthy labors sometimes feel a great sense of frustration and even inadequacy to the task. "I can't do this," is a commonly heard refrain in the final throes of labor. Yet, when the time comes to bear down and push the baby out women almost always find resources of energy that are quite equal to the need.

For the great majority of women labor also is painful. Most women deal with this discomfort quite well. They do so vastly better in the presence of an active, warm, and sympathetic support system such as can be provided by their partner, labor coaches, labor room nurses, and the attendants they have chosen to help with the process. For some women, however, the process seems to cause almost intolerable pain. A great deal of obstetrics, thus, is devoted to pain relief.

The History of Pain Relief in Obstetrics

Throughout most of human history, pain has been taken for granted as an accompaniment of labor. Using only the Western world as an example, early in the first book of the Old Testament it is said to women that "in sorrow thou shalt bring forth children." The authoritative obstetrical texts from the sixteenth century through the first half of the nineteenth century make no reference to the use of drugs in the relief of pain in labor, despite the fact that pain-relieving drugs were known and used in medicine and surgery. The greatest obstetrician of renaissance France, Francois Mauriceau, noted in 1668 that when asked to see a kinswoman who had injured her back when 6 months pregnant, he prescribed "at two different times a small grain of laudanum (the available preparation of opium at the time) in the yolk of an egg, a little to ease her violent pains." However, in the same authoritative textbook he makes no comment on easing labor pain. Many pages are devoted in these early books to the proper management of very long, very uncomfortable labors, whose conclusion was achieved by crude surgery that must have been the source of extreme pain, without any mention of pain relief as part of the care.

In a fabled episode in the late seventeenth century, Dr. Pierre Chamberlen, the physician who invented obstetrical forceps, was invited to demonstrate them in the delivery of a woman with severe pelvic deformity due to rickets (vitamin D deficiency). He struggled unsuccessfully for 3 hours in a woman who had nothing to help with her pain, before having to admit failure to deliver the baby. Physicians in that era took for granted that survival of the baby itself was not a consideration, and we are not told whether the mother survived.

The credit for bringing this dreary epoch to an end goes to Sir James Young Simpson of Edinburgh, the intrepid innovator who conducted the very first delivery under anesthesia as we know it today. Simpson himself searched the medical literature fruitlessly in an effort to find any reference to pain relief during childbirth. He administered the first obstetrical anesthetic for the delivery of a woman in the slums of Edinburgh. She was "etherized shortly after 9 o'clock," on the evening of January 19, 1847. Simpson had experimented on himself with the primitive anesthetic agents available at that time before using them on this woman. By coincidence on the very same day he was informed of his appointment as one of Queen Victoria's Scottish physicians. He considered this appointment the less important of the two events. He wrote to his brother that "flattery from the Queen is perhaps not common flattery, but I am far less interested in it than having delivered a woman this week without any pain while inhaling sulphuric ether. I can think of naught else."

Simpson was vigorously attacked for having given pain relief in violation of the proscription in the Bible. His prompt reply to this criticism was that before Adam produced Eve from his rib, God caused him to fall into a deep sleep. Theological arguments aside, anesthesia quickly became established for use in delivery. Queen Victoria herself served as a role model for women wishing anesthesia for delivery.

The use of medication to relieve pain during labor, prior to the delivery itself, was introduced by Carl Friedrich Gauss of Freiberg, Germany. In 1907 he combined two drugs, morphine and scopolamine, for this purpose. The morphine relieved pain and the scopolamine impaired memory. Under the influence of these drugs, women remained in a dream state somewhere between consciousness and unconsciousness. Gauss called this technique *twilight sleep* (*dammerchlaf* in German). Interestingly, the drug that has been most commonly used for pain relief in obstetrics in the United States is Demerol, a name derived from the German name for twilight sleep. At the time it was introduced, twilight sleep was seen as a humane advance, supported by the medical and feminist communities. It was only later that the potential for adverse effects on mother or baby was addressed.

Although there are newer drugs available for pain relief, the only significant addition to the medical alternatives for the relief of pain in labor and in delivery since the contributions of Simpson and Gauss has been the development of regional block anesthesia. In the quest to counteract any possible detrimental effects of medications, however, a wide array of nonmedical relief measures has been developed.

Methods of Pain Management

Pain relief in labor can be achieved in a number of ways. Techniques for prepared childbirth including relaxation and breathing can be effective for many women. Support, position changes, and simple comfort measures help women to cope. Massage and immersion in warm water can be anxiety relieving and may contribute to pain reduction. Alternative therapies such as hypnosis, acupuncture, acupressure, and aromatherapy have been used. Recently, a relatively noninterventionist method involving the injection of sterile water papules under the skin has become popular for back labor, especially among midwives. More medical approaches include administration of drugs to change the woman's threshold for pain and the use of nerve-blocking agents that interrupt the transmission of pain from the abdomen and lower back to the brain.

No pain relief method using drugs is entirely free from the potential of causing undesirable side effects for both mother and fetus. The choice of whether to use these medications is a highly individualized one. Risks must be weighed carefully against benefits.

General Considerations

Numerous considerations come into play when an individual woman or couple decides whether to use pain medication, and, if so, which to use. Some of these issues can be resolved in advance of labor, others depend on the nature of the labor itself.

Your personal belief system is one such consideration. Some helpful questions to ask yourself and your partner while planning for labor follow:

- What is your attitude toward the use of medications in general?
- To what extent do you wish to experience the sensations of labor?
- Although medication types and dosages currently used are not known to cause serious damage to the baby, they may have subtle effects. How do you feel about this? How does your partner feel?
- Review in advance your previous experiences with pain. How did you react? How would you rate what is called your threshold for pain?

Discuss the decision with your partner and others who will be with you in labor:

- What is their feeling about pain and pain relief?
- How comfortable will they be seeing you in pain?
- What role do they expect to be able to play in helping you relieve the pain?

Discuss your feelings and desires about pain medication with your physician or midwife:

- What are your care provider's attitudes toward pain medication?
- Does he or she share your values?

• What types of pain relief is your physician or midwife most comfortable using? Is it consistent with what you want?

You ought to be in agreement about this in order to avoid conflict in the throes of labor.

A woman may have a deeply personal desire for a nonmedicated labor. She may want to avoid exposing her newborn to medications or may desire to experience labor and birth fully—to be not only awake and aware but also connected to the experience with its many bodily sensations. If her physician or midwife is less committed to this, there may be some conflict in the throes of labor, a situation best avoided. Conversely, if a woman really wants the option of medication for labor, either given as an injection of a drug or via an epidural catheter, and her midwife or physician is opposed to the use of medication, this too will cause conflict.

Think about the consequences of utilizing pain medication. These include the need for an intravenous line. Although "walking epidurals" are now available, any kind of pain medication will limit your mobility. Narcotics will make you sleepy and most hospitals limit the amount of walking you can do even with a walking epidural. You may be kept on bedrest except to go to the bathroom.

Learn about the options available where you have chosen to deliver. If you have chosen a home or birthing center birth, you won't have the option of getting an epidural unless you transfer to a hospital in labor. If the availability of the full scope of obstetrical *analgesia* (pain relief) and *anesthesia* (complete pain removal) is important to you, you should choose a hospital birth. If the advantages of either home or birthing center are so important to you that it is worth limiting your choices of pain relief, that, too, is a reasonable decision. If you choose an out-of-hospital birth, but find that you must have greater pain relief than is available in your birth place, you can be transferred in order to get the medication you require.

Several things that you cannot determine in advance of labor may influence your ultimate decision regarding medication use. These include the length of your labor, the intensity and frequency of your contractions, and the position of your baby. *Back labor*, for example, occurring when the fetus is lying with the back of its head against the small of your back, may be more difficult to tolerate. The progress you make in labor may influence your decision. You may, for instance, decide you want to have an epidural, but make such rapid progress that by the time you feel the need for pain relief, you may be almost fully dilated—a time when having feeling in the vaginal and perineal areas is beneficial for pushing. Or, you may think you want to labor without pain medication but have a very long and difficult labor. Your own tension may appear to be contributing to slow progress. Something to "take the edge off" may help you relax enough to allow the labor to proceed more efficiently.

In general, a good rule is to discuss the medication decision in advance of labor with your support persons and physician or midwife, to make a decision based on your personal beliefs and desires, and then be flexible enough to change that decision if necessary. Let your support team know how much they should be prepared to "talk you out of it" if you start asking for medication when you had decided you wanted a nonmedicated birth. Do you want them to go with your labor wishes, or to remind you of your original choice? To what extent do you want to be persuaded in any given direction? Of course, the exact circumstances of labor and your response cannot be entirely predetermined, but at least you can set up some guidelines. You may choose to put your feelings about medication into a written birth plan (which will include other choices as well, such as whether you want routine electronic monitoring, what positions you want to be able to assume for labor and birth, who you want with you for labor and birth). Some midwives and physicians have forms for such plans and you can simply check off your choices; others will write your preferences into your prenatal chart.

Several recent authors have pointed out the distinction between pain and suffering. You can feel the pain of labor without truly suffering. For women for whom the experience of pain causes undue suffering, use of the most effective means of pain relief may be in order.

Nonmedical Means of Managing Pain

An extensive discussion of managing pain in labor is beyond the scope of this book. Entire books have been devoted to this topic. There are even books exclusively about one method of pain relief, such as relaxation or hypnosis. We summarize a variety of coping strategies here and refer you to the Appendix for a listing of books that deal with pain management in greater detail.

Support

The value of support cannot be stressed enough. Imagine, for example, having an injury and going to the emergency room by yourself. From the early part of the twentieth century, when labor and birth were moved from the home to the hospital, through the 1960s, women labored mostly alone, without the comfort of having a familiar person with them. This is probably one reason why heavily medicated labors and births became the norm.

Today, nurses in obstetrical units are experienced in caring for non-medicated women or women who are medicated but still fully conscious. They provide one source of support. However, nurses are often strangers and you may have several different nurses attending during the course of your labor and delivery. Partners, as well as mothers, sisters, and friends are now accepted members of the labor support team and provide emotional support that compensates for any lack of extensive training or familiarity with labor.

Whether you wish to have your children with you is a personal decision. Siblings are welcomed in many institutions. Certainly, they may be present at home birth or a birthing center. Consider your child's age and temperament. If you want a child present, then he or she should attend a childbirth class for siblings. Check with your hospital, birthing center, or local childbirth education organization for such a class (see the Appendix). Also, your child should have a personal support person. Many children get bored with the process of labor, or find it difficult to see their mother in pain. For these reasons, they tend to wander in and out of the labor room and need someone to provide care for them. You will need to delegate this responsibility to someone who is not part of your support team—assisting you in labor. Although they need care, your children can be a source of love and support for you—but their ability to do this is something you must evaluate in advance.

Your physician and midwife, of course, will be another source of labor support for you. Midwives are particularly known for providing attentive and supportive labor care. A new type of obstetrics professional has entered the scene in recent years—the *doula* (also called the *monitrice*). This is usually a woman whose job is to be "on call" for laboring women. While not an intimate family member or friend, doulas meet women and families before labor. Recent studies have shown that the continuous presence of a professional support person such as a midwife, nurse, or doula can lead to shorter labor, less use of pain medication, and a reduced need for intervention such as forceps and vacuum births.

Most doulas and midwives have an extensive "bag of tricks" for labor support. They give massages, help with position changes, work on relaxation and breathing with you. They also work with your support person or team, helping them find the best ways to help you.

Discuss in advance with your midwife or physician how busy their practice is and the extent to which you can expect them to be available to you during your labor. Also find out the usual nurse-to-patient ratio if you will deliver in a hospital. If it is low (1 to 1 or 1 to 2), a doula may not be necessary. Remember, however, that you can't plan the day or time of your birth, and that staffing patterns cannot be guaranteed. Resources for locating doulas are listed in the Appendix.

Relaxation, Positioning, Breathing, Yoga, Visualization

The pain of contractions comes from involuntary muscle tension. The more you can keep all your muscles in a relaxed state, the more comfortable you will feel in labor.

Practicing relaxation before labor will help you learn to relax yourself most effectively during contractions. *Relaxation* is a part of most childbirthing classes, regardless of the specific method offered. One technique of learning relaxation is called *progressive relaxation*. Lying in a comfortable position, with lots of pillows to support all joints, have your partner or a friend speak you through relaxing each muscle and joint. Your helper can test your relaxation by lifting each limb. If you are truly relaxed, the limb is loose and heavy. It will drop down if your helper lets go. To prepare for labor, you can practice tensing one body part, such as an arm or leg, while keeping the rest of the body relaxed. You can tense and then relax each body part. Remember to include not just the large muscles of the arms and legs, but your facial muscles and the smaller muscles in your hands and feet.

In labor, your support team can watch out for tensed body parts. During the prenatal practice sessions, you can develop a code that will let you know that you need to relax. Merely telling you to relax doesn't often work. You might practice responding to a gentle touch so that in labor, for instance, if your partner sees you frown, he or she can touch your brow and you will almost instinctively relax it. A word that induces relaxing thoughts might be equally effective; try something like "sunshine," "love," or "baby."

Music, positioning, and the environment all can add to relaxation. You can choose soothing music before labor and become used to relaxing to it. Bring a cassette or CD of this music to labor, with the tape deck or CD player, of course. During the pushing stage of labor, you may want to change the music to something more energetic.

You may relax more easily if the lights in the room are dimmed or turned off, or the shades or blinds pulled down. You may find the room too hot or too cold. Ask if the temperature can be adjusted. If not, you may find that extra clothing or less clothing helps with your comfort. You may need to ask your support team or the hospital or birthing center staff to be quiet in your presence, especially during contractions. Side conversations can be very distracting and annoying to you.

Breathing also contributes to relaxation. Deep abdominal breathing provides the best oxygenation for the fetus and helps the whole body relax. Some pregnant women attend yoga classes (check if there are special classes in your community for pregnant women) or practice yoga with the aid of books, tapes, or videos. *Yoga* concentrates on relaxation, with an emphasis on breathing, and its teachings can be very helpful in labor.

Although hospital staff may be quick to offer medication to a woman who makes noise during labor, allowing yourself to vocalize may be a release. Some women chant, hum, or moan. This should not be discouraged if you find it helpful.

You will find that your pain may increase or decrease according to the *position* you assume in labor. Of course, if you need fetal monitoring, your ability to change position will be restricted. If you can move around freely, experiment with various positions. Never lie flat on your back as it interferes with blood flow to the fetus. Use pillows to support your joints. Find out in advance if your facility for birthing allows you to bring extra pillows as you may get only one, two if you are lucky. Use the bed or your partner as a leaning post. Try the hands and knees position if you have back labor. Change positions frequently if this helps. Try walking and rocking back and forth or swaying during contractions.

Some women use *birthing balls* in labor. These are big inflatable rubber balls that are also used in exercise classes or children's play groups. They can be ordered via many children's mail order catalogues. The large size is usually best for labor. You can sit and relax your back against the ball in labor (with the ball leaning on the wall or your partner supporting it) or lean your belly over the curve of the ball from a hands and knees position. This is especially comforting for back labor. You can find out in advance whether you can bring a birthing ball to the labor unit, or whether one is available there.

Another aid for relaxation is *visualization*. This is also part of hypnosis for childbirth. Visualization is one of the techniques that should be practiced during pregnancy. It involves creating mental images of the body letting go, the cervix doing its job of thinning and opening, the baby moving down in the pelvis. There are tapes available to help with visualization, or you can make a tape for yourself, or ask your partner or somebody whose speaking voice you find soothing to make a tape for you. You can talk to your body and the baby as part of the visualization.

Use familiar images of opening: a flower, a butterfly emerging from a cocoon, a chick hatching.

You can play your visualization tape at various times during the final weeks of pregnancy. You can incorporate it into relaxation sessions, use it to help you unwind at the end of the day, or fall asleep listening to it. You can bring the same tape to labor with you.

You might want to use relaxing images other than labor—a great vacation you recently took or would like to take—or as Peter Pan told Wendy, John, and Michael, think any happy thoughts—and include them on the tape. Think about the baby soon to enter the world, how you will feel cuddling and holding your new child. Imagine its smell, its softness, the noises it will make. Some people include *affirmations* in their visualization tapes and repeat them before and during labor. "I will birth my baby." "So many women before me have had babies; I can do it." "Childbirth is a normal process." "My body is uniquely adapted for labor and birth." "Labor will bring my baby to me." "I am strong and competent." Make up your own affirmations. Be creative and use phrases that will have meaning for you.

Heat and Cold

Although some hospitals have regulations about the use of heat and cold during labor, they can be used at home in early labor, before you leave for the hospital. They may also be used liberally during home births or in birthing centers. Applications of heat or cold are especially soothing for back labor. Some women prefer heat, others cold. There is no particular rule about which to use. You can use a heating pad—wet or dry—or ice packs against your lower back. Sometimes alternating heat and cold works best. A heating pad on your lower abdomen may be soothing. Be careful not to burn yourself. This may happen if you apply heat to skin that is covered with lotion or ointment.

Massage

Massage is distracting and relaxing. Several types of massage can be used in labor. *Effluerage* (meaning "feather touch") is a gentle massage. It is done with the tips of the fingers in an up and down or circular motion on the uterus, from fundus to pubic bone. Effluerage can be used during or between contractions. It can be self-administered, although late in labor, even effluerage may be too much for the uterus to bear.

Back massage is good for back labor and general relaxation. Your partner or doula can be the masseuse. You will need to guide them, however, instructing them on whether you prefer light or deep strokes,

or a combination. Deep pressure can be applied with the palms of the
hand, the thumbs, or the fist. Muscles can be kneaded between the thumb
and fingers. Massage strokes should be continuous, going from up to
down and down to up without lifting the hands off the back. Strokes
should be rhythmic and definite, even when gentle. The masseuse's hands
may glide more easily over a thin T-shirt or nightgown than over bare
skin. Lotion, powder, oil, or witch hazel can help the hands move on skin.

Don't forget the neck, head, face, feet, and hands. They tend to tense
up during labor and this tension contributes to overall pain as well as to
fatigue and frustration. Massage of any of these areas can be wonderful.

Water Immersion

A warm bath or Jacuzzi is very comforting and recent research has
shown that it does not increase the chances of an intrauterine infection.
Don't try getting in or out of a tub without assistance! A shower can be
comforting if a tub is not available, or not clean. If you are in bed, a
sponge bath may be soothing or invigorating. Soaking your feet may be
relaxing, even if you can only sit at the side of the bed and immerse
them in a basin.

Hypnosis

Gayle Peterson, a strong advocate of hypnosis for childbirth, states
that "body-centered hypnosis . . . facilitates prenatal bonding, noninter-
ventive birthing, and healthy postpartum adjustments . . . , it creates a
bridge between the unconscious bodily processes of pregnancy and
childbirth and the emotional and psychological growth required during
this sensitive time in a woman's life cycle" (www.parentsplace.com). The
hypnosis for birthing advocated by Dr. Peterson does not involve "disso-
ciation from bodily experience," as some forms of hypnotherapy do, but
rather "deepens a woman's bodily sensation . . ." The main goal of hypnosis during labor is to reduce maternal anxiety, which in turn facilitates
labor and relieves pain. Exactly how hypnosis achieves its effects is not
known.

Dr. Peterson's book on hypnosis as well as other books and tapes on
this topic are listed in the Appendix. Some of the resources provide
guides to self-hypnosis for childbirth, teaching you to put yourself into
a trancelike state for labor.

No form of hypnosis works for everybody. Certain individuals are
more susceptible to hypnosis than others. For this reason, the technique
should be tried out before labor, unless you have had experience being

hypnotized for reasons other than childbirth. If you use a hypnotherapist, make certain the person is reputable.

Aromatherapy

Aromatherapy utilizes soothing and healing scents provided by essential oils. These oils are extracted from flowers, plants, trees, roots, and fruit.

Lavender is recommended for relieving tension and aiding in relaxation during labor. Sandalwood, chamomile, melissa, geranium, rose, and orange oils also may be relaxing or refreshing. You may not be able to bring the scented oils to a hospital, but you can use them in a tub, for massage, or as a compress before you leave your home. The oils should be diluted before being used on the skin. Be careful not to overdo the use of these oils; some women (and partners) get headaches from too strong a scent. Six drops in a bathtub is sufficient, and half that amount makes a good compress.

It's a good idea to try the oils before labor to make sure you don't have an unpleasant reaction to them. Use a patch test on your skin to see if you are allergic to the oil before you immerse yourself in it.

Acupuncture and Acupressure

Acupuncture is a Chinese healing technique involving the placement of needles to stimulate and heal the body. It must be applied by a licensed practitioner. Acupressure or *shiatsu* is a massage technique in which the body is stimulated by touch. The Ho-ku and Spleen 6 points on the body correspond to the uterus and cervix, respectively. Stimulating these specific points is said to help relieve the pain of labor. The Ho-ku point is on the back of the hand, at the "V" formed where the base of the thumb and the index finger join. Pressure is advised with the thumb for 10 to 15 seconds, three times, with a brief rest between each application. The Spleen 6 point is about the width of four fingers above the inner ankle on the shin. You press with the tip of the thumb from behind the mother's leg, in and toward the front of the leg. The timing of application is the same as for the Ho-ku point. These acupressure techniques can be repeated as frequently as every few minutes if the laboring woman wishes them repeated.

Transcutaneous Electrical Nerve Stimulation (TENS)

TENS is the application of small doses of electrical stimulation to nerve fibers. This is believed to cause the body to produce its own pain relieving substances. The electrodes through which the low-voltage current travels are taped to the lower back. The effectiveness of TENS in labor is not completely known, but it does not produce more than moderate pain relief. If it works, the advantage is that there are no known ill effects. TENS is considered most effective in early labor. Some hospitals have TENS machines available and some childbirth organizations will rent them to you.

Sterile Water Papules

Sterile water papules are used for the relief of back labor. This technique, administered by midwives, nurses, or physicians, involves the injection of sterile water just under the skin of the lower back. It is thought to provide nerve stimulation, distracting you from the back labor. The injections themselves are painful, but their pain is of short duration and they provide relief for an extended time period.

Medical Means of Managing Pain

Drugs for Labor

Several types of drugs are used in labor for the reduction of pain and anxiety. Chief among these are drugs classified as *narcotics*. Narcotics are *analgesic,* or pain relieving, drugs that are related to the opium poppy. Morphine is a natural opiate. Demerol (generic name, meperidine), the narcotic with the longest history of use in labor, is a synthetic opiate. Nubain (generic name, nalbuphine) and Stadol (butorphanol) are closely related and also used in labor. Narcotic drugs are carried by the bloodstream to the pain centers in the brain.

Narcotics used in labor are more likely to encourage drowsiness than *euphoria,* the technical term for a "high." The goal of narcotics in labor is to provide relaxation and assist the laboring woman in tolerating the pain. The medications are not meant to "knock you out" or to wipe out the memory of labor. In the past, an amnesiac, scopolamine, was used in labor to prevent women from experiencing delivery, by blocking their memory of labor. Rather than having a relaxing effect, this medication actually increased a woman's agitation. Stories are told of laboring women on scopolamine needing to be restrained so as not to climb out of bed. Such a medicated woman might scream in terror during labor, but remember none of this behavior.

The great majority of women now wish to be active participants in their labor and delivery. Pain relief today concentrates on reducing the unpleasant aspects of the process without removing awareness and memory.

This is not always done easily. Individual women react quite differently to identical doses of medication. With the customary narcotic dose, some fall asleep for an hour or two and others have only a slight response. Most women are alert during uterine contractions and doze off between them. They are awake enough to follow instructions from their birth attendants.

All narcotic drugs can slow breathing in both the mother and the newborn infant. For this reason, they are used in modest doses, given so that their peak action will not be at the time of birth, and combined with other drugs, principally the tranquilizers Phenergan (promethazine) and Vistaril (hydroxyzine). The tranquilizers relieve anxiety and increase the effectiveness of the narcotics. The tranquilizers also prevent nausea and vomiting, otherwise common narcotic side effects.

Narcotics usually are given only when you are in active labor. If given too early, they may reduce the effectiveness of the contractions, slowing labor. In active labor, they shouldn't affect contractions. In fact, the relaxation achieved with medication may help contractions work more efficiently.

In early labor, if you are having difficulty coping or losing sleep, a sedative such as Seconal (secobarbital) or Nembutal (pentobarbital) may be prescribed. Sedatives induce sleep without altering respirations, and are rapidly eliminated by the liver. If you are in false labor, they often will stop the contractions, but they don't interfere with real labor. These can be given by mouth or as an intramuscular injection. The usual dose is 100 mg.

In active labor, narcotics and tranquilizers must be given by injection. Depending on the medication, the injection can be given under the skin (*subcutaneously*) or deep into a muscle. Any of the medications can be given directly into the veins. A subcutaneous (SQ) or intramuscular (IM) injection will take 15 or 20 minutes to take effect, but its effect will last longer than the intravenous (IV) injection. The IV dose will act almost immediately, but it will be of shorter duration. Most often, these drugs are given intravenously. Commonly used dosages for pain relief in labor are:

Demerol: 50–100 mg IM or 25–50 mg IV
Nubain: 10–20 mg SQ, IM, or IV
Stadol: 1–2 mg IM or IV

Phenergan: 25–50 mg IM or IV
Vistaril: 50 mg IM

When the lower doses are given, the dose can be repeated after its effects wear off.

There has always been concern about the effect of labor drugs on the fetus and newborn. These drugs do cross the placenta. They may reduce the variability in fetal heart rate patterns. After an intravenous injection of Demerol, for instance, reduced variability may be seen in the fetal heart within 5 to 10 minutes. It can last for 60 or more minutes, depending on the medication dosage.

If narcotics are given so that their peak action coincides with the birth, the infant may have difficulty breathing. The IM dose peaks about 45 minutes after injection and the IV dose peaks shortly after its administration. If the newborn has trouble breathing, he or she can be given a narcotic "antagonist" called naloxone (Narcan).

By-products of narcotic metabolism can exist in the bloodstream of the newborn for days, possibly affecting behavior in the early days of life. If this occurs, it usually is a subtle effect, one believed to cause no lasting damage. If the baby is premature, shows signs of distress, or is otherwise at risk (such as if it is growth restricted), then these medications should not be used, or used with extreme caution.

Recently, narcotic drugs have been used as part of epidural anesthesia, described in the next section. They also are used for what is called *intrathecal injection*—injection directly into the spinal fluid as a one-time dose, without the indwelling catheter that is used for epidural anesthesia. The narcotics fentanyl (25 micrograms) and morphine (.25 mg) are usually used. Fentanyl, another synthetic opiate, acts rapidly, but its duration is limited to 1½ to 2 hours, whereas morphine has a slow onset but works for 2 to 8 hours. The advantage of intrathecal injection over epidural anesthesia is that it does not cause motor block, thus allowing the woman to move her legs. The advantage over IM or IV use is that intrathecal injection causes sensory nerve block without inducing drowsiness. Onset is rapid and duration relatively long. Side effects include itching, nausea, urine retention, decreased blood pressure, headache, and rarely, respiratory depression. The fetal heart may slow following intrathecal narcotic administration. Intrathecal medication is administered by an anesthesiologist.

Regional Block (Epidural) Anesthesia in Labor

Epidural anesthesia has become a very popular form of pain relief in labor. In some hospitals the majority of laboring women receive epidural anesthesia. In most cases, epidural anesthesia provides more pain relief than any other method. It's estimated to relieve 90 percent of pain in 85 percent of women who choose this form of anesthesia.

An advantage of epidural anesthesia is that should a cesarean delivery be necessary, the epidural can provide sufficient anesthesia for the surgery. In this case, a stronger dose of medication will be injected into the epidural catheter. If you need stitches after a vaginal birth, the epidural will provide anesthesia for that as well. Although it might seem to be an almost perfect method of pain relief, there are a number of controversies surrounding epidural use, particularly because it has become so widespread. Epidural anesthesia involves drugs that, like most drugs, cross the placenta. The nerve-blocking drugs used in epidural anesthesia are synthetic offspring of cocaine, with names ending in "-caine." Chemists have developed forms that are rapidly broken down in the body, thereby increasing their safety. The drugs are similar to novocaine used for dental work.

The most commonly used local anesthetic in epidural anesthesia is bupivacaine (trade name Marcaine or Sensorcaine). Among this group of drugs, bupivacaine has high potency and a slow onset of action. Its anesthetic effect lasts for 3 or more hours. In some situations, it may be combined with a narcotic, usually fentanyl.

HOW AN EPIDURAL IS ADMINISTERED   The epidural space is located within the bony ring that forms the spinal canal. The backbone is made up of twenty-four vertebrae, which rest on one another like a stack of checkers. The bodies of the vertebrae have cartilage pads between them and are connected to one another by dense ligaments. Behind each vertebral body, there is a bony ring. The spinal cord comes down from the brain through this series of rings, encased in a dense membrane named the *dura mater*. Nerves emerge from the dura and go out through the spaces between the rings of the vertebrae to the entire body.

The spinal fluid in which the nerve tissue of the spinal cord floats is within the dura. This fluid communicates with the fluid of the brain inside the skull. There is a space between the spinal cord and dura and the spinal canal. The size of this epidural space is greatest at the level of the two vertebral bodies just below the rib cage in the lumbar region (*epi*, from the Greek, means around, indicating that this space is around the dura).

Before an epidural is administered, you may be examined by your physician or midwife. You should be more than 3 centimeters dilated, but less than half an hour from full dilatation—to the extent that this can be determined—for the technique to be utilized. You will be visited by the anesthesiologist who will ask you questions to determine that an epidural is appropriate anesthesia for you. If you don't have an intravenous line, one will be started. You will receive a large amount of fluid through the intravenous line before epidural insertion. This guards against lowered blood pressure, a common side effect of epidural anesthesia. A dose of oral antacid may be given to help prevent the contents of your stomach from being acidic.

The technique for epidural anesthesia is to insert a fine catheter through a needle into the epidural space, inside the spinal canal but outside the dura. The woman remains in her labor bed and usually lies on her side, with her back curved, knees bent to her abdomen and chin tucked to her chest. This is called a "C" or "cat" shape. It separates the vertebral bones to increase the space into which the needle must be passed. Sometimes the epidural can be placed with the woman sitting up. The skin into which the needle will go is cleansed with an antibacterial solution and the area numbed with an injection of a local anesthetic. You will feel a brief sensation like a pin prick or bee sting. The anesthesiologist may take a few minutes to identify the epidural space. Inserting the catheter into the correct area is very important. Once the catheter is placed, it is taped to your back so that medications can be infused continuously through it or given in repeated doses.

Some anesthesiologists will ask your partner or other support persons to leave the room during the insertion of an epidural. This is something you might want to discuss in advance with your care provider so you know the routines of the anesthesiologists in the hospital where you will deliver. If you take childbirth education classes at the hospital, an anesthesiologist may come to one of the sessions and you can ask about this. You can certainly request that your support team, or at least one member, stay with you during the epidural administration.

The success of an epidural is dependent on the skill of the *anesthesiologist*, the person administering the block. The anesthesia must be given with care not to accidentally introduce the anesthetic agent into the spinal fluid in the *intradural space* (*intra* = within). The doses of drugs given in the epidural space are substantially larger than those given with direct spinal anesthesia. On occasion, despite all precautions, the drug given through the catheter can leak into the intradural space and engender a profound spinal anesthetic. The effect can extend up the spinal cord and, by paralyzing the muscles of the chest, interfere seriously with respirations. Epidurals therefore must be given slowly and deliberately, with a test dose injected before the full pain relieving dose is administered. Establishing an effective epidural ordinarily takes 20 to 30 minutes; the method cannot be used in a hurried situation.

As the test dose is given, you will be asked if you are dizzy, have any unusual tastes in your mouth, experience rapid heart palpitations, or feel sudden numbness. During and after epidural insertion, blood pressure is taken frequently and continuous electronic fetal heart monitoring usually is used. Pain relief occurs within 3 to 7 minutes, with full relief taking 10 to 20 minutes. The nerve-blocking agents flow through the catheter and bathe the nerves as they emerge from the dura. This stops the pain sensation from reaching the brain. It may also remove the brain's control over the muscles served by the nerves.

Because of the lower extremity weakness that is produced by epidural, the woman who has a traditional epidural will almost always have to remain in bed. She should lie with her right hip elevated on a pillow to take the weight of the uterus off her major abdominal blood vessels. Sometimes, the woman can still maintain some muscle control, an asset to pushing in the second stage of labor.

THE WALKING EPIDURAL   Today, a new type of epidural has been developed with the specific purpose of relieving pain without blocking the nerve signals to the muscles. This is the *walking epidural*. A walking epidural is more accurately called a *combined spinal epidural* (CSE), sometimes referred to as an ultra low dose epidural. This means that some analgesic medication is injected for a one-time dose into the spinal fluid as described above as intrathecal narcotic administration, while a catheter also is placed into the epidural space. The needle to be placed through the dura is called a *spinal needle*. It is placed through the epidural needle, so there is no additional discomfort in the insertion procedure for a CSE. The medication injected into the spinal fluid is an opiate, like those given intravenously. The medication injected through the catheter into the epidural space is a combination opiate and local anesthetic. The local anesthetic is given in a weaker dose in CSE than in a traditional epidural because the spinal injection provides additional pain relief. The combined spinal epidural is technically more difficult to administer and therefore available only in institutions where the anesthesiologists are familiar with the technique. This is something to find out about in advance of labor so you know the available options.

CSE works more quickly than a traditional epidural, with pain subsiding within 2 minutes. In theory, it numbs only the abdominal nerves, leaving the woman with control over her lower extremities. In reality, however, many women do not have full muscle control and mobility is limited, often to moving around in bed and sometimes going to the bathroom.

Some combined spinal epidurals and traditional epidurals are set up so that the woman can regulate her own dosage, with a limit set on the patient controlled pump so an overdose cannot occur. This is known as *patient-controlled analgesia* (PCA).

SIDE EFFECTS OF REGIONAL BLOCK ANESTHESIA   Neither traditional epidurals nor combined spinal epidurals, unfortunately, are without side effects, creating some of the controversy around their use. An epidural block may cause the blood to pool in the woman's legs and tissues below the level of the block, as the blood vessels in this area are widely open. The consequence of the pooling can be a drop in maternal blood pressure. This, in turn, can diminish the flow of blood to the uterus and bring about undesirable changes in the fetal heart rate. The blood pressure drop can be prevented by giving the woman at least a half liter (a little over a pint) of intravenous fluids shortly before administering the anesthetic agent. Therefore, use of epidural anesthesia requires an intravenous line.

Sometimes an epidural anesthesia is not wholly effective. In some women, a *patchy block* occurs, meaning there is an area, usually on one side, in which the anesthesia has not taken effect. This may be related to the skill of the person administering the epidural.

When narcotics are used, as they are in the combined spinal epidural, side effects include itching and respiratory depression. With either traditional epidural or combined spinal-epidural analgesia, urine retention may occur. This means you have difficulty urinating, sometimes necessitating the use of a urinary catheter, a thin tube inserted into the urethra to draw out the urine. This can lead to a urinary tract infection, although strict adherence to sterile technique by the staff reduces this risk. Nausea and vomiting may occur. Shivering is common. Sometimes epidural anesthesia causes the mother to develop a fever. Unfortunately, differentiating this fever from the fever of an intrauterine infection may be difficult, so treatment usually is initiated. This exposes the woman and her fetus to antibiotics, and the newborn to tests for infection (called a *sepsis workup*). In the rare occasion that the epidural anesthesia is accidentally injected into a blood vessel, seizures and irregularities of the maternal heart beat can occur. This is one reason for a test dose to be administered before the full dose of anesthetic agent is injected through the catheter.

One of the most controversial issues surrounding the use of epidural anesthesia is the extent to which it slows labor and causes an increase in interventions, including forceps, vacuum, and cesarean deliveries. Evidence is conflicting on whether the anesthesia slows the first stage of labor, but strong evidence shows that it slows the second or pushing stage. This is because the local anesthetic numbs the *perineum*—the area below the vagina where the pushing sensation is usually felt. This makes push-ing more difficult, although the difficulty can be overcome in several ways. The medication dose can be lowered or discontinued during the second stage, although for some women the sudden experience of pain in the pushing stage can be hard to tolerate after an almost pain-free first stage. A midwife or labor and delivery nurse can assist with pushing so that even without a strong urge, a woman can be guided to push effec-tively. Or, pushing can be delayed until the fetus descends on its own to at least a +2 or +3 station (see the previous chapter). This will shorten the overall amount of time spent pushing. Finally, the physician or mid-wife attending the labor simply can allow a longer second stage before intervening.

Because of the slowing of labor, oxytocin is used more often to aug-ment or assist labor in women who have epidurals (see Chapter 22 for more discussion of augmented labor). As the muscles of the vagina and perineum are numbed and relaxed with epidural anesthesia, the resis-tance of these muscles is lost. This resistance ordinarily would help the fetus turn during its descent into a favorable position for birth (see Chapter 19). This effect on fetal position, along with prolonged labor, results in an increased use of forceps and vacuum extractors for birth, also discussed in Chapter 22.

Whether or not there is an increased rate of cesarean deliveries with epidural use is less clear. Earlier studies tended to show an increased rate of cesareans, but it was never clear whether this was due to the epidural anesthesia or to the fact that women who received epidural anesthesia were more likely to have longer, more difficult labors to begin with—labors that would ordinarily lead to an increase in cesarean rates. More recent studies, which included *randomized trials*—meaning that women were assigned randomly to a group receiving epidural or to a group not receiving such anesthesia—have not shown significant differences in ce-sarean rates between women receiving epidural anesthesia and those not receiving this type of anesthesia. The issue is not entirely resolved by the currently available data. There is also debate on whether combined spinal epidural (CSE) is associated with fewer instances of prolonged labor than traditional epidural.

Some side effects of epidural or CSE anesthesia are not experienced until the postpartum period. Although any woman can get a backache in the postpartum period, women who have had epidural anesthesia are more likely to experience this problem. A small percentage of women get headaches following epidural anesthesia. This is due to a small, slow leak of spinal fluid and usually occurs if the dura mater was punctured during the insertion of the catheter. Puncture of the dura is most common in obese women or women with severe curvature of the spine (*lumbar lordosis*).

Because the combined spinal-epidural technique involves deliberate puncture of the dura, a headache is more likely following this technique. Still, headache is limited to less than 1 percent of all women who have had epidural anesthesia.

The headache may resolve if you lie flat on your back for a day or two—not an easy thing to accomplish with a new baby to care for. Drinking lots of fluids may help, especially fluids high in caffeine. Other methods may be used, if the pain is intense. Two or more quarts of intravenous fluid may be infused for the purpose of restoring a normal amount of spinal fluid volume. A clot of the woman's own blood can be used as a patch over the hole in the dura.

Very rarely, women will experience postpartum weakness or decreased mobility in the lower extremities. This also occurs in less than 1 percent of all women receiving epidurals.

Another controversy about the medications used in epidural anesthesia is the extent to which they affect the newborn. Both narcotics and local anesthetics pass through the placenta regardless of the route they are given. Fetal heart rate changes may be seen on the monitor tracing. As already noted, because of the increased likelihood of maternal fever, the newborn may receive antibiotics through the placenta and then may be subjected to a workup for infection. This can include invasive tests such as a spinal tap. The most obvious newborn problem is interference with nursing from poor rooting and sucking reflexes (see Chapter 26). This certainly does not make nursing impossible, but may make its initiation more difficult. When narcotics are used, the effects described earlier in this chapter may be experienced by the newborn, including drowsiness at birth and breathing problems.

Some women cannot have epidural anesthesia. These include women who have had previous back surgery, who have heart disease, a skin disorder of the back, or women who are allergic to the local anesthetics. If you ever have had an injection for dental work, you should know whether or not you have an allergy to the type of medication used. Rarely, the anesthesiologist finds that placement of the catheter into the epidural space is not possible.

Paracervical Block for Labor

There used to be some enthusiasm for paracervical block for pain relief in labor. This block is produced by injecting a labor anesthetic agent alongside the cervix, using a vaginal approach for the injection, with the intention of blocking the nerves near the uterus. This technique is no longer widely used for two reasons. One is that its effectiveness is not entirely predictable. The other is that every once in a while there has been severe slowing of the fetal heart rate after the drug is given. This is probably due to passage of the drug into the placenta and thereby into fetal circulation, and also to spasm of the uterine arteries from its local effect.

ANESTHESIA FOR BIRTH

Normal spontaneous vaginal delivery does not require anesthesia. Anesthesia for birth is limited to cesarean, forceps, or vacuum extraction births. Anesthesia to the perineum, however, may be used to cut an episiotomy, or to repair an episiotomy or tear. Such anesthesia is discussed in Chapters 19 and 22.

A Guilt-Free Experience

No woman can entirely anticipate what her labor will be like. No woman can entirely predict what her reactions to labor will be. The value of support—for women choosing either nonmedicated or medicated labor—is now widely recognized. While no medication can be guaranteed entirely safe, the possibility of serious or long-term consequences from medications used in labor today is small. Labor is painful; labor is hard work. Labor should not cause suffering beyond a woman's ability to endure. Your level of endurance is a personal, even private, issue. Only you can be inside your own body. Medication should be a choice you make for yourself. It is a personal decision. Knowing the pros and cons of various choices allows you to make an informed decision, based on your own assessment of your needs. No choice should lead to regret or guilt.

CHAPTER TWENTY-ONE

Difficult Labor

Most labors and births occur without difficulty or undue medical assistance. Many complications seen in the past rarely are encountered today. Contraction of the pelvis, once the usual cause of obstructed labor, has been virtually eliminated by improvements in nutrition. Diseases such as diabetes and high blood pressure that used to nearly preclude normal pregnancy are now managed so well that most women with these illnesses have healthy babies. While survival of the mother was once considered the main medical goal of a pregnancy and birth, today that is almost assured. Attention has turned not only to newborn survival but to the quality of its life. Interventions often are implemented in an effort to prevent lifetime neurological damage.

This chapter reviews possible problems that can occur during labor and birth, as infrequently as they are seen today. The next chapter describes the interventions that can be applied when these problems arise.

Dystocia (from the Greek, meaning "difficult birth") is due to three principal causes:

- Inadequate uterine contractions
- Fetal problems, including unusual positioning
- Birth canal narrowing

These have been called the *3 p's*: the powers, the passenger, and the passage. Dystocia also can be caused by a combination of these factors—a pelvis that would be adequate in size for a baby in the usual position, for example, but is too small for a baby unusually positioned in the uterus.

THE POWERS

No one can predict entirely how a woman's body will respond to the forces of labor. In one woman, what seem to be strong and frequent contractions may accomplish little in the progress of labor. In another woman, contractions that appear mild to moderate produce rapid progress. To an experienced observer, the frequency and intensity of contractions and the pain they create tells a lot about the efficiency of labor, but in an occasional woman, these observations lead to an inaccurate conclusion. Electronic equipment does no better than human observation in this prediction. The final criteria for the adequacy of uterine force are the descent of the presenting part and the progressive dilatation of the cervix.

As determined by vaginal examinations in a first labor, once the cervix is more than 3 to 4 centimeters dilated, it opens at about 1.2 centimeters (one half-inch) an hour. For second and later labors the rate is about 1.5 centimeters an hour. The pace tends to increase as the first stage continues. Of course, labor is not mechanical and this rate of progress does not occur in a clocklike manner every hour. Starts and stops in progress are common. If, however, the cervix fails to dilate over a period of several hours, we must consider the diagnosis of inadequate contractions or uterine dysfunction, although other causes of delay in progress are possible.

Hypotonic and Hypertonic Uterine Contractions

There are two types of uterine dysfunction. In one, the uterine contractions are ineffective because they are too weak, perhaps too spaced apart. This is called *hypotonic labor* (Greek: *hupo* = beneath; *tonos* = tone). In the other, the contractions are very strong, perhaps unusually so, but ineffective. They do not last long enough and are too irregular in pattern. The uterine muscle may contract more strongly in its midsection than in the fundus or upper section. This is called *hypertonic labor* (Greek: *hyper* = above) or, less commonly, *incoordinate uterine dysfunction*.

Uterine dysfunction may occur with another problem such as an unusual fetal presentation or an anatomical defect of the uterus, described later.

Hypotonic Uterine Contractions
Hypotonic uterine contractions are too weak, too infrequent, and/or too short to effect cervical dilatation. Labor must be clearly established for

this condition to be diagnosed. Latent phase contractions are naturally mild and widely spaced. Once the contractions have become stronger, more frequent, and regular, and the cervix has dilated to at least 4 centimeters, then a slowing of contractions without further progress can be designated hypotonic labor.

In the absence of signs of fetal problems such as a nonreassuring fetal heart rate pattern, hypotonic labor can be corrected in a number of ways. Simple measures are worth trying before more medical interventions are utilized. Emotional support, for example, has been shown to reduce the duration of labor. Although the exact nature of the effect on labor of a woman's stress level cannot be stated, sometimes allowing the woman to express anxieties and fears will result in more efficient labor. If the woman is dehydrated, fluids are helpful, given either orally or intravenously. Walking or showering or immersion in a tub may stimulate labor. Some practitioners try using enemas in this situation, but their value is dubious at best. Rupture of the membranes often will speed up labor, as will nipple stimulation because of its effect on the release of *oxytocin*, the hormone that produces uterine contractions.

If hypotonic contractions without cervical dilatation or fetal descent continue over time, medical interventions become necessary. Labor can be stimulated with oxytocin (Pitocin). When labor has already begun and oxytocin is used, it is called *augmentation of labor*. The use of oxytocin in labor is discussed further in Chapter 22.

Hypertonic Uterine Contractions

Besides being ineffective, hypertonic, or extra-forceful, uterine contractions also may be an added stress for both mother and fetus. They may lead to maternal exhaustion and fetal distress.

Hypertonic labor is a latent phase dysfunction. Hypertonic contractions can be misinterpreted as false labor because they do not cause cervical dilatation. However, they are excessively strong and painful, and occur more frequently than contractions in false labor usually do. Their irregular pattern, however, is similar to false labor.

Hypertonic labor usually is treated with medication to stop or slow the contractions. A barbiturate (sleeping pill) like Seconal or Nembutal (see previous chapter) or a strong narcotic like morphine may be prescribed in a safe dose. The goal of this treatment is to help the mother sleep with the expectation that she will awaken in a better, more effective labor pattern.

Uterine Rupture

Uterine rupture is an infrequent but serious complication. It rarely occurs in the absence of certain complications or risk factors. Previous surgery to the uterus may have weakened an area of its muscle, making it susceptible to rupture. In a type of cesarean section called a classical cesarean, for example, the incision is made into the body of the uterine muscle—its most contractile part. Fortunately, classical cesarean section is an outdated procedure for routine cesarean delivery. Today, most cesareans are done through the lower uterine segment which thins but does not contract in labor.

Occasionally, a woman will have had a classical cesarean for a premature baby because early in pregnancy the lower part of the uterus is not formed well enough to cut into it. Very rarely, a lower uterine incision may lead to a rupture in a subsequent labor. For this reason, the American College of Obstetricians and Gynecologists recommends hospital as the place for delivery following a previous cesarean birth. Surgery for fibroids may weaken the uterine muscle as well. Aggressive use of oxytocin can cause a uterine rupture. Very high *parity*, meaning the woman has had many previous term or near-term pregnancies, somewhat increases the possibility of a rupture.

With uterine rupture, the fetal parts are felt easily on an abdominal examination. These parts are more movable than previously. The uterus itself may be felt as a hard or contracted mass next to the fetal parts.

The woman experiencing a uterine rupture may have severe pain. She may show signs of shock: rapid pulse; decreased blood pressure; extreme paleness; cold, clammy skin; extreme fear; shortness of breath; restlessness; visual disturbances. Changes in the fetal heart rate may also signal a rupture. There may be decelerations or a slowing of the heart rate (*bradycardia*).

When rupture occurs, the woman must receive intravenous fluids. Blood must be made ready for a transfusion and the baby delivered via emergency abdominal surgery.

THE PASSENGER

Abnormalities in Fetal Position

The previous chapters discussed normal labor. In normal labor, the fetus is head down (*vertex*). This is called its *presentation*. There are two other possible presentations besides the vertex. These are the breech and shoulder. In the breech presentation, the baby's buttocks or feet are the first part to be born. In a shoulder presentation, the baby's shoulder is at the cervix. The fetus lies side-to-side or transversely in the mother's uterus. A breech presentation presents difficulties for the birth but a fetus with a shoulder presentation must turn in order to deliver vaginally. On occasion, the fetus may be in an oblique or diagonal lie during pregnancy, but this always becomes either a transverse or longitudinal (up and down) lie in labor. Oblique lie may therefore be called an "unstable" lie.

Even when the vertex or head is presenting, there are some positions of the head that make the birth easier, others that make it more difficult, and a few that make it impossible. The head may change position in labor, but occasionally will not.

Each of these problems involving the "passenger" or fetus can be termed *malpresentations* or *malpositions*.

Breech

It is not unusual for a fetus to be in a breech presentation from time to time until the last 4 to 6 weeks of pregnancy. In a breech, the buttocks are down into the pelvis and the head up toward the mother's ribs. Most fetuses finally settle into a head-down position. Left to their own devices, however, about 3 to 4 percent of all babies come to rest as breeches and remain so at the onset of labor.

There is no particular cause for most breech presentations. They are simply accidents of posture of the baby. There are, however, certain conditions which make a breech presentation somewhat more likely. These include relaxation of the uterine muscle after a woman has had many children; twins or other multiple pregnancies; extra or insufficient amniotic fluid (*polyhydramnios* or *oligohydramnios*); and certain fetal anomalies. When a woman has had a delivery by the breech, there is a slightly increased likelihood that she will have another. A woman with a partial or complete duplication of the body of the uterus, itself an unusual event, may have all her babies by the breech. A breech presentation is more frequent in a premature fetus than a fetus at term.

A breech can be felt on abdominal examination and confirmed by vaginal examination and ultrasound.

In a breech presentation, most commonly the legs are alongside the baby's trunk, with the feet near the face and the baby presenting by its buttocks. This is a *frank breech*, and the likelihood of normal labor and birth in this position is very close to that of the baby presenting by the vertex. Less frequently the baby sits in the yoga position, with knees

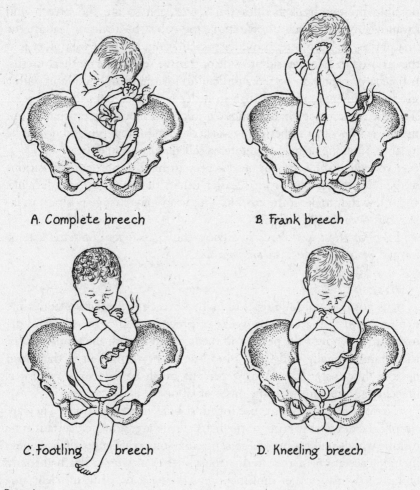

A. Complete breech

B. Frank breech

C. Footling breech

D. Kneeling breech

Breech.

bent and buttocks and feet presenting. This is a *complete breech*. In other cases one or both of the legs may be extended so that the feet occupy the lowermost portion of the uterus and the buttocks are relatively high. This is called a *footling breech*—either single or double.

The principal problems with breech presentation are difficult delivery of the fetal head and umbilical cord obstruction or *prolapse*. In a vertex presentation, the least pliable and largest part of the baby is born first; in a breech, the least pliable and largest part is born last. The head may not have molded (or narrowed) during labor as it does in a vertex presentation. It may need time to mold after the breech is born, delaying delivery and possibly causing the baby to lose oxygen, or it may have difficulty fitting through the pelvis, causing trauma and damage to the baby. These usually are not dangers to the mother. The main danger to the mother with a breech presentation is the increased possibility of a cesarean delivery.

In an occasional breech presentation, the head of the fetus is *hyperextended*. This means the chin is up and the head bent backward, rather than forward. This can be a danger to the fetus at the time of birth. If the breech baby has a hyperextended head at the time of labor, usually a cesarean is necessary. Hyperextension of the head usually is diagnosed by ultrasound. It also can be diagnosed with an X ray or C-T scan. Whether or not the mother's pelvic measurements should be taken with X ray or C-T scan is controversial as it exposes the fetus to additional radiation.

If you visualize a newborn baby you will realize that the navel, which is where the umbilical cord attaches to the abdominal wall, is very much closer to the buttocks than it is to the head. With a vertex presentation the head and the shoulders ordinarily are born before the navel itself enters the pelvis. At that moment cord blood flow may be obstructed, but since the head is born, the rest of the baby usually is born easily.

With a breech presentation the cord is low in the uterus. Indeed, with footling breeches, about 1 time out of 8 the cord *prolapses*—or falls through—the cervix into the vagina during labor. When this occurs early in labor the likelihood of vaginal birth of a healthy baby is remote. However, even if the cord behaves well and remains up in the uterus during most of labor, as the breech descends through the pelvis at the time of birth, the chance of cord obstruction remains greater than with a vertex presentation.

The route of delivery for breech presentations is a continued source of controversy within the obstetrical community with some arguing that cesarean birth is safest for all babies presenting in the breech. Many medical centers, however, individualize the method of delivery and deliver a fair number of breech babies vaginally. Breech babies that pose the least risk are those that are neither too small nor too big and in the frank breech position. With large babies, the danger of the head becoming trapped increases. With small babies, the danger of cord prolapse increases. In premature babies, the difference between the size of the buttocks and the size of the head is particularly pronounced. The buttocks even may pass through an incompletely dilated cervix, adding to the possibility of the head's being trapped or damaged following delivery of the breech. Recently, a large study, conducted in a number of medical centers and involving thousands of births, showed that infant outcomes were better when babies in the breech presentation were delivered by cesarean.

Other studies, however, have showed excellent outcomes for breech babies in favorable circumstances, as described. Undoubtedly, this controversy will continue, with the expectation that since the publication of this study, more breech babies will be delivered by cesarean.

Vaginal breech delivery may be easy, requiring little assistance, or more difficult, requiring hand maneuvers known as *assisted breech delivery*. Vaginal delivery requires that physicians experienced in the technique of breech birth be available to perform the birth or assist with it. This may not always be possible as physicians become used to performing cesarean section for all or most breech births.

The reasons generally agreed upon for cesarean delivery for breech babies include:

- A premature fetus when delivery is necessary (possibly due to maternal illness) or impossible to stop (except in the rare instance of such extreme prematurity that survival is highly unlikely)
- Severe fetal growth restriction
- A very large fetus
- Any question about whether or not the pelvis is adequate in size
- A hyperextended head
- A history of a perinatal death
- A previous child with a birth trauma

If there is a need for delivery (such as with pregnancy induced hypertension), but the woman is not in labor, an induction (discussed in the next chapter) is not advised with a breech, so this is another reason for a cesarean birth.

EXTERNAL CEPHALIC VERSION   One way to reduce the number of babies that enter labor in a breech presentation is to turn the baby manually during pregnancy. This procedure is called *external cephalic version*. The goal is to change the presentation through the mother's abdomen from breech to *cephalic* (head).

External version is most successful early in the pregnancy, but there is also a strong possibility that the breech will turn on its own before term. Most versions, then, are performed between 37 and 39 weeks of gestation. Today, versions are carried out under ultrasonic guidance. The amount of amniotic fluid is measured and the placenta localized. If there is reduced amniotic fluid, the version is less likely to be successful. The woman lies in bed, with her legs slightly elevated, and the baby is turned under ultrasound direction by the care provider's hands. The external fetal monitor is applied to make sure the heart rate remains normal during and after the procedure. Often, medication is used to relax the uterine muscle before the version is attempted. This is the same medication that might be used to relax the uterus that is contracting prematurely (see Chapter 15). An example is terbutaline (Brethrine), which is given just under the skin (subcutaneously) in a dosage of 0.25 mg. The entire procedure, including monitoring the fetus after the version is completed, takes several hours. External version usually is done in the obstetrical monitoring unit of a hospital. Women with Rh negative blood should receive an injection of Rh antibodies or RhoGAM after an external version (see Chapter 5).

SELF-HELP MEASURES   Earlier in pregnancy, several self-help measures can be tried at home to turn the breech. The effectiveness of these have not been studied, but they do no harm. One is to place a radio or other source of music at the pelvis to lure the baby's head to the music. Another is to use gravity to turn the fetus. This involves assuming an "upside down" position several times a day in the last few weeks of pregnancy. The easiest and safest way to do this is to lie in a bed that is next to a wall, with a pillow under the hips and legs extended and resting on the wall. There is no hard and fast rule about how many times a day to play the music or assume the breech position or how long to use the methods each time. Ten to twenty minutes several times a day seems reasonable.

Transverse Presentation

When the fetus lies with its long axis (the line of its spinal column) at right angles to that of the mother, the position is called a *transverse lie*. The fetal head is at the mother's left or right side, rather than up or down. If the fetus is transverse when labor starts, normal birth is not safe for either the mother or the baby. For the infant the risk is that the cord may *prolapse*, or fall past the baby, who, in this position, does not fill the lowermost part of the uterus. The cord thus becomes obstructed, endangering fetal circulation. The risk to the mother is that a live term infant in a transverse position cannot fit through the birth canal. The possibility of rupture of the uterus in such a case, if labor continues, is prohibitively high. The only time a live fetus in a transverse lie can deliver is if the baby is extremely small, usually less than 2 pounds, and the mother's pelvis is large. The treatment for transverse lie in labor, with very few exceptions, is cesarean.

A transverse lie is a rare event, seen in far less than 1 percent of all labors. There are certain situations in which it is more likely, though never common. These situations include:

Transverse lie

Transverse lie.

- A lax abdominal wall, which occurs in women who have had many births
- Prematurity
- Placenta previa (when the placenta presents over the cervix)
- Excess amniotic fluid
- A uterine abnormality
- A contracted or small pelvis

The last two of these are described later in this chapter in the section on "The Passage."

A transverse lie may be suspected on observation alone as the uterus will be unusually wide, but not as high up in the woman's body as expected for the weeks of the pregnancy. The lie can be confirmed by abdominal examination as the head and breech are felt on the side of the uterus rather than at the top and bottom. It can be diagnosed definitively by ultrasound.

A transverse lie discovered during pregnancy usually converts to a *longitudinal* (up and down) lie. However, spontaneous turning becomes less likely as pregnancy advances. An attempt can be made to turn the baby with external cephalic version after 37 weeks of pregnancy or even at the onset of labor, if the membranes are not ruptured. Although the version can be done earlier in the pregnancy, the lie will most likely revert back to transverse, often to turn later on its own. As placenta previa may be the cause of a transverse lie, mechanically blocking the fetus from moving down toward the cervix, the placenta must be located by ultrasound before version is attempted. The procedure is described on page 578, as it is essentially the same as the version performed when the baby is in the breech presentation.

If the lie reverts to transverse after external version, or if external version is not possible or successful, then a cesarean delivery is the safest choice for both mother and baby.

Occiput Posterior

A baby in the occiput posterior (OP) position lies with its *occiput* (back of its head) at the mother's back, its face toward her pubic bones. As mentioned in previous chapters, if this position persists until birth, the part of the head coming through the birth canal is wider than it is in an anterior position, in which the baby's occiput is toward the front of the mother's body. An occiput posterior position that persists through the second or pushing stage of labor may prolong pushing. Alternatively, if the baby changes positions during labor from left or right occiput posterior to direct occiput anterior (OA), then the rotation that the head undergoes during labor (see Chapter 19) is a longer rotation—135 degrees compared to 45 degrees—so that either the first or second stage of labor may be slowed. If the physician or midwife is aware of the baby's position and demonstrates patience, the increased length of labor is not a problem, just a slightly more difficult variation of normal. Rarely, if labor is unduly delayed, causing unusual stress for mother or baby, forceps delivery or a vacuum extraction may be performed.

Face Presentation

In a head-down position, if the fetal head is hyperextended rather than flexed, the neck is bent backward and the occiput lies against the fetal back. The chin (called the *mentum*) is the presenting part. This occurs in about two-tenths of 1 percent of deliveries or even less—1 in 600 to 1 in 900 births. A face presentation may occur with a fetal anomaly or with a very large fetus. It is more common in women with lax abdominal muscles.

A face presentation usually is diagnosed on vaginal examination. The examiner may feel the mouth (which can be mistaken for an anus) or an eye.

In a face presentation, the chin may point toward the front or back of the mother's body. If it is pointing toward her back (*mentum posterior*), labor may become obstructed because the brow of the fetus gets pushed against the pubic bones. The baby cannot be born in this position. Most mentum posterior positions rotate during labor to mentum anterior positions and the baby's head can be born. Rotation can even happen late in labor.

During crowning, the baby's face can be seen in the birth canal, presenting a very different picture from the back of the head seen in the vertex position. The chin is born first, followed by the nose, eyes, brow, and back of the head. The face may be quite swollen. This will resolve within a few days.

Sometimes a face presentation occurs when the pelvis is contracted. Labor does not then progress and a cesarean is needed for delivery.

Brow Presentation

A brow presentation is the rarest of all presentations. In one hospital with thousands of births per year, the brow presentation was seen in 0.03 percent of these.

The brow (or *forehead*) presents when the fetal head is neither flexed (with chin on chest) nor extended (with chin up and the back of the head against the mother's back). In a brow presentation, the neck is straight. This is sometimes called the *military attitude*.

A brow presentation usually is diagnosed on vaginal examination. The eyes and nose may be felt, along with the large fontanelle or soft spot in the front of the baby's head. Unlike with a face presentation, however, the mouth and chin are beyond reach.

The brow presentation is called an *unstable presentation* because it rarely persists throughout labor. The head almost always flexes or hyperextends so that either the occiput or chin presents. This is fortunate, as the head will not be able to fit through the birth canal when the brow presents, except when the fetus is unusually small and the pelvis unusually large. Once the brow changes to an occiput or face presentation, vaginal birth is possible. There is no reason for interference as long as labor progresses well.

Transverse Arrest (Persistent Occiput Transverse Position)

When the *vertex* (fetal head) enters the pelvis, it is usually in the *oblique* (diagonal) position or the *transverse* (side-to-side). It must eventually rotate or turn to a direct front to back position—either anterior or posterior. Occasionally, the head does not complete its rotation and gets "stuck" in the transverse position. Usually, in this case, it does not descend fully into the pelvis. This may be a consequence of *hypotonic uterine contractions* (see above).

There are three ways of dealing with transverse arrest. If the cervix is fully dilated and the head low enough, the physician can administer an anesthetic and assist the birth with either a vacuum extractor or forceps. (Some midwives perform vacuum extractions, but many do not.) Oxytocin can be used to increase the force of uterine contractions. If the head is too high for forceps or vacuum, the physician may perform a cesarean delivery. Whether and when to administer these therapies depend on the force of the labor, the *station* or level of descent of the head, evidence of maternal and fetal well-being, and the size of the pelvis. Ultimately, this is a matter of obstetrical judgment. These interventions are discussed in Chapter 22.

Fetal Anomalies

Hydrocephalus

Some fetal abnormalities cause parts of the baby to become very large. The commonest of these is *hydrocephalus* (Greek for "water in the head"). In this condition the drainage of the fluid that is normally inside the brain fails, but the formation of the fluid continues. The brain steadily swells, spreading the movable plates that compose the skull to a size that may not fit through the birth canal. The diagnosis of hydrocephalus can be made with considerable accuracy by ultrasound of the fetus, and plans for management determined in advance of labor.

There recently has been an intense effort to save babies with hydrocephalus, although proper management of birth for babies with hydrocephalus is somewhat controversial. For many years, the practice was to drain the excess fluid from the baby's head in order to decompress it to a size that would pass through the birth canal. This was done during labor, with a long needle passed through the vagina and open cervix or through the mother's lower abdominal wall. With a breech presentation, the fluid was removed abdominally or vaginally after the birth of the breech, before delivery of the head.

As this procedure can result in fetal death, many experts no longer advocate using it, except in instances were there are other severe abnormalities. This cannot always be determined. Cesarean birth is advised instead. Delivery of a hydrocephalic fetus by cesarean, however, requires an unusually large uterine incision because of the size of the head, unless drainage can be done safely at the time of the cesarean. Sometimes, the baby is delivered early so it can be treated with neurosurgery to minimize damage.

Fetal Masses

On rare occasions, a fetus may develop a tumor that reaches great size and obstructs delivery. Recently such fetuses have survived with appropriate surgical intervention when the correct diagnosis has been made by ultrasound. The fetal abdomen can be enlarged due to an accumulation of fluid (*ascites*) or enlargement of any of the abdominal organs— the bladder, kidney, or liver. In this event, a decision must be made whether or not to use a cesarean for delivery. This is based on the likelihood of newborn survival.

Nonreassuring Fetal Heart Rate Patterns and Meconium

Sometimes, the fetus has a difficult time tolerating the stress of labor. The first signs that this might be happening are changes in the fetal heart rate, called nonreassuring fetal heart rate patterns, or the presence of meconium in the amniotic fluid. Fetal heart rate changes can be picked up by a simple instrument called a *fetoscope* or by *electronic fetal monitoring equipment*. These changes are described in detail in Chapter 20. Meconium is the contents of the fetal bowel and may be seen in normal term deliveries as well.

Meconium may be a sign of distress or may itself lead to a problem in the neonatal period if the baby *aspirates,* or breathes, it into its lungs while in the uterus or during birth. The likelihood of aspiration may be reduced if an *amnioinfusion* is performed in labor. In this procedure, described in the following chapter, the meconium-stained amniotic fluid is diluted. The benefit of this procedure is controversial.

Today, we have the ability to measure the oxygen content of the fetal blood, increasing the ability to determine whether or not the fetus with meconium or with a nonreassuring heart rate pattern is having a real problem. Labor can proceed on its own even when the baby is having problems, but obstetrical care today focuses on a healthy baby, one without future damage. The extent to which nonreassuring fetal heart rate changes in labor actually causes future neurological damage, such as cerebral palsy, is an area of considerable controversy, but even without a clear resolution to this issue, if the fetus appears to be having difficulty tolerating labor, this is considered a reason to deliver the baby. Once delivered, the pediatric staff can provide expert care.

The nature of the intervention to deliver the baby in the presence of nonreassuring fetal heart rate patterns will depend on the severity of the problem, the progress of the labor, and the likelihood of a rapid delivery. If the fetal heart rate change occurs in the second stage, for example, delivery may require only an episiotomy to speed it up or some assistance to help ease the baby out. This can be done with a *Ritgen maneuver*, which simply means the birth attendant will reach through the mother's thinned out perineum for the baby's chin, and gently use it to guide the head through the birth canal. These maneuvers may speed up the birth by several contractions, sparing the baby added stress. If signs of fetal problems occur earlier in the second stage, but the baby is low in the birth canal, then forceps or a vacuum delivery might be appropriate. If nonreassuring fetal heart rate patterns are seen early in labor, a cesarean may be necessary. This will depend on the severity of the heart rate problem, the progress of the labor, and the oxygen content of the baby's blood.

How to deliver the baby who appears in distress calls for clinical judgment. This is one reason to choose a physician or midwife carefully. Although the midwife will, in these instances, collaborate with the physician, perhaps calling him or her into the hospital to perform a cesarean birth, or transferring the mother from home or birth center to hospital, the midwife's judgment is critical at this time in labor. Ultimately, in this situation, you place your trust in your care provider.

Prolapsed Umbilical Cord

A prolapsed umbilical cord is an obstetrical emergency. It occurs rarely, but causes serious fetal distress. The cord *prolapses* when it becomes caught between the baby and the pelvis. Blood cannot flow through the trapped cord and the baby will eventually lose its oxygen supply. Almost always, a rapid cesarean delivery is warranted.

Most often a prolapsed cord occurs in predictable situations, although even with identifiable risks, prolapse is not common. In most risk situations, the baby does not fill the pelvis, leaving room for the cord to literally fall into the pelvis and get trapped. These include a footling breech; a transverse lie; a premature or very small baby; a high presenting part, especially when the membranes rupture and especially if the practitioner ruptures them. In most circumstances, the membranes should not be ruptured before the head has engaged, which means it has made its way at least to the midsection of the pelvis from which it will not move up again.

Certain signs suggest the possibility of cord prolapse. On a rare occasion, the cord may be seen protruding from the vagina. More likely, the fetal heart will drop, especially after the membranes rupture. A vaginal examination will reveal a soft pulsating part next to the fetus. This is the cord.

Although a serious emergency, cord prolapse does not have to lead to a poor outcome for the fetus. The baby can be saved, as long as the prolapse is diagnosed quickly and steps taken immediately. The physician, midwife, or nurse can push the baby's head or presenting part off the cord during the vaginal examination. Sometimes the mother may be assisted to assume a knee-chest position, which relieves some of the pressure against the cord. This will be done with the examiner's hand remaining in the vagina. This creates an awkward, but lifesaving, situation. Even if a prolapse were to occur in a birth center, for instance, requiring transfer, the midwife or nurse would transfer the mother without releasing the pressure she or he is placing on the fetal head to keep it off the cord. In the meantime, the hospital will make preparations for an immediate cesarean. (Of course, a prolapse in a birth center would be rare, as any of the risk factors for prolapse preclude anything but a hospital delivery. Practitioners in the home and birth center are especially careful not to rupture membranes with a high head.)

Shoulder Dystocia

After the fetal head is born, the shoulders must make their way through the birth passage and be born. In some fetuses, especially large ones, the shoulders have difficulty being born. They become entrapped against the pubic bones.

Shoulder dystocia is an obstetrical emergency, as the baby eventually will die if it is not delivered. A systematic series of steps has been developed, which are eventually successful in delivering the baby. These include cutting an episiotomy and repositioning the mother, either by bending her legs up against her chest (called the *McRoberts maneuver*) or moving her into a side-lying or knee-chest position. These position changes often will free the shoulder from its locked position against pubic bones. If these are not successful, then an assistant is asked to apply downward pressure just above the *pubic bones* (the bones behind the vulva or pubic hairline) while the physician or midwife delivering the baby applies gentle traction on the already delivered head. If this maneuver doesn't work quickly, then the physician or midwife will attempt to rotate the shoulders, in what is called a *Woods screw maneuver*. This is a further attempt to free the shoulder from its impacted position. Other procedures to help with delivery in the case of shoulder dystocia include manual extraction of the fetal arms, purposeful fracture of the fetal *clavicle* (collarbone), and, rarely, replacing the fetal head into the uterus and performing a cesarean.

There is a risk of fetal injury with shoulder dystocia, from a fractured clavicle which heals relatively easily, to a paralysis of the arm (*Erb's palsy*) or hand (*Krumkie's palsy*). Treatment consists of time, physical therapy, and possibly surgery. Usually, healing is complete, but some degree of permanent damage is possible. Whenever a shoulder dystocia is antici-

pated (as it might be when the fetus is very large), or when one is encountered unexpectedly (as many are), a pediatrician should be called
for the delivery to attend immediately to the newborn. If a midwife is
performing the birth, he or she will call the collaborating physician to
assist with the birth, although all midwives are prepared to deal with
this obstetrical emergency.

THE PASSAGE:
DIMINISHED PELVIC CAPACITY

The Bony Pelvis

The bony pelvis is a complex structure, made up of seven bones: the
sacrum, the two iliums (or *ilia*), the two ischiums (or *ischia*), and the
two pubic bones, joined together to form a ring. The *sacrum* consists of
the lowermost five segments of the spinal column, different from the
vertebrae above because they are fused together to form a solid bone. Attached to the lower end of the sacrum with a flexible joint is the three-
segment *coccyx*, a remnant of the tail and quite without function.

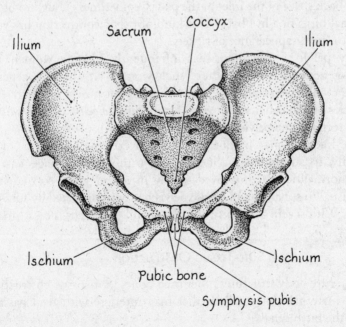

Bones and joints of the pelvis.

The circle of pelvic bones surrounds the lower part of the uterus. In its passage through the birth canal, the fetus must fit through this bony ring. First, it must enter the pelvis. The place where the fetus enters is called the *pelvic inlet*. Entry usually occurs before labor, especially with a first baby. Next, the fetus must *engage* or become fixed in the pelvis. This happens when the bones of its skull reach a place in the middle of the pelvis called the *ischial spines*. The "spines," as they are commonly referred to, are tiny projections from the ischial bones into the right and left sides of the pelvis. In effect, the presenting part becomes wedged between them. Finally, at the time of birth, the fetal presenting part must pass through the *pelvic outlet* to leave the mother's body. The ischial tuberosities, better known as the *sitz bones*, because we sit on them, are prominent protrusions of the ischiums. With the pubic bones, they form the front arch of the pelvic outlet. The lower end of the sacrum is the back boundary of the outlet.

A hundred years ago vitamin D deficiency was common. It resulted in *rickets*—a softening of the bones. When toddlers with this deficiency disease began to walk, putting the weight of the trunk on the sacrum, the effect of rickets was to push the sacrum forward toward the *symphysis pubis*—the cartilage between the two pubic bones. This narrowed the front-to-back space of the inlet of the pelvis, sometimes enough to block the vaginal birth of a live baby. This kind of pelvic contraction has vanished with the disappearance of rickets.

Today, pelvic contracture is seen infrequently. In some women, the pelvis is genetically small. Because such women are small in general, they often will have small babies, so this does not pose a problem. Abnormalities due to pelvic fractures and from rare *congenital abnormalities* (birth defects) of the pelvis are possible.

Pelvic fractures may be due to falls from extreme heights or, more commonly, to automobile accidents. The orthopedic management of these abnormalities has improved greatly in recent years, so that it is now unusual to see a woman whose pelvis has been distorted by such an accident. With severe deformity, the obstetrical treatment is cesarean.

Soft-Tissue Obstruction

Soft tissues are body structures other than bones. Soft-tissue obstruction refers to maternal abnormalities that may interfere with fetal passage through the birth canal.

Tumors

Soft tissues do not often obstruct labor. On occasion, a common type of benign uterine tumor called a *fibroid* (myoma or leiomyoma) may lodge between the presenting part and the bony pelvis. This may occur with fibroids that grow within the cervix or within the uterine wall. Even fibroids that have grown out from the body of the uterus can drop into the pelvis below the presenting part and cause obstruction. Most times, whether this will be an obstacle to delivery cannot be decided before labor begins. Most women with fibroids, however, do not have problems in labor.

A similar obstruction may result from large ovarian cysts and the occasionally misplaced kidney, called a *pelvic kidney*. Either of these may be felt in the pelvis below the presenting part. In this event the treatment is cesarean delivery. An ovarian cyst can be removed at the time of the surgery; a kidney is left undisturbed.

If ovarian tumors that warrant removal are found early in pregnancy, they can be removed promptly to avoid the possibility that later they will obstruct labor. If a pelvic mass is found during pregnancy, it should be followed with pelvic examination and ultrasound. If the mass is large or has characteristics on ultrasound that suggest malignancy, then it must be removed. Pregnancy does not preclude such surgery. It is generally unwise, however, to undertake removal of fibroids at any time during pregnancy. The risk of excessive bleeding—*hemorrhage*—is considerable, due to the richness of the fibroid blood supply, a consequence of the hormone effect of the pregnancy.

Congenital Abnormalities of the Reproductive Organs

A number of *congenital abnormalities,* or birth defects, can occur during the development of the reproductive organs. Some abnormalities, like the absence of a uterus, make pregnancy impossible. Others do not stop a woman from becoming pregnant, but may interfere with the pregnancy or labor.

The reproductive structures are formed early in embryonic life from paired tubes, which fuse together in the midline. Occasionally this junction is accomplished imperfectly. In some cases, there is no fusion, resulting in two separate vaginas, cervixes, and uteri. In other cases, the wall between the right and the left sides does not vanish entirely. Such a wall, called a *septum,* may be found in the vagina, cervix, and uterus, or any of these organs. The septum can form an obstruction to labor.

Congenital malformations of the reproductive organs may be discovered on simple vaginal examination, or they may not become apparent until labor has been obstructed and a cesarean section is performed. They may be seen on ultrasound examinations, but can be missed in a routine ultrasound.

Reproductive organ abnormalities may lead to uterine dysfunction or abnormal presentations of the fetus, such as a transverse lie. External version attempts may be unsuccessful. Some types of abnormalities result in *spontaneous abortion* (miscarriage) early in pregnancy, or preterm labor. In some of these situations, surgical repair before a subsequent pregnancy may be beneficial.

A number of reproductive abnormalities are associated with a synthetic hormone called *DES* (diethylstilbestrol), taken by the woman's mother during her pregnancy. In some DES daughters, fertility is impaired, and some women may have trouble carrying their pregnancies to term. Fortunately, DES use stopped in the early 1970s, so within another decade or so, these problems will no longer be seen among women in the childbearing years.

Previous Surgery or Disease

Occasionally, surgery to the cervix results in scarring such that normal dilatation of the cervix is difficult. Labor in a woman who has a history of prior surgery in the upper vagina and the cervix should be monitored carefully for its progress. Extensive cancer of the cervix is another condition that can prevent normal dilatation of the cervix, with a chance of tears and bleeding. With invasive or advanced cervical cancer, the usual mode of delivery is cesarean. Precancerous conditions or *carcinoma-in-situ* of the cervix, a cancer that remains only in the cervix without spreading, does not preclude labor or vaginal birth.

The concept of *cervical dystocia*, in which unusual rigidity of the cervix prevents it from dilating despite what seems to be strong labor, cannot be verified. The management is no different from that of inadequate uterine action.

THE RELATIONSHIP AMONG THE POWERS, THE PASSAGE, AND THE PASSENGER

Cephalopelvic Disproportion

Cephalopelvic disproportion is a term commonly used when labor does not progress because the cervix fails to dilate or the fetus fails to descend. The phrase was originally meant to describe the condition in which the pelvis was too small for the size of the fetus. Experience has shown, however, that, not infrequently, women who have cesarean deliveries for cephalopelvic disproportion (CPD) can deliver an even larger fetus vaginally in a subsequent pregnancy. As true pelvic contracture due to rickets has vanished, this diagnosis has become much harder to make definitively. Many cases of so-called CPD are really a malpresentation or malpositioning of the fetus or a lack of strong enough contractions. True CPD only can be assumed if the cervix has dilated fully and the baby is not able to descend, yet sometimes a cesarean is performed and attributed to this diagnosis before full dilatation.

Failure to Progress

In recent years, a less precise term has been used to describe labors in which the cervix fails to dilate or the baby to descend. This catch-all term is *failure to progress*. The American College of Obstetricians and Gynecologists recommends calling abnormalities in the progress of labor either *protraction disorder* to mean slower-than-normal progress or *arrest disorder* to signify complete cessation of labor's progress.

Sometimes one of these designations is erroneously made before the active phase of labor has begun. If the woman is not at least 3 or 4 centimeters dilated, then she is in the *prodromal* or latent stage of labor and none of these terms or their concomitant interventions should be applied.

THE THIRD STAGE OF LABOR

Failure of the Placenta to Separate

Occasionally the normal mechanism of placental separation and expulsion does not function and the placenta has to be peeled away from the uterine wall. The procedure may be quite uncomfortable, especially if the cervix has had time to start to close. If epidural anesthesia is still in place, no further anesthetic is required, although additional dosing may be necessary. If an epidural has not been used, the woman may need pain medication. A narcotic like Demerol may be given intravenously. If an anesthesiologist or nurse-anesthetist is available, general anesthesia may even be used, if only for just a few minutes.

The physician puts a gloved hand into the vagina, using sterile technique. With it, he or she follows the umbilical cord through the cervix and up into the uterus. If the cervix has begun to close, the hand may meet some resistance, but this will yield to firm, gentle pressure. With the hand in the uterus, the physician feels for the plane of separation between the placenta and the uterine wall, sweeps around this plane, separates the placenta, takes hold of it, and withdraws the hand. The other hand firmly holds the uterine fundus. This is a simple and safe procedure if it is done early, before serious hemorrhage can take place, by one who has had experience with the maneuver. Usually a manual removal is performed by a physician, but in an emergency it may be performed by a midwife. Antibiotics often are prescribed after a manual removal to prevent infection.

Some physicians wait only a brief period of time for the normal separation of the placenta before delivering it manually. Others will wait at least 30 minutes, and even then may try measures to encourage natural placental separation before manual removal. Certainly everyone intervenes quickly if the placenta has partly separated and hemorrhage is taking place.

Natural measures to effect separation including nursing the baby or using nipple stimulation if the mother does not wish to nurse or the baby requires pediatric care. This releases oxytocin which causes uterine contractions. Sometimes repositioning the mother will work. She can sit up in bed, for instance. In births at home, some midwives report that the mother's walking helps with placental separation by the force of gravity. This may not be considered an acceptable procedure in the hospital, but if the mother is not bleeding and her *vital signs* (pulse, respirations, and blood pressure) are normal, there is no particular reason she cannot walk.

Placenta Accreta

An extremely rare cause of failure of the placenta to separate is *placenta accreta*—a condition in which the placenta or part of it adheres to the uterine wall. Hemorrhage may or may not occur with placenta accreta. Hysterectomy (surgical removal of the uterus) is the lifesaving treatment for this rare occurrence. If hysterectomy is unacceptable to the woman, and she is not bleeding profusely, the placenta can be left in place or as much of it removed manually as possible. Sometimes a *currettage* (scraping) of the uterine wall is done and some *sutures* (stitches) placed to control bleeding. The uterus may be packed with gauze for about 24 hours. This nonsurgical treatment requires careful follow-up observation and antibiotic therapy as it carries some risk for the woman. The placenta may eventually be resorbed by the body. In the presence of active bleeding, however, an emergency hysterectomy may be the only lifesaving option. Often, blood transfusion is required.

Postpartum Hemorrhage

Postpartum hemorrhage (PPH) is an excessive blood loss following delivery. The exact amount of blood that must be lost before the bleeding is called a *hemorrhage* is hard to quantify exactly. The clinical judgment of the birth attendant usually determines whether a hemorrhage is occurring or not. Hemorrhage is an emergency situation requiring prompt attention.

There are two types of PPH. Early PPH is hemorrhage that occurs within the first 24 hours after birth and late PPH is hemorrhage that occurs after the first 24 hours following birth. Postpartum hemorrhage is due to one of three causes:

- Uterine atony or failure to contract
- A tear or laceration
- A retained placental fragment

Failure of the uterus to contract over the site where the placenta has separated or partially separated is the most common cause of PPH. Excess bleeding from a laceration or tear in the vagina, perineum, or cervix is seen less frequently. If a part of the placenta is retained, hemorrhage may occur when the uterus contracts to the point where that piece of placenta is attached. This may occur immediately or days or weeks after delivery. The placenta always is inspected carefully after a birth so the physician or midwife may suspect that a fragment has been left inside, and take measures to expel it, but sometimes a placenta appears complete despite a retained fragment.

Immediate postpartum hemorrhage can occur during the *third stage of labor*—before the placenta has delivered—or afterward. If hemorrhage occurs before delivery of the placenta, prompt delivery will usually stop it. If the placenta has separated, it can be delivered easily. If it has not separated, then a manual removal is appropriate.

If hemorrhage occurs shortly after delivery of the placenta, the first thing to check is whether the uterus is contracted or not. This is a simple procedure, requiring only *palpating* (touching) the *fundus* (top) of the uterus. If the uterus is contracting well, the fundus will be firm. If the uterus is not contracting, the fundus will be soft or boggy.

There are several ways to help the uterus contract. Oxytocin can be added to the intravenous fluids or given as an injection into a muscle. Of course, if an intravenous line is not in place one should be started immediately. At the same time, the uterus can be massaged externally. This may be uncomfortable as the massage must be vigorous for it to bring about uterine contractions. If external massage doesn't work, *bimanual compression* of the uterus is the next step. This involves putting one hand into the vagina and squeezing the uterus between that hand and the external hand, which presses on the fundus. Bimanual compression is very effective. Additional medications can also be administered. Methylergonovine can be given either as an injection into a muscle or into the intravenous fluids. A type of prostaglandin (carboprost, tromethamine, Hemabate, or Prostin/15M) can be given intramuscularly.

If these measures do not help, and the uterus is not contracting, a uterine exploration may be necessary. This is done in a fashion similar to a manual removal of the placenta, except that the fingers are searching for possible retained parts. Rarely, the uterus may be *packed*. This means that gauze is placed inside the uterus to control bleeding. Finally, in the extremely rare event that true uterine atony exists and all measures fail, an emergency hysterectomy or removal of the uterus is needed. Blood transfusion may be necessary.

If hemorrhage occurs despite a firm uterus, the birth attendant will look for possible unnoticed lacerations or tears and *suture* (sew) them.

There are a number of risk factors for postpartum hemorrhage, alerting the physician or midwife to the increased likelihood of this event. This awareness will result in faster action if excess bleeding occurs. An intravenous line could be placed during active labor, for instance, and a midwife could alert her or his consulting physician that a hemorrhage may occur postpartum. This way, the physician can be available if necessary. The usual risks include:

- A very large fetus or multiple pregnancy leading to an overdistended uterus
- A very long or very rapid labor
- High parity—having had many babies previously
- An infection in the uterus or fetal membranes (chorioamnionitis)
- Use of oxytocin
- Ruptured uterus
- Difficult delivery leading to trauma or lacerations to the vagina, perineum, or cervix

A REMINDER

This chapter has reviewed some situations that can be rather frightening. Anticipating any of them can make any woman nervous about labor and birth. We urge you to reread the previous three chapters, which describe normal labor and birth. Remember, always, that labor and birth are without incident for the overwhelming majority of women. We believe that women should have information about possible problems and have presented this information in the spirit that the informed user of health services is an empowered user. We believe that this empowerment should make women approach labor and birth with confidence, not trepidation. You should have confidence in your care providers, your support persons, and, most important, your own body.

CHAPTER TWENTY-TWO

Obstetrical Interventions

Nature does an excellent job bringing new life into the world. But, as discussed in the previous chapter, occasionally something does go wrong. Complications and problems do occur, although only in a small minority of births. Fortunately, most of these complications are treatable.

This chapter discusses the interventions that are used in obstetrical practice today. Most often, these are implemented in response to a problem. Although few, if any, interventions are without risk, most are utilized carefully, often to save the fetus or spare it damage, and, on occasion, to save the mother. Sometimes, however, certain procedures such as amniotomy or rupture of the membranes will be performed even in the absence of a complication. Some physicians and even some midwives believe in *active management of labor*, which means that their patients will receive medication simply to speed up the process of labor. The key to effective and safe use of obstetrical interventions is a thoughtful physician or midwife, one who exercises extreme care in clinical judgment and decision making.

The significant interventions in contemporary labor care include:

- Induction and augmentation of labor
- Active management of labor
- Amniotomy
- Amnioinfusion

Interventions for birth are:

- Episiotomy
- Assisted breech delivery

- Internal version for a second twin
- Forceps
- Vacuum extraction
- Cesarean section for birth

Interventions for the third, or placental, stage of labor may include:

- Active management of the third stage
- Cervical inspection
- Manual removal of the placenta
- Uterine exploration

If your labor and birth are planned for a birthing center or your home, transfer to a hospital might be considered an intervention.

INDUCTION OF LABOR

Induction of labor means bringing on labor before it has begun on its own. Labor may be induced for reasons related to the mother's health, the baby's health, or the health of both. Although inductions have been performed for the convenience of either mother or physician, the medical ethics of this practice are questionable, at best.

Maternal Reasons for Induction of Labor

A common maternal reason to induce labor is *preeclampsia* or pregnancy-induced hypertension (discussed in Chapter 12). Mild cases of this disease of pregnancy may be treated prior to term with bed rest and observation alone, but severe disease usually requires delivery. An induction is considered safer than a cesarean birth, although if the induction is not successful, a cesarean may become necessary.

When the membranes rupture prematurely, the risk or presence of infection may be a reason for induction. *Premature rupture of the membranes* (PROM) is defined as rupture that occurs before the onset of labor. If it also occurs before the fetus is at term, it is called *preterm premature rupture of the membranes* (PPROM). Labor almost always ensues within a few days to a week after rupture, with its onset more rapid the closer to term the rupture. At term, more than 60 percent of women will be in labor within 24 hours and more than 95 percent within 72 hours.

Some practitioners believe that inducing labor within 12 to 24 hours after rupture will prevent or reduce the risk of infection for the mother and the fetus. Many practitioners will induce routinely when the fetus is at term or near term, but only induce when there is evidence of infection if the fetus is preterm. In fact, in a small number of women whose membranes rupture before term, there is only a small leak rather than a large rupture. In these cases, the membranes may reseal themselves and the fluid will stop leaking.

Usually, fever in the mother is the symptom that indicates infection. When the membranes rupture, your temperature must be taken frequently—at least once a day if you are not in labor. If you are admitted to the hospital, as some women are whenever the membranes rupture, your temperature will be taken every 4 or 8 hours. If you are at home you must take your temperature and call your physician or midwife if there is a rise or if you have chills or feel feverish.

Whether to induce or not when membranes rupture without labor is an area of some controversy within obstetrics. Studies are not entirely consistent, but seem to show that while there are more infections when the woman is not induced, the newborn is infected in less than 20 percent of maternal infections. There also may be more cesarean deliveries when induction is used routinely. The most important preventive measure against infection once the membranes rupture is to avoid vaginal examinations.

You may have feelings regarding induction or watchful waiting in the situation of ruptured membranes at term. This is a topic to discuss with your physician or midwife. Find out his or her beliefs and practices. You should feel comfortable with them.

Fetal Reasons for Induction

The common fetal reasons for inducing labor are related to problems that occur with maternal diabetes, hypertension or pregnancy-induced hypertension, or prolongation of pregnancy past the expected date of childbirth. Fetal anemia related to *isoimmunization* (Rh incompatibility) has become a less usual reason for induction, because the routine use of RhoGAM prevents the occurrence of the disease (see Chapter 5).

Your physician or midwife will determine whether and at what point to induce labor in each of these conditions. Their decision will be based on their experience and clinical judgment. Hard and fast rules cannot always be established. How to manage the pregnancy that goes beyond the expected due date is a particular area of controversy. Although the due date is only an estimate, studies have shown an increased chance of perinatal death in pregnancies that extend beyond 42 weeks gestation. This means the baby dies before birth or shortly afterward. Usually, the problems seen in this group of pregnancies, which constitute about 10 percent of all pregnancies, occur during labor and delivery. They are often associated with the presence of *meconium*—the contents of the fetal bowels. The fetus may breathe in the meconium, causing *meconium aspiration syndrome*, a serious and sometimes fatal disorder. Problems also may be associated with *oligohydramnios*, or a reduction in the amount of amniotic fluid in the uterus. This can result in cord compression during labor. Controversy surrounds two areas:

1. When to begin to test the fetus for its well-being with fetal surveillance tests (described in Chapter 17).
2. When to induce labor if it hasn't occurred.

Many physicians and midwives begin fetal testing at 41 weeks, although there is no evidence that the fetus is at any increased risk at this point in pregnancy. Having the mother count and record fetal movements is completely noninterventionist and can certainly be begun by 41 weeks, and weeks earlier in pregnancies considered at risk. Using ultrasound to check the amount of amniotic fluid is also a relatively easy test. This, too, can be begun at 41 weeks. It is usually repeated twice a week.

The American College of Obstetricians and Gynecologists (ACOG) recommends induction at 42 weeks if the cervix is ripe. A *ripe cervix* means it will be readily dilated with medications that bring on contractions. If the cervix is not ripe, which means an induction is likely to fail and possibly lead to a cesarean birth, ACOG recommends one of two choices: continued fetal surveillance or medically induced cervical ripening followed by induction. Fetal surveillance can continue as long as the tests are reassuring and the mother reports adequate fetal movement. The techniques for determining cervical readiness, for ripening the cervix, and for induction are described in the sections that follow.

Determining Readiness for Induction: Cervical Ripeness

The more ready or *ripe* the cervix, the likelier that the induction will succeed. Of course, if conditions exist that make it essential that the baby be delivered in a timely fashion, induction may be undertaken even when the cervix is not ripe, but the risk that a cesarean will be needed is increased in these situations. Today, methods exist to prepare the cervix before uterine contractions are induced. These are discussed in the next section.

Cervical ripeness is evaluated with a *Bishop score* (named after Edward Harry Bishop, the person who developed it). This score evaluates five characteristics of the cervix or fetus that indicate readiness for the changes that must occur in labor. The extent to which these changes have begun is part of the Bishop score.

The Bishop score is calculated according to the criteria shown in the table.

THE BISHOP SCORE					
Score	Cervical Effacement	Cervical Dilatation	Cervical Consistency	Cervical Position	Station of the Fetal Presenting Part
0	0–30%	Closed	Firm	Posterior	-3 or higher
1	40–50%	1–2 cm	Medium	Midposition	-2
2	60–70%	3–4 cm	Soft	Anterior	-1 or 0
3	≥80%	≥5cm	NA	NA	+1, +2

A Bishop score of 4 or less is considered evidence of an unripe cervix. If, for example, the cervix were 40 percent effaced, closed, medium consistency, and *midposition* (in the middle of the vagina, neither toward its back nor its front), and the fetus –3 station (high in the pelvis), the Bishop score would be 3. This cervix most likely would have difficulty effacing and dilating in response to oxytocin-induced uterine contractions. Cervical ripening usually would be performed before labor induction.

When the Bishop score is intermediate, between 5 and 7, cervical ripening may be beneficial. Medications given for ripening may, in these situations, actually stimulate labor contractions without a later need for oxytocin. Such a score might occur when the cervix is 70 percent effaced, 2 centimeters open, medium consistency, midposition, and the fetal head is –2. This score would be 6.

A Bishop score of 8 or higher implies that the cervix will respond readily to oxytocin administration and labor induction should be successful. This woman's cervix might be almost completely effaced, 3 centimeters open, soft, and *anterior* (toward the front of the vagina). The baby would be at least +1 station (past the midpoint of the pelvis). Of course, the score is not entirely predictive in any given woman in any given labor.

Ripening the Cervix

Today, a number of techniques exist to make the cervix more readily *inducible*, more ripe. These are used when induction is the safest choice for the woman, her baby, or both, but the cervix doesn't know this yet. A woman whose fetus is only 32 weeks gestational age may need to be induced because of severe preeclampsia. Her cervix is unlikely to be ripe. Another woman, despite a due date that is past, also may have an unready cervix. Unless birth must occur imminently, requiring a cesarean delivery, in each of these instances attempting to ripen the cervix before contractions are brought on is a logical step. Theoretically, ripening will shorten the length of labor and increase the chance that the induction will lead to a vaginal birth.

The following sections make a distinction between techniques commonly used to ripen the cervix and techniques commonly used to induce labor. Some of these techniques, however, may actually accomplish both goals.

Methods of Cervical Ripening

LAMINARIA OR SYNTHETIC HYGROSCOPIC DILATORS   *Laminaria* are made from seaweed that is cut, dried, and sterilized. *Hygroscopic dilators* (openers) are synthetic or artificial. Both of these work in essentially the same way. They are inserted into the cervical canal and held in place with pieces of gauze. They absorb the secretions of the cervix and, in so doing, expand. As they expand, they dilate the cervix. This also stimulates the production of prostaglandins, which help in the initiation of labor. The dilators are inserted the night before the labor induction is planned, and they are removed in the morning.

PROSTAGLANDIN E2   Two preparations of prostaglandin E2 (also called *PGE2* or *dinoprostone*) are used for cervical ripening. One is a *gel* (trade name: Prepidil) that is inserted into the cervix and the other a vaginal insert (Cervidil). This chemical causes changes in the cervix that are similar to the usual changes seen in early labor, making the cervix more amenable to induction.

Sometimes, the prostaglandin gel or insert actually causes uterine contractions. *Hyperstimulation*, or excessive uterine contractions, occur occasionally. For this reason, the vaginal insert is preferable, as it can be removed in the case of hyperstimulation. In most cases, the hyperstimulation will be reversed within minutes of removal. Hyperstimulation after insertion of gel may require the use of medication to quell contractions (as discussed in Chapter 15 on preterm labor). Occasionally, such medication is needed even after removal of the vaginal insert.

Recently, another form of prostaglandin—prostaglandin E1 or misoprostol—has been used for cervical ripening. This drug is approved and marketed to prevent the formation of ulcers in persons taking anti-inflammatory medication, but it also causes cervical ripening. It comes in a tablet form that can be inserted into the vagina. Misoprostol (trade name: Cytotec) is much less expensive than dinoprostone. However, the manufacturer of these tablets recently has warned physicians and midwives that the drug is not considered safe in pregnancy as it causes miscarriage. Of course, when the drug is used to induce labor, the issue of miscarriage is moot. The manufacturer also noted that the safety of misoprostol for labor induction has not been assessed adequately in clinical trials. However, many clinical studies have demonstrated its safety. Many physicians continue to use misoprostol for cervical ripening and induction of labor. The American College of Obstetricians and Gynecologists (ACOG) supports this use. Prostaglandin E1 is *contraindicated* (not to be used) in women with prior cesarean sections.

Rare side effects of prostaglandin insertion are fever, nausea and vomiting, and diarrhea. Hyperstimulation or excessive uterine contractions occur in 1 to 5 percent of women in whom these medications are used. The drugs' manufacturers advise caution in women with *glaucoma* (increased pressure in the eye), severe liver or kidney disease, and asthma.

The woman usually lies in bed for 2 hours after the insertion of the prostaglandin. The fetal heart rate is monitored during this time. Contractions may occur. If they do not, and the fetal heart rate is reassuring, the woman can be transferred out of the labor and delivery unit or discharged home. The vaginal insert should be removed at least 30 minutes before induction with oxytocin is started.

Induction of Labor

A few nonmedical methods can be tried to bring on labor. These include nipple stimulation, sexual intercourse or orgasm, and castor oil. More medical means include a technique called *stripping the membranes*, amniotomy or artificial rupture of the membranes, and the administration of oxytocin in one of its synthetic forms (usually Pitocin). These must be done by a midwife or physician. Generally, a midwife will consult with a physician before initiating a medical means of labor induction.

NIPPLE STIMULATION   Nipple stimulation is a relatively simple and noninvasive way of inducing labor. It brings on contractions by stimulating the release of the woman's own oxytocin. Nipple stimulation may or may not induce sufficient contractions for labor to begin. This will probably occur only if the cervix is ready. It can, however, induce excessive uterine contractions, a condition known as *hyperstimulation*. The same method of controlled nipple stimulation used for a *contraction stress test* (see Chapter 17) can be used for induction of labor:

Apply a warm moist towel to each breast for 5 minutes. If this does not produce an adequate number of contractions, you can massage one nipple for 15 minutes or stroke one breast through your clothing with your fingers for 2 minutes, rest for 5 minutes, and repeat the cycle until contractions are achieved.

SEXUAL INTERCOURSE/ORGASM   Because semen contains prostaglandins, sexual intercourse may help ripen the cervix or even bring on labor. You should not have sexual intercourse if the membranes have *ruptured* (your bag of waters has broken) because of the risk of infection. Orgasm also can induce uterine contractions. This does not require sexual intercourse. As with nipple stimulation, the contractions of intercourse or orgasm will likely only be strong enough to bring on labor if your body is otherwise ready.

CASTOR OIL   We do not know exactly how or why castor oil brings on labor, but it may. The usual dose is two ounces and can be taken in juice. You can expect to have diarrhea and cramps once the castor oil takes effect. If you take the castor oil at night, you may not get any sleep. Since it can have severe effects, and its value is uncertain, speak to your physician or midwife before using castor oil.

STRIPPING THE MEMBRANES   Stripping the membranes is done by a physician or midwife. It may be done at a routine prenatal visit at about 41 weeks, in an effort to avoid the need for induction. The practitioner will insert her or his index finger into the vagina and through the cervical *os* or opening, as far as possible. The goal is to loosen the membranes from the uterine wall. The technique is to move the finger in a circle between the membranes and the lower part of the uterus. Stripping the membranes probably works by stimulating the woman's own cervical production of prostaglandin. It feels like a usual vaginal examination, although a bit longer and with more pressure.

Stripping the membranes must be done under sterile conditions to minimize the risk of infection, with care taken not to rupture the membranes accidentally. This procedure is done fairly commonly but has not been subjected to extensive research regarding its effectiveness or safety.

In one study, two-thirds of women whose membranes were stripped entered labor spontaneously within 72 hours of the procedure without an increase in ruptured membranes, infection, or bleeding.

AMNIOTOMY (ARTIFICIAL RUPTURE OF THE MEMBRANES)   *Amniotomy* is a means of both inducing labor and augmenting or assisting it (see below). Amniotomy is the medical term for artificially rupturing the membranes. The midwife or physician does this either before or during labor.

Amniotomy itself is a painless procedure, with no more discomfort than the vaginal examination it requires. The physician or midwife usually uses a long plastic hook to make a small hole in the membranes through which the fluid escapes. As there are no nerve endings in the membranes, neither you nor the fetus feels pain when the hook pierces them. You will feel a gush of fluid and may have continuing leakage of the watery fluid afterward.

If the membranes are ruptured before the onset of spontaneous contractions, then the same danger of infection applies as when the membranes rupture on their own before labor. When amniotomy is used alone to induce labor, the usual procedure is to add oxytocin (see the next section) if labor has not begun within a specified period of time— typically 12 to 24 hours.

The membranes generally are not ruptured unless the fetus is in the vertex position, and engaged in the pelvis. If it is not engaged, the membranes may sometimes be ruptured if the head can be pushed into the pelvis during the procedure with external pressure applied to the uterine fundus. This pressure may be applied by an assistant.

Amniotomy sometimes is performed for reasons other than induction or augmentation of labor. It may be used to check for meconium in a fetus at risk for having difficulty tolerating labor. If the fetal heart is questionable and the physician or midwife wishes to place an internal fetal heart rate electrode on the presenting part, the membranes must be ruptured artificially if they have not already done so on their own.

One objection to amniotomy is that the amniotic fluid provides a cushion for the umbilical cord. Once the membranes are ruptured, the fetal heart rate patterns may show cord compression. Usually this is not harmful to the fetus. Another objection is that the membranes function as a wedge to dilate the cervix. When they are ruptured, the fetal head is pushed against the cervix to help dilatation. This may increase both the *molding* of the *fetal skull* (the overlap of bones that occurs normally in labor) and the formation of *caput succedaneum* (the swelling underneath the scalp that also occurs naturally).

OXYTOCIN   The hormone oxytocin has been used since the early part of the twentieth century to induce or augment labor. It has been available since the mid-twentieth century in a synthetic form. The most commonly used brand name is Pitocin. In fact, obstetricians and midwives may use this word in an abbreviated form, as in, "Can you get the Pit ready?" or even as a verb, such as when somebody might say, "It's time to Pit her." This may not sound nice to a layperson, but it is meant merely as a description of labor induction or augmentation.

The most critical element in a safe induction of labor is continuous observation by an experienced attendant. Once oxytocin is begun, a laboring woman should have someone in constant attendance. This may be a nurse, midwife, or physician. We commonly say they are "sitting with the Pit." Of course, they are really sitting with the woman who is getting the Pitocin. The reason for such close attention is to make sure that the uterus does not become hyperstimulated with the use of the medication. Hyperstimulation is considered present when there are more than five contractions in a 10-minute period or contractions last longer than 1 minute. The presence of nonreassuring fetal heart rate patterns also may denote hyperstimulation.

When hyperstimulation occurs, the appropriate action is to discontinue the oxytocin. For this reason, oxytocin is always given via an intravenous line. The medication is mixed into a bottle of an intravenous solution that contains electrolytes. This way, small amounts of medication continuously enter the woman's body and the flow can be stopped at any time. If the oxytocin is given with sugar water, it can cause the body to retain fluids, even leading to a dangerous condition called *water intoxication*. Sugar water, called *D5W* (dextrose 5 percent in water), is therefore avoided an as intravenous solution when oxytocin is used.

Today, most institutions have special electronically regulated pumps that infuse the oxytocin at a steady, set rate. The rate is increased over time until an adequate number of moderate contractions are achieved. In this way, the labor somewhat simulates natural labor—with contractions usually starting within a few minutes of oxytocin infusion and gradually increasing. Typically, however, induced labor is more rapid and less gradual than spontaneous labor.

In addition to one-to-one monitoring of the laboring woman receiving oxytocin, electronic fetal heart monitoring is used to assess the fetal heart and the uterine contractions. This monitoring may be external or internal. Internal monitoring is considered more accurate for interpretation of both the fetal heart and the strength of the uterine contractions, but requires that the membranes be ruptured. Internal monitoring of contractions also is associated with a small possibility of infection in the mother or fetus, as well as an even smaller possibility of rupturing a vessel in the placenta or otherwise damaging the placenta, thereby interfering with fetal blood supply. While these complications are not common, they are considerations when determining appropriate monitoring of contractions.

Oxytocin can be given in various regimens—low or high dose. Oxytocin is measured in milliunits. In a low-dose regimen, the medication usually is started at ½ to 2 milliunits per minute and increased every 15 to 20 minutes by 1 to 2 milliunits. Several high-dose regimens have been described. In one, the oxytocin is started at 4 to 6 milliunits per minute and increased by 6 milliunits every 40 minutes. Hyperstimulation may occur with the high-dose regimen. If it does, the infusion is stopped, and restarted only if needed. When it is restarted, it is set at half the dose that was infusing at the time it was stopped, and slowly increased. Another high-dose regimen is a 4 milliunit per minute starting dose, followed by 4 milliunit per minute increases at 15-minute intervals.

Regardless of the oxytocin regimen, once strong regular contractions are achieved, the dose need not be increased further. Regular contractions are defined as three in 10 minutes. Most regimens include a limit on the amount of oxytocin infused per minute.

When Labor Should Not Be Induced

Certain conditions make induction of labor a potentially dangerous procedure. Labor generally should not be induced in the following circumstances, called *contraindications*. Many of these are discussed in detail in the previous chapter:

- Contracted pelvis
- Fetus in a transverse lie
- Very high presenting part—above the pelvis
- Fetal distress, including a nonreassuring fetal heart rate pattern
- Prolapse of the umbilical cord
- *Placenta previa*—placenta covering the cervix, in part or completely
- Unexplained vaginal bleeding
- Previous classical uterine incision (see later in this chapter)
- Active genital herpes infection
- Invasive cervical cancer
- *Grand multiparity*—having had 6 or more previous births

AUGMENTATION OF LABOR

Augmentation means assisting labor once it has started. Augmentation is used when labor has slowed down or stopped, as described in the previous chapter. Augmentation can be done in the first or second stage of labor.

Labor generally is augmented in a series of steps—from the least to the most invasive. For example, when labor first slows down, a woman may be asked to walk to see if this will help. An intravenous line to treat or prevent dehydration may be started. Amniotomy may be done. Finally, oxytocin may be used.

When medication is given, the same precautions apply as described above for induction of labor. When labor is slowed or stopped, the physician or midwife evaluates the nature of the woman's pelvis as oxytocin augmentation should not be used if there is pelvic contracture (which could be a reason for ineffective contractions). Of course, as noted in previous chapters, this is rare. The fetal position should be carefully assessed as well, since a malposition also may slow labor, yet make augmentation unwise.

ACTIVE MANAGEMENT OF LABOR

Active management of labor is a term used to described a specific approach to labor. The goal of this approach is to make labor as efficient as possible, in an effort to reduce the number of cesarean deliveries performed. Whether or not active management actually reduces the number of cesarean deliveries is unclear, as different studies have reported different findings. What seems to be true of this approach, however, is that it does shorten labor.

In a large study funded by the National Institute of Child Health and Human Development, the length of labor was decreased with active management, fewer women experienced labor longer than 12 hours, and fewer women developed fever in labor. However, active management did not reduce the number of cesarean operations performed.

In active management, once active labor is diagnosed, the woman is examined vaginally every hour for the first 3 hours of labor, and then every 2 hours. At each hourly examination, the cervix is expected to dilate at least 1 centimeter. If it does not, first amniotomy is performed, and then high-dose oxytocin started. A nurse or midwife must be in constant attendance.

Some medical centers use a variation of this management, also calling it active management of labor. The key point is that the woman is given a limited time from the onset of active labor to delivery. Labor is monitored frequently by vaginal examination—every 1 to 2 hours. If labor does not progress within a specified time frame, intervention is begun.

You should ask your physician or midwife whether they use active management of labor as a routine procedure. If they do, you must decide whether or not you wish this type of management. While detrimental effects have not been shown, many women prefer to allow nature to take its course. Hastening labor is not the goal of every woman.

AMNIOINFUSION

Amnioinfusion is a technique introduced relatively recently into obstetrical care. In this technique, a physiologic fluid, usually saline (salt water) is infused into the uterus. It may be infused as a one-time dose, or continually throughout labor. Amnioinfusion has been recommended in three situations:

1. When fetal heart rate decelerations indicate cord compression
2. When there is reduced amniotic fluid (*oligohydramnios*)
3. When there is thick meconium

In the first two instances, the purpose of the amnioinfusion is to provide cushioning for the umbilical cord for optimal blood flow through it. Reduced fluid may occur when the membranes have been ruptured for a long time before labor and sometimes in pregnancies that are 2 weeks or more past the due date. In the third situation, the purpose of the infusion is to dilute the *meconium* (the often thick and sticky contents of the fetal bowel). This is an attempt to prevent *meconium aspiration syndrome*, in which the fetus breathes in some of this thick substance and subsequently develops pneumonia and breathing difficulties.

The research on amnioinfusion has shown conflicting results. Although researchers have documented fewer variable decelerations after amnioinfusion, studies have not always shown that this has reduced the need for cesarean delivery or improved the condition of the newborn. The same can be said for research on the effect of amnioinfusion on meconium aspiration syndrome. Studies have shown beneficial effects and no effects.

Amnioinfusion is not without risks. It can cause an increase in pressure inside the uterus, leading to abnormalities in fetal heart rate patterns. It also has been associated rarely with infection, rupture of the uterus, heart or respiratory problems in the mother, *placenta abruptio* (the tearing away of the placenta from the uterine wall), and, most rarely, a fatal problem called *amniotic fluid embolism* in the mother.

Amniotic fluid embolism (or clot) is an extremely rare occurrence, usually believed to be unavoidable in obstetrics—a true "act of God." It occurs in 1 out of 8,000 to 1 out of 30,000 pregnancies. Although only two case reports have appeared of this fatal complication with amnioinfusion, this is a relatively large number of women having an amniotic fluid embolism for the number of amnioinfusions that are performed. Amniotic fluid embolism has been considered to be the result of solid material in the fluid, such as fetal cells, somehow getting into the maternal *pulmonary* (lung) circulation. Today, an alternative explanation is that the embolism is a result of a type of maternal allergic reaction to the fluid. Although it is thought that the maternal and fetal tissues are separate, it is possible for fluid to get into the mother's circulation during procedures, in this case amnioinfusion, and even during normal labor and delivery as tiny tears occur in the lower part of the uterus or the cervix.

EPISIOTOMY

Episiotomy is a surgical cut into the vagina and perineum that may be performed during the second stage of labor. For many years, most physicians and many midwives cut episiotomies almost routinely for normal births. This was done to avoid lacerations or tears in the vagina and perineum. It was believed that a straight surgical cut was easier to repair and would maintain the muscular strength of the perineal floor through the rest of the woman's life.

Most research does not support the use of routine episiotomy. The pros and cons of this procedure and the reasons when it might be an appropriate intervention are discussed in detail in Chapter 19.

BREECH BIRTH

The previous chapter discusses problems associated with the breech presentation. It outlines the situations in which cesarean is the delivery of choice. Vaginal delivery of a breech baby is considered safe only when the baby is in a favorable position for vaginal delivery. The buttocks, rather than the feet, present and the breech is low in the pelvis at the on- set of labor. The baby is neither too small nor too big. The fetal head is well flexed, making its birth following the birth of the buttocks and body more likely to succeed without problems. The flexion of the head usually can be ascertained with ultrasound. If this is inadequate, a *com- puterized tomography scan* (C-T scan) often can tell whether the head is flexed. As a last resort, because it exposes the fetus to more radiation, or in the absence of C-T scan equipment, an X ray can be done. Even with X ray, the radiation exposure is small.

Anytime labor is tried when the baby is in the breech presentation, the labor must be monitored carefully for progress and signs of cord prolapse. Careful attention must be paid when the membranes rupture as this is the time the cord may come down or *prolapse*.

For a vaginal breech birth, the birth attendant should be experienced in delivering a breech. Some midwives deliver breech babies, usually with as- sistance of an obstetrician. An anesthesiologist or nurse-anesthetist should be available as should a physician or neonatal nurse practitioner who can provide immediate infant resuscitation, if that becomes necessary.

There are three types of vaginal breech deliveries:

1. In a **spontaneous breech delivery**, the fetus is born without assistance, except for support of its body.
2. In an **assisted breech delivery** (or partial breech extraction), the fetus is born without assistance until the umbilicus, or navel. The rest of the fetus is born with assistance of the birth attendant.
3. In a **total breech extraction**, the entire body of the fetus is taken out with assistance. Today, this is done rarely for a liv- ing fetus, except for a second twin.

Most times, the breech can deliver by itself or with minimal assistance. The woman will be placed in what is called the *lithotomy position*—on her back, with her legs raised. Usually, the legs are supported in stirrups or leg holders. Breech deliveries will take place in a delivery room that has facilities for infant resuscitation in case that is needed.

There are a variety of maneuvers that the birth attendant may use to help a breech baby deliver through the vagina. Delivery of the breech baby, however, is easier if the baby delivers without assistance, at least to the level of its *umbilicus*, or navel. In a spontaneous breech delivery, the birth attendant will support the body after the breech itself has delivered, often wrapping it in a warm moist towel. Sometimes, the arms may be swept up behind the baby's head, rather than folded over its chest. The birth attendant may then need to rotate the baby's trunk in the direction of the arm behind the head. This often allows the arm to deliver. Otherwise, the attendant's hand can bring it out from this position. The baby's other arm may have to be delivered by the same maneuvers.

Often, the head will need help to stay flexed. This help is provided with a maneuver called the *Mariceau-Smellie-Veit maneuver*. In this maneuver, an assistant will provide gentle pressure just above the pubic bone (*suprapubic pressure*) and the birth attendant will insert a hand into the vagina and apply pressure to the infant's upper jaw bone (the *maxilla*) to flex the head. The attendant's other hand will be used to support the rest of the baby's body.

With a complete extraction for a second twin, the obstetrician may convert the breech into a footling breech. The obstetrician puts a hand alongside the breech and into the upper vagina or the lower uterus, and grasps one or both of the baby's feet. The foot or feet are brought down and wrapped in a towel. The obstetrician can then exert traction on the feet. This ordinarily will bring the breech down and the remainder of the delivery will proceed without difficulty.

For assisted breech deliveries, the mother needs adequate anesthesia. She may already have been given an epidural. If not, a pudendal block may be utilized, or the mother may be given nitrous oxide plus oxygen. Alternatively, the mother can be given general anesthesia and a muscle relaxant. The relaxation of the pelvic muscles makes the manipulation necessary in a breech extraction easier for the obstetrician. Many practitioners advocate episiotomy for a vaginal breech delivery so that if manipulations become necessary, there is more room in the vagina for the hands of the birth attendant to move around.

The best way to deliver babies who present by the breech is an area of obstetrics marked by shifting practices. For many years, almost all breech babies were born by cesarean delivery, especially if it was the woman's first baby. As the cesarean rate soared, however, some obstetricians more frequently delivered selected breeches vaginally. This is limited to those babies in the most favorable circumstances, as described earlier. A large study, published in 2000, that took place in twenty-six countries and involved several thousand births of breech babies, found that infant outcomes were better when a planned cesarean was done. The outcomes for the mothers did not differ between those who had cesarean births and those who had vaginal births. With the publication of this major study, it is likely that the incidence of cesarean birth for babies in the breech presentation will rise again. However, many other studies have reported good outcomes with vaginal breech births in selected instances. Besides the position and size of the baby, a successful breech delivery depends upon experience of the birth attendant, monitoring in labor, and meticulous attention during the second stage.

VERSION

Version is the term for the procedures used to turn a fetus from the *transverse*—or breech—presentation into a *vertex*—or head-down—presentation. External version is done during the last weeks of pregnancy. Internal version is performed through the uterus after the membranes have ruptured. Both are described in the previous chapter. In obstetrics today, internal version is reserved for delivery of a second twin, and even then is performed infrequently.

Internal version is correctly termed *internal podalic version* (Greek: *pous* = foot) because the obstetrician inserts a hand into the uterus and grasps the fetus by one or both feet to turn the baby—usually from a transverse presentation into a footling breech. While the baby's feet are grasped, the upper body is turned through the abdomen. The fetus is then delivered by breech extraction.

Internal version was used in antiquity, lost for intervening centuries, and reintroduced in 1550, prior to the development of forceps. At that time, if labor was obstructed, the only way to extract the baby without using hooks was pulling it out by its feet. Cesareans were not done because mothers were not expected to survive major surgery.

Internal version should be done only by those experienced in its performance. Nowadays, the indication for it is the extraction of a second twin, soon after the birth of the first child, when this twin is not in a breech or vertex presentation. If a second twin presents in a transverse lie, internal podalic version ordinarily is not difficult. The uterus is relaxed since the first twin has recently been delivered. Twins are usually smaller than other term babies and the foot or feet are readily grasped. The mother must be given appropriate anesthesia, but profound general anesthesia usually is not needed.

FORCEPS DELIVERY

The forceps has been used in delivering babies for about 400 years. The instrument consists of two separate thin steel blades with inner surfaces curved to fit the sides of the infant's head. The blades are inserted separately into the vagina, opposite each other. When their handles are brought together, the child's head is securely grasped between the blades. With moderate traction on the handles, exerted in the axis of the vagina, the head is delivered.

The word *forceps* in Latin means "a pair of tongs." It is said to have been derived from the earlier Latin words *fornus* = oven and *capere* = to take. The obstetric forceps, in variations of its modern form, have been used since the early seventeenth century to deliver a living child without injury to it or to the mother. Prior to this, single-bladed and even double-bladed instruments, called *hooks*, were in use, but probably only for the extraction of a dead child. The old double-bladed instruments had a permanent articulation so that the blades could not be inserted separately. They looked like ice tongs.

History of the Forceps

The history of the forceps is a story worth telling, calling attention to great changes in the practice of medicine and medical ethics over the past 4 to 5 centuries. The inventors of the modern obstetrical forceps were a singular medical family—the Chamberlens. In 1569 the first of the English line, William, emigrated from France to England to escape persecution. Most of the Chamberlens were royal surgeons or royal physicians, and they attended the labors and births of several queens. This obstetrical dynasty of Chamberlen extended uninterrupted from Peter the Elder's admission to the Guild of Barber-Surgeons in about 1596 to the death of Hugh, Junior, in 1728.

The forceps was probably invented in about 1600 by Peter the Elder and kept as a hereditary family secret to be buried with Hugh, Junior, more than 100 years later. The retention of an important medical secret transmitted from generation to generation for a century and a quarter is unique in history. The Chamberlens were crafty (and by modern medical standards, unethical) enough to exclude all others from the room when they used the forceps and they used the instrument unassisted.

How was the secret finally revealed? The existence of the forceps was hinted at as early as 1616 at a meeting of the Royal College when a reference was made to the boast of Peter Chamberlen the Younger "that he and his brother, and none others, excelled in the management of difficult labors."

Hugh Senior emigrated to Holland in 1699 under suspicion of debt. While in Holland, he sold the secret of the forceps to Hendrik van Roonhuyze, the leader of Dutch obstetrics. William Giffard of London used the forceps openly in April 1726, calling it "extractors." He is generally considered "the altruistic and honorable physician who should receive full credit for introducing the forceps into general use in England." By 1733, when Edmund Chapman published the first account of the forceps, there were already several models, and their use "was well known to all the principal men of the profession, both in town and country."

Types of Forceps

For many years every skilled obstetrician felt obligated to design his own forceps and to name them after himself. However, only a few basic types have survived to present-day use. All forceps have two blades that are readily separated from one another but can be joined together, much as the two blades of a pair of kitchen scissors are joined. The length of the handles and blades varies, and there are a number of curvatures. Some of the blades are solid where they wrap around the baby's head and some have openings.

All forceps have two curves—one to fit the curve of the birth canal and the other to allow the blades to wrap properly around the baby's head. These curves vary slightly from one forceps to another. The Simpson forceps, the Tucker-McLane forceps, the Luikart forceps, an instrument more slender and delicate than the first two, and the Kielland forceps, the most delicate of all, are most commonly used in the United States. The experience of an individual operator with a particular pair of forceps is probably more important to successful use than the particular variety of instrument used for a given delivery.

When Are Forceps Used?

The reasons for forceps delivery are divided into two broad classes, the fetal and the maternal.

Fetal Reasons for Forceps

The fetal indication for forceps is evidence of fetal distress appearing in the second stage of labor. This might be a persistent nonreassuring fetal heart rate pattern, with the awareness that some decelerations are perfectly normal in the second stage of labor. It might be a prolapsed umbilical cord or a separation of the placenta.

Maternal Reasons for Forceps

Maternal indications for forceps are not very clear-cut. A woman with a disease of the heart or lungs may have difficulty pushing. Sometimes a woman is able to bring the baby's head into view at the entrance to the vagina but somehow lacks the strength for the final pushes. Women who are unfortunate enough to have had a long latent labor, especially if they have gone without solid food and sleep, may reach the second stage of labor fatigued and distraught, and may have difficulty pushing well. If contractions are strong and the baby is in a good position, usually they can manage. However, if the baby is posterior, for example, second stage may be prolonged, and maternal exhaustion may become great. If the head is low enough, forceps may be worthwhile in such a situation.

Safe Conditions for a Forceps Delivery

Delivery by forceps is safe only if specific conditions are met. The fetus must be in a vertex or face presentation. In a face presentation, the chin must be *anterior* (facing the mother's front). The head of the child must fit deeply into the pelvis without serious obstruction from the mother's pelvic bones. To ascertain this, the head must be *engaged*— wedged between the ischial spines of the mother's pelvis. This also is called 0 (zero) station. The membranes must be ruptured, and the cervix completely dilated. The physician applying forceps must be certain of the position of the fetal head so the forceps can be applied properly. When the baby is presenting as a breech, forceps can be used, but only for the *aftercoming head*—after the breech and body have been born.

Classifications of Forceps Deliveries

Forceps deliveries are categorized into four types:

1. **High forceps** refers to a delivery in which the fetal head is above 0 station or unengaged. This procedure is no longer used as it is too dangerous for mother and fetus.

2. **Midforceps** are forceps deliveries when the head is higher than +2 station, but is engaged or at least 0 station.
3. **Low forceps** describe a forceps delivery when the baby's head is at least at +2 station.
4. **Outlet forceps** are used when the baby's head is visible in the entrance to the vagina but has failed to deliver, either because of resistance by the perineum, inadequate contractions, or the mother's difficulty bearing down.

With low or midforceps deliveries, the fetal head may not have rotated into the occiput anterior (OA) but may be in one of the transverse or oblique positions (see Chapter 21).

Outlet or low forceps can be done easily under pudendal block or even with local infiltration of the perineum (see Chapter 19). Midforceps call for more potent anesthesia, not only to relieve the pain of the procedure for the mother, but also to relax her muscles and facilitate the birth. A significant variable in the outcome from midforceps deliveries is the experience and skill of the operator, both in deciding when to deliver and how to do it.

Performance of a Forceps Delivery

Except for outlet forceps, anesthesia is administered to the mother before the forceps are applied. This may be a general anesthetic, putting the mother to sleep, but a regional anesthetic is used more commonly. A pudendal block, an epidural, or a low spinal block (called a *saddle block*) may be given. The pudendal block is inserted through the skin of the perineum or more usually through the vaginal mucosa and is therefore put into place after the woman has been prepared for delivery. Epidural or saddle block anesthesia is placed before the woman is put into position on the delivery table. For delivery, the woman lies on her back, knees apart, with her legs supported either by stirrups or by the hands of members of the support team.

The saddle block is a very low spinal anesthesia, administered with the woman sitting up. The saddle block allows the most intense portion of the anesthetic to be in the perineum and the lower part of the abdomen, while it minimizes anesthesia in the legs. Its name refers to the anatomic parts that would make contact with a saddle if the woman were horseback riding—these are the parts most anesthetized by this technique. The woman usually continues to be aware of uterine contractions, although she will not feel discomfort in her vagina or perineum.

She can bear down as requested by the obstetrician who is doing the forceps maneuver. The safety of forceps delivery is enhanced by the improved relaxation available with epidural or saddle block as compared with the more limited anesthesia provided by a pudendal block.

Before the forceps are applied, the vaginal area receives an antiseptic preparation, and the woman is draped with sterile towels or disposable paper drapes. The obstetrician then performs a careful vaginal examination to determine the position of the fetus's head by feeling for the two soft spots (*fontanelles*) at the front and back of the head. The front fontanelle, where four bones join, is relatively large and diamond-shaped, while the one in back, where three bones join, is much smaller and triangular. Sometimes, because of the way in which the bones have shifted against one another in the course of labor (*molding*) or because of the *caput succedanum* (a normal swelling of the baby's scalp), these landmarks are difficult to identify reliably. The obstetrician can then slide fingers alongside the baby's head and feel for an ear. Since the front of the ear is fixed and the back of the ear is loose and floppy, the examiner can tell from the ear which direction the baby's head is facing.

After determining the position of the head, the obstetrician picks up one blade of the forceps and slides it into the vagina alongside the baby's head in such a way that when the two blades of the forceps are brought together, the *maternal* (pelvic) *curve* of the forceps will be in the same direction as the curve of the vagina. Minor adjustments are occasionally needed in the position of this first blade of the forceps against the baby's head. When application of the forceps is completed, each blade should be resting over an ear of the baby. This is especially important when the baby is presenting in the occiput transverse (OT), in which the back of the baby's head is pointing toward the mother's side. It may be necessary with OT to introduce the first blade of the forceps over the baby's face and then jiggle it around (a technique called *wandering*) until it falls over the side of the baby's head. When the first blade is properly in place, the second blade can be readily applied and the forceps brought together (*articulated*). If the application of the forceps is not correct, the blades do not lock properly. They then need to be removed and adjusted. Once the obstetrician is satisfied with a proper application, delivery of the baby can begin.

If the baby's head is not in the occiput anterior, where it should be as it is being born, efforts may be made to turn or rotate the baby into that position with the forceps. Some obstetricians pull the baby's head down as they accomplish this rotation, while others rotate the baby's head before pulling. Once the baby's head is in the appropriate position, the obstetrician exerts traction on the forceps. This means that he or she holds the handles of the forceps and pulls down in the direction of the birth canal. Exactly how this is done varies from obstetrician to obstetrician.

Many obstetricians try as much as possible to mimic the forces of labor. The traction is exerted when the uterus is contracting, if it is possible to feel the uterus or if the woman is awake and can feel contractions. If the woman can cooperate, she may be asked to bear down along with the pulling. If this is not feasible due to anesthesia, then the obstetrician may pull for about 10 or 15 seconds, release for a moment, then pull again, and a third time, trying to simulate the bearing-down efforts that occur with a uterine contraction. Mimicking the forces of labor also involves pulling for under a minute at a time, at intervals of about a minute and a half, repeating this cycle as often as necessary to achieve delivery. Most forceps deliveries last no more than 5 to 10 minutes. If the obstruction to birth is so severe that it requires more time or unusual force, the obstetrician should consider abandoning the effort and delivering the baby via a cesarean.

Sometimes the physician assesses that there is only a chance of performing a successful forceps delivery. In this instance, a cesarean may be set up so that if, in fact, the attempt at a forceps delivery fails, the surgery can be performed immediately.

With success, the baby's head crowns within the forceps. From that point on, the mother usually can push the baby's head out by herself. Once the head is born by forceps, the remainder of the birth of the child is exactly the same as it is with a spontaneous birth.

Most physicians perform an episiotomy for a forceps delivery, since more space is required in the birth canal when the baby is born inside forceps, making lacerations of the vagina more common.

In a breech birth, once the navel is delivered, the head has to be delivered within a few minutes. Delay can occur because the head is the largest part of the baby. If simple maneuvers fail to deliver the head, forceps may be applied for the delivery of what is called the "aftercoming head." The Piper forceps was especially designed for this purpose, although Simpson forceps can be used as well. Whichever forceps is used, the help of a second attendant is needed to hold the baby's trunk in position while the forceps are applied. Once the baby's mouth is brought down low enough in the birth canal to allow the baby to breathe, the rest of the forceps delivery can be done slowly and deliberately.

Prophylactic Forceps

From the 1920s to the 1960s the concept of *prophylactic forceps* had considerable acceptance. The thought was that the baby would be spared the stress of the last half hour or so of labor and, delivered in forceps, would be born under complete control of the physician. The mother also was spared a period of hard work in bearing down. It was additionally thought that if a large episiotomy was done, difficulties related to vaginal relaxation later in life would be prevented.

These arguments for prophylactic forceps have proven false. The stress of half an hour of labor on the head of the fetus is no greater than the stress produced by a forceps delivery. Although the mother may be spared some pushing effort, she is subjected to pain or anesthesia with a forceps delivery. Furthermore, an episiotomy does not prevent injury to the muscles and tissue that support the bladder, rectum, or uterus. Studies have shown that women who have had episiotomies are more likely to have problems resulting from pelvic muscle relaxation, such as involuntary loss of urine, than women who had deliveries without episiotomies.

Incidence of Forceps Deliveries

Fewer and fewer forceps deliveries are being done in the United States today. The rate of forceps deliveries varies according to the type of hospital in which the delivery takes place, the training and expectations of the physicians and of the women delivering at the institution, as well as the proportion of women having a first baby. It also depends upon the extent to which women are educated for natural childbirth and whether the physicians in a given institution still practice prophylactic forceps deliveries. It's been estimated that forceps and vacuum deliveries in the United States together comprise no more than 10 to 15 percent of births. Use of forceps varies widely by state.

Complications of Forceps

As high forceps deliveries are no longer performed, injuries to mother and baby from forceps delivery have decreased in recent years. Most complications are associated with *midforceps deliveries,* or deliveries in which the baby's head must be rotated more than a quarter turn (45 degrees).

Maternal Injuries

A forceps delivery is likely to involve an episiotomy, and there is a greater likelihood of extensions of the episiotomy than with a spontaneous delivery. There is more blood loss associated with forceps delivery. Some women experience difficulty urinating or controlling the anal sphincter after a forceps delivery. These problems most often resolve over time.

Fetal Injuries

Pressure injuries where forceps are applied to the fetus's head usually are limited to simple abrasions of the skin. When the orientation of the forceps on the skull is not ideal there may be a bruise over an ear. If the tip of the forceps makes pressure on the cheek just ahead of the ear it can produce a temporary paralysis of the muscles served by the seventh cranial nerve. In that case, the baby's mouth will be pulled away to the other side and the baby will blink inadequately on the side of the paralysis. This injury clears up quickly, within the first few days after birth. Forceps applications that are badly done, particularly if excessive force is added, have been known to produce skull fractures. Fortunately, these ordinarily heal without doing any injury to the baby's brain and without leaving any later evidence of the event.

Some researchers have raised the question of whether there are any long-term infant consequences from forceps delivery. The questions of whether there is an increase in cerebral palsy with forceps deliveries and whether a such a delivery has an effect on later-life intelligence quotient (IQ) have been raised. Neither has been answered adequately.

VACUUM EXTRACTION

Many efforts have been made over the years to replace the steel forceps with a gentler instrument that can deliver the baby without putting as much pressure on the sides of the baby's head. The first such instrument to gain widespread use was the vacuum extractor, introduced in Sweden in 1954.

The vacuum extractor uses a metal cup about 3 inches in diameter and about 1 inch deep. The original metal cup has been largely replaced in the United States by a soft cone-shaped cup of a synthetic material, which works on the same principle. The vacuum extractor is used for much the same reasons as forceps are used.

To use the vacuum, the cup is placed over the baby's scalp and a carefully controlled vacuum is created inside the cup with a pump. This gradually sucks the baby's scalp into the cup and holds it there, forming an artificial *caput succedaneum* or swelling between the scalp and the bones of the skull. By maintaining this hold on the scalp, the birth attendant can use the instrument as a handle on the baby's head. The scalp is quite loosely applied to the skull, and the artificial caput is as harmless as the caput that normally forms on the head of most babies. With this handle, the birth attendant can rotate the head into a more favorable position and then make traction by pulling on the suction cup with a chain attached for that purpose.

It is important to palpate around the edges of the cup to be certain that no vaginal tissue has been sucked into it along with the baby's scalp. This will make the cup pop off and may cause lacerations and bleeding in the mother.

An advantage of the vacuum extractor is that it is attached at the leading part of the baby's head, rather than the sides of the baby's head. Thus, it does not take up any space in the vagina or pelvis and can be applied with less discomfort than the forceps. The baby's head can adapt itself to the pelvis instead of adapting to the delivery instrument. There also is less chance of traumatizing the mother's tissues.

Bearing down by the mother facilitates progress during traction with the vacuum extractor. With local anesthesia to the perineum, pudendal block, or a low epidural block, the mother can bear down in cooperation with the traction made by the physician or midwife. A vacuum birth can in fact mimic spontaneous birth. An episiotomy can be done but may not be needed.

In some European countries, the vacuum extractor has virtually replaced forceps, and obstetricians there are quite satisfied with its safety and efficiency. It does produce a conspicuous purple bruise on the top of the baby's head at the site of the artificial caput, and can cause bleeding under the skin. This can lead to the baby's developing hyperbilirubinemia. *Hyperbilirubinemia* is an excess of bilirubin in the blood, which occurs when red blood cells are destroyed, as happens with this extra bleeding. Hyperbilirubinemia can lead to newborn jaundice. These complications are more common with the metal cup than with the soft cup.

As with forceps, a vacuum delivery may not be successful, and a cesarean may be necessary.

CESAREAN BIRTH

A cesarean delivery is the birth of a baby via surgery performed through the abdominal and uterine walls. Cesarean is the most common operation in the United States. Since the latter half of the twentieth century, the operation has increased in safety, in part because of the availability of trained anesthesiologists and obstetricians, and capable pediatricians to care for the newborn after the operation. The use of better surgical techniques, blood transfusion, and antibiotics also have helped.

Rates of Cesarean Birth

In 1965, approximately 4.5 percent of births were cesarean deliveries. By 1988, this had risen spectacularly to almost 25 percent of all births. A small but steady decline followed, persisting through 1997. In 1998, the cesarean rate in the U.S. was 21.1 percent, rising to 22 percent in 1999. The recent rise in rate is mostly among women who had not had a previous cesarean, although there also has been a decline in the rate of *vaginal birth after cesarean* (VBAC).

The reasons for the upward, downward, and again upward trends in cesarean births are varied. Specific changes that took place in both society and obstetrical practices in the second part of the twentieth century were responsible for the increase in cesarean rates, in addition, of course, to the continuing increased safety of the surgery itself.

One societal change was that women began to have fewer babies, meaning a higher percentage of births occurred to *nulliparas*—women who'd never had a child before. These pregnancies tend to have more complications, or to be treated as more at risk by physicians. In addition, women are having babies at older ages than previously. This does not necessarily incur increased risk, but some of these women have medical problems such as diabetes and high blood pressure that are less common in younger women.

A major change in obstetrical practice has been the use of electronic fetal monitoring. This has led to the performance of more cesarean deliveries for fetal problems, although it has not improved newborn outcomes. In addition, babies in the breech presentation have been delivered more and more frequently by cesarean. In 1990, 83 percent of all breech babies were born by cesarean. During this same time, the use of forceps has decreased. High forceps, as discussed earlier, are no longer practiced. Some babies that would have been delivered by forceps are now delivered by cesarean.

In looking at whether the rate of cesarean birth is appropriate, one must consider the fact that the surgery does incur significantly increased risks to the mother: discomfort, due to an abdominal operation and an increased likelihood of infection; the need for more extensive anesthesia; hemorrhage from unavoidable surgical accidents; and the increased need for a repeat cesarean in subsequent pregnancies.

The risk of maternal death from cesarean is several times that of vaginal birth. Still, it is extremely small—about 1 in 10,000 births. If this is weighed against the chance of fetal injury from a delay in delivery or a difficult birth—both events avoidable by cesarean—the decision in equivocal situations is likely to be in favor of cesarean.

Yet, once the cesarean rate reached one-quarter of all births, there was a public outcry against so many surgeries performed for what is usually a normal body function. In the publication *Healthy People 2000*, the federal government called for a lowering of the cesarean rate. The rate of cesarean birth in the United States is much higher than in a number of developed countries in Europe, especially for cesareans attributed to previous cesarean and *dystocia*—difficult labor. Dystocia is often a somewhat subjective diagnosis and how quickly a physician or midwife intervenes in the case of slow progress of labor can vary greatly among practitioners.

Reasons for Cesarean Birth

There are four reasons cited most commonly today for the performance of a cesarean delivery:

1. Repeat cesarean
2. Dystocia or failure to progress in labor
3. Breech presentation
4. Fetal distress, or the desire to avoid fetal distress

History of Cesarean Birth

Origin of Name

There are several sources credited as the originators of the term *cesarean*. The historian Pliny the Elder (A.D. 23–79) mentions the cesarean operation. He states that it is the source of the surname of the Roman emperors, since "Caesar" is related to the Latin word for "cut."

A romantic version of history tells us that Julius Caesar (c. 100–44 B.C.) was "cut" from his mother's womb. It seems highly improbable that he was born in this way; first, because his mother survived his birth for many years, and cesareans in his day almost certainly were never done on living women; and, second, because the ancients favored a very different origin for the name of their emperors. In the Punic language, *caesar* meant elephant, and since Julius once slew an elephant he was probably given this heroic sobriquet, which passed on to his successors.

Another improbable derivation for cesarean section is the claim that at about 750 B.C., during the reign of Numa Pompilius, a law was passed which made it obligatory to open the belly of any woman who died near term in order to rescue the infant from its uterine grave. Originally codified as *lex regia*, under the emperors it became *lex caesarea*. It would have been a most remarkable law if it had been enacted in this, the earliest period of Roman history, and its authenticity is highly questionable. And so it remains totally uncertain as to how the operation got its name.

Early History of the Operation

The early history of the cesarean operation is equally vague. What did Pliny know about it? Was it ever done in his day? Was there a law in antiquity in regard to postmortem cesarean sections? There are uncertain references to cesarean sections in the Talmud, the book of Jewish post-Biblical law and lore written between A.D. 76 and about A.D. 200. Do these references in the Talmud to women who survived after being delivered by *yoce dofan*, a "cut in the side," mean that women actually lived after cesarean delivery almost 2,000 years ago?

Postmortem (Latin: afterdeath) cesarean probably was freely practiced in antiquity; unquestionably it was widely used in the late medieval period and the early Renaissance.

It is somewhat apocryphally reported that in 1500 Jacob Nufer, a swine gelder, wiped his butcher's knife on his Swiss Alpine trousers and, before a gallery of thirteen midwives, delivered his own child by cesarean. His wife, Frau Nufer, is said to have survived the operation and subsequently presented the bold Jacob with two more children, born vaginally. Of the thirty-eight cesarean operations performed in Great Britain from 1739 to 1845, only four women recovered.

The first detailed report of a cesarean on a living woman was the account of an operation done in Germany in 1610. According to the research of the preeminent medical historian, Colonel Fielding H. Garrison, the first cesarean in the U.S. was performed by Dr. Jessee Bennett in rural Virginia in 1794. Mrs. Bennett was confined in her first pregnancy. Labor was difficult because of a contracted pelvis, and neither her husband nor the consulting doctor was successful in the attempt at delivery by forceps. The choice lay between a destructive operation on the child and a cesarean delivery. The woman chose to save her baby and, since the other doctor refused to have anything to do with so dangerous a procedure, the unpleasant task fell to the husband. Mrs. Bennett was put under the influence of a large dose of opium. Assisted by two women, Dr. Bennett laid open his wife's abdomen and uterus with a single stroke of the knife and rapidly delivered his daughter, who was still alive. He paused long enough to remove both of his wife's ovaries, remarking, according to one witness, "This shall be the last one." The wound was closed with stout linen thread and, contrary to expectation, mother and child did well. The first cesarean-section baby in this country lived to be 73.

The surgeon-husband did not publish a report of the remarkable feat, and several years later, when asked why, he replied that no doctor with any feelings of delicacy would report an operation that he had done on his own wife. He added that no doctors would believe that operations could be done in the Virginia backwoods with the mother's surviving, and he'd be damned if he would give anybody a chance to call him a liar.

Before 1876, few women survived a cesarean birth by many days, partly because of the crude surgery of that period and partly because the operation was reserved for desperately ill women—those who had labored for days and who were already profoundly infected. In that year, Professor Edoardo Porto of Pavia contended that it would be best to remove the whole uterus at the time of the operation, for with the removal of the large wounded organ the chance for postoperative hemorrhage and inflammation would be lessened. The wisdom of Porto's teaching soon became obvious; however, the great drawback to his technique was the fact that it rendered the woman permanently sterile. Today this type of cesarean section, with removal of the uterus after its incision to deliver the baby, is referred to as *cesarean hysterectomy*. It is rarely performed, reserved only for the emergency situation in which the woman is bleeding profusely and other methods to stem the hemorrhage fail.

In 1882, Max Sanger, then a 29-year-old lowly *Privatdocent* in Leipzig, published an epoch-making two-hundred-page treatise on *Der Kaiserschmitt* (The Cesarean Section). He called attention to the importance of sewing the uterine incision firmly together after delivery of the baby. It had always been customary to *suture* (sew) the wound in the abdomen, but previous to Sanger's contribution the unsutured uterus was dropped back in the abdomen, to remain a constant source of danger—from hemorrhage and growth of bacteria out of the open uterine wound into the abdominal cavity. An American, Robert Harris, and others too, had suggested stitching the uterine incision together, but they did not suggest the orderly and thorough way that Sanger did. Since Sanger's operation was only a refinement of the old type of cesarean, and since it did not remove the uterus, it is referred to as either the *classical* or the *conservative cesarean* section.

Because of the dissatisfaction with the results of Sanger's operation if performed on women who had been in labor for several hours, Fritz Frank of Cologne developed the *low cervical cesarean* in 1907. Frank's new technique consisted of freeing the bladder from its flimsy attachment to the lower portion of the uterus (the low cervical segment), pushing the bladder down in the pelvis, and opening the uterus through the area from which the bladder had just been freed. After child and placenta are removed, the wound in the uterus is sewn together, and then the bladder drawn up and tacked by sutures back to its original position. This seals off the uterine wound from the abdominal cavity by plastering the bladder entirely over it. It is like putting a large rubber patch over an inflated ball whose edges previously had been cemented together.

Modern Results

The results of cesarean section today are a far cry from those of 100 and even 60 years ago. We no longer wait to operate until all else has failed. Many of the operations are done to protect the welfare of the fetus. Most of the mothers are in excellent condition and well prepared to withstand the rigors of a major operation. The use of blood transfusion, improved techniques of anesthesia, and antibiotics have all done much to reduce the serious risks of cesarean birth.

Another significant feature contributing substantially to the present safety of cesarean section is the use of a uterine incision in the thin, lowermost portion of the uterus. This is commonly called a *transverse* or *lower-segment cesarean* section. This operation has almost completely replaced the classical section, in which the incision is made in the muscular, thicker body of the uterus. Both bleeding and uterine infection are more common with a classical incision, and disruption of the uterine incision in a subsequent pregnancy is much more of a threat than when the incision is made in the lower segment of the uterus. Finally, the recovery from a lower-segment cesarean is much quicker and easier than with the classical cesarean.

Classical cesarean sections are used when the lower uterine segment is judged to be unsuitable for a safe delivery of the infant. Examples include:

- Some preterm births where the lower segment is underdeveloped
- When the fetus is in a transverse lie with the back down
- Large fibroids in the lower segment
- Dense adhesions in the pelvis involving the lower segment and bladder (usually from previous surgery)
- Placenta previa/accreta when there is a high likelihood of the need for hysterectomy to be done with the cesarean (*cesarean hysterectomy*)

The lower-segment operation is done through either a longitudinal skin incision (up and down from the pubic area to the navel) or a transverse incision (from side to side across the lowermost portion of the abdomen). The important incision is not the one in the skin but the incision in the uterus itself. Some surgeons call the transverse skin incision the *bikini cut*. Of course, this overemphasizes the cosmetic aspects of the incision. Nevertheless, the transverse (*Pfannenstiehl*) skin incision hurts less and heals more dependably.

The classical cesarean can also be done with either type of skin incision—*Pfannenstiehl* or up and down. Although the up and down incision may be preferable for a classical cesarean, often the decision to do the classical cesarean is made after the skin has already been opened and the lower uterine segment is evaluated as unsuitable for a transverse cesarean.

Cesarean delivery offers the baby as good a chance as a normal vaginal delivery and a better chance of survival than does a difficult vaginal delivery.

Family-Centered Cesarean Birth

Today, whether the woman is awake or asleep for the delivery, partners often are invited into the operating room so they can experience the birth of their child. If the mother is awake, of course, a partner can provide support for her as well. Usually, a drape is hung across the woman's chest so she does not see the surgery. A partner may not wish to look at the operation, but instead focus on the needs of the woman undergoing the surgery. Of course, some women having a cesarean delivery are awake and would like to see the birth of their baby. If you would like this, you can ask the nurse to bring you a mirror or ask the physician to take down the drape at the time of the birth.

The Operation

Before the Surgery

A cesarean delivery usually takes about 45 minutes. Before the surgery, an intravenous line is placed, if it had not been in place before. A *catheter* or thin tube is inserted into the bladder to keep it empty and out of the way during the operation. This is done under sterile technique and usually causes no pain. The catheter may or may not be removed at the conclusion of the surgery. If it is kept in, it usually will be removed when the mother can walk to the bathroom, unless there are bladder complications, generally the day following the surgery. Your doctor may wish to have your hair shaved or clipped with clippers before the surgery, to make it easier to put the skin edges together after the operation. However, research has shown that shaving is not necessary to prevent infection.

Once these preparations are made, you will be taken to an operating room, and placed on a flat table. An electrocardiogram machine will be attached to your chest with sticky pads. An automatic blood pressure cuff will be wrapped around your arm. The skin of the entire abdomen will be cleansed and sterile drapes placed over it. If regional anesthesia had already been in place, a greater amount of medication will be placed into the catheter. If a general anesthesia is to be used to put you to sleep, it will be administered at this time.

The Surgery Itself

With a transverse incision, the skin is cut at the upper margin of the pubic hair. A *longitudinal* (lengthwise) skin incision takes a few minutes less than the preferable low-transverse incision. In either event, the operator makes an incision with a surgical blade through the skin and the fat down to the glistening tough white connective tissue of the abdominal wall, called the *fascia*. In a longitudinal incision the fascia is divided from a point slightly below the navel down to the pubic bone. If the incision is transverse, the fascia under the skin is divided with scissors to either side. The muscles beneath this incision are pulled apart gently. Using scissors, the operator divides the peritoneum, bringing the uterus into view.

If a classical incision is done in the uterus, the operator cuts the uterine wall up and down with a scalpel or scissors for a distance of about 6 inches. If this incision comes down on the placenta, the placenta is either pushed out of the way or cut.

With the lower-segment incision, the operator identifies the point where the bladder lies loosely low down over the uterine wall. The flimsy attachment makes it possible for the bladder to fill and empty. The thin peritoneal covering of the uterus just above the bladder attachment is cut and opened with scissors in a transverse direction. The bladder can easily be pushed off the wall of the uterus, down into the pelvis, and tucked away behind an instrument called a *retractor*. In the area cleared of the bladder, an incision approximately 6 inches in length is made transversely in the lower segment of the uterus. If necessary, the

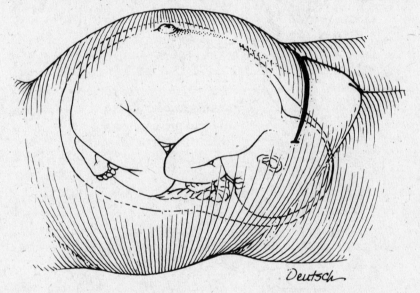

A semitransparent sketch of mother and fetus on the operating table to show the location of a transverse skin incision for cesarean. The mother's head is to the right. Sometimes the incision in the skin is lengthwise, from the mother's navel (seen in the drawing over the baby's back) down to the level of the mother's pubic hair line.

incision can be enlarged with the operator's fingers or with scissors, to make it large enough to bring the baby through.

When membranes have been ruptured previously there may not be much fluid. If the membranes are still intact, they will bulge into the uterine incision. Intact membranes are incised with a gentle flick of the scalpel and the fluid allowed to drain.

Delivery of the Baby

The operator, using a hand or a single blade of a forceps, gently shoehorns the infant's head out of the incision and then delivers the rest

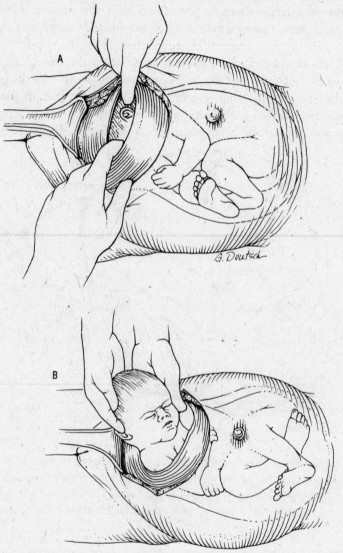

In these two illustrations, the mother is on the operating table in the same position and her navel is shown. The abdominal wall has been cut and is held out of the way by the instrument seen inside and low in the mother's abdominal cavity. The bladder has been pushed down off the uterus, and in A the surgeon's fingers are enlarging the uterine incision by stretching it to the right and left. In B the baby is being delivered through the uterine opening thus created.

of the child. If the cesarean is done when labor is well advanced and the baby's head is deep in the pelvis, an assistant may need to reach into the vagina and push the baby's head up from below.

If the baby presents as a transverse or a breech it is delivered by breech extraction or internal version followed by breech extraction, discussed earlier, through the incision in the lower uterine segment.

The baby's umbilical cord ordinarily is clamped and cut promptly and the baby handed to a pediatrician or neonatal nurse practitioner, so that the operating team can devote its attention to the uterine incision, which commonly bleeds quite profusely. Surgical clamps are placed on the wound's edges to limit the bleeding. The placenta is removed from the opened uterus through the incision from which the baby has just come. Oxytocin is administered at this time to enhance uterine contractions. It usually is given through the intravenous line.

Closing the Incision

The uterine incision is carefully inspected for bleeding vessels. The wound in the uterus ordinarily is closed with one or two rows of sutures to bring the edges of the uterine incision together and to stop the bleeding. There are almost as many ways of repairing the uterus as there are surgeons who know how to do cesareans, and no one way is superior to any other.

The incision made in the peritoneum to push the bladder off the uterus is closed with the simplest kind of sewing. The operator next inspects the fallopian tubes and ovaries to be certain they are normal.

Closure of the abdominal wall is done in the same way as in other abdominal surgery. A simple suture can be used in the peritoneal layer of the abdominal wall, although this step may be unnecessary. The muscles are allowed to fall together, and the fascia carefully repaired with sutures. The skin can be closed with a layer of stitches, which are subsequently removed, or with a fine suture placed just under the skin. The sutures placed under the skin are absorbed over time. Some surgeons use stainless-steel staples. Healing is extraordinarily rapid in the absence of infection. Skin sutures and staples can be removed almost painlessly a few days after the operation.

Anesthesia for Cesarean Delivery

Today, epidural anesthesia is used most frequently for cesarean. Spinal and general anesthesia are also suitable. Both regional and general anesthesia produce the needed relaxation of the mother's abdominal wall.

Local anesthesia, hypnosis, and acupuncture have also been used, but only seldom.

General Anesthesia for Cesarean

A general anesthetic for cesarean ordinarily is begun with a very short-acting drug such as a barbiturate, given intravenously, to put the woman to sleep. This alone will not result in sufficient pain relief, however. In order to provide pain relief, muscle relaxation, and sleep, without causing undue depression of the newborn's breathing, several medications are used together for general anesthesia. Because muscle relaxants may stop breathing as well as all other body movement, the anesthesiologist passes an *endotracheal* (Greek: *endon* = within; *trachea* = windpipe) tube through the woman's mouth and vocal cords, and into the upper portion of the trachea. A small balloon wrapped around this tube is inflated to fill the trachea, thus greatly reducing the possibility of breathing in food or gastric juice, a major complication of general anesthesia. The anesthesiologist connects the tube to the anesthesia machine, which artificially breathes for the woman while she is paralyzed by drugs. The anesthesiologist maintains continuous observation of the woman's heart rate and blood pressure.

General anesthesia often is preferred when a cesarean needs to be done in a hurry or when it is done for hemorrhage. The anesthesia can be established in a few minutes, in contrast to 20 to 30 minutes for an epidural. Epidural and intradural (spinal or saddle block) anesthesias tend to result in the pooling of blood in the lower half of the body, which aggravates the effect of blood loss by further reducing the amount of blood available for the heart, brain, and kidneys. General anesthesia does not have this effect and thus is safer in the presence of hemorrhage.

The obvious disadvantage of general anesthesia is that the mother is asleep during the birth of her baby. She also tends to be in a somewhat detached dream state for varying periods of time after she has begun to awaken from the anesthesia. This may interfere with early bonding with her newborn.

Spinal and Epidural for Cesarean

Spinal, which can be given in 2 to 3 minutes, is the anesthesia of choice in some institutions when cesarean has to be done in a hurry and there is no maternal hemorrhage. The mother loses all sensation below the rib cage for the duration of the spinal anesthetic, which may last for several hours. Since this is a so-called *one-shot technique*, enough anesthetic drug must be given in the initial injection to last the expected duration of the procedure.

The margin of safety with anesthesia such as a spinal that goes through the dura (therefore called an *intradural*) is not as great as it is with an epidural, in which the injection is outside the dura. The *dura mater* is the dense membrane that encases the spinal cord. With an intradural insertion, the drug is put directly into the spinal fluid and can spread farther in that fluid pool than intended. The drug may then weaken the muscles of the chest, decreasing breathing activity. The woman, as she realizes her inability to breathe deeply, may experience considerable anxiety. This complication usually gives a warning with a drop in blood pressure and a speeding up of the pulse rate. The treatment is early support of the woman's breathing, making use of oxygen and the anesthesia machine.

Epidural is now firmly established as the anesthetic of choice for cesarean section. Most hospitals today have the skilled anesthesiologists necessary for its safe performance. Epidural anesthesia for cesarean is more intense and rises to a higher sensory level in the abdomen than epidural for labor and vaginal delivery, but the technique of giving it is identical. This is described in Chapter 20.

With regional anesthesia the woman remains awake and alert. She can see and hear and hold her baby. She may feel motion and pressure in her abdomen, but pain is eliminated. The loss of muscle control wears off in a matter of a few hours, and all functions return to normal. With epidural anesthesia, the catheter can remain in place after the surgery and provide excellent postoperative pain relief.

Blood Loss from Cesarean Delivery

The blood loss from a cesarean delivery is between a pint and a quart. Pregnant women tolerate blood loss of this magnitude remarkably well and ordinarily do not require blood transfusion. When the operation is done for a bleeding problem such as placenta previa or separation of the placenta (*abruptio placentae*), blood loss may be much greater and transfusion may become necessary. A quart of intravenous solution often is given rapidly to the mother prior to cesarean as a preventive measure to help assure an adequate volume of maternal blood.

Complications Due to Cesarean Delivery

Cesarean is a major abdominal operation. The usual complications of surgery such as hemorrhage or infection may occur, but as almost all mothers are young and healthy, these difficulties are encountered infrequently.

In the United States today, a significant fraction of the deaths in childbirth are due to anesthesia, most often associated with cesarean birth. There are no completely safe anesthetics. Still, the operation is considered reasonably safe. In the rare event of an emergency, the greatest safety factor is a skilled and careful anesthesiologist.

The most common worries following cesarean are excessive bleeding (*hemorrhage*) and infection of the uterus and of the incision in the abdominal wall. Infection is more likely when the cesarean was done to treat intrauterine infection (*chorioamnionitis*) or when labor was advanced before the cesarean was done. Treatment with antibiotics ordinarily leads to prompt and rapid recovery. Today, many obstetricians will give preventive or *prophylactic* antibiotics to all women undergoing cesarean deliveries. Research has found consistently that such prophylaxis helps prevent fever, uterine infection, wound infection, and urinary tract infection following the surgery. Most often, one dose of an antibiotic is given after delivery of the infant, although if the surgery was prolonged, a second dose may be recommended. The antibiotics chosen do not preclude breast-feeding. The additional pain and fatigue that follow a surgery, of course, may make infant feeding and care somewhat more difficult than usual.

Recovery from Cesarean

Right after surgery, you will be observed carefully in the recovery room. Your blood pressure, temperature, pulse, and respiratory rate will be monitored frequently. The dressing will be checked for abdominal bleeding, and your sanitary pad for vaginal bleeding. Although you have not had a vaginal birth, the discharge from the vagina will be the same. The catheter in your bladder will be checked for an adequate amount of urine.

Now that the virtues of early ambulation are known, if the cesarean is done early in the day, you will be encouraged to get out of bed and move around on the same day. If the operation is done late in the day or at the end of a long and uncomfortable labor, getting up may be postponed until the next day. Abdominal dressings have become smaller and smaller. Some surgeons do not use any at all or remove the bandage quickly. This makes it possible for you to take a shower the day after the operation. The urinary catheter typically is removed within 12 hours of the surgery or the morning following the surgery if that is more convenient. The intravenous line usually is removed the day following surgery, assuming you do not have a fever or excess bleeding.

You can care for your baby and can begin breast-feeding whenever you feel up to it. The abdominal incision might be uncomfortable if you hold the baby over it, so the "football hold" might be easier at first. In this position, the baby is tucked under an arm, with its head facing the breast. You can also put a pillow over the incision and rest the baby on the pillow. You can later try nursing in a side-lying position.

Of course, you will need pain medication following the surgery. If an epidural was used for anesthesia, it can be maintained for pain relief. Otherwise, meperidine (Demerol) or morphine can be given as injections into your muscle for the first day following surgery. A drug to quell nausea may be given with these narcotic pain killers. Some hospitals provide pumps for patient-controlled analgesia (PCA). This allows you to administer your own pain relief medications through the intravenous line. The pump is set so an overdose cannot occur. This provides for smaller doses of medication at more frequent intervals than is provided by giving medications via injections every 4 hours. Milder, oral medications are most often sufficient after the first 24 hours.

After surgery, you usually will have only ice chips or sips of water for 12 to 24 hours. A nurse, midwife, or physician will then check for bowel sounds using a stethoscope on your abdomen. Once bowel sounds return, you may have a liquid diet, followed soon by a regular diet. Some physicians prescribe a regular diet as soon as you have an appetite.

The stay in the hospital has become shorter following a cesarean just as it has following vaginal birth. Women who have recovered rapidly may choose to go home as early as the third day after cesarean.

Advice on activity, exercises, and resumption of sexual activity is the same for a woman following a cesarean birth as it is for a vaginal birth. See Chapter 25 for these instructions. As noted, there may be substantial blood loss at cesarean. This may result in anemia, which is treated by oral iron tablets or liquid preparations and a good diet (see Chapter 10).

There is no medical reason now known to delay starting a new pregnancy following a cesarean birth. The uterine wound will have plenty of time to heal.

Vaginal Birth After Cesarean (VBAC)

It used to be held in obstetrics that "once a cesarean, always a cesarean." This is no longer considered true, although one of the commoner reasons for cesarean is still that the last delivery was by cesarean. Most reasons for cesarean are present only for that pregnancy and are not likely to recur. This is true even of *cephalopelvic disproportion* (CPD), or a baby considered too large for the pelvis of the mother. In subsequent pregnancies, women often deliver babies as large as or even larger than the baby for whom this diagnosis was given. For this reason, CPD is used less often today as a diagnosis than "failure to progress." Failure to progress can be caused by any of a number of reasons, none of which will necessarily recur.

Ninety years ago, virtually all cesareans were done through a classical incision. The risks to mother and fetus from the rupture of a classical cesarean incision exceed by far what is acceptable in obstetrics today. The classical scar in the upper muscular body of the uterus can tear directly into the peritoneal cavity. About 40 percent of the time the placenta is implanted on the front wall of the uterus under the scar and the rupture therefore initiates placental separation and consequent hemorrhage. Contractions of the uterus tend to push placenta and baby out through the defect whether or not the woman is in labor. If the placenta is on the back wall of the uterus, the baby is pushed into the peritoneal cavity and the placenta follows. The separation of the placenta cuts the baby off from its maternal support system and the fetus is likely to die of asphyxia before it can be rescued by an abdominal operation. The inevitable serious hemorrhage in the mother due to this calamity results in a hundredfold increase in the maternal death rate. A planned, or *elective*, repeat cesarean will be scheduled at about 36 to 37 weeks of pregnancy in the few women who today have had classical cesarean deliveries.

When a previous low transverse scar ruptures, the body of the uterus usually remains intact. Uterine contractions, instead of causing the fetus to erupt into the peritoneal cavity, simply continue to push the baby down further into the birth canal. Since the placenta and its blood supply are in the body of the uterus, placental separation does not take place and bleeding usually is negligible. The baby remains in a position from which it can be delivered readily. The risks to mother and baby are only slightly greater than those of a normal pregnancy. The previous incision is not likely to be disrupted by a later twin pregnancy, by the presence of hydramnios, or by the stretching of the uterus to accommodate a baby much larger than the previous one.

Many studies do not make a distinction between serious and minor rupture of the uterus. Thus, the rate of dangerous rupture cannot be evaluated completely, but most studies report that less than 1 percent of VBACs result in uterine rupture. In most cases, this is not dangerous to mother or baby.

Today, women who have had previous cesarean deliveries are given the option of a vaginal birth for their next pregnancy. Often, this is referred to as a "trial of labor," meaning that a cesarean will be performed if the labor is not successful. Studies have shown that women who have vaginal births have lower rates of fever, infection, and bleeding, although there is the small increased risk of uterine rupture with a trial of labor. For this reason, the American College of Obstetricians and Gynecologists advises that women with previous cesarean deliveries have their subsequent deliveries in a hospital with the capacity to perform an emergency cesarean operation if necessary.

Generally, in order to have a trial of labor, there will have to be documentation of the type of incision used in the cesarean. If you are delivering at the same hospital or with the same obstetrical practice, this is no problem. If you are not, you should request that your medical records be sent to your new physician or midwife early in your pregnancy. If, for whatever reason, you cannot get this documentation, then a careful history will be taken. If your cesarean was done for a baby that was premature, then it will be assumed to have been a classical incision, and you will not be able to labor. In most other cases, the scar will be assumed to be in the lower uterine segment and you will be able to labor, with close observation.

In most of the studies in which women with previous cesarean deliveries have gone into labor, 60 to 70 percent delivered vaginally and uneventfully. Some researchers have attempted to predict which women will experience successful vaginal delivery after cesarean and which will need a repeat cesarean. To date, this prediction has not been possible. The only consistent variable that seems to make VBAC more successful is having had a previous vaginal birth in addition to the previous cesarean. Some researchers have tried measuring the thickness of the lower uterine segment with ultrasound prior to the trial of labor. This may be promising for the future, but currently there is not enough data on this technique to use it to select women for a trial of labor.

Some practitioners examine (with gloved fingers) the scar inside the uterus immediately after the birth of the baby in a woman who has had a vaginal birth following a cesarean to be certain that it has remained intact. Unless active bleeding is present, however, a separation of the old scar, called a *dehiscence*, does not need to be repaired. This examination, then, may be unnecessary unless unusual bleeding is present.

Women who have delivered previously only by cesarean and who then deliver via the vagina are naturally pleased to find that the recovery from a vaginal birth is more comfortable and speedier than recovery from an abdominal delivery.

Elective and Emergency Cesareans

Cesareans that are planned in advance and done by appointment are referred to as *elective operations*. Those that are decided upon after the woman has gone into labor or done without advance plan, for events such as hemorrhage from placenta previa or prolapse of the umbilical cord, are classified as *emergency operations*.

Elective cesarean should be done as late as possible, either at term or as close as can be managed, to give the infant a chance to achieve maximum maturity. In the past, elective cesarean deliveries led to an increase in the rate of premature babies because sometimes a baby thought to be at term was actually not. The American College of Obstetricians and Gynecologists has established specific criteria to document that the fetus is at term. At least one of these must be present for an elective cesarean to be performed without first testing the fetal lungs to be sure that the baby will be able to breathe outside the uterus. (Fetal lung maturity tests are described in Chapter 17.) If the woman goes into labor before the surgery, then the cesarean is performed at the onset of the labor.

Documentation that the fetus is at term can be provided by:

- Documentation of fetal heart tones for 20 weeks by fetoscope or for 30 weeks by Doppler
- The elapse of 36 weeks since a positive blood or urine pregnancy test was performed by a reliable laboratory
- Gestational age documented to be 39 weeks by an ultrasound performed at 6 to 11 weeks, using crown-rump length as the fetal measurement
- Gestational age documented to be 39 weeks by an ultrasound performed at 12 to 20 weeks and confirmed by clinical findings, including uterine size

These criteria speak to the importance of early prenatal care in women who have had previous cesarean births.

The Debate over Elective Cesarean Delivery

Recently, a debate has emerged in the obstetrical community regarding whether all women should have the choice of vaginal delivery versus elective cesarean birth.

The proponents of elective cesarean delivery cite preservation of the pelvic floor as the main advantage. Their claim is that by electing to have a surgical delivery, women avoid problems later in life with involuntary loss of urine or uterine prolapse, also called *uterine descent*. Both can be uncomfortable and interfere with quality of life as one ages.

Certain labor and delivery factors have been associated with pelvic floor relaxation. These include cutting an episiotomy and actively pushing for a long period of time. If episiotomy is avoided as much as possible, the fetus is allowed to descend on its own until the woman feels a strong urge to push, and the laboring woman is encouraged to push *physiologically*—as her own body guides her—then many of these later problems can be avoided.

Opponents of elective cesarean argue that the increased rate of maternal complications, including a risk of death, however small, exceeds the risk in a vaginal birth.

How Many Cesarean Deliveries Can a Woman Have?

It used to be accepted as a truism that a woman who had had a cesarean section could not have more than two more cesareans. This has turned out to be an incorrect belief. At present there is no limit to the number of cesarean operations that can be done safely. The operation generally heals so well that, on occasion, the surgeon has difficulty at repeat operations finding a scar in the uterus. The abdominal wall withstands repeated incisions remarkably well. The limiting factor on the number of cesareans now appears to be the woman's willingness to experience repeated operations.

Many people think that a new incision is made with each cesarean delivery. This is not the case. The surgeon usually will go through the site of the previous incision and, if there is a substantial skin scar, remove it. There is no external evidence of the number of cesareans that have been performed.

INTERVENTIONS FOR THE
THIRD STAGE OF LABOR

The third stage of labor is the placental stage. It begins after the birth of the baby and ends with the birth of the placenta or *afterbirth*. It can be managed in one of two ways: *expectantly* or *actively*.

Expectant management means watchful waiting for signs of placental separation followed by delivery of the placenta through the mother's pushing efforts. It may also include giving natural assistance to separation of the placenta by using nipple stimulation or taking advantage of gravity.

Active management is advocated by many physicians and some midwives and involves three steps:

1. Giving medication to help the uterus contract before delivery of the placenta
2. Early cord clamping and cutting
3. Controlled traction of the umbilical cord for delivery of the placenta

Research has shown active management to result in less blood loss and fewer episodes of postpartum hemorrhage for the mother. It is also associated with nausea and vomiting, and possibly high blood pressure, depending on the medication given to cause uterine contractions.

Even with expectant management, many practitioners will give oxytocin in the intravenous line or as an injection routinely following delivery of the placenta. This may cause unpleasant uterine contractions. Other physicians or midwives will use this medication only if there is excess bleeding, a soft (*noncontracting*) uterus, or a risk for postpartum hemorrhage. (Risks for postpartum hemorrhage include a very large baby or multiple pregnancy, very rapid labor, induction or augmentation of labor, or a history of postpartum hemorrhage.)

Cervical Inspection

Some physicians and midwives routinely inspect the cervix for bleeding after delivery. Others use this intervention only in the case of excessive bleeding that is not due to another cause, such as a noncontracted uterus or blood vessels torn in a lacerated area of the vagina or perineum. In this procedure, clamps are placed on the cervix, which is soft and easy to grab right after delivery. The cervix is pulled into the vagina and each

area inspected for tears. Suturing may be called for if any tears are bleeding. Of course, the vagina and perineum always are inspected. This usually requires manipulation of the tissues. Blood will need to be wiped
away and the tissues gently separated for better exposure. This can be
uncomfortable, but generally is brief.

Manual Removal of the Placenta

Manual removal of the placenta is discussed in the previous chapter. It is
done with the hands, using sterile technique. It is sometimes an emergency procedure if bleeding is heavy and the placenta cannot be delivered easily with traction and maternal pushing. It is also a procedure
utilized by some practitioners after a set period of time if the placenta
has not yet delivered. The time period before manual removal is utilized
varies from institution to institution and practitioner to practitioner,
but 30 minutes is an acceptable time to wait for placental separation
without intervening. In out-of-hospital births, this time period is often
stretched, if the woman is not bleeding excessively.

Uterine Exploration

The question of whether to check routinely for a nonsymptomatic uterine rupture after a VBAC is controversial. Usually such a rupture, called
a *dehiscence*, requires no treatment and whether or not it is significant
for a future vaginal delivery is not established. This intervention, then,
is utilized with a good deal of variation among physicians and institutions. It is done after delivery by feeling the lower portion of the uterus
through the vagina. The physician or midwife performing the inspection will wear long sterile gloves or regular sterile gloves and a sterile
gown. This is an uncomfortable, but brief, procedure.

TRANSFER

While perhaps not technically an intervention, women need to realize
that if they choose a birthing center or home birth, the possibility always exists that they may need to be moved to a hospital. The reasons
for this are varied. You may want more pain relief than is safe in an out-
of-hospital setting. Your labor may fail to progress and you may need
augmentation. You may have thick, meconium-stained fluid. Your baby

may not rotate into a good position for birth or there may be nonreassuring signs in the fetal heart rate patterns.

Moving to a hospital does not necessarily mean that you will have an intervention for the rest of labor or for birth. Sometimes, a labor that progresses slowly starts to move more quickly after transfer. Sometimes a little pain medication is all you need for the rest of the labor to go smoothly.

Transfer is included in this section on interventions because it can be traumatic for the mother. The actual physical reality of transfer can be stressful. The emotional disappointment can be great, if you have not adequately prepared yourself for the possibility that your labor and birth plan has to change.

Every birthing center and midwife or physician who practices home birth has policies for transferring the mother, or the baby after birth. You should become familiar with these. Everything you want for birth—a healthy baby and a healthy mother—are independent of the birth site. With this in mind, your experience can be satisfying and happy after transfer.

A Bit of Advice

Labor might be easier to handle, and certainly more convenient, if it could be planned. Child care arrangements or work-related activities would be more manageable if you knew exactly when labor would start. Pain might be more tolerable if you knew exactly when it would end. You might have more energy for pushing if you were certain it would last no more than 47 minutes. Women today are used to being in control of their lives, scheduling things well in advance, living by their weekly, even monthly, calendars.

The process of labor, fortunately or unfortunately, was not designed for convenience. Predictability is not a word that can be used in its description. Most pregnancies classified as at-risk or even high-risk actually need few interventions. An occasional pregnancy considered perfectly normal may require several interventions, even a cesarean delivery. Since you cannot plan or predict, all you can do is be prepared. Be aware that an intervention may become necessary, even one you assumed you would never need.

Know your physician's or midwife's practices in advance. Go through this chapter with your care providers. Be sure you are comfortable with their answers to the following questions:

Will they induce at 42 weeks with a cervical ripening agent if your cervix is not ready, or continue fetal surveillance?
Do they use prophylactic forceps?
Do they prefer forceps or a vacuum extractor?
Will you be admitted to a hospital if your membranes rupture before labor or will you stay at home, taking your own temperature?
Will they induce labor within a set period of time if your membranes rupture, or will they practice watchful waiting?
Do they do a cesarean for all babies in the breech presentation? If not, what is their experience delivering vaginal breeches?

Remember, many of these questions have no absolute right or wrong answers. What is right is that you and your physician or midwife have similar feelings and attitudes. In the final analysis, your care provider should be someone you are comfortable trusting.

CHAPTER TWENTY-THREE

Twins and Other Multiple Births

The number of multiple pregnancies and the number of babies born in these pregnancies have risen dramatically over the past few decades. From 1980 to 1997, twin births in the United States rose by 52 percent while triplet and what are called *higher order births* rose 404 percent. In 1997, there were 104,137 twins born compared to 68,339 twins born in 1980.

Biologically, the likelihood of a woman's having a multiple birth increases in her thirties, but decreases after age 40. With the current use of assisted reproductive technologies (see Chapter 13), which enhance the chances of a multiple birth, the twin rate for women 40 to 44 years old soared by 63 percent from 1980 to 1997 and by nearly 1,000 percent for women age 45 to 49. The triplet rate rose almost 400 percent for women in their thirties and more than 1,000 percent for women in their forties. Of course, even such huge jumps in triplet and higher order births does not translate into large numbers of live births. In 1997, there were 6,148 live triplets born in the United States and 589 live babies born in quadruplet, quintuplet, and higher order multiple births.

MULTIPLE BIRTHS IN HISTORY: FACT OR FANTASY?

The subject of multiple birth has been a source of myth and fable. We can read in history books of "Dorothy, an Italian who had 20 at 2 births. . . ." and of Lady Margaret, Countess of Hagenau, who delivered 365 children in 1313. Her plight was brought upon her by the wrath of God.

God heard her ask a woman who begged for alms, "Why should I give you alms?" When the beggar replied, "Because of all the children I have begot," Lady Margaret responded, "Fie upon you, you've had the pleasure of begetting them."

Sometimes, fact and fable become indistinguishable. In the German town of Hamelin, which the Pied Piper made famous in 1248, the following tablet is attached to the front of a house: "Here on this spot dwelt . . . Thiele Romer, and his helpmate Anna Byers. It came about that in the year 1600 . . . at 3 o'clock in the morning on the 9th day of January, she was delivered of 2 small boys and 5 small girls . . . All peacefully died by 12 o'clock on the 20th of January and were given the beatitude which is guaranteed to those who believe." That is all we know about the possible, perhaps even probable, Hamelin septuplets.

We come now to undisputed facts outside the realm of the fabulous and the pseudo-fabulous. The first set of quintuplets to survive were the five Dionne sisters of Canada in 1933—not even a single quintuplet ever had survived before. As of December 2000, a quintuplet webpage showed 235 sets of quints from births around the world, with most of the babies surviving. There are quite a few authentic cases of *sextuplets* (six babies) in which all lived. In 1997, the birth of *septuplets* (seven babies) to the McCaugheys in Iowa made international news. Born by cesarean, all seven babies survived. Another set of septuplets—the Qahatanis—were delivered 12 weeks early by cesarean at Georgetown University Hospital in Washington D.C., in July 2001. The birth itself was uncomplicated, but the newborns weighed only about 2 pounds each. In 1998, a set of *octuplets*—eight babies—was born in Houston, Texas. The first baby was born vaginally, and was 15 weeks premature. The other seven infants were delivered by cesarean, 2 weeks later. The smallest one, who weighed just over 10 ounces at birth, died a week after she was born. The other five girls and two boys survived.

Unfortunately, the subject of twins and higher order multiple births is not important merely as a source of folklore. It is important because, even today, multiple births are more likely to be premature, with the babies low birth weight. Appropriate care for twin, triplet, and other multiple pregnancies during the prenatal period and in labor and delivery is of utmost importance. Fortunately, with such care, babies of multiple gestations most often do just fine.

MULTIPLE BIRTHS
OCCURRING NATURALLY

In 1895, Dyonizy Hellin, a Polish pathologist, stated that twins occurred once in 89 births, triplets once in 89 squared (7,921), and quadruplets once in 89 cubed (704,969). Considering that he used no information concerning the varying incidences of multiple births in different ethnic groups (see box on page 649), or the impact of loss of some or all of the babies in high order multiple births, his estimates were surprisingly accurate. In an analysis of 80 million births in the United States between 1928 and 1955, twins were found to occur once in every 90 pregnancies, triplets once in every 9,300, and quadruplets once in every 490,000.

TYPES OF TWINS

There are two types of twins. One variety originates from a single fertilized egg cell that divides into two very early in its development. In this circumstance, one egg is fertilized by one sperm, and the chromosomes of the two offspring are therefore *identical*. Consequently, the twins must be of the same sex and exactly alike in skin, hair, and eye color. They also bear a striking resemblance to each other in body build and facial features and possess exactly the same blood factors. Such twins are termed identical, *one-egg*, or *monozygotic* (Greek: *mono* = one or single; *zygotos* = yoked).

The other type of twinning results from the fertilization of two eggs by two sperm. The eggs may come from the same ovary or from opposite ovaries. Twins of this variety, known as *fraternal, two-egg*, or *dizygotic* (Greek: *dis* = two), bear no greater resemblance to each other than brothers or sisters at exactly the same age. They may be of the same or opposite sex and may or may not have the same blood type.

Triplets and higher order multiple births may be monozygotic, dizygotic, or a combination. In other words, triplets may be formed from one to three eggs. Two of the three may be identical, with the other fraternal. All three may be identical, or all three fraternal. Ovulation induction may produce either monozygotic or dizygotic twins. Multiple births from in vitro fertilization (IVF) or gamete intrafallopian transfer (GIFT) occur as a result of implanting more than one embryo (see Chapter 13). These then are not identical.

Identical twins may occasionally, though very rarely, undergo developmental influences in utero that cause them to be physically different from one another. For example, one twin may have lost one of its two sex chromosomes at a very early embryonic stage and therefore may develop a female external appearance. This phenomenon is known as *Turner syndrome* (45X). The co-twin, always larger, is clearly male. Unless the problem is suspected and laboratory work is done, the smaller twin will be assumed to be female, and the genetic problem may not be noted until the child reaches the age of puberty and secondary sexual development fails to take place.

Another possible developmental deviation in one identical twin may be the retention of an extra chromosome 21. This manifests itself as *Down syndrome*.

Pairs of twins in which either Turner syndrome or Down syndrome has occurred in one twin may nevertheless be identical in all other genetic characteristics. All their other chromosomes, their blood groups, and their HLA tissue types are exactly the same. HLA stands for *human leukocyte antigen* and is the genetic information in white blood cells (*leukocytes*). This is important because when the HLA types of one individual match that of another, successful organ transplants are possible between them without destructive immune reactions. A transplant between fraternal twins behaves like a transplant between nontwin brothers and sisters, which have a lower rate of success.

Knowing whether twins or other siblings born of one pregnancy are identical or fraternal may thus have an important health implication in their future.

Can You Tell One-Egg from Two-Egg Twins?

If the twins are normal and appear to be one male and one female, they must necessarily be from two eggs and not identical, with the uncommon exception of Turner syndrome, noted above. If they are of the same sex, an answer often can be obtained from a careful inspection of the placenta and membranes. The findings will differ, however, depending on when in the pregnancy the egg divided.

If the egg divides very early in the pregnancy, the pregnancy will develop with two separate sacs (*amnions*) for each fetus and two separate membranes (*chorions*) on the maternal side. This only happens when the egg divides within 3 days after fertilization. These types of twins are called *diamniotic, dichorionic, monozygotic twins*. In this case, there may be two placentas or the placenta may fuse to form one large placenta.

These twins may be difficult to distinguish from fraternal twins by post-partum inspection of the placenta and membranes.

If the egg divides between 4 and 8 days after fertilization, the chorion will have already formed, but the fetuses will still develop in separate amniotic sacs. These twins are called *diamniotic, monochorionic, monozygotic twins.* Very careful inspection of the placenta and membranes is required to distinguish these twins from fraternal twins. If the egg divides later than 8 days after fertilization, the fetuses will develop in the same amniotic sac. These twins are called *monoamniotic, monochorionic, monozygotic twins.* These twins are most easily distinguished from fraternal twins by inspection of the placenta and membranes.

These distinctions also are important because different types of twins are at greater risk for certain complications. Monoamniotic twins, which represent only 1 to 2 percent of all twins, are at risk for complications such as intertwined umbilical cords. Monochorionic twins are at risk for *twin-to-twin transfusion syndrome* (see page 660).

If division of the egg occurs after 12 days following fertilization, the division may be incomplete and the twins conjoined. This is a rare event.

Sometimes the type of twins can be determined during pregnancy by ultrasound. If the gender is different, the twins are presumed to be fraternal, although in the rare instance that one develops Turner syndrome, they may be identical, as described above. With specialized equipment, called high-resolution ultrasound, a skilled ultrasonographer may be able to tell whether there are more than one amnion and/or chorion. This is more accurate in the first half of pregnancy, when the membranes are dividing. About one-third of the time, the only way to tell whether twins are identical or not is to perform blood typing or more sophisticated genetic testing after birth.

Frequency of the Two Types

In the United States, in the Caucasian population, about 37 percent of all twins are identical, the other 63 percent fraternal. In the African-American population, identical twinning accounts for only about 30 percent of twin births. In contrast to this, the twins in Asian populations are overwhelmingly of the identical type. The difference in the proportion of each type of twinning from one racial or ethnic group to another depends upon a difference in the frequency of multiple ovulations in the women in each population, leading to more or fewer conceptions of fraternal twins. One-egg identical twinning occurs with the same frequency in all people and is indifferent to ethnicity, age, parity, and family history. Approximately 1 set of identical twins is born per every 250 births.

Conjoined Twins

In rare instances, the splitting of an embryo to form identical twins is incomplete and results in conjoined twins. Recent advances in pediatric surgery have improved our success in dividing these twins from one another and allowing them to grow up separately.

In the past, the commonly used term for conjoined twins was *Siamese twins*. The name is derived from a pair of male children (Chang and Eng) born in Siam in 1811, who were united only by a narrow bridge of tissue in the upper abdomen. In 1829 they came to America and were exhibited all over the country by the showman P. T. Barnum. They married sisters, had many children, and lived to the age of 63, never separated.

Whether conjoined twins can be separated depends principally on the extent to which they share internal organs. If the twins are joined head to head, and share only the bones of the skull, both can be saved when they are surgically separated. The commonest kind of joining is back-to-back in the pelvic region. Most conjoined twins are female and surgical separation of such twins is apt to be complex, as they often share a rectum, an anus, and a vagina.

The extremely difficult question of whether to separate conjoined twins when separation means one twin will not survive or has a poor chance of survival has been pondered recently by ethicists and the public as reports of such surgery have appeared in the media. The issues of what constitutes normalcy and quality of life arise when this question is considered.

Your Chances of Having Twins

- **Race/Ethnicity.** Historically, there have been marked racial differences in the incidence of multiple births. For example, in Japan twins occur about once in every 154 pregnancies, and triplets once in every 17,200. At the other end of the spectrum, in Nigeria twins occur about once in every 42 pregnancies. In the United States twins occur naturally about once in

every 73 African-American births and once in every 93 Caucasian births. However, assisted reproductive technologies have
increased the rates for twins and especially higher order multiples largely among Caucasian women, the group most likely to
use these infertility services. As a result, the rates of twin births
are now similar for African-American and Caucasian women.
Triplet and higher order multiple births are now most common in non-Hispanic white women.

• **Age.** In the United States Caucasian women below the age of
20 have a twinning incidence of 1 in 167 births. As age increases so does the frequency of twins. At about 40, the rate is
about 1 in 55. Past this age the frequency declines, for reasons
not understood, although, again, with assisted reproductive technologies, this decline has been eliminated.

• **Parity.** *Parity* is the number of term and preterm births you
have had, and it exerts an influence on the likelihood of multiple pregnancy independent of age. For example, if you are a
Caucasian woman in the United States age 35 to 40 having
your first pregnancy without using assisted reproductive technologies, your chance of twins is about 1 in 74; if you are in the
same age group on your seventh pregnancy, your chance increases to 1 in 45. A study in Nigeria found that twinning increased from 1 in 50 births (2 percent) in first pregnancies to
1 in 15 (6.6 percent) in sixth or later pregnancies.

• **Size.** Large and tall women have a greater likelihood of having
fraternal twins than small women.

• **Heredity.** Multiple births clearly run in some families in which
the women tend to produce more than one egg from their
ovaries in any particular menstrual cycle. This produces fraternal twins. A familial tendency to produce identical twins has not
been shown. A tendency to twinning does not skip generations.

SUPERFETATION

Superfetation is a conception after an existing pregnancy is already well
established in the uterus. This can take place only if a woman ovulates
despite the presence in her body of estrogen, progesterone, and hCG
concentrations so high that they ordinarily would inhibit ovulation.
Superfetation also requires the passage of sperm cells through the preg-

nant uterus up into the tube, an event that is out of the question by about the end of 3 months, when the pregnancy completely fills the uterine cavity.

In the past, a great disparity in weight between newborn twins, or a great delay in the birth of a second twin after the premature birth of a first twin was considered evidence for superfetation. We now know that disparity in weight between twins—called *discordancy*—can occur in twins of exactly the same gestational age. And, for the most part, a prolonged interval between twin births occurs in women with double uteri, and has nothing to do with superfetation.

It should be possible, using ultrasound as a diagnostic tool, to prove the occurrence of superfetation if in fact it takes place. To date, no such observation has been made and the phenomenon remains only a theoretical possibility.

SUPERFECUNDATION

Superfecundation is the fertilization of two egg cells or ova during a single menstrual cycle by sperm cells from separate sexual exposures. This can be proven only if a woman has had intercourse, in a single cycle, with two different partners and becomes pregnant by each. When the babies are born, a wide difference in appearance between them may suggest the diagnosis, and blood and HLA typing may show conclusively that one man could not have fathered both offspring.

The first authentic case of superfecundation was reported in 1810 by Dr. John Archer who, by alphabetical accident, was the first person to graduate from an American medical school. He described a delivery in which a woman gave birth to a Caucasian child and a co-twin with distinctly African characteristics. She stated that in her fertile cycle she had had intercourse with a Caucasian partner and an African-American partner within a short span of time.

A sufficient number of other credible instances have been documented since that report, so that there can be no doubt that superfecundation does in fact take place. With superfecundation, the co-twins are within a few days of one another in gestational age.

PREGNANCY AND DELIVERY

The Diagnosis of Twins

In the not-too-distant past, twins were identified prior to labor in about 7 out of 10 cases. Today, with widespread use of ultrasound, few twin births occur as a surprise, although this still does happen. Ultrasound can demonstrate two fetal sacs as early as 6 or 7 weeks of pregnancy. Not long after that, the two embryos can be separately identified. The second ultrasound should be done because it is possible to be mistaken before the two heads can be seen clearly.

Some obstetricians believe that the detection of twins or other multiple gestations is a reason for routine ultrasound. Studies have shown that when ultrasound is routine, all multiple gestations are discovered, compared to about the two-thirds discovered when ultrasound is used only for other clinical reasons. Clear benefits have not been shown, however, for routine ultrasound in terms of the outcomes for the babies.

If an ultrasound is not done for another reason, diagnosis of twin pregnancy is most likely to take place when something calls attention to its probability. The larger the infants grow and the closer they get to term, the less likely that they will be missed. If either twin weighs 5½ pounds (2.5 kilograms) or more, chances are that your physician or midwife will suspect twins and ask that you have an ultrasound. Of course, anytime ovulation is induced or assisted reproductive technologies have been used, the chance of multiple gestation is increased. These pregnancies are followed by ultrasound so the number of fetuses will be known.

The following circumstances also raise suspicions of a twin pregnancy:

• **Unusual weight gain,** particularly when the uterus is substantially larger than would be expected for the duration of pregnancy. However, a multiple pregnancy is not the sole possible explanation for an unusually large uterus. Other possibilities are one very large baby, an overweight woman, *hydramnios* (excess amniotic fluid), *fibroids* (benign tumors of the uterus), and *hydatidiform mole* (a tumor growing in the pregnant uterus). With multiple gestation, there is usually rapid growth of the uterus in the second trimester of pregnancy.
• **A family history of twins,** especially on the mother's side.
• **More than the expected amount of fetal movement.** This is not the strongest of clues, since fetuses vary considerably from

one to another in their intrauterine activity patterns. Still, it's definitely worth mentioning to your physician or midwife if you think your fetus is moving enough to be more than one.
• **Palpation, by physical examination, of extra fetal parts,** especially two heads. This usually is possible only in late pregnancy and if you are not overweight.
• **A relatively small presenting part in the pelvis,** with the cervix starting to prepare for labor 4 to 6 weeks prior to term.

If two fetal heartbeats can be heard distinctly, two separate observers can identify them and count them. To be certain that there are two fetuses, the heartbeats must be counted simultaneously. There should be a difference of fifteen to twenty beats per minute between the two.

Length of Pregnancy

Many studies show that twin pregnancies average about 36 weeks in length. The average age at birth for triplets and higher order multiples is even younger—32 to 33 weeks gestation. This means that prematurity is a major problem in multiple gestations.

Most twins are born within a very short time of one another. Attempts have been made, however, when one twin or multiple is born very prematurely, to allow the other fetus to mature in the uterus as long as possible. A gap as long as 143 days between the birth of the first and second twin from a single uterus has been reported. This requires, of course, that labor has stopped after the first birth. This strategy has produced healthy, live, term infants in several reported instances.

Very long intervals between births of twins occur naturally if one twin is in each horn of a double uterus, an anatomic variation that occurs in an occasional woman. In such uncommon instances, even at term, the two horns of the uterus may go into labor at separate times. A recent report of the delivery of twins from a double uterus describes the normal labor and delivery of one twin. The second twin was not born until labor had been induced in the other half of the uterus, after which the second baby was also delivered without problems.

Discomforts of Multiple Pregnancy

For obvious reasons, the mechanical discomforts with a multiple pregnancy are considerably greater than they are with a singleton. Shortness of breath, pressure on varicose veins, hemorrhoids, inability to sleep because of fetal movement, swelling of the legs, and just plain difficulty getting around are all more common. For many women or couples, psychological stress is increased with the anticipation of having more than one baby. The situation may also pose unexpected financial burdens, leading to additional stress.

Care During Multiple Pregnancy

Certain complications of pregnancy are more frequent with multiple pregnancy. These include *preeclampsia* (pregnancy-induced hypertension), *maternal anemia* (low red blood cell count), and *hydramnios* (excess amniotic fluid). The diagnosis of twins or higher order multiples calls for increased surveillance during the prenatal period to check for these problems. Prenatal visits may be more frequent in the third trimester. Amniocentesis may be used to drain the fluid if hydramnios becomes very pronounced, but the condition is likely to recur until delivery.

Fetuses in multiple pregnancies are watched carefully for growth. Many practitioners recommend serial ultrasounds during the third trimester because uterine measurement or *palpation*—the usual way to check for growth of the fetus—does not differentiate growth among fetuses. Ultrasound can tell whether all babies are growing well. The question then arises of what to do when discordant growth is discovered by ultrasound. The risks of discordancy include fetal and newborn loss. These risks seem to increase with the degree of differential growth among the fetuses. Prematurity, however, is also a major risk for multiple fetuses. Delivery is only advised if the fetal lungs are found to be mature, with testing described in Chapter 17.

As noted, the length of pregnancy is considerably shorter with twin and higher order multiples. In the past, women were hospitalized in the third trimester and placed on strict bed rest in an attempt to prevent premature labor. Studies have found that this is not beneficial and routine hospitalization is no longer the norm. However, women carrying twins or other multiples are advised to increase their periods of rest as early as 24 weeks of pregnancy. If possible, women pregnant with twins or other multiples should stop work early to ensure rest. How early depends on the type of work you do, how you travel to get to your job, whether you can both rest and walk around while at work, how you feel, and whether you start to show signs of labor or cervical thinning or opening. Certainly, heavy lifting and prolonged standing should be avoided. Chances are, you will find that you must rest and cut down or discontinue work sometime in pregnancy if you are carrying more than one fetus.

You may also benefit from help at home if you have an infant or toddler (or more than one). Heavy cleaning is not something you should do. Try not to be shy about enlisting the help of friends and relatives. If you can afford it, household help or a loving nanny may be a worthwhile investment.

Prevention of prematurity is discussed in greater detail in Chapter 15. Signs and symptoms of premature labor are outlined in that chapter. Any of these signs should be reported immediately to your physician or midwife if you are carrying twins, triplets, or higher order multiples.

The caloric needs of pregnancy are increased with multiple pregnancies. A total weight gain of 35 to 45 pounds is recommended for full-term twin pregnancies. Weekly weight gain, therefore, should be about 1.5 pounds during the second and third trimesters of pregnancy.

For each additional fetus, you should eat about an extra 300 calories a day. This is, for example, the approximate equivalent of four glasses of skim milk or two glasses of regular milk each day, three ounces of beef (a normal-sized hamburger), or six ounces of chicken or fish (about half a small chicken or a large salmon steak). Of course, as your uterus gets larger and larger, your appetite may get smaller and smaller. To obtain adequate calories, eat frequently during the day as large meals may be too much to handle. A good intake of iron rich foods (see Chapter 10) and iron and folic acid supplementation are also recommended.

Twin Labor

Most twin labors proceed without problems because of the small size of the fetuses and the fact that the cervix is often shortened (*effaced*) and partially opened (*dilated*) before labor begins. Most plural labors are shorter than single labors. However, there may be sluggish labors among multiple births. The uterus, overdistended by the great volume of its contents, may not work as efficiently as a regular-sized uterus. If all else is normal, labor may be stimulated by the careful use of intravenous oxytocin (see Chapter 22).

The continuous presence of a nurse is advised during labor with multiple fetuses. Twins can be monitored by two listeners with fetoscopes or with two external electronic monitors. If the membranes have ruptured, the first twin can be monitored with an internal monitor and the second twin with an external monitor. An intravenous line is usually begun because of the increased chance of a cesarean delivery and of increased postpartum bleeding because of the *distended* (overly large) uterus.

In regard to fetal position, one finds all the possible combinations for two fetuses, either of which may assume any of three positions: *cephalic* (head first), *breech* (buttocks first), or *transverse* (side-lying). Both twins presenting head first, followed by one presenting head first and the other breech, are the two most frequent combinations.

If the first twin is in the breech position and the second in the cephalic, then there is a possibility that the twins will lock. This means the chin of one twin locks in the neck and chin of the other. Cesarean usually is advised when this possibility exists.

Twin Birth

The birth of the first infant is managed in precisely the same way it would be if it were a singleton. If there is a reason for delivery of the first baby by cesarean, then both babies are delivered by cesarean.

Delivery of twins calls for the presence of at least four attendants: one neonatal health care provider for each of the newborns; one obstetrician with experience in the procedures necessary to make certain that both babies are born safely in the *longitudinal lie* (head or breech coming first); and one anesthesiologist—even if only to stand by. Many midwives are experienced in twin births, although the physician will be present with a midwife for a twin birth.

Some obstetricians suggest that if cesarean delivery of the second baby is anticipated, perhaps because it is in a transverse lie, the delivery of both babies be carried out by cesarean. A more measured approach, however, is to deliver the first baby vaginally and then address the birth of the second child as a separate entity. In fact, because the fetuses are so small, the fetal position may change during labor. Their lie is called *unstable*.

Usually, after the birth of the first twin, the birth attendant will ascertain the presenting part of the second twin by vaginal examination. An ultrasound may even be used. The heart rate of the second fetus will be monitored and as long as a nonreassuring pattern is not present, labor can continue. Perhaps most important is to make sure that the clamp on the cut end of the cord of the first newborn is secure, since identical fetuses have a common circulation and the fetus still in the uterus can bleed from the cord of its co-twin. If the second twin is in a longitudinal lie (not transverse), oxytocin may be given intravenously if uterine contractions do not resume after the first baby has been born.

In the past, it was common practice to carry out an internal podalic version and breech extraction for all second fetuses who were not about to be born by the *vertex* (head). For such a delivery the woman is ordinarily given a general anesthetic. The physician then introduces a hand into the uterus, grasps the feet of the infant, and turns it into a breech presentation before it is delivered. Internal podalic version has largely fallen out of favor, except in serious emergencies when there is not enough time to deliver the baby by cesarean.

If the second fetus is not in a longitudinal lie, the physician may choose to do an *external version* (turning the long axis of the baby 90 degrees by gentle manipulations through the abdominal wall). When the first infant has just delivered and the uterus has not yet accommodated to the decrease in its volume, its wall is relaxed and the version may be quite easy.

There has been considerable discussion about the interval between the birth of the first and second baby. In the not-too-distant past, it was believed that the second baby did better the sooner it was born following the birth of its co-twin. A study published in 1984 of 115 women 34 or more weeks pregnant with twins, however, described a wide range of intervals between the births of the two babies, from 1 to 134 minutes. About 60 percent of second twins were born within 15 minutes of the birth of the first twin. The greater the delay between the two fetuses, the greater was the use of cesarean birth for the second fetus, but the occurrence of poor outcomes was no greater for baby number 2.

As mentioned previously, when the first baby is born quite prematurely, an effort sometimes is made to keep the second twin or other fetuses in the uterus as long as possible. Generally, this is done only when contractions are absent following the birth of the first twin, and there are no signs of infection. The mother will be observed *expectantly*, meaning there is no active effort made to stop labor should it begin, as it may be a sign of an infection that could be dangerous to mother and fetus. The mother is carefully observed for signs of labor and/or infection. She will be kept on bed rest in the hospital. Vaginal examinations are avoided, and the fetal heart rate is monitered for signs of distress. Reports have appeared of second and later babies born weeks, even months, after the first birth. Many times, unfortunately, both babies are lost in this situation.

Pain Relief for Labor and Birth

The methods of pain relief during labor with twins do not differ substantially from those with single births (see Chapter 20). Certain circumstances or possible complications, occurring more commonly in multiple pregnancies, may make the choice of pain relief somewhat more difficult. If the babies are premature, for instance, care is taken not to depress them in any way, as may occur with narcotic analgesics. If the mother has hypertension, epidural anesthesia may cause a serious drop in blood pressure, leading to inadequate blood delivered to her vital organs. If extensive manipulation is needed at delivery, such as in the case of an internal podalic version (done infrequently today), then an epidural will not provide adequate uterine relaxation and a light general anesthetic may become necessary.

Birth of Triplets and Higher-Order Multiples

With increasing numbers of fetuses, the potential risks of delivery increase. The position of each fetus may vary and delivery may be difficult for some or all of them. Because they are so small and may not be head down (cephalic), prolapse of the cord is possible. Despite these difficulties, the outcomes for multiple births have improved so that today most are born alive and survive. In the United States, most physicians will deliver triplets, quadruplets, and others by cesarean. One of the reasons for the recommendation for cesarean delivery is the difficulty (if not impossibility) of monitoring more than two fetuses should labor take place. In some European countries, however, triplets are most often delivered vaginally. If you are carrying a high order multiple pregnancy, discuss the options for delivery with your physician. Certainly, if you have more than triplets, you can anticipate a cesarean birth (see Chapter 22).

Postdelivery Care

Except for extra vigilance for postpartum hemorrhage, care after delivery is the same as for a single birth (see Chapter 25). All natural processes go on as scheduled. Breast-feeding is still the preferred method for feeding the babies, although it poses some challenges. Twins and even high order multiples can be fed one after the other, simultaneously, or sometimes together, sometimes separately. The milk supply will respond to the demand. There are excellent resources and supports for nursing mothers, including books and groups such as La Leche League. A number of them are listed in the Appendix.

THE BABIES

Size

Twins and other multiples are more likely than singletons to be both growth restricted and preterm. Growth restriction is more common in *monozygotic* twins (those from the same egg cell) than in *dizygotic* twins (those from two different egg cells). Sometimes, only one twin is growth restricted, and the babies are born with remarkable differences in weight.

Not all twins are small at birth, however. In one group of 1,000 twin infants, 3 percent weighed 8 pounds and 0.4 percent weighed over 9 pounds. The largest twin of this group was 9 pounds 2 ounces; the heaviest pair totaled 17 pounds. This hardly competes with a pair reported by Holzapfel in 1935; these twins together weighed 20 pounds 4 ounces.

Sex Ratio

Of a series of 126,328 pairs of twins born in the United States, 42,923 were both male, 42,557 male and female, and 40,848 both female. The total of 128,403 male twins and 124,253 female twins produces a sex ratio of 103.3 males per 100 females, instead of the usual 106-to-100 ratio in singletons. With triplets and higher order multiples, even more females are seen. Two explanations are possible. One is that the zygote destined to be female is, for an unknown reason, more likely to divide. The other is that fewer female babies die in utero (see the next section).

Special Fetal Problems in Multiple Pregnancy

Loss

Early ultrasound has shown that many more twin pregnancies are conceived than are delivered. One fetus often dies early in the pregnancy and is either miscarried or resorbed into the mother's body. An unrecognized miscarriage of one twin may have occurred, for example, when there is early bleeding, but the pregnancy continues. A resorbed fetus may leave no trace during pregnancy or at birth that the pregnancy had been a multiple. Sometimes, at the birth of a singleton baby, a tiny, long-dead co-twin may be uneventfully passed by the mother before the birth of the placenta. Such an early loss has no ill effects on the remaining fetus.

Occasionally, a situation exists in which there are two pregnancies in different locations in the reproductive tract. There may be two ectopic pregnancies, one in each tube, or, more commonly, a normal intrauterine pregnancy combined with an ectopic pregnancy. This is called a *heterotypic pregnancy*. The fetus in the uterus experiences an increased mortality risk in the first trimester of pregnancy when a heterotypic pregnancy occurs.

Even in the third trimester, there is a greater mortality among babies in multiple pregnancies than among single infants. This is most commonly because of premature labor and the problems attendant on severe prematurity.

Since most twins are light in weight for their physiological maturity, which is determined largely by how long they spend in the uterus, the prognosis for a twin at any given weight usually is better than for a singleton of the same weight. In other words, a twin born alive weighing three pounds has a greater chance for survival than a single baby weighing three pounds because it has typically spent more time in utero. This effectively demonstrates that the chance of survival of a live-born baby is dependent more on its maturity than on its weight.

Ordinarily, when both twins are alive there is no consistent difference in survival between the first twin and the second twin, unless one of them has been subject to an unusual amount of birth trauma.

The Twin-to-Twin Transfusion Syndrome

The identical *twin-to-twin transfusion syndrome* (abbreviated as TTTS) is a serious problem that occurs mostly in monochorionic, diamniotic twins, but also occurs in the less common monochorionic, monoamniotic twins. TTTS apparently comes about because of an unusual arrangement of the two circulations in the placenta such that the blood pumped out by one twin returns to the other. One fetus becomes the donor of blood and the other the recipient.

With TTTS, the recipient fetus develops a very high blood count and grows substantially larger than the donor co-twin. An excessive amount of fluid may accumulate in the amniotic sac of the recipient twin. This hydramnios is due to the unusual amount of urine that the recipient twin passes in response to the extra blood it receives. The donor twin may develop the opposite condition—*oligohydramnios,* or too little fluid. This is because it gets so little blood that it urinates only minimal amounts. With oligohydramios, fetal movement is restricted so the donor twin has been called the "stuck" twin. Hydramnios may further complicate the situation by bringing on the premature onset of labor.

Either twin may experience difficulties in the newborn state, the donor because it is very small in size and anemic, the recipient because it is so overloaded with blood that the blood may become almost too thick for normal circulation.

When hydramnios occurs in the presence of twins, TTTS should be suspected. A number of prenatal treatments are now available, although invasive. Many times both twins will die in utero or shortly after birth without treatment. Treatment options include serial amniocentesis to drain the fluid from the amniotic cavity of the recipient twin, laser photocoagulation of the vessels that communicate between the twins, and umbilical cord ligation.

Serial amniocentesis is a relatively easy procedure, but requires repeat interventions and does not cure the syndrome. In *laser photocoagulation*, after the communicating vessels are identified, they are interrupted with a laser. This treatment is available only in a few major medical centers in the world. It is done under general anesthesia with a small incision through the mother's abdomen. Survival of at least one fetus is high with this technique. *Umbilical cord ligation* is conducted only when one fetus is about to die. Its death may cause brain damage or death in the surviving co-twin. Ligation (or cutting) of the umbilical cord of the dying fetus spares the co-twin about 90 percent of the time. Cord ligation also is done through a small incision in the uterus through the mother's abdomen.

Congenital Abnormalities

Congenital malformations are slightly more common among twins. Two-egg or fraternal twins never show the same malformation except through sheer coincidence. Conversely, an identical twin is more likely to suffer from a defect shared by its co-twin. Such abnormalities may appear on the same side of the body of each twin or, through the biological mechanism of *mirror-imaging*, common in one-egg twins, may occur on the opposite side. This same process of mirror-imaging is responsible for the high frequency of opposite-handedness found in adult pairs of identical twins. In 30 to 45 percent of identical twin pairs, one twin is right-handed, the other left-handed.

With the use of ultrasound, early genetic studies on each of a pair of twins are now possible. When one of the two has been proven to have a major abnormality, the question of selective abortion (also called *selective reduction*) arises. This can be carried out without injury to the healthy co-twin. It is, of course, a difficult decision to be made by parents. See Chapter 13.

Even more difficult, perhaps, is the decision to perform reduction before genetic testing is done. The purpose of such reduction, also discussed in Chapter 13, is to increase the chances of a successful pregnancy when there are quadruplets or higher order multiples. They are usually reduced to twins. As the fetal and newborn loss increases with the number of fetuses in any pregnancy, the advantages of this procedure are evident. Nonetheless, the personal and ethical issues posed can be heart wrenching. This is an individual decision to be made by each woman or couple facing a high order multiple pregnancy.

A Happy Note

Although this chapter has concentrated on the special needs of multiple pregnancy, there also are multiple joys involved. Twins, especially identical twins, often share a unique bond, a bond that extends beyond time and distance, that is lifelong. While there are challenges associated with raising multiples, there are supreme pleasures and delights. The best advice is to be organized!

The Appendix contains several resources available for parents of twins and other multiples. There are books, support groups, and websites for your various needs. When you become a parent of twins, triplets, quadruplets, or other multiples, you become a member of a national supportive community.

CHAPTER TWENTY-FOUR

The Newborn

All of us envision newborn babies as cute, cuddly, darling, and angelic. They are, of course, but some babies have their appearance temporarily altered by the processes of labor and delivery. If you aren't prepared, this might be worrisome. Within a few days, your baby will look more like the idealized image of the newborn.

IMMEDIATE NEWBORN CARE

In a normal birth, the baby can be handed to the mother immediately. Usually, the baby is placed on her abdomen or chest. Skin-to-skin contact between baby and mother is nature's way of preventing the baby's temperature loss after birth. A warm towel over the baby further reduces heat loss, and a little stockinet cap on the baby's head is an excellent preserver of heat. If, for some reason, the mother cannot hold the baby, then the baby can be wrapped in warm blankets and handed to the mother's partner or labor support person or put under a radiant heater.

Babies placed in a warm, comfortable environment with their mothers ordinarily initiate breathing quite promptly but may not cry vigorously, probably because they are right back near the mother's heartbeat where they have been for the previous 9 months. Babies treated in this gentle and loving way continue to look blue for a substantially longer period than babies rubbed and dried off with towels or otherwise stimulated to cry. They are nevertheless vigorous and alert and in no difficulty. Although their Apgar score may be reduced because of their color, this is not a cause for concern. (Apgar scores are discussed in Chapter 19.)

Cutting the Cord

With a normal birth there is no hurry to clamp and cut the umbilical cord. The ordinary length of the cord is sufficient to permit the baby to be held by the mother. There have been debates in the childbirth literature for at least 30 years as to whether the cord should be clamped early or clamped late and whether the baby should be above or below the placenta during the time before cord clamping. This question is reviewed in greater detail in Chapter 19.

Although the issue remains unresolved, current research favors cutting the cord after it has stopped pulsating. As long as the cord continues to pulsate, blood will be pumped to the baby even if the mother is holding the baby on her abdomen, higher than the placenta. More blood will go to the baby, however, if it is held lower than the placenta. Since there is no way of knowing how much of this extra blood is helpful or not, giving the baby to the mother, which we know has benefits, makes sense. Once the cord stops pulsating, however, it should be cut if the baby is higher than the placenta, because gravity will then cause the blood to flow back to the placenta. If you have a preference for early or delayed cord cutting, discuss this in advance with your physician or midwife so a plan in accordance with your wishes can be made.

To cut the cord, a clamp is placed a short distance away from the baby's *navel* (belly button). A second clamp is attached nearer the baby, about half an inch from the first one. The cord is cut between the two clamps. Many times the father, grandparent, or other friend or relative will cut the cord. This symbolic gesture has great meaning for somebody close to the baby. If you think this will be important to you, your partner, or your support person, discuss it with your physician or midwife before the birth.

Each clamp prevents the cord from bleeding. The critical one is the clamp closer to the baby. The exact clamp used varies from place to place. Some hospitals or birthing centers use a metal clip, some a plastic device. The clips or plastic clamps can be removed in 36 to 48 hours. This is done before discharge from the hospital. If your discharge from the hospital or birthing center is earlier than 36 hours, or if you have a home birth, the clamp can be removed at the follow-up visit for the newborn. This visit, which may be with a nurse, midwife, or physician, usually occurs within 2 days after the birth. The stump of the umbilical cord ordinarily falls off in 1 to 2 weeks. Occasionally, it takes somewhat longer.

The area of the cord attachment will sometimes look a bit unclean and may have a small amount of *exudate* (discharge), which gets on the diaper. The only care needed is washing and drying the area. If there is some pus in the discharge, you can swab the area with a little hydrogen peroxide followed by alcohol, but routine use of these or other antiseptic solutions is not necessary. Folding the diaper so it doesn't cover the cord will help the area stay dry and heal more quickly. Some newborn diapers are now specially constructed with a cut-away area around the navel. If the discharge increases and becomes filled with pus, the area develops an odor, or the skin around it reddens or feels warm, you should call the baby's physician or nurse practitioner.

When the birth has been by cesarean, the cord is clamped and cut promptly, and the baby given to the waiting pediatrician or neonatal nurse practitioner who will make certain that he or she is in good condition. After the pediatric examination, the baby can be wrapped in warm blankets and handed over to the mother or her partner. If the mother has delivered under regional anesthesia and is awake, there is no reason she cannot see, touch, feel her newborn with her free hand, and even hold the baby with help from her partner or a nurse. She and her partner can share the baby's first few moments.

Identification

Babies are identified carefully in the delivery room immediately after birth. In most hospitals, identification includes fingerprinting the mother and footprinting the baby and attaching name bands to the mother and the baby. Identification can be carried out while the baby is on the mother's chest or while he or she is held by the mother's partner. At home, of course, this step is not necessary, although you may wish to have baby footprints as a memento.

Procedures for newborn care vary from hospital to hospital. In some, the parents are shown the baby, who then is placed in a newborn baby warmer. Someone will dry and clean the baby up a bit. The identification procedures will then be completed.

Once this housekeeping is done, the baby may be wrapped and returned to the mother or placed in a closed baby warmer before being transported to the nursery. Sometimes, the baby may be placed in the warmer and kept alongside the mother until she is transferred to a nearby recovery room. Some hospitals keep the baby with the mother in the recovery room for varying periods of time, while others transport the baby directly from the delivery room to the newborn nursery. Others have labor-delivery-recovery-postpartum rooms (LDRPs), so nobody needs to move anywhere. Birthing centers have no newborn nursery, so the baby doesn't leave the mother's side. At home, babies may stay in bed with their mother or be placed in a bedside bassinet.

As the benefits of early bonding of baby and parents have become known, the trend has been to keep the baby in close contact with them in the immediate newborn period. Competent studies show that keeping an alert infant in proximity to an alert mother establishes bonds between them that help facilitate newborn attachment in the subsequent days and weeks. If you plan to deliver at a hospital, you should find out what its practices are in the immediate care of the newborn and make certain they are compatible with your wishes.

A Baby with Breathing Problems

When babies are born after experiencing problems during labor or delivery, they are promptly turned over to pediatric care. For instance, if there has been thick meconium-stained fluid in labor, the physician or midwife attending the birth may suction the baby's mouth and nose *on the perineum*—before the shoulders are born. After the birth, a pediatrician or nurse practitioner will apply further suction to remove the meconium. If the baby is vigorous, this may be all that is done. If the baby is not breathing well, the pediatric care provider will look at the baby's vocal cords with an instrument called a *laryngoscope* to see how far down the passages the meconium has gone. As contact with meconium irritates the trachea and bronchi, it is suctioned out of these passages as rapidly as possible.

A baby who has trouble breathing may need *positive-pressure ventilation*—oxygen pumped into the lungs with a *respirator*. This can be facilitated in the delivery room by passing a tube down into the baby's *trachea* (windpipe). Babies who do not breathe well on their own, premature babies, and sometimes those born to mothers with certain illnesses, such as diabetes, are taken to special-care units for further observation. These are called *neonatal intensive care units* (or NICUs).

EXAMINATION OF THE BABY

Shortly after birth, your baby will have a complete physical examination. An abbreviated examination is done right after delivery by the physician or midwife attending the birth. This is to make sure the baby is breathing properly, has a normal heart rate, and has no obvious abnormalities. The examiner will check to make sure the baby is mature. The baby may be weighed in the delivery room or later in the nursery. Soon after birth, the baby will have the most comprehensive examination he or she will probably ever have as every body part is checked for normalcy.

The baby's heart and breathing rates are counted. The temperature is taken. The baby's color, muscle tone, and physical activity are observed. The skin is thoroughly surveyed and its texture and temperature felt. Every feature on the baby's face is examined. The head is looked at for its general shape, the condition of the *fontanelles* (soft spots), the consistency of the bones, the fineness of the hair, and for any bruises, especially if internal fetal monitoring was done. The head and chest are measured for normalcy, and for the size relationship between them. The baby's nails are examined for their color and any abnormalities. The limbs are looked at and assessed for range of motion and hip dislocation. The heart is listened to and several pulses are checked to assess for any heart abnormalities. The lungs are listened to. The abdomen is palpated to feel for the kidneys, liver, and spleen (they may not be felt). The anus is checked for *patency* (although if meconium has been passed, the anus is known to be open). The genitals are examined for normalcy.

The baby will also have an examination for gestational age. Certain physical characteristics such as the condition of the genitals, the amount of breast tissue present, the number and depth of the creases on the soles of the feet, and the amount and firmness of the cartilage in the ear are part of this assessment. Body posture, the condition of the baby's skin, and the presence or absence of certain reflexes (see page 675) also contribute to the determination of gestational age.

The physical examination can be done in the newborn nursery or at your bedside. Discuss this with your baby's care provider at your prenatal visit and let him or her know if you wish to be present for this examination.

APPEARANCE OF THE NEWBORN

The Head

The skull of a newborn baby consists of seven separate bones, connected to one another by pliable tissue called *sutures*. This allows the baby's head to "mold" to the shape of the mother's pelvis. Molding may result in a head that at birth looks more like a loaf of French bread than like the idealized image of a perfect baby, but this process is rapidly reversed. The baby's head resumes an almost spherical shape within 24 to 48 hours after birth.

The part of the baby's head that leads into the cervical opening during labor sometimes becomes *edematous*—swollen into what is called *caput succedaneum* (Latin: *caput* = head; *succedaneus* = substituting). This often looks like a somewhat distorted skull cap on the top of the baby's head. When scalp electrodes have been used in monitoring or blood samples taken from the scalp during labor, the puncture marks made will be found somewhere on the skin of the caput.

More conspicuous distortion of the shape of the baby's head can occur when there is bleeding under the *periosteum*, the connective tissue covering of each of the skull bones. This mass of clotted blood (known as a *cephalohematoma*) does not extend across the suture lines that separate the bones of the skull. This means that the swelling occurs on only one side of the head and either in front or in back. It is therefore asymmetrical and gives the baby's head a lopsided appearance. A cephalohematoma (Greek: *kephale* = head; *aima* = blood; *oma* = swelling) has a fluctuant feel much like that of a plastic bag full of liquid.

Cephalohematomas may last for several weeks or even a few months. The baby's body, however, is very efficient in eventually removing the clot of blood and making use of the material in it for the formation of new blood.

Babies Born in the Breech Position or by Cesarean Birth

The baby born by the breech may have swelling and bruising on the buttocks similar to that on the scalp of the baby born head first. Occasionally, the skin looks purplish and the external genitalia may be swollen. This is much more noticeable on the scrotum of boy babies than on the labia of girls but is present in both. The head of a baby born by the breech does not undergo molding and is therefore nice and round like a picture of a classic newborn.

Breech babies very often lie in the uterus with their legs extended and their feet right in front of their faces. They may continue to occupy this position in the first hours of life. This position is strikingly different from that of the baby born by the vertex, whose legs usually are flexed in the well known "fetal position."

The heads of babies born by cesarean delivery, except for those delivered late in labor, exhibit none of the changes associated with labor. Like breech babies, they look more like the idealized newborn.

Newborn Skin

Vernix

Vernix caseosa (Latin: *vernix* = varnish; *caseus* = cheese) is a fatty material, which looks like soft cream cheese, spread over the surface of most newborns, except those who are born past their due date. Vernix is just about the best skin cream ever. Although most babies are bathed shortly after birth, if the vernix weren't removed, it would remain for a few days. An excellent moisturizer for the baby's skin in utero, it would function in the same way in the first days after birth. The baby's skin otherwise tends to dry out in the newborn period.

Color

When babies are first born, before they have established much gas exchange through their lungs, their skin color is a somewhat dusky purplish, particularly in the hands and feet. This is followed by a bright red color when the blood vessels of the skin open up widely in response to the sudden exposure to the air and to a drop in temperature. After a day or two, as the baby becomes accustomed to being out at room temperature, this red color gradually fades to the more familiar ordinary skin color, although the hands and the feet often remain rather blue. The feet may be somewhat cold. These changes are entirely natural and require no treatment. Dark-skinned babies may be born lighter than they ultimately will be. Sometimes, you can look behind their ears to see their eventual skin color.

Rashes

Newborn skin is subject to a variety of rashes and irritations, most of which clear up on their own. A common newborn rash is called *erythema toxicum* (Greek: *erythema* = redness; *toxikon* = poison). This possibly frightening name actually describes a totally benign condition in which there are red blotches in the skin with tiny pustules in their middle. The spots of erythema toxicum appear in one place, disappear, and reappear in other parts of the skin.

Extensive rashes, particularly with spots in the creases of the skin that do not go away spontaneously, can represent a true infection that requires medical attention. These rashes ordinarily are due to infections with *Staphylococcus*, commonly called "staph."

The best way to limit the likelihood of infection is careful hand washing by all who have contact with the baby. Fortunately, skin infections are seldom serious.

Another skin infection of the newborn is caused by a common fungus, *Monilia* (*Candida*). It appears in the diaper area and surrounding skin as small, bright red, raised patches. When it occurs in the mouth it is called *thrush*, and it appears as a white coating on the palate, gums, and tongue.

The treatment for candidal diaper rash is an application of a topical antifungal cream. Thrush can be treated by either giving the baby an antifungal medication by mouth or painting the mouth with a solution called *gentian violet* twice a day. An antiyeast medication, nystatin, comes in a powdered form and can be mixed with breast milk. It is a very benign medication. Gentian violet is usually effective, but very messy. It will stain clothing, so dark colors are best worn during the treatment, which lasts for about 2 to 3 days.

If the mother develops a candidal infection on her nipples, she will have pain, itching, or both. She may need to apply the antiyeast cream to her nipples after breast-feeding. If the infection persists, the mother may use an oral antifungal preparation—fluconazole (brand name: Diflucan). She may need repeated doses.

A variety of herbal medications are available to treat thrush, and many are effective, but usually take longer to work. A good summary of herbal treatments is available at www.lifepassages.net/ArticlesandInfo .htm. Of course, speak to your baby's pediatrician or nurse practitioner before using any over-the-counter preparations, including herbs.

Simple diaper rash differs from the rash caused by *Candida* in that it is less likely to involve the skin folds and the irritated areas do not extend as far outward from the diaper area as they do in a candidal infection. Diaper rash not caused by a fungus rapidly clears up with exposure to air. A zinc oxide barrier cream may be used if the skin is very irritated.

Powders and creams are not necessary to prevent diaper rash. Preventive measures include changing diapers frequently, making sure the diaper area is dry before putting on a new diaper, and exposing the diaper area to air for a short time each day.

Cradle Cap

Some infants develop *cradle cap*—dry scaly patches on the scalp, possibly with a crusty yellow cover. Cradle cap can be treated by massaging the scalp with vegetable or olive oil and then combing out the scales with a fine-toothed comb. Usually, frequent shampooing keeps cradle cap from returning. Even the rare times that cradle cap is resistant to treatment, it resolves itself by the time the baby is a year old. It is not a dangerous condition, although parents find it distressing.

Mongolian Spots

Some babies have dark brown to blue-black pigmented areas on the low back or over the buttocks. These flat markings, called *Mongolian spots*, are of no particular significance. They may be large but will fade, although not for one or several years. They are most common in dark-skinned babies.

Hemangiomas

Babies may show patches of *dilated* (opened) blood vessels (*hemangiomas*) of a variety of shapes and sizes. These are usually slightly raised and bright red and fade out with pressure on the skin. The vast majority of these hemangiomas are quite benign. Even if they appear on the face, they constitute a cosmetic rather than a medical problem. Very often, they will get bigger during the first year of life, but eventually regress. Larger ones may not resolve completely. They may be called *strawberry hemangiomas* because they look like a strawberry. They may not appear until a few months have passed. They are more common in premature babies and in girls.

Port Wine Stains

Port wine stains are flat discolored birthmarks. They may be red, pink, or purplish in color. They are caused by dilation of tiny blood vessels and usually occur on the head or neck. They may be small or large. Port wine stains do not fade or blanch when they are pressed and they do not disappear or regress. They may even become darker as the child gets older. If small, they can be covered with cosmetics. If large, they can be treated with a special laser when the baby is older. This is usually done by a plastic surgeon.

Milia

Many babies have tiny hard spots on the nose, chin, or forehead. They look like pimples. These are called milia and are blocked oil glands. Milia is nothing to worry about. The spots will disappear. When these blocked glands occur in the mouth they are called *Epstein's pearls*.

Hands, Feet, Fingernails

One of the first things a parent will check out about a new baby is whether or not the baby has all its fingers and toes. In fact, *syndactyly*— or fusing of the fingers or toes—or *polydactyly*—an extra finger or toe— is a common minor anomaly. These often run in families. They may need no treatment, a simple treatment such as tying off an extra finger that is attached by a skin tag, or surgical treatment.

A newborn baby has very fine fingernails. Babies that are born past term generally have rather long nails. In their unguided random activity, babies may scratch themselves and make themselves unsightly and uncomfortable. Rather than allow this to happen, you should keep the baby's fingernails trimmed, using baby nail scissors or clippers. You might find this a little daunting the first few times you try, but you really cannot inflict harm in cutting the nails, even though the baby is tiny and wiggly, and you may cut a bit too deep at first. Some people cut the baby's nails while the baby is sleeping. Still, be careful—the baby might wake up and start wiggling the fingers again.

Body Hair

Newborn babies ordinarily have hair on their head, eyebrows, and eyelids. There may be some fine hairs over the trunk, called *lanugo* (Latin: *lana* = wool). These generally vanish quite soon after birth and do not reappear. Babies born early have more lanugo than babies born at term.

Some babies come from families with a strong tendency toward hairiness and these babies may have dark hairs over their shoulders and on their foreheads. These hairs disappear fairly early in the newborn period.

The hair on the head does not tell the hair color the baby will ultimately have. First, hair may change dramatically at about 3 months, when the baby loses its newborn hair. Second, hair color may change in childhood. Many brunets were blond as babies, for instance, and some were blond through a great deal of their childhood.

The Eyes

Eye color is almost always a uniformly dusky gray in the newborn, with the exception of albinos, whose *irises* (colored eye part) have no pigment and are bright pink from the blood circulating in them. The newborn gray color does not predict the eventual eye color of the baby, as the definitive pigment in the iris does not appear until about 6 months of age. Newborn babies, no matter how hard they cry, do not form tears until they are about a month old.

If a mother is a carrier of gonorrhea in her vagina at the time of the baby's birth, the baby's eyes can become infected in the *conjunctival sac*, the space just under the eyelids, and in the *cornea*, the clear transparent structure through which we see. Given a foothold, this infection can scar the cornea badly enough to produce blindness. Every health department in the country has a regulation requiring that some sort of medication be put into the baby's eyes to prevent this condition, known as *gonococcal ophthalmia*. Most hospitals now instill an antibiotic ointment in the baby's eyes. This is effective and free of the undesirable irritating effect of the silver nitrate drops that were formerly used.

Recently, we have observed a different sort of eye infection in newborns, caused by another sexually transmitted organism—*Chlamydia*. This generally does not appear until the baby is a week or 10 days old. It is characterized by the formation of a *purulent* (pus) discharge from the eyes. It also responds to antibiotics. Fortunately, mandatory gonorrhea *prophylaxis* (preventive treatment) reduces the incidence of chlamydia infection as well. Should your baby develop a discharge from the eyes, however, you should report it promptly to the pediatrician or pediatric nurse practitioner.

Some parents object to routine eye treatment, as they are certain the mother does not carry sexually transmitted organisms. You can find out in advance whether the regulations in your state will permit you to sign a waiver refusing this medication. This should only be done when you are sure both partners are free of both of these sexually transmitted infections, which may have no symptoms. You should have tested negative during the pregnancy and both partners should be sexually monogamous.

The *lacrimal system* that produces tears is not fully developed at birth. Therefore babies do not produce enough tears to flow out of the eyes. When tears do flow, they are collected in small ducts found at the inner corner of the eyelid. The tears enter the lacrimal sac and flow through the lacrimal duct into the nose. Up to six percent of healthy newborns may have blocked tear ducts. When the tear duct is blocked, the eyes may appear excessively teary and have a mucous discharge. They may be swollen and possibly reddened. The baby may seem uncomfortable or even in pain. Untreated, a blocked tear duct can result in infection. Call your baby's care provider if you notice any of these symptoms. Most often, simple massage of the ducts combined with warm moist compresses and clearing the discharge out of the eye are sufficient treatments. Always wash your hands before touching the baby's eyes and make sure all the soap is rinsed off. If infection occurs, antibiotic drops or ointments may be prescribed. Rarely, an ophthalmologist may need to be consulted and surgery may occasionally be performed. Most of the time, however, the measures used at home will clear up the problem by the time the baby is a year or a year and a half old.

Do not become alarmed if you see your baby's eyes moving independently of each other. Many newborns can do this, so that they look cross-eyed some of the time. This often occurs when the baby is half asleep and not paying attention to what it is doing. When the baby actually looks at something the eyes work together.

The Face

The baby's nose at birth does not have fully formed cartilage and therefore may appear temporarily pushed out of shape. The chin of a normal newborn is small by adult standards and this may sometimes give the baby an odd appearance. These features will straighten themselves out before long, and more esthetic proportions will appear.

There may be small hemorrhages or broken tiny blood vessels in the skin of the face and neck. These flat little red marks are called *stork bites* because, when they occur on the back of the neck, they look like they are the marks made when the stork picked up the baby to deliver it. These will eventually disappear. Hemorrhages also occur in the retina, at the back of the eye, and can be seen with an ophthalmoscope. They occur with surprising frequency at the time of normal birth, but evidently have no consequences. Unless the baby's eyes are examined by a skilled ophthalmologist we are likely to be blissfully unaware that anything of the kind has happened.

About 20 percent of babies develop "pimples" within the first month of life (different from milia). These appear on the cheeks and forehead and disappear within a few months. They are called *acne neonatorum*— baby acne. Refrain from the impulse to break open or squeeze the pimples because this can cause infection.

Some babies have skin tags in front of their ears. They are usually just a cosmetic issue, but may be associated with some hearing problems.

Occasionally, a baby will be born with a tooth.

Breast Engorgement

All babies in the uterus are exposed to the mother's high levels of female sex hormone. As a consequence newborns usually show some enlargement of breast tissue. This rarely is conspicuous, but on occasion the breast may become *engorged* (distended or excessively enlarged) for a brief period. Left alone, this clears up without problems. There even may be a small amount of secretion, picturesquely called "witch's milk," which is of no concern.

The Genitals

The genitals of both girl and boy babies may be swollen at birth. Girls may have a small amount of whitish discharge or even blood-tinged mucus from the vagina in the first few weeks of life. This is normal and is due to the mother's hormones in pregnancy.

NEWBORN REFLEXES

Reflexes are involuntary actions. Certain reflexes are present only in the newborn period. Their presence indicates normal brain and nervous system activity. Testing for these reflexes is part of the complete physical examination that a newborn receives. The following reflexes are normal:

- **Rooting reflex.** When the baby's mouth is stroked or touched, the baby will turn or "root" in the direction of the touch. This helps the baby find the breast to begin nursing. This reflex persists for several months, by which time the baby can turn voluntarily.
- **Sucking reflex.** The baby sucks when the roof of the mouth is touched. Sucking is not fully developed until about 36 weeks of gestation, explaining why premature babies may have a difficult time with feeding. Sucking also becomes a voluntary action after a few months.
- **Grasp reflex.** The baby will close its fingers in response to stroking of the palm. The grasp reflex is stronger in premature babies. It disappears within a few months.
- **Startle reflex.** Also called the *Moro reflex*, this is the baby's response to a loud sound or sudden movement. The baby will throw back the head, extend the arms and legs, cry, and then pull the arms and legs back in. Babies can be startled by their own cries. This reflex disappears at about 5 or 6 months of age.
- **Tonic neck reflex.** When a baby's head is turned to the side, the arm on that side extends out and the opposite arm bends at the elbow. This is also called the *fencing reflex* because it looks like the position of a fencer. This reflex disappears at about 6 to 7 months.
- **Stepping reflex.** This is also called the *walking* or *dance reflex*. The baby will take a step or walk when it is held with the feet touching a solid surface. This persists for several months.
- **Babinski reflex.** When the foot is stroked, the big toe will bend

back toward the top of the foot and the other toes will fan out. This reflex lasts about 2 years.

NEWBORN BEHAVIOR

Most babies cry briefly after they are born. This helps expand the baby's lungs and provides for an adequate exchange of gases. Once this is accomplished, babies tend to doze off and sleep a great deal in the first 8 to 12 hours. They are more likely to sleep if the mother initiates breast-feeding right after birth. This seems to be reassuring to the baby.

Babies have their individual sleep-and-wake cycles, which may be a continuation of prenatal behavior. Some babies may not seem to have a pattern at all to their sleeping and waking. Most newborns sleep most of the time, waking only for feedings. It takes a long time before babies become accustomed to the social cycles of older children and adults, which are related to the periods of light and dark.

Newborn babies have episodes of sneezing and hiccoughing. Occasional babies go through periods of snorting. All these phenomena are perfectly normal, and do not persist past the newborn phase. The ordinary rolling and wiggling movements that newborn babies make are probably similar to their acrobatics in the uterus.

In the past, newborns were believed to be like blank slates, not capable of anything more than eating and sleeping, and without personality traits of their own. It was also thought that they did not see or hear for several weeks. We now know that not only do babies learn in utero, but they also are born familiar with their mother's voice. Once born, full-term babies can hear, see, mimic facial expressions, cry, suck, swallow, grasp things with their hands, move their hands, turn their heads from side to side, and, placed on a flat surface, move around, unless they are restrained.

Newborns show a preference for high-pitched voices. Many adults are subconsciously aware of this and speak to newborn babies in a squeaky voice. Babies will turn their head toward a voice and follow it for 180 degrees. They will follow a light. As a baby exposed to a light in utero will blink, it is not surprising that a baby does this very soon after birth. Babies have a preference for looking at stripes. They prefer black and white patterns or bright colors like red and orange over subtle colors even though there is evidence that color vision is not fully developed until 4 to 7 months of age. The baby also has a preference for human faces, and the combination of a face and a familiar voice is particularly alluring. Most of these accomplishments are expressed best when the infant is in a quiet, alert state, neither asleep nor fully awake and crying, but with the eyes open and searching.

The infant's instinct to suckle is very strong. Most babies are able to nurse shortly after delivery, making use of the rooting reflex. When a newborn's cheek is stroked, the baby will turn its head in the direction of the stroke, open its mouth, and suck on almost anything that will go into it. There is a protective *gag reflex* that prevents babies from choking. If by any chance they happen to get any material into the trachea, which is the "wrong tube," they cough it up promptly.

Most babies urinate very shortly after birth with no embarrassment whatever. Some babies, especially those who have been stressed, may pass meconium before birth. The unstressed newborn usually pushes out meconium sometime in the first 12 or 24 hours. This initial meconium is gluey and dark green. It is followed by what are called *transitional stools*, when bacteria get down into the lower intestinal tract from the initial feedings. The pigment changes to a greenish yellow and the consistency becomes seedy.

Babies who are formula-fed have stools that are larger, more formed, and chalky yellow. These stools have an odor. The stools of breast milk–fed babies are smaller in volume, usually wetter, and odorless. The greenish color of the meconium tends to persist a little longer. This kind of stool should not be confused with the diarrhea stool, which is very watery and has a strong smell. If the baby has a milk allergy, there might be blood in the stool as a reaction either to formula or milk in the mother's diet. If your baby has blood in the stool, talk to your pediatrician or nurse practitioner.

Almost all babies experience weight loss in the first few days of life as they lose the fluid they accumulated in the uterus. They will regain this by the tenth day of life. Afterward, babies gain about an ounce a day, doubling their birth weight by 5 months of age and tripling it by one year.

Newborn Temperament

Newborns demonstrate characteristic temperaments from the time of birth. These have been described on a spectrum ranging from very easy to very difficult. Such terms are not meant to be judgmental in any way. No baby is a "good baby" or a "bad baby," although some people do talk about babies in this way.

Such behaviors as the fraction of the day spent crying, the amount of motor activity, sleep and feeding patterns, and any feeding difficulties contribute to a baby's temperament. Parents will have an easier time if they try to understand their baby's temperament and adapt to it. Thinking of the baby as a blank slate on which you write all your shortcomings as a parent can lead to unnecessary feelings of guilt.

FEEDING THE NEWBORN

Breast-feeding

Human milk provides perfect nutrition for the full-term infant and for most premature infants. In addition to its nutritional elements it contains antibodies to viruses and bacteria and also white blood cells that help to prevent many diseases. These immunizing mechanisms are very important, because they assist in the prevention of the diarrheas that are the major cause of disease and death of infants throughout the world. Intolerance of mother's milk is a great rarity.

While we support choice in all aspects of birth, we must take a position in favor of breast-feeding. This does not mean that babies in developed countries cannot be fed adequately by the bottle. Formula is simply not the best in most circumstances.

Many books have been written about breast-feeding; support organizations such as La Leche League have formed; and a new professional called a *lactation consultant* has emerged. While all these provide information, assistance, and support for nursing mothers, they might have the negative side effect of making women think that breast-feeding is terribly difficult—something you must get help to be good at. In fact, breast-feeding is rather simple. The problem is that an entire generation or two almost completely gave up breast-feeding in this country several decades ago. As the advantages of mother's milk became known, many women resumed the practice. Unfortunately, as their mothers, perhaps even grandmothers, aunts, sisters, and friends had not breast-fed, nursing women couldn't easily get help for the problems that sometimes occur. They also were often ridiculed for being "old-fashioned," or chastised for exposing what had become a body part associated with sexuality. Like many other groups of mavericks, these women joined together to help each other and provide support for other women.

We have decided to emphasize breast-feeding in a separate chapter; here we present a brief discussion of bottle feeding. For more information about nursing, see Chapter 26.

Bottle-feeding

There are several standard prepared formulas available, most of them made from a cow's milk base. Plain cow's milk, however, should not be given to a baby before it is a year old. Cow's milk has hard-to-digest protein and does not supply adequate vitamins or iron. It is hard on the infant kidneys.

Formula also may be made from soy. This may be more acceptable to strict vegetarian (vegan) families. However, soy protein is not quite as good for infants as the protein in milk, and babies don't absorb some minerals from soy milk, such as calcium, as efficiently as they do from cow's milk. Nevertheless, soy is a good alternative for infants who develop an intolerance to cow's milk. There are also special formulas made with hydrolyzed protein for babies who cannot tolerate cow's milk. These are made from cow's milk with the protein broken up into its parts. Basically, this is like drinking predigested milk, which decreases the chances of an allergic reaction.

Prepared formulas usually are supplemented with vitamins and iron and are available in ready-made liquid form, as a liquid concentrate to which you add water, or as a powder, also to be mixed with water. If you use non–iron fortified formula, the baby should get an iron supplement by 3 months of age. Do not give both iron-fortified formula and an iron supplement as this will constipate the baby. Although in the past, parents made their own formula from evaporated milk, water, and sugar, this is no longer recommended as today's commercially made formulas are closer to breast milk than this homemade variety and provide substantially more nutrition.

The pendulum on whether or not to sterilize water used in making infant formula has swung back to recommending sterilization. This is because of bacteria found in some water supplies in recent years. Water can be sterilized by bringing it to a bubbling boil, boiling for 1 to 2 minutes, and then allowing it to cool. Bottled water can be used, but it too should be sterilized. The standards for bottled water are no different from the standards for tap water in the United States. Very hot soapy water and a bottle brush or a dishwasher will clean the bottles and nipples well enough, although these also can be sterilized in a pan of boiling water for 5 minutes.

If you are using reusable bottles for artificial feedings they should be emptied as soon as the baby finishes drinking, rinsed at once, and then run through a wash before they are used again. This step, of course, is not necessary with the collapsible disposable plastic bags that are sometimes used for bottle-feeding. Neither type of bottle is better, although the baby may show a preference.

Nipples are now available that are close in shape to that of the human nipple. These also are available as pacifiers.

There is no need to follow a prescheduled feeding pattern with formula or with breast milk. Bottle-fed babies, however, will sleep for longer periods between feedings. Breast milk is more easily digested, so infants will awaken more frequently to nurse.

ROOMING-IN

Rooming-in is the name given to the practice of keeping the baby in the mother's room during the hospital stay. All in-hospital and out-of-hospital birthing centers have rooming-in. Delivering at home is, by definition, rooming-in.

Rooming-in facilitates bonding between the baby and the parents and at the same time assists in the establishment of breast-feeding. It was started in the late 1940s but had only sporadic acceptance. Now, most hospitals have some provision for rooming-in. Babies in some hospitals may room-in 24 hours a day, but in other places round-the-clock rooming-in may conflict with local health rules or hospital policies designed to protect the babies from too much contact with visitors. There is no persuasive evidence of any more risk to the baby from visitors at the hospital than there would be at home, but hospitals often adopt a conservative course.

Some hospitals provide modified rooming-in, in which the baby is placed with the mother whenever she requests it and is taken back to a central nursery during visiting hours and during times when the mother is away from her bedside, such as for hospital classes in newborn baby care.

Some hospitals return the baby to a central nursery at night, which has the merit of giving the mother an opportunity for some sleep, but may have some risk for the babies. Specifically, the concern is for the spread of infection from one baby to another when one of them is exposed to hospital visitors. The usual precaution against this is careful hand washing by everybody who handles the baby. Returning the baby to the nursery to allow the mother sleep at night also might interfere with the initiation of breast-feeding. If the baby is given a bottle, nipple confusion may develop. Some of the benefits of breast milk may be diminished as these are more pronounced with exclusive breast-feeding (see Chapter 26). If the baby is returned to the mother to be fed when he or she awakens, then this disadvantage is eliminated, but so is the advantage of providing the mother with sleep. In the long run, facilitating breast-feeding is the more humane approach, as kind as allowing mothers to sleep may seem.

Bathing the Baby

Rooming-in gives the mother an opportunity to gain experience in changing diapers and in bathing the newborn. The newborn bath is an extremely simple process. Until the umbilical cord falls off, a sponge bath is recommended.

Before you begin the bath, assemble everything you need. For a sponge bath, this includes a bath cushion or soft towels on which to place the baby, a soft washcloth, a basin or clean sink, baby soap and shampoo, a hooded towel, and a clean diaper and change of clothing. The water should be at room temperature. Test it on the inside of your wrist or with your elbow.

Wash the baby's face first, using a washcloth without soap. Start with the eyes, washing outward from the nose. Clean the outside of the baby's ear folds with the washcloth. Do not use cotton swabs in the ears. Gently bathe the baby's body from the neck down, rinsing with a clean washcloth or cup of warm water. Shampoo last, also using a washcloth. Holding the baby is the real trick—keep your arm behind the baby's back and use your wrist and hand to support the baby's neck. Do not use a hot hair dryer on the baby's hair.

A tub bath is very similar to a sponge bath. You can use a special infant tub and a bath thermometer, or a regular large basin (you can place a folded towel on the bottom to provide padding and traction) and your elbow to test the water. The water should be room temperature. Most important, never leave the baby in the bath unattended; don't even let go to answer a nearby telephone.

Lotions and powders are not needed after the bath, although you may use a baby lotion if the skin is dry. If you do use powder, use corn starch, not talc, and don't shake it into the air as this releases small particles that the baby can inhale. Put a bit on your hand and apply it to the baby's skin with your hand.

Since a newborn baby hardly has an opportunity to become dirty, except in the diaper area, daily bathing is probably more a luxury to keep the parents happy than a necessity for the baby's health.

PROBLEMS IN THE NEWBORN

The overwhelming majority of babies are born healthy. Most often, when a baby is born with a problem, it can be anticipated. Many babies with problems are born to mothers who have illnesses such as diabetes or high blood pressure. Sometimes genetic testing or ultrasound reveals an abnormality, so the parents are prepared. On a rare occasion, however, a baby may be born with an illness that is completely unexpected. While this will be upsetting, many newborn difficulties resolve and many others can be treated in infancy or early childhood. Sometimes babies look like they have something wrong, but the condition they show is a perfectly normal variation. It may reverse itself spontaneously during the newborn period or later in infancy or childhood.

Injuries in the Course of Childbirth

Injuries Due to Instruments

When forceps are used to deliver the baby they may cause superficial bruises over the cheekbones or over an eyebrow and sometimes on an ear. These marks disappear within a few days after birth. They result in no long-term complications.

Occasionally a forceps blade will put pressure in front of the baby's ear and cause swelling of the facial nerve on one side. A baby with this injury, a newborn form of *Bell's palsy*, will be able to move the unaffected side of its face quite normally, but on the affected side the eye does not close properly and the corner of the mouth tends to sag. This condition is transitory and heals without later consequences, although occasionally, if the injury is severe enough, surgery may be needed.

When a baby is born by vacuum extraction there is a round swelling at the top of the head similar to caput succedaneum. There also may be a purplish discoloration due to leakage of blood into the skin of the scalp at the point where the vacuum cup was placed. The swelling itself clears up rapidly, at about the same speed as does a caput succedaneum. The circular area of purple, however, takes at least a week or 10 days to disappear.

Injuries Due to Shoulder Dystocia

A baby whose shoulders are considerably broader than its head may have difficulty with the birth of the shoulders. This is called *shoulder dystocia*, discussed in Chapter 21. Sometimes, in the course of delivering such broad shoulders, birth injuries occur.

There are obstetrical maneuvers to use when shoulder dystocia occurs. These include providing pressure in the area of the pubic bone to free the shoulder from beneath that bone. This pressure can be sufficient to fracture the clavicle, the bone that runs from the shoulder to the midline of the chest, commonly called the *collarbone*. Sometimes, fracturing the clavicle is a deliberate lifesaving procedure used as part of delivering the shoulders when other maneuvers don't help.

Clavicular fractures heal completely, without later consequences, although the mother may notice a lump or bruising on the clavicle while the fracture is healing. The babies ordinarily will not move the arm on that side. Immobilizing the arm and shoulder may be recommended.

With difficult delivery of the shoulder, there may be stretching of the bundle of nerves that runs from the spinal column in the neck down to the arm and consequently temporary loss of function of that arm. This can also occur with a breech birth if an arm becomes trapped behind the baby's head and has to be brought down by the obstetrician. The vast majority of these losses of motor function in the arm heal by themselves. A brace or splint may be needed. Physical therapy may be advised.

Diseases of the Newborn

The most important problem of the newborn calling for special care is prematurity. Any of the conditions below can occur in any newborn infant, but all are more common in premature infants.

Jaundice

Most babies are born with an incompletely mature liver. This may cause a problem because the baby depends on the liver for disposing of the breakdown products of the extra blood that the fetus has had in utero. This breakdown is normal. In the process, *bilirubin* is produced. Bilirubin is the pigment responsible for the yellow color of the skin in jaundice. More than half of all babies develop jaundice, and almost 80 percent of premature babies develop jaundice. Most of the time, in healthy term babies, jaundice resolves on its own. When the level of bilirubin in the blood gets too high, however, especially in a baby who is ill or premature, it can lead to brain damage.

There are two types of newborn jaundice: *physiological jaundice* and *possibly pathological jaundice*. Physiological jaundice generally does not reach dangerous levels and does not require treatment. It is seen more frequently in breast-fed infants.

Physiological jaundice is not apparent in the first 24 hours of life whereas possibly pathological jaundice will appear this soon after birth. Physiological jaundice rises slowly, peaks on the third to fourth day of life, and disappears after the tenth day. Possibly pathological jaundice rises quickly and, unless treated, will persist for a longer time than physiological jaundice.

Babies with a blood incompatibility with their mothers are most likely to become jaundiced. Serious blood incompatibility occurs when the mother has Rh-negative blood and the baby has Rh-positive blood. This can be prevented with treatment during and after pregnancy. Its preventive treatment is discussed in Chapter 5. Less serious blood incompatibilities occur when the baby has A, B, or AB type blood and the mother has type O blood. In any of these cases, the mother may make antibodies against the baby's blood. These antibodies pass to the baby and "attack" the baby's own blood.

Other babies with an increased chance of developing jaundice include:

• Babies born to mothers with diabetes
• Asian male babies
• Babies living at high altitudes
• Babies exposed to oxytocin in labor
• Babies with bruising or cephalohematoma
• Babies with a family history of neonatal jaundice

Jaundice can be seen under natural daylight or in a room with fluorescent lights. An easy test for it is to press gently with your fingertip on the tip of the baby's nose or forehead. If the skin looks yellowish with or without the applied pressure, the baby's pediatrician can test the baby's blood for its bilirubin level. The extent of jaundice and whether it is worsening or resolving can be monitored with blood tests.

Nursing ten to twelve times a day is recommended with jaundice as it will result in frequent *stooling* (bowel movements). Bilirubin is passed in the stool. This may help bring down the bilirubin level without other treatment. If there is difficulty with nursing, short-term supplementation using a small cup or other feeding device can be tried. The baby should have two to five stools (bowel movements) per day. Giving water will not decrease the bilirubin level because bilirubin is passed only in stools.

Placing the baby in indirect sunlight, wearing just a diaper, may help break down the bilirubin. Be sure that the sun doesn't shine directly on the baby as this may cause sunburn.

Medical therapy to reduce the bilirubin level usually is recommended when the level reaches 15 to 20 milligrams per deciliter of blood. The value at which treatment is started will depend on when the jaundice first occurs, with jaundice that occurs within 24 hours after birth usually treated at the lower level. It will also depend on the gestational age and general health of the baby, with premature or sick babies receiving treatment at a lower blood level of bilirubin.

Medical treatment is accomplished most easily by exposing the skin of the baby to bright blue lights, with the eyes carefully shielded. The blue light acts on the bilirubin in the skin to change it into a harmless form. Treatment with *phototherapy*, as this is called, recently has been instituted in the home, as long as the bilirubin level is under 18 milligrams per deciliter of blood and the baby otherwise is healthy. Phototherapy does not need to be continuous, so the mother can continue frequent nursing during this treatment. The lights may make the baby sleepy, so the baby will have to be awakened to nurse.

A few babies may need more aggressive treatment. This involves exchange transfusion. In this process, a *catheter* (or very thin tube) is placed through the vein of the umbilical cord into the baby's central circulation. The baby's own blood then is removed little by little, to be replaced by equal amounts of compatible blood from a blood bank or donor. This brings the bilirubin count down quite rapidly. Several exchanges may be necessary before the baby is out of danger from long-term injury.

Most breast-feeding advocates believe that nursing should not be stopped if the baby has jaundice. If your pediatrician asks you to stop nursing for a day or two, you can pump your breasts during this time so that the milk supply continues.

Respiratory Problems

RESPIRATORY DISTRESS SYNDROME (RDS) RDS is a complication in premature newborns whose lungs are not sufficiently developed to remain open with natural breathing. The babies lack sufficient amounts of a chemical called *surfactant*. The role of surfactant is to keep the air sacs in the lungs expanded after each breath. Without it, the air sacs tend to collapse after each breath, and their lining cells to stick together, creating resistance to inhaling. Each breath in essence is like the first breath.

Babies with RDS frequently require assistance from breathing machines attached to tubes put down into the *trachea* (windpipe). Today, babies can be given surfactant. The tremendous strides that have been made in improving the treatment of RDS have played a major role in reducing death among premature babies.

TRANSIENT TACHYPNEA OF THE NEWBORN , Transient tachypnea of the newborn (TTN) is a mild respiratory problem of babies. TTN begins after birth and lasts about 3 days. The terms mean *temporary* (transient) *rapid breathing rate* (tachypnea). TTN is seen in about 1 to 2 percent of newborns and is most common in babies born by cesarean. It is thought that TTN occurs when the fluid that is normally in the fetal lungs is absorbed more slowly after birth than usual. In a cesarean birth, the lung fluid is not forced out as it is in a vaginal birth when the chest is squeezed in the vagina just after the head is born.

Babies with TTN have a breathing rate greater than sixty breaths per minute, may grunt with breathing, have flaring of the nostrils, and pulling in at the ribs (*retractions*). A chest X ray may be ordered when these symptoms are seen. Blood may be drawn to check for its oxygen level. Usually, however, the diagnosis of TTN is made when the symptoms suddenly go away after about 3 days.

Babies with TNN may need oxygen, possibly delivered by *positive pressure*—with a respirator pushing the flow of oxygen into the lungs. Occasionally, tube feedings are necessary if the breathing rate is so high that there is a risk of *aspirating* (breathing in) food. Once the condition disappears, no further problems remain.

Intracranial or Intraventricular Hemorrhage

Another handicap of the small premature infant is that the blood vessels of the brain are very fragile and may bleed under the least stimulus. This is occasionally a fatal event. There is no simple relationship between the signs of such bleeding and its amount. Ultrasound and C-T scanning have markedly improved the ability to diagnose intracranial hemorrhage (Latin: *intra* = within; Greek: *kranion* = skull).

The prevention of intracranial hemorrhage is one of the reasons that normal newborns are routinely given a small dose of vitamin K. This vitamin is essential to blood clotting. It is not made by the body until the intestinal tract is exposed to bacteria. Vitamin K administration is discussed in detail in Chapter 19.

Seizures

The baby who has had decreased circulation through the placenta and umbilical cord during labor has an increased risk of seizures. All babies who seem to be asphyxiated at birth must be kept under observation for seizure disorders, and if necessary, treated promptly with antiseizure medications. Whether or not these seizures will continue and whether there will be any other problems are related to the cause of the seizure and are not absolutely clear in the baby's first few weeks or months.

Some newborns need to be withdrawn from dependence on drugs taken by the mother during pregnancy. These babies are susceptible to seizures if drug withdrawal at birth is abrupt. The pediatrician must know if the mother is a drug user to make proper provision for gradual withdrawal of the baby from dependency. This ordinarily is done by giving the baby a sedative drug and gradually tapering its dosage until the baby can become drug free.

Newborns born to drug-using mothers may be irritable and difficult to comfort, making mothering an even more difficult task than it is ordinarily. Such babies should be kept in environments without excess stimulation, swaddled, and provided with nonnutritive sucking as a comfort measure. Thumb sucking may be encouraged or a pacifier used. If you use a pacifier, never tie it around the baby's neck, as this might cause strangulation.

Infants of Mothers with Diabetes

A baby of excessive size born to a mother with inadequately controlled diabetes is susceptible to periods of *hypoglycemia* (low blood sugar), which can be quite dangerous. Such babies are put under special observation during the first 12 to 24 hours of life, with repeated determinations of their blood sugar and administration of glucose when the sugar drops too low. Blood sugar is tested by obtaining a tiny blood sample through a heel stick of the newborn. Symptoms of hypoglycemia include jitteriness, *cyanosis* (blue coloring), *apnea* (periods when breathing is stopped), *hypothermia* (low body temperature), feeding difficulties, and lethargy. Seizures may eventually result.

If control of the mother's diabetes has been poor, infants tend to be born with high red blood cell counts. They then develop jaundice due to breakdown of the excess blood. This results in *hyperbilirubinemia*, which requires treatment either with blue lights or, in resistant cases, exchange transfusion.

When women with diabetes have had poor blood sugar control early in pregnancy, there is an increase in congenital heart disease among the infants and abnormalities of the lower limbs and skeletal system. With improved treatment for diabetes, these complications are seen less frequently than in the past. Almost always, both the mothers and babies do fine.

Newborn Infection

As mentioned above, the liver is not fully mature at birth. The whole newborn immune system, in fact, is developed incompletely. They have not been exposed to infectious organisms, so they have not built up antibodies to fight infection. Because of the immature immune system, the newborn is more susceptible to infection than it ever will be again in life.

Babies can get infections from bacteria, viruses, or fungi. They can acquire infections while still in the uterus, during birth, or after birth. Many newborn infections occur when the mother has group B strep in her vagina. This is not harmful to an adult woman, but can cause a devastating infection in a newborn. Preventive measures are now advised for this type of infection. As infection with group B strep is a more frequent and serious problem in the premature baby, it is discussed in detail in Chapter 15.

Newborns are not able to limit infection to local areas as can older children and adults. Infections can become rapidly generalized throughout the body and serious. Because of this, pediatricians are quick to test for evidence of *sepsis* (infection in the blood), and frequently begin antibiotic treatment on a strong suspicion without waiting for definitive test results. More than one antibiotic is often used to cover various organisms. The medications are given through an intravenous line.

In the newborn, a suspicion of infection can be raised by either unusually high or unusually low body temperature, poor feeding, lethargy, irritability, breathing difficulties including periods of no breathing (*apnea*), otherwise unexplained jaundice, vomiting, and abdominal *distension* (swelling). If the baby has meningitis (infection of the fluid that surrounds the brain), seizures may occur. When these signs appear, a workup or partial workup for infection may be undertaken.

A variety of tests are used in an infection workup. A white blood cell count tells whether these infection-fighting cells are present in unusually high numbers. An increased white blood cell count is evidence of bacterial infection. Test results are available rapidly. Samples of body fluid are sent to the laboratory to see if organisms grow in them. These are called *cultures*. Cultures may be taken of the blood, spinal fluid, urine, and, if intrauterine infection is suspected, the amniotic fluid and the placenta. If the baby has any discharge, such as from the eyes or umbilical cord, this may be cultured. Cultures can show the specific organism causing the infection and determine which medications are effective against the particular organism, making treatment more appropriate. Culture results usually take 2 to 3 days. A chest X ray may be ordered if the baby is having breathing difficulties. This is to check for pneumonia.

Some of these tests are rather invasive. Spinal fluid, which tests for *meningitis* (an infection of the fluid surrounding the brain), is obtained through a *spinal tap* (also called a *lumbar puncture*). Urine may be collected through a *suprapubic tap*—aspirating the urine with a needle put into the bladder, just above the pubic area. To put some fears to rest, a spinal tap will not cause paralysis because the needle is inserted into the space beneath the spinal cord, below all nerve endings. The tap, however, may cause a baby who is already oxygen deprived to become more oxygen deprived. This test may be postponed if the baby is having respiratory difficulty.

You should thoroughly discuss with your baby's pediatrician the reasons for each of the tests used. Remember, however, that newborns are not merely smaller versions of adults. Infection in the newborn is very different from infection later in life. It can become systemic and dangerous quite quickly.

Herpes simplex is a viral infection that the infant may acquire from an infected mother. It is passed rarely through the placenta, usually only if the mother has the infection for the first time during pregnancy. It can be acquired through a vaginal birth if the mother has a herpes blister on the vagina at the time of the birth. (For this reason, women with active herpes blisters at the time of labor usually have a cesarean delivery.) The infant born to a mother with active herpes needs close observation.

Treatment for newborn herpes may be begun even before symptoms appear if the mother is known to have had an active herpes blister at the time of birth and either a vaginal delivery occurred over the blister or the membranes were ruptured for more than 4 hours before a cesarean was done. The antiviral agent acyclovir (brand name: Zovirax) is the usual treatment. The dosage is based on the infant's weight and the medication is given through an intravenous line for 14 days. If not treated, neonatal herpes is a very serious systematic infection, unlike the local infection seen in adults.

As the hepatitis virus can pass through the placenta, the baby born to the mother with the active carrier state of hepatitis B virus requires treatment. The Centers for Disease Control and Prevention recommend treating the baby within 24 hours after birth with hepatitis B immune globulin (HBIG) and with the first dose of the hepatitis B vaccine. The second and third doses of the vaccine are given at 1 and 6 months of age, with testing for antibodies done 3 to 6 months after the third injection.

Congenital Anomalies

Few babies have congenital anomalies and most are treatable today. The following are some of the more common abnormalities that occur in newborns. This is in no way a complete discussion of any anomaly nor does this section cover all possible problems in newborns. We remind you that we use the terms *anomaly* and *abnormality* only to refer to the particular problem that the baby has. These terms in no way diminish the value of any newborn or the potential of any human being.

Hearing Loss

Hearing loss is the most common congenital abnormality. Between 1 and 3 babies out of every 1,000 born are estimated to have serious loss. Another 1 to 3 per 1,000 have lesser degrees of hearing loss. Most hearing loss is *congenital*—present at birth. The National Institutes of Health (NIH), the American Academy of Pediatrics, and the National Association of the Deaf now recommend screening for hearing loss for all babies before hospital discharge or shortly after birth for those born out of the hospital.

Two types of tests for hearing loss are available. They may be used alone or together. Both tests take a few minutes, are done while the newborn is asleep, and do not appear to cause pain. Babies may be fussy after the tests, however, and may wish to be held and fed.

- The **evoked otoacoustic emissions** (EOAE) test sends sounds through a small, flexible plug inserted into the baby's ear. A microphone in the plug records responses of the ear (the *otoacoustic emissions*) in reaction to these sounds. If the baby has hearing loss, there will be no emissions.
- The **auditory brainstem response** (ABR) test uses *electrodes* (small wires) attached with adhesive to the baby's scalp and earphones in the baby's ears. Clicking sounds are made through the earphones. The brain's activity in response to the sounds is recorded through the electrodes.

If these tests show possible hearing loss, the infant is referred for further testing. Early intervention can be implemented if results of more definitive tests indicate that this is necessary.

Hypospadias and Cryptorchidism

Some male infants are born with the urethral opening at the *base* (underside) of the penis rather than out at the end. This condition is known as *hypospadias* (Greek: *ypo* = under; *span* = to draw). It occurs in about 1 in 250 male babies. It is more of a practical cosmetic difficulty than a threat to health. Hypospadias may be corrected by later plastic surgery.

Another problem of male infants is undescended testicles (*cryptorchidism*). This means that one or both testicles have remained in the abdomen, where they formed in the fetus, rather than moved down into the scrotum. This condition is much more common in premature infants. Up to 17 percent of infants weighing less than 5 pounds have cryptorchidism and just about all babies weighing less than 2 pounds have this problem. In full-term infants, the problem occurs in 3 to 5 percent of male babies. Both testicles are undescended about 10 to 15 percent of the time.

Most often, the testicle or testicles will descend within the first year of life. Sometimes the testicle can be felt during physical examination in the groin and brought down easily into the scrotum. If this is possible, treatment is not required.

If the testicle remains in the abdomen, several problems can result. The warm temperature of the body can interfere with sperm production. Studies show that when testicles remain undescended past the first year of life, later fertility problems are likely. Also, hernias are more common where there is an undescended testicle. Finally, there is an increased chance—although still rare—of a tumor developing with an undescended testicle. To prevent these problems, treatment is recommended sometime between 6 and 12 months of age. Treatment for an undescended testicle can be hormonal, surgical, or a combination of both. Usually a pediatric urologist is consulted. Hormonal treatment consists of intramuscular injections of *hCG* (human chorionic gonadotropin) several times a week for 4 weeks. Usually, surgery is a more effective treatment. The type of surgery will depend on whether or not the testicles can be felt.

Umbilical Hernia

Not uncommonly, babies are born with umbilical hernias. They occur in about 10 percent of all babies, and more frequently among African Americans. Umbilical hernias are seen more often in girls and in premature babies.

The presence of an umbilical hernia means that the tiny opening in the abdominal muscles, which allowed the umbilical cord to pass through, has not closed completely.

Most umbilical hernias eventually heal without treatment. However, a loop of intestine could get trapped in the opening in the muscles and become cut off from its blood supply. Therefore, if the hernia does not heal, usually by the time the child is school age, surgery is recommended. The surgery is done on an outpatient basis. While it requires general anesthesia and recovery involves pain, the children heal remarkably quickly.

Dislocation of the Hip

All newborns should be examined carefully for the presence of congenital dislocation of the hip. This occurs when the head of the *femur* (the long bone in the thigh) fails to remain properly in its socket. Congenital hip dislocation is seen in 1 or 2 of every 1,000 babies born. It is more common in girls.

Hip dislocation is readily diagnosed by the presence of a "hip click" felt when the legs are gently supported and moved in a backward circle as part of the physical examination. (Don't try this yourself—it has to be done correctly so as not to cause damage.) A variety of treatments are available to return the femoral head to its socket. The baby can wear a special harness, *traction* (weights) can be used, or the baby may be placed in a cast. Rarely, surgery may be needed.

Cleft Lip and Palate

A cleft lip, cleft palate, or both occur in about 1 in every 700 births. This happens early in fetal development if the sides of the lip and possibly the roof of the mouth (the *palate*) fail to fuse together. The condition may create sucking and feeding difficulties, but, with assistance, mothers can feed their babies. Special nipples are available for bottle-fed babies. The assistance of a lactation consultant (see the next chapter) will be most helpful if you wish to nurse a baby with a cleft lip or palate.

Surgery is very successful at repairing these problems. Cleft lips are repaired within the first several months of life and cleft palates are repaired when the baby is somewhat older, but usually before the age of 2. A small scar remains above the lip after repair of a cleft lip, which adult men can cover with a mustache and adult women with cosmetics.

Clubfoot

A clubfoot, technically called *talipes equinovarus*, affects the bones, muscles, tendons, and blood vessels of one or both of the newborn's feet. This problem occurs in about 1 in 1,000 births and affects boys twice as often as girls. A baby with clubfoot will have one or both feet turned in. About half the time both feet are affected. Treatment to straighten the foot usually involves casting and perhaps surgery.

Trisomy

Careful examination of the baby is desirable to identify the occasional newborn with some type of trisomy, the commonest variety of which is *Down syndrome* (see Chapter 5). Physical examination will reveal characteristics that are highly suggestive of this genetic disorder. Genetic studies are required to make a definitive diagnosis, however. Although there is no cure, appropriate counseling for the parents and supportive therapies for the newborn can be initiated.

NEWBORN SCREENING

All states mandate newborn blood tests for several disorders, the number varying from state to state. Some states screen for two or three disorders while others have programs that screen for twenty to thirty disorders. The March of Dimes currently recommends screening for at least nine disorders—called inborn errors of metabolism—in newborns. These are phenylketonuria (PKU), congenital hypothyroidism, galactosemia, sickle cell anemia, maple syrup urine disease, homocystinuria, biotinidase deficiency, congenital adrenal hyperplasia (CAH), and dehydrogenase medium chain acyl-CoA deficiency (MCAD). This advocacy organization also recommends routine newborn hearing testing.

Newborn screening tests require a sample of the baby's blood, usually obtained via a heel stick. The heel stick may cause redness and bruising, but this heals within a few days. To minimize the pain of the heel stick, the heel should be warmed first so that the blood flows easily. This avoids the trauma that occurs if repeated sticks are needed, or a lot of pressure is put on the heel to cause the blood to flow. Feeding the baby just before the heel stick may help with blood flow as well. Doing the stick when the baby is in a sleepy state, and swaddling and holding the baby during and right after the heel stick, may also help reduce pain.

For some of the screening tests to be accurate, several days of feeding are required. With early discharge from birthing center or hospital, or if the birth took place at home, arrangements must be made for the tests to be performed. Waiting until the baby is 5 or 6 days old to perform the screen may increase the likelihood that the blood will flow easily from the heel. The following describes the nine conditions for which screening is recommended by the March of Dimes:

- **Phenylketonuria** (PKU) is an abnormality of *amino acid* (protein) metabolism that causes serious mental retardation. About

1 baby in 10,000 to 1 in 25,000 (average 1 in 12,000) will have this disease. With early dietary intervention, the consequences of PKU can be prevented. Although a rare condition, all states mandate screening for PKU.

• **Hypothyroidism,** or thyroid deficiency, occurs in 1 in every 3,600 to 1 in 5,000 babies (average 1 in 4,000). Untreated, it can lead to mental retardation as well as poor growth. All states mandate screening for hypothyroidism.

• **Galactosemia** is a disorder in which the baby cannot metabolize *galactose*, a milk sugar. This is rare, occurring in 1 baby in every 60,000 to 1 in 80,000 (average 1 in 50,000). Without treatment, however, it can be quite serious, even life-threatening. Symptoms may be seen within the first 2 weeks of life.

• **Sickle-cell anemia** is a disorder of red blood cells that causes severe anemia. It may occur in 1 in 375 to 1 in 1,700 babies, with the frequency of occurrence dependent upon on the population. Sickle-cell disease is most common in African and Mediterranean populations or those with African ancestry. It is seen in 1 in 400 African-American babies and 1 in 1,000 to 1 in 30,000 babies of Hispanic descent.

• **Maple syrup urine disease** (branched-chain ketoaciduria) affects only 1 in 250,000 to 1 in 400,000 babies, but is more common in the Mennonite population, where it occurs as frequently as 1 in 760 births. It is caused by an inability of the body to process amino acids. It is called "maple syrup urine disease" because it causes the urine to smell like maple syrup. If this disease is not treated, it can be fatal within the first few weeks of life.

• **Homocystinuria** occurs in 1 in 50,000 to 1 in 150,000 babies. This rare disorder is an inability to digest the amino acid *methionine*. It causes mental retardation, bone disease, and blood clots.

• **Biotinidase deficiency** is a rare deficiency of the enzyme biotinidase. This enzyme metabolizes biotin, a B vitamin. Biotinidase deficiency occurs in 1 in 70,000 to 1 in 126,000 babies, mostly in the Caucasian population. Problems can be prevented if the baby is given extra biotin early in life.

• **Congenital adrenal hyperplasia** (CAH) is a group of disorders in which there is a deficiency of certain hormones. CAH occurs in approximately 1 in 5,000 babies. It affects genital development and, if severe, can interfere with proper kidney function. This disease can be fatal, but lifetime treatment with the missing hormones suppresses CAH.

• **Dehydrogenase medium chain Acyl-CoA deficiency** (MCAD) is a disorder in which babies cannot burn fat when they deplete their stores of sugar. This can cause sudden death in infancy and serious disabilities in survivors, such as mental retardation. MCAD affects about 1 baby in 15,000. When diagnosed early, the disorder can be successfully treated with regular food intake and avoidance of fasting so the body always has glucose to burn.

Screening tests are not conclusive. A positive test does not mean your baby has the disease. The tests ordinarily pick up far more positives than there are cases of disease but they do serve as an early warning system and allow for further testing to confirm the diagnosis.

The March of Dimes also recommends hearing tests for all newborns. Approximately 1 in 1,000 to 3 in 1,000 well babies have hearing loss. In intensive care nurseries, this rate is much higher—2 in 100 to 4 in 100. Early detection and intervention can prevent speech and language difficulties later in life. Newborns can be tested for hearing loss with one of two tests that measure response to sounds. These tests use either a very small, soft earphone or a microphone in the baby's ear. When the test result is abnormal, the baby may need additional hearing testing to determine if there really is a hearing loss.

CIRCUMCISION OF MALE NEWBORNS

Urine comes out of the penis at the urethral opening, which is normally at the tip of the spongy erectile structure, the *glans penis*. The glans is covered at birth by a fold of skin, the *prepuce* or foreskin. The foreskin is not firmly attached to the glans. The opening in the foreskin through which the urine passes is adequate for the purpose, and infection in this area in babies is rare. As the boy becomes older and experiences erections from time to time, this opening is stretched gradually until the foreskin can be peeled back off the glans without discomfort. In the ordinary course of events, the child learns to keep this area clean as a part of his general hygiene.

Certain ethnic groups have practiced *circumcision*—removal of the foreskin—for several millennia. A good deal of anthropological evidence suggests that the practice derives from a sacrificial fertility rite and did not originate as a medical procedure.

Without circumcision, a few boys or men will develop *phimosis*—an inability to retract the foreskin—and sometimes may develop inflammation of the glans due to this condition. If needed to correct this problem, circumcision becomes a more difficult procedure.

Recent research has shown that circumcision lessens the chances of urinary tract infection in boys and penile cancer in men. Neither of these conditions are common, however. Some experts, including the Canadian Pediatric Society, have suggested alternative strategies for preventing urinary tract infection in newborns. These include deliberately exposing newborns to certain germs found in the mother that might protect against infection, and encouraging rooming-in. Rooming-in provides close contact between mothers and newborns, promoting colonization with the mother's bacteria as a protection against infection. The extent to which these efforts prevent urinary tract infection warrants research.

The issue of whether or not female partners of uncircumcised men are more likely to develop cervical cancer has been debated for decades. A study published in the *New England Journal of Medicine* in 2002 showed that for men with a history of multiple sexual partners, circumcision reduced the risk of cervical cancer in their current female partners.

About 63 percent of boys in the United States are circumcised. This means that your son will find other boys whose penises look like his regardless of whether or not he is circumcised.

When circumcision is properly done, complications are extremely rare. Hemorrhage and infection occur infrequently. Disfigurement occurs even more rarely.

For years, it was believed that infants did not experience pain with circumcision. Today it is recognized that infants do experience painful sensations. Several types of anesthesia are available for pain relief during circumcision. A pacifier soaked in sugar water can provide some relief, but if this is all that is given, infants still cry considerably during and after circumcision. A *nerve block* is more effective. It involves the injection of a local anesthetic agent, lidocaine, into the base of the penis in two places. The nerve block has some potential side effects, however. Most commonly, bruising is seen, but sloughing off of skin is possible, though rare. Anesthesia also can be delivered via a procedure called a *subcutaneous ring block*. This also involves an injection of lidocaine, but into the midshaft of the penis, rather than the base. A subcutaneous ring block is highly effective and complications have not been reported. A *local anesthetic cream*, EMLA, can be applied noninvasively to the skin, but takes 60 to 90 minutes to become effective and appears less soothing during the most traumatic moments of the procedure than the nerve block or the ring block.

Some people have strong opposition to circumcision, believing it is a violation of the child's rights, removing a part of the body without his consent and without sufficient medical reason in the absence of a problem. Some claim that later sexual pleasure may be diminished through desensitization of the exposed glans, although this is difficult to prove. Some groups have formed to lobby for laws against this procedure.

With these considerations in mind, circumcision remains an individual decision to be made by parents who receive complete information regarding its advantages and disadvantages. In its most recent review of circumcision, reported in 1999, the American Academy of Pediatrics stated: "Existing scientific evidence demonstrates potential medical benefits of newborn circumcision; however, these data are not sufficient to recommend routine neonatal circumcision. In circumstances in which there are potential benefits and risks, yet the procedure is not essential to the child's current well-being, parents should determine what is in the best interest of the child."

If your son is not circumcised, do not try to retract the foreskin. It will eventually retract on its own. Until it can retract, it is not necessary to clean the cells that accumulate under the foreskin. These cells, called *smegma*, look like white beads and will work themselves out. Once the foreskin is retractable, your son can be taught to clean under it with soap and water during his regular shower. No other hygienic measures are necessary.

If your son is circumcised, the penis will be wrapped in gauze to which petroleum jelly or an antibiotic ointment has been applied. This is removed with the first diaper change and may or may not be replaced. The person performing the circumcision (a physician, midwife, or practitioner from a religious community) will advise you whether or not another dressing should be placed. Once the dressing is removed, the only care needed is washing with soap and water. The penis may be reddened and raw looking and there may be bit of blood or yellow discharge. Your son may feel discomfort for several days with diaper changes. Healing takes about 1 to 2 weeks.

RELATIONSHIP BETWEEN PARENTS AND INFANT

The relationship between the parents and the infant starts during the pregnancy. It may begin as soon as the first missed menses, the positive pregnancy test, the first perceived fetal movement (*quickening*). Sometimes, it may not begin until you start to "show" and other people comment on your obvious pregnancy. The relationship may be enhanced when an ultrasound allows you to see the fetus in motion. Certainly by the time the fetus is about 6 months and can be readily seen and felt through the pregnant woman's abdominal wall, there is an ongoing relationship.

Still, a uniqueness exists to the moment of birth and the period immediately following it. The newborn, now actually to be seen and felt and held, going through phases of crying and wiggling and then to a peaceful alertness with open eyes searching around the room, always seems like some kind of miracle. The parents are very sensitive to the baby at this point. The baby sees and hears and feels and is receiving a tremendous barrage of new images and experiences. If the baby is kept close to the parents during these immediate moments, very strong and long-lasting attachments occur in a process that has been called *bonding*.

The bonding process can be facilitated by closeness between the baby and the parents in the first few moments following birth, skin-to-skin contact between baby and mother or father, stroking movements by the mother, warmth and relatively dim lighting with a reduced amount of noise, early nursing, and a minimum of interruptions for such procedures as footprinting. Newborn babies remain alert for half an hour to an hour after birth and then usually fall off into a peaceful sleep from which they awake only when hungry.

These represent ideal circumstances, which cannot be achieved fully if the baby is born by cesarean birth, if the mother has been under general anesthetic for the delivery, or if, for any reason, the newborn has to be taken to a special care nursery for observation. The various features of bonding can be initiated as soon as the mother and the baby can be brought together, however. Mothers should go to the special care nursery where their babies are. The staff there are very good about encouraging the mother to handle the baby, to stroke the baby and feel the baby, to talk to the baby, to establish eye contact, and all the other things that enhance bonding. If the baby is able to suck, breast-feeding can be started then and there. If not, the mother can pump her breasts and the milk given to the baby.

A number of special care nurseries or neonatal intensive care units (NICUs) promote *kangaroo care*. This refers to a way that mothers (or fathers) hold babies with skin-to-skin contact. The baby wears only a diaper and is held against the mother's bare chest. The baby can be covered with blankets for warmth and screens used for privacy.

Kangaroo care is so named because it mimics the way kangaroos and other marsupials carry their newborns—in their pouches. It has been found to help stabilize the baby's temperature, heartbeat, and breathing. It also facilitates breast-feeding, especially in premature babies. Research has shown that kangaroo care may help with brain development as well, even with only 10 minutes a day of such close contact with parents. Kangaroo care usually can begin once the baby is no longer on a respirator. It may start for 10 to 30 minutes a day and increase to several hours each day. Monitoring of the baby's vital signs can continue during kangaroo care.

Kangaroo care also has benefits for the parents. It increases milk supply and makes parents of tiny infants or infants with problems more comfortable. It gives them a sense of participating in a meaningful way in their baby's care and eases fear and tension about the care. Instead of hovering and worrying over the incubator, the parents are themselves keeping the baby warm. It promotes parent-infant bonding.

Interestingly, kangaroo care began in Bogota, Colombia in South America in 1979, in response to a shortage of incubators and staff to care for premature babies. The benefits were so apparent that it spread, first to several countries in Europe and then to the United States.

Bereavement

When a baby is stillborn or has serious congenital anomalies the parents are destined for a terrible letdown. Fortunately, unexpected stillbirth in normal situations has become an extremely rare event and, with genetic screening and ultrasound, it is most unusual for a baby to be born with unexpected problems. Nevertheless, there are still occasions for the parents to go through a period of great grief. For many years, in an effort to guard the mother from this, abnormal and stillborn infants were hidden from her.

We have learned that this leaves a mother with an empty feeling, compounding her disappointment at the outcome of her pregnancy. It strengthens the mother's groundless suspicion that she has done something wrong, and it denies her an opportunity to express her feelings. When a mother of a stillborn infant is allowed to see the child, even if the baby is deformed, she is able to focus on what is beautiful to her about the baby.

Many hospitals now have bereavement groups consisting of professionals who are attuned to the needs of mothers and fathers under these painful circumstances. Individual counseling may be worthwhile as well.

There is no particular medical reason to wait to become pregnant once you have a menstrual period after a pregnancy loss. It is desirable, however, for the woman and couple to complete the process of grieving before starting another pregnancy, so as to maximize the chance of having a happy pregnancy and delivery. How long this takes is very individual. Some women find that grief is not concluded until they are pregnant again.

CHOOSING A HEALTH CARE PROVIDER FOR THE BABY

Newborn and infant care ideally is provided by pediatricians, family doctors, and pediatric or family nurse practitioners who are motivated to deliver this kind of service. You need not choose a physician or nurse practitioner on the staff of the hospital where you intend to have the baby, or at the hospital that provides backup services for the birthing center. All hospitals provide temporary pediatric consultation during the period that the mother and baby are hospitalized, and there are no difficulties in transferring care to the pediatrician selected by the parents when the baby leaves. If the doctor or nurse practitioner you have chosen is on the staff of the hospital where you deliver, however, examination of your baby at the time of birth is by someone that you have already begun to trust.

Most pediatric care providers agree to meet with you for a pre-birth visit. Topics to discuss include:

- Hours of services for well baby care
- What kind of coverage is provided for nights, weekends, and emergencies
- With what hospital the provider is affiliated
- What health insurance is accepted
- What fees will be involved

As many new parents are understandably nervous about the health of their baby, availability and accessibility are among the most important characteristics of the person you choose to provide health care for your child. Most important, you should make sure that the physician or nurse practitioner holds attitudes compatible with yours on such matters as breast-feeding and the relationship between the parents and the care provider.

You might wish to find out whether a physician is certified by the American Board of Pediatrics or the American Board of Family Practice.

You can find out if a pediatric nurse practitioner holds a certificate from the National Certification Board of Pediatric Nurse Practitioners. Family nurse practitioners are certified by either the American Nurses Association or the American Academy of Nurse Practitioners. Contact information for these organizations is found in the Appendix.

TAKING THE BABY HOME

Going home used to be a formidable undertaking. For one thing, it was thought that an elaborate layette was called for. Babies were considered fragile and an extraordinary amount of protective clothing was considered necessary, to shield them from strangers and from large crowds of relatives. For babies who were to be bottle-fed, parents had to provide a host of paraphernalia for preparing formula and sterilizing feeding equipment.

These aspects of life with baby have been simplified greatly. There is no question that the baby can be costumed in a frilly dress and booties or a sweater and a knit cap, but a baby can go home just as happily in a cotton shirt and a disposable diaper, wrapped in an appropriate soft, warm blanket. At home, you probably will find that a crib or even a bassinet and a convenient-sized basin for bathing the baby are the only baby furnishings you will need, at least at first.

Disposable diapers have largely supplanted an immense trousseau of cotton diapers. But modern laundry equipment and easy-to-use outside coverings have made cloth diapers less of a chore, and diaper services are widely available. The decision whether to use disposable or cloth diapers is one worth thinking about. There are advantages and disadvantages to each. Disposable diapers save time. Most are not biodegradable, however, and even those that will degrade will take millennia to do so. Questions have been raised about whether the chemicals used in disposable diapers are harmful to the infant's young skin. This has not been studied, and there are no known detrimental effects, but possible long-term problems have not been examined. Disposables are more expensive. They absorb the urine so well that you may not know whether or not the baby has urinated.

If you choose to use cloth diapers, you can get a diaper service or wash them yourself. It's a good idea to wash diapers (and all baby clothes) before they are used. They should also be put through an extra rinse with each washing. Extensive instruction on laundering cloth diapers is available on the internet at www.childbirthsolutions.com/content/postpartum/caringdiapers/index.html.

Many states have laws requiring that all newborns, infants, and young children sit in car seats. If you are taking the baby home by automobile, you must have a car seat. Carrying the baby in your lap is not safe. Make sure the car seat meets safety standards and that you use it appropriately. Newborns should be in rear-facing car seats in the back seat. Babies less than 37 weeks gestation and those with respiratory problems should be assessed for breathing difficulties in car seats before discharge.

Be sure you have an appointment for follow-up care for your infant with a pediatrician, family practitioner, or pediatric or family nurse practitioner before you leave the hospital or birthing center or make one shortly after you arrive home. In a home birth, call the physician or nurse practitioner soon after the birth.

SAFETY TIPS IN THE EARLY WEEKS

Eventually, most parents find it necessary to *baby-proof* their homes—using special gadgets to lock cabinet doors and cover all sockets. You have several months to do this. Certain simple actions will keep a new-born safe:

- Never leave the baby unattended on a flat surface such as a changing table or any other table, dresser, or bed. Babies can roll off.
- Don't ever leave the baby alone in a bath. Don't take your hands off the baby in the tub—not even just to answer the phone or the doorbell. If you forget to bring something for the bath, like a towel or soap, pick the baby up, wrap the baby, and take it with you to get whatever you need.
- Don't keep pillows, stuffed animals, or any soft items in the baby's crib. They can cause suffocation.
- Don't use quilts or unnecessary blankets. If you use a blanket, tuck it in around the crib mattress, and pull it up only as far as the baby's chest.
- Do not place the baby on a waterbed, sofa, soft mattress, pillow, or other soft surface to sleep.
- If the baby sleeps with you, observe several precautions: do not have soft items in your bed and move it away from the wall and other furniture to keep the baby from becoming entrapped between the bed and the wall or another piece of furniture. Do not smoke in bed. Do not use substances such as drugs or alcohol that impair your ability to awaken.

• Don't let the baby sleep on his or her stomach as this has been associated with *sudden infant death syndrome* (SIDS). Sleeping on the back is the safest, although side-lying is better than lying on the stomach. Babies can be placed on their stomach when they are awake.

• Babies should not get overheated at night. They should be lightly clothed for sleep and the room at a temperature that would be comfortable for an adult wearing light clothing.

• Never never shake the baby. It can cause serious injury to the baby's brain. If the baby is crying incessantly and you cannot provide comfort, you will be naturally frustrated. Try feeding, changing the diaper, burping the baby. Undress the baby if he or she seems overheated, or swaddle the baby in a blanket for extra comfort. You can rock the baby, sing to the baby or play music, walk with the baby in a sling or carrier, put the baby in a swing or stroller. Take a warm bath with the baby. Try noise like a washing machine or vacuum cleaner. Go for a ride in the car (with baby in an appropriate car seat, of course). If the baby is still crying and you are feeling angry, remember, the baby is not fussing on purpose. If somebody is available, let them take the baby, even just for a few minutes. If you are alone, if necessary put the baby in the crib or another safe place and walk away. Count to ten. Call a sympathetic friend. But don't shake the baby.

NEWBORN WARNING SIGNS: WHEN TO CALL YOUR PEDIATRICIAN OR PEDIATRIC NURSE PRACTITIONER

You should never feel "silly" calling a pediatric care provider if you have a question about your newborn. Most often, the purpose of your call will be to provide you with reassurance, but this does not make the call unimportant. Normal newborn behaviors may seem unfamiliar and strange to you at first. As you become more confident and get to know and interpret your baby's signals, you will not need as much professional support.

Most babies are quite healthy, but there are a number of warning signs that should prompt a telephone call to your pediatrician, family physician, or pediatric or family nurse practitioner. These are listed below.

Warning Signs in the Newborn

If you notice any of the following call your physician or nurse practitioner immediately:

- The baby is listless.
- The baby's behavior seems unusual.
- The baby will not eat.
- The baby has had no bowel movement for 48 hours.
- The baby's umbilical cord has a bad odor or is oozing pus or blood, or the skin around the cord is reddened and warm.
- The baby's temperature—taken rectally for 2 minutes—is below 97.5 degrees or is 100.4 degrees or higher. (Note: Don't take an infant's temperature orally.)
- The baby's eyes or skin looks yellow. Check near a window with good light. Press on the baby's nose or breastbone. If the baby is jaundiced, the skin will look yellow when you release the pressure.
- If you have had a home birth, call if the baby does not urinate within the first 24 hours. This may be difficult to assess with disposable diapers as they absorb all the urine. You may need to keep the baby undiapered for a period of time, or use cloth diapers during this observation period.
- The baby is breathing rapidly—over 60 breaths per minute—or has a blue coloring that does not go away. Breathing should not pause for more than 5 seconds between breaths.
- The baby has *retractions*—pulling in of the ribs with respirations.
- The baby has wheezing, grunting, or whistling sounds during breathing.

CHAPTER TWENTY-FIVE

After Childbirth

The period of six weeks or so after delivery is called the *puerperium*, a Latin word meaning "having brought forth a child," or, more commonly, the postpartum period. Traditionally, this period ends when the reproductive tract has returned fully to its nonpregnant state. If you consider the psychological and family adjustments made after birth, however, this period lasts much longer.

Physically, the puerperium is a time when the body undergoes many rapid changes in its readjustment from pregnant to nonpregnant. The most obvious changes are the return of the uterus to its nonpregnant size and condition, and the appearance of milk in the breasts. Many other events occur, however, including a reduction in blood volume and a loss of the extra body fluid that had accumulated in pregnancy.

While fatigue and some discomforts are common during the postpartum period, most women feel well and recover quickly from the work of childbirth. But don't expect to be able to follow your usual routine or perform strenuous tasks during the first few weeks following childbirth. You should continue the healthful eating patterns established in pregnancy and allow friends and family to help with tiring tasks.

During the last several decades, many hospitals and birth centers have revised policies on postpartum discharge. Hospital stays, routinely five days in the 1950s, were reduced to three days by the 1970s. During the 1980s, women were sent home within 12 to 48 hours after birth. In the early 1990s, many managed-care organizations mandated 1-day discharges. Although the advantages and disadvantages of early discharge have not been researched well, the practice of health organizations determining length of postpartum hospital stay stimulated responses from the public, the medical community, and legislatures—both statewide and nationally.

In 1996, the federal government passed the Newborns' and Mothers' Health Protection Act (NMHPA). This act mandates that group health insurance plans and health insurance carriers that offer maternity care provide for a 48-hour hospital stay after a vaginal birth and a 96-hour stay after a cesarean birth. Pre-authorization is not to be required for these minimum stays, although the mother, in consultation with her physician or midwife, may choose to go home sooner.

For births that occur in a hospital, the stay begins at the time of delivery. For multiple births, the 48-hour count starts at the birth of the last baby. If the birth has occurred elsewhere, as when a woman transfers from a birth center to a hospital in the postpartum period, the beginning of the hospital stay is considered the time of admission.

Under this legislation, insurance plans cannot offer monetary payments or rebates to a mother or a provider who chooses earlier discharge. The plan can provide follow-up services for a mother and newborn who leave early. These services are limited to those that the woman or newborn would have received in the hospital—such as nursing care—had either or both stayed the 48 or 96 hours.

We support the intent of the NMHPA—that mothers and care providers, not health insurance plans, determine how long a woman needs to be hospitalized following a birth. We also support the advantages of early discharge; families are reunited and the woman and her baby adjust to their own rhythms, not to hospital routines.

Yet, with early discharge, new mothers lose the opportunity to learn from experienced hospital staff. If you will be on your own shortly after birth, learn as much as possible in the months *before* delivery about postpartum care of yourself and your baby. You need to become aware of symptoms in the newborn that might indicate common conditions, such as jaundice and infection, which could be missed with early discharge. These are discussed in Chapter 24. For your own sake as well as your baby's, you must also be certain that you can reach your physician or your midwife or the hospital staff. Your baby will need a checkup shortly after discharge if discharge is earlier than 48 hours after birth.

The American College of Obstetricians and Gynecologists and the American Academy of Pediatrics have issued guidelines for early discharge, for both the mother and the newborn. These organizations also suggest that women who will go home early should attend prenatal classes. They suggest early discharge be implemented only when the following conditions have been met:

• Pregnancy, labor, birth, and the immediate postpartum period must be without complications.
• Screening tests for hemoglobin or hematocrit, blood type and Rh factor, syphilis, hepatitis B, and blood sugar if necessary are available (see the tables on pages 168 to 172, Chapter 7). These must be reviewed before discharge.
• The mother must have knowledge of how to feed an infant, care for the newborn's skin and cord, and take the baby's temperature.
• The mother must be able to assess the infant's well-being and to recognize common problems.
• Family members who will help with care must be available.
• A source of ongoing medical care must be available.

For you to assess your own well-being in the postpartum period, you must understand the changes your body will go through.

PHYSIOLOGIC CHANGES

You can expect certain fairly predictable changes to occur in your body following pregnancy and birth. These changes are very similar in women who have had vaginal or cesarean births.

Involution: The Uterus Shrinks to Nonpregnant Size

Right after birth, the uterus weighs about two pounds; by six weeks after birth, it weighs about three ounces. Shortly after birth, the top of the uterus, called the *fundus*, rises and then gradually, day-by-day, descends. This process is called *involution*.

The cycle of growth followed by involution, which the uterus undergoes in each pregnancy and postpartum period, is unique in the human body. No other organ enlarges itself more than tenfold and then regresses back to its basic size. The growth is caused by a vast increase in the size of each individual muscle fiber forming the uterus, not by an increase in the number of fibers. Involution occurs as each cell rids itself of excess *cytoplasm*—the material within the cell. Exactly how this happens is not understood.

Immediately after delivery of the placenta, the fundus is approximately two-thirds to three-quarters of the way from the vulva to the navel. Within a few hours, it rises to just below the navel. Because uterine muscles are contracting strongly to prevent bleeding from the area where the placenta has detached, the uterus feels hard, even rocklike. During the first few postpartum days it can be felt as a smooth, firm, gourd-shaped organ.

Health care providers measure uterine descent in fingerbreadths below the navel; each day it moves approximately one fingerbreadth lower in the abdomen. By the end of the first week after birth, the uterus weighs about one pound and the fundus is about two inches (or about three fingerbreadths) above the top of the vulva. By the tenth postpartum day, the fundus can be felt just above the *symphysis pubis*—the bone forming the front of the pelvis that can be felt by pressing on the vulva. The uterus then sinks into the pelvis and by the end of the second week, it can no longer be felt in the abdomen. At the end of 4 to 6 weeks, the uterus is once more the weight and size of a pear. This process of involution occurs more rapidly in a woman who nurses. This is because nipple stimulation releases the hormone *oxytocin*, responsible also for uterine muscle contraction.

Immediately after birth, your physician or midwife will check your fundus and keep a close watch on it for several hours to make sure it stays contracted. Your provider or a nurse may massage it or even express a few clots by pressing down heavily on the fundus. This may be uncomfortable but lasts only a few moments. If you remain in the hospital for a few days, a nurse or your care provider will likely check your fundus daily by pressing gently to measure its firmness and descent.

Puerperal Vaginal Secretion

You can expect to experience a vaginal secretion for about three to four weeks following delivery. Called *lochia*, from the Greek "pertaining to childbirth," the secretion is not menstrual blood. It is composed of shreds of the specialized lining of the uterus that had developed for pregnancy, as well as other cells, bacteria, and some blood. For the first 3 or 4 days, there is enough blood in this secretion to make it a bright red color. It is called *lochia rubra*. From the fourth to the tenth day it becomes paler and pinker and is called *lochia serosa*. Starting about the tenth day, it is yellow-white, sometimes with a little blood mixed in. This is called *lochia alba*.

Occasionally, the lochia may maintain a reddish color for longer than expected. If the bright red lochia persists for two weeks or more, you should call your physician or midwife. A small part of the placenta may have been retained in the uterus.

Although lochia may have a distinct odor, similar to menstrual flow, and be stronger when mixed with perspiration, it should not be foul smelling. A bad smell may be a sign of an infection; this is another reason to call your physician or midwife. Since the lochia comes from the uterus, vaginal douches or deodorant sprays will not affect its odor.

In addition to changing color, the amount of lochia should diminish as the days and weeks pass. Often, the flow will decrease when you are lying down and become heavy when you arise. Sometimes, clots may be passed; while this is usually normal, you should notify your physician or midwife if at any time the flow seems much heavier than what you were accustomed to before pregnancy on the heaviest day of your period or if it does not diminish over time. Conversely, very scant lochia in the early postpartum period also can signal a problem; contact your physician or midwife if your lochia is practically gone after only a few postpartum days, especially if you notice a foul odor or cramping that seems to be worsening.

Ordinarily, lochia disappears between the third and fourth postpartum weeks. In total, the amount of fluid and tissue lost through the lochia is about eight to nine ounces.

During the first few days after delivery, a large-size perineal pad probably will be needed. This is always supplied in the hospital or birth center; women delivering at home should make sure to purchase maternity or large-size pads to use in these first days. Later, a regular-size pad should be sufficient. Because of the increased risk for toxic shock syndrome in the postpartum period, vaginal tampons are not recommended during this time. While you are in the hospital a nurse or your physician or midwife may make "pad checks" each day to ascertain that you are not bleeding too heavily.

The Return of Menstruation

True menstruation returns at variable times after a birth. If you are not nursing, you usually will have a menstrual period within 4 to 8 weeks. If you are nursing, the variability is extraordinary; menstruation may return at any time from the second to the eighteenth month. Its return may depend on whether you nurse exclusively or give formula or other supplements along with breast milk. Many women have their first menstruation shortly after introducing solids to the baby.

Whether you nurse or not, the amount of bleeding and the interval between periods may be irregular for the first several cycles. Painful menstruation, called *dysmenorrhea*, often is improved by a pregnancy; in many women, the pain never returns.

Bleeding before real menstruation begins is sometimes erratic. Your postpartum bleeding may come to a quiet end, only to resume a few weeks later for a day or two. Even as late as 6 months after delivery, brief periods of unusual bleeding may appear without warning. If the bleeding appears unduly heavy, however, or persists in a sporadic and irregular way, you should consult your physician or midwife.

Increased Sweating and Urination

One of the more striking phenomena of the postpartum period is how the body sheds itself of excess fluid that has accumulated during pregnancy. This is done through perspiration and urination, both of which may be profuse from about the second to fifth postpartum day. You may find that you need to change your nightgown or sheets frequently.

Although the body is losing fluid, your feet and ankles may puff up on the second or third day after the baby is born. Why this happens is not known, but the swelling is harmless and goes away quickly. Do not limit liquids in an attempt to reduce this swelling or to stop urinating or sweating so much. In fact, your body needs lots of fluids at this time to prevent dehydration; a glass of water an hour is not too much. Some women just put a glass of water or water bottle by their beds and sip continually throughout the day. It's just about impossible to drink too much.

Vaginal Dryness

Women in the postpartum period, especially nursing women, often experience vaginal dryness. This is due to the hormonal changes—a lack of estrogen in particular—that occur after pregnancy and before the resumption of menstruation. While this is a normal and temporary occurrence, it can be bothersome and interfere with sexuality. Over-the-counter vaginal lubricants, such as K-Y jelly or Astroglide, can be used.

Postpartum Loss of Hair

Another troublesome postpartum complaint for some women is hair loss. Body hair, particularly head hair, grows in two phases. The *anagen phase* lasts three years, and about 90 percent of scalp hair is in that phase at any one time. The *telagen phase* is a resting period and usually lasts three months, after which those hairs fall out. In pregnancy, however, all hair may enter the telagen phase, resulting in increased hair loss for a few months after delivery. Sometimes, especially in nursing women, gobs of hair seem to fall out with normal brushing. Rest assured, however, that the hair lost is only a small fraction of all body or scalp hair, and that the excess loss will stop within 6 months.

LACTATION

The advantages of breast-feeding are compelling. We do not mean to imply that the health of mother or baby is dependent on nursing, but it is certainly an influence. Because the physical and psychological benefits of lactation are considerable and because today's mothers did not always grow up around nursing women, as mothers of past generations did, we have devoted an entire chapter to breast-feeding. In this chapter, we briefly cover the immediate benefits of lactation on postpartum adjustment.

Breast-feeding as an Aid to Involution

Immediately after the placenta separates from the uterus and is "born," the uterine muscles contract down on the site of separation to stop its bleeding. These contractions prevent postpartum hemorrhage and over time cause the uterus to return to a nonpregnant size. It has been known for centuries that suckling helps to control postpartum hemorrhage by inducing uterine contractions. We now know that the contractions occur under the influence of oxytocin, released from the anterior pituitary gland. Suckling stimulates a nervous reflex that releases oxytocin. Oxytocin has the dual effect of making the milk ducts release their milk into the nipple and of causing the uterus to contract.

Sometimes, even if a mother is not planning to nurse, the health care provider will ask her to put the baby to the breast right after birth. This may be helpful when the birth of the placenta is occurring slowly, as contractions caused by suckling also can help push out the placenta.

Because of these ongoing contractions, the nursing mother's pelvic organs return quite rapidly to their nonpregnant state. Now that the mechanism is understood and drugs that will cause contractions are available, they can be given when the mother cannot nurse her baby and the uterus is not contracting well on its own.

Suppression of Lactation:
Natural vs. Medically Induced Suppression

Of course, not all women choose to breast-feed. More detailed information that will help you choose a method of infant feeding is provided in Chapters 24 and 26. Some women breast-feed for a short period of time only, stopping for a variety of reasons, from family pressure to wanting to return to work without dealing with the issues of nursing while working. We admit to a strong bias in favor of nursing, especially for its benefits to the newborn, but we also believe that how to feed an infant is a personal decision that a woman and her partner make for a myriad of reasons. While breast-feeding almost always ensures good nutrition, babies can be fed adequately with formula. Warm and loving feedings can be achieved with bottle-feeding, and for some families that option simply works better.

Whether nursing or not, some milk forms in the breast during and immediately following pregnancy. Medical science sought for years to develop a lactation suppressant in an injection or pill. While hormonal measures are effective, they have undesirable side effects. Recently, a nonhormonal medication, bromocriptine (Parlodel), was found to inhibit the secretion of *prolactin*, a hormone necessary for milk production. Unfortunately, bromocriptine has a high likelihood of side effects including nausea, dizziness, headaches, fatigue, light-headedness, and vomiting. Because it also lowers blood pressure, some women have fainted from it. It has even been associated with seizures, strokes, and heart attacks in postpartum women. For these reasons, its use is highly discouraged.

The safest and surest method of suppressing lactation is simply not to nurse. This usually involves enduring an 18- to 24-hour period of discomfort due to engorgement of the breasts. This can be relieved by good support of the breasts in a well-fitting bra, moderate analgesics (such as acetaminophen—Tylenol, for example), and ice packs. Ice can be applied intermittently for about 20 minutes at a time. Hospitals and birth centers may have ice packs available or an ice pack can easily be made by putting ice into a plastic bag and covering it with a cloth or towel.

Some women find it helpful to bind the breasts tightly, although this doesn't always work better than a supportive bra. Some hospitals provide ready-made breast binders. In her classic text for midwives, Helen Varney describes making a fairly simple binder out of a pillowcase. Cut it into one long rectangular piece and two shorter, narrower pieces to be used as straps. Tie the longer piece around your breasts, overlapping it slightly in front, and close it with safety pins. Pin the two straps to the long piece. They go around each shoulder. A tuck taken under each breast gives extra support. Two maternity pads can be placed under the binder if your breasts are large and need even more support; one goes under each breast and curves along its outer edge. The less ambitious woman can simply wrap and pin a towel tightly around her breasts or use a wide Ace bandage as a binder.

While you are in the hospital, a nurse or your physician or midwife may check your breasts on daily "rounds" to see if they are becoming hard or uncomfortable. You can ask for a breast binder if you don't have a well-fitting bra or feel as though you could use extra support. With today's early return home, however, engorgement generally occurs after you are home. Always remember, as uncomfortable as it may be, it doesn't last longer than a day or so.

For a few days after the immediate period of discomfort has passed, your breasts will be full but no longer painful. During this period you should not manipulate them nor express milk from them. Even running hot water from the shower over them may be stimulating to milk production. Sexual stimulation of the breasts should be avoided in this early postpartum period. Trying to empty the breasts by squeezing the nipples only makes the body think the baby is suckling and in response, it produces more milk. Milk production is a supply-and-demand system. If there is no demand—that is, no nursing or breast stimulation—the supply will dry up shortly.

WEIGHT LOSS

One hour after delivery the average woman weighs about 12 to 14 pounds less than before. This is due to the loss of the baby (about 7–8 or more pounds), the loss of the amniotic fluid and placenta (another 3–4 pounds), the beginning loss of the extra blood and body fluids that accumulate in pregnancy, and the beginning involution of the uterus. Several additional pounds are lost between the first postpartum hour and the twelfth day, much of it from the loss of increased body fluids. At the sixth postpartum week, if a woman weighs more than her prepregnant weight, the gain is of fat and, in those who nurse, breast tissue.

With a healthful diet and moderate exercise all pregnancy weight can be lost by the sixth postpartum week, although breast-feeding mothers may retain a bit of weight until they wean the baby. In reality, however, rates of postpartum weight loss are quite variable among women. In one study of almost 800 women, 22 percent had returned to prepregnancy weight or less by 6 weeks postpartum and 37 percent by 6 months postpartum. The average weight loss at 6 months in this study was 27 pounds, which meant that the average woman weighed just about 3 pounds more than she did at her first visit for pregnancy care. Another large study, the 1988 National Maternal and Infant Survey, showed that women who gained more weight in pregnancy retained more after delivery and that African-American women retained more weight than Caucasian women did. At 10 to 18 months following delivery, Caucasian women who kept within the recommended weight gain for pregnancy (see Chapter 10) were likely to retain less than 2 pounds above their prepregnancy weight while African-American women retained an average of 7.2 pounds.

CARE DURING THE EARLY POSTPARTUM PERIOD

A woman who has had a normal labor and delivery is able to get up and walk away from it. No special medical measures are needed. The internal organs resume their appropriate relationship immediately. The new mother can consume a hearty meal half an hour after delivery if she is not too excited to eat or still nursing or playing with the baby. In short, delivery is not a disease state.

If she has delivered in a hospital that provides family-centered care, or in a birth center or at home, the new mother's partner will have been present at the birth and may wish to stay at her side for the next few days. This often can be arranged for women who are in private hospital rooms. Birth centers facilitate family bonding and the family goes home within 6 to 24 hours to begin their new life together as a family or an expanded family in the privacy of their home. Of course, delivering at home allows this from the moment of birth.

It is certainly true that labor is hard work and the new mother has earned a period of rest. If she happens to have spent a good part of the night in labor and awake, she may need privacy for catching up on sleep. She may have had an episiotomy or a tear in the vagina or perineum and may be quite uncomfortable. On the other hand, the mother may wish to share her achievement with her other children or with her parents or her friends. There is no medical reason for restrictions on visitors, nor is there any need to isolate the newborn from relatives and friends as long as they do not have any contagious diseases.

New mothers can take showers and wash their hair. Bowel and bladder function return rapidly to normal, especially if the new mother is active. Women are clearly able to leave the hospital or birth center shortly after delivery, to return to their supportive and familiar home environment.

Women with medical complications will have to proceed more gradually. Other women will need time to recover from the effects of anesthesia used at the time of delivery. Those who have delivered by cesarean birth have to manage the discomforts of an abdominal incision, but there is no medical reason to restrict their activity.

If the baby is born prematurely, is of low birth weight, or has any other problems, he or she might need a longer hospitalization. Some hospitals provide facilities for mothers to remain in the hospital when the baby needs to stay beyond the usual time of discharge for the mother. In other institutions, the mother is discharged at the usual time, but is welcome, along with the father, to return at any time to see and care for the baby, depending on the newborn's condition. This policy might be a good thing to check in advance when you are choosing a hospital for birth, especially if you suspect that your baby might have a problem (such as when you have had a child born with a familial problem or one who was born prematurely).

Nutrition

Women who have delivered without general anesthesia can resume eating normally as soon as they are hungry. Women who had difficult cesarean births and those who had general anesthetics may have to deal with some degree of stomach upset, which usually manifests itself by nausea and an absence of appetite. Such women should simply refrain from eating until normal appetite returns. Usually, the physician or midwife will order a *progressive diet* after surgery—starting with clear fluids (water, apple juice, clear broth, Jell-O), sometimes progressing to full fluids, and within one or two days to a regular diet.

Postpartum Exercises

The woman who has had an uneventful delivery can resume exercise as soon as she feels motivated to do so. There are a number of books available that describe exercises to be practiced before and after delivery. Exercises of the abdominal wall and the pelvic muscles provide the most specific postpartum benefit. The abdominal muscles are inevitably stretched and spread apart by the growth of the fetus in the uterus. This is called *diastasis recti—*

a separation of the muscles. The abdominal wall suffers substantial loss of strength in the midline immediately after birth. The new mother can demonstrate this for herself by lying flat in bed and raising both feet off the bed with the legs stiffly extended. This will make the midline muscle separation readily visible.

Sit-ups are excellent exercises for the abdominal muscle. At first, you can do an isometric exercise consisting of simply tightening and holding in your tummy. As you exhale, tighten the abdominal muscles. Do these for a number of repetitions several times a day. As soon as you feel able (even as early as the first or second postpartum day, depending on how your labor went), you can do head lifts. Remember to always bend the knees to spare the lower back when doing any type of sit-up. Any other exercises can also be done if you enjoy them. There is no urgent medical reason either to do them or not to do them, except for the same benefits to health that exercise has at any other time of life. Regular exercise, at least three times per week, is preferable to sporadic exercise.

The American College of Obstetricians and Gynecologists recommends the pelvic tilt, described in Chapter 11, as a good exercise to continue after birth to counteract back pain and injury that can occur with the bending, lifting, and carrying that is involved in the care of an infant and toddler. Walking is always a good beginning exercise. Mother-infant exercise classes are available in many communities and some women feel ready to begin these as early as the third or fourth postpartum week.

Following a cesarean birth, exercises should be done to help with circulation. Wiggling the toes is a good starting exercise. Hospital nurses should help you with deep breathing, coughing, or huffing to clear your lungs and prevent pneumonia. You can use a towel to splint the incision to ease the discomfort of the cough. Walking is really important and you will be assisted in getting out of bed very shortly after the birth. This will help prevent the formation of a blood clot, always a risk following surgery. Abdominal exercise should be delayed until the incision has healed.

Don't exercise to exhaustion in the postpartum period. Stop well before you are really tired. Drink a lot while you exercise. For the first several weeks, if vaginal bleeding increases after exercise, chances are you've overdone it. This should stop with a little bed rest. If it doesn't, call your physician or midwife.

Excessive stretching, jerky or bouncing motions (*ballistic movements*), heavy weight lifting, and working on resistance machines may be a problem for the first 12 postpartum weeks. This is because the effects of the pregnancy hormone *relaxin* often persist for this length of time. Relaxin loosens the connective tissue in joints, making them more lax. This facilitates delivery through the pelvic bones, but makes other joints more subject to trauma.

If you are anemic, you may need more rest, and strenuous exercise should be postponed until your blood count has returned to normal.

You can gradually increase the intensity and length of your exercise periods and, by the end of the sixth postpartum week, can do most anything you did before the birth, if you feel strong enough. By the twelfth postpartum week, you can safely resume or begin weight training and vigorous stretching.

After a vaginal birth, the pelvic muscles are usually quite stretched. These muscles also can be exercised and conditioned to prevent future problems such as losing urine when you cough or laugh or jump. You need not set aside any special time to do this exercise—called the *Kegel exercise*, after Arnold Kegel, the physician who developed it. You can try the Kegel exercise as soon as a few hours after birth. Then, do it whenever you remember—it can't be overdone. Feeding the baby is a good time to remember to exercise the pelvic muscles as babies eat often. Just tighten and pull up the muscles of the vagina and pelvic floor. It's the same motion you do when you are trying to hold in your urine—you can practice when you are urinating just to see how it feels to contract these muscles. When you are not urinating, try to hold the muscle contracted for increasingly longer periods. You may only be able to hold the contraction for a few seconds at first; after some time exercising you should be able to hold it much longer. Repeat for at least ten repetitions each time.

Afterpains

During the first few days of the postpartum period most multiparas and some primiparas complain of *afterpains*. These usually begin soon after delivery but seldom last more than 3 days. They consist of painful contractions of the uterus, recurring irregularly and lasting about a minute. They are stronger in a woman who has had a number of births as the decreasing uterine muscle tone seen in each pregnancy causes the uterine muscle to relax and then contract. In a woman having a first baby, the muscle simply stays contracted, causing less cramping. Afterpains are often initiated by the act of sucking, as noted earlier; whenever the baby is put to the breast, the uterus reacts by contracting. Such contractions may cause a spurt of lochia or the passage of a small clot.

For most women no treatment is required for afterpains. Remember to urinate frequently as keeping an empty bladder is crucial in helping the uterus work more efficiently and therefore less painfully. Lying on your abdomen may help. Placing a pillow under the lower part of the abdomen (near the vulva) puts even more pressure on the uterus, helping it stay contracted. When you first lie on your stomach, you may have an increase in pain for a few minutes, before the pain goes away.

If the pains are really uncomfortable, analgesia can be used. Usually, acetaminophen (Tylenol, for example) or a nonsteroidal anti-inflammatory drug (NSAID) like ibuprofen (Advil or Motrin, for example) will be enough. NSAIDs also block the production of prostaglandin. *Prostaglandins* are a family of chemicals made from fatty acids that are involved in many aspects of reproduction—including the induction of uterine contractions. Occasionally, a woman may need a prescription for codeine (such as Tylenol 3, which is Tylenol with 30 mg of codeine). If the pain increases during nursing, you can try to time the medication dose to be about a half hour before feeding so the peak effect will be during nursing. These medications are not considered dangerous for the baby.

Severe, persistent cramps can be a sign of infection, so inform your physician or midwife if these afterpains don't go away within a few days or seem unusually strong or if you have pain that is constant, rather than intermittent.

The "Blues"

Emotional changes after delivery can be quite disturbing. Despite the sense that birth "should" make a woman happy, many women experience postpartum blues. Such women have mood swings that are sometimes intense, feelings of ambivalence toward motherhood, mild depression, and bouts of tearfulness, with no apparent reason. Science to date has not explained what causes the blues. We do not even know how prevalent this phenomenon is, but know that it is quite common. Possible explanations vary and include hormonal changes, negative experiences of labor and delivery, and the isolation often associated with having a newborn. For sure, lack of sleep is involved.

Despite the fact that the blues can be expected and are considered normal, they can become severe. New mothers should not feel guilty for feeling down; it isn't something they can control. Most times these feelings pass and cause no problems, but if they persist beyond the first postpartum week or feel debilitating, or if you have a history of depression or previous postpartum depression, you should discuss this with your physician or midwife. You may benefit from psychological counseling or other treatments.

Both hormone therapy (the estrogen skin patch, for example) and antidepressant therapy (such as Prozac—fluoxetine) have been used to treat serious postpartum depression. Estrogen is not advised in nursing women as its use may adversely affect milk supply, especially in the first several months of lactation. Prozac has not been shown to have adverse effects on the newborn or milk supply, but reports are scarce. Medications should be taken only if you are under the care of a qualified health care professional who can prescribe them and follow your responses. For mild depression, exercise, getting out, and getting together with other adults can be of help.

Occasionally, symptoms similar to depression, such as overwhelming fatigue, can be caused by a condition known as *postpartum thyroiditis*—inflammation of the thyroid gland. If depression is prolonged, especially with severe and sudden fatigue occurring without physical exertion, and if the woman experiences unusual weight loss, followed later by weight gain, tests for thyroid function should be performed. For this reason alone, severe or prolonged postpartum depression should never be ignored.

Bathing and Shampooing

There is no reason for a new mother not to take a shower or shampoo her hair as soon as she feels steady on her feet. A woman can take a bath as well, although in the first weeks it is usually a good idea to tub bathe only when someone is home who can help you in and out of the tub should you find that you need assistance. Women who have had cesarean births may have an abdominal dressing that should be protected from getting wet, but if the dressing has been removed or none has been put on, there is no reason not to shower.

Care of the Vulva/Perineum

The *vulva* is the term used to describe the area of skin surrounding the entrance to the vagina. It includes the lips of the vagina—the outer *labia majora* (Latin: larger lips), which are covered by hair-bearing skin, and the inner *labia minora* (Latin: smaller lips), covered by hairless skin. Both have sweat glands. It also includes the pubic hair. The perineum is the relatively hairless skin and the muscles beneath it found between the vagina and the anus. Some degree of pain is expected from the stretching, cutting, or tearing that occurred during birth, or from pressure and pulling caused by stitches if any were used to repair a cut or tear.

Immediately after delivery, whether or not you had an episiotomy or a tear, an ice pack to the perineum both numbs the area and prevents or reduces swelling. Ice packs can be used for about twenty minutes intermittently during the first 24 hours, although if there has not been a cut or tear, they probably aren't needed past the immediate postpartum hour. Commercially prepared ice packs may be available where you deliver, or you can simply put ice into a plastic bag. An examining glove filled with crushed ice works especially well, if available, as the different fingers can be used to cover the vulva, the labia, and the perineum. Always wrap a plastic ice pack with a cloth or towel before applying it to sensitive skin or mucous membranes (like the vagina).

After the first 24 hours, warm soaks are better to reduce pain and swelling. Hospitals usually have portable sitz baths available for women to soak in. Soaking two to three times a day for as little as 10 minutes can bring much relief. Walking also helps minimize discomfort by reducing the swelling of the area and stimulating circulation to aid in healing.

Other remedies include witch hazel compresses and a variety of numbing medications available in the hospital. Called *topical anesthetics*, these include Americaine, available as a spray or ointment, and Nupercainal anesthetic ointment. Wash hands before applying the ointments. Witch hazel compresses—such as Tucks—can be purchased or made at home by soaking small gauze pads in witch hazel. Wring them out gently before placing them on your perineal area. You can buy witch hazel very inexpensively before birth. Numbing medications can be ordered for you in the hospital or purchased over-the-counter in most drug stores.

Perineal exercises can also aid in healing. If you are uncomfortable sitting, you can do the Kegel exercise before you sit down, keeping the muscles contracted until you have sat. Some women find it easier to simply put extra pressure on one buttock, sitting slightly to one side, thus relieving direct perineal pressure.

After delivery, the vulva requires only simple washing, most easily done in the shower. Wipe gently from front to back after urination. If you have stitches, you may prefer to gently pat yourself dry, rather than wiping. Sometimes women who've had stitches find it more comfortable to urinate standing up in the shower as this keeps the urine from running over the stitches. After a bowel movement the area can be washed off with a soapy washcloth and patted dry with a towel. Antiseptic washes are unnecessary. The care is the same whether or not there has been an episiotomy or repair of a perineal tear.

If you have unusual pain in these parts of your body, you should bring it to the attention of the hospital nurses or your physician or midwife. While you are in the hospital, a nurse or physician or midwife may ask you each day to turn to your side so she or he can check your perineum, especially if you have had stitches. Your bleeding can be assessed this way too.

If you have a mirror, or your nurse or midwife or physician has one, use it to look at your perineum. Even with an episiotomy or laceration and stitches, you will be surprised how quickly it looks normal. Swelling resolves rapidly. Since stitches are rarely put into the skin, but rather into the layer just under the skin, you barely will be able to see the scar where they were placed, even as early as the first or second postpartum day.

The Abdomen

The skin and the muscles of the abdominal wall are considerably stretched by pregnancy. The larger the uterus and its contents—for example, with twins, excessive amniotic fluid, or a very big baby—the greater the likelihood of permanent changes in the skin and the muscles. However, both of these have a built-in tendency to return to the condition they were in prior to the pregnancy. As stated previously, the muscles usually require exercise, and that is particularly true when they have been severely stretched. The skin, being more elastic, has a tendency to snap back by itself sooner or later, although the stretch marks of pregnancy may never vanish. Girdles and corsets fortunately are entirely out of fashion for postpartum wear. They functioned only as crutches and perpetuated the muscle weakness, which is much more effectively dealt with by a conscientious exercise program.

The Bladder

Urinary retention frequently occurred in the days when forceps deliveries were common and were done under spinal or general anesthesia. The new mother was unable to urinate, and her bladder became severely stretched. It was in that era that hospitals instituted the routine, which many still follow, of measuring the amount of urine passed in the first one or two urinations immediately following childbirth, and keeping track of the output in the first 24 to 48 hours postpartum to ensure proper bladder function. However, with the switch to minimal and local anesthesia and away from forceps deliveries, urinary retention as a problem following normal deliveries is an unusual event.

Among women who have had surgical deliveries or difficulty in vaginal birth, however, measures to protect against urinary retention are still necessary. A small tube (*catheter*) is placed in the bladder to drain urine continuously until the woman has fully recovered from anesthesia or from the effects of a difficult delivery. After 18 to 24 hours, the catheter comes out and the woman ordinarily has no problems.

A catheter might be used when a woman is unexpectedly unable to urinate after delivery for some other reason. Usually, the midwife, physician, or nurses will first make every effort to help a woman urinate on her own. Privacy, walking to the bathroom if possible, drinking, hearing running water or putting one's hands in water, and pressing down on the area just above the pubic bone where the urinary bladder is located can help with urination. If these fail, a woman may be *straight cathed*. This means a catheter is placed just to let the urine pass and then is removed. In the rare event that the woman still cannot urinate on her own, however, an indwelling catheter may be needed. This may be kept in place for as long as 48 to 72 hours to allow the bladder wall to recover from the stretching it has undergone. Then, when the catheter is removed and the bladder again begins to fill, the woman experiences the normal sensations associated with the urge to urinate, and will be able to do so without difficulty.

The presence of a foreign body such as a catheter in the urethra and the bladder sets the stage for a urinary tract infection. For this reason some physicians or midwives will administer antibiotics preventively. Drinking lots of water and wiping from front to back are also good preventive measures against a urinary tract infection. In any case, after a birth, if you experience *dysuria* (painful urination), especially internally in the bladder region at the end of urinating; *urinary urgency* (a very strong urge to go); *frequency* (going to the bathroom much more often than usual), especially if you actually urinate very little, or notice blood in the urine, you should notify your physician or midwife.

Bowels

Early ambulation, minimal trauma, and minimal anesthesia have virtually eliminated the severe postpartum constipation of decades back. The fact that women can rapidly return to normal exercise and eating habits allows them to return to ordinary toilet habits. This is true even when a woman has had a cesarean delivery. Women with abdominal incisions and episiotomies find it difficult to believe that they can move their bowels without aggravating pain in the incisions, but they really can.

Because of manipulation of internal organs during any abdominal surgery, women who have had cesarean births may experience fairly intense gas pains. These usually occur during the first 3 days after delivery. Once your intestines start working again, the pains will ease. Walking, changing positions frequently, and rocking in a chair will help to get rid of any trapped gas and reduce the pain.

As with urinating, the hospital staff will ask you whether you have had a bowel movement but no longer routinely provide milk of magnesia or another laxative to all postpartum women. Women often go several days after birth without having a bowel movement. This makes logical sense when you consider that the digestive system slows down during labor, that most women eat little if any solid foods in labor, and that the bowel is most likely emptied during pushing. Yet even after going several days without a bowel movement, most women will be able to have one easily and spontaneously once the intestinal tract returns to its normal level of activity.

Women who have had a long history of constipation, of course, may need some help postpartum, but it is hardly an emergency. The help may consist of milk of magnesia or other laxative or a small enema or suppository. Stool softeners can be taken, but medications are probably less useful than stimulating bowel activity by resuming normal activity and normal eating habits. Plenty of fluids, fresh fruits and vegetables, and whole grains are the best laxatives available. Prunes or prune juice and bran cereal work wonders! Ask your partner or another visitor to bring some to the hospital or your home.

Hemorrhoids often increase in size in the postpartum period and may be quite uncomfortable, making the idea of a bowel movement somewhat worrisome. These hemorrhoids will shrink with time, but until they do, witch hazel compresses or various preparations available over-the-counter provide relief. Ice packs numb the area and reduce swelling, although some women prefer warm compresses or soaks after the first 24 to 48 postpartum hours. Your physician or midwife can order Anusol suppositories or a stool softener, if necessary.

The most effective remedy for painful hemorrhoids is to gently replace them into the rectum, using a finger. The hospital or birth center can give you a rubber glove or a covering for one finger to use and you can put some lubricant like K-Y jelly on your finger to ease the insertion, although neither is necessary. Squeeze your rectal sphincter muscle tight afterward to help the hemorrhoids stay inside. This can be done after each bowel movement. Remember to wash your hands thoroughly after touching your rectum.

If you find yourself uncomfortable from postpartum constipation or haven't had a bowel movement within about a week, do call your physician or midwife.

Sleep Deprivation

Probably the most consistent complaint heard in the postpartum period is, "I'm tired." Probably one of the most consistent questions new parents get asked is, "Is your baby sleeping through the night yet?"

Sleep deprivation is a very real situation in the first weeks, and often months, after a baby is born. Babies simply need to eat more frequently than anyone else does and parents have to feed them. Remember—all babies eventually will be able to sleep through the night although this reminder may feel hardly comforting at 4 A.M.

Remember, also, that newborns spend a lot of time sleeping. New mothers should try to take naps when the baby is napping—even if the nap is brief. This may mean that certain tasks remain undone. The postpartum period may not be the time to plan gourmet meals or have a spotless house or apartment, unless you can afford to hire other people to do these jobs.

Whether or not you can afford household helpers, don't be afraid to ask friends and relatives for assistance. Most new mothers get a lot of visitors in the early weeks—everybody wants to see and cuddle the new baby. If someone calls to arrange a visit, don't be shy about saying, "Could you please pick up some milk and eggs (or prune juice and bran cereal) on your way over," or whatever else you need. Nobody expects a new parent to prepare an elaborate meal for them. Again, you can ask guests to bring something, order out, or invite them between meal times.

If one parent—in our society usually the mother—undertakes the bulk of the responsibility for child care, the second parent can provide after-work relief or help with the nighttime feedings. If the baby is bottle-fed, the father or partner can do the nighttime feeds, or share them. If the baby is nursing, the father or partner can get the baby from the crib and bring it to the mother. Some families find that having the baby sleep in a bassinet or cradle in their bedroom or even in bed with them reduces the problem of sleep deprivation. This is a personal decision that each family makes for itself. Friends, relatives, and even professionals may have strong feelings about the *family bed* but it is really a private matter.

Family Adjustment

A new baby has a very strong presence in a household. If it is a couple's first baby, their roles are changed dramatically by the birth. Their relationship is affected, forever. If it is a second baby, the older child's relationship to the family is changed as well. While these changes can bring joy and fulfillment, and ultimately enrich relationships, they can also bring incredible stress.

The entry of a new person into established relationships can cause major upheaval. This stress may begin during the pregnancy as the woman begins to focus on her bodily changes and the new life growing within her. Identities change. Fathers or partners may feel neglected as a woman moves into motherhood. Differences may emerge in child rearing philosophies. Some degree of conflict is almost inevitable.

As with most problems in life, open communication is the best way to resolve these conflicts. Ideally, discussions about child rearing should begin in advance of pregnancy and continue during pregnancy. After birth, both members of the couple will undoubtedly feel interruption in their old routines and a lack of enough time to take care of their own needs, let alone each other's. But it is crucial that some time be set aside for you to take care of each other—to express affection not just toward the baby but toward one another, to listen to each other, to provide support and comfort, not criticism. Each partner will have to make compromises as you will never agree on every decision that will need to be made. Couples should spend some time alone together whether this means asking a friend or family member to watch the baby or hiring a baby-sitter. It may be difficult to leave a newborn, but the time you spend together need not be long—an hour can work wonders. Some couples find this is not possible in the first few weeks, even months, but it should happen eventually.

The transition to family life may be eased somewhat if both members of the couple are involved in the pregnancy and birth and in making preparations for the newborn. If there is an older sibling, she or he should be involved also. Discussion of having a sibling at the birth is provided in Chapters 18 and 19, but even if you choose not to have your first child or other children present for the birth, they can visit soon after. During the pregnancy, they can come to some prenatal visits, help choose furniture, clothes, or toys for the baby, and afterward assist with care of the baby. With supervision, older children can hold the baby and be taught to change the diaper. Younger children can assist with tasks, even if it makes you do them less efficiently.

Sexuality

Sex is a major concern of postpartum couples. With the assumption of new roles, the old image of the couple as a sexual dyad changes. Women may experience perineal discomfort, postpartum blues, and, if nursing, leaking breasts. Weeks or months may elapse before a woman returns to her usual weight. She may have stretch marks on her abdomen or breasts. The hormonal changes of the postpartum period, especially in lactating women, may cause vaginal dryness. Both parents may have lost a day or more of sleep during labor and may be awakened several times each night by the crying baby. All these conspire against sexual feelings. Yet, like other forms of communication, the expression of physical love is important to most relationships.

Like other postpartum adjustments, sexual changes require time and patience. A couple's sexual relationship may never be exactly the same as it was before the baby was born, but certainly it can be equally satisfying.

Resumption of Intercourse

In the past, doctors advised women to wait 6 weeks before resuming intercourse. Today, most midwives and physicians suggest a more flexible approach—that a woman's body be her guide to when she is ready to resume intercourse. As long as there is no pain and bright red bleeding has stopped, intercourse is not dangerous. Of course, for the bright red bleeding to stop and for the vaginal and perineal areas to be touchable without pain may take several days to several weeks.

Certainly, the need to postpone intercourse does not preclude other ways of lovemaking. Touching, kissing, and caressing are alternate ways to show love and affection. Of course, having a new baby in the house means that a couple's relationship to sexuality will change. In the early days and weeks, there are many distractions to resuming a sexual relationship. Parents may be distracted by their need to listen for the baby to cry. Many new parents tell stories of how they finally fall into each other's arms after a long day, only to be interrupted by the cry that insists, "Feed me now!" Possibly most distracting of all is the fatigue that accompanies new parenthood. Too many new parents are just too tired to do anything but fall asleep the moment they lie down. Try to remember that this will pass and there is sex after baby. It will take time, but sexuality will return and intercourse will be comfortable and satisfying.

Contraception

Since it is impossible to predict exactly when the first postpartum menstruation will occur, and since ovulation occurs *before* menstruation, fertility can return without warning. Even in women experienced in using natural methods of family planning, the postpartum changes may be difficult to interpret. Therefore, most providers recommend that all heterosexual women use contraception as soon as they resume intercourse if they do not wish to become pregnant right after a birth.

Lactation has been found to be an effective contraception for approximately the first 6 postpartum months or until you get your first menstrual period, assuming you breast-feed exclusively. This means giving no formula feedings, no solids, not even supplementing with water. The less the newborn relies exclusively on breast milk, the less effective nursing is as a method of birth control. Since the norm in the United States is to supplement in some way, lactation generally is not considered a good contraceptive for American women. If you know that you are breast-feeding exclusively, however, you will be reasonably well protected against pregnancy for up to 6 months. After 6 months have passed or after your periods resume, even women who are totally breast-feeding should use another method to be protected against pregnancy.

Many methods of birth control are acceptable to use in the early postpartum period. Diaphragms and cervical caps are not to be used before the sixth postpartum week as toxic shock syndrome may be associated with these methods and the risk of acquiring this serious disease is increased in the postpartum period. Adding risk to risk is not advisable. This is true of the vaginal sponge as well. This method is currently off the market, but may someday make a comeback as its removal was voluntary on the part of the company that produced it and not due to adverse health effects. If a couple wishes to use a barrier method, the male or female condom is appropriate. These methods also have the advantage of protecting against sexually transmitted diseases, should a couple require such protection.

Some chemical methods of birth control are acceptable to use postpartum, although acceptability differs between nursing and non-nursing women. For nursing women, oral contraceptives that use both estrogen and a progestin (called *combined pills*) or the newer *vaginal ring* or *contraceptive patch* are not advised in the first 3 postpartum months. This is

because estrogen reduces the milk supply. Once lactation is fully established, which usually takes about 3 months, combination pills do not
have a detrimental effect on milk supply. While the hormones in the
pills do reach the baby through the breast milk, they are not considered
to have adverse effects. In women who choose not to nurse, combined
oral contraceptives are acceptable to use in the postpartum period. Because they are associated with a slightly increased risk of blood clots,
which is also a postpartum risk, some providers prefer not to prescribe
them until after the woman has experienced her first postpartum period.
In the meantime, condoms can be used.

Progesterone-only contraceptives are appropriate for both nursing
and non-nursing women. The synthetic progesterone-like hormones
(called *progestins*) in the mini-pill, shot (Depo-Provera), or the implant
(Norplant) are not considered to adversely affect either the milk supply
or the developing newborn. While the progestin in these methods does
reach the baby through breast milk, no effect on infant growth has been
demonstrated over time and no other side effects have been documented in newborns whose mothers use these methods. Most practitioners advise starting these methods after the first postpartum period or
at least after the sixth postpartum week, but others see no detriment in
prescribing them in the immediate postpartum period for women who
are not breast-feeding. If they are not to be prescribed in the immediate
postpartum period, a condom can be used until they are started.

The intrauterine device (IUD) can be inserted at the 6-week postpartum checkup. Either the Mirena, which secretes a synthetic form of
progesterone called levonorgestrel, or the copper-containing IUD (the
Copper T 380A or ParaGard) is acceptable. The copper-containing
IUD can be kept in place for 10 years and the Mirena 5 years. Chapter
27 gives more details on each of these methods, including situations or
medical conditions that would make each one inadvisable.

COMPLICATIONS AFTER DELIVERY

The overwhelming majority of women experience normal pregnancies
and births. They feel just fine during the postpartum period and return
to normal activities very soon. A small minority, however, will have a
postpartum problem or complication.

Postpartum Hemorrhage

When the placenta separates from the uterine wall, open blood vessels remain. Severe hemorrhage can occur in this area. In addition, in the early postpartum period, bleeding can come from tears in the uterus, cervix, vagina, and perineum. The main reason that women are kept in recovery rooms for periods of time following childbirth, even when it appears to be completely uneventful, is to watch carefully for such hemorrhage. This is the reason to remain in the birth center for at least 6 hours after birth and why practitioners who attend home births stay for several hours after the birth.

Many postpartum hemorrhages can be anticipated and either prevented or prepared for so that emergency equipment and medications are on hand. Women with known risks for postpartum hemorrhage should have their babies in a hospital, not at a birth center or at home. Risks include a previous postpartum hemorrhage, a placental problem such as placenta previa or abruptio placentae (see Chapter 12), and an overly enlarged uterus such as occurs with multiple gestation or polyhydramnios (see Chapter 12). Induction or stimulation of labor with oxytocic agents also makes hemorrhage more likely, and should therefore only be used in the hospital setting.

In the event of a totally unexpected postpartum hemorrhage, which occurs rarely, the midwife or physician in the birth center or at home is able to institute emergency measures to control the bleeding until the woman can be transported to the hospital. In a midwife-assisted delivery, regardless of the place of birth, the midwife is well prepared to institute these emergency measures until the physician arrives.

When hemorrhage occurs, the first step is to put a hand on the abdominal wall to be certain that the uterus is contracting adequately. If it is not, the next step is to try vigorous massage to see if this helps the uterus contract. It often does. It may involve what is called *bimanual compression*—with one hand inside the vagina, up against the uterus, and the other on the abdomen. The uterus is compressed firmly between these two hands. Although very uncomfortable, this can be a lifesaving procedure.

If massage and bimanual compression do not stop bleeding, the next step is to administer medications. An oxytocic agent (the natural oxytocin or the synthetic Pitocin or Syntocinon) is commonly used. Oxytocics are added to intravenous fluids or given as an injection. The ergot preparation, Methergine, is another medication that causes uterine contractions. Methergine results in sustained contractions, rather than intermittent ones, and is therefore used only after delivery. It is usually given as an injection. Methergine should not be given in a woman with high blood pressure, so a nurse or birth assistant will most likely take your pressure before this medication is used. A newer method to control postpartum bleeding is administration of prostaglandin deep into the muscle. *Prostaglandins* are chemicals made in the body that are involved in contraction of the uterine muscle. Prostaglandin (Prostin) can be injected directly into the uterine muscle, either through the abdominal wall or the vagina. It should not be used in women with high blood pressure or symptomatic asthma. Diarrhea may result.

If medications produce uterine contraction and thereby stop the bleeding, the problem is under control. If good uterine contractions occur and the woman nevertheless continues to bleed, the next step is a careful examination of the reproductive tract. The examiner starts with the perineum and lower vagina and proceeds to the upper portions of the vagina and cervix. If necessary, some light sedation can be helpful in carrying out this examination, as it can otherwise be quite uncomfortable. Most women are able to tolerate it, however. The cervix is brought down into view with special instruments and inspected throughout its entire circumference to ascertain whether it is the source of the continued bleeding. If the structures so far examined are not actively bleeding, and the blood is coming from the uterus, the examiner puts a hand—covered by a long, sterile glove—into the uterus and palpates to determine whether there is a tear in the uterine wall or, more likely, a fragment of retained placenta. Such a placental remnant can prevent the uterine muscle from closing down on the blood vessels and halting the bleeding.

If tears are found to be bleeding, steps are taken immediately to sew them closed. If, however, there are no identifiable sources of the bleeding and the uterus continues to relax and bleed, the very bleeding process itself can begin to interfere with the ability of the body to form clots. This condition is generally referred to as *disseminated intravascular coagulation* (DIC), which describes the fact that fibrinogen, platelets, and other factors required for adequate clotting are depleted in the course of the hemorrhage and the woman loses the ability to clot her blood. Treatment consists of administration of the clotting factors and continued other efforts to stop the bleeding.

If uterine hemorrhage continues, the next move is abdominal surgery. If the woman wants the surgeon to preserve her ability to have additional children, the initial step is to tie off the major arteries supplying the uterus in order to cut down the force and rate of blood flow. This form of *blood vessel ligation* occasionally will allow clotting to take place. Although it does reduce the blood supply to the uterus, this is not to a point that the uterus will fail to function normally thereafter. Should tying off the blood supply not result in stanching the hemorrhage, the final recourse is removal of the uterus. The decision to carry out these procedures requires experience, good judgment, and rapid decision making.

A postpartum hemorrhage also can occur later in the postpartum period, when the woman is at home. This may be due to *subinvolution*—a condition in which the uterus stops contracting before it has reached its nonpregnant state. This may be the result of an infection (see the next section). Another reason for a late postpartum hemorrhage is retained placental fragments. Although all physicians and midwives inspect the placenta after birth, a minute fragment might have been left in the uterus—one that even the most experienced practitioner can fail to appreciate through placental inspection. In this case, when the contracting uterus reaches the site of the placental fragment, it cannot close down over that area, stops contracting, and bleeding ensues.

At any time in the postpartum weeks, a woman should call her practitioner whenever her bleeding seems unusually heavy—more than a normal menstrual period—or increases or becomes redder instead of decreasing and becoming paler. Call your physician or midwife also if you pass large clots or experience signs of uterine infection: foul smelling lochia, fever and chills, or severe abdominal pains.

If you are experiencing a late postpartum hemorrhage, your physician or midwife may institute a number of therapeutic measures. He or she may prescribe antibiotics to treat the infection. If the uterus is subinvoluted, you will be given a Methergine series—Methergine pills to be taken by mouth over 3 days, three times a day. If there is any question about a retained placental fragment, you will be sent for a uterine sonogram to look for such a fragment. A physician will be consulted if your care has been with a midwife. In the recent past, this was usually treated with *dilatation and curettage* (D & C)—a procedure that opened the cervix (*dilatation*) and scraped the lining of the uterus with a sharp instrument or suction tube (*curettage*). As this may traumatize the uterus and even cause more bleeding, it is reserved today for those instances in which bleeding persists or recurs after treatment with medications.

Puerperal Infection

This term refers to conditions caused by the introduction of harmful bacteria into the postpartum uterus. The area where the placenta was attached offers rich nourishment for any bacteria that may intrude. These bacteria ordinarily come from two sources. One is the outside world, introduced by doctors, midwives, nurses, and anyone else who comes into intimate contact with the woman's reproductive tract either during labor or in the immediate postpartum period. The other is the woman's own bacteria, which take advantage of any reduction in her normal resistance to her own germs. Cesarean birth, for example, establishes a wound in the uterine wall; difficult delivery may result in maternal tissue damage and retention of fragments of placenta or membranes in the uterus. Puerperal infection is thus most common after cesarean birth, and when there has been hemorrhage. It is also more common after prolonged labor, especially if the membranes had been ruptured for a long time and especially if a woman has had many vaginal examinations after her membranes ruptured.

Puerperal infection makes itself known by a general sensation of fatigue, headache, chills, and elevation of temperature. We consider it to be present whenever the woman's temperature taken orally reaches 38° centigrade or 100.4° Fahrenheit on 2 or more days in the first 10 postpartum days after the first 24 postpartum hours. The fever can be much higher than this.

Care for puerperal infection begins with a physical examination to search for sources of the infection. Added to this is a study of the white blood cell count, which normally is below 12,000 white blood cells for every cubic centimeter of blood. If it goes above that—even as high as 35,000—it confirms the diagnosis of infection, although your care provider still may not know where the infection is located. Bacteriological cultures are obtained from the uterine cavity, the bladder, and the bloodstream in an effort to grow and thus identify the causative bacteria. This requires that the woman provide a urine specimen and that she have a sterile pelvic examination, with a small cotton swab on an applicator placed gently into the cervix and removed rapidly. She will also have several tubes of blood drawn, usually from her arm.

If the physical examination confirms the diagnosis of puerperal infection, a combination of several broad-spectrum antibiotics will be given, even before the results of the cultures are available. Rapid developments in the field are constantly producing safer and more effective antibiotics. Whatever drugs are used, they are given intravenously, unless the infection is very mild.

With proper treatment, puerperal infection should clear up within a few days. Following treatment, a woman can go home after she has been without a fever for 24 hours. She may be prescribed antibiotics to take orally for a short period of time after discharge, depending on the recommendation of her physician or midwife.

If puerperal infection does not resolve within a few days, a suspicion arises that the infection is complicated. Complications might include areas of pus formation in the broad ligament—which extends outward from the uterus—or the formation of abscesses in the pelvis. There also might be inflammation of blood vessels and clot formation in the pelvic region—a *pelvic thrombophlebitis* (see the next section). Complications are most likely to occur following cesarean birth.

Ongoing fever after antibiotic treatment requires another abdominal and pelvic examination. A sonogram may show the areas of pus or abscess, but *computed tomography* (a C-T scan) is usually more useful and can also reveal a thrombophlebitis. These rarely occurring complications need to be treated promptly as pus can cause the infection to spread to the abdominal cavity, causing a serious condition called *peritonitis*, or to the bloodstream, causing a generalized infection. A pelvic abscess may require surgical drainage. A thrombophlebitis can lead to a blood clot in the lungs. With appropriate treatment, these consequences are avoidable.

An uncomplicated puerperal infection—as the vast majority are—does not have any consequences for a woman's overall health or for her future childbearing, nor is it likely to repeat itself in the future.

Several components of health care have contributed to a large reduction in the number of puerperal infections caused by the woman's own bacteria. One is the careful avoidance of tissue injury at the time of delivery. Another is good prenatal care, starting early in pregnancy, since the maintenance of good nutrition improves the immune system's ability to fight disease.

Even more spectacular has been the reduction of infection from bacteria transmitted to the woman by those giving her care. Birth attendants now wear readily disposable caps, masks, shoe covers, suits, and sterile gowns when they enter a delivery room. Antibacterial preparations are used to wash off the mother's external genitalia prior to birth whenever any operative maneuver is considered. The lower genital tract is sturdily resistant to infection from its own bacteria, but it must be protected against infection with organisms foreign to the mother.

When women deliver normally in a labor room, a birth center, or at home, the likelihood of infection is exceedingly low and therefore the precautions need not be quite so strictly enforced as for more complicated deliveries in the delivery room.

Thrombophlebitis

Thrombophlebitis—an inflammation of the veins with possible formation of a blood clot—may occur as a complication of puerperal infection or without an infection. With infection, the thrombophlebitis usually occurs in the pelvic area, and may be diagnosed with the use of *computed tomography* (C-T scans). It might be suspected when a pelvic infection does not resolve after appropriate antibiotic therapy. Blood thinners (*anticoagulants*), such as heparin, then become necessary. These are generally given intravenously. Without infection, thrombophlebitis is most often seen in the legs, although it is increasingly rare.

Without infection, symptoms of thrombophlebitis include fever, leg pain, warmth, tenderness, and redness where the vein is inflamed, swelling of the ankle, leg, and thigh, and possibly tenderness along an entire vessel. A hardness may be felt in the vein, sometimes called a *cord*.

Thrombophlebitis may be superficial or deep. If it is superficial, it can be treated with bed rest, elevation of the leg, hot packs, elastic stockings, and pain medication as needed. If it is deep, antibiotics and anticoagulants may be used. Anticoagulants are given intravenously, and antibiotics may be given this way as well. The leg should not be massaged as this could send a clot into the circulation, possibly to the lungs. Difficulty breathing, shortness of breath, sharp chest pain, and apprehensiveness are symptoms of a *pulmonary embolism*—a blood clot in the lungs. A rare complication of thrombophlebitis, this is a life-threatening condition and must be treated immediately.

Engorgement/Inflamed Breasts/Mastitis

There are three different and distinct conditions that can produce painful changes in the breasts. In the first and most common of these, the lacteal ducts fill with milk and then, for whatever reason, do not empty, and the breasts become *engorged*. There is no sign of infection, and there are no bacteria and few white blood cells present in the milk if it were to be looked at under a microscope or sent for culture. The woman feels diffuse discomfort in both breasts, with no signs of inflammation in any particular area. If she receives local treatment, as described below, the condition does not last long and has no further complications.

The second condition is *noninfectious inflammation* of the breast. One or two areas in one breast are tender. The skin is reddened over them. Chills do not occur and fever is not high. Under the microscope, the milk of these women shows a moderate increase in the number of white blood cells, but few bacteria.

Both engorgement and inflammation should be promptly treated with supportive care. Inflammation may require antibiotics if it doesn't clear up within a day. The breasts should be emptied often by nursing or pumping or both. Warm soaks can be applied to the painful area of the breast and the hot water in the shower can be run over the breasts. During nursing, massage of the painful area will help empty the ducts around it. Engorgement generally resolves within a day, but the symptoms of noninfectious inflammation are likely to last seven or eight days and 50 percent of untreated women develop *frank infectious mastitis.*

The third condition is infectious mastitis, the development of localized inflammation of the breasts. Mastitis seldom occurs prior to delivery. In the postpartum period, it is seen almost entirely among nursing women. It rarely occurs until the third or fourth week after delivery and may occur as late as when the baby is several months old.

Ordinarily, mastitis is due to *Staphylococcus aureus* bacteria, which are found in the nose and throat and on the skin of apparently healthy people. The *Staphylococcus* is probably transmitted to the mother from the baby, through some crack or abrasion in the nipple, even one that may be so small as not to be noticeable.

Typically, the nursing woman with infectious mastitis develops sudden and unexplained fatigue, malaise, headache, and aching of the muscles and joints, sometimes with chills and almost always with an elevation of temperature that may go as high as 40° centigrade or 104° Fahrenheit. She may confuse this with the flu, but there is an obvious local tenderness in one breast. Inflammation commonly occurs in the outer and lower areas of the breast. On examination, this tender area is found firm and the skin overlying it is red and hot. If the skin appears blue tinged, it may mean there is an underlying abscess filled with pus.

The baby is not sick with the bacteria but may have patches of skin infection, also due to the same organism. In hospitals, nursery personnel are required to wash their hands frequently to minimize the transfer of these organisms from one baby to another. At home, where public bacteria do not intrude, the family need not follow this rigid cleanliness discipline.

In cases of infectious mastitis, the milk contains many *inflammatory cells* (white blood cells) and large numbers of bacteria. Ideally, sending a sample of milk to the laboratory for culture from women with infectious mastitis would provide absolute proof of the bacteriologic diagnosis. The clinical diagnosis, however, is usually quite unmistakable even without laboratory findings.

With therapy, mastitis clears up in 2 to 3 days. The treatment includes frequent nursing to empty the breasts, applications of heat, breast massage, and antibiotics that are effective against *Staphylococcus*. At present, the drug of choice is dicloxacillin. Small doses of antibiotic will get into the milk, but these will not do anything much more than change the odor of the baby's bowel movements.

Untreated, mastitis continues for long periods of time. In the breasts, as elsewhere, infections with *Staphylococcus* tend to produce abscesses, which may appear as early as a few days after the onset of the mastitis. For this reason, antibiotic therapy should begin early. If it doesn't, and an abscess forms, surgical draining of the abscess may become necessary. The process then is prolonged considerably and recurrences are not at all uncommon. This can make breast-feeding very difficult. The likelihood of infectious mastitis can be reduced by following simple measures discussed in the next chapter.

Hematoma

A *hematoma* is a collection of blood that causes tissue swelling. Following a delivery, a hematoma can develop in the vulva, vagina, rectum, or even the *broad ligament*—the ligament that surrounds the uterus. Occasionally, the bleeding from a hematoma will extend into deeper tissues.

A hematoma is usually associated with a difficult delivery, such as a forceps delivery. It may occur if there has been a torn blood vessel that wasn't repaired from an episiotomy or laceration.

If a woman has a hematoma, she will have extreme pain and discomfort. She may not be able to walk. Urinating may be very painful or impossible.

When the physician or midwife hears such complaints, he or she will do a pelvic examination and possibly a rectal examination. Initial treatment for a small hematoma might consist of warm soaks to help the blood be absorbed. If the hematoma continues to grow or is large when first noticed, treatment might include an incision and drainage. Antibiotics may be needed.

Urinary Tract Infection

Cystitis or urinary tract infection (UTI), an inflammation of the bladder, generally makes itself known by an urgency to urinate frequently in small amounts and severe sensation of pain in the bladder area on the completion of urination. The discomfort is not generalized and there is no fever, although it is a genuine infection, most commonly due to the bacillus that is ordinarily found in the colon and rectum (*E. coli*). It can be responsible for blood in the urine, resulting from the opening up of small blood vessels in the wall of the bladder, which is part of the body's effort to combat the infection.

Prompt treatment of cystitis with a variety of currently available antibiotics given by mouth will ordinarily clear up the initial attacks quite reliably. The drug is usually given for seven days. It is desirable to obtain urine culture studies at the time of the initial symptoms, before the initiation of antibiotic therapy.

The organism responsible for UTI may also produce infection of the collection systems of the upper urinary tract: the *kidney pelvis*, where urine briefly collects; and the *ureter*, which is the tube from the kidney pelvis to the bladder. Infection in the kidney is called *pyelonephritis* (Greek: *pyelos* = pelvis; *nephritis* = inflammation of the kidney). It is usually accompanied by bacterial cystitis, but the infection of the upper tract dominates the clinical picture. Its symptoms include back pain over the kidney area on one side or both, chills, fever up to 40° centigrade or 104° Fahrenheit, and a general sensation of being ill. There is also burning on urination and loss of appetite. Prompt diagnosis is established through the clinical presentation and by demonstrating tenderness in the kidney area—called *costovertebral angle tenderness*—as this is the area where the ribs (*costo*) meet the spine (*vertebral*). The examiner will gently hit this area; invariably a woman with pyelonephritis will jump. The diagnosis is confirmed by a urine culture and a microscopic examination of the urine for pus cells (*white blood cells*) and bacteria.

The woman usually responds quickly to treatment with antibiotics, given intravenously and in larger doses for pyelonephritis than for a simple bladder infection. Oral treatment should be continued for 7 to 10 days, and a follow-up culture of the urine is imperative, to detect the continuing presence of the organism even after symptoms have completely disappeared.

To some extent, with the best of intentions, medical personnel themselves in the past contributed to the incidence of urinary tract infection. That incidence was markedly reduced as soon as it was realized that organisms could be introduced into the bladder by the catheters used for taking urine samples. Today, specimens are obtained by having the woman urinate after washing herself carefully—the *clean catch technique*. This has reduced the occurrence of infection. Other improvements in care, not obviously related to the urinary tract, have also reduced the incidence of urinary retention and subsequent infection: better anesthesia, early ambulation, less frequent operative delivery, and wider use of antibiotics.

Anemia

Anemia is a condition in which there is a reduction in the oxygen-carrying chemical in the blood—*hemoglobin*. As iron is the main mineral needed for the body to make hemoglobin, insufficient iron in the diet is a major cause of anemia. It also may be due to inherited disorders such as sickle-cell anemia or to blood loss. Postpartum anemia is usually related to blood loss of delivery. Many women experience a mild anemia with a rapid return to normal. Some women, especially those who have had cesarean or difficult births, develop more serious anemia with symptoms. The most common symptoms are pallor and fatigue.

We do not treat anemia with blood transfusions nearly as frequently as we did several decades ago. The blood volume normally expands in pregnancy as a protection against acute blood loss. Thus, a woman does not need additional blood unless she has lost enough to cause circulatory difficulty, characterized by a marked increase in the heart rate and a drop in blood pressure. In that case, intravenous fluids are the first step in treatment, followed by transfusion if her bleeding has not come under control or her symptoms continue.

A woman who is anemic postpartum but who has normal blood pressure and pulse rate may find that she fatigues easily. Her anemia is rapidly and safely corrected by oral iron supplementation and iron-rich foods. Both iron supplements and foods containing iron should be taken with vitamin C–rich foods. The vitamin C helps the body absorb the iron.

Foods high in iron include green leafy vegetables (the greener the better), dried fruit, egg yolk, and organ meats, especially liver. Vitamin C is found in many fruits and vegetables, especially citrus fruits and juices. There are a variety of available iron preparations on the market. These are discussed more fully in Chapter 10. The amount of hemoglobin in the blood will return to normal in about 3 weeks—the fatigue vanishes in less time than that. Iron therapy should be continued for up to 6 months in order to rebuild iron stores.

Postpartum Danger Signals:
When to Call Your Physician or Midwife

Although almost universally marked by fatigue, the postpartum period usually proceeds without problems. The body is designed beautifully to return on its own to the nonpregnant state. Occasionally, one of the complications described above does occur. However, prompt treatment and proper follow-up result in rapid return of health and energy. For timely treatment to be initiated, women need to be aware of the danger signals—those symptoms which should prompt a call to a physician or midwife, clinic or emergency room. Make sure you have a source of care, with a readily answerable phone number, before you leave the birth center or hospital or before your midwife or physician leaves your home.

Postpartum Danger Signals

- **Fever** ($\geq 100.4°F$) and **chills**
- **Excessive bleeding**—bleeding that is greater than a usual menstrual period or that has large clots or increases rather than decreases over time
- **Abdominal pain**
- **Severe pain in the perineum**—difficulty with walking; swelling; or pain that increases over time
- **Foul-smelling discharge**
- **Pain with urination** or at the end of urination and the urgent need to urinate frequently, especially with small amounts
- **Pain, tenderness, swelling, redness, or warmth in the breasts**
- **Pain, tenderness, swelling, redness, warmth, or a feeling of a "cord" in the leg**

POSTPARTUM EXAMINATION

Those who have cared for you during pregnancy, labor, and delivery do not consider their job complete until they have seen you through the period of recovery and the return to ordinary activity. We assume that you will return for at least one follow-up examination (and for later care as necessary).

While you are in the hospital, each day you may get a brief postpartum check from a nurse, your care provider, or perhaps both. They will ask you questions about your general sense of well-being, how you are eating, urinating, and moving your bowels. They will inquire about how much bleeding you are having and how your infant's feedings are going. Your nurse or provider may check your breasts for fullness, swelling, or hardness; your fundus for firmness and position; your bleeding for odor and amount; your perineum for healing; and your legs for signs of blood vessel inflammation or clots. They may check the status of your abdominal muscles by asking you to raise your head while they press on your abdomen, seeing how many fingerbreadths actually fit into the space where your muscles have separated naturally. They may gently hit your back to check for tenderness in the costovertebral angle area, to examine for a possible kidney infection.

Traditionally, a postpartum visit occurs 6 weeks after childbirth. The basis for this particular timing is the belief that the involutionary process takes approximately 6 weeks. Seeing somebody toward the end of this process allows the physician or midwife to assess the status of involution. Of course, involution is a variable process and many women are well involuted before the sixth postpartum week. There can be flexibility in planning the time of this visit.

Often, after a cesarean birth, a 2-week postpartum visit will be planned. This is mainly to assess the healing of the incision and the woman's general well-being.

Since all organ systems of the body go through changes during pregnancy, they all need to go through changes after the pregnancy is over. A postpartum visit will, therefore, often consist of a head-to-toe physical examination, starting with palpating a woman's thyroid, listening to her heart and lungs, checking her breasts, her back, her abdomen and legs, and doing a pelvic examination. After a cesarean birth, the abdominal wound will be checked again at 6 weeks.

The purpose of the pelvic examination at this time is to be certain that the internal organs have returned to their nonpregnant size and to check on any repairs that were made in the vagina or perineum. A Pap smear or cultures of the genital tract may be necessary, depending on when these were last done. Muscle strength will be checked and Kegel exercises may be taught if you haven't been doing them.

If you have had a vaginal birth, many physicians and midwives will follow the vaginal examination with a rectal-vaginal examination. This is to make sure the *recto-vaginal septum*—the tissue separating the back wall of the vagina from the front wall of the rectum—is intact and healing well. It is very thin at the time of birth and can be traumatized. A rectal-vaginal examination is not usually painful, although it may be uncomfortable. It can be done in the same position as you are in for the vaginal examination and is very brief and gentle. Only one finger need be inserted into the rectum.

The postpartum visit is also a time to discuss any of your concerns with your physician or midwife. Your care provider may initiate such discussions, or you may. Sleep deprivation, nursing problems, family relationships, exercising, nutrition, body image, returning to work, child care—any and all of these are appropriate topics to discuss. You can ask any and all questions about your labor and birth experience if you have lingering concerns. Your physician or midwife may choose to make a referral for you to another health care professional, such as a lactation consultant in the event of nursing difficulties, or a family therapist when family relationships have become strained.

The postpartum visit is often a time to initiate birth control, if this hasn't been accomplished already. Any birth control method that is appropriate for you (see Chapter 27) can be used at this time, although combination hormonal contraceptives (the pill, the patch, or the vaginal ring) are not advised this early if you are nursing.

Most physicians and midwives love to see the newborn at the postpartum visit and can accommodate the baby during the examination of the mother. An office nurse can hold the baby, some settings provide cribs, the mother can sometimes hold the baby during the examination—assuming the physician or midwife is comfortable with this and feels that it will be safe. After all, your physician or midwife has seen you frequently during your pregnancy, been involved with your birth, and feels a special relationship with you and the baby. This visit is usually a time for pleasant sharing of memories, experiences, and of recounting the birth experience.

CHAPTER TWENTY-SIX

Breast-feeding

How you feed your baby is a personal choice, with many considerations going into that choice. Yet, breast milk is beyond doubt the best food for newborns. Although several generations in the United States survived on formula, and many infants are still formula-fed, no formula exactly matches human milk. No formula provides the protection against infection, allergy, and illness that breast milk provides.

Breast-feeding need not be difficult. It requires no preparation during pregnancy. It requires no equipment. It is one of the few things in life truly free of charge.

ADVANTAGES OF BREAST-FEEDING

Advantages for the Baby

Human breast milk is uniquely designed to feed human babies. It contains all the nutrients they need. Nutrients are more easily absorbed from breast milk than from formula. Iron, for example, is present in breast milk in low levels, but 50 percent of the iron is absorbed from breast milk, compared to 7 percent from formula and 4 percent from infant cereal.

Breast milk has several infection-fighting properties. First, breast milk inhibits the growth of disease-causing bacteria. Second, it provides antibacterial and antiviral agents. Third, it stimulates the infant's own immune system. These properties protect against infections of the *gastrointestinal* (digestive) and respiratory systems and help prevent ear infections. When breast-fed babies do get infections, they tend to be less severe than infections in bottle-fed babies. Recovery is more rapid.

Breast milk protects babies against food allergies and eczema. Breast-fed babies are less likely to develop certain chronic diseases later in life. These include *lymphoma* (a type of cancer), *Crohn's disease* (a type of inflammatory disease of the bowel), and insulin-dependent or *type 1 diabetes*.

The type of sucking involved in breast-feeding helps develop the mouth and jaw muscles.

Supplemental formula-feeding may interfere with some of these advantages. Iron-deficiency anemia, for example, is sometimes seen in partially breast-fed babies under the age of 6 months but not in totally breast-fed babies before 6 months. Once formula or foods other than human milk are introduced, the infant's exposure to disease-producing bacteria increases.

Advantages for the Mother

In the immediate postpartum period, breast-feeding helps the uterus contract and so prevents bleeding.

Lactation delays ovulation and menses. In fact, exclusive breast-feeding decreases the chances of a pregnancy for 6 months, or until you get your first menstrual period, whichever comes sooner. Exclusive breast-feeding means no supplements are given and babies are fed on demand. This isn't a foolproof contraceptive method, but for families that don't use contraception for philosophical, esthetic, or religious reasons, breast-feeding is a helpful way to space children.

Studies suggest that breast-feeding may be protective against breast cancer that occurs early in life.

Finally, breast-feeding is fulfilling. While a mother's relationship with her infant can be as close and satisfying if she bottle-feeds, with as much touching and stroking, a special physical bond exists between breast-fed babies and their mothers.

GETTING STARTED

Getting started with breast-feeding shouldn't be intimidating. In the best circumstances, the baby is placed on your chest immediately after birth. The brand new baby is alert and ready to nurse. Babies actually will find their way to the breast on their own at this moment. If immediate nursing isn't possible, getting started may be a little more difficult, but, still, it should not be daunting. Of course, this is a new activity—for you and your baby. Some learning and patience will be required.

If you nurse right after delivery, you may not be able to get into the most comfortable position, but proper positioning of the baby at the breast is important to prevent sore nipples. The baby's mouth should be at the level of the nipple and straight in front of it. This way, the baby's sucking will not pull the nipple down or up. Tummy-to-tummy is a good rule. If the baby's tummy is facing yours, the baby's mouth will face the nipple.

To begin, hold the breast in your hand, with your thumb on top and the fingers on the underside. Use the rooting reflex—stroke the baby's lips with your nipple. The baby will open its mouth wide. Don't push on the baby's face because the rooting reflex will cause the baby to turn toward your touch. Guide the baby gently toward you with your hand on the back of the baby's head.

The baby should take a good deal of the *areola* into the mouth—the darkened area around the nipple. This way the baby's mouth is not clenching directly on the nipple. The baby is properly latched onto your breast if you can see the baby's mouth open, the lips curled out, and the chin pressed into the breast.

Since babies will suck for a long time, they are all nose breathers. Their flat noses are designed to allow them to breathe even when they are pressed up against the breast. However, if you are worried, you can use your finger to press down on your breast in front of the baby's nose to allow air to pass more easily to the nostrils. Also remember, your breast size has nothing to do with your ability to nurse. Large breasts are large mostly because of fatty tissue, not functional breast tissue.

The first food the baby gets is not milk. It is *colostrum*, also called "first milk." This yellowish fluid is full of infection-fighting ingredients, just what the baby needs for the first 3 to 5 days of life. Colostrum is a very important part of your baby's nutrition.

After newborns nurse in the first half hour or so of life, they drift off into a calm and deep sleep. They awaken when they are ready to nurse again—several hours later.

Some women find the atmosphere in a hospital less than encouraging for breast-feeding. Although you may have a private or semiprivate room, and all rooms have curtains around each bed, you may be disturbed by hospital routines. People may come in to take your temperature, change your wastebasket, or give you a meal tray. One of the positive aspects of shorter stays following birth is that you return to the

relative tranquility of your own home, where you can give your attention to nursing free of hospital schedules and interruptions by strangers.

A hospital, however, may employ a lactation consultant. The obstetrical or nursery nurses may be knowledgeable about breast-feeding.
Don't be shy about asking for help, even if you feel you don't need it. An
extra eye to check on the baby's position is always useful. This is especially true if you have had a cesarean birth or have an intravenous tube
in your arm for any other reason.

POSITIONING

Breast-feeding should not be painful. When breasts do become tender, a
common cause is less than optimal positioning. The baby should be
square on the breast—the mouth facing the nipple, not above or below
it. You should use a variety of positions to keep pressure from being
placed continually in the same area of the breast.

There are at least four basic nursing positions:

1. **The Cradle Hold:** sitting up, with the baby lying across your
   lap, the baby's head can be nestled in the crook of your arm
   on the same side as the breast at which the baby is sucking.
   An arm chair and footstool might increase your comfort.
2. **The Cross-Cradle Hold:** similar to the cradle hold, but the
   baby's head is held with the hand on the side opposite to the
   breast at which the baby is sucking. Your elbow supports
   the baby's bottom. This is a good position for a baby who is
   having a bit of trouble latching on.
3. **Side-lying:** the baby lies next to you, with its head in the
   crook of your arm on the same side as the nursing breast.
4. **The Football Hold:** one of the positions recommended for
   breast-feeding right after a cesarean birth. In this position,
   the baby "sits" on one of your hip bones, circled by the arm
   on the same side. The baby's feet point toward your back.
   The baby's head is held in the palm of your hand and the
   baby's back rests on your forearm. This is similar to the way a
   football player (the running back, if that helps you picture
   this) holds the ball, hence its name.

THE SOCIAL REALITY OF NURSING

Because it is so specially designed for human babies, breast milk is easily digested and nursing babies will get hungry quickly. This does not mean you are not making enough milk. Nor does frequent feeding use up your milk supply. Quite the opposite is true. The more the baby nurses, the more milk you will produce. It's a supply-and-demand system. If you compare your baby to a bottle-fed baby, however, you may get worried, thinking the baby isn't satisfied at each feeding. Don't worry. Babies almost always drink enough to meet their hunger and nutritional needs.

The idea that babies should be fed every 4 hours by the clock derived from research on the emptying time of the stomachs of babies fed formula. It also relates to the work schedule of personnel in hospital nurseries and to housekeeping needs at home, rather than to physiological processes in the baby.

When left to determine their own schedule, babies will nurse eight to twelve times a day, every 1½ to 3 hours. They may *cluster feed*. This means they may have many short feedings in a few hours, followed by a longer sleep. There may seem to be no pattern to the baby's hunger. The baby may nurse especially frequently during growth spurts. These tend to occur when the baby is about 3 weeks, 6 weeks, 3 months, and 6 months old. At times, a nursing mother may feel literally latched onto the baby.

Yet, ultimately, if you allow the baby to let you know when he or she is hungry, breast-feeding will be easier for both of you. Frequent sucking will bring the milk in best and may also help prevent *engorgement*, a condition in which your breasts become very full of milk, feel hard, and may even be painful. Frequent feedings assure the baby an adequate amount of fluid and help with bowel movement and urinating. Additional water or supplementary formula is unnecessary, and may interfere with the milk supply as well as diminish some of the benefits of breast-feeding.

If you wait until the baby is crying to nurse, the baby may be so upset that latching on may be difficult. Signs that the baby is hungry are fast eye movements under the eyelids as the baby begins to wake up; sucking movements of the lips; licking movements; putting the hands into the mouth; stretching and body movements; baby sounds.

The duration of breast-feeding sessions may vary. Babies will nurse for anywhere from 15 to 45 minutes. They suck most at the breast given first, so alternate the breast that you offer first. The easiest way to tell which breast to give first is to feel your breasts. Start with the one that feels fuller. Don't take the baby off one breast to place him or her on the other breast. Let the baby stop nursing before offering the second breast. Burp the baby after he or she finishes at each breast, just as you would when giving formula.

You cannot measure the amount of milk the nursing baby is taking. For some parents, this is frustrating, especially if you have bottle-fed one baby and then choose to nurse, or if you have friends or relatives who are bottle-feeding. There are ways other than measuring what's left in a bottle to tell if the baby is getting enough milk. Your breasts should feel soft after a feeding. This means they are being emptied. After the first 5 days, the baby should have six to eight wet diapers daily and the urine should be pale and nearly odorless. The baby should have two to three large stools a day for the first month, although some breast-fed babies have a bowel movement after each feeding. After a month, the stools may not be as frequent. Other signs of a well-nourished baby are active moving, a loud cry, a wet and pink mouth, and alert-looking eyes.

When the baby sucks, you experience a reflex called *letdown*. Some women feel the letdown, others do not. Your breast may letdown even when the baby isn't sucking—at the sound of your baby's cry, or any baby's cry, at the time you usually feed, even at just a thought of your baby.

CARE FOR THE NURSING WOMAN

Producing breast milk requires energy. If you breast-feed, you should eat about 500 more calories than you ate before you were pregnant, about 200 more calories than during pregnancy (see Chapter 10). Two hundred calories is about one-quarter of a chicken, two ounces of cheese (two slices in most packaged cheese), or two and a half to three slices of the average sliced bread. Follow the balanced dietary pattern outlined in Chapter 10 as much as possible.

You may be advised by the well meaning to force fluids to increase the milk supply. Common sense teaches that you will need the additional fluid that you are providing to the baby. Your thirst is the best guide, however. You need not force yourself to drink. Usually, 6 to 8 glasses of fluid are sufficient. Cow's milk is a suitable beverage but not a requirement. Occasionally, a baby will have an allergy to milk. The allergic baby may react to the milk or other dairy products in the mother's diet with fussiness; colic; spitting up or vomiting; frequent stools, sometimes with blood in them; or rashes. If your baby has these symptoms, speak to your pediatrician, family doctor, or nurse practitioner, but also try eliminating dairy from your diet.

No particular foods should be avoided during nursing unless you notice that the baby has an unusual amount of gas or seems unusually fussy after you eat a certain food.

In addition to good nutrition, rest is important. Try to rest when the baby sleeps.

INCLUDING THE FATHER AND OTHER FAMILY MEMBERS

Today, involvement of fathers in infant and child care is commonplace. Breast-feeding may seem to discourage this involvement, but there are many ways fathers and other family members can stay involved with their nursing newborns. They can perform other infant care activities, such as diapering and bathing. They can hold and comfort the baby. If the baby does not sleep in the parents' room, the father can bring the baby to the mother for feedings, change the diaper after the feeding, and return the baby to the bassinet or crib.

You can pump your breasts and when you are not available, the father or other family members can give your milk in a bottle. (Pumping is described on page 759.) If you choose to supplement with water or formula, someone else can give the baby the supplement in a bottle. However, supplementing or giving breast milk in a bottle is not recommended for at least several weeks—preferably longer. Any supplement may interfere with the baby's appetite for breast milk, possibly leading to a diminished supply of milk and interfering with optimal nutrition. The suck on an artificial nipple is different from the suck on the breast. This can lead to a problem called *nipple confusion*, which can make nursing more difficult for the baby and, in turn, the mother. Eventually, babies can take either an artificial nipple or the breast without this problem, but not in their earliest days.

HANDLING DISCOURAGEMENT

Breast-feeding still may be seen by some individuals as unusual. Even well-meaning friends and relatives may make inappropriate comments to nursing women. This becomes even more pronounced as the infant becomes a toddler. Although the World Health Organization recommends nursing "well into the second year of a child's life and for longer, if possible," women often find little support for nursing beyond the first year of life.

Nursing, especially at the beginning, is easier if you are relaxed and comfortable, physically and psychologically. For this reason, support is valuable. You should choose a pediatrician, family physician, or nurse practitioner who supports breast-feeding fully. You should have the support of your partner. You should have reference materials to help you through any trying times. The Appendix lists a number of reference books for breast-feeding. It's worthwhile to have the phone number of your local La Leche League and possibly a lactation consultant in your community. Your obstetrician or midwife may be a source of good support. Some women attend breast-feeding classes, usually given during pregnancy, or breast-feeding support groups. These may be run by nurses at the hospital or birthing center where you gave birth, La Leche League, or your childbirth instructor.

BREAST-FEEDING AND CONTRACEPTION

Lactational Amenorrhea

Under certain circumstances, breast-feeding has a contraceptive effect. This can last up to 6 months, or until you get your first menstrual period, whichever comes sooner. This only works when you are exclusively breast-feeding. *Exclusive breast-feeding* means giving no supplements and feeding on demand. Anytime you add supplements, including fluids, you can no longer consider nursing as a contraceptive. Once you get a menstrual period, then you know the contraceptive effect of nursing is no longer working. You cannot depend on this method beyond 6 months, which is the time your baby needs solids. If you want to be sure not to get pregnant, you can use contraception even if you breast-feed exclusively and do not menstruate.

If you do not breast-feed exclusively, then lack of a menstrual period does not mean you can't get pregnant. You ovulate or release the egg cell *before* your first period, so you can be taken by surprise.

Appropriate Contraceptive Choices

Most contraceptive methods, described in Chapter 27, are appropriate during lactation. These include *barrier methods*—male and female condoms, the diaphragm, the cervical cap. They can be used with spermicides—cream or jelly or spermicidal lubricants. The IUD (intrauterine device) can be used in breast-feeding women who are in mutually monogamous sexual relationships. Hormonal methods that supply only *progestin* (a form of progesterone) do not interfere with breast milk. Adverse effects on the newborn have not been shown, although the hormone does get to the baby. These include the "mini-pill," injectables (the "shot," or Depo-Provera), and implants (Norplant).

The "combination pill," which delivers both a progestin and estrogen, may interfere with milk supply if it is started before the supply is established firmly. This is also true for the newer progestin/estrogen contraceptives—the patch and the vaginal ring. Wait until you've nursed for about 3 months before using these methods. The hormones in these contraceptives do get to the baby through the breast milk, but they are not considered harmful.

Natural birth control can be used during nursing, but it poses a number of difficulties in interpreting the cervical mucus and temperature charts. If you wish to use this method, consult your gynecologist or midwife. If necessary, they can refer you to somebody with expertise in use of this method. If you meet the requirements for lactational amenorrhea, then no other method of natural family planning is needed for 6 months.

COMMON PROBLEMS:
PREVENTION AND CARE

Breast-feeding can continue for months, even years, without any problems. Sometimes, however, a woman encounters a situation that interferes with her comfort. The following sections provide tips on prevention of common problems and their treatment. If the simple measures below don't help, consult any of the specialized books on nursing, your local La Leche League, or a lactation consultant.

Inverted Nipples

Some women have flat nipples. Most of the time these can be *everted* or pulled out during pregnancy and certainly by the baby's suck. They pose no problem.

A few women have truly inverted nipples. This means the nipple points inward toward the breast rather than outward. Sometimes, inverted nipples reverse themselves during pregnancy or the immediate postpartum period.

If your nipples appear flat or inverted, try during pregnancy to see if they evert. Gently squeeze the area of the breast immediately around the nipple—the *areola*—between your thumb and forefinger. If your nipples evert, even if they return to their inverted position afterward, they will evert when the baby sucks. If the nipples do not evert, ask your midwife or physician to see if she or he can evert them. If this isn't possible, then breast shells might help.

Breast shells, also called *breast shields* or *breast cups*, are plastic dome-shaped cups placed inside your bra. They are available from La Leche League. They can be worn in the third trimester of pregnancy and during the first few weeks of breast-feeding. The shells have a small opening in their center. They exert a constant and painless pressure which gradually brings the nipple through the opening in the shell. During pregnancy, you can start wearing the shields for 1 to 2 hours two times daily. Over time, you can increase the length of time you wear the shields, until you wear them all day. There is no research available to demonstrate whether or not they are effective. Discuss with your physician or midwife whether they think the shells will help you. You also can check with a lactation consultant. In the early weeks of nursing, the shells are worn for half an hour before feedings. They are not to be worn when you are lying down. You will probably need a larger-sized bra to accommodate the shells comfortably. (Do not confuse these breast shells with nipple shields, which are marketed to prevent or relieve nipple soreness and are not considered beneficial.)

Engorgement

Engorgement (French: *engorger* = to obstruct) is common in the early days of nursing, shortly after the milk comes in. Engorged breasts are filled with milk. They are hard and painful.

To prevent engorgement, nurse on demand. Don't limit the baby's sucking time. Don't take the baby off the breast to switch breasts. Let the baby stop nursing on her or his own. Start each feeding with the breast that feels heavier.

If, despite all your best preventive efforts, your breasts become engorged, take comfort in knowing that engorgement usually lasts only about 2 days. Unfortunately, when the breast is so full, the nipple may become flattened, making it difficult for the baby to latch onto the nipple. You can pump or express a little milk with your hands before feedings to take some of the pressure off the nipple.

To pump with your hands, first put a warm wet towel over your breasts and massage them. Place your thumb, your forefinger, and middle fingers on the breast, just beyond the areola. The thumb is above the nipple and the fingers below the nipple. Push back toward your chest and then roll your fingers together and slightly forward. If you have a breast pump, you can use that. Breast pumps are discussed briefly on page 759. During the feeding, you can continue to use the warm towel on the breast and massage it while the baby sucks.

Between feedings, an ice pack or cold towel may help reduce the swelling of your breasts and relieve the pain. Many women report that placing cabbage leaves on the breasts helps relieve engorgment (even to the extent of helping dry up the milk during and after weaning). How cabbage leaves work in relieving engorgment is not understood.

The cabbage leaves should be peeled off the head of cabbage and washed. Green cabbage is recommended. The veins can be cut out or crushed (using a rolling pin, for instance). The leaves can be placed on the breasts or into a bra. Do not place them directly on irritated skin. Keep the leaves on your breasts until the engorgement subsides or until the leaves wilt. This should be about 20 to 30 minutes. (Don't leave them on after you feel relief as this might cause reduction in your milk supply.) Some women prefer the cabbage leaves to be chilled, but others have found that relief occurs whether they are chilled or not. You cannot use cabbage leaves if you are allergic to cabbage or to sulfur.

Taking a warm bath or shower before feeding may be soothing and may help the milk flow. Don't attempt a bath in the early postpartum days without help, however. Continue to nurse frequently.

Leaking Nipples

Leaking is usually a problem of the first few months of nursing, when your body is still figuring out how much milk to produce. Leaking actually isn't a problem. It just means you have a lot of milk. But, don't become alarmed if your breasts don't leak—it doesn't mean you don't have enough milk. Insufficient milk is an extremely rare problem as long as your baby feeds frequently.

When you nurse your baby, your opposite breast may leak. Your breasts may leak when you hear your baby cry, or even when you hear another baby cry. Some women just need to think about their babies, or look at a picture of any baby, and their breasts leak. If you are away from the baby, your breasts may start to leak at the time you'd generally be nursing.

Commercially made breast pads are available to absorb leaking milk or you can use any cotton cloth inside your bra. You may want a bra that is one size too big so you can fit the pad inside without being uncomfortable. A sweater or jacket can cover any possibly embarrassing wet spots, so carry one with you in any kind of weather. Print clothing hides wet spots better than solid clothing. You can cross your arms over your breasts and press inward for about 30 seconds to try to stop any squirting leaks.

Sore Nipples

Like other nursing problems, sore nipples are better prevented than treated, although they can be healed. You need not discontinue nursing when your nipples are sore, even if they become cracked.

Preventing Sore Nipples

1. **Use a variety of positions** for nursing. Make sure the baby's mouth is always at the level of your breast and facing the nipple squarely. Your nipples should go deeply into the baby's mouth, so be certain that much of the *areola* (the dark part around the nipple) is within the baby's lips. You can use your forefinger to pull down the baby's chin. This causes the baby's mouth to open as wide as possible, allowing enough of the areola to go into the mouth.

2. **Expose your nipples to the air** and, if possible, to sunlight between feedings. Rub a little of the breast milk around the nipple after a feed and wait until the milk is dry before putting on a bra. You can dry the milk around the nipple with a hair dryer. Use a medium setting for just a few seconds on each nipple. Hold the dryer at least six inches from the breast.

3. **Wash your nipples only with water.** Soap will dry the skin and make it more susceptible to cracking.
4. **Avoid bottle-feeding and pacifiers** in the first month or two. This can create nipple confusion for the baby and make it difficult for the baby to latch on. If the baby has difficulty, this can lead to sore nipples or painful nursing.
5. If you want to take the baby off the breast, **put your finger into the baby's mouth to break the suction.** Never pull the baby off the breast.
6. If your nipples still become sore, you want to avoid their becoming cracked. Use the breast milk as an emollient cream, air-dry the nipples, and expose them to sunlight. Try the following as well:
   • Start to nurse on the less sore side.
   • Get extra rest.
   • Speak to your physician, midwife, or lactation consultant.

Yeast Infection

A yeast infection may cause pain and itching in the breasts. The baby may or may not show symptoms of *thrush*—a yeast infection of the mouth. The baby with thrush has a white coating on the palate, gums, and tongue. If the baby has thrush, you should both be treated (see Chapter 24). You can use an antiyeast cream on your breasts after nursing or take fluconazole (Diflucan) by mouth. These treatments will not harm the baby.

Clogged Duct

The breast is composed of many ducts, with milk flowing through each toward the nipple. One or more of these ducts can become clogged with milk. This usually appears as a tender, swollen area, often near the armpit. When the area is very swollen, the skin may be shiny. If the area is also red and warm or you have a fever, you might have *mastitis* (see below), and should call your physician or midwife.

Nurse frequently when you have a clogged duct. Use different positions so the baby drinks from all the breast ducts. Start feedings with the breast that has the problem. Take a hot shower and let the water flow over the tender area before nursing. During nursing, use a warm, wet towel and massage the area of the clogged duct. Gently press toward the nipple to help the milk flow from the duct. Get lots of rest and drink lots of fluids to prevent mastitis.

Mastitis

Mastitis is an infection of the milk-forming glands. It requires immediate attention.

Mastitis usually is due to a *Staphylococcus* bacteria that ordinarily resides on the skin. All of the measures discussed above will help prevent mastitis as it most frequently occurs where the milk pools (with engorged breasts or a clogged duct), or where there is a crack in the skin, allowing bacteria to enter the breasts.

You may get mastitis if you don't effectively treat other breast problems or it may appear without warning. You may notice that one small area of one breast is tender and the skin over it reddened and possibly warm. You will be extra tired and achy, and may have chills. You may think you have the flu. Take your temperature. With these symptoms it is almost certain to be elevated. Report this promptly to your physician or midwife.

Mastitis is treated by antibiotics. If caught early it need not interfere with breast-feeding. It may take a few days of antibiotics for the disease to relent but you should feel better in 24 to 36 hours after starting medication. Of course, the baby will get some drug, but your physician or midwife will choose an antibiotic that is not harmful to newborns. The medication may alter the odor of the baby's stools but otherwise will not have known adverse effects.

NURSING IN SPECIAL SITUATIONS

Almost all babies can be breast-fed. Prematurity, illness or disability in the mother or baby, multiple birth, birth by cesarean, and a new pregnancy may present challenges to successful nursing, but you can nurse in any of these situations. Motivation, patience, personal support, and professional help are the keys to this achievement.

After a Cesarean Birth

Mothers who have delivered by cesarean usually spend a longer time in the hospital than those who have delivered vaginally. You will have access to people who are knowledgeable about breast-feeding and who can provide the follow-up support that might not be as readily available to a woman who has left the hospital one or two days after the birth. However, the hospital, with its routines and noises and interruptions, is not always ideal for nursing. If the baby rooms-in, you enlist support, and, whenever necessary, you close your bedside curtains for privacy, you should be able to initiate nursing without difficulty.

The mother who has an abdominal incision may be somewhat uncomfortable holding the baby for breast-feeding. There are a number of simple techniques to minimize the discomfort. One is to rest the baby on a pillow on the abdomen. Another is to hold the baby in the football hold (see page 745). As you get more mobile, you can use the side-lying position.

With a Multiple Birth, a Premature Baby, or a Baby with Problems

Some premature babies and babies with certain congenital problems such as a cleft lip or palate may have difficulty sucking. Breast milk is still the best food for these infants. Sometimes, such as with transient tachynea of the newborn (see Chapter 24), there is a danger of *aspirating* (breathing in) oral intake. When this possibility exists, the babies usually are fed through plastic tubes passed through the nose or mouth and then down the esophagus to the stomach.

When a baby has a congenital anomaly, mothers often need assistance with breast-feeding. A special nurse in the hospital or a lactation consultant will be a great help in these situations. In other situations and with tiny babies, the mother may have to pump her milk until the baby is big enough or strong enough or well enough to nurse. Sometimes, babies can suck, but will have to undergo procedures or surgeries that make taking in oral fluids impossible for a period of time.

If your baby is in a neonatal intensive care unit (NICU), talk to the baby's pediatrician and the nurses on the unit about bringing breast milk for the baby's feeds. They will advise you whether this is possible and what is the best way to supply your milk.

Pumping is described in the section on returning to work, below. We refer you to the resources in the Appendix for help in special situations such as these.

When there is more than one baby, feeding the babies is a challenge— whether it is by breast or bottle. Babies can be nursed one or two at a time. This may depend on your personal preference or whether the babies are on similar schedules. Some women nurse one at a time if the babies wake up at different times, and two together if the babies awaken

at the same time. Newborns sleep soundly so the awakening of one infant will not necessarily wake the other or others. The more babies you
have, the more challenging it will be to nurse them.

Illness or Disability in the Mother

Most mothers who have illnesses or disabilities can nurse. Again, there
may be special challenges such as which positions you can and cannot
assume. Nearly all women on medications can nurse, with a few exceptions. The benefits of breast milk to the baby outweigh any possible side
effects of most medications.

Medications that may be harmful to babies and preclude nursing
include:

- Certain anticancer or chemotherapeutic agents
- Radioactive nuclear medicine tracers (used in diagnostic testing)
- Lithium carbonate
- Chloramphenicol
- Phenylbutazone
- Atropine
- Thiouracil
- Iodides
- Mercurials

If you take or have been advised to take any of these medications,
discuss with your physician whether or not there are alternative treatments or if you can postpone treatment until you wean the baby. If neither of these choices is possible, you should not breast-feed.

If you take any other medication for a chronic or acute illness, check
with the baby's pediatrician or nurse practitioner or your obstetrician or
midwife to see if it is harmful to a nursing baby. It is likely to be fine.

If you become ill while you are nursing, or require a medical, dental,
or surgical procedure, remember to tell your physician or other care
provider that you are breast-feeding. Most times, medication can be
chosen that is compatible with nursing. On occasion, you may have to
pump and discard milk for a short period of time and use formula for
some feedings.

Women who test positive for HIV (human immune deficiency virus)
or who have AIDS (acquired immune deficiency syndrome) are advised
not to nurse as the virus can be passed through breast milk to the baby.

Some communities have milk banks that provide donated breast milk for babies whose mothers cannot give them their own milk. If you are nursing, you can donate to such a milk bank by expressing milk, starting a few weeks after birth. Ask your care provider or the lactation consultant where you deliver to refer you to this resource or contact your local La Leche League.

AVAILABLE SUPPORTS

The La Leche League (Spanish: *la leche* = the milk) is an organized group of experienced women dedicated to furthering breast-feeding. Its members will give support, advice, and practical assistance over the telephone, and when necessary with home visits, to mothers who need help and encouragement. Branches of the organization exist in a great many communities. They are listed under the name of La Leche League in the business section of the white pages of the telephone directories of the communities where they operate. The La Leche League International offers support groups led by trained volunteers, and a 24-hour hotline for breast-feeding problems. Contact numbers are listed in the Appendix.

Frequently, the hospital or birthing center where you gave birth can provide support after you leave. There might be a breast-feeding expert affiliated with the obstetrical department who can talk to you or even see you after you are home.

In recent years, the lactation consultant has emerged as a new health care professional. The International Lactation Consultant Association certifies lactation consultants and can give you a referral. Contact information for this organization is listed in the Appendix.

There are a number of helpful and well-organized books on breast-feeding available. Several are listed in the Appendix.

RETURNING TO WORK

Today, many mothers of young children work outside the home. In an ideal society, all workplaces would allow breast-feeding women to take breaks to go home to nurse, to have a nanny bring the baby to you to nurse, or to nurse in the child care center in the workplace. Working at home, or *telecommuting*, would be another option. A third possibility would be for workplaces to provide break time to pump the breasts, and offer private, comfortable areas for pumping, as well as refrigerators for milk storage. Despite the fact that few work situations support breast-feeding in any of these ways, nursing can be combined with working. You have the option of preparing formula for the baby to drink while you are at work, or pumping your milk, storing it, and leaving it for the baby.

If you choose to combine breast milk and formula, then start substituting one feeding at a time with formula before your work start date. This way, your breasts will adapt gradually to the changed need for milk production. Your milk supply will adjust eventually even if you shift schedules abruptly, but you may suffer painful, engorged breasts during work hours for at least several days. When you get home, it may be difficult for your baby to latch on if the breast is engorged.

Pumping Breast Milk

As milk is a supply-and-demand situation, pumping the breasts is important to maintain the supply when you are temporarily separated from the baby. It is also a way to provide breast milk when you return to work. You will find pumping helpful if your breasts become engorged at any time.

If possible, you should be in a warm and comfortable area to pump. This helps with the letdown reflex.

Milk can be stored in glass or hard plastic containers with tight lids or in special breast milk freezer bags. You should store about two to four ounces in each container so that you don't waste milk as it can't be reused from a bottle once the baby has sucked on it. If you pump less than this amount at any one sitting, cool the milk before adding it to already cooled or frozen milk.

Put a date on the bottle of pumped milk before you refrigerate or freeze it. Fresh milk can be kept in the refrigerator for up to 3 days. Milk can be frozen for up to 2 weeks in a freezer of a one-door refrigerator, 2–3 months in a freezer of a two-door refrigerator, and 6 months in a deep freezer. You can thaw frozen milk in the refrigerator for 4 hours or by running the container first under cool water, then under warm water once it has begun to thaw. Do not thaw milk at room temperature. Once milk has been frozen and then thawed, it can be kept in the refrigerator for up to 24 hours.

To use the breast milk, warm it by placing the container in a bowl of very warm water. Do not heat milk (or formula) in the microwave. Test the temperature of the milk on your wrist.

Do not refreeze milk once it is used. If the baby does not drink everything that is in the bottle, throw the rest of the milk away, just as you would with formula.

Breast Pumps

There are four types of breast pumps: your hands, manual pumps, small battery-operated pumps, and larger electrical pumps.

Pumping by hand can be tiring and time consuming. It is usually done to relieve engorgement, or when you only have to pump a bit of milk to relieve pressure. The technique is described earlier in the section on engorgement on page 752.

A manual hand pump is inexpensive and easy to carry. It may be operated with one or both hands. A manual pump can be tiring to the hands and wrists. If you have a problem such as carpal tunnel syndrome, you will not be able to use this kind of pump. It usually is used by women who pump only occasionally. Don't use a pump with bulb suction. It applies too much pressure to the breasts.

A portable, battery-operated pump can be used with one hand and is easy to carry. Some can be plugged into outlets so you can use them if the battery runs out. These are not as efficient as larger, electrical pumps. Like manual pumps, they are best used by women who pump infrequently. They are generally more expensive than manual pumps, but not as expensive as electrical pumps.

Electrical pumps can be purchased or rented. They are best if you need to pump over a period of time, such as if your baby needs tube feedings, has surgery, or if you will be away for a period of time. You can pump both breasts simultaneously with these types of pumps so you can get a lot of milk quickly. Electrical pumps are large and heavy, however, and you would not want to transport one back and forth to work every day. You should try to store your pump at work if that is where you will be using it. In most communities, you can rent a pump from the local La Leche League chapter, some pharmacies, and many lactation consultants.

A WORD ON WEANING THE BABY

There is no right or wrong time to wean. If you wean before the baby is 1 year old, you need to replace the breast milk with formula. After 1 year, babies can tolerate cow's milk. They need whole milk, not fat free or low fat milk, for at least another year.

Although nursing can be combined with work outside the home, some women wean before they return to work. Others wean when the baby can take a cup, usually about 9 months of age. Some women follow the recommendation of the World Health Organization to nurse "well into the second year of a child's life and for longer." Some women allow their babies to wean themselves. You'll be surprised how long a child nurses if left on his or her own. Over time, your child will reduce the number of feedings, perhaps to just one in the morning and one at night, eventually just to one at bedtime. Older toddlers nurse as much for comfort as for nutrition.

Both you and your baby will be happier if you wean gradually. Substitute formula or milk for one feeding at a time. This way, your baby won't feel sudden deprivation and you won't become painfully engorged.

A Happy Note

Breast-feeding is a gift you give to your baby. It is also a gift your baby gives to you. It should be joyful and happy. Seek help if it is anything but.

CHAPTER TWENTY-SEVEN

Family Planning

Throughout history, human beings have attempted to control their numbers. Some method of family limitation has always been employed. These methods have included celibacy, often through taboos, abortion, or simple means of contraception. The average woman who begins her reproductive life as young as age 17 or 18 and makes no effort at family planning will have thirteen children. In recent years this degree of unrestrained fertility has been met only occasionally. Today in this country it is seen largely in religious groups such as the Hutterites and Hasidic Jews.

The ability to control reproduction effectively, however, and the freedom from fear that your children will die in childhood are relatively recent occurrences in the history of our species. These advances have changed the lives of human beings as significantly as any medical or technological innovation.

EARLY REFERENCES TO CONTRACEPTION AND ABORTION

Early references to contraception and abortion both condone and condemn such practices. Among the medical treatises written on papyrus by the priest-physicians of the ancient pharaohs 4,000 years ago, seven of which survive in part or in whole, three are gynecological works that contain contraceptive and *abortifacient* (abortion causing) recipes for ladies of the court. When the Babylonian Code of Hammurabi was drawn up in about 1800 B.C., abortion was important enough to be discouraged through the penalty of death by crucifixion. By the time the first book of the Old Testament, Genesis, was written in about 1500 B.C., contraception by *coitus interruptus* (withdrawal) was sufficiently widespread among the early Hebrews that four verses (Genesis 38: 7–10) were devoted to its interdiction through the parable of Onan.

We do not know with any certainty whether abortion or contraception is the older form of family limitation. Soranus, the famous gynecologist of antiquity, in Chapter XIX of his *Gynecology*, written in about A.D. 130, discusses the question: Which is the better method to limit childbirth: abortion or contraception? He concludes that it is safer to prevent conception than to destroy its product. However, this decision was made on the basis of the substantial physical and psychological trauma that resulted from the inept and dangerous methods of abortion that were the only recourse in his day.

In the centuries that followed the pronouncement of Soranus, abortion continued to present extreme hazard to the life or health of a pregnant woman. This was true until the twentieth century, when practitioners began to invest their ingenuity in developing safe and effective abortion methods. One of the safest of these methods is *suction aspiration*. The use of this technique in the first few months of pregnancy as a backup in case of a failure of a *barrier method* (such as the condom or the diaphragm) results in the lowest health risk for sexually active women. This, of course, assumes conscientious use of the barrier method and, if it fails, timely resort to abortion. Abortion thus may be part of an overall approach to family planning, although reliance on it as a contraceptive method is not considered appropriate in this country.

BRIEF HISTORY OF BIRTH CONTROL IN THE UNITED STATES

Before 1873, there were no laws in the United States concerning contraception. In that year, Anthony Comstock, secretary of the New York Society for the Suppression of Vice, persuaded Congress to pass an anti–birth control law. He then convinced many state legislatures to pass their own statutes. The federal law was enforced nationwide by a prohibition on mailing contraceptive devices and information. As is often the case, these laws principally penalized the poor.

Margaret Sanger

The first American evangelist to fight full-time for the liberalization of birth control was a trained nurse, the mother of three children, Margaret Sanger. She had good training in fighting for causes on the picket lines of the trade union movement and in the struggle for women's suffrage. Her interest in birth control came through her experiences nursing among Jewish and Italian immigrants in poor neighborhoods in lower Manhattan. She saw firsthand the misery resulting from unplanned and unwanted pregnancies, which led to either life-threatening abortions or families with many children who could not be well provided for.

In 1912, at age 33, Margaret Sanger defied the United States Postal Department regulations by writing articles on birth control for the *Call*, a socialist paper widely distributed by mail. Indicted, she fled abroad, where she used her self-imposed exile to study birth control in England, France, and Holland. When she returned to the United States, she brought with her knowledge and appreciation of the usefulness of the diaphragm. Ms. Sanger's motivation in the espousal of *birth control*, a term she coined, was single-minded—prevention of unwanted conceptions among the married poor.

Margaret Sanger opened the first birth-control clinic in the United States in an impoverished community of Brooklyn in October 1916, which immediately led to her arrest—the first of eight. Under her leadership, federal and state anti–birth control statutes were eroded by public and judicial opinion. In November 1921, the dispersal by the police of a public meeting that she was to address in New York's Town Hall brought the American press to her side.

Legal Emancipation of Birth Control

In 1936, a landmark decision was made by the New York Circuit Court of Appeals in the case of *The U.S. v. One Package*, the package being three diaphragms imported from Japan. The favorable opinion of the three-judge court legalized prescription of contraceptives by the medical profession for health indications. In this day of widespread condom advertising and birth control distribution at some public high schools, it is sobering to realize that the final blow against the statutory ban on birth control occurred as recently as 1965. In that year, the United States Supreme Court declared the prohibitory law of Connecticut unconstitutional, largely as an invasion of privacy.

REASONS FOR EFFECTIVE CONTRACEPTION

There is no longer any reason (if one ever existed) to deny women the right to be sexually active without the threat of unwanted pregnancy. Pregnancy and childbirth carry a health risk for women, however safe they have become. Furthermore, responsibility for childrearing continues to fall largely upon the mother, and this has a major impact on how she spends the rest of her life. Children, too, have the right to be wanted and loved. Today, of course, in what might be called "The Age of HIV," freedom from sexually transmitted infection is as primary a concern as freedom from unwanted pregnancy. This has given men a more personal interest in having protected sexual relations.

METHODS OF CONTRACEPTION: AN OVERVIEW

There are many methods of contraception, some relatively new, some pre-dating written records. More than 1,500 years ago, the Talmud recommended a "cup of roots" to prevent pregnancy. One such prescription was to dissolve in beer Alexandrian gum, alum, and the bulb of the crocus and "to drink thereof." Throughout the folklore of most peoples are stories of plants reported to diminish fertility. The American Indians made tea from *Lithospermum ruderale*, which grew on the Western slopes of the Rockies, and each spring both women and men who sought to prevent pregnancy drank it. Temporary lodgment of a foreign body in the uterine cavity was first used by sixteenth century Arabs to prevent their camels from becoming pregnant. A long, hollow reed loaded with a small stone was introduced through the vagina and cervix and the stone blown into the uterine cavity. When pregnancy was desired, it is said, the stone was milked out.

Most Popular Contraceptive Methods in U.S.

A survey conducted in 1999 showed the popularity of various contraceptive methods in the United States. The most widely used methods, in order, were:

- Oral contraceptives and sterilization (use tied at 23 percent of all women aged 15 to 50)

> • The male condom (used by 16 percent of women)
> • Withdrawal and "rhythm" (7 percent)
> • Injectables (accounting for 3 percent of contraceptive use)
> • Spermicides
>
> Other methods, including the intrauterine device, implants, and several types of female barrier methods are used by relatively few American women today.

In the discussion of each method of contraception, several concepts are introduced. These are effectiveness, continuation rate, and safety.

Effectiveness of a contraception method means the extent to which the method prevents pregnancy. Estimates of effectiveness are usually measured by the number of pregnancies that would occur among 100 fertile women using the method for 1 year. As a comparison, in the absence of contraception and without suppression of ovulation by breast-feeding, 85 out of every 100 fertile women who are sexually active would be pregnant within a year.

There are two measures of contraceptive effectiveness. One is the effectiveness if the method were used perfectly by everybody using it. No method has a 100 percent effectiveness rate, although several methods have effectiveness rates of more than 99 percent if they are used perfectly. These include combination oral contraceptives, the patch and the vaginal ring, copper IUDs and the levonorgestrel IUD, the injectable (Depo-Provera), the implant, and female and male sterilization. If two barrier methods such as a condom and spermicide are used together, effectiveness is similar to these other methods. (A male and female condom, however, should not be used together as they can get stuck together.)

The second type of effectiveness measure is the percent of actual pregnancies prevented. This is called the *typical use effectiveness*.

For some methods, perfect use effectiveness and typical use effectiveness are almost the same. These are methods that need little input from the user, such as injectables and implants, sterilization, and the IUD. For methods such as barriers, that require intensive user input, these two rates can be rather far apart.

Effectiveness measures also can be expressed as *failure rates*—the percent of pregnancies theoretically possible or actually occurring with any particular method.

Effectiveness rates are based on research studies, often carried out when the manufacturer of a method is seeking marketing approval from the Food and Drug Administration. Studies of effectiveness vary in how they are conducted, in the mathematical method for figuring out the effectiveness rate, and in the interpretation of the findings. Although the numbers given in this chapter are reasonably accurate, they are not exact measures.

The *continuation rate* of a contraceptive method tells how many women who are still trying to avoid pregnancy use the method at the end of 1 year. This is an important rate because, even with high effectiveness, if the continuation rate is low, many women probably do not like the method. A low continuation rate makes a particular method less likely to be adopted for widespread use.

The *safety* of a contraceptive method involves how many side effects it has and how serious a threat to health they are. Some methods, like condoms, have few side effects and in fact have health benefits beyond their contraceptive effect. Other methods, like the pill, have a number of side effects, but also have some added health benefits. In general, today's methods pose few serious health problems.

The choice of a contraceptive method is highly individualized. A couple must choose a method that has a high degree of acceptability for both partners. There is therefore no best method of contraception in use, but there is a best method for an individual partnership. The large psychological component in sexual satisfaction makes it unwise for couples to choose a contraceptive method in which they lack confidence, which they fear because of side effects, or which is unaesthetic or objectionable to either the man or woman. For some women or couples the effectiveness of the method is most important, for others the lack of side effects is more important. The amount of *user input*—how much bother they perceive the method to entail—may be a key consideration. For some women, medical complications such as a history of blood clots make one or more methods possibly unsafe.

A final consideration today is the extent to which a method protects against sexually transmitted infections (STIs), including HIV. Some women and couples will combine methods to achieve the highest protection against pregnancy as provided by hormonal methods or the IUD and also use a condom for disease prevention. Any sexually active person who is not in a mutually monogamous relationship in which both partners are sure they are disease-free at the beginning of the relationship is at risk for an STI. Because of the nature of human beings, some experts consider anybody who has sexual relations to be at risk for STIs, regardless of whether they themselves are monogamous. The extent to which couples, even those in marriages or long-term relationships, choose to trust each other is a personal decision, perhaps difficult to make.

INFORMED CONSENT

Before deciding on a contraceptive method, you should have complete information about all choices. If you are seeking a method available only by prescription or that requires a procedure performed by a health care provider, you must receive what has become known as *informed consent*.

Most health and legal experts agree that informed consent consists of the following information, provided in language you understand:

- How the method or procedure works
- Advantages and disadvantages of the method or procedure. For family planning methods, this includes information about effectiveness and safety
- Common side effects and possible risks, including risk to life
- Alternative methods
- The risks of pregnancy and how likely you are to become pregnant if no contraceptive is used
- Cost of the method

You must be given the opportunity to ask questions and the opportunity to change your mind.

CONTRACEPTIVE METHODS FOR THE WOMAN

Oral Contraceptives: The Birth Control Pill

How the Pill Works

The birth control pill, or oral contraceptive, if taken as directed, is among the most effective reversible contraceptives known. There are two types of pills—combination pills and mini-pills. Combination pills have two active ingredients—the hormones estrogen and progestin, both synthetically produced. The mini-pill has only one active ingredient—progestin. These manufactured hormones are similar to, but more potent than, naturally occurring estrogen and progesterone. (The word *progestin* refers to a synthetic form of the hormone progesterone. There are a number of different types of progestins, with varying strengths and side effects.) This section discusses the combination pill. The mini-pill is reviewed starting on page 772.

The hormones in the pill are related to the hormones found in high doses during a pregnancy. In essence, when you take oral contraceptives, the body thinks you are pregnant, so the hormones that stimulate the ovary to ovulate are suppressed. Without ovulation, or the secretion of an egg cell, a pregnancy cannot occur.

Normally, hormones secreted by the pituitary or the body's master gland control the ovaries. These hormones are called *gonadotropins*. One is FSH (follicle-stimulating hormone) and the other LH (luteinizing hormone). These hormones cause an ovarian follicle to grow and release an egg cell each month. FSH and LH are in turn controlled by a hormone secreted by the hypothalamus, a specialized area on the underside of the brain. This hormone is called GnRH or *gonadotropin-releasing hormone*. With menstruation, the levels of natural estrogen and progesterone in the body drop. This signals to the hypothalamus to secrete GnRH, causing the pituitary to secrete FSH and then LH. Estrogen and progesterone levels then gradually rise, suppressing the control hormones. When a woman takes the pill, the estrogen and progesterone levels are high for 3 weeks, thus preventing the pituitary from secreting FSH and LH.

A secondary action of the pill prevents the cervical mucus from entering its midcycle profuse watery phase, a phase that creates a perfect fluid medium for penetration by sperm cells. Instead, under the influence of the pill, the cervical mucus remains scant, thick, and difficult, if not impossible, for the sperm to pass through.

A third action affects the lining of the uterus, the *endometrium*. For a fertilized egg to implant successfully the endometrium must present a specific pattern of cells, glands, and blood vessels. The pill alters this endometrial pattern.

The pill may interfere with the normal transport of the egg down the tubes. It also may cause the corpus luteum to degenerate, if one develops at all. The *corpus luteum* is the part of the ovary formed from the follicle that ruptures to release the egg cell. After ovulation, this structure secretes progesterone. Progesterone is necessary to maintain pregnancy. If the corpus luteum degenerates, there is insufficient progesterone.

The main action of the pill is to prevent ovulation. However, its other actions provide backup should a woman ovulate occasionally while taking the pill. This helps explain the pill's contraceptive effectiveness.

Pill Effectiveness

The pill has a failure rate of 0.1 percent, if used perfectly. This means there will be no more than 0.1 unplanned pregnancies per year per 100 women using the pill (1 pregnancy per 1,000 pill users). The actual effectiveness is somewhat lower than this, about 95 percent. This is because women forget to take pills or discontinue the pills due to unwanted side effects and don't use another method immediately. Approximately 50 to 75 percent of all women starting the pill continue to use it after one year.

Starting the Pill

Although there are health care providers who believe that oral contraceptives should be made available over the counter, in this country the pill is available only by prescription. Before starting the pill, you will have an examination. A thorough health history will be taken to check for reasons not to prescribe the pill, such as a history of stroke, heart disease, or *deep vein thrombosis* (blood clot). You will be asked about smoking. Your family history will be considered, although family history is not a reason to preclude pill use. It can, however, be a reason for caution. The physical examination will include breast and pelvic examinations and a Papanicoloau (*Pap*) *smear* (a test for cancer of the cervix). Blood pressure and weight should be taken. In women over 35, the blood may be tested for cholesterol ("good" and "bad" cholesterol—called HDLs and LDLs), triglycerides (another fatty substance in the blood), and possibly sugar.

When the pill is first begun, if it is started on day 1 of a menstrual period, you are protected against pregnancy from the time you take your first pill. An alternative way of starting is the Sunday start. You take the first pill on the Sunday following the beginning of your period (or on the first day of your period if it starts on a Sunday). With a Sunday start, you finish your twenty-one pills on a Saturday and start bleeding about 3 days later. Since periods when you're on the pill are short, you will almost never bleed on a weekend. If you prefer the Sunday start and it's not the first day of your period, or if you get or fill your prescription after your period has begun, use an additional means of contraception for the first 7 days you are on the pill.

You can adjust yourself to a Sunday start at any time by continuing to take the pills until a Saturday, using an extra package for the extra pills. This adjustment may be complicated if you are on a triphasic pill such as Ortho-Novum 7/7/7 or Triphasil, as one or both of the hormone doses change through the cycle. If that is the case consult your physician, nurse practitioner, or midwife for advice.

There are many brands of oral contraceptives available. Some of these, like Ortho-Novum 1/35 and Norinyl, are composed of the same exact hormones, while others are different formulations. While most pills combine estrogen and progestin, two types of estrogen and a variety of progestins are used. The dosages of each hormone also vary among pill brands. Each woman, then, should be able to find a pill that has few side effects for her. Several combinations, such as Ortho-Novum 7/7/7, are called *triphasic* pills. These increase the amount of progestin over the 21-day cycle. Another pill, with the brand name Triphasil, varies the estrogen and progestin dose throughout the cycle. Yet another, Estrostep, varies the estrogen only.

One of the newest birth control pills is called Yasmin. This pill has a different kind of progestin than most other birth control pills. This progestin works like a diuretic (water pill) so women shouldn't experience the fluid retention and bloating that they sometimes do with other pills. They are less likely to gain weight (although with today's low-dose pills most women do not gain significant weight on any pill). The progestin in Yasmin has the effect of "sparing" potassium in the body— meaning you maintain potassium even as you lose fluids. For this reason, women who use Yasmin should not regularly use other medications that have the same effect on potassium. Such potassium-increasing drugs include the non-steroidal anti-inflammatory drugs (NSAIDs) such as ibuprofen (Motrin, Advil) or naproxen (Naprosyn, Aleve, Anaprox). These can certainly be used occasionally for headaches or cramps when you are on Yasmin, but may cause a problem when taken long-term and daily for conditions such as arthritis. If you take any of these drugs every day, inform your care provider and have your potassium level checked in the first month of taking Yasmin. Other potassium-increasing medications include certain diuretics (spironolactone and others) and, of course, potassium supplements. Certain medications used to treat high blood pressure— ACE inhibitors (such as Capoten, Vasotec, Zestril) and angiotensin-II receptor antagonists (such as Cozaar, Diovan, Avapro)—also increase potassium levels. (Women with high blood pressure shouldn't be on oral contraceptives anyway.) The anti-clotting drug Heparin is another potassium-increasing drug, but women who are at risk for blood clots should not take birth control pills.

Some pills, such as Micronor and Ovrette, consist of progestin only. These are somewhat less effective, but may be best for women who cannot take estrogen (see page 778). Progestin only pills are called mini-pills.

How to Take the Pill

The pill (in reality a tablet) is taken every day for 21 days. No medication is taken then for 1 week. Most brands provide a different-colored *placebo* (fake pill) for you to take daily for 7 days before restarting the 21-day (real pill) cycle. Some have iron in the placebo pills. Many women find it easier to take a daily pill rather than go through the routine of 21 days on and 7 days off. The pill preferably is taken at the same time every day. This helps you remember to take it on a daily basis and maintains its effectiveness.

All birth control pills are packaged so that each pill is marked with a day of the week. This way you never have to remember whether or not you took your pill for the day. Develop the routine of checking the pill pack every morning to make sure you took the previous day's pill.

About 72 hours after taking the last active pill, you will have vaginal bleeding, which can be considered a menstrual period. It actually differs from a regular period, since pill bleeding is from a different type of uterine lining than the bleeding of normal menstruation. A pill period is usually briefer and scantier than a true period and is almost always free of cramps.

Occasionally, no bleeding occurs after the last pill. If you've taken the pill correctly without missing days, and you haven't used any medication that might interfere with the pill's effectiveness (see page 778), you are unlikely to be pregnant. Despite absence of bleeding, you can start your new pack at the usual time. If you have missed pills, have been irregular in your taking of the pills, or have been on medication, then consult your physician, nurse practitioner, or midwife, or perform a home pregnancy test. You can also check your basal body temperature (see the section on Natural Family Planning on page 813). If it is 98° Fahrenheit or less for three consecutive mornings, then very likely you are not pregnant.

If you have no bleeding for two successive cycles, consult a physician, nurse practitioner, or midwife to rule out the unlikely possibility of a pregnancy. Occasionally, periods may stop completely on the pill or be so scant as to be just a bit of spotting. If not having a period is not worrisome for you, it is not a health problem when you are taking pills. If you are bothered by not having your period, however, or unduly worried about a possible pregnancy without the reassurance of a monthly period to tell you that you are not pregnant, then speak to your physician, nurse practitioner, or midwife about trying a pill with a different hormonal formulation. You might have to use trial and error until you find a pill that will work without causing *amenorrhea* (absence of menses or periods).

If you wish to postpone bleeding for an event such as a trip or an athletic meet, there is no harm in taking the pill continuously for 30 or 40 days instead of 21. Some women who have severe menstrual headaches or cramps can take the pill continuously for three cycles to better avoid these problems. You stop, then, only every 63 days or 9 weeks. This is called *tricycling*.

There is no time limit on how long the pill can be used. There is no need to discontinue it after several years and substitute another contraceptive method for a few months before resuming its use. Such a pill "vacation" has no health benefits.

If pregnancy should occur because of either improper use or pill failure in a woman taking ordinary doses of oral contraceptives, there are no known adverse effects on the fetus.

What to Do If You Miss a Pill

As the dosage of hormones used in pills has decreased, the safety of the pill has increased. The effectiveness has remained the same if you take the pill correctly. However, if you miss pills, effectiveness decreases. You can even decrease effectiveness if you take the pill every day, but more than 36 hours apart.

If you use mini-pills (progestin-only pills), effectiveness is reduced if you are even a few hours late in taking the pill. A backup method (such as a condom or diaphragm) is advised for 48 hours anytime your mini-pill is 3 or more hours late. You should always have a barrier contraceptive like male or female condoms on hand for emergencies. (If you forget the pill for the entire day, use the backup for 7 days, as you would with the combination pill.)

To keep from missing pills, develop a routine. Take the pill at the same time every day. You can associate pill taking with something else you do daily, like brushing your teeth. If you use this reminder, keep the pills near your toothbrush. If this isn't private enough, keep the pills at your bedside and associate them with going to bed. If you use a 21-day pack, mark your calendar to remind you when to start a new pack.

If you use a 28-day pack and you miss any of the last seven pills, don't worry. These are placebo pills. They have no active ingredients. If you miss one of the first 21-day pills, those with hormones, use a backup method for 7 days, or don't have sex for 7 days. Take the missed pill as soon as you remember it, and take the regular day's pill at the usual time. If you only realize that you missed the previous day's pill when you are about to take the regular day's pill, then take two together. If you miss more than two pills, take two, and throw out the other missed pills. Use a backup contraceptive or abstinence for 7 days. If you miss two pills on the mini-pill, take 2 pills for 2 days and use a backup or abstinence for 7 days. If you've had unprotected intercourse after missing 2 mini-pills, you should call your physician, nurse practitioner, or midwife for possible emergency contraception.

If you miss pills in the last week of hormone pills (numbers 15 to 21) in addition to using a backup contraceptive for 7 days, don't wait 7 days to start a new pack. If you use a 28-day pack, throw out the seven placebo pills and start your new pack the day after you take the last active pill. If you use a 21-day pack, start your new pack the day after the last pill. Most likely, you will not have a period that month.

Advantages and Disadvantages of Oral Contraceptives

The pill is a highly effective method of birth control. The combined pill is among the most effective reversible contraceptives available.

Use of the pill is completely separate from the sexual act. However, because pill use requires that you take a pill every day, at approximately the same time for optimal effectiveness, the typical use effectiveness of oral contraceptives is somewhat less than the perfect use effectiveness.

The pill bestows a number of health benefits. Important benefits include a reduction in cancer of the ovary and *endometrium* (lining of the uterus). Protection increases with increased time of pill use and persists for years after the pill is stopped.

The pill decreases menstrual pain and bleeding. Some women have fewer premenstrual symptoms (such as anxiety, depression, and fluid retention) when they are on the pill, but other women have more of these.

The pill reduces the likelihood of developing benign breast cysts and higher dose pills reduce the frequency of some types of ovarian cysts. Because of reduced uterine bleeding, pill users have a decreased likelihood of becoming anemic (having low hemoglobin or low red cell count in the blood). Women who have unwanted facial hair usually find that the pill improves this problem (called *hirsutism*). Certain types of pills can be used to treat acne. The pill is protective against some types of pelvic inflammatory disease. It prevents not only intrauterine pregnancy, but also *ectopic pregnancy* (a pregnancy outside the uterus, which can be a dangerous condition).

Because the hormones in the pill act on many body organs, there are also some health disadvantages to oral contraceptives. Some of these are considered minor problems, also called *nuisance problems*. They do not have serious effects on health, but they may make you unhappy. Some, like nausea and vomiting, are common but temporary. They are mostly seen in the first few months of pill use. If you can stick it out, they will go away. If you vomit within 1 hour after taking your pill, you will need to take another. Always have an extra pack on hand as the pills are clearly marked for each day to keep you on schedule. The extra pill should be taken from your spare pack. (If you are sick and vomit or have diarrhea for more than 24 hours, besides contacting your physician, nurse practitioner or midwife, use a backup method for the duration of the illness and 7 days afterward.)

Although scant and pain-free periods are an advantage for many women, the pill may cause some unwanted spotting or bleeding, especially in the first few months of use. You might skip periods or have periods that consist of just a small amount of staining. For some women, these changes are disturbing.

Some women gain weight on the pill. This may be cyclic and mostly due to fluid retention from the estrogen in the pill. It may not be cyclic but due to an increased appetite from the progestin. The pill may cause breast fullness and tenderness and skin changes such as *chloasma* (the *mask of pregnancy* or darkening of the skin on the face). Most side effects reverse once the pill is stopped, but chloasma may be permanent. If you had this problem with pregnancy, you might want to consider another contraceptive method or stay out of the sun, use sunscreen, and wear wide-brimmed hats whenever sun exposure is unavoidable.

If you are nursing, the combined pill will interfere with milk supply. The baby will be exposed to the hormones in both the combined pill and the mini-pill, but these are not known to have adverse effects. However, the combined pill should not be used until the milk supply is well established. The earliest time would be 6 weeks after childbirth, but most experts recommend at least 3 months. The World Health Organization, noting that milk production increases for 6 months, recommends waiting 6 months to start combined oral contraceptives.

Oral contraceptives do not offer any protection against sexually transmitted infections (STIs). This includes HIV (human immunodeficiency virus), which causes AIDS (acquired immune deficiency syndrome). If you are at risk for STIs and want to use the pill for its effectiveness, you should use condoms along with the pill. Anyone in a relationship that is not mutually monogamous in which both partners are sure they are disease-free at the start of the relationship is at risk for an STI.

The pill may have beneficial or nonbeneficial effects on mood. In some women, depression is improved during pill use. Other women feel more depressed. Because of decreased worry about pregnancy, the pill increases sexual drive for many women. Occasionally, however, it may decrease sexual desire. Sometimes the particular formulation of the pill is responsible for depression or decreased sexual drive and a change in pill might relieve either problem.

Women may get headaches while using the pill or have worsening of pre-existing headaches. If there are visual changes with the headaches, the pill should not be used.

The pill may increase the development of gall bladder disease for susceptible women. Symptomatic gall bladder disease is considered by the World Health Organization as a reason not to use the pill. The pill does not increase the risk of gall bladder cancer.

Although studies have shown conflicting results, a recent analysis of many of the reports on pill use and breast cancer showed that women on the pill are slightly more likely to have breast cancer diagnosed than women not on the pill. The risk is increased during pill use by about 24 percent, the risk dropping to 16 percent 1 to 4 years after discontinuing the pill, and to 7 percent 5 to 9 years later. Ten years after stopping the pill, the increased risk is eliminated. It is possible that this small increase in risk is actually due to increased detection, not increased disease. This means that since women on the pill may have more frequent physical examinations, they are more likely to have an early breast cancer discovered than a woman using a method which doesn't require frequent health checks. This is supported by the fact that the breast cancers among pill users tend to spread less quickly than cancers in women not on the pill, meaning that perhaps these cancers are found earlier. There is also a small increased risk of developing cancer of the cervix while on the pill, especially with long-term use.

The pill may cause an elevation in blood pressure, which is reversible when the pill is stopped. Increased growth of uterine fibroids may be noted, also reversible. Long-term oral contraceptive users have an increased frequency of *hepatocellular adenoma*, a nonmalignant tumor of the liver. This is an extremely rare condition in women not on the pill and only slightly less rare among pill users. This problem has not been found to date with low-dose pills currently in use.

The most serious health problems associated with pill use are diseases of the circulatory system. These include blood clots, heart attack, and stroke. A blood clot often starts in the legs but if it travels to a major organ such as the lungs or the brain, it can be very serious, occasionally resulting in death. None of these complications of pill use, however, are common with the low-dose pills in use today.

When you have one or more health problems that also increase the risk for circulatory problems, pill use may be unwise. These problems include:

- Sedentary lifestyle (lack of exercise)
- Obesity
- Age (over 50)
- Hypertension (high blood pressure)
- Previous heart disease ·
- Diabetes
- High cholesterol
- Smoking

The World Health Organization (WHO) considers age 35 and heavy smoking (twenty or more cigarettes a day, or at least one pack per day) as a reason not to use oral contraceptives. WHO considers age 35 and light smoking (less than twenty cigarettes a day) as a reason for caution. (See the section below for other precautions recommended by WHO.)

Some pill side effects diminish over time. Others can be corrected with a change in the specific pill prescribed. Still others will require you to use a different contraceptive. If you wish to continue using a hormonal method, you may be able to use a progestin-only contraceptive, (see pages 782–787). Whenever you have a side effect due to the pill, or one that you think may be due to the pill, discuss it with your physician, nurse practitioner, or midwife, who will help you decide the best way to deal with the problem.

The Pill and Subsequent Fertility
In most individuals pill use has no effect on subsequent fertility. Ordinarily, a true menstrual period—not the immediate withdrawal bleeding—resumes 4 to 6 weeks after stopping the pill. Most women who have sex without contraception after stopping the pill get pregnant within 3 months. About 1 or 2 percent of women have *amenorrhea* (absence of periods) for 6 months or longer after discontinuing the pill. In general, the pill does not help or hurt fertility, although the pill does help prevent some causes of infertility including pelvic inflammatory disease, uterine fibroids, and ectopic pregnancy.

Drug Interactions with Oral Contraceptives
A number of medications interact with the pill. The medication will either make the pill less effective, or the pill will make the medication

less effective. These include several anticonvulsants and some antibiotics. Possible drug interactions are listed in the table.

Drugs That Interfere with Pill Effectiveness	Drugs That Are Affected by the Pill
Anticonvulsants: Phenytoin (Dilantin) Phenobarbital Topirimate Primidone Carbamazepine (Tegretol) *Antibiotics:* Rifampin Griseofulvin Ampicillin Doxycycline Tetracycline	*Drugs That May Be Cleared More Slowly:* Tranquilizers Corticosteroids *Drugs That May Be Cleared More Rapidly:* Acetaminophen (Tylenol) Aspirin

If you take medications that interfere with pill effectiveness for a
short period of time, you can use a backup contraceptive during the
treatment and for 7 days afterward. If you take any of these medications
for a long period of time, you might need a higher dose pill. You can
also increase pill effectiveness by *tricycling*—taking the pill continuously
for three cycles. You do not take the placebo pills if you use a 28-day
pack or don't stop for the fourth week if you use a 21-day pack. After
completing three packs, you stop for only 4 days. Discuss this method
with your care provider.

If you are prescribed any medication, you should mention to the
prescriber that you take oral contraceptives. If the medication is cleared
more slowly in the body when you take the pill, its dose may have to be
reduced. If the medication is cleared more rapidly, the dose may need to
be higher for the drug to work.

Pill Precautions

There are a few reasons not to use the pill (called *contraindications*).
As mentioned, one is early breast-feeding, before the milk supply is well
established. At 6 weeks postpartum, however, the mini-pill, containing
only a progestin, can be started. It does not interfere with milk supply.
Although the infants are exposed to minute quantities of hormones,
there are no known ill effects.

Other contraindications include:

- Pregnancy
- Breast cancer
- A history of *phlebitis* (inflammation of a vein)
- *Deep vein thrombosis* (blood clot) or *pulmonary embolism* (blood clot in the lungs)
- A history of *stroke* (cerebrovascular accident)
- Coronary artery disease or other heart disease
- Headaches with neurological symptoms, such as visual disturbances
- Longstanding or severe diabetes, including disease with kidney, eye, or nervous system complications
- Liver problems
- Planned surgery that will involve immobilization or any surgery of the legs
- Age 35 and heavy smoking
- *Hypertension* (high blood pressure)

Caution should be used in women with undiagnosed abnormal vaginal or uterine bleeding; women over 35 years of age who smoke less than twenty cigarettes a day; past history of breast cancer, but without recurrence for 5 years; use of drugs that interact with oral contraceptives; and gall bladder disease.

Pill Warning Signs

The most serious problems with the pill often present warning signs. If any of these occur, call your physician, nurse practitioner, or midwife as soon as possible:

- Pain, tenderness, or warmth in the legs. There also may be a hardened, ropy-feeling area in the calf or thigh. This may indicate the start of a blood clot.
- Chest pain, shortness of breath, or any difficulty breathing. This may mean the blood clot has traveled to the lungs or heart.
- Severe abdominal pain. Rarely, this may indicate a liver tumor.
- Severe headache, dizziness, weakness, or numbness. This is especially significant if it is one-sided. Difficulty with speech.
- Eye problems, such as vision loss, sudden blurry vision, spots or lights in front of the eyes.

Oral Contraceptives as Emergency Contraception (The "Morning-After" Pill)

The pill can also be used as a "post-coital" or emergency contraceptive. This means it can prevent a pregnancy after unprotected sexual intercourse. Without a corpus luteum to secrete progesterone, pregnancy will not occur. Using the pill in this way, it has been called a *morning-after pill*, although in fact it is effective up to 120 hours (5 days) after unprotected intercourse—4 or 5 mornings after. The mechanism of action is thought to be primarily an interference with fertilization, with the corpus luteum, or with implantation. This is different from the so-called abortion pill (RU-486 or mifepristone) which is taken after a missed period and does cause an early abortion.

The likelihood of pregnancy resulting from one act of unprotected intercourse is about 8 percent, as the odds are well against a woman's being in her fertile period at any given time. This means about 8 women out of every 100 women having unprotected intercourse would become pregnant. Using emergency contraception reduces the pregnancy rate by about 75 percent of the unprotected level. This means about 2 out of every 100 women having unprotected intercourse would become pregnant if they all used emergency contraception.

Unprotected intercourse could mean no contraceptive was used or a method failed. The condom might have broken, for example.

Emergency oral contraception consists of two doses: The first is taken within 120 hours of unprotected intercourse, the second is taken 12 hours later.

Pills used for emergency contraception contain either the estrogen ethinyl estradiol with the progestin levonorgestrel, or just levonorgestrel. As the morning-after dose greatly exceeds the routine daily dose of oral contraceptives, it cannot be used on a regular basis. The two-hormone pill causes nausea in about 30 to 50 percent of all women. Vomiting occurs in 15 to 20 percent. The progestin-only pill results in less nausea and vomiting—20 percent and 5 percent, respectively—and therefore may be more effective. Other side effects include breast tenderness, fatigue, headache, stomach pain, and dizziness. These subside within a few days.

If you don't have birth control pills, or have a different type of hormone in your pill, you can be given a prescription for emergency contraception. (If you are a pill user, the only time you might need emergency contraception is if you miss three or more of the active pills and had sex without a backup method, such as a condom, during the days of missed pills or within the first 7 days afterward.) Today, emergency contraceptive pills are marketed under the trade names Preven and Plan B. In England, emergency contraception has been approved as an over-the-counter medication and some experts support this in the United States.

If you are already using pills with these hormones, the number of pills to take at each dose for emergency contraception appears in the box below:

Recommended Number of Pills to Take at Each Dose for Emergency Contraception

Ovral, 2 white pills
Lo/Ovral, 4 white pills
Nordette, 4 light-orange pills
Levlen, 4 light-orange pills
Triphasil, 4 yellow pills
Trilevlen, 4 yellow pills
Alesse, 5 pink pills
Ovrette, 20 yellow pills

With all but Ovrette, an antinausea pill should be taken 1 hour before the first dose. Your care provider can prescribe something or you can take an over-the-counter medication like Dramamine II or Benadryl. You can take these pills in repeated doses, according to the instructions on the package. They may make you drowsy, so don't drink or drive while taking these antinausea medications.

Emergency contraception does not prevent pregnancies from intercourse occurring after you take the pills—only intercourse that occurred 120 hours or less before you take the pills. You can use a barrier method immediately or start your usual pill pack after the emergency pills are completed or with your next menstrual period. Other hormonal methods can be started with the next menstrual period.

If you cannot reach your care provider, or do not have a regular person to call, you can contact the emergency contraception hotline at 1-888-NOT-2-LATE, run by the Reproductive Health Technologies Project. This hotline will provide you with phone numbers of care providers near you who will prescribe emergency contraception, even if you are not their usual patient.

If you don't get a period within about 3 weeks after using emergency oral contraception, call your physician, nurse practitioner, or midwife, or do a home pregnancy test. You might be pregnant.

Other Hormonal Contraceptives for Women

Injectables

Hormonal contraceptives can be given by injection, with long intervals between doses. The hormone most used in this way is another synthetic progestin, called *medroxyprogesterone acetate* (Depo-Provera). Depo-Provera is injected every 12 weeks. More recently, monthly injectables have been developed. These combine Depo-Provera with estrogen. Brand names include Lunelle, Cyclofem, and Cyclo-Provera.

Injectable contraception works similarly to the way oral contraceptives work. It inhibits ovulation, changes the cervical mucus so the sperm cannot navigate through it, and thins the endometrium (lining of the uterus) so that implantation is not possible.

INJECTABLE EFFECTIVENESS   The perfect use effectiveness of injectables is close to that of oral contraceptives, with less than a 1 percent failure rate. The great advantage of injectables is that you do not have to do anything other than return for each dose. Therefore, injectables have a typical use effectiveness that is about the same as their perfect use effectiveness. In cultures where male partners restrict women's access to contraception, the man need not know that the hormone has been injected. In the United States, approximately 40 to 60 percent of all users continue with Depo-Provera after the first year. It has the added advantage of continued effectiveness even if you are 1 to 2 weeks late for the next injection, although it is preferable to stay on the 12-week schedule.

HOW TO USE THE INJECTABLE   There is little to do should you decide to use Depo-Provera. You must see a physician, nurse practitioner, or midwife. A health history will be taken and a physical examination performed. Women who cannot take oral contraceptives for a health-related reason cannot use the combined injectable. It may be a good choice, however, for women who can take estrogen but have trouble remembering to take a daily pill.

If the first Depo-Provera injection is given within 5 days after your period begins, you will be protected immediately. If you have the first injection later in your cycle, use a backup method such as a condom for

1 week (7 days) after the injection. The company that markets injectable contraceptives advises giving the first injection only within the first 5 days of a period, but if you have not had unprotected intercourse since your last period, many providers will give you the injection anytime in your cycle. You should not have an injection beyond 5 days after your period starts, however, if there is any chance you are pregnant.

Injections of 150 mg of Depo-Provera are given into the arm (*deltoid*) or buttocks (*gluteal*) muscle. You may prefer the injection in the arm as it is a body area many people are more comfortable exposing, but deltoid injections may be a bit more painful than gluteal injections. Once you receive the first injection, return to your care provider or birth control clinic every 12 weeks for repeat injections of Depo-Provera or every 4 weeks for repeat injections of the combined injectable. If you are more than a week late for a 3-month injection or more than a few days late for a monthly injection, your care provider will need to make sure you are not pregnant before giving you a repeat injection.

INJECTABLE ADVANTAGES AND DISADVANTAGES   Because Depo-Provera is only one hormone, the estrogen-related side effects of combined oral contraceptives, such as fluid retention, growth of uterine fibroids, and a reduction in milk supply during early breast-feeding are not problems with injectable contraceptives. Serious cardiovascular problems have not been seen with progestin-only contraceptives. With the combined injectable, however, estrogen side effects are possible. Women who cannot take estrogen for reasons such as high blood pressure should not use the monthly combined injectable.

The most common side effect of Depo-Provera is irregular and unpredictable bleeding, which contrasts with the regularity that most women enjoy on oral contraceptives and the monthly injectable. This occurs mostly in the first few cycles of use. Over time, periods become very scant and may disappear eventually. Depo-Provera use eliminates pain associated with periods and, for some women, with ovulation. It also helps prevent *anemia* (low hemoglobin or low red cell count in the blood).

Women using the combined injectable are more likely to have regular periods. About 50 percent of women using the combined injectable have regular periods about 20 to 25 days after receiving the injection. Periods may be more or less than before injection use, longer or shorter. Some women experience spotting during the cycle, especially in the first few months of use.

An often undesirable side effect of injectables is weight gain. This averages 4 to 5 pounds the first year, 8 pounds after the second year and almost 14 pounds after the fourth year. Headaches and breast tenderness may occur. Some studies have found that some women using Depo-Provera experience depression, but not all studies have confirmed this. Other side effects include unfavorable changes in cholesterol levels (a reduction of "good" cholesterol) and decreases in bone density.

While using an injectable contraceptive, be aware of an increased appetite. Make wise food choices such as fruits and vegetables to satisfy your needs. Because of Depo-Provera's effect on bone mass, you should do weight-bearing exercise while taking this medication (such as weight lifting, jogging or running, bicycling). Exercise, especially aerobics, also will help with weight control. Eat foods that contain calcium, such as dairy products (but choose low-fat or fat-free dairy products), or take calcium tablets. The average American diet contains only about one-quarter to one-third the recommended calcium requirement. Unless your daily intake is at least four glasses of milk (preferably skim or 1 percent), or the equivalent (about six ounces of cheese, for example), you should supplement with calcium. If you have about two glasses of milk per day or its equivalent, then you should take at least 600 mg of calcium each day. The only common calcium side effect is constipation, so increase fluids, fruits, vegetables, and whole grains.

When Depo-Provera was initially used internationally, concerns were raised because beagle dogs given the shot had increased rates of mammary gland (breast) cancers. The World Health Organization conducted a widespread study that did not find an increased rate of breast cancer among women using Depo-Provera. However, one study found that the hormone may accelerate the growth of breast cancer in women between the ages of 25 and 34, especially after 6 years of use, although this was not documented in the larger World Health Organization study.

Unlike oral contraceptives, Depo-Provera does not interact with other drugs. For women with seizure disorders such as epilepsy, Depo-Provera reduces the number of seizures. Like oral contraceptives, it has a protective effect on cancer of the lining of the uterus (*endometrium*). Like oral contraceptives, Depo-Provera provides no protection against sexually transmitted infections.

One of the major disadvantages of Depo-Provera compared to other contraceptives is that the medication stays in the system long after the last dose. Side effects may linger for as long as 6 to 8 months after you are no longer getting injections. Normal menstruation and fertility also may take up to 6 to 12 months to resume. This same side effect makes injectable contraceptives "forgiving" of human error. If you are late for an injection, you will be protected for quite a while afterward. By 18 to 20 months, the return of fertility among those wishing to have a child is the same as with all other methods of contraception. With monthly injections, periods and fertility return for most women about 2 to 3 months after the last injection. (Of course, after any contraceptive use, about 8 percent of women will be unable to get pregnant—the natural level of infertility in the population.)

Injectable Contraceptives: Warning Signs

The warning signs of a possible serious problem when you are taking Depo-Provera are:

- Recurrent painful headaches
- Heavy vaginal bleeding
- Depression (may show itself with insomia, fatigue or lack of energy, mood change)
- Severe pain in the pelvic area (may indicate an ectopic pregnancy)
- Signs of infection where the injection was given—a discharge with pus, ongoing pain, or bleeding

If you are using the combined monthly injectable, the warning signs are the same as those for oral contraceptives, listed earlier in the chapter.

Implants

Another way to administer long-acting hormonal contraception is to implant a rod containing *levonorgestrel*, a potent progestin, just under the skin. These are marketed under the name Norplant. The rod is made of *silastic*, a porous synthetic material. Small amounts of the hormone are released daily from the rod into the circulation and suppress ovulation.

Until recently, an implant consisting of six small rods was implanted, usually in the underside of the upper arm. Unfortunately, sometimes one or more of these rods would move and removal would then prove difficult. A newer implant has been developed, which consists of only one rod. Unlike the six-rod implant, which could remain in place for 5 years, the single rod implant is effective for only 3 years—which still makes it a long-term contraceptive.

Because there is absolutely nothing that a woman must do for 3 years once the implant is in place, the perfect use and typical use effectiveness rates of implants are equal, making these the most effective contraceptive available. Because its hormones are released in such low doses, however, the implant is slightly less effective among women who weigh more than 154 pounds. At 1 year, almost 90 percent of all women continue to use implants, and half continue for 3 years.

Implant Insertion and Removal

Implant insertion is a simple procedure. Usually the implant is placed on the inner part of your upper arm. Most of the time it cannot be seen under the skin or is barely visible. Local anesthesia is used for insertion so the procedure should not be painful. A tiny incision (less than a quarter of an inch) is made and the implant is inserted with a needle. Some practitioners use the needle to puncture the skin without making an incision.

Following insertion, your arm will be wrapped in a bandage that you should wear for 3 to 5 days because of tenderness at the site of insertion. You may have a bruise for several days after you remove the bandage.

Removal of the single-rod implant is not difficult; however, your arm may be bruised for a few days after removal and may be tender. You can take nonsteroidal anti-inflammatory drugs (NSAIDs) such as ibuprofen (brand names: Motrin or Advil) or naproxen (brand names: Aleve, Anaprox, or Naprosyn) for the pain. Having removal done by a practitioner with experience removing implants is essential.

Implant Advantages and Disadvantages

The great majority of women using the implant will have menstrual changes. You may stop menstruating entirely. If you are bothered by continued spotting, you may be given a low-dose birth control pill for several months or a low dose of estrogen to take with the implant. This shouldn't cause undue side effects since the dose of the hormone in the implant is extremely low. In fact, it is so low that certain medications, including rifampin and antiseizure medications (except valproic acid), interfere seriously with the effectiveness of the implant. If you take any of these medications you must use a backup barrier contraceptive if you want to use the implant.

Other undesirable implant side effects include:

• Inflammation or infection where the implants are placed
• Headaches

- Depression
- Breast tenderness
- Acne
- Possible weight gain

Weight gain averages about five pounds in 5 years of use, so it is not clear the extent to which this reflects normal weight gain over time rather than gain related to the implant. Some women develop cysts in the ovary while using Norplant. These are not cancerous and usually regress without any treatment.

Implant Warning Signs

Call your physician, nurse practitioner, or midwife if you experience any of the following while you are using implants:

- Heavy vaginal bleeding
- Pain in the arm of insertion
- Bleeding or a discharge with pus where the implant was inserted
- Expulsion of an implant
- Delayed menstrual period after having regular periods (with Depo-Provera, periods may stop after long use, but with the implants, if you have *amenorrhea* (lack of periods), it will occur earlier in use of the method)
- Headaches, especially if migraine, very severe and recurrent, or accompanied by changes in your vision, such as blurry or double vision
- Severe pain in the pelvic area (may indicate an ectopic pregnancy or ovarian cyst)

Unlike the injectable, once the implant is removed, side effects are relieved and fertility restored immediately. Unlike many other methods, however, discontinuation requires a health care visit.

Contraceptive Patch and Vaginal Ring

The two newest methods of birth control available in the United States are the contraceptive patch and the vaginal ring (Ortho Evra and NuvaRing, respectively). Both of these are new ways of delivering types of estrogen and progestin to the body. They are especially good for women who have trouble remembering to take their pill. They work similarly to the pill, and have similar side effects and contraindications. The patch may cause a bit more breast tenderness than the pill and occasionally may irritate the skin.

The contraceptive patch is worn on the outer upper arm, the buttocks, the abdomen, or the front or back of the torso, except for the breasts. The patch is applied to clear dry skin. Its effectiveness is over 99 percent. The patch, which is a thin beige square, 1¾ inches on each side, is changed weekly. Studies have shown that only about 4 percent of patches come off the skin, even in hot weather and with exercise or sauna use. Often, they can be reapplied, or replaced with a new patch. Patches, available by prescription only, come in packages of three as they are applied once a week for three weeks, followed by a patch-free week. You can also purchase a single patch in case a patch does come off.

The vaginal ring is a very thin, pliable open ring, made as a one-size-fits-all device. It is about 4.5 centimeters in diameter (approximately 2 inches). It is worn for 3 weeks and removed for 1 week—requiring even less user involvement than the patch. If you or your partner feel it during sexual intercourse, it can be removed for up to three hours. Although it does not need to be fit, it is available only by prescription because of its hormonal content.

Intrauterine Devices (IUDs)

The intrauterine device (Latin: *intra* = within) is used by relatively few women in the United States. In contrast, this method of birth control, most often called the IUD, is used by many women throughout the world, especially in China and several European countries. A number of years ago, IUDs were taken off the U.S. market because of lawsuits claiming that the device caused women to develop pelvic infections. These infections led to infertility in some cases and even a few deaths. In fact, only one marketed IUD was responsible for this problem. This IUD was called the Dalkon Shield and its string was made in such a way that it encouraged the movement of bacteria upward through the cervix and into the uterus and the tubes. The infections caused by the Dalkon Shield gave all IUDs a lot of "bad press."

This is most unfortunate, as many experts in the field of contraception agree that the newer devices come as close to the perfect reversible contraceptive as we have available today. Users have a higher level of satisfaction with them than with any other methods.

Today, three IUDs are available in the United States. All are smaller than most previously available devices, and include copper or a hormone to enhance their contraceptive effect. One of the three (the Progestasert) is less effective and needs to be changed annually. Its advantage over the copper IUD is that the progesterone in it reduces the amount of menstrual bleeding and bleeding between periods. However, the Mirena, the newest IUD, has these same advantages, but is more effective and can remain in place for up to 5 years. The Progestasert is likely to become obsolete very shortly.

The Copper T 380A or ParaGard is a small plastic device in the shape of a T and wrapped with copper. It has been available in the United States since 1988. The progesterone-releasing IUD or Progestasert, in use in the U.S. since 1976, is a similarly shaped device that releases a small amount of progesterone into the uterine cavity. The newest IUD (brand name Mirena) has been used in Finland since 1990 but has been available in the U.S. only since 2001. It looks like a curved T. It releases a synthetic form of progesterone called *levonorgestrel*. The manufacturers of Mirena call it an intrauterine system or IUS, but many physicians, nurse practitioners, and midwives still refer to Mirena as an IUD.

The IUD can remain in the uterus for varying periods of time: 1 year for the Progestasert; 5 years for the Mirena; and 10 years for the ParaGard. As previously mentioned, the need for annual reinsertion of Progestasert is a big disadvantage. Now that a progestin-releasing IUD is available for 5 years, it is doubtful that any providers will continue to insert Progestasert.

How the IUD Works

Each of the IUDs works in a slightly different way. The copper IUD or ParaGard appears to work by a direct effect on sperm, making fertilization highly unlikely. If a rare sperm does manage to get to the tubes and fertilize an ovum, ParaGard will then prevent implantation.

The exact way the levonorgestrel-releasing IUD or Mirena works is unclear. It appears to affect the cervical mucus so that sperm have a harder time getting into the cervix and also to prevent implantation.

IUD Effectiveness

The new IUDs are very effective at preventing pregnancy. The levonorgestrel-releasing IUD is the most effective of the three types of IUDs. In the first year of use, its pregnancy rate is approximately one-tenth of 1 percent. In fact, it is one of the most effective methods of birth control available, with the copper IUD close behind. The copper

IUD has a first year pregnancy rate of about one-half of 1 percent. Over 10 years, the cumulative rate of pregnancy is between 2 and 3 percent. IUDs have high continuation rates, with 78 to 81 percent of women still using the method at the end of the year following insertion.

Although the IUD does not increase the likelihood of having an ectopic pregnancy, if a pregnancy does occur it is more likely to be ectopic than a pregnancy occuring in a woman not using an IUD.

If pregnancy occurs with an IUD in place, the IUD should be removed as soon as possible. However, if the strings cannot be seen, the IUD cannot be removed because probing the cervix or uterus to find the strings could interfere with the pregnancy. In that case, the pregnancy may continue, although there is about a 50 percent risk of miscarriage. There is no increase in fetal malformations. If you choose not to keep the pregnancy, the IUD can be removed at the time of abortion.

IUD Insertion

An IUD can be inserted at any time. It can be inserted at your first postpartum visit, usually 4 to 6 weeks after childbirth. It can be inserted immediately after an abortion. An IUD can be used as emergency contraception, so even if you have had unprotected intercourse, it can be inserted up to 5 days afterward.

Once you decide that you want to use an IUD, schedule a preinsertion visit. At this time, your health history will be taken and a pelvic examination performed. Tests for sexually transmitted infections including chlamydia and gonorrhea may be taken. Some practitioners perform these tests routinely, others do them only if you are at risk for an STI. If an IUD is placed into the uterus in the presence of such an infection, the infection could spread into the tubes and become serious. At this preinsertion visit, you may be given literature to read at home.

If tests are done, once results are available, you will return for your insertion visit. But if there are no signs of infection, and you have no risks for an STI, many providers will insert the IUD at the first visit. You will be asked to sign an informed consent form.

About 30 to 60 minutes before the IUD insertion, you may be given a nonsteroidal anti-inflammatory drug (NSAID) to reduce the cramping of insertion, although cramping is usually minimal. You can also take this pain relief for a day or so after insertion if necessary. These over-the-counter medications include ibuprofen (for example, Motrin or Advil) and naproxen (for example, Aleve).

The person inserting the IUD will first perform a pelvic examination to determine the size and position of your uterus. All the procedures following the examination are done under sterile technique and are described below.

Since the uterus is almost always tipped either forward or backward, an instrument called a *tenaculum* usually is placed onto the cervix. The person inserting the IUD will pull on this instrument to straighten out the uterus, making insertion safer. You will feel pinching or cramping when the tenaculum is placed. The uterus will be measured with another instrument, called a *sound*. Again, you will feel cramping. This step is important as the IUD cannot be placed if your uterus is too large or too small. The sounding also tells the practitioner how far to insert the IUD so it will sit properly in the uterus.

For insertion, IUDs are drawn into a hollow tube, the *introducer*, which is much like a thin drinking straw. The introducer is passed through the cervix into the uterine cavity. Most women experience some cramping, usually mild, as the introducer is placed and the IUD takes its shape inside the uterus, but the actual IUD insertion usually is less uncomfortable than the sounding.

IUDs have strings attached to their lower end. After insertion, the strings are cut so that a few inches will protrude from the mouth of the cervix into the upper vagina. The protruding thread permits you to examine yourself to make sure the IUD is still in position and has not been unknowingly expelled. The thread can be grasped easily by the physician, nurse practitioner, or midwife using an instrument designed specifically for the removal of the IUD called a *ring forceps*, which looks like long-handled tweezers with rounded ends. Removal usually is simple, quick, and painless but requires a health care visit.

The risk of IUD insertion is that in the hands of inexperienced practitioners, the IUD can be thrust through the uterine wall. This is called *perforation* and is a very rare event with today's IUDs. The IUD should be retrieved if perforation has taken place. This retrieval requires a laparoscopic procedure, but occurs very infrequently.

The IUD cannot be inserted in the following circumstances:

- Pelvic infection
- Risk factors for STIs (such as multiple partners)
- Postpregnancy infection
- Uterine fibroids if they distort the uterine cavity, or other distortion of the uterine cavity (such as a septum or divider)
- Uterine or cervical cancer, or a Pap smear that is abnormal, without having had further testing showing that it is not cancer
- Abnormal vaginal bleeding

- Untreated vaginitis or cervicitis
- Increased susceptibility to infection
- Allergy to copper or Wilson's disease (only for the Copper T 380A or ParaGard)

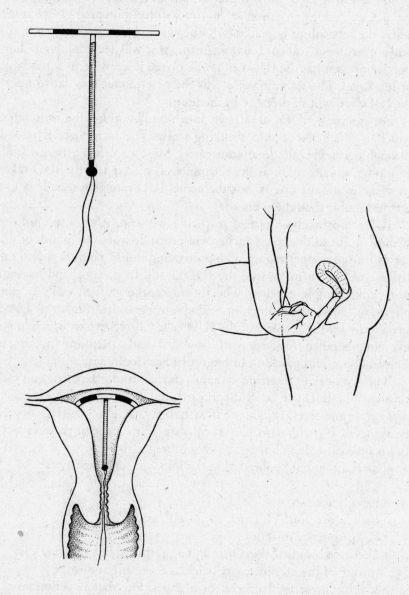

(Clockwise) The Coppper T or ParaGard IUD; checking for the IUD strings; the IUD properly placed inside the uterus.

IUD Advantages and Disadvantages

Today's IUDs are extremely effective methods of contraception, with few side effects. Their use is completely separate from the act of intercourse and requires almost no effort on the part of the user. All a woman need do to use an IUD is to come for several health care visits, check the strings about once a month, and keep up regular annual visits. The health care visits may include a preinsertion visit and always include an insertion visit and a postinsertion checkup about 1 to 3 months later. Of course, annual visits for health maintenance should be continued, but the IUD will work even if your visit is late or you miss an examination.

The IUD provides immediate protection against pregnancy after insertion and its action is reversible immediately upon removal. It does not provide any protection against sexually transmitted infections, but can be used with a barrier method such as a male or female condom. The IUD can be used by many women who cannot use the pill for health-related reasons.

The copper IUD is likely to increase slightly the amount of blood flow during your periods. It is also likely to lengthen your period as well as cause some increase in menstrual cramping in some women. NSAIDs like ibuprofen and naproxen can relieve menstrual cramping and decrease the amount of bleeding. If possible, start these medications a day or so before your period and continue for the first day or several days of bleeding.

The levonorgestrel-releasing IUDs (Mirena) decrease menstrual bleeding and cramping. They may cause irregular bleeding. About 20 percent of Mirena users stop having periods. This is not a health problem when you have an IUD, but some women do not like this side effect. For others, this is very desirable, especially if their periods have been painful, long, or heavy.

Occasionally, an IUD can be expelled spontaneously from the uterus. Sometimes you will feel this or see the IUD in the toilet after you urinate or have a bowel movement (if you look). For this reason, you should regularly check your IUD strings. You will be shown how to do this when your IUD is inserted. Most practitioners advise you to check the strings once a month. You can check after your period, if you continue to have periods, or at any time during the month. If you do not feel the strings, call your physician, nurse practitioner, or midwife to schedule a visit. In the meantime, if you have sexual relations, use a backup method such as a condom.

If you miss a period, especially if you don't feel the IUD strings, you can do a home pregnancy test. With Mirena, however, missed periods are normal. The first time you miss one, a pregnancy test is a good idea, just to be certain. There is no need after that to continue to perform pregnancy tests if you keep missing periods, unless you don't feel the strings.

Missing strings may mean either that the IUD has been expelled, even if you haven't felt this, or that the strings have moved up into the cervix or uterus. Rarely, it means the IUD has perforated through the uterine wall into the abdominal cavity. Perforation can only happen at the time of insertion, but it may take awhile for the strings to move up through the cervix to the point where you can no longer feel them.

If you are definitely not pregnant, your care provider may use a long cotton swab (like a Q-tip) to check if the strings are in the cervix. He or she may use a long type of *forceps* (an instrument like a tweezers with long handles) to check inside the uterus. If the strings cannot be found easily, an ultrasound can locate the IUD. Rarely, an X ray will be used, although ultrasound has largely replaced X ray in this situation.

The copper and progesterone-releasing IUDs cause no side effects outside the reproductive system. The Mirena, however, may occasionally cause side effects similar to those caused by other progestin contraceptives such as mini-pills or Depo-Provera. These are less common with Mirena as the progestin works mostly in the uterus. In rare instances, you might experience acne, depression, breast tenderness, nausea, or headache.

A rare type of pelvic infection is caused by an organism called *Actinomyces*. This type of infection is very severe. Sometimes a Pap smear may show the possibility of *Actinomyces* in the cervix. If your Pap smear reports *Actinomyces* and you have any symptoms such as pelvic pain, a foul-smelling discharge, or abnormal findings on pelvic examination, you should be treated for infection, and the IUD removed shortly after treatment is begun. If you do not have symptoms, the IUD does not have to be removed and you do not need treatment, but you should watch for any symptoms of infection such as pelvic pain, discharge with a bad odor, or both.

IUD Warning Signs

Contact your physician, nurse practitioner, or midwife for any of the following IUD-related problems:

- Missed period with a copper IUD (with Mirena, you can do a home pregnancy test and if negative, consider this normal. You

need not continue to do pregnancy tests each month, except
if the IUD strings are missing.)
- Pelvic pain, pain with intercourse
- Abnormal vaginal discharge and/or odor
- Missing IUD string
- String shortening or lengthening
- Feeling the IUD protruding from the cervix

The IUD as Emergency Contraception

Although the IUD works primarily by interfering with fertilization, it can also work by interfering with implantation. Therefore, insertion of the copper IUD also will provide protection against pregnancy for up to 5 days after unprotected intercourse. The IUD works very well as emergency contraception, with a failure rate of about one-tenth of 1 percent. Because of expense, however, you may not want to choose the IUD for emergency contraception unless you plan to continue using it for birth control. If you seek emergency contraception within 5 days after unprotected intercourse, the pill is a more frugal method and does not necessarily require a visit to a health care practitioner.

The Diaphragm

Since ancient times, people have known that when semen is ejaculated into the vagina, pregnancy cannot result if an obstruction blocks the seed. In preliterate societies gums, leaves, fruits, and seedpods were used for this purpose. The Hebrew Talmud, compiled in the fifth century, recommended stuffing wool into the vagina. None other than Casanova suggested that a half lemon, squeezed of its contents, be inserted into the vagina as an obstructive cup.

One hundred and eighty years ago a German physician created a removable, individually molded cap for his patients to insert over the cervix. Over 100 years ago a Dutch physician published a study on a rubber, domed cap attached to a circular watch spring, which occluded the cervix and the upper vagina. Known as the *vaginal diaphragm*, it was prescribed routinely in all birth control clinics in the days before the pill and IUD.

Today's diaphragm is made of latex in the shape of a shallow cup with a metal spring forming its circular rim. It comes in sizes ranging from 55 millimeters to 105 millimeters in diameter. When properly placed, the diaphragm covers the cervix. The diaphragm is held in position by the muscles and tissues of the pelvic floor and the bones forming the front part of the pelvis, the pubic arch.

Like gloves and shoes, a diaphragm must be fit carefully to each individual woman. Diaphragms differ both in size and in the type of spring used in their construction. Stronger springs, called *arcing springs*, can be used by all women, even women with weak vaginal and pelvic muscles. Flat and coil springs, which may be more comfortable for some women as they are softer, require strong muscular support to stay in place.

In Canada and some European countries, a one-size-fits-all device similar to a diaphragm is available. Called Lea's Shield, this device may be approved at some future time in the United States. It probably will be available over the counter as it will not need to be fit, although a practitioner may help you place and use it correctly.

How the Diaphragm Works

The diaphragm is only in part a barrier method. It is used with contraceptive cream or jelly specifically made for use with a diaphragm. An important part of the diaphragm's action is to keep the cream or jelly up against the cervix. The contraceptive creams and jellies contain a potent agent that destroys sperm. They also are called *spermicides* (Latin: *cidus, caedere* = to kill).

About a teaspoonful or a bit more of the diaphragm cream or jelly is placed inside the rim before the diaphragm is inserted. This provides a chemical seal against semen and also acts as a lubricant for diaphragm insertion. Some creams and jellies contain perfumes. Others are odorless and tasteless.

Effectiveness of the Diaphragm

Theoretically, the diaphragm is highly effective. Its failure rate, if it is used exactly as instructed, is about 6 percent. However, the typical use effectiveness of the diaphragm is considerably lower than the perfect use effectiveness as it requires a lot of user involvement. It must be used every time you have sex. This means remembering and planning. Failure rates as high as 20 percent have been reported. More than half of all women fit for a diaphragm continue using it 1 year later.

When deciding whether or not to use the diaphragm, consider your sexual practices. In general, diaphragm effectiveness is higher for women having intercourse less than three times a week.

Also think about your willingness to use the diaphragm. You need to place it inside your vagina whenever you think you may be having sex within 6 hours. If you haven't done this, you may have to place it during sex. It needs to be removed 6 to 8 hours after the last act of intercourse, washed, dried, and stored. For many women, this leads to a satisfying sense of control over their bodies and reproductive capacity. They enjoy the rituals of diaphragm use. Other women consider diaphragm use a nuisance, but are willing to put up with the bother because of the diaphragm's high perfect use effectiveness and its few side effects and absence of risks to health.

The Diaphragm Fitting

When you are fitted initially with a diaphragm you should be given the opportunity to practice inserting it before leaving the office or clinic so that you know you are inserting it in the right place and that it is not uncomfortable. You should learn to feel your cervix with your fingers inside the vagina so that you can be certain that the diaphragm covers the cervix. In fact, before going for a diaphragm fitting, you can practice feeling your cervix. Put a finger or two (usually the long middle finger and sometimes the index finger as well) deep into the vagina. You may at first only feel the vaginal walls. They have a somewhat "mushy" feeling. If you reach far back enough (although occasionally, the cervix is rather forward or even upward in the vagina), you will encounter something that feels somewhat like the tip of your nose, or like pursed lips. It is smoother, harder, and more noticeable in feel than the vaginal walls. You may feel a slight indentation in its center. This is your cervix.

Don't be afraid to push back into the vagina with your fingers. You cannot do damage (unless you have long nails—then be careful). The vagina is what is called a *blind pouch*. It does not lead into the internal organs. It simply ends. If you are used to feeling your cervix, then you will more readily feel it when it is covered by rubber.

Because the vagina enlarges in response to sexual stimulus, practitioners often fit women with the largest size diaphragm that is comfortable. A common side effect of the diaphragm, however, is irritation to the urinary tract as the rim presses against the *urethra*, the tube through which urine flows. Many practitioners have begun to fit women, especially those with a history of urinary tract infections or who develop an infection while using the diaphragm, with a smaller diaphragm or one with a softer rim. If your practitioner changes your diaphragm, you should again practice insertion and removal. A smaller diaphragm may be more difficult to grasp to remove. The softer rim, since it does not arc when folded together, can more easily be placed incorrectly—so that it doesn't cover the cervix.

There is a common opinion that the diaphragm needs to be refitted if the woman has either gained or lost weight. This is rarely if ever the

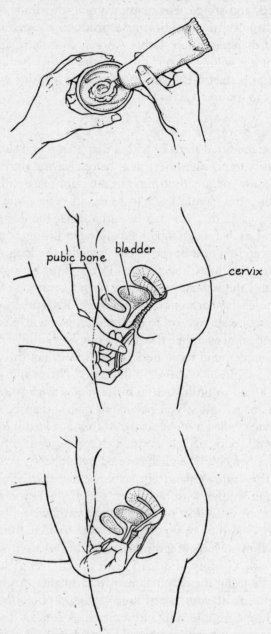

(Top to bottom) Adding cream or jelly to the diaphragm; placing the diaphragm; checking the diaphragm for proper placement.

case, since external weight gain does not particularly affect internal measurements. Many women can accommodate a larger diaphragm after they have delivered a baby, however, and will need to be refit at their postpartum visit.

How to Use the Diaphragm

The diaphragm with cream or jelly must be in place before there is any penile penetration. Some men have a discharge of fertile semen, capable of causing pregnancy, prior to ejaculation. The diaphragm can be inserted during sex, but if you prefer that it not interfere with spontaneity or sexual practices, you can insert it up to 6 hours before intercourse.

Wash your hands before you insert the diaphragm. Place about a teaspoonful or a bit more of the spermicidal cream or jelly into the cup of the diaphragm. Rub a fingertip's worth of the spermicide around the inner edge of the rim. You can use any finger for this, but they become gooey and should be wiped off before inserting the diaphragm. Try not to get any cream or jelly on the outer side of the diaphragm as this makes the device slippery and harder to hold.

You might want to try both cream and jelly before deciding on one or the other. Women who need vaginal lubrication may prefer the jelly. Do not use any oil-based lubricants such as petroleum jelly (Vaseline). They corrode the rubber.

Hold the diaphragm from above with your dominant hand and squeeze it closed between your thumb and middle finger. You can place your index finger on the back of the rim to help guide the diaphragm. If you have an arcing spring, the folded diaphragm will look like it is frowning. If you have a flat or coil spring, the folded diaphragm will be straight across. With the arcing spring, the diaphragm almost automatically follows the curve of the vagina and covers the cervix when placed inside. With the other two types of springs, you have to be more careful to point the diaphragm toward the small of your back to place it correctly over the cervix.

You can use an applicator with the flat or coil spring diaphragm, but it's one more device to keep track of. If you have difficulty with insertion, your practitioner can show you how to place the diaphragm onto the notches on the applicator and how to twist the applicator off from the diaphragm once it is deep inside the vagina.

Practice insertion in a variety of positions. Many women find it easiest to insert the diaphragm with one foot resting on a stool, a chair, the toilet seat, or the bed, the other leg slightly bent. You can also try squatting, sitting on the toilet, or lying in bed with both legs bent up toward your chest.

The arcing spring, although easiest to place correctly over the cervix, is the hardest diaphragm to hold closed because the spring is so firm. Women tell stories about the diaphragm flying out of their fingers and landing on the floor, the opposite wall, inside the toilet bowl. Don't worry. With practice, insertion will soon become an easy task. At the beginning, however, give yourself time.

After insertion, check to see that the diaphragm is placed correctly. First, check under the pubic bone. The rim should be resting just behind this bone. If it seems to be protruding from the bone, try pushing it up. If you can't place the front rim properly, the diaphragm either may not be covering the cervix or may be too large. If the front of the rim is properly placed behind the pubic bone, then follow the rubber backward with the ball of your finger. You should feel the cervix behind the rubber. If the diaphragm is not covering the cervix, you may have to remove and reposition it. If you have difficulty inserting the diaphragm, return to your physician, nurse practitioner, or midwife for help. Until you are comfortable with inserting and positioning the diaphragm, use a condom or other method of birth control.

The diaphragm should be left in place for at least 6 hours after the last act of intercourse. If you have intercourse more than once during this time, insert additional spermicidal jelly or cream into the vagina without removing the diaphragm. Use an applicator. When you buy cream or jelly for the first time, look for a package with an applicator.

To remove the diaphragm, place your index finger on the rubber just behind the rim. Pull the rubber toward the rim and then pull on the rim. First, pull downward to release the rim and then outward to pull the diaphragm out. Alternatively, you can hook your finger inside the rim to release it and then pull downward and outward. You can remove the diaphragm in any of the same positions you used for placement. After intercourse or wearing the diaphragm for several hours, the diaphragm may have moved back in the vagina, so the rim may be farther back than when you placed it. You can bear down a bit to bring the rim closer to your fingers.

If you have long fingernails, be careful not to puncture the rubber. Use the balls, rather than the tips, of your fingers.

After removal, the diaphragm can be washed with soap and water and dried with a towel or tissue or left to air dry. A light dusting of cornstarch may help absorb excess moisture and odor and prolong its life. Don't use talcum powder.

Before you put the diaphragm away, check for holes or areas where the rubber appears to be thinning. You can do this by holding the diaphragm up to the light or filling the diaphragm with water. If it is thin, ripped, or leaks, you should immediately replace it. As it can only be purchased with a prescription, call your physician, nurse practitioner, or midwife. At your initial fitting, you can ask for some refills on your prescription, although they will run out over time. If you would like to keep your diaphragm at more than one place, ask for a prescription for two or more diaphragms.

A diaphragm can be used during your period, however, you must remove it promptly when the requisite 6 hours have elapsed as the risk of toxic shock syndrome is increased during menstruation. Although toxic shock syndrome is not commonly seen with diaphragm use, it is a potential risk. Some women prefer to avoid intercourse when they have their periods or use a condom. Some women do not use any contraceptives during this time, but unless they are carefully using methods of natural family planning (see later), they may not know whether they are safe from pregnancy during the entire period.

Diaphragm Advantages and Disadvantages

The spermicide used with the diaphragm confers some protection against gonorrhea, chlamydia, and trichomonas, which are types of sexually transmitted infections (STIs). Spermicides cannot be advocated for protection against HIV, however, as their effectiveness against this virus is unclear. If you are at risk for sexually transmitted infections, condoms are the best protection.

Some women or their partners are sensitive to rubber or to the chemicals in contraceptive jellies or creams. In such individuals the diaphragm may cause irritation or itching, with or without a rash. If this happens, you can try another type or brand of spermicide. If you use jelly, for instance, try cream. If this doesn't help, you may not be able to use this method, or you may have an infection not related to the diaphragm, so check with your physician, nurse practitioner, or midwife.

Rarely, the man will feel the rim of the diaphragm and be uncomfortable during intercourse. The diaphragm may increase the frequency of urinary tract infections (*cystitis*), because of both pressure against the urethra and the use of the spermicide.

Diaphragm Warning Signs

The warning signs with diaphragm use are:

- Vaginal or pelvic pressure
- Irritation
- Itching
- Discharge
- Odor

Call if you have any signs of a *urinary tract infection*—pain or burning with urination or increased frequency of urination. You may want to urinate, but may pass little urine or be unable to urinate. If you have an infection, you may need antibiotic treatment. You can be fit with a smaller diaphragm or one with a softer rim if these infections recur. Sometimes a diaphragm user finds relief from recurrent infection only when she changes her birth control method. Other preventive measures include:

- Drinking lots of fluids, especially water and cranberry juice (to acidify the urine, increasing its resistance to infection)
- Urinating after intercourse (to flush out any germs)
- Taking vitamin C (also to acidify the urine)
- Wiping from front to back (to avoid bringing germs from the anus into the vagina and urethra)
- Avoiding contact with the vagina after contact with the anus during sex, unless your partner first washes his hands or penis

The warning signs of toxic shock syndrome are important to know when you use the diaphragm. They are:

- Fever, usually with a sudden onset
- Vomiting
- Diarrhea
- Feeling weak, dizzy, or faint
- A sunburnlike rash
- Sore throat
- Muscle aches
- Joint pain

Call your physician, nurse practitioner, or midwife immediately if you develop any of these symptoms while using the diaphragm. If you cannot contact somebody, you should go to the nearest emergency room.

The Cervical Cap

The cervical cap is a rubber cup that fits securely over the cervix, much as a thimble fits on a finger. The cap is held in place by suction. It works primarily as a barrier, with contraceptive cream or jelly added for additional protection.

The cevical cap is a good contraceptive choice for women who want a female barrier method but either get urinary tract infections while using the diaphragm or find the diaphragm inconvenient. The cap can be left in place for 48 hours—compared to 24 hours for the diaphragm—and you need not add additional spermicide with repeated acts of intercourse. As you use less spermicide, the cap is less messy and costs for the spermicide are less over time than they are with the diaphragm. However, cap insertion may be more difficult to learn than diaphragm insertion.

Cap Effectiveness

The cervical cap is about as effective as a diaphragm. Since cervixes vary considerably in size, the cap, like the diaphragm, must be fit by an individual who has experience with this method. About half of all women who've never had a baby still use the cap at the end of the first year after being fit. Among women who have had a baby, for whom the cap may be somewhat less effective, just over 40 percent continue use at the end of the first year. In a small percentage of women, the cervix may have an unusual shape or position, making use of the cap difficult or impossible.

Cap Fitting

As there are currently only four sizes of cap, not all women can be fit. The sizes are measured in millimeters around the diameter and are 22, 25, 28, and 31 millimeters. A cervical cap that could be molded to an individual cervix has been long considered, and is still under investigation.

Even with a good fit, in some women the cap will be dislodged during intercourse. For this reason, some practitioners advise a cap practice period of at least eight sexual encounters or 1 month, whichever takes longer to occur. During this period you use a condom with the cap and check the cap's placement after each act of intercourse. Also check the cap after each bowel movement. Occasionally, it can dislodge with straining.

When you are fit with the cap, your practitioner should make sure you can tell correct and incorrect placement so you will know if the cap has dislodged. If it gets dislodged one time, you can continue with the backup method and see if it dislodges again. Try using the same position for intercourse as you used when it dislodged. If the cap doesn't dislodge again, perhaps you had inserted it incorrectly the time it dislodged. If it gets dislodged more than once, you can return for a refit, choose a different method of contraception, or continue to use a condom with the cap. Occasionally, the cap dislodges in only one position. In that case, you can either avoid that position or choose another birth control method.

Self-insertion and placement of the cervical cap may be more difficult for some women than they are with the diaphragm. The diaphragm is placed in the vagina. It fits behind the pubic bone and against the vaginal walls. The cap fits directly over the cervix. Placement of the cap requires reaching the cervix, which can be located deep in the vagina. Some women may have more difficulty removing a cervical cap than inserting it. It helps if you know exactly where your cervix is, so if you are interested in a cervical cap, practice finding your cervix (see the instructions in the section on the diaphragm, page 797). With practice, most women find they can readily insert and remove the cap.

How to Use the Cap
Wash your hands before inserting the cap. Fill the cap about one-third full with spermicidal cream or jelly. Spermicides are not marketed for cap use, so buy the kind whose package states that it is for use with a diaphragm. Don't use extra spermicide, thinking it will be extra protective. It may interfere with the cap's suction.

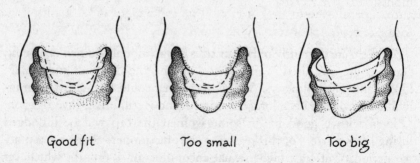

Good fit   Too small   Too big

Correct and incorrect cervical cap placement.

Hold the cap from above in your dominant hand and fold it in your fingers. Open the vaginal lips with the opposite hand and put the cap into the vagina, with the open end leading. Aim the cap toward the small of your back. Once the cap has passed the vaginal lips, you can let go of the lips and use the hand that had been holding them to help push in the cap. You can use the same positions as you would for diaphragm insertion.

Once the cap is in place, check to make sure that it covers the cervix. You will not be able to feel the cervix through the cap as you can with a diaphragm because the cap is a thicker rubber and because it does not fit up against the cervix. There is always a gap between the cap and the cervix. You can tell that the cervix is covered in two ways. One is simply that you do not feel the cervix anywhere in the vagina. Another is to slightly dislodge the cap with your fingers and feel inside of it. If you feel the smooth surface of the cervix entering the cap, you know it is covered. You must remember, then, to push the cap firmly back onto the cervix. Practice with your cap fitter to find the best way for you to tell correct placement.

The cap can be kept in place for up to 48 hours, according to the Food and Drug Administration guidelines. As the cap works as a better barrier than the diaphragm, additional cream or jelly is not necessary when you have intercourse more than once during that time. The cap should remain on the cervix at least 6 to 8 hours after the last act of intercourse.

To remove the cap, break the suction by placing your long finger between the rim of the cap and the cervix. Then pull the cap outward from the cervix.

Wash the cap with soap and water. Turn it inside out as there is a groove on the inside in which spermicide and cervical secretions can accumulate. Turn it right-side out to store. Do not use talcum powder on the cap, but you can dust it with a bit of cornstarch. It can be dried with a towel or allowed to air dry. Hold it up to the light or fill it with water to check for holes or tears. With proper care, a cap can last for years. If the cap develops an odor, you can try soaking it in apple cider vinegar for up to 20 minutes, or replace it. Caps are dispensed through your practitioner.

Advantages and Disadvantages of the Cap

The cap is a convenient barrier method. It need not relate to the act of sexual intercourse. Once placed, it can be undisturbed for 48 hours. It is a very inexpensive birth control method.

The cap has almost no side effects, but does not protect against HIV, although, like the diaphragm, it may provide some protection against gonorrhea, chlamydia, and trichomoniasis through the action of the spermicide. You or your partner may develop an allergy to the rubber or the spermicide. Occasionally, your partner will feel the cap and be uncomfortable.

The cap will not hold menstrual flow, and because of the possible risk of toxic shock syndrome, use is not recommended during your period. You can use a condom during that time or avoid intercourse. Although many women think they are protected from pregnancy during menstruation, this may not always be true. Toxic shock symptoms are listed in the section on the diaphragm, page 802.

The Female Condom

The female condom is the newest available vaginal barrier contraceptive. Unlike the diaphragm and cervical cap, it need not be fit by a health care practitioner. It is readily available over the counter, without prescription. Like the male condom, the female condom prevents semen from entering the vagina, providing protection against STIs, including HIV.

The female condom is made of polyurethane. It is stronger and more tear resistant than the latex used in most male condoms. The condom is marketed under the name Reality.

Female Condom Effectiveness
The female condom has a perfect use effectiveness of about 95 percent, but a typical effectiveness of just under 80 percent. Like all barrier methods, it must be used consistently. Over half of all women continue using the female condom at the end of the first year of use.

How to Use the Female Condom
The female condom can be inserted into the vagina up to 8 hours before intercourse, or during sexual relations. It has two rings. One goes inside the vagina and helps with insertion and keeping the condom in place. The other remains outside the vagina and helps with removal. It twists to form a seal so that semen doesn't leak out when you remove the condom.

The female condom is lubricated on the inside and the package contains additional lubrication for the outside. The lubricant is not spermicidal.

The condom package comes with directions and illustrations for use.

You squeeze the inner ring with your middle finger and thumb and use your index finger between them to push the condom into the vagina. Use your other hand to spread open the vaginal lips. It's a good idea to place the condom the first time before you are sexually aroused as it can be a bit tricky to follow the directions until you have done it at least once.

You must take care when the man's penis enters the vagina that it goes into the condom. Sometimes, it can slide into the space between the condom and the vaginal wall. It might help if the woman guides the penis with her fingers as she can feel the condom opening.

Like the male condom, the female condom is good for only one act of intercourse. A new one is needed each time you have intercourse. The condom should be taken out right after intercourse, before you stand up. To prevent semen from leaking, squeeze and twist the outer ring before you pull out the condom. Pull on the outer ring to remove it. Discard the condom. Do not flush it down the toilet. Male and female condoms cannot be used together as they can get stuck to each other.

Female Condom Advantages and Disadvantages

The main advantage of the female condom is its protection against STIs. Women may prefer the control it affords them compared to the male condom. Unlike the male condom, the female condom can be put on before intercourse so it need not relate to the sexual act. Like the male condom, it can be purchased over the counter. Its use does not require any health care visits. Like all barrier methods, of course, its effectiveness depends on use with each act of intercourse.

Over-the-Counter Vaginal Spermicides

Vaginal foam, jellies, creams, film, suppositories, and tablets are available without prescription. These products, sold under various trade names, depend on the chemical nonoxynol-9 to destroy sperm. Only the base that carries the nonoxynol varies among them. In some preparations, such as some jellies and foam, the base also acts as a barrier, covering the cervix to some degree. For ideal effectiveness, they must be placed in the upper vagina against the cervix.

Spermicides also are used, in some formulations, with the diaphragm or condom to provide additional protection. Some of the bases used in the spermicides, however, can corrode rubber, so make sure, if you use a particular spermicide with a diaphragm or cervical cap, that the package specifies that it can be used with the diaphragm.

Spermicide Effectiveness

The reported pregnancy rates of spermicides depend upon consistent use and vary widely from one study to the next. Pregnancy rates with various spermicides have been reported as low as 5 percent or less and as high as 50 percent.

How to Use Spermicides

Spermicides should not be used more than 1 hour before intercourse. If you are using foam, shake the can of foam about twenty times before filling the applicator. Place the tip of the applicator onto the top of the can and then push down. This will automatically fill the applicator. Applicators for foam, creams, or jellies should go deep into the vagina.

If you use film, tablet, or suppository, you must slide it with your fingers far into the vagina, so it rests near the cervix. These contraceptives usually must be inserted at least 15 minutes before intercourse so they will melt in the vagina. Read the package for any special directions.

If you have repeated intercourse, you need a new application of any spermicide. After you use an applicator, wash it with soap and water. If you douche, which is not recommended, wait at least 6 hours after intercourse.

If you don't use a spermicide regularly and don't buy new supplies frequently, check the expiration date on the can, tube, or package before you use it. Don't wait until you are having intercourse to check.

Advantages and Disadvantages of Spermicides

Spermicides reduce the risk of contracting gonorrhea and chlamydia by about 25 percent. They are not considered effective against HIV, although a number of alternative chemicals are being studied for their effectiveness at preventing both pregnancy and HIV infection. Some may become available in the near future.

Some women or their partners are sensitive to nonoxynol-9. Spermicides are best used by women who have intercourse infrequently and those who try to increase the effectiveness of barrier methods. They share the great advantage of the condom that they are readily available without a prescription, but they should not be used as a solo contraceptive when maximum effectiveness of the contraceptive is a crucial consideration.

Douching

Douching is not an effective method of contraception. Sperm swim up the cervical canal shortly after intercourse so douching in the vagina, even with a spermicidal solution, doesn't destroy them.

Although women who douche do so for purposes of cleanliness and hygiene, douching actually interferes with the normal environment of the vagina and makes women more susceptible to pelvic inflammatory disease. It is not recommended as a routine practice and is not needed at all.

CONTRACEPTIVE METHODS FOR THE MAN

Research has been conducted on several chemical and hormonal methods of contraception for men. The male hormone testosterone is being evaluated as one such contraceptive. Currently it involves weekly injections, which are considered impractical and unduly unpleasant. Today, only two reversible male contraceptive techniques are available. They are the condom, a barrier method, and withdrawal, a behavioral method.

The Male Condom

The derivation of the word *condom* is uncertain. It is claimed without strong evidence that a certain Dr. Condom was attached to the court of the seventeenth-century English king Charles II, who perhaps holds one of the world's records for creating royal offspring with many women. Dr. Condom is said to have invented the sheath for the welfare of his monarch, who had become alarmed by the number of children he had fathered. For the relief his device supplied, it is said, the grateful sovereign knighted Dr. Condom. Doubt is cast on this intriguing story by evidence that animal bladders were probably used as penile sheaths in the days of imperial Rome and that, as early as 1564, an Italian physician, Gabriel Fallopius, in his poem on syphilis, mentions the value of a linen penile sheath in the prevention of venereal disease. The less romantic but more likely etymology of the word "condom" is that it derived from the Latin *condo*, meaning "to sheathe."

The male condom is a thin sheath shaped like the finger of a glove. It is placed over the erect penis to collect semen. It prevents sperm from entering the vagina. Although today many condoms are made with spermicide, condoms provide an effective barrier with or without the spermicide.

Most male condoms are made of latex. As some people are allergic to latex, and some men complain of a lack of sensation with latex condoms, condoms made from the intestines of lambs (called *natural* or *lambskin* condoms) also are available. This material may not afford as good protection against STIs as latex, however, so if prevention of infection is a reason for you to use condoms, latex is a better choice. *Polyurethane* (plastic) condoms are now available and can be used by people sensitive to latex. These condoms are thinner and stronger. They may be more acceptable to some men who complain of reduced sensations with condom use. Other plastic condoms are in development.

Condom Effectiveness

When used properly and regularly, male condoms provide a high degree of protection against unwanted pregnancy. Their perfect use effectiveness is about 97 percent, although the typical use effectiveness drops to about 85 percent. Over 60 percent of couples continue condom use after 1 year.

Instructions for Condom Use

Male condoms are placed on the erect penis before intercourse. They can be purchased without prescription in drugstores and supermarkets.

Condoms are about 7½ inches in length and are made of such thin material that each weighs only about ⅟₂₀ of an ounce. They are packaged rolled in aluminum foil, cardboard boxes, or metal containers in quantities from three to a dozen. Packaged condoms have a *shelf life*—the period of time during which a packaged product can be kept before it deteriorates—of about 5 years if the condom is not lubricated with spermicide and 2 years if it has spermicide in it. Always check the date on the package to see if the condom is expired. The date may be the manufactured date or the expiration date, so be careful when you check. If it says "Exp.," then it is the expiration date. Latex condoms are heat sensitive so they should not be kept in hot places or in sunlight. Don't carry a condom in your wallet for more than a month.

The condom should be put onto the penis before it comes into contact with the vagina, as there may be pre-ejaculatory secretion containing sufficient sperm to cause pregnancy. The penis must be erect for the condom to be placed onto it.

Open the condom package carefully to avoid damaging the condom. The upper, open end of the condom is surrounded by a rubber rim. Unroll the condom a bit to make sure you have it right-side out. The rim should be on the outside when you unroll it. If you have difficulty un-rolling the condom onto the penis, it may be inside-out. If so, remove it and use another condom as there may be pre-ejaculatory fluid on the ac-tual outside of the one removed.

The condom's closed end may have a pocket or *reservoir tip* for trap-ping semen. The reservoir tip variety is considered less likely to burst with ejaculation. If the condom you use doesn't come with a reservoir tip, leave about half an inch at the tip to catch the semen. Press this tip to release air.

If you use nonlubricated condoms, you may want to put some sper-micidal cream or jelly or a water-based lubricant on the penis after the condom is in place. This will help prevent breakage. You can use one of the many contraceptive jellies or creams or any water-based lubricant, such as saliva, K-Y jelly, or Astroglide. Don't use Vaseline, cold cream, mas-sage oil, or other oils with latex condoms.

You can do all this for your partner, making it part of sexual foreplay, or he can do it himself.

A new condom is needed if the condom breaks before ejaculation and with every new act of intercourse. Make sure you have enough con-doms on hand. Discard them in the garbage, not the toilet.

To prevent the condom from slipping off, the penis should be re-moved from the vagina shortly after ejaculation. You or your partner should hold onto the condom while he withdraws the penis.

If the condom breaks or slips off the penis, wash the area around the vagina immediately with soap and water if you are at all worried about an STI. If you don't use a vaginal spermicide routinely with the con-dom, then insert an applicatorful right after you wash. Make sure you have spermicide on hand. You can also contact your physician, nurse practitioner, or midwife for emergency contraception if you've had such a condom "accident."

Advantages and Disadvantages of Condoms

Male condoms have the great advantage of protecting each partner from sexually transmitted infections (STIs). This includes protection against HIV. Condoms are harmless, have virtually no side effects except in the case of allergy, are simple to use, and can be purchased relatively in-expensively without a prescription. They can and should be used with other methods such as female hormonal contraceptives whenever there is a question as to whether one partner has such an infection, is not *monogamous* (has other partners), or has other risks for certain STIs such as intravenous drug use.

Despite the advantages of the condom, some couples do not like to use it. One objection is that love play must be interrupted to put on the condom. With imagination, however, this can be made part of the pleasurable preparation for intercourse. The woman can place the condom as a signal of her readiness. Some men claim that the condom interferes with normal sexual response by dulling sensation, and others tend to ejaculate prematurely while the condom is placed. Conversely, condoms may help some men maintain their erections.

Many couples use condoms perfectly happily in preference to all other methods. They may find the condom reassuring because they can see clearly that it works by preventing semen from entering the vaginal canal. By containing semen, condoms reduce what some people consider the messiness of sex. Certainly, for casual sexual encounters, the condom's protection against STIs is a special benefit.

Some condoms are ribbed, which their manufacturers claim increases sexual pleasure for either partner. You can try a variety of condoms to see if you or your partner has a preference.

Coitus Interruptus (Withdrawal)

Coitus interruptus has many synonyms in the vernacular including *withdrawal, pulling out,* and *taking care.* A man might say, "I won't come inside you." Coitus interruptus may well be the oldest method of birth control, since it is mentioned in the Old Testament (Genesis 38:9), and worldwide it may be the one used most extensively. The decline in birth rates in the developed countries in Europe in the eighteenth and nineteenth centuries is largely attributed to the practice of coitus interruptus.

Withdrawal Effectiveness

In the United States at the present time, withdrawal is used by few couples as their principal method of birth control, although many more employ it occasionally. This makes it difficult to state the method effectiveness of withdrawal. With perfect use, it might be as effective as 95 percent. However, it is a difficult method to use perfectly. Some men do not know when they are about to ejaculate, others find that their impulse is to penetrate more deeply during ejaculation rather than pull out. Certainly, it requires conscious thinking at a time when many people find themselves overwhelmed by physical sensation, not conscious thought.

Spilling even the initial drop of semen in the vagina is dangerous, since the first portion of the ejaculate contains the greatest bulk of the sperm cells, the latter part being mainly a diluent. This method places a great responsibility on the male partner. There is also the problem that some pre-ejaculatory fluid contains sperm and some women do get pregnant from these sperm. This accounts for the failure rate of this method even with correct and consistent use.

Withdrawal Advantages and Disadvantages

Withdrawal is a simple method requiring no equipment or preparation before the sex act; it costs nothing and is always available. And although it requires intercourse to be terminated rather abruptly by the male, it permits full contact between the sex organs of the partners. Withdrawal also may help prevent the transmission of HIV exposure, although not as well as a condom.

Spermicides can be used as a backup to be inserted immediately in case of a withdrawal "accident." Emergency contraception is now also available by prescription, so contact your care provider if you think you need it.

METHODS FOR THE COUPLE

Natural Family Planning (NFP)

The theory of natural family planning (NFP) is that your own body can tell you when you can and cannot become pregnant. This method can be used in two ways: you can restrict intercourse to infertile times or you can use a barrier method during fertile times. Some people call this method *natural family planning* when intercourse is restricted and *fertility awareness* when a barrier method is used. Either way, this is a "couple method" because it requires the understanding and cooperation of both partners. Nevertheless the woman must do most of the bookkeeping required by the method.

Natural Family Planning Effectiveness

Natural family planning has a typical use effectiveness of about 80 percent, although its perfect use effectiveness is higher than this. Depending upon which specific technique of natural family planning is used, the perfect use effectiveness is 90 to 98 percent. The most motivated couples use NFP the most effectively. The continuation rate is over 60 percent, attesting to the commitment of couples choosing this method.

How NFP Works

Normally a woman ovulates once each menstrual month. The egg cell survives for about 12 to 24 hours, during which time it can be fertilized. A man's sperm has a fertile life of 72 hours and possibly longer following ejaculation into the vagina. This means that a woman can become pregnant as a result of intercourse only during about 96 hours or somewhat longer each menstrual month, approximately 3 days before ovulation and up to 1 day afterward. In order to utilize natural family planning, a woman needs to determine when ovulation is going to take place, and that is where the difficulty lies.

There are five ways for a woman to identify her fertile period:

1. **The calendar method,** which works best when the woman has regular and predictable menstrual cycles and is therefore the least reliable of these methods
2. **The temperature method,** based on the rise and fall of basal body temperature throughout the menstrual cycle
3. **The cervical mucus method**
4. **The sympo-thermal method,** which is a combination of the temperature method, the cervical mucus method, and observation of other possible signs of ovulation
5. **Over-the-counter home urine tests.** These kits are based on estimation of levels of the hormone LH, detectable the day before ovulation or the day of ovulation. Use of these kits is expensive compared to the first four methods, but may be more accurate in determining fertile days, especially for women with irregular cycles or irregular life schedules, making basal body temperature difficult to implement

Most women and couples find these methods easier to use if they seek help from a professional experienced in guiding people through natural family planning. Ask your physician, nurse practitioner, or midwife to assist you if you want to use NFP. If he or she does not have experience with these methods, request a referral. You may want to check with the Catholic church in your community as the church often offers classes in natural family planning. Usually, these classes are only for engaged or married women or couples.

How to Use Natural Family Planning Methods

THE CALENDAR METHOD   The calendar method was the original rhythm method. Women normally ovulate 12 to 16 days before their next menstrual period begins. If you menstruate every 28 days, you should ovulate halfway through the cycle—on the thirteenth to the seventeenth day after menstruation begins. If your cycle is regularly 33 days, your egg would be released between 18 and 22 days after the first day of your period.

The difficulty is that few women ovulate or menstruate with clocklike regularity. In most women, the cycle can—and does—vary considerably. The following calculation makes allowances for cycle irregularities:

1. Keep a written record of your menstrual cycles for 12 consecutive months. Count the first day of your period as the first day of the cycle, and the day before the next period as the last day of the cycle. At the end of 12 months, choose the shortest and the longest cycles for that year. (If you wish to use the method before 12 months, keep a menstrual calendar for 6 months. If you already have a record, you can use the method immediately.)
2. Subtract 18 from the number of days in the shortest of the twelve cycles. This determines the first fertile, or unsafe, day of the cycle.
3. Subtract 11 from the number of days in the longest cycle. This determines the last fertile day of the cycle, or the day before the safe period begins.

For example, Jane's shortest cycle was 27 days and her longest 30.

$$
\begin{array}{cc}
27 & 30 \\
-18 & -11 \\
\hline
9 & 19
\end{array}
$$

Jane should not have intercourse between days 9 and 19, inclusive.

The "18 and 11" rule will help a woman determine with some degree of accuracy which days of the month are "safe" and which are fertile. As time passes and each month is ended, substitute its length on your menstrual calendar for the same month the previous year. This keeps the 12 menstrual intervals current and permits for changes in cycle length that normally occur throughout reproductive life.

Using the calendar method means a lot of abstinent days. Many couples practice methods of lovemaking other than vaginal intercourse during abstinent days. Alternatively, you may choose to use a barrier method such as a condom or diaphragm during the unsafe days. As barrier methods do fail, even if used correctly, the effectiveness of this method is reduced somewhat when you use a barrier method rather than abstinence.

Approximately 15 percent of women menstruate with such irregularity that they cannot use the calendar method at all. This method is difficult to use during the months immediately after childbirth, since the first several postpartum menstrual periods may be very irregular. However, if you exclusively breast-feed on demand, your fertility is substantially reduced for up to 6 months, as described in Chapter 26.

THE BASAL BODY TEMPERATURE (BBT) METHOD   The basal body temperature (BBT) method depends on the fact that, if taken first thing in the morning, your body temperature changes in a predictable pattern through the menstrual cycle. During the first half of the cycle, the days preceding ovulation, your temperature is relatively low. With the occurrence of ovulation it rises about 4/10 to 6/10 of 1 degree Fahrenheit, remaining elevated until just before menstruation. If you become pregnant, the temperature stays elevated and does not show the premenstrual drop.

The reason for the temperature rise is that ovulation causes a wound in the ovary with the rupture of the follicle. The wound is immediately filled in by a rapid growth of cells forming a new gland, the *corpus luteum*. This gland manufactures the chemical *progesterone*, which has the effect of causing a temperature rise. Therefore, in the absence of any other cause for temperature elevation in midcycle, such as the flu or a sore throat, you can safely assume ovulation has occurred.

To use the BBT method, take your temperature each morning when you wake up, before getting out of bed. You need to purchase a special basal body thermometer, which calibrates temperature in one-tenth of a degree, rather than two-tenths. This is easier to read to detect the small rise that signifies ovulation. You can use a rectal, vaginal, ear, or oral thermometer, but take your temperature in the same way each day.

After the thermometer is kept in the necessary number of minutes (based on the kind of thermometer used), you can read it immediately or put it aside to read later. You chart the temperature daily, preferably on wide-spaced graph paper. Connect the dots each day, to make the graph easier to interpret. When your temperature has risen about half a degree or more and remains elevated for three consecutive mornings, ovulation has occurred and intercourse is unlikely to result in pregnancy.

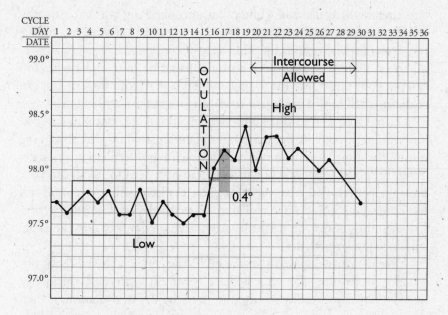

A sample month's Basal Body Temperature chart

Some women notice a slight drop in temperature just before ovulation, but not all women have this drop. Some women do not ovulate every cycle, so will not always show what is called the *biphasic* temperature pattern. A bad cold or tonsillitis or even a sleepless night may interfere with the method's accuracy for that time.

BBT is superior in effectiveness to the calendar method, but it usually restricts the days for intercourse to the last 10 or 11 days of the menstrual month, with no intercourse permitted during the entire cycle before the third day of elevated temperature. BBT tells you when ovulation has occurred, but does not tell you which days from menstruation to ovulation are safe. If you do not wish to abstain or practice lovemaking without vaginal intercourse, you can use a barrier method in the first part of the cycle or combine the BBT method with the calendar or cervical mucus method.

With meticulous use of the temperature method, using abstinence, perfect effectiveness is about 98 percent. In practice, for many women and couples, the actual effectiveness is much less.

THE CERVICAL MUCUS METHOD   The cervical mucus method depends on a woman's study of the amount, consistency, and color of her cervical mucus. Cervical mucus changes throughout the menstrual cycle. At the time of ovulation, cervical mucus becomes copious, clear, and stretchy. It is like the white of an uncooked egg and has a quality called *spinnbarkeit*, which means it can be stretched between two fingers for several inches without breaking apart.

You can see cervical mucus on toilet paper or your underwear. You can put your finger into the vagina and feel it with your fingers. You can sometimes tell how wet you are when you are walking.

During your period you cannot tell what kind of cervical mucus you have. Some experts in natural family planning recommend abstaining during this time as you cannot be sure you are not fertile. For instance, if you have a 21-day cycle one month, and have bled for 6 days in your previous period, you may very well have ovulated while you were still bleeding. (You would have ovulated 12 to 16 days before the twenty-first day; this means you might have ovulated on day 5 or 6 of the cycle, still during your period.)

After menstruation, early in the cycle, the cervix is dry, without observable secretions. The mucus next becomes sticky and thick, but scant. It increases steadily in amount up to the day of ovulation. It then becomes clear and liquid, with the raw egg white quality. Immediately after ovulation the cervix starts to dry again. The secretions once again are thick and sticky, if there are any.

To use this method, observe the cervical secretions daily once your menstrual period is over. You can check your secretions when you urinate. Look at the toilet paper you use to wipe yourself. Record the amount and quality of the secretions on a chart. If you use this method with the basal body temperature method, you can write the information about the secretions at the bottom of the temperature graph.

Once the dry days have passed, consider yourself fertile, especially as sperm can lie in wait for a number of days before ovulation. You are no longer fertile once 4 days have passed after the peak mucus day.

As both semen and the secretions of sexual arousal can be confused with cervical mucus, some experts advise abstinence during the first cycle that you check cervical secretions, so you can become familiar with your pure secretions. If you do not want to abstain, you can use a condom. Alternatively, you can have intercourse no more frequently than every other day, allowing you to check your secretions on alternate days without confusion. Abstaining from intercourse every other day is necessary for the duration of use of this method unless you use condoms or combine the mucus method with another natural method.

Not every woman can use the mucus method. Women who are nursing, those with vaginitis, and women who sometimes use contraceptive chemicals may find it difficult to interpret their cervical mucus. The success rate of the cervical mucus method is about 97 percent in women who meet all the requirements for effective use of the technique and use it absolutely correctly and conscientiously. Like the BBT method, the cervical mucus method requires daily record keeping. It does not depend on regular cycles for its interpretation.

THE SYMPTO-THERMAL METHOD   The sympto-thermal method combines several ways of determining fertile days. It uses both cervical secretions and basal body temperature. Some women also learn to feel the position and consistency of their cervix throughout the cycle and know when ovulation is close. Many women experience pain at the time of ovulation, a phenomenon called *mittelschmerz*. This is felt as a cramping or sharp sensation in the lower abdomen, often on one side. Gwen Gentile, a very experienced family planning physician, recommends that women take a few jumps in place every morning to help them feel ovulation. Other women have breast tenderness around the time of ovulation or afterward. Some women spot with ovulation. All of these are recorded on the fertility awareness chart. These signs help you identify the time of ovulation with greater accuracy.

TESTING KITS   As described in the discussion of in vitro fertilization in Chapter 13 (see pages 370–377), precise techniques now exist for determining ovulation based on measures of pituitary hormones in a woman's blood, combined with ultrasound of her ovaries. The expense and inconvenience of such testing takes this out of the realm of natural family planning. However, easy-to-use kits that test for hormones in the urine are readily available and are very reliable in detecting ovulation or impending ovulation. These kits indicate only the end, not the beginning, of the fertile period, although a urine test kit that detects both is under investigation.

Advantages and Disadvantages of Natural Family Planning

NFP is the least expensive of all techniques, as it requires little equipment and devices, and it is physically harmless. In addition to using NFP for family planning, awareness of the fertile and nonfertile times can help a woman achieve pregnancy, know when she is pregnant, and notice abnormalities that might signal a need for care. Fertility awareness also can be used to help find the cause when a woman has trouble becoming pregnant. NFP is the only contraceptive other than abstinence with the approval of the Catholic Church.

A special advantage of NFP is its cooperative nature. It facilitates communication, understanding, and trust between sexual partners. Lovemaking and pleasuring each other in ways that don't involve vaginal intercourse can encourage couples to share thoughts and feelings, needs and desires. The disadvantage is that in general use, the overall failure rate is high.

RESEARCH IN CONTRACEPTION

As no contraceptive method is appropriate or perfect for everybody, and as prevention of sexually transmitted infections is an increasing public health issue, research continues into contraceptive methods. Although some research focuses on male methods, more research is carried out on methods for women. Chemicals that would kill both sperm (*spermicides*) and germs (*microbicides*) are being investigated. New types of cervical caps and diaphragms made of silicone are under investigation. A cervical cap that could be molded to an individual cervix has long been considered.

The male hormone testosterone is being evaluated as a contraceptive for men. Currently it involves weekly injections, which are considered impractical and unduly unpleasant.

Another direction of research is into vaccines that would prevent fertilization in the woman or prevent sperm production in men. These are years away from realization.

There are many possibilities building on newer molecular and cellular biologic research approaches, but the pharmaceutical industry, for a number of complex reasons, is not investing in very much basic contraceptive research.

PERMANENT CONTRACEPTION (STERILIZATION)

Sterilization is any procedure that permanently prevents the union of the egg and sperm. Today, safe and effective methods of sterilization are available for both women and men.

In almost all sterilization procedures, the surgeon blocks the pathway of the egg or sperm without removing the testes in the man or the ovaries or uterus in the woman. In men a portion of the vas deferens, the passageway for sperm, is interrupted. In women the procedure is done upon the fallopian tubes, preventing the upward passage of sperm and downward movement of eggs. Female sterilization is also called *bilateral tubal ligation* or *tubal ligation* and male sterilization is called *vasectomy*.

These sterilization operations leave the sex glands intact. Tubal sterilization for women does not bring on premature menopause. Menstruation continues. Neither male nor female sterilization changes an individual's sexual drive or performance. In fact, because the surgery eliminates the possibility of pregnancy, it may result in a more spontaneous and enjoyable sexual relationship.

Legal Status of Sterilization

In the 1920s, there was a drive to "improve" the human species by compulsory eugenic sterilization of the "unfit." This received the approval of the United States Supreme Court in 1927, and many states thereafter passed laws mandating sterilization for loosely defined "defects" such as mental retardation. In the 1950s, with vastly improved understanding of the complexity of genetics and the revulsion of forced sterilization in the Nazi concentration camps in the 1940s, compulsory sterilization appropriately fell into total disfavor and was abandoned.

Voluntary sterilization of competent adults, however, on medical, personal, and social grounds is legal. No state completely prohibits voluntary sterilization.

Consent is required only of the individual to be sterilized. Although until the 1970s, hospitals or physicians required the consent of a spouse, this is no longer the case, and such consent cannot be mandated legally. Nonetheless, in counseling, it is recommended that both partners discuss the option. Coercive sterilization ordered by local courts for women who have had children out of wedlock has been held illegal by the federal courts. Roman Catholic hospitals do not sanction operations whose purpose is sterilization, but removal of diseased organs where sterilization is a secondary effect is not prohibited.

To safeguard against coerced sterilization, especially among poor women, federal legislation covering Medicare recipients mandates waiting 30 days after giving consent for sterilization before the operation can be carried out. Two exceptions exist. One is emergency surgery occurring 7 days or more after the consent has been given if the surgical procedure is such that the sterilization can be carried out at the same time. The other is an early birth if the consent was signed 30 days before the expected date of delivery. Medicare also requires that the woman be over 21 years of age regardless of her medical and childbearing history and be mentally competent. Counseling must be provided at the time the consent is signed and the counselor must not be the person performing the surgery.

Effectiveness of Sterilization

Although sterilization is considered permanent, it does have some failures. A large-scale study of sterilization called the Collaborative Review of Sterilization (CREST) found that there were approximately 5.5 pregnancies for every 1,000 female sterilization procedures performed in the first year after the surgery. This is a first-year failure rate of just over half of a percent. Over 10 years, the failure rate increased. The cumulative 10-year pregnancy rate was 18.5 per 1,000 procedures, or a failure rate of close to 2 percent. This is similar to the failures of long-term contraceptive methods such as the IUD, Depo-Provera, and Norplant.

Pregnancy rates are related to a number of factors. Younger women are more likely to become pregnant after sterilization than are older women. Occasionally, a woman is unknowingly pregnant at the time of the procedure. Sterilization will not interrupt the pregnancy as the uterus and hormone producing organs are not removed or changed. Different methods of sterilization have different failure rates, but if the surgeon is experienced in the method used, he or she may have a lower failure rate than if the surgery is performed by a less experienced surgeon. This is true even if the technique used by the less experienced person is considered generally more effective.

The failure rate of male sterilization is difficult to evaluate since the person sterilized is not the person who becomes pregnant. However, experts report that the rate of pregnancy in the first year after vasectomy is about one-tenth of 1 percent—a very low rate. Sterilization does not occur immediately after a vasectomy as sperm already in the reproductive tract are not removed by the procedure. Some failures may be due to reliance on the technique before the man's semen has been examined to be sure that it is sperm free. Therefore, it is generally recommended that another method for birth control be used until the man has ejaculated at least twenty times.

Making the Sterilization Decision

You must assume that sterilization is irreversible when deciding whether to undergo the procedure. Success rates for reversal of female sterilization vary from 43 to 88 percent of attempts. The operation to reconnect the tubes is major surgery with health risks. It is expensive and difficult to perform. *Ectopic pregnancy* (pregnancy outside the uterus) is more common in women attempting pregnancy after a tubal reversal than it is in women who have not had a sterilization procedure.

Success rates for reversal of male sterilization vary as well. Although sperm are found in the semen following more than 80 percent of reversal procedures, pregnancy is not achieved this frequently. A reasonable estimate of the success rate for vasectomy reversal is somewhat higher than 50 percent.

The decision to be sterilized should be made carefully, without coercion from professionals or family members. Research reveals that women less than 30 years old at the time of sterilization are most likely to have regrets. Making the decision when you have marriage problems, right after a birth, following a divorce, or at other times of personal or family crisis or change may lead to regret.

Although the consent of a spouse is not required for a sterilization procedure to be performed, if you are in a relationship, you should discuss the decision fully with your partner. Consider the number of children you have and how many you each want. Although difficult even to think about, consider how you would feel if your relationship ended through separation, divorce, or death. Would you wish to be able to have more children with a new partner? How would you feel if something happened to your children? Of course, if you are close to the end of your reproductive years, these issues are less relevant.

Consider also your own decision-making pattern. Do you have a pattern of making quick decisions that you later regret? Or are you really good at sticking to the decisions you make? Think about your age. If you are in your twenties, you might want to postpone the decision, even if you think you eventually will choose sterilization. Of course, this is not a hard and fast rule. Many women in their twenties are in stable and close relationships with the desired number of children, and, facing many years of contraceptive need, choose sterilization as a reliable and simple option. Of primary importance always is that you do not make the sterilization decision because of persuasion by anyone else, and you earnestly desire the procedure.

Today, several long-term contraceptive options may be preferable to permanent surgical sterilization. These options share the advantages of sterilization in that they require no or little user input, are totally separate from the sexual act, allow for complete privacy, and, following an initial expense, become very inexpensive over time. The IUD and implant provide protection against pregnancy that is as effective as that provided by sterilization. Of course, these methods may have side effects, discussed earlier, that sterilization does not have.

Once a couple makes the decision to seek permanent sterilization, the next question is: "Which partner should be sterilized?" There is consensus in the health care field that male sterilization is a simpler procedure. It has virtually no risk of death compared to a risk of 1 to 2 deaths per 100,000 sterilizations performed for women. It is as effective as female sterilization, possibly even more effective, and does not increase the risk of ectopic pregnancy should the method fail. Vasectomy is less expensive than tubal ligation and usually results in fewer days of missed work. Despite these vasectomy advantages, more than twice as many women in the United States have been sterilized as men.

Female Sterilization: Bilateral Tubal Ligation

Most female sterilizations involve operations on the fallopian tubes. While removal of the ovaries or uterus (*oophorectomy* or *hysterectomy*) would achieve sterilization, these operations carry more risk and side effects and should not be done unless there is a clear health need.

Sterilization may be accomplished by the complete removal of both tubes but a much simpler operation, consisting of interrupting the passage through each tube, is the procedure of choice. Such surgery takes only about 20 or 25 minutes.

There are a variety of surgical techniques to interrupt this passageway. These vary in the technique used to reach the tubes and the technique used to block the tubes once they are reached.

Each of these techniques has advantages and disadvantages. The training and experience of the surgeon in a particular technique is extremely important. If you have a preference for a particular technique, discuss with your surgeon her or his prior use of that technique. You may have to choose an alternate surgeon if you are committed, for example, to a laparoscopic technique, but the physician you usually see does not perform laparoscopy. If you do not have a preference, then the recommendation of the surgeon is a valid way to make your decision, as the surgeon will likely use the technique with which he or she is most comfortable. This increases the success rate of the procedure. The surgeon performing the tubal ligation may be an obstetrician/gynecologist or a general surgeon.

Sterilizations can be performed at any time, including the first few postpartum days, during a cesarean section, and immediately after an abortion. (A cesarean operation, however, with its risk, should not be performed just because you want a sterilization and have consented to it. A vaginal birth followed by a postpartum sterilization is much safer, unless you need the cesarean for other reasons.) The timing of the sterilization might determine the surgical technique used.

How the Tubes Are Reached

The tubes can be reached in a variety of ways, depending on the preference of the surgeon and of the woman, and when the operation is done. The tubes are located high in the abdomen immediately after a birth and very readily accessible, so the incision, which can be quite small, will be made higher up if the sterilization is done at this time. It will be just under the navel, a little half moon (*semilunar*) cut that will barely show over time. This is called a *subumbilical laparotomy* (laparotomy is any surgical incision into the abdomen and *sub* is Latin for under).

The postpartum period is a safe time for a tubal ligation. The abdominal wall is relaxed. Minimal anesthesia is needed. The tubes are found easily and tied and cut. The hospital stay may be no different from the stay for a normal birth.

If you are not postpartum, your tubes can be reached with an incision made just above the pubic hair. This is called a *suprapubic* (Latin: *supra* = above) *laparotomy*. The incision can be just under an inch to just over two inches. Immediately after an abortion, the incision may be made slightly higher in the abdomen. This procedure is often called a *mini-laparotomy*.

Another procedure to reach the tubes is *laparoscopy*. Laparoscopy literally means looking into the abdomen. It involves a very small opening in the abdominal wall. A specially designed needle goes through the abdominal wall into the potential space just under the abdominal wall. This is called the *peritoneal cavity*. A gas, usually carbon dioxide, is pumped in through this needle to blow up the cavity, much as you blow up a balloon. It generally takes about two or three quarts of the gas to lift the abdominal wall away from the internal organs. A small incision then is made just below the navel and a thin tube is put through it. A viewing scope, called a *laparoscope*, is placed into the thin tube. This is fitted with fiber optics that deliver cold light by which the surgeon can get an excellent view of the abdominal contents. Slender operating instruments can be passed alongside the viewing scope or through another tube inserted into a second small incision.

The complications of laparoscopy are infrequent but may be serious.

The blind insertion of the tube can cause accidental injuries to the major blood vessels on the *posterior* (back) wall of the peritoneal cavity. This accident necessitates immediate abdominal operation to repair the vessels.

Sterilization by laparoscopy cannot be done in the presence of multiple previous operations in the lower abdomen, which may have caused adhesions or scar tissue to form in the tube. Laparoscopy is also more difficult in markedly obese women.

The tubes also can be reached through the upper vagina. Some women think this is a good idea as it leaves no external scar. However, the rate of infection is high with this method so it is used rarely.

Efforts have been made for years to block the tubes where they enter the uterus. This point can be seen by passing an instrument called a *hysteroscope* through the vagina and cervix into the uterine cavity. Like the laparoscope, the hysteroscope consists of a slender viewing scope equipped with fiber optic cold light. Chemicals or devices are injected through the hysteroscope into the tubes to close them. Chemicals are injected as liquids but very rapidly solidify to form a plug. The advantage of these injection methods is that they do not involve abdominal surgery. These procedures, however, are still experimental and their success and failure, safety and reversibility are still being evaluated.

How the Tubes Are Occluded

The tubes can be *occluded*, or blocked, by cutting and tying the cut ends, by electrocautery, or by placing clips, bands, or rings on them. There are three techniques for cutting and tying:

1. The Pomeroy method
2. The Pritchard (or Parkland) method
3. The Irving method

Several types of clips are manufactured including the Hulka, Rocket, Wolf, and Filshie clips. Bands made of silastic or a ring called the *Falope-Ring* can be inserted. Electrocautery introduces heat into the abdominal cavity. This can cause accidental burns to other body organs. Electrocautery has a lower reversal success rate and a higher risk of ectopic pregnancy following reversal procedures than the other methods. Some surgeons no longer use electrocautery for these reasons.

The method used to occlude the tubes depends on the training and experience of the surgeon, and whether the procedure is done in the postpartum period or not. It also depends on the method used to reach the tubes, as certain occlusion techniques cannot be used with all incisions.

The tying and cutting procedure called the *Irving method*, for example, requires a good deal of exposure of the abdominal cavity as it involves placing the end of the tube into the uterine wall. The Irving technique, then, is reserved for tubal sterilizations performed as part of a cesarean operation. It is one of the most effective methods available and has a low risk of future ectopic pregnancy, but generally is not practical or possible.

The *Pomeroy* and *Pritchard methods* both involve placing *sutures* (stitches) on the tubes. The Pomeroy technique consists of raising a knuckle of fallopian tube and placing a tie around the base of the knuckle on each tube. The knuckle is then cut off, the tie having been tightly drawn so that, when cut, each of the two severed ends is squeezed together. This controls immediate bleeding. Catgut suture is used for the tie. Body enzymes dissolve the catgut in 4 or 5 days. The cut ends of the tube then pull away from each other so they will not rejoin. The Pomeroy method is the method used most frequently when the tubal sterilization is done in the postpartum period via subumbilical laparotomy.

The Pritchard technique differs from the Pomeroy technique in that two sutures are put on each tube and the tube cut between them. Less of the tube is cut than with the Pomeroy method and the ends are not close to each other right after the procedure. Chromic catgut suture is used. This suture, treated with chromium salt, dissolves more slowly than plain catgut. Some surgeons consider this a superior method.

With a suprapubic laparotomy, performed anytime except in the postpartum period, the Pomeroy or Pritchard technique can be used, or bands, rings, or clips can be applied to the tubes. With laparoscopy, band, rings, clips, and electrocautery are options, but there is not enough exposure for cutting and tying.

Sterilization by laparoscopy or mini-laparotomy at the time of early abortion does not increase the complications of either procedure.

Anesthesia for Tubal Sterilization

Female sterilizations often are performed under general anesthesia, which means you are put to sleep. This eliminates the pain of the procedure and allows your muscles to relax to make the surgery easier to perform. However, local anesthesia with intravenous sedation often achieves both goals adequately, with less potential risk. Unlike general anesthesia, local anesthesia, even with heavy sedation, does not block the protective gag reflex. A sedative may be given by mouth or injection 30 minutes to 1 hour before the procedure. You will sleep through the procedure, but continue breathing on your own.

Recovery from Tubal Sterilization

Recovery from sterilization is almost always uneventful. You usually can have the procedure as an outpatient and go home within 8 hours. You can resume normal activity as soon as you feel up to it. The incision will be uncomfortable for a few days. You can take pain medication as needed, although you should avoid aspirin as it can increase bleeding.

You can take a tub bath after 48 hours. Avoid strenuous lifting and sexual intercourse for 1 week. Most of the time the stitches placed are absorbable. This means they do not need to be removed. Most surgeons will ask you to return after about 1 week to make sure you are healing well.

Advantages and Disadvantages of Tubal Ligation

Once you have a tubal ligation, there is nothing more you need do to protect yourself against pregnancy.

Tubal ligations are subject to the risks that attend other abdominal operations. Infection and bleeding are possible following any surgery. Injury to nearby organs can occur.

Respiratory complications from anesthesia are infrequent, but can be severe. In fact, there is a very small risk of death from a tubal sterilization. Approximately 1 to 2 women die from complications for every 100,000 sterilization operations performed. This is less than the rate of death from pregnancy, but there are many ways to prevent pregnancy that carry no risk of dying.

For many years there has been debate about whether there is "post-tubal ligation syndrome." This term refers to a variety of menstrual disturbances that some researchers have found after tubal ligation. Although research in this area has shown inconsistent findings, the largest studies have not supported such a syndrome.

If a pregnancy does occur following tubal sterilization, there is an increased possibility that it will be an ectopic pregnancy. Tubal ligation does not protect against sexually transmitted infections. If you are at risk, use a barrier method for disease protection.

Warning Signs After Tubal Ligation

You should call your surgeon if you have any of the following problems:

- Fever
- Dizziness
- Fainting
- Severe abdominal pain or pain that increases rather than lessens
- Bleeding from the incision site not stopped with pressure
- Pus or foul-smelling discharge where the incision was made

If at any time after a tubal ligation you miss your period or experience other signs of pregnancy, contact your physician, nurse practitioner, or midwife promptly as there is an increased possibility that your pregnancy might be *ectopic* (outside of the uterus). This could happen years after the surgery.

A Note About the Term "Tying the Tubes"

Many people call female sterilization "tying the tubes." This name has given rise to some misconceptions, most notably about the ease of reversal.

Fallopian tubes are not tied in a bow like shoelaces, nor in a knot like a string around a package. Both the shoelaces and the package string can be untied, and are then in much the same shape they were in before they were tied. The tubes, however, are tied with suture material and are then cut between the tied off sections. The suture material dissolves and disappears after a few days. This leaves two separate segments of tube, which do not rejoin if the operation is successful. We therefore cannot untie the tubes that we have tied. If we hope to reverse the operation and reestablish the continuity of the passage through one or both tubes, we must put the open ends of the segments together, using very delicate and meticulous surgical techniques that are much more difficult than the initial ligation.

Reversal of Female Sterilization

Reversal of female sterilization is done by removing the scarred portion of the tubes and reconnecting the two freshened ends. A large abdominal incision is necessary. The best results are obtained by experienced surgeons working under magnification with very fine suture material. It requires skill and experience to sew the muscle and the lining of each cut end of the fallopian tube to the other with precision. Often, the continuity and patency of the tubes is restored, but women do not achieve uterine pregnancies.

As an alternative to surgical reversal of tubal sterilization, some women choose in vitro fertilization (IVF). IVF is discussed more fully in Chapter 13. It, too, has limited success and is costly.

Male Sterilization: Vasectomy

Sterilization of the male is carried out by a procedure called *vasectomy* (Latin: *vas* = vessel; Greek: *ektome* = excision). Vasectomy consists of blocking the vas deferens—part of the passageway from the testicle, where sperm are manufactured, to their point of exit, the penis. Since there are two testicles, the operation must be done on both sides.

Vasectomy is a relatively simple surgery since no body cavity is entered. The procedure is done either in a doctor's office, a clinic, or a hospital outpatient surgery unit. It is performed ordinarily by either a *urologist*, who specializes in male reproductive and urinary problems, or by a general surgeon. Occasionally general practitioners or family physicians perform vasectomy.

A local anesthetic is injected into the operative site to eliminate pain. Some men and a few physicians prefer general anesthesia, but this adds risk to the procedure and is very rarely used.

There are a variety of surgical techniques available to reach the vas. Some surgeons make two small incisions in the upper portion of the scrotum, one on each side of the penis. Other surgeons make only one incision, in the midline of the scrotum, using this incision to reach both testicles. Still other surgeons do not make an incision at all, but reach the vas with a puncture in the skin. This seems to have fewer complications, although no procedure carries a high risk of complications.

The incision in the scrotum is extended about a quarter-inch downward from the skin until the vas is reached. The vas is then cut. It can be cauterized to keep the cut ends from reuniting, or each end tied with a suture. Some surgeons cut out a section of the vas, but others consider this unnecessary. A few surgeons perform what is called an *open-ended vasectomy*, which means one end of the tube (the end closer to the testicle) is kept open. This is thought by some surgeons to increase the chances of a successful reversal and to decrease pain following the procedure.

The skin incision is closed with one or two stitches or with small bandage strips, and a dressing applied. The operation requires 15 to 20 minutes, a good deal of the time spent in injecting the local anesthetic. After an observation period of about an hour, the man goes home.

Since there is storage of sperm in the ampulla of the vas deferens, sperm cells do not disappear immediately after vasectomy. The *ampulla* is a slightly enlarged part of the vas that connects to the seminal vesicle. The seminal vesicle empties into the *urethra* of the penis, where ejaculation takes place.

It may take as many as twenty ejaculations before all fertile sperm are washed out of the system. Contraceptive methods should be continued until the man has ejaculated at least twenty times. Even then it is advisable to have a semen specimen examined under the microscope to be certain that the operation was successful. A man can masturbate to get a specimen or his partner can stimulate him with her hands. If the semen still contains sperm, you will be asked to return for repeat testing periodically until it is sperm free.

Vasectomy does not change either sexual drive or sexual performance. The sperm cells constitute a negligible proportion of the semen and the volume of the ejaculate is not diminished. Sperm continue to be produced after the procedure, but with their passage blocked, they disintegrate and are reabsorbed by the body. Over half of men who have had a vasectomy subsequently develop sperm antibodies as a response of the body's immune system to these reabsorbed sperm. As far as is known, however, these do no harm, except that they may possibly interfere with the success of later efforts to reestablish fertility.

Following vasectomy, the man should rest for 48 hours. He should use an ice pack on the scrotum for at least 4 hours after the surgery. To avoid undue pulling on the incision, he should wear jockey shorts for 2 days. He may take pain medication if necessary. He can shower or bathe after 2 days. Normal activities can be resumed within 1 or 2 days, although strenuous activity should be avoided for about a week. This includes lifting or other activity that places undue pressure or strain on the scrotum.

Sexual relations, with birth control, can be resumed within 2 to 3 days if the man feels comfortable. If there are noticeable stitches, they usually don't have to be removed unless the surgeon used a non-absorbable suture material on the skin. This type of suture usually is removed at an office visit 5 or 6 days after the operation.

Advantages and Disadvantages of Vasectomy

Following vasectomy, once the semen is sperm-free, there need be no further worry about contraception. Vasectomy does not protect against sexually transmitted infection, however, and use of a barrier may be wise if there is any question that either partner is at risk for an STI.

Immediately after the surgery, leakage from the artery that runs alongside the vas deferens can introduce some bleeding into the scrotum, producing a painful hematoma. This heals itself unless it becomes infected, in which case it must be drained. Infection also requires antibiotics, rest, and the use of moist heat compresses. Swelling of the scrotum may occur occasionally, requiring extra support and application of heat. Swelling usually subsides within about a week. Occasionally, when sperm leak out of the cut end of the vas, a painful nodule develops, called a *granuloma*. This usually resolves on its own, although it may require pain medication. Rarely, it needs surgical treatment. Each of these complications occurs in less than 2 percent of vasectomies.

Questions have been raised regarding whether vasectomy has an effect on heart disease or prostate cancer but further studies have clearly demonstrated no such complications.

Prostate cancer has increased in recent years and researchers have examined whether the increased rates of vasectomy have contributed to this. Studies on this subject have had conflicting results. No definitive association has been shown. In 1993, the National Institutes of Health studied the question. They did not recommend discontinuing the performance of vasectomies nor reversing them in men who had already had them. Recommendations regarding screening for prostate cancer do not differ for men who have had vasectomies and those who have not. Research in this area is continuing.

Warning Signs After Vasectomy

While some pain and swelling are normal, the man should notify the surgeon if:

- Pain is not relieved with the medication prescribed
- The scrotum is more than twice its normal size
- Bleeding does not stop with pressure applied for about 10 minutes
- A fever develops
- There is pus or foul-smelling discharge at the site of the incision in the scrotum
- There is a particular area of swelling that is larger than the diameter of a nickel

Reversal of Vasectomy

Like fallopian tubes, the vas deferens can be reunited. This calls for meticulous surgery, often carried out under magnification and employing very fine sutures. About 75 percent of reversal operations result in the presence of sperm in the ejaculate and approximately 50 percent of the men subsequently impregnate their partners. As is the case with the original vasectomy, this second operation has minimal risk.

A Final Word on Choosing a Method of Family Planning

As contraceptive options have increased and contraceptives have become safer to use, couples today have a variety of choices. Except for sterilization, which must be considered a permanent method, you can try various methods to see which feels most comfortable for you. Most people, in fact, use a number of methods over the course of their reproductive lives. At one time in life, effectiveness might be the most crucial consideration in making a choice. At another time, absence of side effects might become more important. In some circumstances, prevention of sexually transmitted infections is key. In other situations, lack of interference with the sexual act becomes the primary concern.

Couples should be open about discussing contraceptive methods and together come to a decision that is acceptable to both members of the partnership. Remember, you can change methods if either of you is dissatisfied. Effective use of any method relies on respect for each other's feelings and needs.

CHAPTER TWENTY-EIGHT

Induced Abortion

A BRIEF HISTORY OF ABORTION

Induced abortion or termination of pregnancy by artificial means is an ancient procedure long predating recorded history. Abortion was practiced by primitive people on every continent. A 5,000-year-old Chinese herbal medical manuscript mentions abortion. The priest-physicians of the pharoahs, in papyri written 4,000 years ago, evidenced knowledge of induced abortion.

Nineteenth-Century Western World Abortion Laws

Before 1803, England had no specific abortion law. The English Common Law had jurisdiction over abortion. It held that abortion was legal until the fetus moved. That year, an English statute made all abortions a crime, but abortion before fetal movements was a lesser crime than abortion after fetal movements. The American colonies, and subsequently the early United States, were bound in many areas by English Common Law. Connecticut, the first state to pass an abortion statute, made all abortions illegal in 1820, the penalty not affected by duration of pregnancy. In 1828, New York was the first political jurisdiction in the world to introduce an exception, permitting abortion "to preserve the life of the mother."

According to professor Cyril Means, a legal scholar who researched the New York law, the statute was passed not on ethical grounds, but specifically to promote maternal health. This was in the days before anesthesia, sterile technique, antibiotics, or transfusions, and death from abortion was common, even within a first-rate hospital. Therefore, to protect women against the inherent dangers of abortion, the early nineteenth century legislators insisted that its risk be permitted only when the physician involved believed there was no other way to preserve the life of the pregnant woman.

Within several years all states had either copied the exact wording of the New York law or approximated it. In some, the exception was phrased to promote "the safety of the mother." A few states made "illegal abortion" a criminal offense but did not define "legal abortion."

PRESENT LEGAL STATUS OF ABORTION

By the late 1960s, widespread dissatisfaction was voiced over antiquated abortion laws. Legislatures began to approve laws authorizing abortion for reasons other than the few medical pretexts that had been accepted previously. In 1970, New York eliminated all restrictions on abortions done by physicians, except for requiring that standards set by the state Board of Health be met. In January 1973, in *Roe v. Wade*, the United States Supreme Court recognized abortion as a privacy right to be exercised by the woman with the aid of her doctor, under no special supervision by local law until the second trimester of pregnancy. Once the fetus reaches the age at which it can survive outside the womb, the state may assert an interest in its welfare.

In 1992, another Supreme Court decision, *Planned Parenthood of Southeastern Pennsylvania v. Casey,* ruled that states could impose restrictive regulations on abortion. This ruling allowed the legal imposition of waiting periods, requirements regarding the content of counseling to be provided for an abortion, and mandatory involvement of parents if the pregnant woman is a minor. It permitted states to specify a need for hospitalization for early abortion.

Today, violent tactics by anti-abortion forces have decreased the number of providers available to perform abortions. Fortunately, the Freedom of Access to Clinic Entrance laws have restricted the intimidation directed toward women seeking abortion.

Women have always had abortions, even when they were illegal and dangerous. Today, approximately 1.3 million abortions are performed in the United States each year. This is approximately 21 to 22 percent of all pregnancies. The most significant change for anyone who has worked in a large public hospital is that physicians and nurses are no longer confronted repeatedly with the need to try to rescue desperately ill women from death due to infection from illegal abortion.

OVERVIEW OF
ABORTION TECHNIQUES

Abortion can be performed by techniques that are called *surgical*, although there is no cutting or sewing. This can also be called *suction* abortion. Abortion also can be performed by medical means—the use of medications to bring about the abortion. Abortion cannot be legally prohibited by state law before 24 weeks of pregnancy, considered the age at which the fetus can survive outside the uterus (the age of *viability*), although some hospitals limit the time they will perform abortion to 20 weeks. Some outpatient facilities perform only first-trimester abortions—those up to 12 or 13 weeks of pregnancy.

The abortion technique used depends on the number of weeks of pregnancy the woman is at when she has the abortion, and the experience and preference of the abortion provider. The woman also has a choice between medical and surgical techniques in many facilities, or she can choose a facility that performs the technique she prefers.

In the first trimester, the surgical abortion technique of choice is *vacuum aspiration*. Medical abortion in the first trimester involves a number of medications given over several days. These can be injected, given by mouth, or placed into the vagina. Some of these medications also can be used later in pregnancy.

In the second trimester, surgical abortion is called a *dilation* (or dilatation) *and evacuation*. A medical abortion may involve removing the amniotic fluid and replacing it with labor-inducing chemicals, although this technique is used infrequently today.

Abortion performed in the first trimester is easier and safer than abortion performed in the second trimester. Unless you are awaiting results of genetic testing (see Chapter 8), you are urged to make the abortion decision as early as possible in your pregnancy.

MAKING DECISIONS
ABOUT ABORTION

For some women the decision to seek abortion is clear and the experience leads only to feelings of relief. For other women the decision is more difficult, possibly leading to delay in seeking abortion. This may result in having to undergo a second-trimester procedure.

The legality of abortion emphasizes that the woman herself has the responsibility for the choice. For many women, legalization and societal acceptance of abortion support their personal belief that a woman has the right to control her own reproductive function. Sometimes, however, knowing that abortion is available on request may not be helpful in dealing with moral qualms arising from personality, upbringing, religion, family attitudes, or philosophical beliefs.

The health care provider's role is largely to give advice on medical aspects of abortion. Some physicians are not willing to do abortions but may be able to refer a woman to another doctor or clinic. If this is not possible, the woman may have to conduct her own search for the help she needs. A good resource is the nearest Planned Parenthood clinic. Unfortunately, you may have to travel outside your immediate area to find a facility that performs abortion.

In some states, abortions are performed by physician assistants, nurse practitioners, or midwives. In all states, these health care providers participate in pre- and postabortion care and provide counseling for the procedure.

PRE-ABORTION CARE

An abortion procedure is scheduled after you have a positive pregnancy test. This may be a home urine test or a blood or urine test performed in a health care office or facility.

A crucial part of providing safe abortion services is an accurate dating of the pregnancy. This is accomplished readily if you have regular menstrual periods and have kept careful records of your periods and contraceptive practices. A pelvic examination is performed in any case.

If the uterus is retroverted or tipped backward (a normal variation), a rectal examination may be performed to help the examiner feel it. If you are very heavy or if for any reason the examiner has trouble assessing the size of the uterus, an ultrasound may be helpful. If you do not know your last period, have irregular periods, or if your uterus on examination is substantially larger or smaller than would be expected for your menstrual dates, an ultrasound can determine the duration of pregnancy. If you have symptoms that suggest an ectopic pregnancy, such as unusual pelvic pain or spotting, or if the examiner finds an enlargement in the area of the fallopian tubes during the examination, you will have an ultrasound.

Many abortion providers routinely perform ultrasound after about 14 weeks past your last menstrual period. There is more variation in uterine size starting at about this time, so an examination may be less accurate. An occasional provider performs ultrasound anytime an abortion is to be performed.

Before the abortion is performed, a complete health history is taken. Some health problems, such as heart disease, blood clotting disorders, or severe anemia, make it necessary to perform even early abortion in a hospital. Some conditions like severe asthma or other respiratory problems make general anesthesia a risky choice.

During the history, be sure to mention allergies you have to any medications. If you've had a reaction to a local anesthetic at the dentist's office, let the physician or other abortion provider know this. You will be asked about exposure to sexually transmitted infections and whether you or your partner has multiple sexual partners, putting you at risk for sexually transmitted infections.

A physical examination will be performed. This will include listening to your heart and lungs and feeling your abdomen. Your blood pressure, pulse, and temperature will be taken.

Certain laboratory tests are necessary before an abortion. Some abortion providers will routinely repeat the pregnancy test. Rh blood typing is needed unless you know for sure that your blood is not Rh negative, or that both you and the man involved in the pregnancy are Rh negative. Women who have Rh negative blood will receive a preventive dose of Rh immune globulin (RhoGAM) after an abortion (see Chapter 5). Most often, a check of your hemoglobin or hematocrit will be done. The *hemoglobin* is a measure of the amount of red-blood-cell-carrying chemicals in the blood and the *hematocrit* is a less direct measure of the hemoglobin. It gives the percentage of *solid* (cellular) material in the blood. These measures tell whether you are anemic.

If you are at risk for sexually transmitted infections (STIs), you will be tested for gonorrhea and chlamydia. This is done by swabbing the cervix during the speculum examination. Some providers do these tests routinely, regardless of whether or not you believe yourself at risk. Although a Pap smear (which screens for cancer of the cervix) is not necessary before an abortion, many abortion providers and facilities will perform this test if you have not had one in the previous year.

If you have a vaginal infection at the time of the abortion or have been exposed to a sexually transmitted infection, you should be treated at the time of the abortion. If any tests for STIs come back positive, you will be notified and treated promptly.

ABORTION TECHNIQUES IN THE FIRST TRIMESTER

Surgical Abortion in the First Trimester

Technically, surgery is any procedure involving manipulation or change of body tissues. By this definition, certain types of abortion are surgical.

The basic technique for early abortion is suction or *vacuum aspiration* of the fetus, placenta, membranes, and amniotic fluid (called the *products of conception*) from the uterus. This is also referred to as *suction curettage*. In the past, *curettage* (scraping the uterine lining) with a sharp instrument was used more commonly. Sharp curettage is still used in other countries, but has more potential for harm. Suction aspiration has made abortion very safe.

When abortion is done up to about the sixth week past your last menstrual period (LMP), it occasionally can be accomplished with *manual vacuum aspiration* (MVA). This requires no electrical suction equipment and is often used in developing countries or as a backup should there be a power failure in an abortion facility.

Before 6 weeks after the LMP, however, certain complications are more common than if the abortion is performed later. These include retained products of conception (an *incomplete abortion*) or a continuing pregnancy (*failed abortion*). Because the cervix has not yet been softened by the hormones of pregnancy, it may be more likely to tear or lacerate. There also may be greater pain if the procedure is performed this early in pregnancy. If you know you are pregnant shortly after a missed period, you may choose to postpone the procedure for several weeks or to have a medical abortion (see later on page 843).

The Suction Procedure

A suction abortion is carried out with the woman lying on her back and her legs in stirrups, similar to the position used for a pelvic examination. The external genitalia are washed with an antiseptic solution. A sterile speculum is placed in the vagina to view the cervix and the anti-septic is applied to the cervix and upper vagina. If you are not put to sleep (see page 841), local anesthetic is injected. The anesthetic is like that used in dental procedures. It is instilled into and around the cervix. This is called a *paracervical block*. Next, the cervix may be held by an instrument called a *tenaculum* while a thin rod, called a *sound*, is inserted briefly into the uterus to verify its position.

With somewhat more advanced pregnancies, usually those over 10 weeks, the cervix may need to be opened or dilated. Dilation increases the woman's comfort during the abortion and makes it less likely that the cervix will tear.

The cervix is most effectively dilated by inserting *laminaria* into it prior to the abortion. *Laminaria* are sterilized seaweed stems that act as *osmotic dilators*. (Osmotic is a word used to describe *osmosis*—the passing of a liquid through a membrane.) A synthetic dilator can be used as well. These tend to work more quickly than the laminaria. One or more dilators are placed in the cervix, and remain there for 4 to 12 hours, depending on the type of dilator used and the duration of the pregnancy. During this time, they draw fluid into themselves through osmosis and thus expand slowly. As they expand, they cause the cervix to open. The dilators are removed at the time of the abortion. Laminaria dilation generally has replaced dilation with metal dilators because there is less chance of damage to the cervix.

Once the cervix is dilated, if it needs to be, a *catheter* (tube) is passed into the uterus. For pregnancies at about 7 weeks the catheter is about the same diameter as an ordinary pencil. For more advanced pregnancies it has to be larger. The catheter's outer end is attached to the vacuum device. Once it is in the proper place and suction has been established, the catheter is rotated. The suction within the catheter draws the products of conception through it into a collecting jar.

The suction abortion takes only a few minutes. Very little bleeding occurs, since the uterus responds promptly with contractions to reduce blood loss.

At the end of the procedure, the vaginal instruments are withdrawn and the woman is allowed to rest briefly to recover from whatever discomfort she may have had. The abortion provider will inspect the tissues in the collecting jar to be reasonably certain that the abortion has been successful. Inadequacy in the amount of tissue might indicate an ectopic pregnancy or an incomplete abortion.

PAIN RELIEF FOR SUCTION ABORTION   Surgical abortions are associated with some pain and discomfort which can be relieved with local or general anesthesia. Both types of pain relief have advantages and disadvantages, but local anesthesia is generally safer.

General anesthesia is given via inhaled or intravenous medications (or both) that cause you to fall asleep. These block the protective gag reflex, causing an increased risk of breathing problems. You may have an airway started with general anesthesia, meaning that after you are asleep, a tube will be placed into your throat so the anesthesiologist can assist your breathing during the procedure. Although it carries a risk, general anesthesia for an abortion is of short duration, unlike the anesthesia administered for more complex and lengthy surgeries. General anesthesia can lead to an increased risk of *hemorrhage* (excess bleeding), *perforation* (penetration with the instruments) of the uterus, *laceration* (tear) of the cervix, and breathing problems.

Local anesthesia is called a *paracervical* or *cervical block*. Numbing medications are injected into the cervix. If you have an allergic reaction, you may experience itching, hives, swelling, sneezing, nausea. If the reaction is severe, it can cause breathing difficulties. An overdose can cause symptoms such as light-headedness, restlessness, anxiety, shakes, numbness, visual disturbances, ringing in the ears, and, if not treated, convulsions and breathing difficulties. A reaction or overdose is rare.

With local anesthesia, the body of the uterus is itself not anesthetized, so you are able to feel the contractions with which the uterus responds to the suction. The suction can be turned off temporarily if the discomfort becomes severe. Remember, though, it is used for only a few minutes.

Narcotics, or pain relievers, may be given with the local anesthesia. They can be given either orally, before the procedure, or intravenously, during the procedure. Sedatives also may be given for their antianxiety effect. Together, these medications can cause an effect called *conscious sedation*, which means you fall asleep, feel very little if any pain, but you can respond to physical and verbal stimulation. Breathing reflexes are not altered.

Recovery is faster and more comfortable after local anesthesia. There is less nausea following the procedure and less need for assistance. Local anesthesia can lead to an increased risk of an incomplete abortion. An allergic reaction or an overdose rarely may occur.

Care Following First-Trimester Surgical Abortion

Recovery following a first-trimester surgical abortion usually is rapid. You will rest for about an hour in a recovery room. A nurse or nursing assistant will take your pulse and blood pressure. Your bleeding will be observed. You will be checked for unusual pain or other symptoms that could indicate a complication. You will be given something light to eat and drink before you leave the abortion facility.

You should have somebody to accompany you home after an abortion, especially if you had general anesthesia. At home, you should rest for at least 24 hours. Most women return to reasonably normal activities the day after the abortion. You can let your body be your guide regarding when to resume more strenuous activities including heavy lifting.

Pain can be relieved with ibuprofen (such as Motrin or Advil) or naproxen (such as Aleve, Anaprox, or Naprosyn) in a dosage of 400 to 800 mg every 6 to 8 hours. Some of these medications are available over the counter, but you may be given a prescription, as the higher dosage is more than you get from two pills in the over-the-counter strength. You can also take acetaminophen (such as Tylenol), two tablets every 4 hours. You can apply a heating pad to your lower abdomen, or take warm baths. There is no danger in taking tub baths, showers, or swimming.

As a precaution against infection, avoid sexual intercourse for 1 week after the abortion. Do not douche for at least a week (although douching is unnecessary at any time). You may use sanitary pads or tampons, but change them frequently. Wash your hands before inserting a tampon. Take your temperature every morning and evening for the week following the abortion and call your abortion provider or facility if it is greater than 100.2° Fahrenheit or if you experience shaking chills. Call if you have vaginal discharge with a foul odor.

You will most likely be given a prescription for antibiotics, as several studies have shown that they reduce the likelihood of postabortion infection. Take all the medication prescribed. Some abortion providers also give you a medication, methylergonovine maleate (or Methergine), to help control excessive bleeding. Women who have had five or more deliveries, who have a history of hemorrhage after childbirth, or who have a cervix that was difficult to dilate usually will be given this medication for a few days. It may cause cramping.

Expect light bleeding for about 3 or 4 days after an abortion. If you take Methergine, you may bleed more heavily after the last dose, starting about when you would have taken the next dose or sometime after that. Many women have an episode of heavier bleeding on day 4 or 5 after the abortion. You may then continue light bleeding for about 3 weeks. Call your care provider if you soak through a maxi-pad each hour for more than 2 hours or if you soak through more than six pads in one day.

You may pass small clots, but call your care provider if you pass a clot the size of a lemon or larger. If you feel faint or weak or have heavy sweating, you may need immediate attention, so don't hesitate to call.

Go to the nearest emergency room if you cannot contact your abortion provider or facility. If you have severe or increasing abdominal pain or cramping without bleeding, contact your care provider as the cervix may be closed and the blood pooling in the uterus.

Feelings of pregnancy, such as breast tenderness, may persist for a few days or even more than a week following the abortion. If these persist for 2 weeks or more, call your care provider. You may have a continuing pregnancy.

Drinking alcohol or using perception-altering drugs is never advised, of course, but these should especially be avoided for at least a week after the abortion or you might miss a danger sign. All women should return after 2 to 4 weeks for a postabortion checkup.

Medical Abortion in the First Trimester

Medical abortion means that an abortion is induced with medications. This avoids the need for a surgical procedure and anesthesia. It can be performed safely as soon as pregnancy is confirmed. The abortion takes place in the privacy of your home. The disadvantages of medical abortion are that the abortion is not completed in one short procedure like surgical abortion, but takes at least several days, occassionally several weeks. You may have more cramping and bleeding than with a surgical abortion, but these usually are not severe. You do not risk uterine perforation, infection, or the respiratory complications of general anesthesia.

A first-trimester medical abortion only can be performed if the pregnancy is 49 days or less (7 weeks gestation or 9 weeks from your last menstrual period). This generally is confirmed by ultrasound.

Most often two medications are used for medical abortion. The most commonly used combinations are methotrexate with misoprostol, or mifepristone (also called RU-486) with misoprostol.

Methotrexate is a drug that is toxic to certain body tissues. It works in abortion by blocking folic acid (a vitamin) in fetal cells. This prevents the cells from reproducing themselves. You cannot take folic acid as a supplement or in a multivitamin tablet if methotrexate is to work properly, although you can stop the folic acid 1 week before the procedure.

Mifepristone works against progesterone, a hormone necessary for pregnancy maintenance. It also causes the body to produce prostaglandins, which have an abortion-causing effect. Misoprostol (brand name: Cytotec) is a prostaglandin whose use increases the success of the abortion.

Mifepristone (RU-486) has been approved for use in abortion. It is used with a prostaglandin. The prostaglandins, however, have not been specifically approved for usage in abortion, nor has methotrexate. Their use in abortion is called *off-label*, because the drug is not manufactured or sold for this purpose. Research, however, supports their effectiveness and safety.

Contraindications of Medical Abortion

Medical abortion generally **cannot** be offered in the following circumstances:

- Kidney or liver disease
- Acute inflammatory bowel disease
- History of blood clotting disorder or use of anticoagulant medications
- Anemia
- Confirmed or suspected *ectopic pregnancy* (pregnancy out of the uterus)
- Breast-feeding
- Uncontrolled seizure disorder (with methotrexate)
- Severe heart disease (with methotrexate)
- Taking folic acid supplement or multivitamin with folic acid (with methotrexate)
- Long-term corticosteroid (cortisone) use (with mifepristone)
- Allergy to the medications used
- Unwillingness to have a surgical abortion should the procedure fail
- Living more than 2 hours away from emergency care or a lack of transportation or telephone for emergency consultation

---

The way these abortions are performed varies from facility to facility and is undergoing change as the procedures are relatively new. The specifics of the procedures may not be followed exactly as described below because of provider variation or refinement over time.

Medical abortion requires two to three visits to the abortion facility. Pre-abortion laboratory tests are the same as for surgical abortion (see page 838).

When methotrexate is used, an injection of the drug is given on the first visit. The dosage is based on body size (weight). The injection is made into the buttock muscle. This injection is followed 3 to 7 days later by misoprostol, taken orally or inserted vaginally. Many facilities give women these tablets to place into the vagina at home. Other facilities require that you return for placement. If you place the misoprostol at home, you can do the insertion just before you go to sleep or anytime you can rest afterward. Wash your hands and insert the tablets deeply into the vagina with your fingers. Drink plenty of fluids or you may become dizzy when you get up. Eat lightly as you may have nausea and vomiting.

Most women experience cramping and vaginal bleeding within 12 hours of inserting the misoprostol. Some women may need a second dose if bleeding has not begun within 24 hours. You might be given a prescription for acetaminophen with codeine (Tylenol 3) which can be taken every 4 hours for cramping. It may make you drowsy, so avoid driving while taking this medication. Avoid anti-inflammatory drugs like ibuprofen because they are also antiprostaglandins which interfere with misoprostol.

Call your abortion care provider if you soak through more than four maxi-pads in 2 hours, six maxi-pads in one day, or if you think your bleeding is unusually profuse. You may also experience headache, nausea, vomiting, and diarrhea.

About two-thirds of women will abort the pregnancy within a week after the misoprostol insertion. You will be told to return to the abortion facility within 3 days to 1 week after you start bleeding. A vaginal examination and/or ultrasound will be done at that time. If there is still evidence of a pregnancy, you will be given another dose of misoprostol and asked to return every week for up to four visits, or perhaps longer. Eighty to 85 percent of women will complete the abortion within 2 weeks of the second dose of misoprostol. About 1 percent of women will take up to 6 to 10 weeks. At that time, a surgical abortion will be needed if there is still evidence of a continuing pregnancy. About 8 to 10 percent of women undergoing medical abortion eventually need a suction procedure to complete the abortion.

With the other regimen—mifepristone and misoprostol—both medications may be given orally, or the misoprostol may be given vaginally. The mifepristone is taken at the first visit to the abortion facility. One or two days later the misoprostol is administered, either at the abortion facility or at home. A very few women (1 percent) may complete their abortions after just the mifepristone dose and do not need the misoprostol. If you have been bleeding, an examination and/or ultrasound will be performed to determine whether the abortion is complete. The majority of women will get misoprostol. About two-thirds will complete their abortions within 4 hours after the misoprostol dose.

You will need to return to the abortion facility 10 days to 2 weeks after a medical abortion. An examination, ultrasound, or both will be performed to make sure the abortion is complete. Women whose blood is Rh negative receive RhoGAM after a medical abortion, just as they do after a surgical procedure. RhoGAM is given anytime before the misoprostol is given.

ABORTION TECHNIQUES IN THE SECOND TRIMESTER

Surgical Abortion in the Second Trimester

The abortion technique most commonly used between 15 and 23 weeks of pregnancy is *dilation and evacuation* (D & E). This allows the uterus to be emptied with vacuum aspiration and is easier, faster, and safer for a woman than a medical procedure at this stage of pregnancy. An accurate estimate of the duration of pregnancy is obtained by ultrasound.

Women are prepared for D & E by methods to soften and open the cervix, at least several hours and sometimes a day or two before the procedure. The most common method is the insertion of natural or synthetic osmotic dilators (see page 840) into the cervical canal. These swell in the presence of fluid. One or more is introduced into the cervix. They absorb fluid from the cervical canal and gradually enlarge, sometimes sufficiently so the cervix may not need to be dilated at the abortion. They also soften the cervix so that any necessary further dilation can be accomplished easily. The dilators are removed before the initiation of the abortion.

As with suction abortion, the woman lies on her back with legs in stirrups, and a speculum is put into the vagina to visualize the cervix. Some sedation generally is given before this, by mouth, by intravenous drip, or both. Unless general anesthesia is used, a local anesthetic of the cervix is injected and the cervix held with a special instrument (a *tenaculum*) to stabilize the uterus. Some abortion providers give intravenous oxytocin before the D & E to help the uterus contract and control bleeding. Others, fearing that the cervix will close with this medication, give the oxytocin after the procedure is completed.

Once the cervical canal has been dilated adequately, the amniotic fluid is drained out of the uterus. This can be done by introducing a catheter through the cervix and applying suction or by allowing the fluid to drain after the membranes are punctured with a long sterile instrument.

Using a special instrument called an *ovum forceps*, the fetus can be grasped and drawn through the dilated cervix. The suction device then can be put back in and the placenta removed by suction.

If a D & E is performed after 20 weeks of pregnancy, many practitioners will inject potassium chloride or digoxin into the fetus 1 or 2 days before the abortion to cause fetal death before the procedure. The injection goes through the uterus, using ultrasound as a guide. This is thought to increase the safety and ease of the abortion.

Dilation and evacuation can be done on an outpatient basis. Its complications are like those described earlier in the section on surgical techniques for first-trimester abortion. You will be observed in the recovery area for a slightly longer time than after a first-trimester abortion, usually 1 to 2 hours, but recovery at home is similar. You should return for a postabortion checkup 2 to 4 weeks after the procedure.

Medical Abortion in the Second Trimester

Second trimester medical abortions are performed very infrequently today. These techniques involve the induction of labor. Several types of medications are used to induce labor. Osmotic cervical dilators as described earlier can be used with each technique to shorten the time from induction of labor to abortion and to reduce the risk of cervical tearing.

The oldest second-trimester abortion technique involves placing a needle through the abdominal and uterine walls into a pocket of amniotic fluid inside the uterus. Because placing a needle into the amniotic sac is more difficult at less than 16 weeks pregnancy, this procedure is usually reserved for pregnancies of 16 weeks or longer duration. Several ounces of fluid are withdrawn in a procedure known as *amniocentesis*. Then, chemicals intended to bring about fetal death and uterine contractions are injected into the amniotic sac in a procedure called *amnioinfusion*.

At some not entirely predictable time after the injection of these chemicals, the fetus dies and uterine contractions begin. Contractions may become quite forceful.

The original chemical utilized for amnioinfusion was a strong salt (*saline*) solution and this is still used. Another chemical, *urea,* has fewer complications. Abortion with *urea* has a higher failure rate than abortion with saline, however, unless it is combined with prostaglandins. Prostaglandins also are used with the saline instillation to shorten the length of the induction. Prostaglandins can be given as vaginal suppositories or as injections.

Instead of using amniocentesis and amnioinfusion, prostaglandins can be given as vaginal suppositories in regimens that vary from every 3 or 4 hours to every 12 hours depending on the type of prostaglandin used. Oxytocin may be given intravenously with prostaglandins.

Oxytocin may also be used as the sole labor-inducing agent, although it is not effective until late in the second trimester. It may be used for abortion performed for genetic reasons as results of genetic testing may not be available until the mid to late second trimester of pregnancy.

Women undergoing late medical abortions are best cared for in a hospital. The majority of women require drugs to alleviate pain. They frequently are unable to eat due to nausea and vomiting during the labor induction and benefit from the administration of intravenous fluids. With saline, excess salt can build up in the bloodstream. A saline abortion is also associated with a complication called *disseminated intravascular coagulation* (DIC). This disease is a complex process, but basically it causes a disturbance in the body's blood clotting mechanisms. The blood clots throughout the blood vessels. This continues until the factors in the blood that cause clotting are essentially used up. Then, hemorrhage begins. While these complications are rare, saline instillation is always an in-hospital procedure.

Fever and diarrhea may occur with prostaglandin use. Fortunately, prostaglandin is destroyed quite rapidly in the lungs as the blood containing it passes through, and these toxic responses are of brief duration.

Once the abortion is complete and bleeding minimal, the woman can be discharged from the hospital to her own care. Most women will need to rest at home after the procedure. Follow the same care guidelines described above for first-trimester surgical abortion. Those women who have more than the usual amount of bleeding are advised to take iron by mouth for 2 or 3 months after the completion of the abortion.

INDUCED ABORTION
AFTER CESAREAN

Previous cesarean does not complicate first-trimester suction abortion. The same applies to D & E. However, since amnioinfusion induces uterine contractions, there have been uterine ruptures at the site of the previous cesarean incision with this method.

ABORTION BY HYSTEROTOMY AND HYSTERECTOMY

Hysterotomy (emptying the uterus by opening it through an abdominal incision) and *hysterectomy* (removal of the uterus) are major operations and present an unacceptable degree of risk when used for abortion. Hysterotomy, by producing a defect in the uterine wall, has the potential of imperiling future pregnancies. These procedures should not be utilized today for abortion.

POSTABORTION CARE

Postabortion care is described in the section "Surgical Abortion in the First Trimester" on page 841. It is essentially the same after a later abortion, although you may find you need to rest for a longer period of time. In 2 to 4 weeks a postabortion checkup is important for all women regardless of the procedure undergone.

EFFECTS ON FUTURE CHILDBEARING

There is no higher incidence of infertility, cervical incompetence, preterm labor, or congenital anomalies after abortion. There is an increase in the risk for ectopic pregnancy only when the abortion was complicated by a postabortion infection. An infection occurs in about 1 in 100 abortions.

DANGER SIGNS FOLLOWING ABORTION

Although legal abortion is a safe procedure, with few complications and less than 1 death per 300,000 procedures, you should be aware of certain danger signs and call your abortion care provider or regular physician, nurse practitioner, or midwife should any of these occur in the first few weeks following abortion.

- Chills and fever
- Pelvic pain, cramping, lower backache
- Tenderness if pressure is applied to the abdomen (stomach, pelvic area)

• Profuse or prolonged bleeding
• Vaginal discharge with bad odor
• Lack of a period for more than 6 weeks

These dangers might signify a pelvic infection, hemorrhage or a blood clot in the uterus, an incomplete abortion, or an ongoing pregnancy. All can be treated if diagnosed promptly.

CONTRACEPTION FOLLOWING ABORTION

You can become pregnant within 10 days following abortion. If you have sexual intercourse, you must use contraception. You can start taking oral contraceptives on the day of the abortion. You can be given an injection of Depo-Provera, have an implant placed, or an IUD inserted at the time of an abortion. Foam and condoms can be used anytime. If you have a medical abortion, you need not refrain from intercourse. You can use any method of birth control, although an IUD cannot be inserted until the abortion is complete. A diaphragm or cervical cap cannot be fit until your cervix is back to its nonpregnant size, usually about 2 to 6 weeks after any type of abortion.

APPENDIX
Resources

————

BOOKS

Expectant and new parents can read hundreds of books. Some are general guides to pregnancy or parenting. Some are more specialized. There are books for specific groups such as teenage mothers, single mothers, working mothers, African-American mothers. You can read books about methods of childbirth and about healthy eating in pregnancy. There are guides to coping with loss from miscarriage, stillbirth, or infant death. Resources are available for women with certain illnesses in pregnancy, such as diabetes. You can find information about homeopathy and herbal remedies, acupuncture, aromatherapy, and hypnosis for childbirth. There are books about the postpartum weeks, about breast-feeding, about infant nutrition. Parents of infants with certain illnesses and special needs can find written information. Fathers can find books and so can expectant siblings. You can read about the emotional development of newborns and about their physical health and common illnesses.

Some authors have written critiques of the medical system of birthing. A few of these books, like *The Immaculate Deception*, by Suzanne Arms, *Giving Birth: Alternatives in Childbirth,* by Barbara Katz Rothman, and *Silent Knife*, by Nancy Wainer Cohen, have become classics and have been instrumental in helping to change childbirth practices throughout the United States. Others, like *Spiritual Midwifery*, by Ina May Gaskin, have helped shape the way we view birth and offer wisdom and insight into childbearing.

The following list is just a taste of what's available for you to read during pregnancy and afterward. It is not intended to be thorough or comprehensive or even representative of all categories of materials. It is just a list of books that we think are useful. In some cases, we are only somewhat familiar with the book itself, but the writer is someone whose work and opinions we respect. This does not mean we endorse the entire content of any book. Nor does it mean these are the only or the best books you can read. It's just a suggestion, a place to begin. We have only included books currently in print, although this can change at any time. We apologize to worthwhile authors we have omitted.

General Pregnancy

The Complete Book of Pregnancy and Childbirth by Sheila Kitzinger. Anything by the English author Sheila Kitzinger is worth reading, even if a bit heavy.

A Good Birth, a Safe Birth: Choosing and Having the Childbirth Experience You Want, 3rd Revised Edition by Diana Korte and Roberta Scaer.

Having Your Baby: A Guide for African American Women by Hilda Hutcherson with Margaret Williams.

The Pregnancy Book: Month-by-Month, Everything You Need to Know from America's Baby Experts by William Sears and Martha Sears. The Searses are a husband-and-wife, pediatrician-and-nurse team and the parents of a large family.

Pregnancy, Childbirth, & the Newborn: The Complete Guide by Penny Simkin, Janey Whalley, and Ann Keppler. Penny Simkin is a well-known childbirth educator.

The Thinking Woman's Guide to a Better Birth by Henci Goer. Questions many standard obstetrical practices and provides understandable research information.

A Personal/Spiritual Approach to Pregnancy and Birth

Active Birth: The New Approach to Giving Birth Naturally, Revised Edition by Janet Balaskas.

Birthing from Within: An Extra-Ordinary Guide to Childbirth Preparation by Pam England and Rob Horowitz.

An Easier Childbirth: A Mother's Guide for Birthing Normally by Gayle Peterson. Gayle Peterson is a nationally prominent figure in birth visualization, hypnosis, and other natural methods of dealing with the pain of childbirth.

Pregnant Feelings by Rahima Baldwin.

Special Delivery by Rahima Baldwin. About home birth.

With Child: Wisdom and Traditions for Pregnancy, Birth and Mothering by Deborah Jackson. A cross-cultural approach.

Exercise in Pregnancy

Essential Exercises for the Childbearing Year: A Guide to Health and Comfort Before and After Your Baby is Born, 4th Edition by Elizabeth Noble. The standard exercise book in pregnancy and the postpartum period by a physical therapist and childbirth educator. Available from Elizabeth Noble at her website: www.elizabethnoble.com.

Yoga for Pregnancy: Safe and Gentle Stretches by Sandra Jordan. One of a number of books on yoga, an excellent pregnancy activity, promoting flexibility, body awareness, and relaxation.

Nutrition in Pregnancy

As You Eat So Your Baby Grows: A Guide to Nutrition in Pregnancy by Nikki Goldbeck.

Before Your Pregnancy: Prepare Your Body for a Healthy Pregnancy—Expert Advice on Nutrition and Exercise (also video) by Amy Ogle. A book by a registered dietitian.

Eating Expectantly: A Practical and Tasty Guide to Prenatal Nutrition by Bridget Swinney and Tracey Anderson.

Nutrition and Pregnancy: A Complete Guide from Preconception to Postdelivery by Judith E. Brown.

Pregnancy Nutrition: Good Health for You and Your Baby by Elizabeth M. Ward.

Vegetarian Pregnancy: The Definitive Nutritional Guide to Having a Healthy Baby by Sharon K. Yntema.

Childbirth Education

Six Practical Lessons for an Easier Childbirth, 3rd Revised Edition by Elizabeth Bing. Any book list about pregnancy and childbirth should include something by Elizabeth Bing, although most of her works are out of print. A pioneer in childbirth education, a cofounder of the American Society for Psychoprophylaxis in Childbirth (ASPO—now called Lamaze International), she helped revolutionize childbirth in the United States almost half a century ago. This book takes you through a series of Lamaze classes.

Pain in Labor

Body Centered Hypnosis for Pregnancy, Bonding and Childbirth by Gayle Peterson.

Creative Childbirth: The Leclaire Method of Easy Birthing Through Hypnosis and Rational-Intuitive Thought by Michelle Leclaire O'Neill.

Easing Labor Pain: The Complete Guide to a More Comfortable and Rewarding Birth, Revised Edition by Adrienne B. Lieberman.

HypnoBirthing: A Celebration of Life by Marie F. Mongan.

Fetus and Newborn

A Child Is Born by Lennart Nilsson. A classic.

Postpartum

Mothering the New Mother by Sally Placksin.

Fathers and Other Birth Partners

The Birth Partner: Everything You Need to Know to Help a Woman Through Childbirth by Penny Simkin. Another guide by this well-known childbirth educator.

Breast-feeding

The Breast-feeding Book: Everything You Need to Know About Nursing Your Child from Birth Through Weaning by Martha Sears and William Sears.

Breast-feeding Your Baby by Sheila Kitzinger.

The Complete Book of Breast-feeding, 3rd Edition by Marvin S. Eiger and Sally Wendkos Olds. An old breast-feeding guide, updated.

The Nursing's Mother's Companion by Kathleen Huggins. Photographs by Harriette Hartigan, an outstanding birth photographer, who is also a midwife.

Nursing Mother, Working Mother: The Essential Guide for Breast-feeding and Staying Close to Your Baby After You Return to Work by Gale Pryor.

La Leche League publications.

Defining Your Own Success: Breast-feeding After Breast Reduction Surgery by Diana West.

How Weaning Happens by Diane Bengson.

Mothering Your Nursing Toddler, Revised Edition by Norma Jane Bumgarner.

Mothering Multiples: Breast-feeding and Caring for Twins or More, Revised Edition by Karen Kerkhoff Gromada.

Twins (and Up)

Twins to Quints: The Complete Manual for Parents of Multiple Birth Children by The National Organization of Mothers of Twins Clubs. Available from the organization's website—see Parent Organizations on page 863.

Having Twins by Elizabeth Noble.

The Art of Parenting Twins: The Unique Joys and Challenges of Raising Twins and Other Multiples by Patricia Maxwell Malmstrom and Janet Poland.

The Parents' Guide to Raising Twins by Elizabeth Friedrich and Cherry Rowland.

When You're Expecting Twins, Triplets, or Quads: A Complete Rescource by Barbara Luke, Tamara Eberlein.

Twins!: Expert Advice from Two Practicing Physicians on Pregnancy, Birth, and the First Year of Life With Twins by Connie L. Agnew, M.D.

The Multiple Pregnancy Sourcebook: Pregnancy and the First Year with Twins, Triplets, and More by Nancy A. Bowers, RN.

Raising Twins: What Parents Want to Know (and What Twins Want to Tell Them) by Eileen M. Pearlman and Jill Alison Ganon.

The Joy of Twins and Other Multiple Births: Having, Raising, and Loving Babies Who Arrive in Groups by Pamela Patrick Novotny.

Double Duty: The Parent's Guide to Rasing Twins, from Pregnancy Through the School Years by Christina Baglivi Tinglof.

Mothering Twins: From Hearing the News to Beyond the Terrible Twos by Linda Albi.

Raising Multiple Birth Children: A Parents' Survival Guide by William Laut.

Two at a Time: Having Twins, the Journey Through Pregnancy and Birth by Jane Seymour.

Twins, Triples and More by Elizabeth M. Bryan.

The Twinship Sourcebook: Your Guide to Understanding Multiples edited by Susan J. Alt.

Pregnancy Loss

Empty Cradle, Broken Heart: Surviving the Death of Your Baby by Deborah L. Davis.

How to Go on Living After the Death of a Baby by Larry Peppers.

Pregnancy After Loss: A Guide to Pregnancy After a Miscarriage, Stillbirth or Infant Death by Carol Cirulli Lanham.

Trying Again: A Guide to Pregnancy After Miscarriage, Stillbirth, and Infant Loss by Ann Douglas.

Infertility

Resolving Infertility: Understanding the Options and Choosing Solutions When You Want to Have a Baby by the Staff of RESOLVE (see Parent Organizations).

Other (History and Social Science)

Birth as an American Rite of Passage by Robbie Davis-Floyd. Dr. Davis-Floyd is an anthropologist who studies childbirth and midwifery in America. She always writes with insight and intelligence.

Midwifery and Childbirth in America by Judith Pence Rooks. A readable, often fascinating, history of midwifery in America.

AUDIO TAPES AND VIDEOS

Pregnancy Exercise

ACOG Pregnancy Exercise Program (1990) A video produced by the American College of Obstetricians and Gynecologists of gentle but effective and safe exercises for pregnant women.

Childbirth

Giving Birth: Challenges & Choices, a film by Suzanne Arms and featuring obstetrician/gynecologist Christiane Northrup, M.D., FACOG, and author of *Women's Bodies: Women's Wisdom.*

Childbirth Hypnosis

Order audio and videotapes at www.mychildbirth.com

Yoga

Yoga for Pregnant Women. A set of yoga exercises, warmups, and meditation for pregnant women.

Multiple Births

Expecting Multiples by Multiple Birth Resources, LLC, www.expecting multiples.com

ORGANIZATIONS

Like the book list, this is not a comprehensive guide to organizations relating to pregnancy, birth, and family planning. The professional organizations listed can offer referrals to practitioners as well as information about licensure or cer- tification of a practitioner. Other organizations offer reading materials, direct assistance, and support groups. Many have local chapters, whose location and contact information are available through the national organization. Where there appears to be missing information, such as a phone or fax number, this is because the organization doesn't readily provide this information. Again, we apologize to worthwhile organizations we have omitted.

Professional Organizations

Medical
American College of Obstetricians and Gynecolgoists (ACOG)
P.O. Box 96920
Washington, DC 20090-6920
(Organization requests e-mail, not phone calls)
www.acog.org
E-mail: See website for specific e-mail addresses

American Board of Obstetrics and Gynecology (ABOG)
2915 Vine Street, Suite 300
Dallas, TX 75204
Phone: 214-871-1619
Fax: 214-871-1943
www.abog.org
E-mail: info@abog.org

American Academy of Family Physicians (AAFP)
P.O. Box 11210
Shawnee Mission, KS 66207-1210
Phone: 913-906-6000
Fax: See website for specific fax numbers
www.aafp.org
E-mail: fp@aafp.org

American Society for Reproductive Medicine (ASRM)
(formerly The American Fertility Society)
1209 Montgomery Highway
Birmingham, AL 35216-2809
Phone: 205-978-5000
Fax: 205-978-5005
www.asrm.org
E-mail: asrm@asrm.org

The American Academy of Pediatrics
141 Northwest Point Boulevard
Elk Grove Village, IL 60007-1098
Phone: 847-434-4000
Fax: 847-434-8000
www.aap.org

The American Board of Pediatrics
111 Silver Cedar Court
Chapel Hill, NC 27514
Phone: 919-929-0461
Fax: 919-929-9255
E-mail: abpeds@abpeds.org

American Board of Family Practice, Inc.
2228 Young Drive
Lexington, KY 40505-4294
Phone: 859-269-5626 or 888-995-5700
Fax: 859-335-7501 or 859-335-7509
E-mail: general@abfp.org

Midwifery
American College of Nurse-Midwives (ACNM)
818 Connecticut Avenue NW, Suite 900
Washington, DC 20006
Phone: 202-728-9860
Fax: 202-728-9897

www.acnm.org
E-mail: info@acnm.org

Midwives Alliance of North America (MANA)
Phone: 888-923-MANA
E-mail: info@mana.org

Nurse Practitioners
The National Certification Board of Pediatric Nurse Practitioners and Nurses
(NCBPNP/N)
800 S. Frederick Avenue, Suite 104
Gaithersburg, MD 20877-4151
Phone: 301-330-2921 or 888-641-2767
Fax: 301-330-1504
www.pnpcert.org
E-mail: See website for specific e-mail addresses

American Nurses Association
600 Maryland Avenue, SW, Suite 100 West
Washington, DC 20024-2571
Phone: 800-274-4ANA
Fax: 202-651-7001
www.ana.org
E-mail: See website for specific e-mail addresses

Childbirth Education
Lamaze International
(formerly American Society for Psychoprophylaxis in Obstetrics—ASPO)
2025 M St, Suite 800
Washington, DC 20036-3309
Phone: 202-367-1128; 800-368-4404
Fax: 202-367-2128
www.lamaze.org
E-mail: lamaze@dc.sba.com

International Childbirth Education Association
P.O. Box 20048
Minneapolis, MN 55420
Phone: 952-854-8660
Fax: 952-854-8772
www.icea.org
E-mail: info@icea.org

Childbearing Centers
National Association of Childbearing Centers (NACC)
3123 Gottschall Road
Perkiomenville, PA 18074
Phone: 215-234-8068
Fax: 215-234-8829
www.BirthCenters.org
E-mail: reachnacc@BirthCenters.org

Breast-feeding
The International Lactation Consultant Association (ILCA)
1500 Sunday Drive, Suite 102
Raleigh, NC 27607
Phone: 919-787-5181
Fax: 919-787-4916
www.ilca.org
E-mail: ilca@erols.com

La Leche League International (LLLI)
P.O. Box 4079
Schaumburg, IL 60168-4079
Phone: 847-519-7730
Fax: 847-519-0035
www.lalecheleague.org
E-mail: See website for specific e-mail addresses or
PRDept@llli.org

Doula
Doulas of North America (DONA)
13513 North Grove Drive
Alpine, UT 84004
Phone: 801-756-7331
Fax: 801-763-1847
www.dona.org
E-mail: info@dona.org

National Association of Postpartum Care Services (NAPCS)
800 Detroit Street
Denver, CO 80206
Phone: 1-800-45-DOULA
Fax: 303-321-4058
www.napcs.org
E-mail: DoulaCare@aol.com

Other Professional
National Society of Genetic Counselors (NSGC)
233 Canterbury Drive
Wallingford, PA 19086-6617
Phone: 610-872-7608
www.nsgc.org
E-mail: nsgc@nsgc.org

Advocacy Organizations
Global Maternal/Child Health Association, Inc.
P.O. Box 1400
Wilsonville, OR 97070
Phone: 503-673-0026
www.waterbirth.org
E-mail: waterbirth@aol.com

Institute for Family-Centered Care
7900 Wisconsin Avenue, Suite 405
Bethesda, MD 20814
Phone: 301-652-0281
Fax: 301-652-0186
www.familycenteredcare.org
E-mail: Institute@iffcc.org

International Cesarean Awareness Network (ICAN)
1304 Kingsdale Avenue
Redondo Beach, CA 90278
Phone: 310-542-6400
Fax: 310-542-5368
www.ican-online.org
E-mail: info@ican-online.org

Midwifery Today, Inc.
P.O. Box 2672
Eugene, OR 97402
Phone: 541-344-7438 or 800-743-0974 (orders only)
Fax: 541-344-1422
www.midwiferytoday.com
E-mail: See website for specific addresses or
Inquiries@midwiferytoday.com

Planned Parenthood Federation of America
810 Seventh Avenue
New York, NY 10019

Phone: 212-541-7800
Fax: 212-245-1845
www.plannedparenthood.org
E-mail: communications@ppfa.org

Research, Educational, Advocacy, and Philanthropic
Organizations
March of Dimes Birth Defects Foundation
1275 Mamaroneck Avenue
White Plains, NY 10605
Phone: 888-MODIMES or 800-367-6630 (for ordering materials only)
www.modimes.org or in Spanish: www.nacersano.org
See webpage for contact form and catalog of materials

Maternity Center Association
281 Park Avenue South, 5th Floor
New York, NY 10010
Phone: 212-777-5000
Fax: 212-777-9320
www.maternity.org
E-mail: info@maternitywise.org

Governmental Agencies
United States Food and Drug Administration
Center for Food Safety and Applied Nutrition
24-hour phone: 800-SEAFOOD (832-3663)
www.cfsan.fda.gov

Environmental Protection Agency—fish advisory
www.epa.gov/waterscience/fish/

Organizations for Ordering Products (for purchase or rental)
Cue Ovulation Predictor
Zetek, Inc.
876 Ventura Street
Aurora, CO 80011
Phone: 800-FOR-CUES (800-367-2837)
E-mail: info@zetek.net

Breast pumps, accessories, and nursing bras
Medela, Inc. (USA)
1101 Corporate Drive
McHenry, IL 60050
Phone: 800-435-8316

www.medela.com/index.html
E-mail: customer.service@medela.com

Ameda Breast-feeding Products
c/o Hollister Incorporated
2000 Hollister Drive
Libertyville, IL 60048
Phone: 877-99-AMEDA (877-992-6332) (USA)
        800-263-7400 (Canada)
        847-680-1000 (International)
www.ameda.com
www.hollister.com
E-mail: us.ameda.feedback@ameda.com

Parent Organizations
National Organization of Mothers of Twins Clubs (NOMOTC)
P.O. Box 438
Thompsons Station, TN 37179-0438
Phone: 615-595-0936 or 877-540-2200
www.nomotc.org
E-mail: info@nomotc.org

International Twins Association (ITA)
6898 Channel Rd. N.E.
Minneapolis, MN 55432
Phone: 612-571-3022
www.intltwins.org
E-mail: ITAconvention@aol.com

Mothers of Supertwins (high-order multiples—MOST)
P.O. Box 951
Brentwood, NY 11717-0627
Phone: 631-859-1110
www.mostonline.org
E-mail: info@mostonline.org

Multiple Births Canada
P.O. Box 234
Gormley, Ontario L0H 1G0
Canada
Phone: 905-888-0725 or 866-228-8824
Fax: 905-888-0727
www.pomba.org
E-mail: office@multiplebirthscanada.org

RESOLVE: The National Infertility Organization
1310 Broadway
Somerville, MA 02144-1779
Phone: 617-623-0744 (Helpline)
Fax: 617-623-0252
www.resolve.org
E-mail: resolveinc@aol.com

Internet Resources

The internet offers a wealth of information. We could list hundreds, even thousands, of websites that you might find useful. However, due to the nature of the medium, websites are often transitory. We've been led astray by many a web resource list—searching for sites that no longer exist. Some websites remain in place for a long time but are not updated. Others are updated frequently, and this is one of the advantages of web-based information. It can be cutting edge in its immediacy, but nothing is guaranteed.

Web resources are also extremely variable in quality. Some are superb, others far from superb. Many have been developed to support a particular person, institution, or idea. These may be excellent, but may present biased information. So, before believing anything you read on the web, check the sponsorship of the site. A fertility group sponsoring the site, for instance, may overvalue the use of certain procedures. A group advocating for or against epidural anesthesia, as another example, may present skewed research data to support its position. Biases, of course, are not necessarily bad as you can learn a lot from an advocacy organization arguing its opinion. It's just important to distinguish opinion from fact, and this isn't always easy.

We encourage you to explore internet resources relating to pregnancy, birth, and family planning, just as we encourage you to go to your local library or bookstore and read as much as you can. If you type in a word like "pregnancy," of course, you will get thousands of responses on many search engines. Have fun, but don't get too carried away!

With this in mind, we offer the following as excellent web resources (in addition to the web addresses included with the organizations listed above).

Centers for Disease Control and Prevention (CDC)
www.cdc.gov
Pages and pages of useful information on many health topics, including pregnancy-related topics.

Occupational Safety and Health Administration (OSHA)
U.S. Department of Labor
www.osha.gov

INDEX